PRAISE FOR A

"4.8 out of 5...An excellent addition to a well-written, high-quality series...A worthy and almost impossible to put down second book in the Archanium Codex saga...McIntire's world-building is excellent - we are made to feel at home here, and to understand the complexities of this world, quite naturally as events unfold...New surprises await around every corner...All in all, this is an excellent addition to a well-written, high-quality series."

— *INDIEREADER REVIEW*

"★★★★★. McIntire expands his magnificent world of magic and shapeshifting, exploring the ways greed, malevolence, and the lust for power and control affect the lives of the protagonists...Dark magic, high action, deadly chases, daring escapades, gruesome torture, and vicious fights, all pose heavily in the story. But it's the deep, soulful love of Jonas and Aleksei that drives the plot. There are heartfelt emotions, tender romance, and burning passion. Despite the book's length (700+ pages), the reader will stay invested in the story. The major twist in the end is as touching as it is unexpected...McIntire's assured language and entertaining storytelling make it a page-turning read."

— *BOOKVIEW REVIEW*

"A vibrant array of colorful characters guides readers through this absorbing fantasy. McIntire's epic tale accommodates an extensive cast. But the story unfolds across a relatively small landscape, making the various subplots easy to follow. The lord captain's indisputable strength fuses well with his devotion to Jonas; even with only a spattering of romantic interludes, his love clearly drives him. But supporting characters don't let the two leads completely steal the spotlight."

— *KIRKUS REVIEWS*

"This darkly escapist, highly readable fantasy is a stunner...An emotional and remarkably inventive fantasy...*McIntire continues his The Archanium Codex series with this emotionally rich, sweeping tale*...The book has everything: a lavish fantasy world, endearing heroes, malicious villains along with the grit and grime of the genre. The fully fleshed-out, multi-dimensional world of McIntire's magical universe sets the tone for a quick, thrilling journey."

— *THE PRAIRIES BOOK REVIEW*

"Nicholas McIntire's dedication to elaborate world-building is more impressive than ever in A Wicked Wind, his sprawling sequel to 2019's The Hunter's Gambit...fantasy fans looking for a carefully constructed universe populated by three-dimensional, compelling characters will find plenty to love here. McIntire's world feels boundless once its dimensions are clear, and he uses this sequel to construct an ambitious universe with unlimited action."

— *BLUEINK REVIEW*

A Wicked Wind

The Archanium Codex: Book Two

NICHOLAS MCINTIRE

Published by Black Dove Press, 1504 Clover Lane, Fort Worth, TX 76107

For information about bulk purchases, either in print or eBook form please contact Black Dove Press at 817 320 2886.

Manufactured in the United States of America.

A First Edition

ISBN 13: 978-1-7338491-9-7

ISBN 10: 1-7338491-9-7

Ebook ISBN 13: 978-1-7338491-4-2

Ebook ISBN 10: 1-7338491-4-2

Map by Erin Lameroux. Interior Illustrations by Sonarix and Erin Lameroux

Interior book design (print and ebook) Nicholas McIntire

Cover created by Sonarix

10 9 8 7 6 5 4 3 2 1

FOR MY MOTHER, MELISSA.
YOUR LOVE AND WISDOM ARE GIFTS THAT I CHERISH EVERY SINGLE
DAY, AND I WOULD NOT BE THE MAN I AM TODAY WITHOUT YOUR
MAGNIFICENT PRESENCE IN MY LIFE.
I LOVE YOU.

The Archanium Codex

The Hunter's Gambit
A Wicked Wind
Book 3 (forthcoming)

Codex Novellas

The Gilded Prince: A Prelude to A Wicked Wind
Novella 2 (forthcoming)

CONTENTS

CHAPTER 1
Herald
1

CHAPTER 2
Out of Time
14

CHAPTER 3
Awakening
27

CHAPTER 4
Sin and Sacrifice
39

CHAPTER 5
A Golden Seal
51

CHAPTER 6
Tangles in the Web
62

CHAPTER 7
Sactuary
74

CHAPTER 8
Phantoms
87

CHAPTER 9
Amongst the Shadows
99

CHAPTER 10
An Eye in the Storm
112

CHAPTER 11
Sweet Sacrifice
124

CHAPTER 12
Traps
137

CHAPTER 13
Stone by Stone
148

CHAPTER 14
Breaking Through
160

CHAPTER 15
Secrets and Lies
172

CHAPTER 16
A Wicked Wind
186

CHAPTER 17
Unexpected Companions
199

CHAPTER 18
Into the Belly of Darkness
210

CHAPTER 19   223
Serpents and Seraphs

CHAPTER 20   235
On a Wing

CHAPTER 21   245
Kindness Can Be Cruel

CHAPTER 22   257
Divine Comedy

CHAPTER 23   265
Reaching From the Abyss

CHAPTER 24   277
Blood Meridian

CHAPTER 25   288
Perfect Illusions

CHAPTER 26   297
Bound

CHAPTER 27   307
An Unexpected Arrival

CHAPTER 28   319
Bloodletting

CHAPTER 29   331
White Light

CHAPTER 30   345
Into Oblivion

CHAPTER 31   361
Closet Confessions

CHAPTER 32   376
Starling

CHAPTER 33   390
A Brotherhood of Bone

CHAPTER 34   399
Impure

CHAPTER 35   408
A Nameless Blade

CHAPTER 36   421
The Pit

CHAPTER 37   431
Anomaly

CHAPTER 38   443
Richter

CHAPTER 39   453
A Blighted Blessing

CHAPTER 40   466
The Claws of Corruption

CHAPTER 41   481
One by One

CHAPTER 42   501
Drippings To Follow

CHAPTER 43   515
Fading Away

CHAPTER 44   536
Greetings and Goodbyes

CHAPTER 45   552
Riddles in Ink, Riddles in Blood

CHAPTER 46   567
Devils and Gods

CHAPTER 47   582
Reveling and Reckoning

CHAPTER 48   595
The Worth of a Good Man

CHAPTER 49   608
Altered States

CHAPTER 50   626
Laws of Illusion

CHAPTER 51   648
Ghost

CHAPTER 52   658
A Rule of Unintended Consequences

EPILOGUE   676
Behemoth

ACKNOWLEDGMENTS   679
CODEX PRONUNCIATION GUIDE   681
ABOUT THE AUTHOR   685

CHAPTER 1

HERALD

The Angel Adam drifted on the wind, staring down into the smoldering southern gate of Kalinor Palace. Smoke billowed from the site, and amidst the char and sulfur Adam detected the rankling odor of burnt flesh.

Were he a mere man, Adam might have wondered at the source of such destruction. As it was, the stink of the Demonic Presence was practically overwhelming. Rebel troops meandered through the thoroughfares of the city, their movements outlined by tiny pinpricks of torchlight.

His chest tightened as he reached into his jacket, withdrawing a slim strip of parchment. The Angelus would *not* be pleased if he returned empty-handed. Adam read over the notes inscribed on the parchment, studying the musical name of his quarry. He closed his azure eyes and took a deep breath, summoning the Song.

As he wove the notes through the Archanium, he opened himself to the gray morass of swirling shadows. A single, brilliant whorl of crimson and turquoise arose, wrapping itself around him and singing its countermelody into his mind.

His eyes snapped open as he twisted in the air to face north. There, at the edge of the horizon, sounded the echo of his Song.

Adam breathed a heavy sigh of relief. His target was alive. He hadn't failed the Angelus. He might even be *redeemed*.

"I'm coming for you, Jonas Belgi."

"We're going in circles."

Roux Devaan regarded his cousin with a mixture of irritation and resignation. "I'm aware, Aleksei. What I want to know is *why*."

Aleksei Drago crouched near the forest floor and sniffed experimentally. His quarry's scent lingered on the underbrush, but it was fast becoming muddied by his own. His feet had passed over this spot multiple times in the few hours they'd been searching.

It should have been impossible. Both men shared deep connections to the Seil Wood; travel under Her branches had never been a challenge for either. For them to be lost in the Wood was incomprehensible.

Aleksei was the Ri-Vhan Hunter. There was no prey he could not track. Nothing had ever evaded him, not since his birthright had awakened the year before. Yet, despite having just sent them into the Wood in the small hours of morning, both the Archanium Magus Aya and Andariana Belgi seemed to have simply vanished into thin air.

"This is maddening," Aleksei muttered, running his hands through his short blond hair.

Roux nodded his confounded agreement.

Aleksei searched the heavy undergrowth blanketing the Wood on either side of the pathway. It was dense, but not significant enough to impede his tracking. Yet they had seen nothing. No sign of Aya or the Queen could be found.

Hunter. Aleksei rose as the motherly voice of the Wood filled his head. *Hunter, someone approaches.*

Aleksei frowned, concentrating. There, just beneath the night-sounds of the Wood, came a deep rumble. One growing progressively louder.

Roux turned to him, "Do you feel that? Something's heading our way."

"We need to get off the road," Aleksei growled, sliding into the underbrush and looking down the path.

Roux joined him, crouching low and squinting into the darkness.

"Volos's Beard," Roux whispered, "what *is* that?"

Aleksei was unable to mask his confusion. "It's a coach and four.

Who'd be dumb enough to bring a coach into the Wood? Especially this *deep?*"

Roux shook his head, "I didn't think anyone but the Ri-Vhan could navigate this close to the Wood's Heart."

As the coach grew nearer, a light shot across the forest floor. The two men started at the sudden presence of firelight, watching in stunned amazement as the air before them *parted*.

A space opened in the air, ripping a jagged hole in the walls of reality, revealing a barren pasture. The forest path wound down into the field, torches lighting the road as it wound its way towards a spindly tower jutting from the field's center.

Aleksei caught a scent on the wind and stiffened. He had only encountered it once before, but that had been memorable enough.

"It's Darielle," he whispered.

Roux frowned, "*Darielle?*"

The Ri-Hnon looked up when no response came, only to find his cousin gone.

Roux shot to his feet, staring out into the forest for any sign of Aleksei. The man had vanished completely.

As the coach drew closer, its pace increased.

Roux stepped back into the forest, not willing to believe his eyes as he watched the coach roar towards the shimmering patch in the air.

There was a flash of movement to his left, and he hardly had time to register Aleksei's form before the man dashed out into the path. A heartbeat before he crashed into the side of the coach, Aleksei rolled.

Roux's entire body braced for the moment of impact, but it never came. One moment his cousin was committing suicide, and the next he was simply gone.

The Ri-Hnon stared as the coach passed him and rolled through the strange expanse. As it rumbled down the torch-lit road, the breach diminished.

And then Roux was standing in the middle of the Seil Wood, alone.

Jonas Belgi collapsed onto his face, panting savagely as he failed to regain his footing. The high grass whipped wildly in the gale surrounding him.

He tried to stand again and stumbled into a crouch.

The sky was black with storm clouds, the air growing rapidly colder. His pursuer was close.

It had been the matter of an instant. He'd been in hot pursuit of Sammul. The traitorous High Magus had staggered from the Voralla in the small hours of the morning, and Jonas had been waiting. But Sammul had no sooner shown his face than he Faded out of sight.

It was not welcome news to Jonas that his suspicions were correct. Somehow, the Demon Bael and his followers had rediscovered the lost art of translocation. It was an incredibly difficult skill to master, not to mention believed lost for an Age, and it gave the other side yet another advantage that Jonas could hardly stomach.

He had followed, though shapeshifting took considerably longer than he would have liked, despite being many times faster than horseback. But Jonas had only managed to make it a dozen leagues north of Kalinor before the windstorm struck him down.

Since landing and shifting back into human form, the wind had risen to a piercing howl. It was all he could do to keep his feet on the ground.

A light shot into the air a hundred paces away, and Jonas's heart staggered. He knew the source of that harsh chartreuse light.

The Demon had found him.

Jonas reached into the Archanium and the air around him stilled, allowing him to stand. If Bael was this close, there was no reason to hide himself any longer. He had no choice now but to fight.

The nimbus of putrid light moved closer. Jonas made out the shadow of Bael's form as he neared.

The prince pulled the Archanium tighter to himself, reaching into the destructive, chaotic Nagavor as deeply as he dared and lashing out.

The air split as a lance of pure white light erupted from the earth.

The spike splashed across the nimbus, but halted Bael only a moment. Jonas cursed and reached out again, this time into a very unfamiliar region of the Archanium.

He dropped to his knees as the spell erupted and the earth heaved.

Huge, jagged stone teeth rose up, yawning open under Bael.

Jonas gasped for air and staggered to his feet, taking in the incredible devastation he had wrought. The crack in the earth yawned ten paces across. At the bottom of the crevasse lay Bael's unmoving form, still wrapped in chartreuse light.

Jonas lashed out again, clapping his hands, forcing the earth back together in a thunderous crush.

The aftershocks threw him on his back, knocking the wind from him. His vision swam as he stared at the storm-black sky.

As he tried to right himself, Jonas found his limbs numb, unable to support his weight. His entire body shook. He had nothing left.

He closed his eyes and breathed in short, shallow gasps, searching for the energy to lift his head.

There was a rumble, and Jonas managed to roll to the side as something exploded from the earth, showering him with stones and soil. He coughed violently in the dust, staring up into the enraged face of the Demon.

"Pity," Bael snarled, extending a hand throbbing with yellow-green light.

Jonas screamed as his vision was overtaken by a burst of corrupted sun.

Aleksei clenched his jaw, every muscle in his body rigid. His hands burned from clutching the leather straps of the suspension while the rest of his body was held in close proximity to the coach's underside by the sheer strength of his muscles alone.

He breathed in short, measured bursts, unwilling to analyze what he'd just done, much less what he'd just *seen*. In the back of his mind, he could tell that they had not traveled to a different part of the Wood. Even as the coach creaked to a halt in front of the tower, he knew he'd only moved a few hundred paces from where he and Roux had been searching.

The door of the coach swung open and the Prophet Darielle stepped out. Aleksei watched her slim legs, intermittently visible among the swirling fabric of her gown. It amazed him that someone so small could fill him with such dread.

As she reached the front of the tower, a very tall, thin man stepped out to greet her.

"This is unexpected, Sister," the man mumbled, scratching at his wild silver hair.

"Azarael, darling, I *thrive* on the unexpected," Darielle laughed as she paused to kiss his proffered cheek.

She swept into the tower and, after briefly gazing out into the night, Azarael followed.

Aleksei found himself staring at the massive double doors in amazement. This shadowy figure who had, mere moments ago, been cloaked in whispers and conjecture was Darielle's *brother*? The implications were as horrifying as they were perplexing.

The coach rolled into motion and Aleksei cursed, releasing his hold on the suspension and landing heavily on the gravel beneath him. The coach rumbled away, leaving him there on his back, staring at the vast sky above.

A short, powerful vibration in the earth alerted him that something huge had landed nearby, and seconds later he found himself staring into the eyes of the largest wolf he'd ever seen.

Aleksei rolled to the side and onto his feet. His sword was already in his hand as he turned to confront the creature.

Rather than a wolf, Aleksei found himself facing a chilling abomination. It was a head taller than he, with the stature of a man. Its body was covered in fur, but the two black raven wings extending from its back sent shivers through him.

He was beholding something wholly unnatural.

The wolf creature snarled and launched itself towards the Archanium Knight. Aleksei leapt back, raising his sword towards its chest. The wolf-raven batted his blade down and raked its claws across his ribcage.

Aleksei fell onto his back, coughing as the shock of the attack struck him. And then he was staring into a snapping maw of fangs that his arms only just kept at bay.

Red tendrils burst from his shoulders, sinking into the wolf creature and feasting, even as it hurled itself away from Aleksei and sought to flee. Aleksei watched in horrified fascination as the wolf creature attempted to fly up into the air, its raven wings flapping in futility.

The tendrils of the Hunter's Mantle reached up, entangling the creature and slamming it back to the ground. It drained away the wolf's life before receding up his arms and settling back into writhing, icy black talons splashed across his flesh.

Aleksei coughed and sat up, gasping for breath and trying desperately to make sense of the last few moments. Any trace of injury was gone, leaving behind the hot throb of vitality that feeding the Mantle provided him.

He came to his feet, pausing only to collect his sword before heading towards the tower doors.

Aleksei slowed as he approached, closing his eyes and concentrating on the cacophony of beating hearts he could hear emanating from within.

He frowned.

On the first level he detected only two pulses, but high above him he could hear a surprising barrage of beats. Equally surprising was the number of flitting animal pulses that intermingled with slower, steadier human heartbeats.

He focused again on the human pulses before him. They were moving upwards.

Aleksei gripped one of the heavy door handles and pulled. Nothing. He gritted his teeth and pulled harder, this time digging his heels into the ground.

The door glided ponderously open.

Aleksei slipped inside, pausing only to pull the door shut. It was remarkably easier to do from the inside.

"Good evening, Captain Drago."

Aleksei spun to stare at the Prophet.

"How'd you do that?" he whispered.

Darielle rolled her eyes, "You are a clever man, Lord Captain, but you've become complacent in your abilities. It's not so difficult to sneak up on you as you may believe."

"Where's Azarael?"

Darielle sighed, "He's tending some of his little...pets. He is diverted for the moment, and thus I would suggest that you act in all haste. You'll find the Queen and the Magus on the uppermost level." She reached into the sleeve of her dress and withdrew a slender key. "You'll also need this."

"Why are you helping me?" he asked warily. "Why betray your own brother?"

Darielle laughed at that, "I doubt he'll even notice. My brother has a rather...*unique* way of seeing the world. The loss of two specimens will hardly be taken into account. But you must go *now*. Otherwise, you risk becoming one of his pets yourself. And I would be *so* sorry to see that."

Aleksei took the key from her. "Thank you."

She sighed, "Captain Drago, the days ahead will be hard enough. Trust me."

The glittering suggestion in her emerald eyes sent a ripple of terror through him.

"*Go*," she commanded.

Aleksei turned and dashed to the stairs, gliding up into the tower like a whisper.

He came to a landing and took a cursory sniff at the air. Azarael was on this level. The only visible door was open, but when Aleksei peeked into the chamber, he found the Magus's back to him.

He stole a second moment to take in all the bizarre cages that filled the room. On a table in front of the Magus lay a series of books and bottles of brightly colored liquid. Aleksei immediately recognized them as Ri-Vhan healing potions.

He slipped across the landing and scaled the stairs, trying to understand exactly what Azarael was doing with all these animals. Each room contained the same curious sets of cages, the same bottles of potion, yet the higher he climbed, the stranger the creatures became.

By the time he reached the pinnacle, Aleksei thought he had a full appreciation for what Darielle referred to as her brother's "little pets".

The man was *insane*, using magic to cross animals with each other to create unholy chimeras. It certainly explained the wolf-raven creature Aleksei had dispatched in front of the tower.

He reached the uppermost door and hurriedly unlocked it.

Aya and Andariana were chained to bolts in the wall. Beside them were a series of skeletons, some possessing bizarre bone structures that Aleksei couldn't begin to understand.

"Aleksei," Aya breathed, her eyes watering.

Aleksei pressed a finger to his lips, gliding over to Aya and slipping the key into her manacles. They popped open effortlessly.

He bent over Andariana to do the same when a wave of confusion washed across him.

"Aleksei?" Andariana whispered, her brow etched with concern.

Aleksei hardly heard his name. He looked into his queen's eyes and opened his mouth. A strangled gurgle was all he managed before he collapsed across her.

Adam plummeted towards the earth. It was foolhardy to fall such an incredible distance, but judging from the ripples he'd felt in the Archanium, he had very little time.

A figure appeared beneath him, wreathed in yellow-green light and black fire.

Adam wasted no time, plunging past the veil of the Archanium and deep into the Angelic magic of the Seraphima.

Blue light enveloped him, filling him with the cold, crystal purity; the beauty of the Host's combined Song.

With an ease born from years of practice, Adam set the Demon in his sights and unleashed a heavenflare.

The Demon vanished a heartbeat before the flare struck the earth, shattering the air with an earsplitting crack and sending up a spray of burning grit and ash.

Adam's wings spread rapidly from his sides, and the angel felt the powerful muscles in his chest and wings strain and tear as he struck the ground. He reached out with the Seraphima, searching for the Demon.

It was gone.

Adam came carefully to his feet, checking over his wings for damaged feathers. While he had managed to slow himself, he knew he hadn't avoided injury.

He flexed his ivory wings experimentally and found them to be sore but functional. The earth he had struck was unexpectedly soft, as though it had been recently turned. A quick glimpse into the Archanium explained everything he needed to know.

As his head cleared, Adam searched for any signs of the Prince. His Song had located Jonas Belgi moments before the Archanium had exploded into the battle he had just interrupted. Adam was still unsure whether the man lived.

He closed his eyes and listened to the still morning around him. He picked out a few songbirds twittering in the high grass, and something else. A faint scratching, emanating from the east.

Adam hurried in the direction of the sound, finally locating a prone form. It was a young man, likely in his twenty-fifth summer, or near enough.

He was wearing fine enough clothes, though not nearly so fine as would befit a prince. His face was contorted in an expression that Adam had never beheld. But by far the most striking feature were his wide, unblinking eyes.

9

His unblinking, jet-black eyes.

Adam knelt over the man and pressed his hand to Jonas's heart. He quickly summoned a song of healing, steeping himself in the Seraphima. The man's face calmed, and Adam breathed a sigh of relief. The prince was clearly submerged within the Presence, though hopefully not too deeply.

Adam silently breathed a curse to the One-God. It was one thing to locate a man, provided he had the proper musical signature. It was quite another to pry someone from the grip of the Demonic Presence.

Of the entire Host, Adam knew of only one angel he could trust with his quarry's life.

He slipped his arms under the Prince's frame and flapped his wings experimentally. He was indeed sore, but he had no other option. With a few mighty wing-bursts, he was airborne, the Prince of Ilyar cradled against his chest.

"Just see me to Shangri-Uun," he pleaded, glancing to the heavens. "*Please*."

Aya was on her feet before Aleksei struck the floor. She raced to his side, straining to roll him off of Andariana as the queen struggled to breathe.

"*Gods*, but that man is heavy!" Andariana panted as she pulled herself up against the wall.

Aya didn't speak. She found the key, which had skidded against the opposite wall of the chamber, and hurried back to the queen's manacles. The iron cuffs snapped open.

"Where did *that* come from?" Andariana asked, massaging her aching wrists and eyeing the key suspiciously.

"I have no idea. Aleksei had it when he came in. There wasn't exactly a lot of time to question him."

Andariana opened her mouth, but Aya shot her a murderous glare.

"With all due respect, Majesty, keep your mouth shut until we get out of here."

Andariana stared for a moment, but then looked at the floor and nodded.

Aya leaned down beside the Lord Captain and touched her fingers to his chest. She frowned.

"What's wrong with him?" Andariana whispered.

"I have no idea, but it doesn't appear to be physical. This is like nothing I've ever felt. But either way, we need to get out of here as quickly as possible."

"How are we going to carry him?" the queen asked, her voice now shy.

Aya shook her head, "We *can't*. He's far too heavy."

"Can you make him any lighter?"

Aya frowned, "I've never tried anything like that before. And besides, I'm not the only Archanium Magus here. I don't want to draw any unnecessary attention to us."

Andariana sighed, "So what's your plan?"

"We'll have to drag him."

The queen arched a chestnut eyebrow, "*Drag* him?"

"Do you have any other ideas?" Aya shot back.

Andariana paused, then shook her head.

They each took one of his hands and backed slowly towards the door.

"How high up are we?" Andariana whispered as they began the agonizing process of dragging Aleksei's limp body down the seemingly endless flight of stairs.

"I haven't a clue," Aya muttered. "I wasn't any more conscious than you when that...*thing* brought us here."

Aleksei's boots and sword made a terrific amount of noise during their descent, and Aya was surprised no one rushed to root out the source of the ruckus.

They passed a number of rooms, but each time they stopped and Aya peered in, she found only animals in cages. At first, the very sight of the creatures had filled her with horror. The animals closest to the top of the tower positively stank of perverted magics. It was as though someone had taken the glorious light that was the Archanium and filtered it through oily smoke.

But as they descended lower and lower, the animals began to lose their impurities. By the time they reached the last door, the cages were stocked with very simple, unaffected forest creatures.

And yet while her panic over the cages had been slowly subsiding, a new fear was inching into her mind.

This tower had to have a master, yet they hadn't encountered a single human. Nothing besides caged creatures. Suspicions began cropping up in Aya's mind, specters of what might be lurking at the tower's base.

Given her charge of a fallen soldier and a semi-useful queen, Aya did not fancy her odds. Especially if the master of this tower was the same Magus performing such bizarre experiments.

Still, they reached the tower's base without meeting a single figure. Rather than relax her, this only increased Aya's trepidation.

"Hold him while I get the door," Aya whispered, hurrying across the chamber to the two massive wooden doors.

As she reached them, one banged open to reveal a man, silver hair wild in the firelight, his face contorted in rage.

"No one takes my *progeny*," he panted.

Aya threw out her hands, diving into the Archanium and lashing out recklessly.

There was an impact in the air, and the crazed man vanished into the night. Aya didn't stop to ponder what she had just done. Instead, she ran back to where Andariana waited with Aleksei.

She grasped his limp wrist again, pulling him as hard as she could.

"Hurry!" she barked. "He'll be back any moment."

It was something of a surprise when they made it out onto the lawn without encountering him again. Surely such a simple defensive spell should be easy enough to recover from by now....

A thunderbolt struck the earth inches from her foot and exploded in a hail of dirt and stone.

Aya searched for the source of the bolt, her eyes finally settling on the figure of the other Magus, his face more terrible than ever to behold.

Her heart froze.

Above his head, a ball of pure swollen darkness roiled. She had never seen its like before, but it was impossible to miss the intention.

Aya gazed helplessly from the Magus to Andariana. There was a hopelessness in the Queen's eyes that echoed her own. Heart sinking, she understood that it was over.

Aya turned and faced the man. If this was to be her end, she would confront it with as much bravado as she could muster. She knelt next to Aleksei's body, her eyes never leaving the Magus.

Whatever he was conjuring, Aya could only hope that she might shield Aleksei; that providence might smile upon him for a few moments longer.

A hand gripped her shoulder painfully and she screamed in surprise.

The Magus across the field smiled. His hands contorted in occult gesticulations and the darkness tumbled towards them, shrieking as it ripped through the air.

"Close your eyes," came a harsh voice.

Aya obeyed, instinctively throwing up her arm to protect her face. She felt incredible heat, and then the world lurched. She thought she might be sick.

Everything was suddenly silent. Surprised to be alive, she realized that her knees ached and hazarded a glimpse at her surroundings. She was kneeling on a great wooden platform.

She turned and found herself staring into the strange golden eyes of the Ri-Hnon.

"Take heart, Lady Magus," Roux Devaan whispered. "You're safe."

CHAPTER 2
OUT OF TIME

A scream rent the air. Jonas winced at the piercing quality of the sound, the hollow pain in pleading for an end, whatever that may be. With a lurch in his stomach, he recognized the scream as his own.

He had long since lost any concept of time in this twisted world. Undulating shades of yellow and green, like pus oozing from a corrupted wound, made up a sky sometimes flirting with absolute darkness. He lay on the dusty earth, the moments in between screams punctured by violent coughing fits. Beside him lay a pool of what he assumed was blood.

A harsh *thrum* filled the air, and Jonas involuntarily tensed. The buzzing always preceded the screaming.

You are different. *We* like *you. You are* sweeter.

Jonas breathed deeply to calm himself, and only served to fill his lungs with another choking cloud of dust. He exploded into fit of coughing.

"Show yourself!" Jonas demanded brashly, his voice ragged.

The buzzing changed pitch, and for some inexplicable reason, Jonas understood that the entity was laughing at him.

A bold one. We like it. We never taste ones like you.

Jonas could hardly describe why, but the admission that he'd somehow *pleased* the entity made him wretch.

He coughed blood and bile into the fine dust, finally dry-heaving when there was nothing left. He coughed, wiping at his mouth and eyes as tears streamed down his face.

Jonas reached for the comfort of the Archanium and immediately felt an incredible weight upon his chest. He gasped to pull in air, but the pressure was too great.

Foolish little fly, the voice droned. *We don't* like *that here. You can't* have *that here.*

Jonas screamed as the burning pain flashed through him yet again. It seemed stronger this time, though at such intensity Jonas wasn't sure that he could accurately judge the measure of agony he was experiencing.

The pain finally subsided, the pressure lifting. Jonas pulled in greedy lungfuls of dusty air, surprised to be alive. It was difficult to scream without being able to breathe but, Jonas reflected bitterly, he'd managed.

The path was becoming clear to him now, lying there on the desolate plain. No matter how hard he pleaded, the entity showed no mercy. Jonas was beginning to suspect that it possessed no such capacity. His mind quickly accepted this and moved on. No point in begging for something that could never be obtained.

Jonas tried to raise his head, but found he lacked the strength even for that. And there was the second revelation. Without strength, he could never challenge the entity, could never rebel, or free himself. Once more, an untenable situation, and one that Jonas found bitterly unacceptable.

"Show yourself!" he barked again, the absence of pain making him bolder, even with his body sapped of its strength. "Only cowards would behave so!"

As his words echoed away, the same searing pain crashed through him, the same screams, but Jonas tried paying closer attention. He knew he was flirting with oblivion. He slowly realized the buzzing changed each time he spoke, and he thought he might even have figured out some of the entity's moods.

The more he interacted with the entity, though his own part was rather passive, the stronger this suspicion grew. A hypothesis was rapidly building in his mind, though his experiment had yet to present him with the answers he sought. All the while, his body was becoming weaker and weaker. This was a losing battle.

The buzzing dropped into a low hum, and Jonas tensed for yet another round of torturous pain that never came.

We will grant your request, the harsh voice intoned. *You believe you want to see us. We will allow it.* The words seemed to be followed by the same hint of mirth Jonas had detected earlier.

He looked up. The empty plain had now been punctuated by a solitary figure. It was cloaked in a white robe, but even from this distance Jonas could detect the presence of something wholly Demonic.

His suspicions were confirmed.

While he'd never read of anything like this, it didn't surprise him. It was impossible to know how many others might have lost their souls in this very same manner. The chance of any one of them escaping to write of their experience struck him as extremely unlikely.

The white figure floated closer, halting several paces from the prince. Jonas struggled to his feet, trying his level best not to display the sheer fear that filled him.

Apparently, the Demonic Presence liked to play with its food.

Feeling emboldened, he tentatively reached into the Archanium. To his great shock, the flood of color and emotion cascaded into him. He spared a moment to wonder what had changed in the last few hours.

"What are you?" he shouted at the white figure.

It was only as the words left his mouth that Jonas realized the buzzing had ceased entirely.

The figure pushed back its hood, and Jonas stared into a very familiar face. The face of his father.

Of course, the Presence hadn't gotten every detail right, and the eyes had a decidedly yellow-green glow to them. Jonas had little doubt that this particular image had been lifted directly from his mind, because it was the only image of his father he'd ever seen. The portrait that hung in his library.

In spite of the dire situation, Jonas laughed out loud.

This display of amusement seemed to give the figure pause. It frowned for a moment, then began to take a different shape.

Yet even as it did, Jonas knew he'd broken its spell. Though terror still rampaged through him, his awe for the Presence was gone. He felt little security being wrapped in the Archanium as he was, yet he had the sense that it needed his fear far more than it feared his magic.

The white cloth around the figure vanished as the image of his father warped into a snarling, mustard-skinned beast. Spikes protruded from its flesh in odd places, giving it the look of a jaundiced porcupine.

Jonas laughed again, believing fully in his power to delude himself.

The creature launched itself towards the Magus, its great jaw snapping hungrily in the air.

Jonas reflexively invoked a spellform and raised his hand. The creature froze in midair.

The Prince stepped up to it cautiously, looking it up and down as he studied its construction, marveling all the while that his spell had actually worked.

The buzzing roared back into the air and Jonas was hurled to the ground. Yet this time his head felt clearer, sharper than it had in hours.

We do not find your behavior amusing. You will be punished.

Jonas snorted against his better judgment. "So, what was all that before if not 'punishment'? Is this the sum of what you do? Or do you have any *other* tricks you'd like to show me?"

The pitch of the buzz changed dramatically, and this time there was no mistaking the roar of fury that reverberated across the desolate plain.

Jonas raised an arm experimentally, then pushed himself to his feet. He had never lost his connection to the Archanium. This all seemed increasingly strange. Why would the Presence allow him to maintain a source of power?

Unless, of course, the Presence wasn't allowing it at all.

"I'll be going now," he called, looking around as he waited for a response.

None came.

Jonas frowned as he considered the best way to leave. While there were writings about Magi attempting to move from one world to another, the only man known to ever enter and return from the Presence was the Magus Cassian.

The *Demon* Cassian.

It was encouraging, in a way, that Jonas was in the same world Cassian had stumbled into a thousand years prior. But, as for exiting it....

A blazing aurora fell across him, and Jonas turned eagerly. A doorway of white-blue light hung in the air before him.

The Seraphima.

Jonas dove into it, before his unexplained luck ran out.

Aleksei sat up sharply, his hand immediately moving to his sword.

Nothing.

It took Aleksei a moment to realize that he wasn't even in Azarael's tower anymore. He was in a hammock, in what he could only guess was the home of the Ri-Hnon.

A second later he realized that he was naked.

"Great gods," he muttered, "what *happened?*"

He threw off his blankets and stumbled to small chest on the other side of the room.

He found his clothes neatly mended, laundered, and folded. As he pulled his trousers on, he reflected on the night before.

Everything had been moving smoothly, if rather strangely. And yet the moment he'd reached Aya and the Queen there had been that wave of...what? Exhaustion? His first thought was that it had been some sort of Archanium trap.

Yet the longer he thought about it, the more Aleksei realized what had felt so peculiar about that sudden, overpowering rush.

It had come across his bond with Jonas.

Even now he could feel Jonas, alive and far to the north.

Gods, what had happened to his Magus to affect him across such a distance? His heart staggered at the thought.

Aleksei pulled his shirt over his head and stepped lightly out into the hallway leading towards the center of the house. Just from waking up in a separate room, Aleksei knew he had to be in the house of the Ri-Hnon. The other dwellings in the village were far too small to afford such luxuries.

As he walked towards the common room, Aleksei kept one hand on the wall for balance. His legs seemed steady, yet every now and again his knees felt on the verge of buckling. It was a queer feeling, and one he tolerated with increasing irritation.

He stepped into the common room and frowned.

Empty.

He kept moving, heading towards the chambers of the Ri-Hnon. Roux spent a great deal of time there, either listening to the concerns of his people, or meditating to discern the needs of the Seil Wood.

But when Aleksei pushed aside the bark netting that served as a door, he found another empty room.

Something was wrong.

With panic steadily rising in his heart, Aleksei hurried to the front of the dwelling, pulling the door open and staring out into the village.

It was the middle of the day. Sunlight filtered lazily through the canopy, casting a mosaic of light across the great platforms that provided the foundation for the village.

And, arranged like statues across the platforms, were the figures of the Ri-Vhan in various stages of activity.

Children were frozen in the air, chasing one another around couples or groups of adults carrying baskets of bread and piles of laundry. One small girl stood only paces away, a small blue ball hovering inches from her outstretched hands.

Aleksei braced himself against the doorframe, his brain racing to make sense of the impossible scene laid out before him. It was like standing in the middle of a dream.

A flash of motion caught his attention.

Across the platform, he saw a thin black shape dodging in between frozen forms.

Aleksei instinctively hurried after the figure. Whatever it was, perhaps it was causing this unnatural twist in time.

Of course, that begged a question. Why could *Aleksei* move? Why wasn't he frozen along with everyone else?

Aleksei pushed the thoughts from his mind and hurried after the shadowy figure, his legs gaining confidence as he moved. He ducked under outstretched arms and leapt over motionless children. It all became a blur as he tracked his prey.

As he ran, Aleksei tested the air for a scent.

Anything.

The figure's movement was the only thing moving the air, and thus Aleksei found the scent easy enough to pick out. It struck him like a thunderbolt.

Azarael.

Aleksei's bare feet pounded the boards of the great platform, gaining speed now that he had the quarry's scent in his nostrils.

Azarael stepped out from the shadows a moment before Aleksei crashed into him.

"Interesting," the Magus muttered. "You're out of time."

Aleksei's eyes immediately shot to the bundle cradled in Azarael's arms. A Healer's bag.

Before the Magus could say anything else, Aleksei's hand darted out and ripped the bundle away.

"Get out of here. Now!" Aleksei roared.

Azarael smirked and raised a hand. Aleksei's throat clenched in fear as the stupidity of what he'd just done came crashing in on him. He might very well have made the last mistake of his life. His hands instinctively rose to ward off whatever spell the Magus was about to level against him.

Azarael cried out.

Aleksei opened his eyes to see three blood-red tendrils leading from his wrist into the Magus's face.

Aleksei recoiled, the tendrils flowing back across the gap between them, splashing back into inky night across his shoulders.

Azarael staggered backwards, staring at Aleksei in what could only be called dread. He raised a hand, and Aleksei felt an impact in his chest as the Magus vanished.

Time slammed back into place. The city came to life in an instant, and Aleksei dropped to the platform as the world lurched around him.

"Lord Captain?"

Aleksei looked up. The world spun around him. He thought he might be sick.

Slowly, Aya's face came into focus.

"*Aleksei?* Are you alright? What are you doing out of bed?"

He waved off the barrage of questions, "Did you see him? Where did he go?"

She frowned, "Who?"

"*Azarael.* He was here."

Aya stiffened, "In the village? When?"

Aleksei grunted in frustration. "Just now. He was right here. He was trying to steal this." Aleksei lifted the Healer's bag.

Aya frowned, "What would he want with that?"

"When I was in his tower last night, I saw Ri-Vhan potions in each of the chambers. I think he uses them to...alter his victims." He was about to continue when he noticed an odd expression cross her face. "What? What's wrong?"

"Aleksei," she said awkwardly, "you've been unconscious for four *days.* I was beginning to wonder if you were *ever* going to wake up."

Aleksei rested his head in his hands. That would certainly explain why his legs had been so unsteady upon waking. He wondered when he'd last eaten. "I think there's something wrong with me," he said finally.

"Are you ill?" she asked, kneeling to look into his eyes. "You look flushed."

He could tell she was doing her best to assess him, but he shook his head. "Not like that. I'm flushed because I just ran across the entire platform."

She arched an eyebrow, "Aleksei, I've been standing here for almost half an hour. I didn't see anything unusual, and I *certainly* didn't see you racing through the village."

"Then where'd I come from?" he snapped.

"Pardon?"

"I wasn't here a moment ago, was I?"

Aya shrugged, "I thought you merely stumbled as you were approaching me."

"I was chasing Azarael. I opened the door to Roux's house, and everything was frozen. It was like time had just *stopped*. But I could move. And so could Azarael."

Aya laughed, but it sounded hollow, "Aleksei, what you're describing is impossible."

"Azarael said something to me," Aleksei muttered. "When I caught up with him, he said I was 'out of time'. I just assumed that meant he was going to kill me."

"And now you think...what exactly?"

He could tell Aya was having difficulty understanding what he was trying to say. Gods, *he* was having a hard-enough time trying to wrap his mind around the implications.

"My bond to Jonas is tied to time," he said in a measured tone, trying to convince himself as much as Aya. "When I collapsed in the tower, whatever knocked me out came across the bond. I think that whatever happened to the bond changed...time. At least around me. Does that sound insane?"

He looked up and could hardly believe what his eyes beheld. Rather than Aya's patient if perplexed face staring back at him, now he saw only blurs. All around him, streaks of color and light were flashing this way and that, buffeting him with an intense whirlwind of motion.

"Great gods," he whispered, "what's *happened* to me?"

Jonas opened a cautionary eye.

The filtered sunlight came as a welcome change from the harsh, putrid light of the Presence.

He breathed a sigh of relief and immediately started coughing uncontrollably.

"Easy, boy," came an unfamiliar voice.

A wave of ice washed through Jonas and he inhaled deeply. Clearly.

Jonas looked up into a face that was at once strange and familiar. The man smiled and Jonas blinked. It was almost like looking in a mirror.

"Who are you?" he managed.

The man straightened, and for the first time Jonas noticed angular gray wings stretching behind him. "My name is Xavathan. And you're Jonas Belgi, lest I'm much mistaken."

Jonas sat up and frowned, "I recognize the name. You're the fourth-born Seraph."

Xavathan's mouth quirked to the side, "You could also just call me 'Uncle'."

"I apologize...Uncle. I'm not accustomed to thinking of my Angelic family as much more than names on a page."

Xavathan's face softened, "And why shouldn't you? God knows we've been absent enough from your life. But take heart. You're here now, among family. And you've survived what I can only imagine to be quite the harrowing journey."

Images tumbled through Jonas's mind, images that should have made no sense, though he knew they were real enough. And with the images came the sounds. The horrific *thrum* of the Presence.

"Come back, boy."

Xavathan's voice broke through the memories like sun through fog. Jonas blinked and looked into his uncle's kind gray eyes. "How long will I be like this?"

His uncle shrugged, "Difficult to say. You're the first one to come through that whole ordeal alive. I had a look at some of the Fallen from Krilya, but they didn't last long.

"To be honest, I'm amazed that you're even conscious. I suppose your survival is less surprising, given your heritage. But angel or no, you've accomplished something unheard of."

A thought struck Jonas, "How did I get here?"

Xavathan smiled, "Ah, yes, you wouldn't be knowing too much

about that, I suppose." He turned from Jonas and raised his voice, "Adam, he's awake."

Jonas frowned. Adam?

"The young man who brought you here has been very anxious to see that you made it through. I finally had to send him to bed in the small hours of the morning. But now that you've come back to us...."

Xavathan's words were interrupted as a young angel burst into the room. His face was contorted in concern, his dark brows shadowing his clear blue eyes.

"Is he alright?" the words were already out of his mouth before he took in the sight of Jonas sitting up, looking back at him.

"He's doing well, considering," Xavathan said softly.

Adam turned to Jonas and dropped to a knee, "Master Cherub, it gladdens my heart to see you well."

Jonas frowned, "Angel Adam, stand. Please. *I'm* the one who should be supplicating myself before *you*. And it seems I owe you a great debt of gratitude."

Adam looked down at the floor, "I only wish I'd found you before the Demon ensnared you."

Jonas froze. Adam had been *looking* for him? Until that moment, Jonas had merely assumed that Adam had felt the Presence and had gone to investigate. There were enough aeries on the Madrhal Plain that it wouldn't have been out of the question for an Angelic scout to be in the general area.

But the angel's words gave Jonas a very different impression.

"You were looking for me?" Jonas asked casually.

Adam stiffened, "I was, Master Cherub."

"May I ask why?"

"The Angelus asked that I find you and bring you to her, Master Cherub. That is all she would tell me. She gave me this."

The angel handed Jonas a thin strip of parchment. At first, he wasn't sure what he was looking at. After turning it over, he realized it was musical notation.

"What is this?" he asked, straining to make sense of the progression.

"It's your name, Master Cherub," Adam said, sounding a touch uncomfortable.

Jonas looked up, startled, "You mean anyone who has this progression of notes can *find* me?"

Adam shook his head, "No, Master Cherub. Only an angel or

someone of Angelic descent like yourself, who can command Song, can find you through the notes on that parchment. Even then, access to something that powerful is a closely guarded secret. I doubt anyone but the Angelus had ever seen your name in Song before she sent me to find you."

Jonas arched an eyebrow, doing his level best to commit the progression to memory. If it was a tool that could be used against him, he might as well make sure he knew it too.

"Sing it for me," he said softly.

Adam glanced about nervously, "Here, Master Cherub? Now?"

Jonas looked at his uncle and the older angel sighed impatiently. "You've shown the boy this much, Adam. You might as well."

Adam paused for a long moment, then nodded. "Yes, Master Seraph."

Jonas shivered as Adam grasped the Archanium. It was certainly different than feeling another Magus do the same thing, yet the change in the air around them was unmistakable.

Adam's soft baritone sent waves of ice through Jonas as he sat there, transfixed by the simple melody that was his name. As the last note faded away, the ice was replaced by a warmth that filled Jonas's entire body. His head felt clearer than it had in ages.

"Did you feel it, Master Cherub?" Adam asked tentatively.

Jonas nodded slowly. "What was that?"

Xavathan placed a gentle hand on Jonas's shoulder. "Your name, boy. And when Sung from a place of magic, it has the power to restore you. Or, in the hands of your enemies, to harm you. This is one reason its secrecy is paramount."

"I think I understand that a bit better now," Jonas whispered.

He considered the piece of parchment in his hand for a moment before looking up at Adam, "Am I supposed to hand this back, or can I destroy it?"

Adam shrugged, "It's yours more than anyone else's, Master Cherub. Do as you see fit."

Jonas reached into the Archanium to incinerate the tiny scrap.

He hardly had a chance to scream before he blacked out.

Lord Simon Declan squinted into the distance. It was still leagues away, but he thought he could make out the rude outline of a country village.

Summoning his remaining strength, Declan forced himself to stagger towards the murky shape on the horizon.

Gods, but it had been days since he'd slept. The haunting memories of Mornj still ricocheted around in his skull, the screams mixed with the stench of burning flesh. It had been harrowing. Worse, it had confirmed his deepest fears.

Declan had never been in favor of the rebellion against the Queen. He was a loyal man, and never one to harbor delusions of grandeur. He had no appetite for power.

Still, there had been little choice at the time. Had he stayed on the side of the Queen, his lands would have been overrun, his people slaughtered. He had been too vulnerable, too weak to stand up to Chancellor Perron.

To stand up to Bael.

But as the garrison in Mornj erupted, Declan had seen his chance to escape. Who was to say he hadn't been killed in the very same explosion? Flight would give him time to regroup, to think things through, and then decide how best to proceed.

That had been before. After losing his way on the southern roads, and a handful of days wandering the wilds on the Southern Plain, Declan was seriously rethinking his decision. He was no hunter. He had no knowledge of survival in the open field, and now his ignorance would very likely result in his death.

The toe of his boot caught a stone, and he suddenly found himself facedown on the ground. With a groan, he rolled over and tried to sit up, but found he lacked the strength. He felt oddly warm.

Perhaps this is a fitting end for a traitor, he thought bitterly, the cold sun glowering down upon him.

A shadow blocked the light and Declan squinted, trying to make out the shape that hovered above him. A halo of light surrounded the form, making its details impossible to distinguish.

"Mother! Mother, come quick."

It was a woman. Her long auburn hair brushed against his face, and Declan wondered if he was not at last being carried to the Aftershadow. Surely this woman was a spirit, come to whisk him away from this wretched world.

A second shadow joined the first.

"Fetch your brothers, dear," the second voice said. Another woman, this one much older.

"Who are you?" Declan rasped.

The older woman looked down at him as the younger one vanished into the grass. "Relax, dear. You look a little worse for wear. Rest now, and we'll see what can be done for you."

Declan let his head lie upon the hard-packed earth. Rest. Yes, rest would be the best thing for him.

The old woman reached out a hand and laid it against his forehead. "Sleep."

Declan hardly heard the command before he sank into blissful oblivion.

CHAPTER 3

AWAKENING

"Lord Captain?"

Aleksei sat a few paces away, staring into the glowing embers of the hearth. Try as he might to focus on his bond with Jonas, the only thing he'd managed to divine was that his Magus was rapidly growing farther away. North.

"Lord Captain?" the voice came again.

With an effort, Aleksei returned to the moment at hand. He looked up into the face of a young Magus. "What can I do for you?"

"Lord Captain, the Ri-Vhan have found a wounded man, a Legionnaire wandering on the forest floor. He is incoherent, but we believe him to be one of ours, Sir. Magus Aya asked that you come see him."

Aleksei rose swiftly, following the young man out of Roux's house and across the platform. A hundred paces away, he saw a crowd of people.

He smelled blood, and something else...odors that only came from deep within the body. If he was picking up these varied notes, the man didn't have long to live.

He ran the rest of the way, pushing past the crowd of onlookers. Most, he noted, were Magi. Their faces were white.

In the center of the gathering, Aya knelt over the prone form of a solider in simple, nondescript Ilyari peasant garb.

Aleksei's frown deepened.

He knelt next to Aya and looked into the man's face.

It was Sergeant Ballard.

Aleksei let loose a curse as he scanned the man's wounds. He looked at Aya and she shook her head.

"I can't fix this. I wouldn't even know where to begin."

Aleksei ran a hand through his hair, "Did you send for the Healers?"

She nodded, "But I don't know if we're in time. Some of these injuries are deep."

Aleksei let out a breath in frustration. He had left Sergeant Ballard in command of the insurrection forces within Kalinor. What could possibly have made the man abandon his post and follow them into the Wood?

Whatever it was, Aleksei knew it had to be important.

"We can't afford to lose him. Whatever his reasons for coming after us, he knows something, and he risked his life to get that information to us. He could have just as easily sent an errand boy, but he came himself. We can't lose him."

Aya's face settled into a resigned mask. "I'm sorry, Aleksei. This is beyond my abilities."

Aleksei gritted his teeth, rapidly assessing his options. Where were the bloody *Healers*?

As the seconds ticked by, his sense of urgency grew. Finally, he leaned forward and grasped Ballard by the jaw, looking into the man's eyes. They were glassy. Even though they were open, Aleksei knew the man wasn't aware of his surroundings.

Aleksei closed his eyes. He removed his hand from the man's face, planting it firmly on the soldier's chest. With as much control as he could muster, Aleksei called the Mantle forth.

A few night-black talons rippled down his forearm and dipped into the man's wounds.

Aleksei's eyes snapped open, and he gasped in shock. His entire body felt as though it had been rent apart. Still, he kept the tendrils of the Mantle where they were, feeding his life force into Sergeant Ballard.

A warning sounded in his head. He ignored it, pouring more of his energy into the sergeant.

The warning intensified into a wail of panic. Aleksei suddenly understood that if he let much more of his energy leech out, he would die.

With a frustrated cry, he ripped his hand away. The Mantle receded up his arm, vanishing beneath his shirtsleeve. He lay back on the platform, his tortured grimace fading as the pain of Ballard's wounds slowly eased.

Aya's face appeared in his vision, and he searched her face for any sign that it had worked. She looked like a vision of grim death itself.

With his remaining strength, Aleksei pushed himself up on one arm. Not far away, Sergeant Ballard was groaning as the Healers painted him with their potions. From his vantage, Aleksei couldn't make out much.

Aya gripped his shoulder angrily, and he looked back into her gold-flecked green eyes. "What in the gods' names do you think you're *doing?*" she shouted.

"Saving a life. Or at least trying to."

"You could have killed yourself. You could have killed *Jonas,* for all you know. For a common soldier," she whispered harshly, suddenly conscious of all the onlookers now staring at the two of them.

Aleksei managed a small smile, "But I didn't, did I? How is he?"

Aya scowled, "He'll live. He's not completely recovered, but the Healers say his wounds are mostly superficial. Now."

Aleksei pushed himself into a sitting position, leaning forward heavily. "Do you even know what I did?"

"I know enough of it. Anyone with a pair of eyes could tell you were feeding your life into him. Do you have any idea how *dangerous* that is? Especially on someone so grievously injured? You came very close to trading your life for his."

Aleksei shrugged his shoulders, "I know what I did, Aya. But thanks for the lecture."

Her face softened a touch, and the anger left her. "I simply wish you weren't so cavalier with your life. Your life means more than any soldier's. You are bound to the Prince. The both of you have gifts that we can't afford to lose. Especially now."

Aleksei nodded, "I know. I just used one of my 'gifts' to save a man with valuable information that, especially now, could make a great deal of difference for us."

"But you don't *know* that. You're simply assuming that this man can help us."

Aleksei shook his head, "I know Tobin Ballard. He's as good a man as we have in the Legions. I'm telling you, whatever his decision for coming into the Wood, he didn't make it lightly."

He finally found the strength to push himself to his feet. Aya caught his shoulder as he stumbled forward. His head was swimming. He felt like he hadn't eaten in weeks.

"I need to lie down a while. Let me know when the sergeant has regained consciousness."

Aya sighed as two strapping Ri-Vhan men came and relieved her of Aleksei's weight. She watched his back as it vanished between people in the crowd.

She hated being so cross with him, but the truth of the matter was that she had been scared half to death. She hadn't told him that, after he withdrew the Mantle, he'd lain on the platform, semi-conscious and barely breathing for almost three minutes.

But beyond even that, she was terrified of the Mantle. The power Aleksei so casually wielded was an instrument of life and death with such breathtaking simplicity and brutality that she could hardly wrap her mind around it.

The Archanium was a vast and complex network of energies that she'd only just begun to grasp in her lifetime of study.

The Mantle was not.

It was a weapon, and yet she had just seen Aleksei tap its power in a completely new way. From the looks on the faces around her, they had been as unaware of the Mantle's second nature as she.

She wasn't even sure they'd witnessed everything it was capable of. And of course, the fact that Aleksei seemed to understand what to do, that he had found that capability, raised even more frightening questions.

A fist-sized hole blasted through the marble vase. It ricocheted off the mantelpiece before falling to the floor and shattering into jagged chunks.

Bael clenched his jaw, flopping back into a plush chair. How could this keep happening? Every time he was about to spring the trap around Jonas Belgi, the man managed to escape in the last moment.

He had even plunged the Prince into the depths of the Demonic Presence. And for what? For some fool angel to swoop down and save him. It was beyond infuriating.

We told you, Pilgrim. We are not strong enough to challenge the Seraphima. We are still recalling this world and its strange magics. You did not release Us only to be bested so soon.

"I know that," Bael snapped. "But do not forget that I sought you out for one reason. To take back what is *mine*."

Yes, Pilgrim, but you must have patience. Time means nothing to you now. You are not vulnerable in this world as normal men are. You are near to a god.

"Gods don't run from flying rats. Gods smite them into oblivion," Bael snarled.

He could feel the deep, buzzing laughter in the center of his chest. They were amused at his insolence, his impatience. He hardly cared. His single-minded determination had gotten him *this* far.

"After all, what was the point of bringing you back if you can't give me what I want?"

We did not say We could not fulfill your desires. We said you must be patient. *We are not strong enough to lay waste to the angels. Their numbers are too great and their power a poison to Us. We are newly reborn. But We can grant your desire in other ways.*

Bael shrugged, "I don't have the time to run off chasing Jonas and his pauper Knight. Not that it would matter if I *did*. It seems every time I'm ready to strike, they vanish into thin air."

The buzz that he had come to understand as amusement shifted to a sharp clicking that pricked underneath his skin like a thousand spider bites.

There are things you must collect for Us, Pilgrim. But should you find them, We will see to your desires.

"I don't understand."

The power you wield through Us has facets beyond black fire. That is but a trifle compared to what you will one day command. There are other facets, other methods to achieving your ends. Bring Us what We require, and We will employ one.

Bael's mind lit with understanding, "We're sending an assassin?"

The buzzing returned, *A limited way of understanding Our thoughts, but you are near enough.*

"And before Jonas knows the trap's been sprung, he'll be dead," Bael chuckled.

The clicking returned, *Not the Prince. He is protected by the angels. His blood alone gives him some protection from Our power.*

"Then who?" Bael demanded. "You said you would see my desires came to fruition. My *desire* is to take everything I can from Jonas Belgi, for taking everything from me."

We know your desires, Pilgrim. And you will see them come to pass. But We cannot send death to the Prince. We will send it to the other, the Hunter.

Bael felt immediately foolish. His single-minded determination was making him blind to basic reason. "Of course," he muttered. "Why make this any harder than we must? So what are we going to do to him?"

The Demonic thrum filled him until he thought he might shake apart.

We will call the wind, and he shall vanish.

Aleksei was marching towards the Healers' quarters when he saw a familiar form stalking towards him. With an inward groan, he slowed his progress to wait for her.

"Lord Captain," Andariana said as she fell in stride with him.

Aleksei gave a deep nod of his head, "Majesty."

"I received word that Sergeant Ballard was awake. I would very much like to speak with him, before you begin your...interrogation."

Aleksei smothered a rueful chuckle, "Majesty, I'm not going to *interrogate* Sergeant Ballard. I'm going to find out why he nearly died abandoning his post. And to be perfectly frank, I'd appreciate it if you remained outside while I speak with him. At least for the moment."

Andariana arched an eyebrow, "I shall do no such thing. I wish to speak with him, and I shall do so."

Aleksei came to a halt. "Majesty, you may speak with him when I am finished, but I need to find out what was so urgent, and your presence would not make that especially easy for him."

She frowned, "What are you talking about?"

Aleksei sighed, "Majesty, with all due respect, your presence won't exactly put him at ease. I don't want him worrying about whether or not he's saying the right things, or the things he *thinks* you want to hear. I don't want him to worry about trying to bow to you. I want him to tell me why he came here.

"I don't completely believe that your presence in the room will cause him that much grief, but he's in a weakened state. After I find out what I need to know, you're free to do as you wish. But for the moment, I'm asking you to wait outside."

She stared up at him for a long while before finally nodding, "Very well, Captain Drago. I will do as you ask."

He smiled, "Thank you, Majesty. I appreciate your understanding."

Without waiting for a response, Aleksei started away again. He could feel her eyes on his back, could hear her following him, but slower this time. Less insistent. Less demanding.

Her reaction didn't really surprise him. It was his job to think like a soldier, hers to think like a queen. And he appreciated that; at least she tried to understand his point of view.

Jonas had certainly given him a wealth of understanding about her thought processes.

He felt a sharp pang at the thought of Jonas. He'd been so busy since the night of the invasion, he hadn't had any leisure time to speak of. Worse, he knew something had happened to his Magus. He didn't know what, precisely, but if it could affect the bond from such a distance, it had to be serious.

More than that, he desperately missed the man. He missed Jonas's wit, the way he made Aleksei feel smart, valued. The only other person who'd ever provided that feeling of worth for him was his father.

But at least he was certain Henry Drago was safe in the hills with General Rysun and a sizable force of men around him. With any luck, they were marching for Keldoan at that very moment.

While not as heavily fortified as Kalinor, Keldoan had sturdy walls. It had been constructed during the Dominion Wars, and its walls still retained the shields imbued by the Magi of the time. It was the next best option for what Aleksei had in mind.

He stepped into the small hut to find Sergeant Ballard sitting upright in a chair near the fire. The man looked pale, and his right arm was bound in a sling. Aleksei didn't remember much about healing him, but he *did* recall an urgent need to put the blood back where it belonged, to seal that which was severed, and restore the natural order of things. He supposed that a broken bone hadn't registered as a big enough threat to the man's life to enter his awareness.

When Sergeant Ballard saw him, his face lit with a weary smile. Aleksei realized that he wasn't looking at the soldier right then; he was looking at the man.

He was glad he'd asked Andariana to stay outside.

Before Ballard could to attempt a salute, Aleksei flashed a smile, "Tobin," he said softly, setting the tone, "it's good to see you breathing."

"Lord Captain," Ballard said with a small nod of his head, "I understand you had something to do with that."

Aleksei shrugged, "I did what I had to, and I'm glad for it." He sat in the chair opposite the Sergeant and leaned forward, "But beyond checking on your health, I think you know why I'm here."

Tobin's smile faded, "Lord Captain," he glanced up at Aleksei's face, "*Aleksei*, you didn't risk your life to save a soldier. I know that."

"You wouldn't have come here unless you had no other choice."

"If I'd felt I had the luxury of time, I'd have arranged a more cautious way to get information to you. I did as you commanded, went into hiding as a peasant. The rebels are mostly tolerant of us. They seem to understand they have nothing to gain from terrorizing the citizens. But they also made it very clear that they were in charge now, and that their idea of rule wasn't going to be quite as...lax as it had been under the Queen."

Aleksei nodded, "If they begin by making you wary, afraid, they have to waste less energy dealing out punishments. It serves to make their lives easier. I'm sure there were one or two examples for effect."

Tobin looked away, "There were. More than were absolutely necessary."

Aleksei reached out and grasped the sergeant's good shoulder, "Don't dwell on it if you don't have to."

Tobin finally met Aleksei's gaze, "I felt so...*helpless*, watching it. It made me angrier than I've been in my life. I wanted to *do* something, but I knew if I pulled my sword I would just end up like the rest of them, with my head on a bloody pike. I could do more good in secrecy."

Aleksei held his emotions in check. It was one of the terrible realities of being a soldier. Sometimes a few had to be sacrificed to save the many. But knowing that didn't make it any easier to endure.

"When everyone had been properly subdued, one of their generals, General Barnes," Aleksei nodded that he knew the man, "came through with a squad of soldiers. He was pulling men from the crowd. Some of them were hardly more than boys, Aleksei. He pulled me along, too."

Aleksei sat back in his chair, listening to the sergeant tell his story, his mind racing at the same time to fit the pieces together.

"When they had perhaps two thousand of us gathered in Butcher's Square, General Barnes addressed us. He said we had been selected to join their forces, and that time was of the essence." Tobin sighed deeply, "His scouts had found signs of a large force of soldiers heading west. We were to be part of a strike team sent after them."

Aleksei's jaw clenched. "This news isn't unexpected, but it's not welcome either."

Tobin nodded, "It gets worse. Lord Captain, they're splitting up their army. They're sending fifty-thousand after Colonel Rysun."

Aleksei almost retched right there. That was nearly twice the size of his force. They would be crushed into oblivion, his father along with them.

"We can't let that happen," he whispered.

Tobin groaned, "I agree, Lord Captain, I do. But I'm not sure what we're supposed to *do* about it. The odds could be worse than two to one, but they hardly favor us. And if that force catches Colonel Rysun, they'll have to fight in the open."

Aleksei shuddered with a renewed sense of panic. He now understood why Tobin had been so desperate to reach him. Still, it had bought them some time. Rysun would be pushing his men at a double march. Twenty-six thousand could move a great deal faster than fifty. General Barnes would have to push his men nearly to death to reach them in time.

And then he paused. It still didn't completely add up.

"Tobin, how did you get away from an army that size? Surely they were watching for deserters."

Tobin drew a deep breath, "General Barnes sent the two thousand he picked out in Kalinor ahead with an expeditionary force. Perhaps another five or six thousand."

And then Aleksei finally understood. General Barnes hadn't been selecting soldiers; he'd been rounding up decoys. "They'll catch Rysun's men and delay them until the larger force arrives. Rysun will waste more time if he thinks they can stomp out a smaller force. By the time they take them out, they'll be tired and wounded, but over-confidant from the victory."

"Exactly, Sir. When they sent us out of Kalinor, I found a few men willing to help me escape. They pulled a diversion while I escaped with two other men in the night. The three of us split up, so that even if they got two of us, the last might make it through."

Aleksei shook his head. The cost of this information was higher than he'd originally thought.

Finally he stood. "Thank you for this, Sergeant Ballard. I believe there's someone outside who would like to thank you for your bravery, and then you need some rest. I'll see to this."

Ballard nodded with a smile, "Thank you, Lord Captain. It's an honor to be of service."

Aleksei gave him a crisp salute, then stepped out of the hut. Andariana was waiting patiently. When she saw his face, her own fell, "How serious is it?"

"We're in great deal of danger, Majesty. I have to leave immediately. After you've spoken with the Sergeant, and that man has done a great service to us all, I want you and the Princess to go to Taumon."

Andariana's eyebrows shot up, "Taumon? Why would you have us go there?"

Aleksei tried to keep his voice calm. He was practically in a panic, "Majesty, Taumon is one of the last cities you'd be expected to head for. The rebel forces are chasing Colonel Rysun's men towards Keldoan. It's the largest force we command. They'll assume you'll be where you're safest, surrounded by the greatest collection of Legionnaires loyal to you.

"The commander of forces in Keldoan is Colonel Walsh. He has an additional three thousand under his command. It's also the most defensible position outside of Kalinor. That is why you and the Princess will hide in Taumon. It's in the opposite direction from Keldoan."

"You can't get any further in the *realm*, Captain."

Aleksei nodded, "It's also on the Autumn Sea. From Taumon, I want you to commission a boat and take it to Zirvah."

"*Zirvah?*" Andariana shrieked. "To the end of the bloody world?"

"The Dalitians will grant you sanctuary. Our enemy's force is two-pronged, Majesty. Once in Zirvah, you can easily get to Kuuran. Krasik would be mad to attack Dalita. It doesn't further his goals, and would only serve to wipe out the force he's carved for himself.

"But that's not even the most important point. The Magus Bael has unleashed the Demonic Presence back into our world, but its magic is still weak. He, however, is not. And neither are his Magi.

"What's more, they're far more capable than your own Magi, thanks to Sammul's lifetime of treachery. Seeking the protection of the angels would thus serve you two-fold. The Demon won't set foot within a hundred leagues of anyone commanding the Seraphima until the Presence is properly established in our world, and his Magi would be fools to attack any Angelic stronghold, much less the Basilica itself.

"And, even if Krasik and Perron suspect that you'll seek the aid of the Angelus, they'll never expect you to take such a circuitous route. They'll be watching the Madrhal Plain, none the wiser while you sail around it. As long as you're alive, they don't get what they want."

"Except my bloody realm," she snapped.

"As long as you're alive," he repeated patiently, "the people of this realm have someone to rally around. At the worst, once they see that Perron's promises of a glorious revolution are full of holes, they'll yearn for the way things used to be. With you alive, they'll have a symbol of that. Without you, it'll be much more difficult to raise an effective resistance. Please, Majesty, I'm only trying to keep you safe."

She sighed deeply, "I know, Lord Captain. And I appreciate your dedication to my safety."

"So, I have your word that you will follow my advice, and leave immediately for Taumon?"

Andariana nodded wearily, "You have my word, Lord Captain. I find now that I would rather be inconvenienced and alive than headstrong and dead. I will go to Dalita and beg the aid of the Angelus. The gods know I hate that woman, but she won't refuse me."

She arched a chestnut eyebrow, "And what of you, Lord Captain? What will you be doing while I'm off on my merry little adventure?"

Aleksei rubbed his temples. His head was beginning to pound something fierce. "Hopefully, I'll be winning your war, Majesty." He looked up into her emerald eyes. Gods, but they made him think of Jonas. With an effort, he quashed the ache in his heart.

"And now I'm off. The Ri-Vhan will see to any needs you may have. I'll speak to Roux first, and make sure you have an escort out of the Wood. It will save you time. Do you have somewhere to go? Someone who can help you look less like...that?"

The woman bristled, but after a long pause she nodded, "I have a...friend in Timurus. She ought to be able to help us look the part again."

Aleksei sighed. At least one thing was going their way. So far, at least.

She offered him a small smile, "Thank you. I'm once again reminded why my nephew loves you the way he does. You have a good heart, Aleksei Drago. A kind heart. Even when some of us are too stubborn to use reason, you won't let us suffer the results. I appreciate that more than I can say."

Aleksei bowed his head, "Take care, Majesty. May the gods watch over you."

And then he was away, running across the platform to collect his things. He was shoveling supplies into his pack when Roux walked into the room.

"Heading out?"

Aleksei nodded, "I've just received some pretty dire intelligence. I have to leave immediately. I need you to get an escort for the Queen and the Princess to the eastern edge of the Wood. If you could personally follow them to Timurus, I'd be even more in your debt."

Roux frowned, "Timurus?"

Aleksei nodded as he strapped on his sword, "I'm sending them to Taumon. Tell Aya that I want the Magi to leave as soon as Sergeant Ballard is well enough. He is to guide them through the hills to Keldoan. Avoid the main roads at all costs. There are few enough Magi that it shouldn't be difficult. I need them to get to Keldoan before Rysun's force reaches it. If we're going to avoid a total slaughter, no one can afford to delay right now."

Roux blinked at the flurry of information. He stood in the doorway, collecting his thoughts as Aleksei finished packing, then followed him outside. "I'll do as you say, Cousin. I'll escort the Princess and the Queen to the edge of the Wood, and then follow them to Timurus myself. I wouldn't trust to it anyone else. And I'll pass your request on to Aya. What if she refuses?"

Aleksei considered, "Tell her that if she wishes to escape the Demon's claws, she'll do as I say. I doubt she wants to be any closer to that vile piece of shit than she absolutely has to be."

Roux shrugged, "Consider it done."

"Can you take me to the southwest? I want to be as far south of Kalinor as possible."

Roux clapped a hand on Aleksei's shoulder and the world melted into a tangle of white and gray.

CHAPTER 4

SIN AND SACRIFICE

Jonas sat up gingerly, supporting himself with one arm while experimentally brushing the front of his face. He felt a hard crust around his eyes and began peeling it away. It felt rough; sticky.

He carefully opened one eye, then the other. He was in a soft bed. He breathed a sigh of relief at waking once again in his own world, rather than trapped in the hell of the Presence.

A quick look at his hand confirmed his suspicions. His eyes had been crusted in blood. *Old* blood.

Gods, how long have I been out? he wondered idly.

Jonas came gently to his feet, relieved to see that, besides being a little shaky, he seemed unaffected. He was nearly to the door when his uncle rushed in and braced him. "You shouldn't be standing. You're far too weak."

Jonas frowned, "I feel fine. And I'd like to wash the blood off my face anyhow. Where's the basin?"

Xavathan sighed and relaxed his hold on Jonas, leading him to the stand and filling the marble bowl. Jonas scrubbed irritably until the water was a cloudy pink.

When satisfied, he made his way to a chair and sat back heavily. Xavathan had been right, he *was* weak. But he wasn't about to spend any more time than necessary covered in his own blood.

"You gave me quite the fright, boy," Xavathan said, stepping back and eyeing Jonas cautiously.

Jonas's eyes narrowed, "Why are you watching me like that? You act like I could burst into flame at any moment."

With a fatherly smile, Xavathan relaxed, "I apologize. It's just that I'm not exactly sure what to expect with you. It was remarkable enough that we brought you out of the Presence. That alone would not have been possible if you hadn't gained some sort of foothold of your own in that world."

"Foothold?"

"Some modicum of autonomy. From what we know of the Presence, it is simply a place your soul is sent to endure horrific torture, seemingly for eternity. Almost like the lowest depths of your blasphemous After-shadow. Those plunged into the Presence can escape through the Seraphima, but from our understanding, you'd have to be aware that help is being offered.

"That you had awareness means you were able to avoid the pain, even if for a moment."

Jonas nodded, "That's about right. How have you learned so much about the Presence if I'm the only one to return from it?"

Xavathan shrugged, "Through healers. Many have devoted their lives to helping those trapped in the Presence. Sometimes, a healer will get a small insight from the other side. After hearing the many visions from different healers, we began to realize that there were common threads running through every account."

Jonas smiled weakly, "Well, you have it mostly right. I wasn't aware of any other people trapped there, just me. But I did manage to stand up and account for myself, at least a little. Before they slapped me down again, the portal opened and I dove into it."

Xavathan frowned, "I've never heard anyone speak about it like that. Never in terms of standing and motion, only pain. I imagined it to be more like a formless void, much like the Seraphima."

Jonas shook his head, "Not exactly. At least, not for me. As I said, I was alone, but it felt real to me. Alien...Other, but real nonetheless. There were voices. A lot of voices, but all saying the same thing. They had an odd speech pattern, and everywhere around me the air was buzzing. I got the impression the buzzing came from the same place as the voices, but I can't remember much more than that at the moment."

His uncle's eyes were wide, "This is remarkable. I've never heard such a clear description of the place before. Jonas, if you can speak to some of the angels in the Basilica, you could teach them more about the Demonic Presence in an hour than we've discerned in the last thousand years."

"I can't," Jonas said automatically. When he saw the hurt in Xavathan's face, he softened, "I apologize. I'm sure that sounds like ingratitude. I would be far worse off without the aid you have provided me, but I have to get to my Knight immediately. There's something going on with our bond. Something is very wrong."

Xavathan pondered Jonas's words for a moment before responding, "I have books here, books of history. I seem to recall several Magi who were lost to the Presence. Some of them had Bonded, even back then. I remember reading about the Bonded, some sort of reaction to their bond having passed through to the other side. We might be able to learn something of value on the way to Kuuran."

Jonas sighed, "Uncle, I *just* said I have to get to Aleksei." And then he realized that Xavathan wasn't offended. He was sad. "What is it?" Jonas growled. "What haven't you told me?"

His uncle fetched a stool from across the room and set it right before Jonas. He sat and pressed his fingertips together for a long moment before speaking.

"To start, for the record, that's the second time I've saved your life."

The prince frowned, "Second time?"

"I healed you moments after Malachai took your wings. I protected you and your mother while your father gave up his life to stop your...the Angelus."

Jonas blinked, suddenly unsure of what was happening. He'd never heard that story, merely that instead of baptizing him as was customary, his grandmother had ordered Malachai to make a baby an amputee. And Xavathan had healed him, protected him and his mother, while his father did...what? Gods, he had so many questions.

Xavathan drew a deep breath, his gray eyes piercing straight into Jonas. "I know you have questions, boy. And I have answers. Believe me when I say I meant to tell you all this before. When you first awoke. Unfortunately, we got sidetracked, and then you had your...episode. So understand that this is the first time I've been in a position to tell you the truth of your...situation."

Jonas crossed his arms across his chest, "Go on then."

Xavathan smiled softly, "Jonas, as I said before, we've never had one come back the way you did. There is an enormous amount about your situation that we don't understand. Letting you go running after your Knight would be beyond inadvisable.

"It could be ultimately fatal for you *and* your...Lord Captain, correct?"

Jonas nodded numbly.

"I don't know exactly *why* you were pulled back into the Presence when you touched the Archanium. The Presence is connected to the Archanium in some fashion, but we don't know nearly enough about the ways those two sources interact. It could be that, because you attempted to destroy that piece of paper with the Nagavor, the Presence latched onto your magic and pulled you through. That is one theory I've come up with while tending your wounds, singing your name in rounds.

"I won't go into what you were like while you were in there, but let me say that you're much happier not hearing of it. It was painful enough to watch, believe me."

Jonas felt a well of panic rise up inside him. "Dear gods, what did I do?"

Xavathan's sad smile returned. "Jonas, it wasn't *you*. It was the Presence acting through you, using you. You weren't in there for long. You were wrapped in the Seraphima almost from the moment you were taken."

Jonas suddenly realized what was wrong. "Uncle, where's Adam?"

Xavathan sighed, "He's recovering in the other room. He's alive, but badly wounded. When you were taken, and before I pulled you out, that young angel caught you. You were falling backwards. You were crying tears of blood. When he caught you, he wrapped his wings around you.

"It's an action we are taught as children. He was shielding you from the Presence with the Seraphima, but invoked in such a way, it adds the power of his connection to the Archanium along with it. It is used as a last attempt at saving someone, usually someone you care deeply about. Deeply enough to sacrifice yourself. It's how I shielded you and your mother."

Jonas squeezed his eyes shut. Adam had only worked to help him since he'd met the angel, and all he'd given him in return was pain.

"So, what happened? What did I do?" he whispered.

"I believe the Presence became enraged when it felt the Seraphima so near. Through your body, it unleashed the full power of the Presence into the boy."

"Then how did he survive?"

His uncle's soft smile returned once more, "Even the Demon, the man who you battled on the Madrhal Plain, the one who now commands the Presence, even he still is limited in his power. The Presence works through a conduit in this world. But it takes time to adapt to the channels of power here. They are very different. That's why the Presence needs a human host. It cannot access this world directly.

"The power you unleashed into that boy, while dangerous, was hardly the full might of the Presence, only the full might it could exert through *you*. Since your connection was so new, it was not enough to obliterate the boy. I was able to save his life."

Jonas grunted his understanding, "Which explains why I woke up covered in blood. The entire time I've been out, you've been healing Adam."

Xavathan nodded slowly.

"Uncle, forgive me. I had no idea that would happen."

Xavathan reached out and placed a comforting hand on his nephew's shoulder, "You did not act out of malice, boy. No one knew it would happen. Just be glad you were both among those who could help you."

Jonas placed his face in his hands. He was starting to feel dizzy. "So this is why I'm going to Kuuran?"

His uncle nodded, "Kuuran is home to healers far more talented than I. I was able to pull you from the Presence, but not completely. That much has been made abundantly clear. You need the help of the Angelus. You need to be exorcised before you can go find your friend."

Jonas smiled, "Aleksei isn't my friend, Uncle. He's my Knight. He's...." Jonas trailed off. Gods, was there a proper word for what Aleksei was to him? Could any word do the man justice? Or convey the depth of love they shared for one another?

Bonded sounded cold, clinical to those who'd never experienced the unrivaled intimacy shared between Knight and Magus. Husband was more apt, though they had both spent the last year too embroiled in the needs of their realm to bother planning a future, much less a wedding.

The idea had never actually come up, now that he thought about it. Not because either of them would have been opposed, simply because it wasn't presently necessary.

Their bond was a far more intimate and personal connection than any ceremony. It was forged in magic, in them, through them, rather than in gold tokens or arcane scripture. Still, Jonas harbored no illusions. It *would* happen someday.

But only if they survived the war; survived the onslaught of the Demon. And here he sat, a pace from Xavathan, listening to his uncle tell him in no uncertain terms that if he refused to listen, if he left and went to Aleksei rather than seeking the aid of the Angelus, he would never make it to that fabled wedding day.

He would never proclaim his love under the gaze of family, friends, of the gods themselves. Never hear Aleksei recite the age-old vows, never bind their hands in the same embroidered cloth that had bound the hands of his own parents, of every wedded couple in the Belgi line for the past four hundred years.

The thought of having to willingly travel farther from Aleksei made Jonas heartsick. More than anything, right then he wished he could have Aleksei's arms around him, even for a moment. Just one confirmation that he wasn't damned.

That it would be all right.

Jonas had seen Aleksei Drago pull off the seemingly impossible before. He had never been so in awe of someone, or more frustrated by them.

"I need to shed this curse as quickly as possible, Uncle. What do I have to do?"

Xavathan nodded. Jonas thought he detected a twinkle of amusement in the corner of the Seraph's eye.

"We leave for Kuuran in the morning."

Jonas rose to head back to his bed, but his uncle placed a hand on his arm. "Jonas, before you retire, there's something you need to see."

Jonas frowned, slowly following the angel into a small library. Xavathan walked past a large, gilded stand mirror and reached high on a shelf. He turned and handed Jonas a book. The words tooled into the golden leather were written in Demonic script, inverted and perverted from the original, but Jonas had little trouble imagining their meaning.

Emblazoned beneath the symbols were two narrowed, midnight eyes, cracked with vivid chartreuse lines. He frowned at the image and then back to his uncle. The angel offered only his sad smile. He gently turned Jonas in front of the mirror.

Those same black eyes, cracked with fissures of yellow-green light, stared back at him.

Andariana turned, gazing at the houses on the street, all seeming to look more or less the same. Gods, which one was Nadja's? The letters her old nursemaid sent her every week for years never described exactly where she lived, more for Nadja's protection than anything else. If some stranger intercepted any of those letters, they might deduce her location, and more importantly the very particular prize buried beneath her cellar.

While she stood there attempting to puzzle it out, Tamara marched towards the first person she saw on the street, a woman in her middle years who seemed just as surprised to see Tamara approaching her as Andariana was at seeing her daughter being so forward.

"Excuse me, madam? We're looking for an old family friend. Her name is Nadja, but I'm afraid we don't know which house is hers. Could you help us find her?"

The woman blinked at her for a moment, and Andariana winced, knowing that Tamara's Kalinori accent was distinctly at odds with her Ri-Vhan attire.

"Aye, she's three houses down from mine," the woman said with a nod of her head, "but I'd be careful knocking on her door. She's older and can be a bit...harsh, being bothered and all."

Tamara bowed her head to the woman, flashing a brilliant smile, "Thank you ever so much!"

The woman nodded back, fixing the princess with a look that Andariana knew all too well. That Tamara was so clearly noble was frightening. Andariana realized she'd need to coach the girl in how not to stick out so obviously in the future. No need to invite curiosity and questions, even from the common folk of Timurus.

Andariana caught up with her daughter, following her to the house the woman had indicated, staying a few steps behind Tamara so any prying eyes wouldn't immediately identify their relationship to one another. It was worrisome, all the different ways people could be identified, and by the least likely of individuals.

Nadja was a perfect example of this, a woman who'd spent the vast majority of her years helping to rear future kings and queens in Kalinor Palace, now living out her remaining days in the sleepy little hamlet that was Timurus. If the locals only knew who she really was, it could make for a decidedly awkward situation. Andariana wanted to avoid detection, and she equally didn't want to bring questions and suspicion onto her old nursemaid.

When they reached the broad porch of the house in question, Andariana stepped past Tamara, knocking on the door as forcefully as she dared. Gods, please let the woman be home.

After what seemed minutes, but was likely mere seconds amplified by Andariana's anxiety, the door swung open to reveal a short young man with a face like a brick. He blinked in surprise to see the two women on the porch, stammering unintelligibly for a moment before he was unceremoniously shoved aside to reveal an elderly woman, back hunched, eyes seeming to bulge out of her skull.

"You again?" Nadja snapped. "What'dya want this time, eh?"

Andariana floundered, searching for words in the face of such a strange question from her lifelong friend.

"Ma'am," Tamara said with a slight bob, "I brought my friend, as you requested. She's quite talented, and I'm sure she can mend your quilt. Good as new, it'll be!"

Nadja studied the two women for a long moment before nodding. "Alright, get in here so I can have a proper look at your skills. I'm not letting some out-of-work gutter tramp touch that quilt until I've seen your needlework firsthand."

"Oh, *thank* you, milady," Tamara gushed, bobbing a small curtsey again.

Nadja rolled her eyes, but stepped aside, "Get in here, the both of you, before you catch a chill. I've no interest in sharing your sickness."

Tamara practically dragged Andi into the warmth of Nadja's home, past the stuttering young man who'd opened the door, who seemed to be as perplexed as she was herself. What was going on? Had Nadja's mind gone soft after so many years?

The door shut firmly and Nadja sighed, standing up straight and smiling warmly at both women. "Word reached us yesterday: Kalinor sacked, the Demon running rampant, the royal family missing. Gave me palpitations, it did!"

She led them deeper into the home, to the blazing hearth. Another young man, looking to be roughly in his eighteenth summer, stood apprehensively at the mantelpiece.

"Relax, Corbin. These are good people."

The youth's face colored, and he turned his eyes away from the study he was making of Tamara.

The young man who'd opened the door joined Corbin at the hearth, the two men standing awkwardly, seemingly unsure of what to do or say in such a circumstance.

Nadja sighed heavily. "Your Majesty," she said softly, "your Highness, I present my grandsons, Corbin and Jacob. They're good boys, just a bit shy around strangers."

Andi smiled as the boys stood suddenly straighter, bowing her head ever so slightly, "A pleasure. Nadja, I'm afraid I've come for the reserve. I made it my life's ambition to never need it, but...." She trailed off, tears blurring her vision.

Nadja nodded as though she'd just heard about inclement weather arriving. "I know, darling. But that's why we put it here. For this exact situation, which I'm sure you'll explain in greater detail while the boys dig it up. Please have a seat, the both of you. Boys, go to the cellar and fetch the box."

Corbin and Jacob started at her demand. They looked to one another uneasily, but both seemed to know better than to question her. "Yes, ma'am," Corbin intoned formally, bowing to Andi and Tamara as he turned and headed out of the room, grabbing his brother's shirt and pulling him along, cutting off Jacob's attempt at speech.

Nadja vanished from the room as Andi and Tamara tried to make themselves comfortable on the rickety furniture. A moment later, the ancient nursemaid returned bearing a tray of earthenware cups and a steaming pot of tea.

"Now then, tell me everything."

A shriek cut through the silence, pulling Bael from the storm of his thoughts.

He glanced to the thin, pale form of Delira, one of Sammul's acolytes. While some of them had been ill-prepared for the world he envisioned, she was a berry in the brambles. Her hands moved with surgical precision as she flayed the flesh from the ragged maid strapped to the blood-soaked table.

The Demonic Presence thrummed greedily within him. *Delicious,* it hissed, as it luxuriated and fed on the woman's agony.

Bael didn't care one way or the other. He didn't particularly enjoy hearing a random woman scream as she was tortured; he was only invested in her eventual demise because it would give him what he wanted.

A soldier.

He corrected himself. So much more than a simple soldier. An assassin, perhaps? He wasn't completely clear on what the Presence promised, only that it would hunt down and kill Aleksei Drago, and far more importantly, Jonas Belgi by extension.

It struck him as oddly sad that Aleksei had to die. The man could have been his champion. He still recalled the visions his sister Darielle had forced into his brain. He and Aleksei could have been truly great together. Unfortunately, the man had chosen Jonas Belgi instead. And that decision would be his undoing. There would be no hiding from the demon, the *karigul* as the Presence called it, that Bael conjured. It would destroy Aleksei as swiftly as anything else that got in his way.

Still, it was a shame.

Yet, that sort of certainty was worth whatever means necessary to summon it. Procuring the elements the ritual required hadn't been easy, even for Bael. Even with the wealth of the Ilyari crown *and* the Voralla at his fingertips. But it was worth every second spent, and *certainly* the life of one measly servant, to give him what he craved.

The woman cried out again, and Delira clicked her tongue. "Magda, darling, it *is* unfortunate that it's come to this. But you *were* late with my dinner dress. *Twice.* If anything, you ought to thank me for my leniency."

Magda stared at Delira's pinched face with wide brown eyes. "You're *mad!*"

Delira cocked her head to the side. "I know you're given to histrionics, but hurling such barbs at me is hardly becoming of a lady, even one of your lowly station."

Bael rolled his eyes. "Delira, stop playing with your food. I know you have a flair for drama, but I just want this done."

Delira turned, her hands red with the woman's blood, a sizable flap of flesh hanging from the pincers in her hand. "Apologies, Lord Bael. I merely thought you'd appreciate some new skin to replace your more... fragile bits."

"When I have need of such things, I will obtain them. For now, I don't need her flesh, just her life."

Delira shrugged, dropping the flayed flesh to the table, beside the rest of the ritual implements. "As you command, my lord."

The Presence within him buzzed angrily, irritated that their meal was cut short. *You should relish this, Pilgrim. You want a being of fear and pain, one that will* kill. *It won't hurt you to speak Our language.*

He ignored it, even as the vibration threatened to splinter his bones. Delira stepped back, bowing her head in reverence as he lifted a gilded chalice from the table, picking up the large ruby in his other hand. Rather than embrace the Archanium directly, Bael directed the Presence's powerful vibrations into the stone.

It fell into the chalice as a fine powder, sinking into the dark wine within, the contents bubbling and bursting with yellow-green fire.

Bael tipped the contents down his throat, shivering at the strange feeling of the tincture sliding into him and splashing in his stomach, now quite dry and cracked so long since the death of his physical body. Yet it was not for his own sustenance or enjoyment that he drank the ruby-tainted wine.

The same chartreuse fire lighting the wine suffused his skin, the flames dancing along his arms and erupting from his lips. He shifted the chalice to his left hand, lifting the ceremonial blade from the Voralla's Vault with his right.

He studied it for a moment. Nithernim? It had been labeled as such, but he wasn't sure he believed it. Such a strange, even legendary metal, fabled to possess so many qualities that Bael doubted even a fifth of them could be true.

But the Presence had been satisfied when he'd retrieved it, and the yellow-green fire dancing across his flesh flowed forth, wrapping around the queer blade. He advanced towards the bleeding, moaning woman, and plunged the burning blade deep into her heart.

The scream she released was exactly what he wanted: piercing, raw, primal. The scream of a woman in the throes of death, truly *comprehending* her mortality, and the ending of her life.

Chartreuse flames spread across her body, intensifying until her features were entirely obscured by the swirling inferno. Yet the table holding her down did not catch fire, and he felt no heat radiating from the woman's corpse.

Rather, he felt something entirely different. He felt her spirit leave her body, and the fabric of reality parting to accept her soul into the Aftershadow.

And just as that small tear appeared, linking his world to the realm of the dead, something slithered out. Something terrible. Something *wrong.* An abomination, summoned by his call. It possessed no physical form, yet it consumed Magda's soul nonetheless. The Presence had assured him that the more magnificent her agony, the deeper her terror in her moment of death, the stronger his conjuring would be.

Delira lifted a blood-stained hand to her forehead, "Exquisite! Such blind hatred, such lust for death, and it's hardly seconds old. Well done, my lord."

The ball of vengeance and death roiled, distorting the air it occupied, and Bael stepped up to it, careful not to get too close. He held up his hand, palm facing his newest assassin.

"Hello, my dear," he cooed, threads of Demonic light dancing in the air between them, runes he recognized but could not read wrapping around the tight torrent of air. "We're going to have such fun together."

CHAPTER 5

A GOLDEN SEAL

"You've put on some weight," Nadja muttered as she helped Andariana into a blue silk riding dress.

"I beg your pardon?" Andariana huffed.

"You were skin and bones back when this was made. It's nice to see you with a bit more meat on you. Not everything is a slight, Andi."

Andariana sighed. Nadja was right. Of *course* she was right.

"If I recall correctly, you'd just lost Seryn when these were made. I ensured the dressmaker added pleats and darts so your gowns could be worn whatever weight you were when they were needed, within reason, of course."

Andariana's face colored at that. Gods, what did "within reason" mean?

"I took the liberty of letting three of them out to fit you now. Tamara *almost* fits the original shape just fine, even with her stays loosened a little, though she's a touch softer than you were. You're lucky she's built like you. Seryn was such a genteel man, but he was a big boy."

Andariana snorted, "You don't know the half of it."

Nadja chuckled, turning to Tamara. The princess had her back to the two women, "I don't imagine you've had much cause to exert yourself, have you dear?"

Tamara turned, her face blazing bright red, her eyes directed at the carpet. "No, Miss Nadja. And as I was being whisked away from the

Palace by...a friend, it became painfully clear how unfit and sadly unprepared I actually am for such situations. I aim to fix that, given the chance."

Nadja smiled and turned back to Andariana, "Well done, Andi. You've raised a smart girl."

Andariana offered a weak laugh, "More like *you* raised a smart girl."

Tamara giggled, finally looking up at them, "You're both right, if I do say so myself."

Nadja beamed, and Andariana couldn't help but smirk. The woman had practically raised not only her and her sisters, but Jonas and Tamara as well. Andi had tried to be more present and hands-on with Tamara and Jonas, especially once it became clear that Rhiannon wouldn't be coming back. But Nadja had ultimately spent a far greater amount of time with the young royals, despite Andariana's best efforts.

Andariana didn't begrudge Nadja those relationships, though. After losing both her sisters and her husband so close together, she wasn't sure she would have been much of a mother without Nadja. It turned out that reconstructing a realm after a bloody civil war was quite time-consuming, especially as the nobility made repeated attempts to grab as much power for themselves as possible. Andariana sighed, all the painful particulars of the revived war tumbling through her mind.

It turned out that her best attempts hadn't been worth much.

Nadja finished buttoning up the back of the riding gown and Andariana walked across the room, delighting in feel of fine Fanja silk against her skin.

She was so grateful to the Ri-Vhan for clothing both herself and Tamara when they'd arrived, resembling drowned rats rather than royalty. Andariana had been held in a dank cellar before Aleksei had rescued her, piling corpses on top of her and pulling off a daring escape from the capitol under the very noses of an invading army. Her brief stint in Azarael's bizarre tower hadn't done her clothes any kindnesses, either. But at least she hadn't had to work her way through a league of sewer tunnels just to reach safety. She glanced at her daughter, now chatting happily with Nadja as the ancient woman did up the back of her gown.

She would never have guessed that Tamara would have been up to the tasks Aleksei had set her to secure her freedom, but according to the Lord Captain, she'd been remarkably stoic and capable in their flight from Kalinor. However long she lived, Andariana doubted she'd ever be able to properly repay Aleksei Drago for everything he'd done for her family.

She mentally corrected herself. While the Hunter and her nephew hadn't been properly married yet, they were Bonded. That alone made him part of her family, as far as she was concerned.

"It looks decent enough," Nadja opined, stepping from behind Tamara to get a closer look at Andariana.

"Thank you for altering it. That must have taken you all night!"

Nadja shrugged her shoulders, "I've spent my life fiddling with such things. It was hardly some heroic display of prowess. I was in bed before midnight."

Tamara walked across the room as Andariana had, offering a grateful sigh, "Oh, thank you, Miss Nadja. It's wonderful. I feel a bit more like myself again."

The old woman turned to the princess, her eyes narrowing, "A fine dress doesn't make a princess anymore than a pile of filthy rags makes a beggar. Don't let such frippery define you, darling. Who you are is something you're born with, not something you wear."

Tamara bowed her head, "Of course, Miss Nadja."

The nursemaid turned to Andariana, "I know you hoped to never have to open that box, but it was an ingenious idea to keep it stashed here. You've got the clothes that name you a queen, and the gold to back it up. I must say, if you'd arrived in Taumon in Ri-Vhan barkcloth, you'd have a hard time convincing the guards that you weren't just another madwoman."

Andariana nodded her head, "My thoughts exactly. But seeing Marra dethroned taught me not to take anything for granted. If it could happen to her, it could happen to anyone. And unfortunately, I know how important it is to look the part. I fear *any* woman in a fine dress could walk up to the Admiralty and get inside without too much trouble. Unless someone was there who'd actually seen me the last time I was in Taumon, how would they even know who I was?

"It's been a long while since I've had to *use* money, too. But in this situation, that bag of silver and gold is the difference between life and death."

"Quite right," Nadja said sadly. "Now, you'll need some horses. Corbin and Jacob ought to be finished packing by now. If you like, you can go with them to the farrier and pick out four decent mounts."

Andariana blinked in surprise, "Corbin and Jacob are packing?

Whatever for?"

Tamara sighed behind her, "Mother, do you think Aleksei would want us traversing several hundred leagues to Taumon alone? Especially with a civil war raging? We'll be passing through friendly territory, it's true, but it would be a greater deterrent to have some young men along with us." The princess turned to Nadja, "Can they fight?"

Nadja shrugged, "Jacob is quite accomplished with both axe and bow. He can't string a sentence together, but he's a dead-eye shot. Corbin's been training with a sword for a few years now, though I'm not a good judge of such things. I've always been far more interested in knives."

Andariana smiled knowingly. She looked at her daughter, and fought back a laugh at seeing Tamara's eyes so wide.

She was just about to inquire further when the young men in question descended the rickety stairway. Both were clad in riding clothes, packs slung across their backs. An axe hung from Jacob's belt, an unstrung bow tied to his shoulders. Corbin wore a short sword at his back.

Nadja went to the window, peering up at the sky. "As much as I'd like to have a longer chat, darlings, you'd best get going. If you leave town by midday, you ought to reach Riplenk Spring by nightfall. I daresay the accommodations there are a sight better than a beggar's camp just off the road. Amenities between Riplenk and Taumon are few and far between. Take advantage where you can."

Lord Simon Declan looked at the substance before him dubiously. "Pardon me, miss. But what exactly is this? I've never seen anything like it."

The young woman smiled warmly, "It's vinegar pie, Master Declan. Try it. It's sweet and a little bit sour."

Declan took a tentative bite. He was quite surprised at how simple and elegant the flavor combination was. Eagerly, he took another.

"I apologize for being uncertain before, miss. This is wonderful."

She smiled again. She was a shockingly lovely girl. He hadn't expected a lowly peasant to have such fine features. "Master Declan, please! My name is Katherine."

He smiled, "I apologize, Katherine. I'm afraid I'm not much used to calling people by their given names."

She frowned at that, seeming lost in thought for a moment. Her big brown eyes brightened. "Are you a lord?"

He stiffened, "What would make you suppose such a thing?"

She shrugged as she sat across from him at the rough farm table. "Your clothes are finer than anything in this village, and they're an unusual cut. If I didn't know better, I'd say you bought them in Kalinor. And you're far too genteel to be from around here. You speak differently than we do." She paused and then gave a soft giggle, "Also, you've never had vinegar pie."

When he frowned at that, she shrugged, "This is peasant food, Master Declan. But it's common peasant food. If you'd been to an inn within a hundred leagues of here, you'd probably have had it before."

Declan stared at her for a moment, until he realized he was making her uncomfortable.

"Well, miss," he caught himself and smiled ruefully, "Katherine, you are quite an astute young lady. But you look too young to have traveled much beyond this quaint little hamlet. Tell me, how could you recognize a Kalinori gentleman's coat? Has a lord been through here? It's not exactly along a major road."

Katherine gave him coy smile, "You have your secrets, Master Declan, and I have mine. Even if you've more gold than the worth of this entire village, it doesn't make your secrets any better than mine. Secrets can be worth far more than gold."

He had to fight to keep from his jaw from dropping. "I must say you've surprised me again, my dear. I've been through small villages before. They are full of hardworking tradespeople and farmers, for the most part, but they're not the usual spot to find intellectual gems."

She shrugged her shoulders, "Perhaps it's different here. After all, since you've clearly never been down around here, I doubt you could throw Voskrin in the same pool with all those other villages you've ridden through."

The name struck him as somehow familiar, but he couldn't place it. He couldn't imagine why he would have heard of this tiny nothing of a community. This was as deep into Lord Perron's holdings as you could get without crossing into the mist-mazes of Yrinu.

Katherine continued, "Now, are you going to answer my question?"

He looked up, confused for a moment, "Beg your pardon?"

She fixed him with an intense gaze, "Are you a lord?"

He decided to trust her, at least a little bit. She had only shown him kindness thus far. "I am, Katherine. Lord Simon Declan of Keiv-Alon, and until quite recently representative of my holdings to Her Majesty, Queen Andariana Belgi of Ilyar."

Katherine nodded and gave him a blank smile. She stood and cleared the empty plates from the table. He decided the poor girl must be in shock. It was highly unlikely she'd ever met or entertained a lord, much less one who'd served as a member of Parliament.

"Can I fetch you another piece of pie, milord?" she asked from the counter.

Declan sighed, "There's no need for that, Katherine. Call me Simon. It is, after all, my name."

"As you say, Simon. Would you like some more pie?"

He smiled, "I would, actually."

As she busied herself in the kitchen, she changed the subject to other matters. The poor harvest, her brothers' trials taking over her father's business. And, of course, the war.

"You know, Simon, my husband was killed fighting in the war," she said noncommittally.

"For which side, if I might be so bold?"

She gave a throaty laugh, "Which side would you imagine?"

Despite her light tone, Declan understood that he was treading on dangerous territory. "Well, Katherine, I'm sure a girl as smart as you can make up her own mind. I'm sure any man who won your hand would be just as attracted to your mind as anything else. I'm sure he fought for the side he deemed to be in the right."

Katherine cleared her throat, "And which side do *you* deem to be in the right, Simon?"

Simon breathed out heavily. "The world I've been living in, Katherine, is unfortunately not made up of right and wrong, or black and white. There are many layers, and sometimes the decisions we want to make would not be the best for the people we're charged to care for. Sometimes we have to make very difficult decisions indeed. Does that make sense?"

"I understand that people of your position have to make choices that affect many. But if you were free of all that, who would you side with?"

Simon thought about his answer very carefully before he gave voice to it. He was taking a huge gamble. But, then again, he had very little to lose at the moment.

"I have only ever supported Her Majesty. I am a believer that our rulers were chosen for a reason. I regret that I have made some desperate decisions to spare my people what abuse I could, and I don't regret those decisions. That doesn't mean I thought they were right."

Katherine placed the plate of pie in front of him before taking her seat again. She carefully lifted a pot of tea and refilled his mug.

He studied her closely as she poured, a bite of pie hanging on a fork inches from his mouth.

"I'm pleased to hear you support the Queen," she said softly. "Down here there's so little difference of opinion. It's beyond dull."

Declan breathed a little more easily. "I'm glad I took a gamble and trusted you, Katherine. I feared you might have poisoned me if you found my views contrary to yours. I didn't think anyone as smart as you could follow a madman like Emelian Krasik."

She watched him for a moment before smiling again, "Lord Declan, I have some secrets I've kept from you too. For the moment, I believe we can agree to trust one another." She took a slow breath before she began.

"I have a friend, a friend I'm very fond of, even if he doesn't know it. He left here last year before Harvest, but we were children together. I would no sooner betray him than my own mother."

Declan nodded slowly.

"My husband went off to war, fighting for that madman. He was killed while guarding a very dangerous place, I believe it's called the Drakleyn. The very idea of my idiot husband standing guard on such a place is laughable, at least to me. I married him in a fit of girlish hurt. I thought he would be more like my friend, as they had been boys together."

Declan was now growing very anxious. There was a new look in her eye. The flirty girl of mere moments ago had melted into a formidable woman.

"My husband, Pyotr, was killed by the very boy he grew up with. I won't go into the details. I believe it to have been an accident of sorts. I know my friend was hurt by it, probably more than he would ever let on to me.

"I felt no sorrow at my husband's death. He made a fool's mistake, and he paid for it with his life. I feel sorry that my friend had to hurt over killing a man of such small worth."

She stood. He could tell she was getting upset. He was now terrified of what she was going to say next, less because of her words and more from the look on her face.

"I learned all of this not that long ago, in a letter," she walked to the cupboard and withdrew a heavy envelope. The letter was obviously of some length, and on fine parchment. His heart sank further when she tossed the letter on the table.

"But more than feeling the hurt of Pyotr's death, I realized once again that, though I've been witless around him, or cold to him, my friend still loves me. Perhaps not in the way I once hoped for, but he cares for me.

"He sent me gold, and told me to look after myself. That we were headed for dark times, and he never wanted to see hurt or sorrow come to my door. He was the dearest friend I have ever had, and now he's probably dead because people like you had to make some 'desperate decisions'."

She was in tears as she sat back down. Declan imagined they were the most bitter tears she'd ever cried. She leaned close to him, her voice just above a growl, "So when I asked you which side you supported in this stupid war, you were wrong to trust me. Had you given an unsatisfactory answer, you would have a knife between your shoulders right now. Because every person who is against him is against me, too."

Declan dared to glance away from her fierce glare, staring down at the seal and signature at the letter's end. He stiffened. The golden wax, imprinted with three bearded heads of wheat, was all the information he needed. Still, he read the inscription in astonishment.

Your loving friend, Aleksei Drago.

From the date signed below, Declan realized that the Lord Captain must have sent this out days before the invasion of Kalinor. This was a final letter begging forgiveness, from a man who knew he was about to die.

Declan felt tears wet his cheeks, and was surprised to find himself crying. He reached out a hand and placed it lightly over Katherine's. "Dear girl, I am so very sorry for your pain. Know that you are one of the people that men of my station are supposed to protect."

She withdrew her hand, "I don't want an apology, Lord Declan. I want my friend back. But I can't have him back, because his life was lost to some 'desperate decisions'. So I'll settle for avenging him any way I can."

Declan nodded his understanding, "I lost a very dear friend of mine to this nonsense, too. His death left me with the choice of meeting the same fate, or throwing my lot in with a bunch of corrupt, foolish, power-hungry old men.

"Forgive me for being yet another foolish old man, one too concerned with power and with survival to have stood up for himself, and for all the people out there like you, who understand the difference between right and wrong. That there is always a difference."

Katherine studied him for a long moment, her deep mahogany eyes boring into him, as though assessing his soul. He felt fear clutch at his heart, fear that he would be found wanting. He had been in the presence of the Demon, and yet he was petrified by this slip of a girl in a way that Krasik, Bael, and Perron combined could have never managed.

The moment dragged on interminably before she finally managed a small smile, composing herself somewhat. "Lord Declan. Simon. I must be the one to apologize. I wrongly took my feelings out on you, but you didn't take Aleksei from me. You helped make it possible, but men like Bertrand Perron and Emelian Krasik would have had their way with or without your compliance."

Declan agreed to the truth of that. He sat there a long moment, staring into his cup before it slipped nervelessly from his fingers.

It shattered, spilling tea across the table and into his lap. He looked up, ignoring everything else but the memory. Gods, how long ago had it been?

She was watching him, caution heavy in her eyes.

"Dear girl, I've just remembered something important. Something about the Lord Capt...your friend."

She straightened in her seat. "What do you know?" she whispered.

Declan closed his eyes. His memory surrounding the destruction of the garrison in Mornj was foggy at best. When he'd awoken in this place, it had all seemed like some horrific nightmare. He'd started to doubt if it had even really happened.

But it had. And now he remembered those screams, remembered that terrible wrath anew.

And he recalled its architect.

"I saw him," he breathed, trying to put the pieces together.

"Aleksei?" she shouted in her excitement, "You saw Aleksei? When? Where?"

Declan shook his head, "No, not Aleksei, child. I saw...." He frowned. How in the name of the gods was he going to explain this?

"I saw Jonas, the Prince, and Aleksei's bonded Magus."

Katherine sat back, confused. "I know of the Prince, but not very much. Aleksei mentions him in his letter. He says Jonas has made him as happy anyone he's ever met. It sounded like he was in love."

Declan sighed. Gods, how was he going to explain Archanium Knights to this girl? "Katherine, I'm afraid it's all very complicated. Knights and Magi form bonds. Bonds of magic. When they do, they become joined."

She frowned, "Like a marriage?"

Declan shrugged, "It's probably as close as you or I will ever understand it. But it's so much more. We are talking about a group of highly secretive people here. People steeped in the Archanium. We're talking about magic."

She nodded, clearly trying to keep up.

Declan continued, "Not all, but most of the Magi and Knights who bond to each other develop deep personal feelings for one another. It's almost impossible not to. *Everything* about them is joined by their shared magic." He gave her a very serious look, "Including their lives."

Katherine stared at him blankly.

Declan tried a different tactic, "Because of the nature of this magic, if one of the pair dies, so does the other. They receive many benefits from being joined in this way, but mutual death is the bond's greatest curse. There are others, but they are less severe."

Her eyes lit with understanding, "So, if you saw Jonas alive, that means Aleksei has to be alive too?"

He smiled, "Exactly right. Or, at least he was when I saw Jonas. Now it's been a few days, and the fighting has been serious. But the last intelligence I received, before I abandoned Perron's fools, was that the Lord Captain had vanished. Almost as if into thin air. They were in a rage about that...and then I saw Jonas."

She leaned forward, "And then?"

The memory flashed across his eyes, and his face grew haunted.

"The world erupted."

Aleksei raced across the plain, pushing his great, black warhorse Agriphon as hard as he dared.

It had taken him longer than he would have liked to pass the rebel force heading towards Keldoan, but he had kept to the hills, watching the column of dust that pinpointed their location move farther and farther behind him.

After a few hours he paused atop a rise, watching a significantly smaller dust cloud work its way across the horizon. He had to be far more careful on this terrain, as it slowly became softer. To the south was marshland, to the north open plains dotted with woods stretched for leagues. His best chance would be to get a large enough lead, ahead of any scouts, before finally joining the road. The cover was too sparse to keep trying to outpace them by going cross-country. Eventually the scouts would see him.

He couldn't afford that.

Aleksei spent the rest of the afternoon threading the dwindling hills, working his way northwest, hoping to reach the road well ahead of the preliminary force.

He reached the road just as the moon was rising. He wondered how long the rebel forces would wait before making camp. Being on the road was far safer for Agriphon than riding across the plains at night, but it put him closer to the enemy's scouts than he'd like.

Still, he couldn't risk Agriphon's life. Aside from simply caring for the warhorse, he *needed* Agriphon's strength and spirit. Without a horse he'd never reach Rysun in time, and even if he found another mount, it would never be Agriphon's equal.

The moon was fully risen when he pulled the great black stallion to a halt. He listened carefully, and caught the sound of running water. They could both certainly use a drink and a break.

While Agriphon was indeed strong and spirited, and was devoted enough to let Aleksei ride him to death, Aleksei had no intention of risking his only source of companionship and transportation because he was overly impatient.

He led the warhorse to the stream. As he bent over, a wave of dizziness passed through him. He sat back on his heels and balanced himself on the bank with a hand. It came again, slower this time.

Aleksei felt a sinking feeling in his stomach. The world around him rippled. At first he didn't understand. And then he looked at the sky and watched the moon fluidly sink back towards the horizon.

"No!" he cried in panic, leaping to his feet.

The dizziness overcame him. He dropped to his knees. He felt his face land in the damp snow as the world darkened.

CHAPTER 6

TANGLES IN THE WEB

When Aleksei opened his eyes, he was in a tent. Outside, a cold wind ruffled the waxed canvas, far too thin for use in the winter. The warmth, he decided, was primarily coming from the number of men currently crowding the tent itself.

He sat up with a start, but was swiftly pushed down by a firm hand. An older man was glowering down at him, frowning uncertainly.

Aleksei looked around the tent and saw three other men staring at him. Their ages ranged from the man holding him, somewhat older than Aleksei's father Henry, to a lad barely entering puberty.

"Where am I?" he asked calmly.

The older man leaned back once he was sure Aleksei wasn't going to try to sit up again. "You're in an army camp, boy. We're chasing after some fellows who escaped the sacking of Kalinor. You're our newest recruit."

Aleksei sat up slowly, and this time the older man didn't stop him. "Where's my horse?"

The other men looked at him in confusion. Aleksei sighed. "I was riding a large black horse. Where is he?"

The older man shrugged, "I'm the closest thing we have to a medic in the camp. I got word from Harold here," a man who looked about Aleksei's age gave a tentative wave from over the medic's shoulder, "that they'd found a boy passed out near the creek. Some scouts figured you were fit enough to fight, so they brought you back. Didn't say nothing 'bout no horse."

Aleksei nodded, "I see. Thank you."

The medic shrugged, "I didn't do nothing. You woke up on your own."

Aleksei sighed. At least time wasn't slipping away anymore.

"If I were you, I'd get some sleep. They're marching us near to death to catch up with those survivors. I don't know how they think we're going to fight if we can hardly stand, but them's the orders. Also, don't think of running. They'll just use your hide for target practice."

Aleksei nodded again. He lay back down, his mind racing as he tried to come up with a way out of this nightmare. The medic and some of the others left the tent. Only Harold remained. Aleksei guessed it must be Harold's tent.

He began to get up, "Sorry, I'll get out of here and let you rest up."

Harold shook his head, "No, sir. Sit right back down. You don't want to go out there right now. Besides, it'd be nice to have the company and the warmth. It's awful cold when the tent's only half full."

Aleksei smiled as best he could. "Why wouldn't I want to go out there? Just curious."

Harold shrugged, "Unless you have business, like old Ben there, they make you stay in. Say we need our rest. They just want to keep us from running is all. None of us want to be here. We didn't get a choice."

Comprehension dawning, Aleksei smiled for the first time in days, "I understand. I don't want to be here either. Look, Harold, I *have* to get out of here. I can't stay in this camp. But in order to get out, I need my horse."

Harold's pale blue eyes widened before he dissolved into laughter. "Stranger, you don't have a prayer. If it was easy to get out of here, the whole lot of us would have taken off three leagues out of Kalinor. They keep all the Kalinori in the center of the camp so they can keep an eye on us."

"How close to their camps are we right now?"

Harold grunted, "They're maybe a hunnert paces that way." Aleksei noted which way he casually pointed. "We're sorta on the edge of the Kalinori. But that just makes it worse. There are guards coming by every five, six minutes this far out."

Aleksei sighed, thinking for a long moment. Finally, he looked up at Harold with a frown, "Harold, do you know where you're marching?"

Harold nodded, "The remainder of the Palace Guard and the Legion are up the road. We're running them down."

Aleksei took a deep breath, hoping he wasn't making a horrible mistake. "Do you know how many men you're up against?"

Harold shrugged, "They didn't say. I figured they picked enough to do the job."

Aleksei's gaze hardened. Harold stiffened, finally seeing a flash of gold in Aleksei's eyes. "Harold, there are over twenty-six thousand men up that road. Behind you is a force of over fifty-thousand. They, Harold, not you, are being sent to deliver the crushing blow to the Queen's Legion. You, and the men like you, are being sent as a diversion, so the larger force can catch up and crush those twenty-six thousand men."

Harold blinked at him, "How'd you know this?"

Aleksei arched a golden eyebrow, "Where do you think I was headed when they dragged me in here? I'm trying to get to those men, to warn them of the force marching behind you. To get them to Keldoan as fast as they can march." He paused, making sure he had Harold's full attention.

The man stared at him with a mixture of fright and confusion.

"Harold," Aleksei said in a slow, measured tone, "I have to get to those men. I have to get out of this camp *tonight*. But the last thing I want is for those men to kill you, and the other Kalinori men here. I want to wipe out the men who forced you to march here. But the Kalinori in this camp don't deserve to fall on the swords of the very men they fought beside a few weeks ago. Wouldn't you agree?"

Harold gave him a wide-eyed but knowing nod.

Aleksei smiled, "I was hoping you would."

Harold frowned, "Mister, why are you telling me this? What if I was with the rebels? What if I went and told the commander right now?"

Aleksei shrugged, "It'd make no difference. I'd be gone by the time you got back and, if anything, it would create a small enough diversion to give me a way out of here. If you tried to take me with you, I'd just kill you and be done with it."

Harold's eyes looked like they were about to bug out of his skull.

"And," Aleksei said offhandedly, "you really wouldn't be telling them anything they didn't already know. You and your comrades are the ones believing a lie, not the rebels keeping watch on you. They're there to make sure you don't run, and then to hold off my men until the larger force arrives as best they can. I'm not sure how much success they hope for. For all I know, the Zra-Uul used his occult powers to make them willing to die for his cause."

Harold started to tremble. Tears welled up in his eyes, and Aleksei felt a pang in his heart for the man. This was no soldier. Though they looked to be much the same age, Aleksei knew he was looking at a boy.

"Mister, what are we gonna do? If we run forward we die, and if we don't run they'll kill us anyways."

Aleksei's eyes twinkled as he leaned forward, "You're going to save them."

Harold laughed nervously, "Now I *know* you're crazy."

Aleksei put his hand firmly on Harold's shoulder, "You've got a few days, two, three at the most, before your force reaches the Legion. In that time, you have to get the word to as many of the Kalinori as possible. You tell two people, have them tell two more. Make it clear that if anyone thinks of betraying the group, he'll only die all the faster. But remember, they don't want to have to kill you. As long as they can push you forward into the van, that's all that matters. That's why you're here."

"And how is that going to save us again?" Harold whimpered.

Aleksei leaned forward as close as he could. Harold's eyes only seemed to get bigger and more terrified as he listened. Finally, when the poor man was shaking, Aleksei sat back.

"Sir," Harold ventured, "I don't know how many men I can get to agree to that."

Aleksei gave him a sobering look. "Harold, if it doesn't work the way I say, or if I don't get through, you will be no worse off than you were when I first arrived in this tent. But I swear on my life, I will get to those men. I've got no other choice.

"Just remember, tell them what I told you. Make sure you tell as many as possible. My men will be ready. It's the only way to save your-self, and the rest of these men."

Harold looked like he just wanted to find a place to hide. But finally he swallowed, then nodded. "I'll do as you say, sir. I wish you safe passage from this place."

Aleksei winked, "Don't worry, friend. I will see you on the other side of this battle. Now, I need my horse. Which direction are the picket lines?"

Harold paused for a moment, considering Aleksei's question. "Well, all the horses are picketed by the officers' tents. They're due north of here. But by the gods, sir, I don't know how you're going to get through all those rebels."

Aleksei clapped a hand on Harold's upper arm, "I'll find a way, friend. Remember what I told you. Save yourself, Harold. *You* have control over your actions, not those men out there. Make the best of what time you have." And then he stood and stepped out into the night.

Gods, but he hoped Harold was up to the task. It wouldn't just save the innocents in the camp, it would decrease the force they had to contend with. It was his best shot.

Aleksei slid through the shadows like a wraith. His hand rested on the hilt of his sword. At least he still had that. That and the darkness were only small advantages in a camp this size, but they were better than nothing.

He hadn't walked fifteen paces when two men with a lantern shouted. He kept walking, north into enemy territory, toward the horses.

A plan formed in his mind. The odds were heavily stacked against him, but he wasn't a mere man. He was an Archanium Knight. He was the Hunter. He had weapons at his disposal these men couldn't dream of. But right then his greatest asset was his head, and he was going to have to use it like a keen blade if he was going to live through this.

The shouts came closer. He waited until they were within a few paces before turning sharply. He opened his mouth to reprimand them, hoping to confuse them with a lie passable enough that they left him alone.

He froze.

Something was wrong. Very wrong. The air felt suddenly different. Tainted.

"Stop!" he shouted, holding up a hand and staring around them.

If he had been trying to confuse them, he would have been successful beyond his wildest dreams. But his mind was blank to that. He was only aware that there was danger.

Unseen danger.

"What are you on about?" a guard barked.

"I'm not joking," Aleksei snapped. He sniffed at the air. He drew on his superior senses until the sound of crickets a league away was deafening. He felt a change in the air around him. It had stilled. But he heard wind. Violent wind.

And then he saw it. In the darkness, just behind the guards. The torchlight was being distorted behind them, almost as though he was looking through intense heat.

One of the men stepped angrily towards him. The man flew apart in a spray of blood and viscera. The other man managed a half-turn before he, too, was ripped into a cloud of gore.

Aleksei sprinted away, listening to the sound of the wind. It was getting closer. It was faster than he was. He could hear it gaining rapidly behind him.

With a curse, Aleksei leapt over a campfire. The men behind screamed as they were ripped to tatters. The fire erupted, logs and coals flying into the air. Aleksei could feel the heat on his back, but he didn't dare turn around.

And then he realized that he had gained a few paces.

He charged through another campfire. But as he landed on the other side, he cut to the right, as close as he could come to a tent without running into it.

A moment later, he heard the tent being torn from the ground. The wind had halted. He risked a quick look over his shoulder to find a ball of fire erupting from the canvas. The men below were screaming and running to either side.

He turned towards the officers' tents, and the horses.

The chaos followed him with a shrieking wail. He could hear men screaming; dying. He could smell other things on fire now. Tents burst into flames as coals and burning logs were flung away from the tumbling knot of air.

Aleksei ran straight towards the biggest tent he saw. The guards scattered at the sight of oncoming death. He ran past a very surprised General Barnes, slashing a hole in the canvas wall and diving through it.

The entire command tent erupted and collapsed around the thing.

Aleksei ran up the line of horses and leapt onto Agriphon's back, cutting the picket line with his sword.

Agriphon turned and raced away, following the line. The panicked screams of horses joined the cacophony of chaos left in his wake. He gritted his teeth at hearing both man and horse ripped apart by the flaming ball.

Gods, what was that thing? And why was it following *him*?

Aleksei raced out into the night, away from the camp and west. He heard it clear the camp. The fire was getting dimmer. It was going out, but the wind was still there, just as deadly.

Ahead he saw the dark towers of trees. He urged Agriphon towards the woods. The wind was getting close. So close. He could feel blades of air on the back of his neck, slashing in every direction.

A ripple of terror ran through him. It was anything but natural.

Aleksei raced past the tree line. The wind would be on him in seconds.

An earth-shattering *boom* nearly threw him from the great warhorse.

Agriphon reared in surprise, and Aleksei fought to stay on his back. With a start, Aleksei realized that they were alive. He strained his senses, listening for the wind.

The night was still.

Panting, Aleksei wiped a sweat-soaked arm across his brow. At the edge of the woods stood a magnificent oak. Or, at least, its splintered stump still stood. The rest looked like nothing more than a sea of sawdust and splinters.

Aleksei listened to the night air again. He heard voles and rats digging just beneath the earth, and a fox in mid-hunt a hundred paces south. The strange wind was gone.

He slipped off Agriphon and walked over to the stump, reverently pressing his shaking fingers to the bark. A jolt of dying agony shot up his arm, tears streaking down his face.

His kissed his fingertips and brushed the bark again. "Thank you for your sacrifice, Grandfather Oak."

Still panting for breath, he took hold of Agriphon's reins and vanished into the lightless depths of the forest.

Tamara sat facing the fire, watching as Nadja's boys and her mother slept. Her offer to stand watch had surprised Andariana and the boys both, but she'd calmly explained that when traveling in such small numbers, that was the protocol. She wasn't exactly sure if that was true, but she'd heard Jonas and Aleksei often took turns keeping watch while on the open road.

Her mother had acquiesced easily enough, especially when Tamara had explained that with three of them keeping watch, Andariana could sleep through the night undisturbed. Corbin and Jacob had agreed after a bit of cajoling, but only after Corbin insisted on taking middle watch.

The boys were sweet, in their own ways, but far too easily awed by her station.

The gods knew, she'd only insisted to have a few moments to herself, without being instructed by her mother on every little thing, or waited upon by two lovely but oddly-uncomfortable young men.

They'd been riding hard all day from Riplenk Spring, and while Tamara could still trace the outline of the Seil Wood in the distance, she knew they'd covered a decent amount of ground. Of course, it was still at least two hundred leagues to Taumon.

Roux had saved them days by taking them to the very edge of the Wood, but she supposed they had at least another week ahead of them, if not more. She'd hoped they might hire a coach in Riplenk Spring, but it turned out Nadja's idea of "accommodations" and her own were quite different. Her legs and backside ached from after days in the saddle.

The fire popped, and Tamara flinched at the unexpected sound, turning this way and that as a tower of sparks rose into the night. Gods, but it was cold. She pulled her fur-lined hood closer to her face and tried her best to soak up as much warmth as she could.

Tamara wished she was still in the Seil Wood, among the Ri-Vhan. She was intrigued by the alien culture, their strange food, the majesty of floating above the forest floor. The fact that it always seemed to be spring. But mostly, she wished she was back with Roux.

The man had caught her off guard with his strange golden eyes, so much like Aleksei's and yet so incredibly different. His manner, while polite, had never been deferential. It had been refreshing to be treated like a human being for once, rather than a title. Only two men had ever treated her like that before.

Jonas had only ever treated her as Tamara, never as a princess. Aleksei had known who she was, but he'd made it painfully clear how little that impressed him. He'd never had any interest in her title or influence. From a farm boy, she'd found that at once galling and unexpectedly charming. Over time, she knew he'd come to feel rather protective of her, almost like a big brother. He'd shown the depth of his devotion the night he'd saved her life in Kalinor.

Roux was different. She couldn't quite place how, but she could tell there was something else there. Something she wasn't entirely comfortable with.

The fire popped and she jumped again. It popped again. Tamara frowned. There had been no sparks that time. She felt the fine hairs on the back of her neck stand out. There was someone, or some*thing*, in the woods behind her.

Tamara reached cautiously for the stick she'd found while gathering firewood. She didn't have a proper weapon, but she figured a stout piece of wood was better than nothing. She turned cautiously, worried she might see a bear or a wolf.

She remembered Aleksei's words, when she'd voiced a similar concern before. She had nothing to fear. They wouldn't come near the fire. Besides, she scolded herself, the bears were hibernating. She should be safe near the flames.

Though he *had* mentioned something about the rules being different when wolves were starving....

Tamara scanned the night, but saw nothing out of place. With a sigh, she turned back to the fire. She idly wondered how she would know when her watch was over. She'd never spent a night like this under the stars.

There was another pop, and Tamara jumped as something fell into her lap. It was a bundle wrapped in loose homespun linen. She tensed, glancing from side to side. Someone had managed to place this bundle precisely without her ever catching a flicker of motion.

She nervously unwrapped the package, finding four skinned rabbits inside. She briefly recalled a time when such a sight would have startled her. Now she simply saw breakfast. She sat there for a long moment, puzzled but grateful for the rabbits and their sudden appearance.

And then she wrapped them up and buried them in the snow to keep them fresh. Tamara stood, clutching her stick just in case, and walked into the trees for a few paces.

"Roux?" she called softly, careful not to wake the others.

There was an impossibly fast flicker of motion, and then he was standing before her, a mischievous grin on his face. She didn't know whether to slap him or kiss him.

"What are you doing here?" she whispered sharply.

He shrugged. She noticed for the first time that he wore a cloak that looked to have been sewn together from wolf pelts. The smell of it almost knocked her off her feet.

"Aleksei wanted me to follow the two of you to Timurus, to make sure you made it in one piece. But seeing you ride out with your... escorts?...I'll admit that I wasn't all that sure of your safety. So I decided to follow you a ways, to make sure you'd be alright. I've been watching all night, just to make sure."

"Why would you do that?"

He gave her a confused frown, "I couldn't very well let you ride off without being sure of your safety. If anything happened to you, Aleksei would skin me alive."

Tamara tried to hide her disappointment. While she was relieved to have Roux there, watching from the shadows, she was a little let down that he was acting out of duty to his cousin. She felt foolish for imagining anything else.

Roux leaned closer, "And, of course, I could never forgive myself if harm ever came to a woman as intelligent and beautiful as you."

Her face flushed scarlet in the darkness, and she prayed he couldn't see it.

Roux's hand flicked under the cloak and returned with a wicked-looking blade. She gasped as he casually flipped it over in his hand and offered it to her by the handle. "Take this," he said grimly. "It'll serve you far better than that twig you're clutching."

She tentatively took the knife. It felt good in her hand, but she also knew it was incredibly dangerous to hold a weapon you didn't know how to use. She looked up at him with wide eyes.

"I've never handled a knife before," she murmured.

He gave her a broad grin, and Tamara was freshly aware of how handsome he was.

"Here," he said softly, "let me show you."

He stepped behind her and placed his hand gently over hers. She thrilled at the feel of his warmth against her, the unexpected heat of his skin. He carefully guided her fingers, turning the knife until the blade's spine pressed against the inside of her wrist.

"Hold it like this," he whispered. "In a fight, you'll have more strength from this angle. If you held it outwards, the impact could either break your thumb or knock the knife from your hand."

Tamara frowned, "I've seen men fight with knives before. I've never seen them hold it like this."

Roux chuckled, "They also likely knew what they were doing. They're stronger and more experienced. For you, this way has the least chance of hurting you, and the greatest chance of cutting your enemy. If you use too much force, the spine of the blade will brace against your forearm, and the edge will still cut. The other way, you could either injure yourself or be disarmed. It's much harder to disarm you like this."

She glanced up at him, watching his golden eyes shimmer in the moonlight, wondering how well he could see in the dark. He smiled down at her, then stepped back, drawing his own knife.

"Alright, now I want you to attack me," he said softly.

She turned in surprise, "What? I'm not going to attack you!"

He chuckled softly, "I'm not too worried. Just try it."

Tamara froze for a moment. She didn't want to hurt him. She thought about it, about how she could try without possibly causing any harm. She lunged forward.

Before she'd even taken a step, Roux caught her wrist and gently spun her around. Her knife dropped into the snow. She knew that if he pulled any harder, it would be incredibly painful.

"Don't be scared," he whispered in her ear. "When you swing, mean it. Commit to it. Otherwise, your opponent will do far worse than this, and you'll be lucky if you escape with only a broken arm." He released her. "Again."

Tamara lost track of time, sparring with Roux, learning how to dodge, how to cut. It was exhilarating. She'd never felt so in control of herself before. Finally, he raised a hand.

"Alright, that's enough for one night."

She frowned, "What do you mean?"

He flashed that broad, handsome smile, "We'll work on it again tomorrow."

"Tomorrow?" she whispered weakly.

He chuckled, "One night with a knife is hardly time enough. You'll need many more lessons before you're fit to even *think* about wielding that blade in a fight."

Tamara wanted to protest, to ask how he could leave his people to tutor her in self-defense. But she remained silent.

She didn't want him to leave.

"Will you at least come back to camp with me?" she asked.

He shook his head, "I'm sorry, Princess, but I doubt your mother would approve. Besides, you've already got an honor guard."

She glanced back at the two young men, both soundly sleeping despite it being well into the small hours of the morning, and she snorted.

"But I'll be here every night," Roux said earnestly. "Even if you can't make it, I'll be waiting for you. Don't worry about finding me. If you can get away from them, I'll find you."

She gave him a shy smile, "Thank you. This means more to me than I can say."

He gave her a roguish wink and vanished. She allowed the giddy grin that had been bubbling inside her to finally surface. Gods! How was she ever going to keep this a secret?

Tamara carefully picked her way back into camp, stepping around the boys and glancing at her mother's sleeping form. She tiptoed past it, slipping into her own blankets. She would let Andariana and the boys sleep, knowing that someone dangerous, someone dear, was watching over them.

CHAPTER 7

SACTUARY

"It's a funny thing, transformation," Bael mused.

There was a lengthy pause, and he finally looked up into the uncertain faces of the two captains attending him. Delira seemed curious, almost giddy, though only the gods knew why. Ethan, a strapping lad he'd picked up passing through a whimper of a village only months before, looked predictably confused. Ethan was enormously powerful in the Archanium, but he wasn't exactly sharp.

Delira cleared her throat, "It seems you and I share similar inspiration."

Bael arched a bronze eyebrow, "Oh?"

Delira stepped closer, her eyes wide and excited, "The *possibilities*, Lord Bael. Seeing that woman's soul *transformed* into your new...soldier. Taking the raw materials of life and then *changing* them to reach the desired outcome. I must admit, the range of potential applications is *astronomical*, and I've only been thinking on it for a few days. I recall Master Sammul speaking of your brother, Azarael, and his *experiments*—"

Bael held up a hand, cutting her reverie short, "My brother was obsessed with his...transformations, it's true. But he never had the vision or power to accomplish anything near my success the other day. He was merely taken with melding two biological forms into one. He had apparent interest in altering his projects beyond it, and was eventually banished for committing crimes against nature. What *I* accomplished, however, is leagues beyond his pathetic 'progeny'."

Delira bowed her head, withdrawing a few steps, "As you say, Lord Bael. It was not my *intention* to offend."

Bael waved away her apology, "As long as we're clear. I am not to be compared to Azarael, even in jest."

She dipped into an awkward curtsy, "Of course, Lord Bael."

"Though there are useful...um, applications for altering the physical form," Ethan said, lightly coughing in his hand to gain Bael's attention. "If we could regrow limbs and fix bones at a much more rapid pace, it would go a long way in keeping our soldiers and Magi alive during and after battle."

Delira let out a trill of a laugh, too high, too pointed. Bael was *so* tired of his underlings trying to impress him.

"What a pointless application, Ox," she sneered. "If soldiers die, we'll just replace them. Perhaps you'd be better off if Lord Bael grew you a functioning *brain*."

Ethan's cheeks colored at the insult, his broad shoulders slumping. "It's an *idea,* Delira, not some academic thought experiment. It has actual *use* in the war we're fighting. And it could help the people fighting for us."

"*Help* people?" she laughed, "What a silly exercise."

"You don't have to work so *hard* to sound like the witch in a faerie story. I'm sure Lord Bael got the point of your simpering and flights of fancy long ago."

This time it was Delira's face that colored, her fragile fingers bunching at her side.

"Interesting," Bael chuckled. "Sounds like Ethan has you figured out, Delira."

He watched the body language of his captains shift, Delira growing all the more enraged, Ethan obviously beaming at the compliment. It was so entertaining, setting them against one another. A game of Stone Tower played amongst his minions, while he studied the ways they interacted, battling for his favor.

Delira relaxed after a moment, "It *is* encouraging to see the Ox bite back, I have to admit. It gives me hope that he may have some purpose yet."

"Certainly not the 'purpose' you first envisioned," Ethan snapped.

"Your loss. I invited you into my bed with the hopes of finding something you were *good* at."

Ethan let out a hearty laugh, "*Me* bed *you*? It'd be like bodging a cricket, all sharp elbows and bony knees. If I ever grow enamored of a stick insect, I'll let you know."

Bael wanted to guffaw with the burly lad, but Delira was too valuable to push away so forcefully. She had definite uses, if not the ones she imagined.

"You're right, you know," he said after a pregnant pause, letting Ethan savor cutting her to the quick. "There are *many* possibilities with transformation and alteration of living beings. What did you have in mind, Delira?"

His words seemed to shake her from her vexation, and Bael made a mental note of how easily she rose to anger. It could be an asset, if utilized properly. But it could just as easily become a liability.

She turned away from glaring at Ethan, seeming surprised at his return to their earlier topic. "Why, Lord Bael, there's a *multitude* of applications. Think of the enemy's Archanium Knights. The entire point of that ridiculous bond is that it alters both Magus and Knight into effectively one being. The abilities the Knights gain are impressive, even if they're never put to proper use. We could potentially alter every soldier in our army to have similar strength and stamina with*out* crafting a death pact with a Magus.

"We could also enhance natural ability. If I could have one of your Magi to experiment on, I might be able to discern a way to enhance their raw power in the Archanium. Such an advancement would make newer recruits like the Ox here practically superfluous."

"Intriguing," Bael allowed.

"We could also both give and take. Removing attributes we don't care for while amplifying others to such a heightened degree that the subject ceases to be human, except in the strictest sense."

Bael raised his head at that.

"What a fascinating concept," he said, a smile slowly creeping across his face.

"I've often wondered how the angels came into being, my lord. What strange differences and similarities they have to us. The fact that they can reproduce with humans indicates that we're not *so* different, yet there are *so* many attributes they possess that we do not.

"Their bones, their height, their *wings*, unlike *any*thing seen in humans, and yet every other element seems to be the same. That can*not* be a simple mutation. If their forebearers were so manipulated and mutated with magic, why can't we do similar things to our people?"

Bael leaned forward in his armchair, "Have you ever studied an angel up close, Delira?"

She hung her head in defeat, "I've only ever dissected two, but I would relish the opportunity to study them closer. And, of course, Jonas Belgi is a hybrid, so dissecting him would be of even greater value."

Bael snuffed out the snarl threatening to overtake his cruel smile. It would not do to allow his underlings a vision of how much he hated that man, to display weakness.

"Indeed," he said instead, trying to force a lighter tone, "and soon enough, you'll have the chance to do whatever you wish, to his corpse of course."

She bobbed her crooked curtsey, "As you will, Lord Bael."

He sighed, relaxing back into his chair. He idly wondered how long it would take his little assassin to complete its mission.

Patience is your friend, Pilgrim, the Presence thrummed in his mind. *The* karigul *will accomplish its task when the time is right. When the Hunter is ripe for harvest. You have only to wait for the right time, and his life will be yours.*

Gods, Bael thought eagerly, *it can't come soon enough.*

The Magus Hade was starving. It had been ages since he'd felt the comfort of a real bed, or the satisfaction of a proper meal. Across the fire, Vadim was scraping the hide from a lean rabbit. It had been a miracle that his Knight had caught *that* much this late in the year.

Vadim glanced up at him, sensing his misery. The Knight offered a heartfelt smile and tossed the hide, along with the innards, into the fire. They didn't want to leave any evidence of their passage. Their position was dangerous enough as it was.

As he did every night, Hade wearily recalled their flight from the village of Drava.

Things had settled down. The people were happy for the first time in a long while. Aleksei had Vadim and Hade remain to make sure that things returned to normal, and they had.

And then the people had been visited by a messenger from Lord Perron. With the announcement of Lord Hugo Malak's death at Aleksei's hand, the people became agitated.

It wasn't that they particularly liked Lord Malak; they loathed him. But to know that the very man who had recently been among them, who had fought and defeated an army of revenants, had murdered their lord unsettled them.

It hadn't taken long for the idea of rebellion to seep into their simple, vengeful minds. Vadim had been smart enough to recognize the danger. They'd left under the cover of nightfall, traveling north through the Relvyn Wood. They'd hoped to get far enough to cut cross-country and follow the Ylik Water north back to Kalinor. Drava's hunters had obviously planned something else.

Vadim had taken two crossbow bolts through his leg. There were ten men. Ten men against the two of them.

Hade killed them all.

He wasn't sure where it came from, but there was a fury inside him that he'd never felt before. In the end, it wasn't much more than the simple fire spell that Ilyana had taught him. Yet he used it to raze those men to the ground. Worse yet, he'd enjoyed it.

It had taken a long time for Vadim to heal. Hade's own efforts kept away infection, but he could do little to knit the flesh together. Day by day he worked on his Knight's wound. Day by day, Vadim grew stronger. Hade was far from a woodsman, but he saw deer and rabbits often enough. He used his limited magic to hold them while he cut their throats.

Vadim was glad for the meat.

Hade allowed his Knight to skin the animals and cook the meat. He started the fires and gathered wood and water. Vadim even managed to sew cloaks from the skins he collected.

Hade was stunned at Vadim's ingenuity, carving bone needles and sewing the hides together with gut. Vadim had grudgingly admitted that Aleksei had taught him the technique.

Hade was grateful. He knew that winter would be upon them the moment they left the protection of the Relvyn Wood, and he was glad to have the added warmth.

Vadim had been intent on reaching Kalinor. He was adamant that they tell Aleksei what was happening. Perhaps he would be able to reason with the people of Drava, help ease their fears.

When they'd finally arrived, Kalinor was on fire.

For days they'd retreated into the hills, searching for their next step. Something unusual had slowly overcome Vadim. He had once been so powerfully opposed to Aleksei Drago, but the events of the last few months had changed his mind. And yet, Hade knew that Aleksei and Jonas were undoubtedly dead. He had seen Kalinor. A Kalinor he didn't recognize, one held by the enemy. A Kalinor defeated.

Hade knew that neither Aleksei nor Jonas would have allowed such a thing to happen as long as they drew breath, but he kept his fears to himself. The hope that they might find Aleksei was sometimes the only thing that seemed to keep Vadim going. Hade wasn't about to take that away from his Knight. Not before they reached safety.

From the smoldering capitol, Hade and Vadim had struck out again, keeping to the back hills, far from the roads. Hopefully, Keldoan still stood. They would find refuge there, even as the winter grew bitter. Vadim was confident that Aleksei would want them to be safe, and to help in whatever way possible.

Hade agreed readily. He was just as eager to have a real bed under his back as a hot meal before him. If Vadim said they'd find such a thing in Keldoan, then that's where they'd go.

Hade watched Vadim spit the rabbit on a stick he'd stripped. He laid the rabbit across the stones of their fire pit, turning it as the flesh sizzled. All Archanium Knights received a particular gift from their bonded Magi, though it was never something that could be consciously chosen. Vadim's gift had made him impervious to fire, which certainly made campfire cooking all the easier. Hade marveled at Vadim's ingenuity.

Vadim glanced up with his midnight eyes and smirked, "You know where I learned this, right?"

Hade sighed, "Aleksei Drago?"

Vadim laughed. Louder than Hade had heard him laugh in a long time. Finally, the man shook his dark head of hair, "Not this time. My father taught me. He took me out onto the plains, on occasion. When we caught game, he taught me to roast the meat like this. Just as he taught me to skin. Aleksei was the one who showed me the value of the rest of beast, but I learned the basics from my father."

Hade breathed a sigh of relief. He'd grown tired of hearing of their amazing savior, Aleksei Drago. Vadim now seemed to have endless faith in the very man he used to hate. Hade still didn't understand Vadim's devotion.

He personally thought Aleksei was a nice enough man, but hardly their savior. After all, the Knights and Magi had faced the revenants *together*. Beyond that, Jonas commanded far more power than Aleksei. The Prince had strength in the Archanium the likes of which Hade had never seen.

Hade ate his dinner in silence. Vadim, still weary from the work of trapping the animal and cooking it, not to mention the wound that still pestered him, finally nodded off to sleep.

Hade had never been so relieved to see Vadim curl up in his deerskin cloak. Hade had something important to do this night.

Tonight was the *beginning*. He rose from his position near the fire, casting a spell over his Knight. It wasn't powerful, merely strong enough to ensure Vadim wouldn't wake unexpectedly.

With an effort, Hade suppressed the fire. He watched it dim into glowing coals, satisfied that Vadim would be warm, and that he would be safe while Hade was away.

Hade hurried into the darkness. He didn't need light to find the way; it was practically drawn across the land in foxfire. Of course, he was the only one who could see it. That made the whole thing all the more perfect. He was the only one.

He had been *chosen*.

When he reached the shore of the small pond, Hade fell to his knees and bowed his head, just as he had each time before.

"What do you command, Master?"

He felt the brief flicker in the Archanium. The Master always appeared in the same way, wreathed in green flame, to announce his presence. To make it clear that he *was* the Master.

Sammul smiled and laid his hand on the back of Hade's head. "Rise my child. I have much to tell you tonight."

"Xavathan."

The middle-aged angel looked up into an ancient face, at once radiant and haunted. The Angelus, leader of the Host, and Empress of Dalita.

He stood on the banks of the Fount, the great lake in the center of the Basilica, on the doorstep of her personal palace. Very few angels were ever allowed this close to the Angelus.

"Mother," he said with a bow.

"And Adam," she said, looking past her son to the young angel kneeling before her. "I didn't expect to see you back here without my prize."

Adam looked up into the ice-blue eyes of Kevara Avlon, seeming a breath away from dissolving into tears. She noted the heavy bandaging crossing his chest. "I have not failed you, Angelus. I have obeyed your orders."

She straightened in confusion. "But...."

"Good to see you again, Kevara," came a cold voice. She pursed her lips as the form of her grandson stepped into the light. He had been standing on the other side of her son, but Xavathan's grand wings had concealed him.

"So, you *finally* decided to do as you were told, then?" she asked crisply.

Jonas looked into her eyes, and a small scream escaped her.

"My other options were less to my liking," he said simply. His nightmare eyes bored into her.

Her eyes flicked to the opposite shores of the Fount, her mouth pursing into a tight twist of anger and fear. "Get inside!" she hissed. "All of you. This instant, before someone sees you!"

Jonas made it a point to take his time. He would submit to this woman's healing, but only because he had no other choice. He certainly wouldn't afford her respect. His grandmother's past actions had made her unworthy of anything save his disdain.

It was because of this woman that his mother had vanished, that he grew up an orphan. It was because of this woman that he was a bloody *amputee*, almost from the moment he was born. While his chest was excessively muscular, his back had come to ache constantly, as he lacked the wings that would have balanced his physiology. Because of her, he could never be whole, in so many ways.

When the door snapped shut, she rounded on her son. "Xavathan, what do you think you're doing? Are you mad? Bringing one touched by the Presence into the Basilica in broad daylight? And a bloody *Cherub*? You're lucky the boy is alive."

Jonas frowned, glancing to his uncle. The Seraph's face had grown pale. "Forgive me, Mother. I was only doing what I believed to be right, and that was to bring Jonas to you as swiftly as possible. We have been flying all night and most of the morning to reach you."

Kevara Avlon scowled at him and turned to Jonas, "And you! What do you have to say for yourself?"

Jonas quirked a smile. How like her, he thought. It was a miracle he was even alive, yet she *blamed* him, as though this had been his intent all along.

"I apologize, Kevara. I'll try to avoid battling demon spawn in the future."

"If you had stayed put," she snapped, "Adam would have found you and brought you here. Before the Demon had the chance to do...this."

He was surprised she didn't spit on him, as much as he obviously disgusted her.

He arched a chestnut eyebrow, "If I had stayed put, *Grandmother*, I would be dead, or imprisoned by the self-same Demon who followed me onto the Madrhal Plains. I was running from him, not the other way around. I hardly sought him out. He nearly killed me once already, but I was spared that fate."

Kevara Avlon glared at him, "It would have been better had you died. You were not supposed to survive that encounter with the Demon."

Jonas stepped forward aggressively and stopped a breath away from the ancient angel, "Is that what you wish, Grandmother? Me dead?"

She glared back at him, her eyes ice. "From the moment of your birth. It would have been better. For *everyone*."

He snorted, "Not for me. Not for Aleksei. And at the moment, there are precious few things I care about more than that man. You? You're not even good enough to lick his boots."

Kevara Avlon's hand came up. He could feel the Archanium swirling around her. He caught her wrist, opening himself to the Archanium in the same moment and allowing the power, and the pungent pollution of the Presence, to fill him.

Her eyes widened.

He smirked, "You can try, Kevara. Go ahead, try to burn me from this world because of your unreasoning faith in your One-God. But this time I *will* defend myself. Last time I tried to use the Archanium, it didn't go so well for me. Worse for someone innocent. I don't view you as innocent. I'm willing to take a gamble. Are you?"

"Enough!"

Everyone's heads turned to Xavathan. Everyone except Jonas. He kept his ink-dark eyes locked on the Angelus.

"Mother," Xavathan snarled, glaring at her as he walked forward, "I brought Jonas here so you could *help* him. So you could take this curse away, and we could all return to our lives. Instead you berate him, and act like a spoiled child. You have shamed yourself, Mother."

Her eyes widened, but he had already turned from her. He glowered down at Jonas, "And you. Wipe that smirk off your face, boy. You are meddling in powers you only think you comprehend.

"You think that your luck with magic makes you superior? You are more a spoiled child than she, yet it becomes you all the less. You are lucky to be alive, much less in a position to threaten an angel of her power. She is your only hope in this. And without her, you'll never see your precious Knight again, so try acting like an adult for five bloody minutes."

Jonas arched an eyebrow at his uncle, but Xavathan was unflinching. He leaned closer, where only the two of them could hear. "I'm not playing around, Jonas. She'd burn you from existence before you could blink. Because she *wants* to. She's afraid, but for all the wrong reasons. Let me talk to her. I've already saved your life twice, and I fear I now must do it again. But you have to stop acting like such a petulant child. Even if she is. Be better than that. What would Aleksei think of your behavior?"

Jonas's smirk faltered and faded. He dropped his hand and walked over to stand by Adam, his hands clasped behind his back.

"I have erred," he said calmly. He bowed to his uncle, "Forgive me. I will let one wiser than I handle this."

Xavathan gave him a warning look, turning to his mother. She looked like she could burn *him* from the room for his impudence. He ignored it. Unlike Jonas, he'd had a lifetime of experience with her temper.

Her tantrums didn't interest him.

He knelt. "Holy Angelus, I bring one before you in need of healing. Healing only the Seraphima can provide. Healing from the Demonic Presence, and its curse upon his soul. As Angelus, I charge you with removing the corruption from this poor boy. I supplicate myself before you, and ask that you bestow your benedictions upon him. I invoke the right to Sanctuary on his behalf."

Beside him, Jonas felt Adam tense. Something important was happening, though he had no idea *what*.

The Angelus looked as though she could have spat nails.

"Rise, child of the One-God, in whose image all things are made," she growled. "For He is merciful. May His benediction fall upon the suffering, that through His ways I might bring comfort to this world of sin and corruption."

Xavathan stood.

She turned to Adam, "You are discharged of your duty. You may return to your penance at the Reliquary. Before you return, go to the healer's cloister. They will tend your wounds."

Adam breathed a sigh of relief and bowed before her. He paused only to grip Jonas's shoulder and offer him a shy smile before stepping out of the small palace and flying to the far shore.

She turned to her son. "I don't know what you think you're playing at, child, but you may have your wish. For now. Take him to the Undercroft. And then I would like to speak with you privately."

The angel bowed to his mother.

"Jonas," he said softly as he passed the Prince, "it's time we were going."

The Seraph carried him easily across the Fount before setting off north towards the Undercroft. Jonas trotted after him, his head spinning. Something had happened in there. Something dangerous, and vastly important, yet he was still in the dark.

"What was that?" Jonas demanded, bracing for the worst.

His uncle waved the question away, "Now is not the time. I must get you to the Undercroft, before anyone sees you. Before they *feel* you."

"I don't understand," Jonas snapped.

Xavathan came to a halt, leaning in close, "There are many beliefs that surround our faith in the One-God.

"Some here would kill you for the color of your eyes. They wouldn't ask questions to determine anything else, they would simply destroy you before you even knew you were in danger. *That* was what had the Angelus in such a state. At least at first."

Jonas hung his head as they continued walking, "I truly do apologize, Uncle. We have a habit of drawing out the worst in each other. My last dealings with her went rather differently."

Xavathan snorted a laugh, "I imagine they did. My mother has great regret and shame in her heart for what has transpired in your life, and her part in it.

"But now it is different. You have become something, in her eyes, that trumps those old hurts in her. You are now not only to be feared, but to be destroyed. You represent all that she abhors. Her shame, her regret have now become loathing, and it all feeds her fear."

Jonas blinked in confusion, "I still don't understand. That doesn't make any sense."

The angel waved his protest away, "And it wouldn't, to you. You are not of the faith. The blood, but not the faith. Even if you were to study our holy texts, our Scripture, they could not convey the level of intense fear and hate that your grandmother now holds for you."

"Then *explain* it to me," Jonas demanded, halting the angel in the middle of an enormous marble walkway. A hundred paces before them, the marble turned black. Jonas could feel something emanating from that jet maw. Magic. Danger.

He knew that was where they were headed. He needed to understand before he went too far.

"We don't have the luxury of time at the moment, child. But to put it bluntly, she believes you are an abomination. Wicked. A being sent to test us, or destroy us. Now, we must go."

Jonas walked behind his uncle, rolling the words around in his mind. So, she thought he was wicked? On further reflection, he supposed it made sense. She had hated his mother, had accused her of murder. Of murdering his father, the third-born Seraph. The third child of the Angelus.

He had little doubt Kevara Avlon would have killed his mother if she hadn't vanished first. But simply believing his mother to be evil didn't necessarily mean that he shared that same trait.

He also knew that her hatred for his mother was paltry compared to what Xavathan had just related to him. This was something altogether different. Seeing his black eyes had changed her, and her view of him, forever. He felt it in his heart.

Any pity he still harbored for her evaporated.

He stopped himself short of driving any feeling for her but hate from his heart. He would not become her. If she hated him, then he would do the opposite. He would make her hate herself for loathing him. He vowed to himself, as he entered that cold, black marble archway, that he would become the very stuff of her nightmares before this was all over.

But not the nightmares she anticipated.

CHAPTER 8

PHANTOMS

Simon Declan pushed away the plate of stew and sat back in his chair. "Thank you, Mother Margareta, that was wonderful."

The old woman smiled at him and took the plate away.

Gods! He wondered if either Katherine or the old woman would ever tire of feeding him. He wondered how they managed to do anything else, as much food as they seemed to have perpetually prepared.

"Now, Lord Declan," Mother Margareta said from her small kitchen, "what are your plans moving forward?"

He frowned, "I beg your pardon?"

She returned to the table and set down a basket of apples. She handed one to Katherine with a knife and both women set to peeling them. "You can't stay in Voskrin forever, sampling our culinary talents, Lord Declan. I know that, and so do you. You have much to do, I'm sure."

Declan sighed, "I fear, my good lady, that in this you are correct. Although I must say, I'm not exactly sure where to begin."

Mother Margareta shrugged, tossing a peeled apple into the basket, "Well, I believe you mentioned that your former friends think you dead, yes?"

Declan found himself fidgeting under the elderly woman's interrogation. "I believe so."

Mother Margareta picked up another apple, "Then you have an opportunity to make some good out of the evil you helped create."

He blinked at her. "Pardon?"

Her knife stopped and she looked him in the eye, "Lord Declan, if your friends think you dead, then you find yourself with an enormous freedom. You may do whatever you like. You can join our Aleksei and help him fight these evil men. Be on the side of good for once."

He stammered for words, but she wasn't finished.

"Of course, heading out to find the people that you betrayed might not be the *best* of ideas. They might have some funny opinions about you and your allegiances by now. And then there's the trifling matter of treason."

Declan realized that he was starting to sweat. He was being led like an ox, but he didn't know where. More amazing still, he was being led by a prattling old woman in a peasant village.

"I don't take your meaning, madam," he said weakly.

She smiled, going back to her apple, "I know my Aleksei. He's a good boy, with a good heart. But he's no fool. His father did a fine job raising that boy. He has a strong sense of right and wrong. Of justice. I doubt he'll be too pleased to see you ride up and beg to be placed under the protection of the people you were trying to kill a scant month ago."

"I can see why he would have reservations," Declan admitted softly.

"So what are you going to do about it?"

"Madam?"

She dropped another apple in the basket and gave a weary sigh. "Lord Declan, if in your heart, you regret the side you chose in this war, then what are you going to *do* about it? Begging for forgiveness so that you can hide behind the Lord Captain's men is hardly going to be of aid to anyone. It just makes you look like a coward, which you may well be."

He stood, his face red. He was willing to listen to this crone, but he would not be insulted by her.

"How dare you?" he snapped.

An unseen force slammed him back into his seat. The wood creaked.

Mother Margareta arched an eyebrow, "Lord Declan, I expect two things in my house. I expect my guests to act appropriately and politely. And I only ever deal in honesty. When I said you might be a coward, you must admit that I might be right, though it may offend you.

"What did you do when faced with an unpleasant situation? When asked to make a difficult decision, you chose the easy way out, abandoning your principles and your queen.

"When faced with danger, you did not rise to the occasion. Did you run to those men in the fire, and pull them from the flames of Jonas Belgi's wrath? Or did you run away out of fear? What is heroic about what you did? I would call such a man a coward, and such a man sits before me now."

She picked up another apple.

Declan gritted his teeth. Her words were galling. Who did she think she was to speak to him this way?

"So what are you going to do about it?" she asked again.

There were a great many things he wanted to say to the old cow right then, and none of them were appropriate speech for a lady to hear. He tried to open his mouth, but found he couldn't.

"It's probably best if you hold your tongue for the moment, dear." She looked up into his eyes, "Or I can hold it for you. It's all the same to me. But you will listen to what I have to say.

"I honestly don't care what you do, Lord Declan. It's your life, not mine. But I would be remiss in my duties to the Goddess if I let you wander about without providing the benefit of my counsel. Now, are you prepared to listen to what I have to say? Or do you need another demonstration?"

Declan took a deep breath, cooling his anger. He tried to open his mouth and found he was no longer hindered. "I will listen to your words, madam," he managed, though it galled him to say it.

She smiled, "Why thank you, Lord Declan. I'm so glad you've come around to the side of reason."

She dropped the last apple in the basket. Across the table, Katherine was still peeling her first apple, and doing so very intently.

Mother Margareta wiped her hands on her apron and leaned towards Declan. "I called you a coward because, thus far, you have behaved as one. That does not mean you will die a coward.

"Perhaps it would be in your best interest to change the course you've set for yourself? Perhaps by doing something equally heroic, to help the very people you now claim to support? That might bring them around to trust you. If you in fact want to change your ways, the opportunity is sitting right in front of you."

He frowned, "I apologize, madam, but I still don't see where you're heading with this."

"Lord Declan, you are in a very special position right now. You are still believed to be the ally of your enemies. This makes you valuable. I think my Aleksei would be most impressed if you were to return to Kalinor, once again as you were, a traitor.

"I believe a man in your station would be privy to some highly sensitive information. As their 'ally', you could also see to it that their information begins to show cracks. Seeds of chaos are easier sewn from within."

"You want me to be a spy?" he asked, aghast.

"I do. I want you to seek out their weaknesses, exploit the chinks in their armor. In their plans, their tactics. And then I want you to give all the information you've been gathering to the Lord Captain, so that he can crush these murderous bastards."

Both Declan and Katherine were staring at Mother Margareta now. Katherine's mouth was hanging open.

Mother Margareta paused for a moment, then smiled, "So what do you say, Lord Declan. Are you ready to be a hero for once?"

Declan swallowed hard. "I can try my best. But I think you'll find that sometimes, a man of my station hears less than you'd think. Secrets are guarded jealously by those who hold them, so they might be used against the others. It is hardly a group of confidants."

She nodded sagely, "I know. That's why Katherine will be accompanying you. In the guise of a maid."

"*What*?" Katherine let out a surprised shriek.

Mother Margareta smiled and reached across the table, resting her hand on Katherine's. The poor girl was trembling.

"Katherine, dear, you said yourself that you wanted to take revenge on the men who hurt Aleksei. Who may have even killed him by now. What better way than to use that sharp mind of yours against the enemy?

"As a mere girl from a tiny village in the Southern Plain, you are far more above suspicion than Lord Declan. Better, you are a native of Lord Perron's lands. The *depths* of his lands. He would be more likely to trust one such as yourself than any man in a fancy coat. You are without guile, or ambition. You are simply a maid. But a maid with *ears*.

"Lord Declan, I'm sure you'll agree that men of your lofty station, or Perron's, seldom notice the help." He nodded grudgingly. It didn't make him sound particularly noble when she phrased it that way.

"Katherine, you'll be a phantom, ghosting through their chambers, their things, their papers. As long as you're not obvious, they'll hardly register your presence. Between the two of you, I believe great good can be achieved."

"But Mother," Katherine whimpered, "it's so dangerous!"

Mother Margareta's smile saddened, "Yes, child. But if you believe in what you're fighting for, what Aleksei is fighting for, then isn't it worth that danger? Anything truly worth having, worth fighting for, has a price."

Katherine considered a long moment before tossing her apple into the basket with the rest. "Very well. When do we leave?"

As they reached the black marble archway, Jonas gave his uncle a sidelong glance, "So what is this place?"

Xavathan sighed, "This is the Cathedral of the Sainted Werenboch, named for an angel martyred trying to convert the northern pagans five hundred years past. He was hacked apart by children, who ate bits of his flesh as he watched and bled out."

Jonas stared at him, trying to judge whether his uncle was joking or not.

Xavathan's face betrayed no hint of humor, "Most people outside just call it the Undercroft. It is impenetrably shielded against any attack."

"From inside or out?" Jonas muttered.

"Both. Nothing harmless goes beyond, and nothing of danger leaves without good reason. Inside, you will be safe from the Demon, and from the Presence. It cannot penetrate our shields, certainly not through you. At the same time, the world will be protected from you. As long as you carry this curse, you must remain behind our shields."

Jonas sighed. The entire setup was an obvious trap, but he wasn't exactly in a position to argue. "Very well. Let's get this over with. The sooner we've dealt with this annoyance, the sooner I can be on my way."

His uncle waved an arm, "You first. I cannot pass through the shields with you. You must pass by the power of your own free will. I will follow you."

Jonas arched an eyebrow, but stepped through the archway.

It was like being plunged into ice water. He gasped as he the magic of Angelic Song passed through every fiber of his being. With a start, he realized he was shivering. He turned and looked at the archway. He could see nothing on the other side but cool darkness.

The archway lit with a gentle blue glow as his uncle stepped through, apparently unaffected by the chill of the shields.

"What was that about?" the prince snapped.

Xavathan shrugged, "The shields had to recognize you, and your magic, for what it was. If I had crossed with you, it would have become confused. It would have been unable to recognize you in the future."

Jonas felt an icy tendril wind its way through him, "And why would you want it recognize me in the future?"

Xavathan smiled sadly, "It saw what you are, Jonas. Every part, including the lingering shard of the Presence lodged deep within you. That was the...unpleasantness you felt. The shield identified the magic of the Presence, and it has marked you. Once that shard is removed, the shield will allow you to pass through again."

Jonas's face darkened, "And what if your healers *aren't* able to remove the Presence? How will I get out then?"

Xavathan looked away from the prince's piercing dead-night glare, "I'm sorry, Jonas. I only did what was required to keep my mother from destroying you where you stood. This was the only way."

Jonas swept forward and gripped the angel's robe, pulling him close, "You mean I might be trapped in here forever?"

Xavathan sighed, "It is a possibility, yes, but a dim one. Our healers are without equal. The Angelus herself will oversee your exorcism. None possess more command of the Seraphima. But had I not sought her benediction, she would have killed you."

Jonas released his uncle, "Is that what you did when you knelt? What was that?"

Xavathan straightened his robes, "That was a supplication. As the leader of the Host, she is bound by the covenants of her office to grant Sanctuary to any who seek it. If the one in need is an outsider, the request can be made by another. If invoked by a Seraph, the request supersedes all other covenants. She had no choice but to accept you into her care. If she violates her oath to heal you, she will be giving up her post as Angelus at the same time."

Jonas managed a reluctant smile, "Then I must thank you, Uncle. You have saved my life three times now. I owe you more than I can say."

The angel's face remained grave, "You will more than repay your debt before you leave this place. You have no idea what you are in for.

And I cannot tell you how long you will be here. Some of the magic employed here is sensitive to external elements. Lunar positions, angles of the sun and stars. Things beyond our control. You may have to wait for some of them to align. This is not a process taken lightly."

Jonas sighed in frustration. "I understand. I simply want this dealt with as swiftly as possible."

Xavathan gripped his shoulder and smiled, "Don't worry, Nephew. I will personally see to it that your case is handled with the greatest of both haste and caution. I will not leave the Basilica until we at least know what we're dealing with."

Jonas nodded soberly, "I thank you for that. May I ask you a question?"

The angel smiled, "My knowledge is at your disposal."

"Am I allowed visitors? Or am I a prisoner behind this shield?"

Xavathan took a deep breath, "You are allowed conditional visitors. This means that you have been declared a risk to yourself and those around you. While the Presence can't reach you within this place, that doesn't mean you aren't dangerous. There are a great many unknowns with your...unique situation. Any who wish to see you must agree to a certain amount of risk, as simply being around you could prove fatal. Young Adam has already learned this lesson, yes?"

Jonas looked away.

"But," the angel said, brightening, "should you have friends or family who are willing to accept such a risk, they will be allowed access to you. Anyone in the Basilica you know?"

"Leigha," he said softly. "If she's around and willing, I would very much like to see her."

Xavathan smiled, "I'll see if I can locate her. I'm sure she'll be glad to have family her own age in the Basilica again. And I'm sure you'll see Adam about while you're here."

Jonas frowned, "Why should I? I imagine he doesn't want to be within a hundred leagues of me, if he can help it."

"Dear boy, the Reliquary is housed *within* the Undercroft. As I said, things of danger are kept here. There are objects in the Reliquary that would make your hair stand on end."

Jonas smiled, "Sounds like the Voralla."

"In a way they're much the same. The Voralla is home to a great many more objects than our Reliquary, but the things we keep have a far greater danger associated with them. They are meant to be kept away from those who would use them for evil, not used by the righteous, like in your Voralla."

Jonas snorted, "The last time an object was taken from the Vault, it was used to break open the Cathedral of Dazhbog and free the Demonic Presence."

Xavathan nodded, "Yes, but it only arrived there after having been foolishly released from this very place. Had our forebearers not been quite so nearsighted, you would not stand here now, in your condition."

Jonas sighed, suddenly tired. "So what do I do now?"

Xavathan walked deeper down the dark marble corridor. Jonas followed, realizing that though there was no source of light, he could still see clearly. He was immediately distracted, trying to discern the source of the illumination.

He finally decided that it might come from behind the stone, though the effect was quite subtle. The result was that the space before and behind them faded into pure blackness. Only the space they occupied was lit, casting light roughly a dozen paces in each direction.

It was decidedly disorienting, and Jonas imagined it was all too easy to become lost in this place. His hopes of ever escaping slowly sank. He was in a prison, a prison he'd entered willingly. He simply hoped his wardens were of a gentle and forgiving disposition.

They rounded a corner and Jonas jumped as the illumination ran ahead of them, blossoming into an enormous chamber. Jonas blinked as they stepped out into a wide atrium. Sunlight twinkled in through a great stained-glass dome. Jonas supposed the dome had to be one, perhaps one hundred and fifty paces high, the glass cast in every hue of the spectrum.

It was a breathtaking sight.

"Xavathan!" came a surprised, silvery voice. "Why, I hadn't expected you back until the Solstice. What brings you...." The words trailed off, and Jonas suddenly realized he was being stared at.

He offered the lovely young angel before him a handsome smile. "Good day, Angelica. My name is Jonas Belgi. Whom do I have the pleasure of addressing?"

She stammered for a moment before finding her words, "Sariel, Jonas. I am the Angel Sariel. I am one of the healers here."

Xavathan regarded the other angel sternly, "Now my dear, Jonas is my nephew."

A hand shot to her mouth, "Oh! Xavathan, I'm so sorry."

Jonas gritted his teeth at being treated like he was invisible. "I don't believe my uncle is afflicted at present, Angel Sariel. Thus far, I don't seem to be contagious."

The angels suddenly seemed to remember him. She turned a crimson face to his and managed a smile, "My *apologies*, Jonas. It's just that, well, I've never spoken to one in your...condition before. I must say, it's a little unnerving." She saw his face darken and was quick to add, "But I'm *sure* we'll all get used to it, in time. And after a bit, you won't seem corrupted at all!"

He turned his back to the both of them, stepping deeper into the atrium. All around, people, both Angelic and human, walked through the lush garden that filled the space beneath the dome. Walkways spiraled up towards the light, giving the impression of a giant spiderweb suspended between the stained-glass dome and the garden. It was a dizzying spectacle.

Jonas turned back to the two angels. They were speaking closely to one another, Sariel nodding as Xavathan spoke in short, concise sentences. From his spot several paces away, Jonas couldn't make out any of the words, but he caught their tone.

His uncle was speaking in a very low, dangerous voice. And from the look on her face, Sariel wasn't missing a word. When they noticed his staring, they straightened.

"Jonas," Xavathan said, speaking up, "I must see to a few other matters. I will see you after evening vespers. Until then, I'll leave you in Sariel's capable hands."

Jonas raised a hand, bidding his uncle farewell. As he watched Xavathan walk away, panic clutched at his heart. His breath constricted in his throat.

He was a prisoner.

Before the panic could completely seize him, he slowed his breathing. It would do no good to waste energy on emotion just then. He simply needed to get his bearings. And then he would see how tightly this trap ensnared him.

Sariel walked cautiously up to him, her forced smile returning. "So, Jonas, I was surprised to learn of your relation to Xavathan. I didn't realize there were any non-Angelic Cherubs. Until now, I was only aware of Leigha."

Jonas's eyes narrowed, "I'm not 'non-Angelic'. My wings were excised when I was a babe. By the Angelus. However, I doubt my name comes up often in the halls of the Basilica. I am the only son of Joel and the Princess Rhiannon of Ilyar."

Sariel missed a step. "I see. Well, it's a privilege having royalty amongst us, even if it is for this unfortunate malady. But take heart, there are no better healers in this world. We will set you to rights."

Jonas noticed that she made no mention of how long she thought that might take. He sighed, wishing he could at least have Aleksei here with him. He smiled, thinking of the Knight's handsome smile and the twinkle in his golden eyes when he looked at Jonas.

It seemed years since he'd spent a moment with the man that hadn't been filled with abject terror or urgency. How he longed for those long, wondrous days they'd spent together in the Seil Wood, where Aleksei had taught him to cut trails and follow tracks.

But that seemed a lifetime ago. His expression sobered. That had been before the Presence had been freed, and before the civil war. Now there was hardly anything else to think about. He gently reached for the bond, wondering where Aleksei was right then.

He stopped short, the panic rising in him again.

"Sariel," he said, fighting to keep his voice steady, "I have a few questions about this place. I was wondering if you might be able to provide me some answers?"

She brightened, "Of course. What would you like to know?"

"Well, my uncle filled me in on a few details. I'm not sure if you're aware, but I'm an Archanium Magus. As such, I have a Knight bonded to me. But since we've been beyond the shield, I can no longer feel my bond with him. Do you know why?"

She put a hand to her mouth, "Oh! I'm so sorry, Jonas. Xavathan must have forgotten to mention it. The nature of the shield blocks all outside magics. While it protects you from the Demonic Presence, it also cuts out any other interference. In the case of your bond, I'm afraid it won't function while you're in here."

Jonas eyes narrowed, "What do you mean, 'won't function'?"

She considered a long moment, "Well, I'm not well-versed on the subject myself. Of your bond, I mean. But I imagine that as long as you're in here, the bond you have with your Knight would be nullified."

"You mean to say it's been *broken*?"

She shook her head, "No, nothing like that. Just as your connection to the Demonic Presence would be a danger were you to return to the world beyond the shield, so too would your bond to your Knight return.

But while in here, the bond has been stripped of its power...its connection to the outside world."

Jonas let loose a curse. Sariel gasped at his vehemence. He wondered if she'd ever heard the name of her god used in such a way.

"Jonas, *please*, you are in a sacred place!" she whispered fiercely. "One in your condition needs all the blessings of the One-God you can get!"

Jonas's gaze darkened, "Sariel, at the moment I couldn't care less. You've just delivered me some *very* unpleasant news."

When she frowned, he realized she had no idea. He sighed.

"If I can't touch our bond, neither can my Knight. And while that does me no harm, protected in here as I am, he is not so fortunate. Without his bond with me, he will be like any other normal man. He will have no benefits to draw on. Worse, without knowing this, I fear he might try to pull on the bond in a time of desperation. It could get him badly hurt. Or killed."

She gasped, "Oh my. Jonas, I'm so sorry. I had no idea."

"Furthermore," he continued, realizing the ramifications as he spoke, "if he were to die out beyond the shield, I wouldn't know it in here. The moment I pass beyond the shield, if he *has* fallen in battle, I could share his fate.

"Or...I'm not sure what would happen if he were to die while I'm in here. The bond might simply fade away, and spare me. Or the backlash could be suspended on the other side, waiting like a viper, to strike me dead the moment I return."

He held back the tears that came with such a thought. The idea of losing one's Bonded was bad enough, since it carried the implied death of both Magus and Knight. But the idea of Aleksei having lost his connection to Jonas, not knowing what had happened to him, of him dying without knowing if Jonas was even *there* anymore...it was almost enough to make him sick on the spot.

Her features were stricken with fear. A thought seemed to occur to her, and the fear melted away, "Those are some dire matters to meditate upon, Jonas. I can see your worry. But take heart, it won't be of serious concern for some time. For the moment, let's spend our energy on seeing you restored."

Something she'd said earlier flashed through his mind. He caught her arm as she started walking.

"Sariel, just how long do you anticipate it will take to 'put me to rights', as you said earlier?"

She frowned, "Well, if the moon and sun line up properly, and the Angelus takes a special interest in your case, you might be able to leave soon. I'd say certainly in the next ten years."

Jonas finally released his hold on his panic. It shot through him, gripping his heart and squeezing the remaining hope from him.

He was lost.

Worse, his bond to Aleksei had been silenced. He was trapped in this place, and Aleksei wouldn't even know where to *find* him. By the time Aleksei realized that the bond had been silenced, he might have tried to draw on Jonas's magic. It could very well cost him his life.

Jonas sank to the cool marble floor, an overwhelming hopelessness tearing into him. He was lost, and Aleksei was more vulnerable than he'd ever been.

And Jonas hadn't even had the chance to tell Aleksei how much he loved him. Aleksei could die without ever hearing the words from Jonas's lips again, or feeling his presence through the bond. Jonas might as well be a phantom, for all the good he could do his Knight now. He felt something warm on his hand and realized tears were streaming from his eyes, finally released.

He didn't have the energy to stop them.

CHAPTER 9

AMONGST THE SHADOWS

Colonel Frederick Rysun glowered at the sky. All through the air, tiny flurries of snow were slowly being replaced by thick, heavy flakes. He brushed them from his eyes as he rode through the ranks of his men, watching their steady progress towards Keldoan.

They were still many leagues from the great city, but they had been making good time. The falling snow only increased his urgency to reach those enchanted walls. Worse, they were gaining elevation. He'd never been to the storied city, but he had heard tales of the infamously bitter Keldoan winters. He didn't want his men caught out in such harsh weather. They were tired and hungry enough as it was without adding "frozen" to their list of complaints.

Beside him, Henry Drago surveyed the sky with a grim face.

The man had been an invaluable guide in keeping Rysun and his men alive out in the wilds. With his help, the men had learned to hunt and scavenge food for themselves in the hills. They'd learned to blend into their surroundings, and to use the land to their advantage.

It had honed them into a force that could survive in harsh conditions. Any softness left from a regimented training schedule in Mornj had quickly given way to the core of steel they'd gained through necessity from life in the hills.

But winter was threatening that resolve, and Rysun yearned for a meal consisting of more than roots, hardtack, and the occasional bit of wild meat. He had little doubt that his men were thinking equally hopeful thoughts. They had put up with tougher conditions than most. The defeat at Kalinor had been galling. To have the crown city overrun without even raising a sword....

"Colonel?"

Rysun looked up from his dark thoughts, "What is it, Sergeant?"

"Colonel, a rider approaches. He's coming on fast."

Rysun shared a glance with Henry, then turned his horse towards the back of the column. "And he's alone?"

The sergeant nodded.

Rysun took a deep breath, "I doubt it's any sort of threat. No one man would be so foolish."

"Could be a Magus," the sergeant ventured.

Rysun waved the concern away, "Even one of their power wouldn't come alone. Come on, let's see what he wants."

The words were hardly out of his mouth when he saw the figure growing larger. He stiffened. He knew that horse.

"Great gods," he whispered.

Henry frowned, squinting into the distance. He recognized the rider a moment later.

"I'm afraid that's no god, Frederick," Henry said with a gruff chuckle. "It's just my son."

Rysun arched an eyebrow at the older man. "Perhaps to *you*. Our men have a slightly different view towards him, as you well know."

The great black warhorse slowed as he approached. Rysun gave a crisp salute as Aleksei rode towards them at a canter. The Lord Captain's face was grim, "We have to move the column. Now!"

Rysun frowned, "What's the trouble, Lord Captain?"

Aleksei glared fiercely behind him. His face was haggard. And something more.

Haunted.

"Frederick, we're about to have a fight on our hands. We have the advantage of speed and surprise right now, but not for long. We're being pursued by the enemy. They're less than half a day's march behind you, and closing fast."

Rysun's black eyebrows shot up, "*Who* is?"

"Eight thousand men, including two thousand conscripts from Kalinor. And Colonel, that's not all."

Rysun shared an incredulous glance with Henry as Aleksei rapidly explained the force that pursued them. Their incredulity rose when Aleksei explained his plan, and the seeds he'd sown in the enemy camp.

"That sounds like insanity. You're taking a lot on faith there, Son," Henry ventured.

Aleksei wiped his forearm across his brow, "I know. But it's our only shot. We'll deal with the smaller force as swiftly as possible, then break to the woods. We don't have the time or the men to attempt an open battle against the main force. We'll have to deal with them later."

Rysun shook his head, trying to figure how they were going to defeat a foe half their size, only to turn around and "deal" with another force twice their size. Even in the most favorable conditions, such a feat was hard to fathom.

"Have the scouts been bringing you reports? Do you know the lay of the land?" Aleksei asked hurriedly.

Rysun nodded, "Two leagues ahead lies a quarry. It should work for what you have in mind."

Aleksei sighed, "Alright, that's where we'll make our stand. We should have enough time to set the trap. I presume the men are up to this, Colonel?"

Rysun managed a smile, "This will be the first test, Lord Captain, but I have the utmost faith."

Aleksei glanced at the men marching away from them. "I hope to the gods you're right, Colonel."

Before Rysun could beg another question, Aleksei was riding past him, rounding up the officers scattered throughout the columns. He gathered them, giving instructions and sending them back to their units to spread his strategy.

Rysun glanced to Henry. The older man's face was set with a grim determination.

"How're you holding up?" Rysun asked softly.

Henry started, then turned, "I have faith in my son, Colonel. Still, I'm always struck when I see him these days. I suppose I forget the man you see.

"I just remember the boy. Every now and then, I find myself hoping I'll see that boy riding back on his old draft horse." A wistful smile captured the man's sun-weathered face.

Rysun shivered in the falling snow. "And one day you may, Henry. But for now, I feel a lot better knowing that man is leading us into battle."

Henry grunted and turned his horse without further comment. Rysun glanced to the horizon, where he could just make out the vague cloud of dust amidst the fluttering snow.

He wondered what they would have done if Aleksei hadn't caught up to them when he did. He suddenly smiled as he remembered what Henry had said. No, Aleksei Drago was no god.

But this day he was no less their savior.

"And these are your chambers," Sariel said as cheerily as she could manage under the circumstances.

A tour of the Undercroft had slowly transformed her charge from a man on the brink of despair to one on the verge of murder. He raged like a thunderhead. The very air crackled around him with unreleased need.

Sariel didn't have the slightest idea what she could do to soothe the situation. She had shown him the archway that led towards the Reliquary. He was, of course, forbidden to go down that way. The infirmary was down yet another spoke in the corridors, but it was best if he stayed confined to his quarters, for now.

When she finally opened the door to his quarters, he stepped in and glanced around in surprise.

"These are nicer than I anticipated," he admitted, some of the power receding from him.

She sighed in relief, "Jonas, you are the third-born Cherub. You are royalty, not only to the Ilyari, but to us. Despite your malady, you could only be afforded the nicest rooms we can offer."

Jonas stepped across the spacious quarters and opened a second door, revealing a large library. Across from the library was yet another room, this time the bedchamber.

He turned back, seeming suddenly suspicious, "I don't understand. Why would you provide me such space?"

Sariel stood in the doorway, smiling nervously. "Well, Jonas, until the healers can begin their work on you, you are still somewhat unstable. We need to make sure you can be monitored."

Jonas narrowed his black eyes, the darkness shattering to reveal putrescent light, "This is my cell, then?"

She shrugged, "In a manner of speaking. But only for a short time. The first healing can begin just as soon as the Angelus is finished with her evening vespers. The closer we come to alleviating your condition, the more freedom we'll grant you."

Jonas crooked a finger and Sariel flew across the room with a startled cry. She settled a pace away, panting in surprise.

"I'm beginning to notice a trend here," the Magus growled. "First, my uncle leads me into a prison without warning me of the consequences. And now you've put the lock on my cage. Tell me, what other surprises do I have to look forward to?"

She was trembling.

He frowned, "While I appreciate that you are here to heal me, Sariel, I don't take kindly to being manipulated. Much less imprisoned. I have enough of that to deal with in my day-to-day life. It's unsettling that the need to control me has only intensified in my compromised state."

She started to weep.

Jonas rolled his eyes, "You're embarrassing yourself."

She flinched before straightening, "What is *wrong* with you? We are only trying to help you, and yet all you've done since you've been here is berate and interrogate me for simply doing my duty."

She shrank back from the demonic glint that shone in his eyes.

"Angel Sariel, when you confessed to having trapped me here for the gods only know how long, and I allowed my emotions to overcome me, what did you tell me?"

She glared at him, "I told you the truth. You were being ungrateful for the sacrifice we were offering. You are being selfish, thinking of only yourself. Angels often *die* for trying to help ones such as you."

He nodded, "And yet when I display the same sort of treatment towards you, it offends you."

Her gaze hardened, "You are a recipient of our magic. I'm shocked the Angelus has even allowed you to live, much less come here. But that was not my decision to make. Despite knowing how many of my brothers and sisters will undoubtedly die in the attempt, we will still heal you of your corruption."

Jonas frowned, "But that's not why you're shaking. That's not the cause for your tears."

She stiffened and backed towards the door. "I must admit, Jonas, that you startled me."

He allowed her to pass through the threshold before speaking, his voice innocent. "Did I do something wrong?"

She passed her hands across her face and smoothed her robes,

"While it's true that we've never had one in your condition quartered here, we have seen cases much like yours. In different ways, you understand. But the shields we place over the doors are always the same, and they never falter. I was simply...taken aback that you were able to use your magic through your shield."

"Shield?" Jonas demanded as he swept aggressively forward. He reached the doorframe and was violently thrust back.

As he clutched his chest, panting for air, he looked up to see her self-satisfied glare. "As I said, *Jonas,*" Sariel spat, now using his first name on purpose, showing him she was in charge, "the shield on this door usually prevents such untoward displays."

Jonas arched an eyebrow, and she yelped as a swath of power struck her backside.

"Don't grow overly confident in your prison, Angelica. I warn you now, this charade will last only as long as it takes to free me from this curse. And then I *will* be free of this place."

She did her best to school her face into one of prim disapproval. "Jonas Belgi, you are at our mercy now. Your life, and the lives of those you hold dear, depend on our willingness to help you. Thus far you have proven to be difficult, and we've not even attempted a purification.

"Were I you, I'd pray to the One-God that we continue to extend our kindness. God knows, without your uncle's intercession, the Angelus would have destroyed you on the spot for the danger you bring to us. To this world."

Her expression softened, "I know this is difficult for you. It's difficult for us too. But in time, you'll come to see that we are only acting in your best interest. We don't wish to bring anyone harm. We only want to give you your life back. But you have to be patient. You tread upon uncharted ground, and we must work to catch up, to understand the nature of your condition. Only then can we truly restore you, and trust you with your freedom."

Jonas snorted. "I'll keep that in mind. But don't forget, the sooner you heal me, the sooner you'll be rid of me. And I promise you, you *don't* want to have to handle me for too long."

She sniffed, "Your uncle told us, too, that you are over-confident in your abilities. I will offer the utmost of our talents, but I'll not be intimidated by a whelp such as you. Not to satisfy your ego, Cherub or not. Good evening, Jonas."

He stood there, allowing the quaking anger to sustain the wall to his emotions far longer than he should have. Finally, when he was certain she was gone, he went to the door and put his hand against it.

He felt the push, the force that had thrown him across the room before. It was a shield woven of the Archanium, but with something else threaded through it. Something he intimately recognized.

A tear trickled down his cheek as he finally understood the magic keeping him in his cell. In its own sweeping melodic power, he felt his name resonate through him.

Well, he thought, *at least I know my enemies.*

Harold panted, desperately trying to catch his breath. They had been running since sunup, and he was about ready to pass out. Still, the farther they went, the more excited his commanders became. Those Kalinori at the back who slowed were whipped into greater speed.

Harold counted himself lucky to be in the van.

Then again, he'd had little say in the matter.

To either side trotted a hulking man, blacksmiths who had been selected to ensure that Harold was not simply trying to divert the Kalinori conscripts' attention so he could make a getaway. He ran in the center of the front line, flanked by the biggest captives.

Gods, but he hoped he wasn't being played for a fool.

What was it the man with the golden eyes had said? If he was lying, they were dead either way. Either they ran into the Legion's blades, or they retreated into the rebels' spears.

Harold forced himself to swallow his fear and replace it with faith. Faith that the few moments he'd had with the golden-eyed man were worth his trust, and his life.

As they came around a fat hillock, a cry went up from the commanders on their horses. The enemy was in sight.

Harold thought he might soil himself at any moment.

"Pull your blades, boys. Blood will flow today!" came a shout from behind.

Harold ran, clutching his bent kitchen knife in one hand, his cudgel in the other. It had taken everything he'd had, every possession he'd brought along and every ounce of strength to convince these men. He'd done his best to use the golden-eyed man's logic, his reasoning. That had swayed most. When a few held out, Harold had accommodated them.

Shockingly, he'd learned that the most successful counter to refusal was to simply walk away. He feigned indifference, and often they came scurrying after him, their true fear finally drawn to the glimmer of hope he was peddling.

Those were the men at the back of the van.

As they ran, he heard grumbles and shouts from behind. The force on the road was smaller than the man had claimed. Significantly smaller.

This was not a force of twenty-six thousand, rather closer to ten. They were still heavily outnumbered, but not by the fearsome margins he'd suggested. His stomach sank as he felt cold dread sweep across him.

He'd been taken for a fool.

"Keep running!" he heard himself shout. "No good in turning back now. Stick to the plan!"

For some reason Harold couldn't fathom, he heard the order sweep back through the other men. If this was to be their end, they would die with dignity, but they would not cut into their allies.

The commanders pulled to a halt, saving those whipping the lines in the back. They would let the Kalinori blunt the blades of the enemy before risking their own skins.

Harold realized he was laughing. He must be going mad, running towards his own end. Or perhaps they would survive this day yet. Perhaps that was the source of his laughter. He glanced at the grim-faced blacksmiths of either side of him.

Perhaps not.

They were within a hundred paces, and closing the gap swiftly. Before them stood a line of tower shields, overlapping to provide an impenetrable wall of protection.

Men began to cry out. Men behind him. Harold risked a glance to his left in time to see one of his blacksmith guards drop with an arrow buried in his neck. The Legionnaires were steady. The arrows were coming from the rebel force behind him.

Harold cursed, feeling a surge of rage and adrenaline as he increased his pace. He started screaming. The men behind him were screaming too.

A heartbeat before he crashed into the wall of shields, the Legionnaires pivoted, opening a passageway through the ranks of men. Harold almost wept with relief as his momentum carried him forward, shadowing through the ranks of the Legion until he found himself out on the road again, panting for air and digging his heels into the dirt to slow himself. Ten thousand Legionnaires now stood between him and the bastards who had pressed him into service.

The other Kalinori men, the ones still alive, flew from the charging ranks of the Legion, panting, some falling to their knees.

They were alive.

Harold found himself weeping tears of joy, even as the men rallied around him, cheering. He looked over their jubilant heads, towards the sound of battle. Even though the odds were in their favor, six thousand men was still a sizable force against one of only ten.

His mouth dropped open as he saw Legionnaires sweep in from either side of the road. Thousands of armed men from both sides. From the northern tree-line surged the cavalry, crashing into the rebel flank. From the south, out of the shelter of a quarry swarmed the footmen.

In mere minutes the rebel force was divided and slaughtered. Harold understood at once that he wasn't witnessing a battle. The rebel men were so taken aback, they could hardly think to raise their weapons. They stood, mouths agape as their heads were cleaved in two and men were broken apart like rotten fruit. Only a few offered hopeless resistance.

The Kalinori men all stood still in the awe and horror of what they'd just witnessed. Some of them, the retired soldiers among their ranks, began moving towards the Legionnaires, clapping them on the back or offering a handshake of thanks. Tradesmen, men like Harold, could only gawk at the carnage.

Even the invasion of Kalinor hadn't been this gruesome, this bloody.

"Harold! Harold?"

He started when he heard his name called. Men all around were pointing a finger at him. He wanted to shrink out of existence. These men were real Legionnaires, real killers. The men he had led to safety, the men the golden-eyed man had saved, were not. Just the sight of all those rebel soldiers, torn asunder, was almost more than he could bear.

A big man with black hair and eyes as blue and pale as Harold's own rode up on a fine roan. "You're Harold? You were the one in charge of getting the word out?"

Harold nodded dumbly. He felt like he must be in a great amount of trouble. Men this dangerous didn't seek out nobodies like him. The man before him was obviously important. He didn't want to know what he'd done to attract the attention of such a powerful man.

"Come with me, if you please. The Lord Captain wants a word."

On hearing that, Harold bit his trembling lip and realized he could feel a warm trickle running down his leg.

The black-haired man watched Harold impassively for a moment, then turned to one of the mounted men behind him, "Sergeant Jeffries, would you escort Harold here to one of the tents so he can get cleaned up and find a change of clothes? I'm sure the Lord Captain would appreciate him being as presentable as possible."

Before the sergeant could open his mouth, another, older man rode forth, "If you will, Colonel, I'll take him."

The colonel arched an eyebrow, "Are you sure?"

The older man smiled and dismounted, "It would be my pleasure."

Harold watched the man approach. By the man's bearing, he couldn't tell if he was facing an officer or a lord. He did his best to bow.

"It's an honor, sir."

The older man scowled at him. "Straighten up. You've just pissed yourself. I can understand under the circumstances, but you don't want to meet the Lord Captain in such a state, now do you?"

Harold looked at the ground in embarrassment, "No, sir."

The man's smile warmed, "Well, it's not a far walk to the tents, and then we can get you set to rights. Come with me."

Harold was surprised the man didn't ride his fine horse. Behind him he could hear the soldiers gathering their wounded and giving orders to the befuddled Kalinori men. They were all headed into the trees.

A few hundred paces into the woods, Harold was surprised to find a military camp camouflaged into the forest fabric. From the road, it had been completely invisible.

The older man led him into a tent filled with warm steam. All around, heated rocks sat in braziers. The older man poured a ladle of water over one of the braziers and steam hissed forth.

"There's some water and some clean toweling. I'll fetch you a change of clothes while you get washed up. I won't be long."

Harold found himself on the edge of tears. What had begun as a nightmare was taking a terrifying, if hopeful, turn towards the better. If only he could allow himself to embrace it.

"Thank you, sir," he managed.

The older man smiled, "Please, lad, call me Henry."

Harold managed a half-smile as Henry ducked out. He was glad he hadn't been led by the sergeant. An officer would have made him feel like a prisoner. Henry seemed just like him, and yet the colonel had yielded to his word. Harold found the concept entirely confusing.

He took his time getting clean. The forced march had covered him with layers of dirt and grime that took repeated rinses to scrub off. When he was done, he found that the hot rocks also served to dry him. It was a marvel, and this deep into winter it seemed more than a luxury.

Harold stood in the heat for a time, waiting for Henry's return, when he suddenly noticed a bundle of clothing lying just inside the tent. He dressed himself, relishing the feel of clean cloth before daring to step outside.

Henry was waiting for him. "Feel better, lad?"

Harold blushed and nodded, "Yes, sir. Thank you."

Henry chuckled, "Don't thank me, lad. I merely led you here. Thank the men who saved your life today. Thank...thank the Lord Captain."

The title sent panic rushing through Harold anew. "Oh, sir, if you please? I'd rather not meet the Lord Captain. I don't do well with formal things, sir. Not at all. They make me nervous."

To his surprise, Henry didn't bring up the shame Harold had brought on himself earlier. "Relax, if you can. The Lord Captain isn't quite such a grand figure as you might believe. He's a man, same as you and me. But he does want to meet you. You would honor him."

Harold nodded, unable to voice a word. He swallowed hard, trying to keep his mind on anything but where they were headed.

To his surprise, Henry stopped outside a modest tent, not much larger than the others. It was nothing like the grand command tent General Barnes had occupied in the rebel camp.

"Are you coming in?" Harold asked, his voice coming out as little more than a whisper.

Henry shook his head, "Not unless I'm invited in, lad. Lord Captain Drago asked for you alone."

Harold nodded anxiously, staring at the tent flaps as though unsure how to open them. He finally took a deep breath and stepped through.

He immediately wondered if he was going to soil himself again.

Aleksei looked up, a grin brightening his features. "Harold!"

Harold could hardly open his mouth before he was swept in a heartfelt hug. The strength of the other man nearly crushed the wind from him.

"L...Lord *Captain?*" he asked, trembling.

Aleksei sat him down, his mirth undiminished. "I *knew* you could do it. I can't tell you how proud I am. You saved a great many lives today."

Harold felt like his world was spinning, "But...I *know* you. You were that boy...that man...in the camp. You told me what to do." He leaned in close, like he was sharing a secret, "You didn't say you was the Lord Captain!"

Aleksei seemed puzzled for a minute before laughing, "Oh, gods, I'm sorry, Harold. You can imagine how important it was for me not to tell you who I was. And to be perfectly honest, my title would have done me little good among those men. Better if I was simply a stranger."

Harold thought it over before realizing that Aleksei was indeed correct. It was intimidating to be in the presence of a man who was so much smarter than he was. He felt tiny in the man's presence. Inferior.

"But you did an amazing thing, Harold. You saved so many lives today, including your own."

Harold found his words again, "No, Lord Captain, Sir, I didn't! *You* did. It was *your* idea."

Aleksei waved the suggestion away, stepping behind his field desk and taking a seat. "It was only an idea, Harold. A tactic. Had you not done your part, a great many more would have died, and all on our side. I only had to escape and tell my men what to expect. I must say, I was a bit nervous about the whole business." Harold wished he could vanish from the glowing praise. "But it went off beautifully. You saved the day, my friend."

Harold sat down on the fine carpet that lined Aleksei's tent. "Sir, you don't know what it was like when you left. Half the camp was destroyed. General Barnes was torn to smithereens, along with a goodly number of the enemy, sir. It was horrible. I've never seen anything like it."

The joy ghosted from Aleksei's face. "I know. The death you saw was following *me*. I was able to escape, but only just. I took a foolish chance to do as much damage as I could, and I suppose it worked. But in the end, I scarcely escaped with my life."

Harold nodded, "The scouts found the tree, and your tracks. But no one knew what to make of it."

"I don't either. Wish to the gods I did. But since it seems to be safe enough amongst the shadows, under the trees, that's where I'll stay until I get a better understanding of what happened."

Harold frowned, "So what now, then? If you're confining yourself to the woods?"

Aleksei smiled, "We're going to head north, through the wooded areas. We'll break cover only when we have to. We'll chuck the rebel corpses into the quarry, where the main force won't find them for a while, and then we'll vanish into the trees. It'll slow the rebels down if they have to search for us, and figure out what happened to their men. Hopefully, we'll make Keldoan before they have the slightest clue where we've gone."

Harold's head was already spinning with the manpower needed to bury so many men, to cover their tracks. Aleksei stood and stepped around his field desk, crouching and placing a hand on Harold's arm.

"Harold, relax. You're among friends now. All the Kalinori men will come with us to Keldoan. Once there, I hope you'll be safe until the day you can return to Kalinor."

A light lit in Harold eyes, "Do you know when that might be, Lord Captain?"

Aleksei sighed, "First off, don't call me that. My friends call me Aleksei, not Lord bloody Captain. Second, no, I'm afraid I don't know when Kalinor will be taken back.

"Until we can find a way, and the manpower, I'm afraid you'll have to stay in Keldoan. And that's assuming we can even hold it against their main force.

"Harold, a very large force of men is coming after us. When they figure out where we're heading, they'll only come on faster. They can't trick us like they did in Kalinor, but many will still die, on both sides. It won't be easy."

Harold swallowed, wondering where Aleksei was heading with this.

"Harold, you have many men with you, *craft*smen. Experienced men. You can help us fight this war when we get to Keldoan."

Before Harold could open his mouth, Aleksei held up a hand. "Not with weapons. With your skills. The city isn't prepared for my men to arrive. We'll need your help to keep everything on an even keel. Can your men help us?"

In the back of his mind, Harold wondered when the Kalinori conscripts had become "his" men. He thought for a moment before offering a tentative smile, "We will do whatever is asked of us, Lord Captain. You saved our lives. It's only fair that we do our part for you."

CHAPTER 10

AN EYE IN THE STORM

The blade flipped through the air, burying itself in the fallen log with a solid *thunk*.

Tamara gave a squeal of excitement. "That's ten in a row!"

Roux gave her that special smile she'd grown so fond of. Ever since he'd first appeared to her, offering her a few skinned rabbits and a knife, she'd made it a point to spend at least a *few* hours "keeping watch", leaving her invariably tired and yet exhilarated the next day. Some days she'd wondered if the promise of seeing him that evening had kept her in the saddle. But every night, he'd appeared just as promised. Some nights he taught her more about handling the knife she now kept strapped to her thigh. Others, they just sat and talked, her greedily drinking in his warmth and humor.

It hadn't taken her long to realize the man was besotted with her. It had only taken her a few days longer to admit that she felt the same about him.

He vanished for a heartbeat, then popped back with the knife in hand. "You've improved tremendously. I'm impressed."

She basked in his praise.

They'd been traveling for weeks, it seemed, and only now was Taumon in sight. She thought they might even reach it by the following evening.

The very idea filled her with dread.

It was going to be much more difficult to find ways out of the city to see him. She had explained in no uncertain terms that his woodland appearance and demeanor would cause too great a disturbance within the city proper, so she would have to find a way out to him.

He nodded to the distant lights of the city. "Will I see you again after tonight?"

She turned back to him, her eyes wide with panic, "Of course! Even if we find a ship tomorrow, that won't mean we'll be *leaving*. Sometimes ships remain in port for weeks before departing. We'll be holed up in an inn at least a few days, but it will all depend on the captain and manner of ship we find."

"But this *could* be the last time I see you?"

She gave him a playful shove. "Certainly not. Perhaps I'll be absent for a while," she could feel his heat radiating against her face, "but not forever."

He lowered his mouth to hers. Every nerve in her body exploded at the touch of his lips, and the tingling waves running through her were electric. Before she'd even found a chance to savor the kiss, it was over.

Roux pulled away, leaving her breathless.

She tried in vain to compose herself, "If I can find a way to you, I will."

He smiled, his eyes twinkling, "I don't doubt that for a moment."

Her knees felt weak, looking into his eyes. Gods, but how was she going to leave this man?

"And you're absolutely certain you can't come with us?" she asked, pleading one last time.

He shook his head, "I'm sorry, Tamara. I don't think I'd be much help to you on the open seas. And I doubt your mother would be too keen on having me along, either."

She frowned, "But you're the Ri-Hnon. You have a title, a position. She *respects* that."

He laughed, "She respects that I have power among my people. But I don't for a moment believe she views me as an equal. I'm not terribly interested in such distinctions at any rate. But she is. And I'd rather lose you for a time than gain your mother's enmity forever."

Tamara sighed. She knew he was right, but she desperately didn't want to admit it. She didn't want to leave him. She *needed* him.

"What will I do without you?" she whispered, resting her head against his chest.

She felt the rumble of his laugh, "You'll soldier on, as you did before you met me, as you always have. Tamara, you don't need me. You have your own strength. You've always had it, you just needed permission to bring it forward. You don't *need* anyone. You can survive plenty well on your own. The trick is not to rely solely on yourself when you don't have to.

"Like now, for instance. Your mother is a strong woman. *Use* her strength, her knowledge. You've always known what to do; I've merely given you permission to trust your instincts."

She looked up playfully, "And how do I know I can trust you."

He smiled, "Don't trust me. Just trust yourself."

Tamara sighed. Gods, if only it were that easy.

Jonas lay on his back, Aleksei's head resting against his bare chest. He felt the warmth of the sun shining down on them, and Aleksei's steady breathing. The air had a strange, tangible quality to it that he couldn't place. He knew he'd seen it somewhere before, but for the moment the recollection was beyond his grasp.

Aleksei stirred against him and Jonas shifted his weight under the Knight. He realized that he didn't really care about the alien feel of the air. Or the sandy beach beneath him. It didn't really matter where he was.

He was happy.

Something about that thought struck him as strange. He didn't recall being very happy when he'd gone to sleep.

But now there was a sense of joy that shone within him. He couldn't remember when he'd felt this content. Simply feeling Aleksei against him, the warmth of his skin, the roughness of his stubble, was enough to satisfy Jonas. More than enough.

He took a deep breath and closed his eyes, trying to just enjoy the moment. When he opened them again, he was in a bed. In his cell, he realized with a sinking feeling.

He was still a prisoner, and Aleksei was nowhere to be found.

Jonas took a deep breath and let out a sigh. And now he recognized the strange feeling of the air. It had been a dream, but one cast by magic. It had been disturbingly similar to the dreams he'd sent Aleksei in the past.

Of course, with his bond neutralized by the Undercroft's shield, such a thing wasn't possible. Gods, but he wished it were. He would have given anything in that moment for his dream to be real. For the reality of Aleksei, rather than the wisp of an image drawn from fragments of his memory.

A wave of anger swept through him. This had been none of his doing. Someone else had done this *to* him. His face flushed as he realized that some other person had seen those thoughts, had crafted that scenario.

He felt violated.

Jonas pushed himself out of bed, shrouding himself in the swirls of the Archanium for good measure. He was immediately aware of another presence in the sitting room.

Gritting his teeth, Jonas thrust his hand outwards. The door disintegrated in a burst of sawdust and splinters, the hollow boom of his power sending cracks through the plaster and the doorframe.

Sariel's startled scream was cut short as he strode into the room. She stared up at him, bare-chested, clad only in soft cotton trousers and wrapped in the light of the Archanium. His black eyes glowered down at her.

"What was that?" he demanded, fighting to keep his tone measured.

Sariel placed a piece of embroidery in her lap, setting her needle delicately atop it. "A gift, Jonas. One of the tiny bits of happiness we can bestow on those housed here. I'm sorry you did not enjoy it."

"In those few moments," he growled, "you managed to give me more pain than I've felt since this ordeal began. I cannot begin to describe how violated I feel. Those thoughts, the memories you accessed belong to me and me *alone*. They are not your playthings. And neither am I. Now get out."

She stood, her mouth pursed angrily, "Why must you turn every kindness into a curse?"

He strode aggressively forward. She tried to raise a shield, but he shredded it before it was even half-formed. He halted only a scant inch from her face. "What you just did to me was unspeakably cruel. If you ever attempt something like that again, I will kill you."

The air around him was crackling with unspent wrath. He fought as hard as he could to refrain from erasing her from existence. He knew he couldn't, but it was only with the greatest effort that he released the Archanium and stepped back.

"Get. Out."

Her eyes welled up with tears as she glared at him, and he felt her hatred as she stormed from the room, slamming the door to his cage firmly behind her.

He dropped to the floor, sobbing. It had felt so *real*. His heart ached so deeply he could scarcely draw breath. He forced himself to breathe through the pain, and the tears. She'd given him a vision of everything he'd ever wanted, only to snatch it away, reminding him of his intractable predicament, his suffocating loneliness.

All his barriers, all the walls he'd erected around himself lay shattered amongst the splinters. He knelt there, defenseless in the torrent of emotion that pounded through him. His hand clutched impotently at his chest as the pain coursed through him.

He hardly heard the door open, but he felt a powerful presence sweep into his chambers.

"Get. Up," his grandmother commanded.

He glared up at her, wishing nothing more than to end her horrid existence. He knew it would do nothing to assuage the pain, but just then it didn't seem to matter. He just wanted to see someone else in agony.

Kevara Avlon smirked, "Well, we're not quite so combative *now*, are we?"

He rose and she gasped, looking at, rather than into, his eyes. He ignored her reaction, "Explain your presence. I am *not* in a mood for your games right now. Do you understand?"

Her smirk faded and she nodded, still staring at his eyes.

"What are you looking at?" he snarled.

"Your eyes...for a moment, they were green. They're black again now, of course. But for just a moment, they were green. I've never heard of such a thing, but with you that hardly surprises me."

"Why?"

She sighed, the fight and the cruelty leaving her briefly, "Sit down, Jonas. Now that you're here, you are not the danger you were out in the world. I suppose that if you insist on continuing your life, I had better explain a few things to you."

Jonas grudgingly took a seat, wiping his tear stained face with the heel of his hand as he attempted to regain some small part of his composure.

She took a seat in a curiously shaped chair, the back cut to accommodate her wings. "Jonas, it may surprise you to learn that you are mentioned prominently in our Scriptures, our prophecies. Given your extraordinary parentage, and your talents in the Archanium, you represent a very unusual combination of...factors.

"As you know, it's rare for angels and humans to interbreed. In fact, before your parents married, I don't believe there'd been such a coupling in centuries."

Jonas sat back and crossed his legs. "Which is why you sawed my wings off?" She grunted irritably, smoothing her robe. "So what do these prophecies say?"

She smiled sardonically, "That no longer matters. They have nearly all been invalidated in the past few weeks."

Jonas arched an eyebrow, "Have they now? And how is that?"

"You're still alive. That alone makes them invalid."

Jonas stiffened. So that was what she'd meant by "if you insist on continuing your life". His mouth tightened.

Kevara Avlon continued, "You were supposed to die in the battle for Kalinor. You were to face the Demon, and it was supposed to destroy you. Impossibly, you had the gall to defy prophecy and survive."

Jonas finally allowed himself a broad grin. It had been Aleksei's magic, his discovery of the Mantle's powers to heal, that had saved Jonas from that fate.

"Wipe that smile away, child. You would have done us all a great service by falling there, as you were supposed to. Instead, you invalidated our prophecies and rendered us *blind*."

Jonas frowned, "There are no books that mention what would happen if I survived? Isn't that a bit short-sighted?"

Kevara Avlon fussed with the skirt of her robe, "The Prophets in the Basilica did not foresee any possibility of your survival...only your death."

Jonas shrugged, "I know of at least two Prophets alive today. Are you suggesting that their gifts will vanish, now that I've outlived your books?"

"Of *course* not. It simply means that we can no longer influence events, help them grow towards the desired outcomes. Those who are important to prophecy will be acting blindly, without guidance."

He snorted, "If it's your guidance they'll lose, I'd say the world is better for it." She opened her mouth, but he fixed her with a night-black glare.

"You had your glorious prophecies, and yet you fatalistically allowed the Demonic Presence to be brought back into this world. Because of your blind faith in ancient texts. They provide a guide, but they're not written in stone. If they were, I'd be dead right now, and your books would still be dictating your life. Has it ever occurred to you that you might think for yourself? Use your head, Kevara. Look at the world as it moves around you, not as it's dictated from beyond the grave."

She sneered, "Your blasphemy aside, your survival has only confirmed a belief that I've long held. One that gives me nightmares. You are an eye in the storm."

Jonas burst out laughing. Kevara's face soured with contempt.

"Don't you *dare* laugh, child. You have no idea how dangerous that makes you."

Jonas's laughter dropped into a low chuckle, "Very well, Kevara. You have my attention. What does it mean to be this 'eye in the storm'?"

Her face was deadly serious, "It means you could destroy us all. You are everything, and nothing. You are the bringer of ultimate destruction, but you can't even see it for the placidity surrounding you. Without even realizing it, your very existence destroys everything in your wake."

Jonas pondered for a moment, running the words through his mind.

"That seems to be a terribly myopic view of the phrase," he said at last.

She scowled, "And how would one with your limited knowledge interpret such a title?"

"It could mean any number of things. It could be, as you said, that I am the calm center, and that this storm of yours radiates from me. That doesn't mean that it destroys everything it touches. Perhaps it simply symbolizes change. Perhaps it means that the decisions I make have a magnified effect beyond how they affect me. That wouldn't be at all unusual for either a prince or a Magus, and I'm both."

He learned forward conspiratorially, "Or perhaps, Grandmother, the whole thing is a cart of horseshit."

She clenched her jaw. "I should have killed you when I first knew what you were. You are like a child playing with lightning. Being an eye in the storm marks you as incredibly dangerous for a *reason*. It is a statement that means much more than the simple interpretation I just provided.

"When a Magus takes a path through the Great Sphere, we expect him to end up in one hemisphere or the other. Those on the outer edges have the most severe power associated with that side. You, on the other hand, have taken *neither* path.

"You have inexplicably found your way into the center of the Great Sphere. The eye in the storm. From your path, you may touch either side with equal ability. You will never have the supreme power of either, but rather the combined power of both. It allows you to accomplish things impossible for other Magi. Your ability to shift, for example."

"I know other shifters," Jonas protested.

Kevara Avlon barked a laugh, "Oh, yes, there may be one or two who can manage it for a short time, but not like you. They can't take as many forms, and they can hardly hold them. But you can maintain such unnatural abominations for hours, even *days* on end. This is unheard of, but it is one of many clues that indicate your true nature."

"I still don't understand why you find this so dire," Jonas snapped. "All you've told me is that I'm a different sort of Magus. I'm afraid I already knew that."

"Listen to me, you little *whelp*." Her voice was low, dangerous. "You have no *idea* the power you're capable of. You sit in the heart of the Archanium, commanding both sides, balanced on the edge of a knife. Commanding Forbidden Realms others only *dream* of approaching. And you do it flippantly, as though it were your birthright."

Jonas crossed his arms, "From what you've told me, it sounds as though I'm right."

The Angelus ignored him, "From your position, you have the opportunity of either being our savior, or our destroyer. My greatest fear was that you might someday be touched by the Presence. Unlike that idiot child Bael, so far on the edge of the Nagavor that he was practically touching the Presence from the start, from your position the demons we've so long held back could be fully unleashed, without restraint.

"If they gain any more strength through you, the horrors of the past will seem like a joke in comparison. Allowing the Presence to infect the Archanium, fully through your connection, could end life itself."

Jonas sat there, frozen by her accusations, her condemnation of what he was.

"There is quite a bit of conjecture in your argument," he said, trying to muster some bravado.

She shook her head, "This is not mere prophecy, Jonas Belgi. This is *fact*. If the Demonic Presence gains so much as a foothold in you, you will bring about the destruction of everything and everyone you hold dear. You will sing the Song that ends the world."

"There's no way for you to know that," he snapped. "As you said yourself, you can only guess. Your last presumption was that I would die in Kalinor. I did not. My very survival has proven your prophecies baseless."

She leaned forward, "Then, for your sake, I pray that we are able to lift this curse from you. We can't contemplate the price of failure. For any of us."

Tamara held her hood tight against her cheek, peeking out the window of their modest carriage. Her bones ached with the cold, but she didn't voice any complaints.

Once they'd reached the safety of Taumon, her mother had sent the boys back with what had to be an unreasonable amount of gold, but in all fairness, though their journey had been uneventful, she had been grateful of their presence during the day.

The night was another matter.

She smiled softly as she recalled her time with Roux the night before, allowing the memory to warm her. She was as content as she could reasonably be, given the circumstances. With an effort, she forced those thoughts from her mind. She had an important task before her, and this was one battle she knew she couldn't afford to lose.

She'd learned a great deal in the last few weeks. A great deal about herself. She had little doubt that before the sun set, she would have to put some of those revelations to a test. She relished the opportunity.

Across from Tamara, Andariana sat with her hands folded in her lap, her expression faraway. Tamara knew her mother would be planning their next move.

On the journey to Taumon, Andariana had started to consider the facets of Captain Drago's orders. In the end, she'd reached different conclusions than he. Tamara had done her best to persuade her mother to keep to the original plan.

She'd had limited success.

At the very least, they were finally in Taumon. They were headed to sea. She'd gotten her mother to agree to that much of Aleksei's strategy.

But she could tell that Andariana was coming dangerously close to changing her mind about everything else.

Tamara looked back out the window with a sigh. Gods, but why couldn't her mother just follow orders for once? Tamara had grown up in awe of her mother's ability to command and manipulate flows of power in the realm. It was a job Andariana executed with effortless precision, and Tamara had always been proud that she would one day succeed such a capable woman.

But ever since half the Lords of Parliament had deserted Kalinor and the war began, Tamara's doubts had been growing, and she had noted that many of the events that had transpired had not been within Andariana's power to control, much less correct.

Tamara knew that, often enough, people did as they liked, whether it was the best decision or not.

Still, she felt deep down that more could have been done to appease the disgruntled nobility. Andariana's fear of being dethroned, just like her elder sister Marra, had crippled the woman's judgment at critical moments.

And now she was in a coach with the same woman, heading to the gods-only-knew-where. She hoped they were heading to the harbor. She prayed her mother had the sense to listen to Aleksei Drago.

Tamara's jaw tightened at that thought.

Hadn't the man proven his wisdom? Were they not both in that coach by his sheer grace and heroism alone? The gods be damned; it was that man who had delivered the both of them from certain death, and now Andariana was questioning his judgment?

Tamara decided that she would put her foot down if her mother attempted anything foolhardy. She was along on this same journey, and right then she didn't *care* if her mother was the bloody Queen of bloody Ilyar.

With a small flush in her cheeks, Tamara suddenly realized that she'd finally caught a tiny glimpse into Jonas's mind. She understood that his defiant nature was what had always made him seem so clever, so brave to her. She wondered if it would be nearly so effective for her as it had been for him.

The carriage rolled to a stop and Tamara looked up. Her heart sank.

Before them towered the grand prominence of the Admiralty. Great white pillars marched in a square around the grand golden spire that flared into the sky. Beneath, a massive golden archway permitted access to the naval offices.

This was precisely what she'd been dreading.

As Andariana turned to exit the coach, Tamara leaned forward and gripped her arm, "What are you doing?"

Andariana arched an eyebrow, "I'm following the Lord Captain's plan. He told me to go to Taumon. Here we are. He told me to get a ship to take us to Zirvah. Where else would I find such a ship?"

As the queen attempted to slide forward, Tamara pushed her back, "He didn't tell you to marshal the navy, Mother. He said a *boat*."

The queen looked at her daughter incredulously, "And what would you suggest?"

Tamara took a deep breath, trying to calm herself, "There are trade vessels that sail the Autumn Sea constantly, regardless of the season. We could book passage on one such ship and go that way, without drawing attention to ourselves ."

When Andariana laughed at the notion, Tamara tightened her grip on her mother's arm. "Think for a minute. Our ships are fast and well-armed, but they don't sail the northern reaches like the traders do.

"No amount of soldiers or ballistae are going to save us if we breach on winter ice and sink. No one will care about our titles. We'll drown like all the others. Please, Mother, I *beg* you. Use your head. Are we even certain of the Admiralty's loyalties?"

Andariana jerked her arm from Tamara's grip, glaring at her. "I daresay I've been dealing in matters of war longer than you, child. I will consult with Admiral Crayne. I suppose it's possible that he'll find some sense in your idea. I'll be sure he hears it."

The queen opened to door into the brisk winter air and started marching towards the Admiralty. As the coach started forward, Tamara hopped out, hurrying after her mother and clutching her cloak tight against the sudden cold.

"I'll tell Admiral Crayne myself, thank you," she snapped bitterly.

Andariana turned in surprise, "What are you doing here? The coach was supposed to take you to the inn."

Tamara kept walking, forcing her mother to catch up with her. When she felt Andariana's hand on her shoulder, she turned sharply. Andariana almost tripped into her, but managed to keep her footing despite the icy cobbles.

Tamara leaned forward and spoke in a sharp whisper. "Mother, I am certainly old enough to speak with an officer. If I am to be queen some-day, I don't think the best time to make a first impression with one of my future officers is after your death. Of course, I'm assuming there will *be* a realm to rule by then.

"Now, would you like to accompany me out of this cold?"

Andariana stared at her for a long moment, then started laughing. Tamara could see tears running down her mother's cheeks. She straight-ened after a moment, wiping her eyes gently on the hem of her cloak.

"Gods, but I'd forgotten what it was like to have Rhiannon around," she managed through her giggling laughter.

Tamara frowned. It was the first time her mother had mentioned her younger sister in years. Andariana looked into Tamara's pale blue eyes, her own green now softer, less panicked. "And I must say, I'm proud that you're showing a new sort of spirit. Jonas would be proud of you."

Tamara felt her irritation and anger melt under her mother's gaze. She didn't allow her façade of fierce resolve to crack, though. She offered a faint smile and gently touched Andariana's arm, "Let's go then. Together. We'll get all this sorted out."

Andariana nodded, resting her hand on Tamara's for a moment before the two women turned and stepped under the great golden archway.

CHAPTER 11

SWEET SACRIFICE

K evara Avlon stood outside the circle of white marble, her hands
out to her sides, palms facing her feet. Angelic symbols were
carefully drawn in ash in a complicated ring around her feet. To either
side stood angels, their ash circles intertwining with her own. All told,
eight angels stood around the circle of white stone, their ash rings inter-
locking, creating an unbreakable chain. In a circle of eight there was no
escape, no corners in which devils could hide.

In the center of the circle, Jonas lay on his back. He was surrounded
by similar symbols, with one crucial distinction. The symbols were
inverted, drawn in straight lines that broke along invisible axes in the
amalgamated array surrounding him.

Demonic.

The prince was already deep in a trance state, prepared for the
Seraphima to sweep into him and purge the corruption of the Demonic
Presence. Kevara Avlon had stopped short of voicing her concern to the
others.

This was unlike anything attempted in the past millennium, since
the Angelus Makar and his own circle of eight had birthed the
Seraphima into this world, and imprisoned the Demon Cassian in the
same moment.

Kevara had already accepted the fact that they might all die in this
attempt. Still, she would rather that than have this idiot boy bring about

the ruin of life itself. If she had to, she would make sure that Jonas never woke from this ordeal.

She looked up, checking the position of the moon again. Winter's edge felt especially keen this evening, but at least it was lacking wind. Wind would be *disastrous*.

She turned to the angel on her right and lifted a finger. The air suddenly vibrated, a melody comprised of her grandson's name in Song threading through the air. Kevara couldn't help but smile at the faint warmth it elicited from her bones.

The Seraphima suddenly burst into her world, showering the circle with a dome of glittering splinters of light. The warmth vanished.

She opened her mouth, adding her own Song, letting her voice intermingle with that of the first angel.

One by one, the others in the circle wove their voices into a rich tapestry of melody and harmony, some diverting at key nodes to create an increasingly complicated and hauntingly beautiful spell.

With the first angel guiding the melody, Kevara Avlon began to alter the harmony, guiding the other six angels as she dove into the icy depths of the Seraphima. The shock of the cold nearly took her breath away, but her voice never faltered.

With great care, she wrapped the other voices around her own, gently allowing herself to leave the Basilica, drawing with her a breathtaking amount of power. A harmony this complex was *always* dangerous. Taking this much of Seraphima into herself could shatter her fragile form in a heartbeat, or in the breadth of a single sonic deviation.

She cast her arms out towards Jonas's form. It was a completely pointless gesture, but it always made her feel in control in a more visceral way.

Jonas's body rose from the lines of ash. The runes surrounding him sank into the stone with an otherworldly yellow-green glow. The air throbbed with the pulse of the Presence, even as the light of the Seraphima swept through her grandson over and over.

He jerked spasmodically, but remained suspended in the air.

Kevara Avlon sent her mind into him.

The mists of the Seraphima lifted, and she gazed into the swirling confusion that was the Archanium. He floated there, in the center of the Great Sphere. What she saw almost shocked her Song into silence.

His form appeared much as it did in her own world, but jutting from his left shoulder was a jagged shard of throbbing chartreuse light, threaded through with impossible darkness. It was nearly splitting his body in two.

She urged herself forward on the tide of the Seraphima. The force emanating from the yellow-green light was practically overpowering. She was so nauseated she could hardly think to keep her Song moving, to do what she must to mend the boy.

Marshaling every ounce of strength she could from the seven on the outside, she poured the light of the Seraphima into her grandson, wrapping him in its sparkling brilliance. The chartreuse light flashed violently, but Kevara refused to relent.

The putrid corruption began to erode. She amplified the power she was channeling, feeling her teeth rattle in her skull.

The shard started to sizzle and shrink.

She didn't stop until she could see only the Seraphima's white and blue luminescence enveloping Jonas.

The Angelus gasped as she dared take a breath. The corruption was gone, and Jonas was intact. She nearly wept with relief, feeling as though she might pass out at any moment.

Kevara Avlon turned to withdraw from the Archanium when a faint, midnight sparkle caught her eye. Expending as much power as she could muster, she drifted closer, peering intently until at the very last she could make it out.

There, in the shadowed form of his shoulder, was a tiny splinter of the Demonic Presence. Her heart caught in her throat, the nausea rising again.

Managing another gulping breath, Kevara Avlon reached out and wrapped her hand around the dark splinter. The touch seared her skin, waves of agony blocking everything else out. Despite the pain, she poured the last of her own power into it.

And then she retreated.

No matter how much power she leveled at that tainted splinter, she knew it would remain. This was more than simple corruption. That fragment was intertwined with Jonas's very being, and no amount of the Seraphima would ever expunge it.

Her eyes slowly opened and she straightened, remembering where she was. Her voice was still strong, but her reserves were nearly spent.

With another signal, the lead angel began to draw the Song to a close, winding his way back towards a uniform cadence. She brought the others back to the first harmony, and then slowly let all but the melody die away.

Above her, the curtain of sparkling light still drifted down like heavenly snow. Kevara Avlon allowed herself a deep breath before turning her gaze on the angel farthest from her.

"Very well, Sariel, bring him back."

Jonas floated in a vacuum. It seemed neither dark nor light, neither hot nor cold. Perhaps there was more to this place, but he couldn't perceive it.

Time passed, though Jonas supposed it might just be his mind making sense of a world not his own. Perhaps he would remain in this place forever, trapped between worlds. The idea didn't particularly upset him, though something nagged in the back of his mind. Someone or something wanted him to return, though its name eluded him.

Light broke across him, and he felt the shock of sight return. How long had it been absent?

A figure appeared in the light, and Jonas recognized the cold precision of the Seraphima. He drifted towards the figure, recognizing her an instant before their forms touched.

"Sariel," he said, equally surprised and apathetic.

She smiled at him. There was a feeling in that smile, but his mind refused to recall it.

"Come, Jonas," the angel said softly, "and I'll bring you back."

Jonas started to reach out, but then pulled his hand back. "Do I need to go back?"

"If you stay in this place, you will die," she said simply.

Jonas didn't much care if he lived or died. Neither mattered in the emptiness of the vacuum.

Sariel laughed, "Oh Jonas, you can languish here if you like, but Aleksei would be forever lost to you."

Aleksei.

The name exploded through him.

He reached out, like a drowning man grasping for a lifeline, and clutched her wrist. She maintained her smile, even as cold light filled his vision. He gasped. His lungs had been empty in that place, but here the air tasted sweet on his tongue, sweet and something else.

Something bitter.

He blinked as the Seraphima faded away.

He was lying on the bed in his cell. Kevara Avlon stood mere paces away, her face grim.

"You've woken at last."

Jonas sat up, trying to gain his bearings. "Did it work?" he managed. His mouth felt like it was full of ash.

She pursed her lips, "After a fashion. But a splinter of the Demon still remains. The barest fingerprint of the Presence, but I fear it will be with you always. No amount of the Seraphima can break your link to the Presence."

Jonas felt his chest tighten, "What happened?"

She sighed, "We cut out the root of corruption. It was consuming you, but we whittled it down to a near-nothing. Yet some still remains. Before the exorcism ended, I wrapped the splinter in the last of my power."

Jonas rested his head against the headboard, "Which means what, exactly?"

She raised a hand, "First, you must hear the rest. The power I left there was meant as a message. It merely marks the splinter."

Jonas raised himself to face her directly, "And why would you do that?"

His grandmother smiled, but there was no joy in her expression. "So that Sariel could find it...and you. To bring you back to this realm."

"She found me, obviously."

"Had she not, you would have died in that place between worlds."

"Where is she?"

"She is with the One-God now."

The words staggered him. Jonas struggled to make sense of them, to fit them into a reality he could accept. As they struck home. Jonas opened his mouth to shout, to say something, *anything*, but found himself speechless. His shock overpowered him.

"How?" he finally managed.

Kevara Avlon folded her arms, "She asked to be the one to bring you back, if that became necessary. She surrendered her life to the Seraphima, binding the splinter in your soul, *protecting* you." Kevara wielded the word like a weapon. "Such a sacrifice is far stronger than anything we could have managed ritualistically. Before we began the ritual, Sariel told me that if she could grant you no healing or comfort in this life, she would use her passage into the next."

"But why would she do that?" Jonas whispered, a tear streaking down his cheek. "After the way I treated her, why would she sacrifice herself for me?"

The sheer insanity of it all threatened to overwhelm him. It didn't make any *sense*. It was as though the world had been turned on its head. Gods, why would she sacrifice her life for his?

Sariel had tried to show him kindness, and in his hurt, in his desperation for some level of control over his own life, he'd lashed out at her. She'd been the only person who had tried to help him since he'd arrived in the Undercroft...the only person who acted like she cared. She'd done nothing but what she'd thought was right, what she'd thought would make him happy, and in return he might as well have spat on her.

Guilt threatened to crush him.

In the end, despite his vitriol, despite the way he'd twisted her every kindness against her, cast her as the monster, now he understood.

He was the monster.

And yet in spite of every offense he'd committed against her, she'd given up the most precious thing she had to protect him.

The very thought made him sick. One of the gods' most beautiful, giving creatures taken from this world, so that his selfish presence might continue to poison those around him. He wasn't worthy of the gift he'd been granted.

"Why didn't you tell me this would happen?" he whispered. "Why didn't you tell me this would *kill* her?"

Kevara shrugged, "There was no certainty that it would. Had you refused her help, she would have returned, and you would have languished there until the end of time. For that reason, we never tell those we heal about such eventualities. Our purpose is to save your life, your soul. Occasionally, it is at the cost of one of ours."

He stared past her, his eyes unfocused. "I would never have allowed such a thing. I would never...." his voice broke before he could finish.

"It was a choice *you* made, Jonas. No one could have made it but you. Some do not return to us. They have no wish to come back. I don't know what she said to you, but it was obviously enough for you to accept her help without considering the consequences."

He wanted to scream at her. He wanted to berate her for manipulating him, for allowing the murder of one of her own people. But he couldn't. He couldn't yet find his way out of the mire of sudden grief. It was all too much.

He just wanted her to leave, to be alone with the pain of what he'd done. He was tired of her lectures. Nothing she could say to him right then could have made him feel any worse, any more undeserving. Once again, his grandmother had betrayed him.

Kevara Avlon seemed to suddenly recognize his feelings. "I'll leave you to your thoughts, child," she said with what he assumed was her take on compassion. "No doubt you have a great deal to ponder."

When she was gone, he lay on his bed in the crushing silence, alone.

"I'm so sorry," he whispered to the void. "Know that I never meant this. I never meant you harm. I only...only...I'm sorry."

His tears threatened to overtake him, but Jonas forced them back. He wasn't sure if Sariel could hear his words in the Aftershadow, but he desperately needed to give them life.

"Thank you," he whispered, over and over, until sleep finally claimed him.

Agriphon trotted through the heavy snowfall, his hooves leaving deep prints in the frost-laden road. Keldoan was still a few leagues away, yet they'd already begun their ascent up the steep incline that led to the mountain city.

Keldoan itself was nestled into the rocky embrace of Mount Richter, thus the main road to the city was the only one that was passable in winter. Any enemy force would have to come up this road. To either side, heavy forests wrapped around the mountain and ran north into Dalita.

Aleksei looked up at the city's snowy prominence. Even this far away he could make out the massive Betrayer's Bastion that dominated the rest of the city. The Bastion was colossal, having been built from a warren of caves that tunneled deep into the heart of the mountain.

The caves contained their own natural springs, providing a seemingly-endless water supply for the city's citizens. Anyone who laid siege to Keldoan would have to wait a very long time. As massive as its edifice was, the interior was larger still.

He heaved a sigh, his breath curling away into the frozen air. He was dead-tired in his saddle, but the end was in sight. And then he could get some rest. Perhaps he'd even have time to *think*.

He'd had little time to concentrate on the bond since it had gone silent. And while he was at first relieved that his connection to time was no longer causing him so much trouble, he now realized that something far worse had occurred.

He had no connection to Jonas at all.

It had been so long since he'd felt like a normal man, with normal abilities, he wasn't sure how afraid he ought to be. His bond with Jonas had saved his life countless times before, yet now he was no more special than the men riding in front of him.

Aleksei banished the thought as quickly as it formed. It wasn't true, and he knew it. He was the Hunter. That alone afforded him more abilities than most men could ever dream of; with the Mantle and his connection to the world around him, Aleksei was hardly powerless.

But their bond meant so much more to him than the sum of gifts it granted him. Before, there had always been that special awareness of Jonas's very existence, his imprint upon the world. Even if the man was hundreds of leagues away, Aleksei always knew he was there. Even if the Magus was unwell or injured, at least he knew he was alive. Without the bond, Aleksei wasn't certain of anything.

Gods, what had become of the man?

Worse, and even more puzzling, why was he still alive if Jonas was dead? That was the only thing that kept his hope intact. If Jonas had died, Aleksei should have fallen with him, no matter the distance. Something else had to be going on.

Aleksei prayed that Aya and the other Magi had beaten his men to Keldoan. He needed her knowledge and understanding more now than ever before.

Even though he'd ordered them to travel cross-country, they were only a few hundred. And besides, he and his men had spent the better part of a week traveling under the cover of the woods.

He stayed as near the trees as he could, even when he had to break camp with the Legionnaires. He didn't know what horror had come after him in the rebel camp, but he couldn't risk unleashing destruction on his own men like that. The strange wind hadn't returned since he'd taken to the trees, and he meant to keep it that way. He wondered if the buildings of Keldoan would protect him as the forest seemed to.

Part of him was starting to doubt whether it had even been real. He was so tired, his memories of the last few weeks were starting to fray. It was increasingly difficult to distinguish one day from the next.

Perhaps it had been real, but it had only followed him. He couldn't think of any reasons the thing would be hunting him.

If it *was* a thing.

Perhaps there had been an enemy Magus in the camp. There was always that possibility. Bael's Magi could cause that sort of destruction. But then how would the Magus have recognized him in the dark?

Aleksei shook his head, scattering the snow building up on his cloak. He desperately needed sleep. Perhaps then he would be able to put some order to his thoughts. He glanced up at the approaching gates and breathed a sigh of relief.

At least they were open. The messenger he'd sent had obviously arrived safely. He hadn't been looking forward to convincing the guards that they were a friendly force, especially not after the debacle in Kalinor. Fortunately, a letter bearing his seal appeared to have served as proof enough.

He offered a weak salute as he rode through the gates.

The city itself was a surprisingly ordered place. Unlike Kalinor's loosely ordered sprawl, Keldoan was built on a very tight set of grids, designed to hinder enemy troop movement through the city. The layout seemed almost labyrinthine, but it was immediately clear every man stationed here knew the streets like the back of his hand.

Each structure also served as a defensive position facing the walls. To either side of the gate, longhouses served as quarters for the guardsmen. Beyond those rose the city proper. It was a city designed for defense, and Aleksei relaxed ever so slightly.

He rode through thoroughfares lined with heavily-fortified buildings evenly spaced on two matrices, each laid out to interlock with the next. No single road ran straight through the city, so unlike Kalinor. This was a city built in a time of war, and as a result it was less concerned with the ease of trade or the flow of traffic and gold than it was with the safety of its populace.

Enemy troops, should they breach the walls, would have to weave their way through blocks upon blocks of cityscape before they could even get a look at the Bastion. The layout also provided any fleeing civilians a head-start to reach the Bastion in time.

Aleksei nodded to himself as he rode. He was building a strategy, and all of this played into it nicely.

Their horses finally broke through the rows of buildings and into sight of the Bastion. On either side of the massive structure stood rows of barracks that also served as outreaching stone walls. If any enemy attempted to breach the fortress, they would be contained and confined within those walls.

Aleksei idly wondered if any enemy had ever gotten far enough to be ensnared by this particular trap. The walls that circled the city were themselves imbued with the essence of the Archanium. He doubted any force since the armies of the Kholodym Dominion had marshaled sufficient strength to take such a fortress.

"Lord Captain."

Aleksei pulled Agriphon to a halt and brushed back his hood. The man saluting a few paces away remained still as stone until Aleksei offered him a salute in return and slid out of his saddle. He thought his knees might buckle as he hit the ground.

"Colonel Walsh," he said, stepping forward and gripping the man's hand.

The colonel, a very tall man with black hair cropped short and deep brown eyes, gave him a firm shake in return. "It's an honor, Sir."

Aleksei had never actually met Walsh before. It had been scarcely more than a year since his promotion to Lord Captain, and in that time he'd found no opportunity to head this far west. Keldoan was a remote place at the best of times. Considering the shocking murder of the previous Lord Captain, Jonas and Andariana had both thought it best that he remain in Kalinor until they knew more. He'd only received the promotion because he was the most likely to survive the position, much to the consternation of the Legion's generals.

He desperately hoped he was going to get along with the man. If not, Aleksei supposed he could simply issue orders and be done with it. The fact that the man had remained loyal to the Queen gave Aleksei at least a small amount of hope.

"Let's get inside, if you don't mind, Colonel. I've had about as much of this snow as I can take."

Colonel Walsh smiled grimly and walked with Aleksei towards the imposing Bastion. It was all Aleksei could do to keep from running for shelter. He knew his paranoia was getting the better of him, but he felt terribly exposed without the comfort of trees, vulnerable under the open sky.

Once inside the cavernous walls of the Bastion's entrance, Aleksei took a deep breath. He handed Agriphon's reins to a stable hand and followed Walsh, marveling at the rich carpets in the corridors and tapestries that adorned the walls.

He'd spent a decent amount of time in several fortresses, but this wasn't like anything he'd been expecting. This didn't look like a place of war.

It looked like a palace.

He stepped into Walsh's office and noted with satisfaction that it was a room of modesty. Aleksei had no doubt that there were far finer rooms and offices in the fortress. The man's humility said a great deal about him.

"Colonel," he began once the door was shut, "I don't suppose any stray Archanium Magi have arrived in the last week or so? The refugees from the Voralla were supposed to be on their way. I was hoping to find them here."

Walsh frowned, "It would be hard to notice a Magus or two slipping through the gates, Lord Captain."

"There should have been around three hundred, Colonel."

The man's frowned remained, "I've received no reports about odd behavior, Sir, but we get a fair amount of traffic through the gates each day. Unless the Magi announced who they were, I doubt they would have been noticed. The woods around Keldoan are dotted with a great number of villages that bring their wares to trade during the day. I could have some men look into it for you."

Aleksei sighed wearily, "Please do, Colonel. I'm afraid I come bearing very bad news."

Walsh leaned back in his chair, "Which bit of bad news? The loss of Kalinor? The destruction of the garrison in Mornj? Or the fifty-thousand men on your heels?"

Aleksei straightened, "You have remarkable intelligence, Colonel."

Walsh shrugged, "This is a pretty quiet city, Lord Captain. Because of our seclusion, I have eyes and ears in the villages surrounding us, and some of *them* have informants of their own. We have a network that conveys information at a...gratifying rate."

Aleksei arched a golden eyebrow, "It would appear so. Well, I'm afraid the destruction of Mornj was our doing."

Walsh leaned forward across his desk, "Sir?"

"Prince Belgi left a particularly...volatile spell in the garrison. We took all the weaponry and supplies and set a trap for the rebels. After

Kalinor, we knew it wouldn't be long before they moved to take it. Seeing how most of the lords are from southern Ilyar, we decided the garrison wasn't worth holding. So we destroyed it."

"Lord Captain," Walsh managed, "that explosion killed tens of thousands of rebel soldiers. No one in Mornj is quite sure *what* happened, but it terrified the entire populace. There were barely any rebel survivors."

Aleksei allowed himself a rueful smile, "What of their leaders? Who was in command?"

"Simon Declan."

Aleksei's smile withered, "Pity, that. He was one of the only nobles I admired. Until he committed treason, of course. Seemed to be at least somewhat sensible."

"Well, Kalinor and Mornj aside, what are your orders concerning this force behind you?"

Aleksei idly ran his fingers over the intricate carvings on the arm of his chair. "I was hoping you might help me with that, Colonel. I have the beginnings of a plan, but it requires Magi. You know your defenses better than I. Any thoughts you have would be appreciated."

Walsh blew out a breath, "Well, there are only three thousand men stationed here. At least, before you arrived. But I know my three thousand could hold off that force on your tail for at least six months up here. We have the supplies and the defenses."

Aleksei immediately shook his head, "We can't become locked in a siege. We don't have anywhere *near* that kind of time. We have to eliminate them to a man."

Walsh burst out laughing before he realized Aleksei was serious. "To a *man*, Sir? Even with the addition of your troops, their force nearly doubles ours. Furthermore, from up here, there's not exactly a lot of room to negotiate. Begging your pardon, Sir, but that only works in our favor. In a pitched battle, we'd be annihilated. I'd think a siege would be our best bet."

Aleksei leaned forward, "Right before we lost Kalinor, I thought the same thing. In that situation, a siege likely would have worked for a while. We were routed by magic we had no understanding of. But Kalinor was a different situation.

"If we fall into a siege, then a large majority of Her Majesty's Legion will be bottled up here. In the six months we'll be trapped here twiddling our thumbs, the rest of the rebel forces will be able to sweep across

Ilyar and take every major city, every port, every village. Eventually, we will be the only ones left, and then they will bring the full force of their might down upon us.

"They have Magi who can command magic of incredible destruction. One such Magus has unlocked an even darker power, the Demonic Presence. With it, he can breach your walls. And then they will sweep into this city like locusts, until they will vanquish every last one of us."

Walsh stared at him with wide eyes, his mouth agape.

"No, Colonel. Were the playing field even close to even, I would whole-heartedly agree with you. But we have no such luxury at the moment. The enemy has abilities we've never taken into account before. This war won't be won with textbook strategy and tactics."

When he saw the colonel's face redden, Aleksei quickly backpedaled. "No fault to you, Colonel. I've told you things only a handful of people know or understand.

"Even with your network of spies, there's no possible way you could've known this. Gods, if I'd heard the things I just described to you from *my* network, I'd have thought they were hitting the bottle or gone turncoat."

Walsh nodded, regaining his composure. "I'm pleased to see that you're not the ignorant rube so many claimed you to be."

Aleksei broke into a broad grin, "I'm glad I've proven that much to you, Colonel. Though it suits our purposes just fine if the enemy still believes that."

Walsh considered a moment. "Alright, then, we can't fight by their rules. What do you propose?"

Aleksei shrugged, sitting back in his chair. "We make our own."

CHAPTER 12

TRAPS

Jonas turned down the hall, running lightly into the seemingly-endless darkness. The corridor lit around him, but gave little indication of what lay beyond. He ran, shrouded in the Archanium, until he could feel two angels approach.

He gripped the Archanium, shrinking down into a tiny brown wood mouse. The exhilaration of shifting again felt dull against the sorrow that pervaded his thoughts.

Despite the pain of what he'd done, and the consuming loneliness of imprisonment, he knew without a doubt that he *had* to get out of this place. He couldn't survive like a caged animal, left with no companions save the specters of his own terrible actions and their consequences.

He had to get to Aleksei. He had spent a good day and half feeling despondent, crippled by the crushing guilt of causing Sariel's death before he'd managed to pull some part of himself together.

They wanted him to give up hope. They wanted him to feel worthless, dangerous. And part of him wanted to believe that too; the fear of such a realization drove him on.

He *had* to get out. He would do anything necessary. His grandmother had said the Presence was shielded from him...within him. Jonas's only hope was that the black archway that led into the rest of the Basilica would allow him to pass. If it no longer viewed him as a threat, he could be out of the Basilica in a matter of seconds.

He prayed Sariel had bought his freedom.

Another part of him was afraid to leave this place. What if Aleksei had been killed while he was trapped inside the Undercroft? But then Jonas had realized that if Aleksei was gone, he didn't much care to live either. He didn't want to experience life without Aleksei. And living in the Undercroft was no life.

Certainly not now.

The two angels he'd sensed moments before rounded the corner. Jonas remained perfectly still as they swept past, and then he was off again, racing through the corridors as swiftly as his tiny mouse feet could carry him.

For the moment, he decided to retain his shape. It was slower, but the chances of detection were almost nonexistent. He thanked the gods that the angels couldn't sense his use of the Archanium. They might be able to tell that someone was using magic, but in the Basilica that was hardly worth mentioning. Besides, he was in a place of *very* dangerous magic.

He closed his eyes and tried desperately to remember the twists and turns of a place he'd only set foot in once. He avoided hallways where he could feel life, instead concentrating on the empty ones.

It seemed to take hours, but finally he turned a corner and spotted the black archway. Holding back a cry, he darted towards it. Jonas hugged the wall, out of fear that someone might pass through the archway unexpectedly and step on him. He wasn't entirely sure what would happen in such a situation, but he decided he'd rather not find out.

Jonas reached the cool blackness and reached out a tentative paw. The shield felt cold. He looked behind him before relaxing back into a man. He pressed his hand against the shield again.

It slid a few inches into the darkness, but a force pushed him back. He reached into the Archanium and gently began to study the construction of the shield. He knew it had been crafted through Song, as its age was vastly exceeded the comparatively paltry millennium the Seraphima had been in existence. There was another magic, something that felt at once foreign and familiar. Kevara Avlon had also said that Sariel had used her connection to the Seraphima to shield him, but this wasn't the Seraphima. From what he could sense, it wasn't even Angelic in origin. There was a quality to it that he felt he should recognize immediately, yet its origin eluded him.

Jonas refocused his attention on the Song of the shield, and the Seraphima that dwelt within him. If he could somehow craft a bridge between the Angelic magic humming through him and the arcane Song....

A violent force threw him back across the corridor. He lay there, panting, trying to get his breath. His vision swam. He was amazed that he hadn't cracked his head on the cold stone.

Footsteps echoed through the corridors behind him.

A heartbeat later he was just a little brown mouse, moving through the darkness. He was almost out of earshot when he heard the sounds of conversation coming from the arch.

"What was that?"

"The sound? I think someone was trying to breach the shield."

"Alone?" came an incredulous voice.

"Everyone tries once, Tarquin. Assuming they're clever enough to *make* it this far."

Jonas shifted from his mouse form and trotted back through the halls, feeling his way through the empty corridors, trying to keep the last of his hope from draining out. He wondered if it was even possible to leave this place once the shield felt your corruption. Perhaps it had all been a lie.

He reached the large, open-air atrium and headed for the Reliquary.

One of the few perks of his exorcism was that Jonas was now allowed greater run of the Undercroft. He wasn't yet allowed into the Reliquary, but after failing to pass through the shield, he was quickly running out of options.

He *had* to find a way out.

Jonas walked close to the archway Sariel had shown him. There was a small pond filled with brightly colored fish not far from the arch. Jonas waited until he was sure he wasn't being watched before he stepped behind a strand of birch trees that hugged the water's edge.

He scurried out a moment later, under the archway and into the Reliquary. As he moved, he passed through yet another shield. It wasn't nearly as strong as the first one, but he definitely felt the resistance as he passed through it.

Jonas hurried under a nearby shelf and waited to see if anyone had been alerted to his presence. When a few minutes had passed, he scurried out and headed towards the back of cavernous maze of shelves and tables. It reminded him of the vaults in the Voralla, but it didn't appear to be nearly as well organized.

Then again, Xavathan had said that the things in here were far more dangerous. Perhaps that meant they were merely kept safe here, but never used. Given what he'd seen of the Undercroft thus far, that wouldn't surprise him in the least.

When he determined he was deep enough into the Reliquary, Jonas allowed himself to transform once again. He stepped out from behind a shelf and looked down one of the long stretches in between rows of shelving. It was empty.

Jonas walked carefully between the shelves, holding his arms to his sides. Gods, but how did angels manage to navigate this place with their wings flowing behind them?

He reached a juncture and held his breath when an angel walked by. He started when he recognized the man.

"Adam!" he whispered.

The angel stopped and appeared in between the shelves. His eyes went wide when he saw Jonas standing there. "Jonas?" he whispered back incredulously, stepping into the row.

Jonas offered him a weak smile, "Sorry to surprise you, I was hoping you had a moment to talk."

Adam's face was white, "Jonas, do you have any idea where you are right now?"

Jonas shrugged, "The Reliquary? Far enough in the back that no one will notice me?"

Adam buried his face in his hands before looking up, "This section is forbidden. Dear One-God, Jonas, everything on these shelves could kill you if you don't know what you're doing. Just by touching it."

Jonas glanced to a shelf on his left. A few odd little statues and rings were scattered about haphazardly. From the power they emanated, he recognized one or two. They had similar objects in the Voralla, but they weren't considered all that dangerous.

"Is this section forbidden because it's dangerous? Or because your people don't know what half of these things *are?*" he asked, deliberately lifting a thick golden ring with a huge purple stone.

Adam could hardly hold in his gasp. Jonas frowned and tapped the stone. It lit with a soft violet glow. Jonas extinguished the light and tossed it back on the shelf with the others.

"That's a trinket," he said softly. "The Magi in the past made them as a training exercise."

Adam's face flushed red and he pulled Jonas out from the shelves. "You shouldn't be *in* here, Jonas. This place is dangerous."

Jonas sighed. He certainly wasn't in any mood to get into an argument with the angel. He just wanted to talk to someone he felt he could trust.

His eyes spotted a ewer across the room. It was carved from golden marble and inlaid with irregularly shaped pieces of wood. He pointed, "You see that?" Adam followed the line of his finger. "*That* is dangerous. Don't touch that. Ever."

The statement confused Adam for a moment before his anger resurfaced, "Come on, I have to get you out of here. Patients aren't *allowed* in here."

Jonas pulled away from the angel's grasp easily, "I'm not a patient anymore, I'm a prisoner. Please? Can you spare a few minutes to talk, as a friend? With all the bookshelves I passed, I presume you have private reading rooms?"

Adam grudgingly nodded.

Jonas sighed in relief. When Adam didn't budge, Jonas looked into the angel's heated blue eyes pleadingly. "Lead the way?"

Adam stormed off in a huff and Jonas followed, looking around, trying to get a sense of the layout. He hated having to beg, but in his current state he wasn't sure what else to do.

When he'd first seen the angel walking past, Jonas had been relieved to finally see someone he knew. Someone he liked. Adam's immediately condescending attitude, even if invoked in the name of Jonas's safety, had quickly returned him to his sullen state. He hated being talked down to, but at the moment he had little defense against it beyond simple logic.

He hardly had the energy to summon his imperious royal façade.

Adam led him to a small room that contained a simple table, a lantern, and two comfortable chairs. Jonas stepped in and had a seat. Adam sat stiffly across from him, but left the door open.

With an inward sigh, Jonas flicked his hand. The door shut gently and a shield surrounded the room, cutting off any chance that those outside might be listening in.

"What's this about?" Adam asked testily.

Jonas leaned forward, his eyebrows drawing down, "First, I want you to tell me why you're so angry. Is it because I made you look foolish? I promise you, that was not my intent."

Adam glowered at him, his icy blue eyes furious, "Hardly. I'm angry because you're needlessly endangering your safety and your freedom by coming here. Why couldn't you have just sent an angel back to fetch me? Why did you *have* to come in here? There are more dangers in this place than any of us truly understand, Jonas. You shouldn't be risking yourself so cavalierly."

Jonas sat back and crossed his arms, "If I believed I was truly risking myself, I wouldn't have come. I'm not in the habit of risking my life unless I absolutely have to. Consider for a moment that behavior you see as ignorant might actually be backed up by knowledge. The Basilica is hardly the only place in the world where objects such as these exist. And just because you don't understand all these items does not inherently make them dangerous."

Adam's face remained flushed for a moment before returning to a normal color, "Alright. I'll take you at your word for the moment. What was so urgent that it couldn't wait until tonight?"

"I wanted to talk."

"About what?"

Jonas shrugged, gesturing with his hand, "Everything. This place. The shields. Everything that happened at the exorcism." He leaned forward, "Since I've been here, I have only spoken to my grandmother or Sariel. My grandmother only comes to lecture me on why I shouldn't be alive, and while Sariel tried to be as nice as possible, I didn't do the best job of reading her intentions, and I treated her poorly."

"You have an odd way of showing gratitude." Adam grunted.

"Please," Jonas said softly, "you have to know that I never wanted her to die like that. I never knew that was even a possibility. Since I've been here, no one has told me *anything* I wanted to hear without telling two more things I didn't. I'd about given up when I decided to escape."

Adam stiffened, "Escape? What do you mean?"

"I tried to pass through the shield."

Adam planted his face in his hands again, "Good *God*, Jonas. You're lucky to be alive."

"I've been hearing that quite a bit. The fact is, I heard two angels talking not long after, expressing their shock that someone might attempt such a thing. Can you explain that to me?"

Adam sighed, "You have to enter of your own free will. But in order to leave, you must have assistance. When you walked through the first time, you made a pact that you would not be released without the consent of the Angelus."

"I was never told anything like that," Jonas muttered. "Much the same way I was never told what would happen to Sariel. You people seem to have a habit of omitting any information on potential consequences when it suits your agenda."

"I know it must seem harsh to you, but we only do it out of everyone's best interest," Adam offered limply.

"So how do I get out of here? Can *you* take me through the shield?"

Adam looked away, "No, Jonas. Even if I could, the guard outside would stop you."

Jonas's emerald eyes flared, "I wouldn't count on it."

Adam groaned, "You have to have someone from both sides. It's usually the guard and one of the healers. They create a bridge through the shield, and you're freed. But it can't be done from one side alone."

"What about Leigha? If I could talk to her, I'm sure she would help me." He reached out and gripped Adam's forearm, "I *have* to get out of here. This place is killing me, and I don't have the time to waste, not now. There are too many other things that are more important."

Adam chuckled humorlessly, "More important than the end of the world?"

Jonas didn't flinch, "What do you think is going to happen if I'm kept in here? There are dangerous people out there, Adam. *Far* more dangerous than I. I can't allow them to rape my realm while I sit on my thumbs in *here*."

"I'm sorry, Jonas, but I can't help you. Leigha has been forbidden from seeing you. The Angelus doesn't want her exposed to your corruption, even in its weakened state."

Jonas's face fell. She had been his greatest hope.

"But she asks about you!" Adam offered, attempting to sound cheerful.

Jonas looked up, "She does? *When?*"

Adam's voice became conspiratorial, "She sends...a friend down here to inquire about you, observe you if he can. Just to see if you're healthy, if you're alright."

Jonas frowned, suddenly disconcerted that he was being watched. "What's his name?"

Adam wrinkled his nose in obvious distaste, "Tarquin."

Jonas froze. "Tarquin? He was in the corridor when I tried to pass through the shield. I heard him talking to the guard. I've been out of my chambers for hours. I've been in the corridors."

Adam blinked at him. He could tell the angel wasn't following his line of logic.

Jonas sighed, "If he was looking for me, and I was nowhere to be found, don't you think he might have started asking questions?"

Adam's face darkened, "If he thought you'd escaped, he wouldn't bother telling Leigha. He'd just go straight to the Angelus. If he was there when you tried to go through the shield...."

Jonas leaned back in his chair and groaned. It felt like everything just kept getting worse and worse. He was about to ask Adam how much time they had when the shield around the room evaporated and his grandmother swept in. She looked like she could have chewed the heads off of nails.

"Apparently," she hissed, "we need to have another little *chat*."

Hade stared at the confusion that was the city of Keldoan. The matrix of buildings and streets completely overwhelmed him, yet Vadim seemed to maneuver with relative ease. Hade kept his eyes fixed on the broad prominence of the Bastion in the distance. That was where he wanted to go, more than anything. He could feel the compulsion deep within him.

He recognized Sammul's spell, but he let it be. His Master would have a reason to place such a piece of magic within him. He trusted Sammul. The man had been like a father since Hade had arrived as a boy, and Hade would *not* let him down now.

He had seen Kalinor. Sammul had told him of the others' corruption by the Demon Bael. Hade knew the affliction that possessed those who would be arriving soon.

Alone with Vadim, Hade had traveled far faster than the others he now knew were struggling to reach the city. With his added knowledge from Sammul, Hade understood the importance of his mission. He would watch the actions of the others, and he would report. There was a chance, he knew, that Sammul could save them from damnation.

He wanted that so much. More than power or safety, Hade wanted the others to be freed from their prison. He knew how fragile they were, how fragile *he* was. But Sammul would save them from themselves. He had said as much night after night. Hade believed that as strongly as he believed the sun would rise at dawn. Sammul had never led him astray.

He would obey.

Vadim glanced at him, a frown on the Knight's face. "Are you alright?"

Hade could feel the genuine concern radiating across their bond. He shrugged, "I'm fine. Just not sure what's going to happen next, that's all." Well, that was true enough. He wasn't. But Sammul was. He would listen to Sammul. Sammul would lead them out of their confusion.

Vadim kept a wary eye on him even as they reached the inn. Hade had been very specific. They shouldn't go to the Betrayer's Bastion. Not until the others arrived. They should lie low.

They had plenty of silver to last them a good long while. They could pose as merchants, brothers. Hade wasn't sure that anyone would buy that, seeing his rust-colored hair beside Vadim's dark complexion, but Hade kept up the pretense. Sammul said that as long as he paid the right amount, no one would ask questions.

So far, his master had been correct.

Vadim was more than ready to put their packs down and find the comfort of a bed. Hade wanted to lie down so badly, but he had a greater need. He could feel it ripple through his bones. And while he could have dispelled the sensation, he decided to follow it. It would be from Sammul. He *trusted* Sammul.

He excused himself, saying he was going down to check on their horses. It wasn't an unreasonable comment to make. He had bound both mounts with a spell that would keep anyone from doing them harm. He knew that, but Vadim didn't.

Had anyone tried to steal the horses, or to hurt them, Hade would have known instantly. He could even control the beasts from a distance. Sammul had taught him that spell. He had told Hade, but none of the others.

Hade knew he was special.

When he shut the door, he paused. He listened, touching the Archanium and connecting to his Knight. When he felt Vadim slip into a weary slumber, Hade cast a sleep spell over the Knight yet again. He had become quite practiced at entrancing Vadim after casting the same spell nightly during their long journey to Keldoan.

He hated having to deceive Vadim like this, but he knew it was for the best. Vadim wouldn't understand. He cared too much for individuals.

Master Sammul continually explained how completely different the world really was from what Hade had been brought up to believe. The world wasn't about individuals and their decisions, but about the common good. Master Sammul was simply working towards the common good.

And he *needed* Hade to act for him. He said his presence would upset the new initiates. Hade didn't understand what that meant, but he did as Sammul said.

He would not fail his master.

Hade followed the sensation out into the city, and past the city walls. He kept walking, even though it was much too far to travel on foot. Vadim was asleep. He would remain asleep until Hade released him. Hade walked down the mountain path and into the woods.

And there he finally saw his master, clothed again in green flame. "Hade, my son, you have answered my call."

Hade dropped to his knees and bowed his head, "Master, *Father*, I will always answer your call."

Sammul smiled, "I foresee a great change, my son. You *must* be a part of it, or you will be swept away."

Hade frowned. This was not the way Sammul usually spoke to him, "Master, the other Magi have not yet reached the city. What should I do when they come?"

Sammul's smile returned, "Stay where you are. Stay out of sight. I will tell you when it is time to return to them. But remember, they are infected by the Demon. You must never let your guard down. When you return to them, you may have to eliminate the worst of them."

Hade stiffened, "Master? Do we not want to *save* these innocents?"

Sammul smiled, "Of course we do, child. But there are many who might stand in your way. Ilyana..."

Hade raised a hand, "Master, I will do as you say, but I *cannot* harm Ilyana."

Sammul growled. The green fire flared around him. "You will incur my wrath if you do not deal with her."

Hade stiffened, "Then take me now, Master. I don't care to live in a world without her."

Sammul calmed his flames. "I may grant you this indulgence, child. But you must bring me something precious in trade."

Hade nodded hungrily, "As you command."

CHAPTER 13
STONE BY STONE

Katherine could hardly keep her mouth closed as she followed Lord Declan into the heart of Kalinor. All around, business was still moving, but a heavy pall hung over the city. The cityfolk seemed drained, colorless. On every street corner stood small contingents of rebel soldiers, wearing the purple and gold of House Krasik.

Banners hung above the thoroughfare, a gruesome scene depicting a black raven picking a white ram's skull clean on a field of violet. The symbol was everywhere. When she whispered to Declan about it, he curtly told her it meant victory and to ignore it.

She lost control of her poise and let her mouth hang open as they passed through another gate. This one was blackened and burnt beyond repair. The wood and stone that remained appeared melted. She shuddered to think of a power that could cause such destruction.

When a guard stepped in front of their horses, Declan leaned forward and flashed his signet ring. The guard studied it for a moment before waving them through.

Katherine breathed a sigh of relief. She hadn't been at all convinced that getting into Kalinor Palace was going to be anywhere near as easy as Declan claimed. So far, though, he'd proven to be a surprisingly clever man.

She hoped his tricks didn't suddenly dry up.

They trotted across a broad, snow-covered lawn. She gasped at the massive cathedral that dominated the lawn. It was breathtaking, like nothing she'd ever seen. She'd seen the Palace from the gates, and while its grandeur was breathtaking, she felt a far deeper appreciation for the cathedral. In the face of all that splendor, it stood powerful and steady, but also reasoned and modest.

"The Cathedral of Mokosh," Declan said softly.

Katherine laughed to herself. Of course it was. Nothing like the ornate temples they'd passed on their way onto the Palace grounds. Those had been at once awe-inspiring and vaguely terrifying.

But this building was the first thing she'd seen since leaving Voskrin that felt like *home*.

"Will I be allowed to go inside?" she asked meekly.

Declan chuckled, "Of course, Katherine. These rebels may be victorious, but they aren't heathens. All who live in the Palace are allowed to worship."

She breathed a sigh of relief.

This journey had been onerous in the extreme, but she was determined that she would see it through. She was determined to help Aleksei. It was beyond reassuring to know that there was a place she might find some restoration, some safety, some true peace when she wasn't mining the halls of Kalinor Palace for secrets. It somehow made the insanity her life had lately become a little easier to bear.

Just before they reached the Palace, Declan led them around to the West Lawn. Katherine was surprised to see more structures emerge as they walked across the grounds. She climbed off her horse, starting when a young man came and took the reins from her.

Declan flipped the boy a silver and spoke briefly to the stable master. It seemed to her that the two men knew each other. She could scarcely believe a lord like Declan would have relationship with such a lowly man. On that journey up, she'd found him to be a perplexing and complicated man.

Katherine smiled at the stable master, who tipped his hat, before hurrying after Declan. He'd told her that once they were in the Palace, he would have to treat her like a commoner.

She'd laughed at that then, but the situation was growing rapidly less amusing.

Katherine followed him through a twisting series of corridors and great rooms, some of which she could hardly believe. As she gaped at her surroundings, a knot steadily tightened in her stomach, and she could feel her sense of dread growing.

To distract herself, she wondered what Aleksei had thought the first time he'd set foot inside the Palace. The thought of sharing such an awe-inspiring experience with him made her feel a bit better and, for some reason, her face flushed.

She found herself so wrapped in her surroundings that she jerked when Declan touched her shoulder, bringing her back to the moment at hand.

"Girl! Are you deaf? Go on with Mistress Leams to the servant's quarters. Go on!"

She flinched at the tone in Declan's voice, more out of surprise than hurt. That, added to her flushed face, seemed to satisfy the stout woman standing a few paces away that Katherine was just what Declan had claimed. She scurried after the little woman, murmuring an apology.

When they were out of earshot, the woman smiled at her, "Don't fret, dearie. You'll have your hands full with his sort, but among the servants you're no different from the rest of us. Come on, now, let's get you some proper clothes."

Katherine allowed a shy smile to cross her face, "Thank you, Mistress Leams. I'm just happy to be in the Palace's employ, what with all that's been happening."

The older woman nodded approvingly, "And rightly so. I've heard there's quite a bit of hunger down in your province, what with all the food going to the army."

Katherine bobbed her head. She had seen the truth of that as they'd traveled. She'd prayed every night that the same fate wouldn't be visited on Voskrin. At least they had Mother Margareta to look after them.

She'd seen Margareta do some miraculous things in their time together, and she felt safer knowing her family was being looked after by such a competent woman.

The reached a small servant's door and Mistress Leams motioned her in.

"Now then, dearie, we've got to get you cleaned up and dressed. I must say, we have been short on staff from the Southern Plain, and there are quite a few who have requested your sort specifically."

"I'm excited to be able to start work straight away," Katherine said earnestly, covering her confusion as to who was requesting her sort specifically and why.

"Good, dearie, good." The older woman paused and glanced Katherine up and down, "You know, most of the ones who come in are just covered in dust and grime. You look clean enough."

"Lord Declan insisted we stay at an inn last night. It was quite late. I managed to bathe this morning, the gods be praised. He said he didn't want to arrive with me smelling like a gutter tramp," Katherine said, staring at a speck on the floor, as though she were ashamed.

Her actual joy would have to remain hidden. A real bath after such travel had been a luxury indeed.

Mistress Leams shook her head, "Gods, but some of these men have filthy mouths. Hardly suitable words for a young lady such as yourself.

"Nevertheless, we must suffer their poor manners, even if they won't suffer ours. Here you are." She pressed a starched pile of livery into Katherine's hands, smiling. "Put these on and then we'll get you straight to work."

Katherine accepted the uniform, "Thank you so much for your kindness."

Mistress Leams patted her cheek, "You just get dressed quickly, girl. There's more work in this place than you could care to imagine."

She shut the door firmly. For the first time in ages, Katherine let out a deep sigh. She offered a silent prayer for safety and guidance to Mokosh as she pulled off her boots.

Aya rushed down the hall, following a very nervous messenger. Sergeant Ballard had hardly explained who she was before she found herself galloping after a young Legionnaire.

Keldoan contained the most confusing labyrinth of buildings she'd ever seen, but she'd felt better knowing her Knight, Raefan, was only paces behind. Seeing the full view of the Bastion itself had nearly made her draw her horse back, but she'd followed the young man to the entrance.

Now, he practically dragged her behind him. Raefan hovered over her like a shadow, hand on his sword. He didn't like anyone presuming to touch her, much less lead her in such a manner.

If not for her strict orders, delivered silently across their bond, she knew Raefan wouldn't have allowed any of this. She wondered what could possibly make the young messenger so frantic. Whatever it was, she decided it must be sufficiently important for him to be so presumptuous and ill-mannered.

He knocked on an unassuming oak door, then stepped inside. She heard muffled words. The door burst open and Aleksei Drago stepped out, sweeping her into a heartfelt hug. He let her go and grasped Raefan's arm tightly. Raefan blinked in surprise, his mouth hanging open.

This was the last thing they'd expected.

"Gods, but it's good to see you!" Aleksei exclaimed with a broad grin, ushering them into the office.

Behind the desk sat a very tall, handsome man with raven hair and brown eyes so dark they bordered on black. He stood out of courtesy, "Lady Magus, it's a pleasure to have you in our city."

She gave him a slight nod of her head before surreptitiously casting a shield on the door. She had a feeling anything that had required this much urgency was important enough to warrant secrecy.

Aya turned, trying her best to not seem taken aback. "Alright Aleksei, care to explain what's going on here?"

Aleksei's face grew grim, his smile vanishing as he took a seat. He beckoned Aya and Raefan to do the same. Raefan went and stood by the door, his hand never leaving his sword.

"You don't know?" Aleksei asked. "Surely you saw the force that's coming towards the city."

Aya shook her head, "We were too far away to be able to gauge their numbers or intent. Sergeant Ballard took us so far southwest that it was difficult to discern which troop movement was which. He said he'd rather take the chance they were the enemy, and not risk our lives.

"As it was, we traveled fast enough to get here well ahead of the other force. Last we saw them, they were still some days away. I suppose that means you didn't get caught by their expeditionary force?"

Aleksei wiped a hand across his face. "I'm afraid we're going to have to catch up on specifics later. A lot's happened since we saw each other last. For the moment, we're planning a strategy, and I need your Magi more than ever."

Her face grew grave, "We'll help in whatever way we can, but I'm not sure what we're going to be able to do against enemy Magi."

Aleksei shook his head, "It's not them I'm worried about. I simply need to know if you can perform specific types of spells, and if so, how effective they'd be."

Aya shrugged, "As I said, we'll help in any way we can."

"When we fought the revenants in Drava, I asked some of the Magi to create shields of air. How big can you make them, and how strong are they?"

Aya's mouth quirked to the side, "Each of us could probably create a field big enough to envelop a man. It would deflect a few arrows at the most, but nothing sent by one of Bael's Magi."

Aleksei waved the last comment away, "That's alright. Can you move these shields?"

"Move them? I have no idea. Why would you want to *move* one?"

"Aya," Aleksei said, exasperated, "please, just tell me if it's possible."

She could tell he was beyond exhaustion. "Catching up" was going to be very interesting indeed. "I believe it might be possible to move them, but not very far. No more than three or four paces."

Aleksei nodded and made a note. He asked her a barrage of questions, most of which made little or no sense to her. Each time she gave an answer, he would make a note. She had never been asked questions like these by a non-Magus. Even as a Knight, his understanding of the Archanium was shockingly limited.

When he was finally satisfied, it was near time for dinner. Aya realized with a start that they'd been talking for nearly four hours. She could scarcely believe it. She dreaded to know why he needed to know all these different specifics. Gods, what was the man planning?

"Alright," he finally said, snapping his ledger shut, "that's about all I can handle for now. I'm going to have to think on this tonight." He stood and stretched his shoulders. "Gods, I'm starving! I need to eat something before I pass out, and I'm sure you're famished after your journey. Colonel, what's the easiest way to get some food around here?"

Colonel Walsh groped for words before finally finding what he wanted to say, "Lord Captain, you're in command here. All you have to do is snap your fingers and we'll have your dinner and anything else you require brought to you."

Aleksei sighed, "Very well. I need a room, and I need dinner brought there for myself, Magus Aya and Raefan. How long will that take?"

Colonel Walsh managed a small smile, "It will be set up by the time you arrive in your chambers."

True to his word, by the time an elderly servant showed them to a palatial suite outfitted with every amenity they could have imagined, there was a table set for three. Aya and Raefan eagerly took their seats, savoring the smell of rabbit stew and mulled wine.

As adept as Sergeant Ballard was at foraging in the wild, they hadn't had real food in weeks. It seemed beyond luxury.

"Let me apologize in advance," Aleksei began after their initial pangs of voracious hunger had been sated, "but I don't have the time or energy, mainly time, to go over everything that's happened in the last few weeks, and I daresay you'd like a bath and a bed as much as I.

"Beyond the things we've already spoken about, there have been some events I find troubling. Things have happened that I don't understand. Aya, you're the only one I truly trust with this information. I have to know what's going on."

She took a deep pull of mulled wine and swallowed, "I'm at your disposal, Aleksei. But as you saw this afternoon, I am far from an expert on everything. Or much of *anything* you need to know, it would seem."

"My bond with Jonas is gone," Aleksei blurted.

It was all Aya could do not to spray wine in Aleksei's face. She coughed, managed to finally swallow, and dabbed at the corners of her mouth with her napkin. "That's impossible," she finally allowed.

"That doesn't concern me. What concerns me is that it's true. I have lost my connection to Jonas. I don't feel him anywhere, and I can't tap my bond to alter time. It's as though the bond never existed. Do you know of anything that could cause such a phenomenon?"

She sat back, finally considering his question. "What do you know about Jonas's situation or location when this happened?"

Aleksei took a bite of stew, "He was moving continually north. At first northwest, away from Kalinor. He came back a bit to the east, but never close. Still hundreds of leagues away. But always north, until he... it...our connection was just suddenly gone."

"North of Kalinor...." she muttered. She suddenly gasped, her hand coming to her mouth. The wine glass beside her flipped and splattered the tablecloth. She didn't flinch. "Oh great gods!"

Aleksei leaned aggressively forward, "What is it? What's wrong?"

She swallowed a few times, tears clouding her vision, "I don't know anything with certainty, Aleksei. Understand that first. But the things you've described to me, first the distortion in your bond, and now this, all point to one thing. I think Jonas is in the Basilica."

Aleksei sat back, obviously disappointed. "It can't be that. Jonas has been in the Basilica before, but nothing like this has ever happened."

"No," Aya corrected, "this is different. The Basilica has many different sections, wings, ossuaries, libraries. They also have a place of great magic called the Reliquary. It's a bit like the Vault in the Voralla. The Reliquary is jealously guarded by the angels. Until a few centuries ago, it housed the Prime Key. It's located in what's called the Under-croft. But the Undercroft serves other functions. It's also a place where dangerous creatures of magic are kept. That includes people. The angels use their magic to 'protect' and heal these creatures.

"Aleksei, whatever caused that distortion in your bond happened to *Jonas*. I don't know what it was, but I know that much. You merely felt the aftershock. He must have been in Dalita when it happened. Since you aren't dead, we know he's still alive. But Aleksei, if they took him to the Undercroft...great gods, I don't know *what* they could be doing to him.

"The Undercroft was created to protect the things inside from outside forces. It has a shield that neutralizes outside magic. It's ancient, older than the Basilica itself. It's possible that it's also neutralized your bond."

Aleksei nodded, absorbing everything she said. "So how do I get him out?"

Aya fought back a hopeless laugh, "I don't know. I've never heard of a Magus going into the Undercroft, and I've never heard of *any*one coming out. That's not its purpose. It's meant to protect the things inside from us, and us from the creatures and items they've locked away. Aleksei, it's a *prison*."

His jaw tightened. He took a deep breath, then met her gaze. His golden eyes glimmered in the lamplight.

"Alright, here's what we're going to do: We're going to wipe out the rebel force coming for us. We're going to kill them to a man, so that not even a single scout makes it back to report what happened here. We'll make them simply vanish, just like the expeditionary force. And then I'm going to Dalita to get Jonas back."

"Aleksei," she began, putting her hand on his arm.

"*No!*" he bellowed.

She knew he wasn't yelling at her, but his vehemence was still shocking.

His eyes were blazing, "I will *not* tolerate this, Aya. Not for a *moment*. I will do what I must here, and then I am going to Dalita, and I am getting him back. The gods themselves couldn't stop me if they tried.

I've suffered too much for him to have that bitch grandmother of his lock him away."

"And if they turn you away?" she managed.

The sound of his voice was painful. She had never heard a more powerful or aching collection of sorrow, misery, and rage. The very timbre of his words made her want to run from the room. When he looked at her, she knew she was gazing at something more than Aleksei.

She was seeing something raw, elemental.

"Then I will bring the Basilica crashing to the ground. I will tear it apart stone by stone, but I will get him *back*."

"So, tell me," Kevara spat, "exactly which part were you unclear on last time?"

Jonas glowered at her, his sorrow evaporating in the fire of his sudden anger. "I'm not interested in your lectures at the moment, Kevara. You made your point quite clear.

"But I'm afraid I wasn't sufficiently impressed with your reasoning. You've failed to make your case, as far as I'm concerned. And as it's my life to live, not yours, I decided I've had about enough of our 'chats'. Now, are you quite finished?"

Livid, she raised her hand and the air crackled as the spell ripped towards him, only to vanish with a dull thud inches from his face. He didn't flinch. His shield had barely been raised in time, but it had the desired effect.

She began to draw power around herself again. He snorted, "You really are a dumb bitch, aren't you?"

She faltered.

"Here you are," he went on, "terrified beyond all reason that I'm going to allow the Demonic Presence into this world by using my magic. And then you decide to assault me with yours? Are you trying to goad me, Kevara? Is this another one of your self-fulfilling prophecies?

"I almost tapped into the Seraphima trying to get past your little shield. I'm pretty sure if I tried hard enough, I might be able to touch the Presence again. Especially if I was driven by uncontrollable rage. Maybe that's your goal. Do you want to be the one who helps me end this world? Because you are *very* close to pushing me beyond reason. Your prison is killing me. If I can't leave, I might as well die here and now. I'm ready. Are you?"

He leaned forward, giving himself over to his anger. It was the only thing that seemed to shield him from his pain, his guilt. "You said your shields prevent others from being affected by outside magic. You also said I'm the 'eye of the storm'. How confident are you that your ancient shields can keep me bound like all your other little prisoners?"

She was fuming, and she was terrified. He'd at least managed that. Her certainty cracked. With obvious effort, she composed herself before she spoke again.

"Perhaps you're right, Jonas. Perhaps you just saved me from making a very grave mistake. Allow me to return the favor. If you allow your power to erupt in here, to kill me, to kill Adam, and destroy every living thing in the Undercroft, you still won't breach the shield.

"If the same happens beyond the shield, you could decimate *every-thing*. You could poison the Archanium for all time, effectively ending life itself."

She stepped forward, "While I'm not proud that my own flesh and blood would have such a flippant attitude towards this world, let me instead bring up something you *might* care about.

"Do you love Aleksei Drago?"

Jonas straightened, "I beg your pardon?"

"Your Archanium Knight. The Lord Captain. The Ri-Vhan Hunter. Do you love him?"

"Of course." His rage burned brighter. How dare she even say Aleksei's *name?*

"Then you want him to live, to be happy, don't you? I doubt destroying the world he inhabits is going to make him very happy. Certainly not as the flesh is stripped from his bones, and his soul is ripped into tatters by the denizens of the Presence. You've felt that pain. Would you wish that on him?"

"Of course not!" Jonas snapped, "But you don't know that will ever happen! That's simply the addled thinking of a mad woman. You're allowing your fear to dominate you."

She arched a snowy eyebrow, "And that is a risk you're willing to take? My belief against yours? If I'm right, and you successfully leave this place, the man you profess to love will be destroyed because of your hubris.

"You have an even chance of destroying him, or sparing him a life of loneliness. Just how confident are you in your own wisdom, in your abilities? You'd be making a gamble, gambling with the price of your love's very soul.

"Do you think so little of Sariel's sacrifice? She returned your soul, her sacrifice keeps it safe. And you would spit in her face, on her memory, by casually ignoring divine prophecy? I always knew you to be a selfish man, Jonas Belgi, but this would be a new level of narcissism, even for you.

"But if you care so little for Sariel, for Aleksei, and you insist on having your way, be my guest. I'll not release you on a whim, but no one will stop you from attempting escape. Try all you want. Burn the flesh from your bones trying to get through the shield. Like it or not, you're here for the rest of your life. The sooner you come to accept how dangerous you are, to all of us, but most importantly to *Aleksei*, the safer we'll all be."

Her face softened slightly, "I know this is a painful sacrifice, Jonas. I know you don't give a damn about the rest of us. But please, care about that young man. I'll be sure that he understands the sacrifice you're making for him in full if he seeks you out.

"He will never doubt how much you love him, or the pain you've gone through to save him, to save all of us. If he's as sensible as I've heard, he will understand, and he will thank you."

"Get out," Jonas hissed through clenched teeth. "Get out of my sight. Now! I don't want to hear another word out of your mouth. Stay away from me." He was shaking. "I will do what you suggest, *Grandmother*. But stay away from me unless you want to test your little theory. Because the next time I see your withered face, I won't hold back. I *will* kill you."

She bowed her head and left the room, shutting the door gently behind her. Jonas managed to throw the shield up again before he dissolved into tears. He didn't know how long he cried. He didn't care. His life was over. She had used the one thing she knew he would respond to.

She had used love to break his heart.

At some point he felt Adam's warm arm and wing wrap around his shoulder. He felt a gentle, reassuring kiss in his hair, and comforting words he could hardly understand. He accepted the warmth, leaning into it as he shook.

What fragile energy he'd mustered was once again washed away by his crippling fear. Fear that his grandmother was right. And she was. He couldn't risk Aleksei's life on his own hubris. That would be a fate worse than death.

He saw himself once more as the thing she'd recognized so long ago. He was an abomination, a monster. A monster in a cage.

"Aleksei," he whimpered, "*please* forgive me."

CHAPTER 14

BREAKING THROUGH

Aleksei stood deep in the shade of a mighty spruce, watching tens of thousands of enemy soldiers march past. Aya stood beside him, taking shallow, panicked breaths. He put a hand on her shoulder.

"It'll be alright," he whispered. "Just do what we practiced."

She nodded, her eyes still wide. Her breathing slowed a little.

Gods, but Aleksei hoped he wasn't lying to her.

He pulled out his spyglass and checked the rebel army's progress. They were just a short distance from the gate. His heart hammered in his chest, but he ignored it.

A clarion call came from the front of the rebel force. Men continued to stream past Aleksei, and he could see there were still a great many more on the road behind them. He prayed that the Magi on the wall would be able to pull this off. If not, they were all in a great deal of trouble.

Aleksei turned back towards the gate, waiting for the signal.

It came sooner than he'd expected.

What had, moments before, been tidy ranks of rebel soldiers arranged before the Keldoan gate suddenly became a tangled mass of men. There were shouts of confusion. Men toppled off the edges of the road on either side. At that height, such a fall was fatal.

A rain of arrows from the wall zipped into the confusion, taking down men by the score. Aleksei allowed himself a grim smile as the air shields did their work, popping up and shoving men here, blocking off sections of men there, before vanishing and reappearing in an erratic pattern. He saw men hack at the hardened air, only for the shield to vanish. More often than not, that swing took down one of their comrades.

The enemy archers tried to return fire, but their own arrows clacked harmlessly off the air before each Magus. Aleksei felt a wave of relief wash over him. He'd had his doubts. But then again, if the entire Voralla couldn't stand and fight as one, if their magic was *that* weak, they weren't going to be much good through the long haul of war. Even as it stood, Aleksei wasn't sure how much longer he could use their limited abilities to his advantage.

He turned his spyglass to the rebel forces still streaming up the road. Some ran ahead to help their fellows, only to strike the wall of air that kept them from approaching. He risked a glance to the hunched group of Magi hiding in the forest a few paces distant, maintaining the shields separating the two halves of the rebel army.

Aleksei waved to Aya and she lifted her hand. A red spark of light flared into the sky above the road.

With a roar, his Legionnaires poured from the forest, crashing into the enemy from either side. Aya sent a second signal. The air above the road seemed to ripple and distort.

Aleksei had only seen that once before, at the invasion of Kalinor. Emelian Krasik was not the *only* man skilled in illusion. The battle before him changed as some of the rebels suddenly saw the Legionnaires as their own. They stopped fighting, even as Aleksei's men cut into them.

A lance of flame incinerated a Legionnaire. A heartbeat later, an arrow zipped out of the trees, taking the enemy Magus down. Each display of the Archanium was met with a swift shaft from the canopy. A few impotent bolts of power struck the canopy, but the arrows continued unabated.

At Aleksei's signal, Aya sent another flare of light into the air. The Legionnaires broke from the melee, vanishing back into the surrounding woods. As the rebels chased after them, arrows rained down from above, dropping hundreds before they could even get under cover.

Aleksei drew his sword. This was his element, and even without his bond he was a force to be reckoned with. He watched as Raefan pulled

Aya towards the other Magi and their Knights. She had her own duty to fulfill now.

Aleksei ducked behind a tree, focusing on the sounds of the men rushing towards him. A heartbeat before one man passed the tree, Aleksei swung outward, cleaving the man in two. The second was so surprised, his head left his shoulders before he even had a chance to raise his weapon.

Aleksei had trained the men to do much the same, and thus far it appeared to be working.

His men had spent months on the march, in the fields and the woods, learning the land from his father. They knew how to vanish, how to take down their prey. Now they performed their tasks with deadly accuracy. Archers in the trees struck down the rebels in droves. Legionnaires lured their foes into carefully set traps, striking them down one by one.

Aleksei lifted a clarion and gave three short calls.

The forest became deathly silent as his men seemingly vanished.

He darted down the tree-line, watching the Magi amass on either side of the road. Legionnaires suddenly converged onto the road, blocking any attempts for the main rebel force to escape. The enemy at the gate had turned, rushing back to help their beleaguered comrades hemmed in by the woods. Seeing the sudden bait at the end of the road, they raced towards it with a savage roar.

With grim satisfaction, Aleksei noted that their numbers had been severely diminished.

A fourth and final signal lit the sky, and as one, the Legionnaires shielded their eyes.

The world erupted with blinding white brilliance as the Magi channeled their abilities into a single ball of blazing white. Rebel men cried out as they were immediately blinded.

The Legionnaires on the road swept forward at the sound of screaming, cutting down the blind men like stalks of wheat.

Aleksei watched it all with suppressed emotion. Only half of his force was on the road. The rest were in the woods, hunting. He'd ordered no survivors, and they would see that his orders were carried out to the man.

Along the road, he watched his men execute the rebels. This was no longer a battle. He turned his eyes from the sight of blind men begging as they were cut down. They'd provided his men no such mercy in Kalinor. He would grant them none now. He *had* to send a message that, while the enemy had won a startling victory in Kalinor, the Legion was by no means defeated.

After the slaughter mercifully ceased, he stepped out onto the road, saluting the men as they passed with the bodies of the dead. He'd ordered the dead to be incinerated by the Magi. The winter this far north made digging mass graves impossible, and thus they were going to have to get creative. He wanted the rebels to vanish, for all signs of the battle to disappear. He didn't want to give the enemy any clue of what had happened to their men.

It might be a sight trickier to convince the rebel army's camp follow-ers, the cooks, blacksmiths, and prostitutes that inevitably joined any large military movement, that the soldiers they'd seen march away this morning had just disappeared into thin air, but he had an idea about how such a feat could be accomplished.

Aleksei headed towards the Magi. They all looked drained, but giddy at the same time. He imagined it was the first time many of them had used their magic for something *useful.*

And certainly, to triumph in the heat of battle against a much larger foe had to be intoxicating. Gratifying. He just hoped they didn't let it go to their heads.

He was signaling Aya when he felt it.

With cold dread, Aleksei felt the sudden violence in the air behind him. There was no mistaking that queer sensation.

The killing wind.

Aleksei darted towards the trees.

It was upon him before he'd gone even ten paces. He could feel it, like tiny razors slashing at his neck and back. Its wail filled his ears. Any moment those razors would tear him to shreds.

The woods were still a good fifteen paces away.

He was a dead man.

At least, he thought, Jonas might survive his death, shielded as he was. It almost made dying bearable, thinking that Jonas might survive.

Aleksei shot off the side of the road, through the scree, dancing over enemy corpses. The wind twisted and cut deep gash through the back of his left thigh, forcing him to stagger with a cry. With his tumbling momentum, Aleksei lunged with his good leg and managed to hurl himself into the shadows of the trees.

He winced, waiting for what he knew was coming, terrified that these woods wouldn't be enough to protect him. After a moment, he sat up and turned back to the road. He shouldn't have survived. He should be dead, and yet he was impossibly alive.

But he still heard the wind. It hadn't dissipated, as it had last time.

He squinted back towards his men and the Magi, and his blood ran cold.

It was heading straight for Aya.

Aya was about to congratulate Aleksei on his brilliant strategy. She was more than impressed with his use of their gifts, limited though they were. She was even reminded of her old master, Sammul. The man had never given them an inkling of the power they commanded, or of the true applications it possessed.

Of course, she now knew that Sammul had been working with the enemy for a very long time. He'd kept them sequestered in the Voralla, away from people who might have benefited from their help. He'd trained them in pathetic, useless talents that had ultimately led an entire generation of Magi on a path through the weakest meridians of the Akhrana. All those who *made* it to the Voralla, at least. Those less fortunate had been swallowed by Bael's hidden coven.

The very thought made her blood boil.

Aleksei raised his hand, then stopped stock-still. Suddenly, he ran for the trees as fast as he could. Aya frowned, trying to make sense of his strange behavior.

And then she saw it.

More than see it, she *felt* it. The strange abomination that had just sprung into existence. It was following him at an incredible speed, shrieking as it shot towards him. Her heart skipped a beat as she realized he wasn't fast enough to escape it.

Without a second thought, Aya hurled a shield around the creature. It seemed to slow the thing, but only by a heartbeat. She threw another, and another. She summoned all the power she could muster and hurled a counter gust of air at it, knocking it slightly off-course.

Aleksei cried out as the back of his thigh split open. Aya screamed. That cut had been aimed at his head. She managed one last feeble air shield before Aleksei dove between the trees.

She closed her eyes, too terrified to watch him be torn to pieces.

How had everything gone so suddenly wrong? What *was* that thing? Where had it come from? It was unlike any spell she'd ever seen.

Raefan's hand was suddenly on her shoulder. She opened her eyes to see Aleksei beneath the trees, still very much alive, though bleeding profusely. The creature had abandoned him.

It was coming for *her*.

Raefan started to step in front of her, but she pulled him back. If Aleksei couldn't fight this thing, how could he hope to?

Her energy was nearly spent, but she had to do *something*. Aya knew, just from touching the creature with the Archanium, that it was far too dangerous to be allowed to wreak havoc amongst the Magi, amongst the Legion.

She lashed out with a whip of air, but the creature casually dodged. It closed in on her with a wail. Raefan grasped her hand and gave it a tight squeeze.

Tears clouded her vision.

No. She couldn't allow this to happen. She couldn't allow this creature to harm Raefan. He was her life, her *everything*. If it killed her, he would fall too.

She had to stop it.

The wail intensified.

With a roar of rage, Aya threw herself into the Archanium. She left nothing of herself behind, responding only to the need of saving her beloved. It was all-consuming. She let it wash over her.

Time froze.

She was aware of the creature, but she was more interested in the swirls of the Archanium immersing her, emanating *from* her. It took an eternity to select the proper spellform and bring it back into her world.

The air split with a tremendous, echoing concussion. The creature shattered into a screeching gale that threw her back against Raefan. The big man grunted, but held his ground. His arms caught her, holding her up.

Aya was glad he was there. She couldn't have stood on her own had her life depended on it. She limply relaxed into his arms as he gently laid her on the road.

"Bring Aleksei to me," she croaked, trying to prop herself up on her elbow.

Raefan started to protest, but then he saw the look in her eyes. He rose and ran flat-out for the other Knight.

The Magi were staring at her from a distance, all apparently terrified by what they'd seen, terrified to come near her. They recognized the immense power she'd invoked. It was still the Akhrana, of that there was no question. She hadn't even brushed the Nagavor. So how had she unleashed such *power*? They'd never seen anything like it.

But Aya knew.

She didn't understand how it was possible, but she knew. It was now an intrinsic part of her, like the color of her eyes or her name. The knowledge was inescapable. She had broken through, and onto a new meridian.

Unlike her peers, who could only access the lower reaches of the Akhrana, Aya was now on the edge of the higher realms. The Archanium still swirled in her eyes, but she could see things she'd never known *existed* before. Forbidden Realms that were now within her reach.

"*Aya!*"

Raefan's shout in her ear brought her out of her daze. She forcefully pulled herself back into the real world. She would have time to explore the newly-opened realms of the Akhrana later.

She gazed up at Aleksei's pallid face, Raefan on his knees, cradling the Lord Captain a handspan from her. The snow beneath him was rapidly stained in a brilliant crimson circle, his blood mingling with that of the dead. She grasped his head in her hands and plunged back into the Archanium, seeking the spell she required.

There. White, deep, scarlet throbbing through it, singular in its purity. It practically *sang* to her.

She wrapped it around Aleksei's shuddering form, acting as a conduit for the spellform. The Archanium swept through her like a wave, crashing and breaking across his body. The wave swept back with startling intensity, pulling at her, threatening to drown her in the torrent of his pain. She pulled it away from him and sent it back into the Archanium.

Aya gasped and fell face forward against the Knight, both of them panting, exhausted. Aleksei opened bleary aureate eyes, managing a grateful smile. She knew he didn't have the energy to speak. Nor did she.

Raefan gently laid Aleksei on the road, lifting her up and away from the Lord Captain. The flow of blood from Aleksei's wound had ceased, but she already knew that. She had never experienced anything quite so exquisitely painful, or profound.

She wondered how she had ever dared claim to be able to heal before. It was the difference between a snowflake and an avalanche.

Before she passed out, Aya managed to grab Raefan's attention. "When he wakes," she mumbled, "he *must* come to me. It's *very* important. Get him inside the Bastion as soon as possible."

Raefan nodded his understanding. And then she let everything mercifully fade to black.

"What about this one?"

Jonas took the tiny piece of bronze, shaped like a mouse carrying a pea across its back. "It keeps vermin away from crops. The user only has to activate it, and leave it in the field. It protects the field for the season."

When he saw their obvious confusion, Jonas threw his hands up. "I apologize, but this is exasperating. Everything you've shown me so far has a completely utilitarian use. In fact, I haven't been presented with one piece that is actually meant for either Magi *or* angels. These are trinkets for farmers and goodwives, made by our kind to make their lives simpler."

Jonas knew that his audience still didn't understand. He searched through the collection of knickknacks until he found a thin piece of jade. When he blew on the tip, it ignited.

The angels standing around him gasped.

"Stop it," he moaned. "Can you not see why this was created? To light fires. Normal fires. Cooking fires. It saves time. The gods only know how the Magi of the past imbued such things with the Archanium, but they're not dangerous to you. In fact," he said with weary irritation, "very few items here are dangerous. Most are little more than simple tools."

Adam coughed, "Jonas, excuse me, but if all these relics are harmless, why are they here?"

Jonas frowned, "I didn't say *all* these relics were harmless. Some are of incredible value and some are, as you believe, very dangerous. But most of what you have here is just slightly useful junk."

There were murmurs. He knew some of his audience didn't believe him, but he wasn't particularly interested in their opinions. He'd been hearing nothing else for hours, and the lot of them had proven to be woefully uninformed and remarkably superstitious.

"With all due respect," he said finally, "I'm an Archanium Magus. I'm the only one here who understands how any of these things work. I have no doubt that many of the mysterious wonders in the Voralla are of Angelic descent.

"We don't understand how your magic works, just as you don't understand ours, and that's fine. What's important is that we can learn from one another. Much has been lost since the Dominion Wars. If we work together, perhaps we can dispel this cloud of fear we all seem to be languishing under, yes?"

There were a few nods.

Jonas lifted a tiny three-pronged twig. "Does anyone know what this does?"

There were more murmurs, but no one spoke up.

"It finds water. When activated, it leads the Magus in question to a source of water, so a well can be dug."

"Why?"

Jonas looked to the angel who had spoken. He was a short, bitter-looking man with ashy blond hair and dull brown eyes. His pale white wings flared behind him.

"*Because*, Tarquin," he said patiently, "simple people need water, and can benefit from our power. And as they aren't brought up in palaces or manor homes, they sometimes need assistance. Wells are life, especially in grassland or in arid climates. My Knight hails from the deep Southern Plain. This trinket would be worth a fortune in such a place."

Jonas pointedly dropped the twig into his coat pocket. "I'm going to send this to the leader of his village. She will be able to use it to aid his people."

"That's a priceless artifact," Tarquin protested.

Jonas smiled softly, "I couldn't agree more. And how much good is it doing gathering dust? You have no idea the value people would find in these trinkets. I'm sure it doesn't concern you, but it should.

"That is what you *should* be interested in, not the supposed whims of your One-God. Do you honestly believe that your god wants you to spend all your time on your knees praying?

"Wouldn't He rather you go out and use the powers He's so wisely granted you to help His children who *are* in need? You would object to people finding water in a dry land? Perhaps you should reconsider the purpose of your gifts."

Tarquin scowled, "You have no right to—"

Jonas snapped and the angel's mouth shut with an audible *click*. A heartbeat after the fact, he groaned inwardly. He was growing increasingly impatient, and these people didn't seem to want to do anything besides argue. He was growing weary of it.

"Lest you forget," he said, mustering his old, familiar façade, "I am the third-born Cherub. You are not. Were I not here, you'd still be cowering in the presence of fire-starters and rabbit repellants. As long as I'm a prisoner here, I will do as I please."

Jonas relaxed his grip and Tarquin coughed. He hoped Leigha wouldn't hate him when she heard of his behavior. He knew he sounded petulant. He certainly sometimes *felt* like the spoiled prince everyone saw him as. But further reflection allowed him to see that he was no longer acting the part of the spoiled child as he once had.

The gods knew he was in the presence of enough such children to see the distinct difference. Jonas knew that without Aleksei's influence, he'd be very much the same as these fools before him. Never so afraid, but juvenile and unpleasant nonetheless.

Now, his indignation came in response to the very same attitude he'd once held. Their unwillingness to challenge their points of view frustrated him beyond all reason. He knew what it was to be a common man, if only after a fashion.

After all, Aleksei had come to him, at once as common and unusual as he could have ever imagined. And Jonas knew it had been good for him. Aleksei had shown him a perspective he'd never stopped to consider before.

To be faced with this cadre of elitists now felt somehow galling. Worse, he knew a time when he'd have fit in perfectly. It wasn't all that long ago, if he was being honest with himself.

"I have spent the last two hours showing you how to activate toys," he said gently. "If you would like to see some of the truly deadly relics, I will show them to you later. But for the moment, I'm tired of playing a trick magician."

Adam leaned forward, "Everything you've been shown has been brought with the greatest of care from the forbidden sections of the Reliquary."

"And who put them there?" Jonas demanded.

Adam frowned, "I have no idea. But any such placement decisions would have to be recorded. There would be a record of each and every piece."

Jonas looked at two elderly angels in the back of the room. He lifted one of the light rings he'd showed Adam earlier, "You two. Could you find out who ordered this relic placed in the restricted section?"

Their faces brightened. "Yes, Master Cherub," one intoned, stepping forward and reverentially taking the ring from him before hurrying off with her colleague.

Jonas managed another sigh. "That will be all for now. I'll come back tomorrow when I've had a chance to rest and think a while."

The staff left, some muttering their disappointment. They'd thought they were protecting hundreds, if not thousands of relics, all incredibly dangerous. To be proven wrong was upsetting. Jonas couldn't have cared less right then. He was so exhausted he could hardly think straight.

He hadn't repeated his escape attempt. It was pointless, and he was dangerous, besides. But he knew Aleksei would have laughed at seeing these pompous fools realize that their possessions weren't near so dear as they'd imagined.

"I think I'm going to head back to my room," he said finally.

Adam stood with him, "May I walk with you?"

Jonas shrugged, "You're free to do as you please."

Adam smiled, accepting the prince's answer.

The angel said nothing until they were inside Jonas's rooms.

"Jonas," he began, "I know you're not trying to humiliate us. But you have to understand that we've been studying some of these relics for thousands of years. It's a little hard to believe that they're just trinkets and farmers' tools."

Jonas sat and rested his head against the chair's back, "And what else would they be? With this multitude, they can't *all* be weapons or healing totems. I always thought the purpose of the Archanium was to help us make life simpler. You're just seeing relics from a time when that belief was shared with those less fortunate that ourselves."

"But then why would someone have flooded the Reliquary with such simple baubles?" Adam asked, flopping down into the chair with the carved back.

"To hide something," Jonas muttered, closing his eyes.

Adam frowned, "Like what?"

Jonas gave a half-hearted shrug, "It could have been the Prime Key.

That was hidden in the Reliquary in plain sight, until it was bartered away."

Adam shook his head, "I doubt it. Half of the things you pointed out to us were received in the last ten to twenty years."

Jonas sat up, "From *where?*"

"I'm not sure. I've been an apprentice for ten years, but they didn't let me touch anything until fairly recently. I just sat in the front and filled out forms and receipts. But I recall the Reliquary receiving acquisitions for a time in my first year. We haven't received any since then that I'm aware of."

Jonas eyed Adam curiously, "You said that there were records, documents of everything in Reliquary. Are there records of your acquisitions?"

Adam frowned, "There are records of just about anything. They're all kept in the libraries at the back of the Reliquary."

Jonas leaned forward, "So you would know what was included in each acquisition? If all those relics arrived together, you could find an itemized list?"

"Of course. As I said, we haven't received any new pieces in the last ten years, so the receipts should be fairly easy to locate."

Jonas stood, "I think we should go back to the Reliquary and have a look. I'd be very interested to see who sent those baubles. I'd like to know what *else* you received."

CHAPTER 15

SECRETS AND LIES

The wind cut through her cloak like a knife, but she didn't flinch. She stood on the hill, a knife clutched in her left hand, waiting. She could hear her heartbeat in her ears like a drum in the icy silence. Her breath whispered away in a ghostly cloud as she loosed another quiet sigh.

The blade was cold against her wrist. Just like he'd shown her. Keep the edge facing out, the spine of the blade lining up against her forearm. He'd taught her how to fight, how to protect herself.

She wasn't nearly as skilled as he was, and likely would never even come close, but she *was* getting better.

Gods, but it was cold. Where *was* that infernal man?

A noise sounded suddenly behind her, tiny twigs breaking underfoot. She kept her body relaxed, ready to pounce if it wasn't him.

With the war, it had become dangerous to wander out of the city alone. Too many brigands and thieves trying to capitalize on people's fear. On their insecurity and unrest. During her journey, she'd seen countless abandoned carts, streams of refugees marching off in whatever direction they'd hoped safest.

She wondered where they were getting their information. As far as she knew, *nowhere* was truly safe. Not from the madman who'd taken Ilyar by the throat. But he would be dealt with. One way or another, even if she had to see to it personally. Whatever it took to bring this gruesome chapter to a close.

The figure behind her took another step. She closed her eyes, listening, just as he'd taught her. She tried to catch his scent, but the air was too still, too cold. She was, after all, only human.

A hand gripped her shoulder. Without a sound, she spun around, raising her knife. She jerked it to a halt a scant inch from his throat.

With a grin, he grasped her in his arms and pulled her to him. The knife dropped from her nerveless fingers.

His golden eyes burned in the moonlight, "I wasn't sure you'd come."

Tamara gave him a coy smile, "Do you honestly believe I'd miss such an opportunity?"

Roux Devaan arched an eyebrow, "Opportunity?"

She nodded, looking away from his face, "To say goodbye."

He started to say something, but before he could put voice to his words, she pressed her mouth against his. He returned her kiss gently, clearly taken aback by her urgency. Tamara didn't care.

She knew what this night was.

When she finally broke away, she could read the questions filling his feral eyes. Gods, those *eyes*. From the moment she met them with her own, she'd felt something...different. He was unlike any man, any*thing*, she'd ever encountered.

After Aleksei left, Roux had escorted Tamara and her mother to the edge of the Seil Wood. She hadn't wanted him to leave. Desperately, she'd wished he'd accompany them further. But if Tamara understood one thing in this world, it was duty. He had a duty to his people, and she had hers.

Her shock had been palpable when he'd appeared to her that first night. She'd assumed he'd left them to make their way alone. Knowing that he'd followed them to Timurus warmed her heart, but she figured that had been on Aleksei's orders. Meeting him that first night after they'd left Seil Wood, though, had been something entirely different.

Since then, he'd come to her every night, when she could get away from her mother and the boys. Those nights spent with him had been the happiest she could recall.

She'd learned about life, rather than duty. She'd learned how to fight, rather than cower. She'd learned how to be a woman, not just a princess.

"So this is to be the night, then?" he whispered into the stillness.

Tamara felt tears drip from her chin. The streaks of water were like ice on her face, but she hardly noticed. "I want you to come with us."

He smiled tenderly, but his voice betrayed him. "I would love nothing more, believe me. It's just...I can't. I can't imagine standing without the earth beneath my feet, without the trees and the soil. Even the trees we inhabit are rooted in the earth. I am part of that earth. The idea of standing on water...being away from my land...I'm so sorry, Tamara."

She was suddenly alarmed at the sound of panic in his voice. This was no idle claim. She understood, for the first time, that the idea of the ocean absolutely terrified him. His life was tied to the earth and the Wood. Going to sea would be the ultimate sacrifice for him, something she couldn't possibly demand.

Tamara reached up and gently brushed his rough face with her hand, "Then I won't ask again. I just wanted you to know my feelings."

He chuckled, "I don't think you've left much room for confusion."

She felt her face heat at that. This entire journey now held a strange, dreamlike quality for her. She honestly feared she would board a ship for Zirvah, only to realize that the entire experience had simply been a phantom or fantasy. She was desperately happy to know that she was awake, that this was real.

That *Roux* was real.

"I'm sorry," she managed finally, "I just don't want this to end."

Roux glanced at the moon. He returned his raptor's gaze to her ice-blue eyes, "The moon's not even at its zenith."

She quirked her mouth in confusion, "And?"

His smile grew devilish, "The night is far from over, my darling girl."

He kissed her, harder this time. She felt a soft moan escape her lips. His heat was intoxicating. Her head was spinning. As he laid her on the ground, he wrapped his rabbit-hide cloak around her, but she felt no need for warmth.

She embraced him, feeling his lean muscles ripple as he pressed against her. It was as though their bodies were melding into one. She opened her eyes and looked up, into the stars.

It was rapture.

Katherine knocked at the door a second time, "Lady Delira?"

"Come."

Katherine took a deep breath, pushing the door open.

The room was just as majestic as she'd expected, rich carpets and draperies rendered in royal blue and green. A massive four-poster bed dominated the center of the room, the heavy quilt decorated with rich embroidery that echoed the rest of the room's colors.

Against the far wall, a very thin woman with long, straight black hair sat at a writing desk, her back to Katherine. Katherine approached cautiously, not quite sure how far she should go before stopping to await orders. The lady kept writing for a good handful of minutes before finally turning to examine her new servant.

Lady Delira's face was as thin and drawn as the rest of her figure. Her nose was narrow and pointed, her mouth small and pursed. Katherine imagined the woman wore an expression of dour dissatisfaction almost perpetually.

But her eyes were a different matter.

While alluring in shape and size, it was the color that shocked Katherine. Rather, the *lack* of color. They were solid black, no white to be seen.

Lady Delira looked Katherine up and down with her ink-eyes, absorbing every detail. Katherine felt like she was being sized up by a wolf.

Or a serpent.

And then, unexpectedly, Lady Delira smiled. "Hello, girl. What is your name?"

"Katherine, milady," she said with a deep curtsey.

Lady Delira tapped her chin thoughtfully, "Katherine. Where are you from?"

"Voskrin, milady. In the Southern Plain."

Lady Delira's smile widened, "I've heard such good things about people from down there. Honest, hardworking peasants, from the sound of it. If you're anything like that, I'm *sure* we'll get along just fine."

Katherine curtseyed again, "Yes, milady. Thank you, milady."

Lady Delira watched her carefully for a long moment, still idly tapping her chin, before turning back to her desk. "I have a letter here that I want you to deliver. It is of the utmost importance, so please don't dillydally."

Katherine took the letter carefully, studying the name.

"You'll find him in the Voralla, dear. Ask anyone there where he is and they'll tell you straight away."

Katherine flushed with relief, "Thank you, milady. I'll see that it gets to him immediately."

When the door closed behind her, Katherine allowed herself yet another long sigh. The Voralla? She'd been in the Palace less than a day and she was already being sent *there*?

As she trotted through the hallways, making her way down the servant's stairs and out onto Lawn, Katherine wondered just how powerful Lady Delira was. There was certainly something about the woman that put Katherine on edge, yet piqued her suspicions.

Perhaps it was just nerves from encountering one of the enemy. That was, of course, who these people were. It would do her purpose here no good to make friends or develop loyalties to the very people she was spying on. But being *too* detached could make her stand out all the more.

The East Lawn was empty, save for the great ivory prominence of the Voralla and the majestic oaks that shaded it. The carvings that ran across its walls sent shivers through her. They filled her mind with unbidden images, but she couldn't put names to the things she saw, only dark, unsettled feelings.

At the moment, she was practically shaking with fear.

As she approached one of the great doors, a young woman came out to meet her. Seeing the envelope clutched tightly in her hand, she asked, "Hello there. Are you here to deliver a message?"

Katherine nodded, wondering if the woman was a Magus.

"Thank you," the woman said brusquely, "I'll take it from here." When Katherine didn't hand the letter over, the woman's face shifted from a smile into an impatient scowl, "Only Master Bael and his Magi are allowed within the Voralla itself. Who is the letter for?"

"Bael Bel–"

Before Katherine could finish saying his name, the woman snatched the letter out of her hand, abruptly turning and starting off towards the door.

"Wait!" Katherine called, reaching after the woman. "I was told to see to this personally. You can't just–"

Just as the started after the woman, something hard struck her in the center of her chest. Katherine hardly had time to register what was happening before she realized she was on her back, staring at the sky. She coughed as the air suddenly returned to her lungs.

Forcing herself to her feet, Katherine stared at the now-empty East Lawn in confusion. Gods, what had that woman *done*? She didn't feel any bruises or broken bones. It hadn't even hurt, exactly. But still, such a cavalier use of power, especially against someone lowly like her, felt inexcusable.

She forced herself to calm down, before she allowed her anger to take over. She wasn't here to pick fights with enemy Magi. She was here to learn as much as she could. And, whether that Magus realized it or not, she'd just taught Katherine something valuable.

Whether the Magus was being paranoid or under orders, it was clear that they were uncomfortable with anyone setting foot in the Voralla. Uncomfortable enough to use force, even when no direct threat was evident.

Katherine filed the information away in the back of her head as she made her way back to the servant's quarters. She quickly changed out of her grass-stained livery and into a clean frock, making sure to right her hair before heading back to Lady Delira's rooms. She wasn't sure if Lady Delira had sent her on an impossible task on purpose or not, but either way, she wasn't about to let on that she'd had a hard time of it.

By the time she reached Lady Delira's door, her breathing had returned to a calm, steady rate, even if her pulse still raced. She knocked.

"Come."

Katherine entered the room with as much grace as she could muster. She could feel her legs beginning to stiffen. She knew she'd be sore the next day, but she refused to reveal anything.

"Did you deliver my letter?" Lady Delira asked, arching a midnight eyebrow.

Katherine curtseyed, "I was forced to surrender it at the door of the Voralla, milady. I'm sorry, but the Magus refused to allow me any further. She assured me she would take it to Master Bael."

Delira watched her for a long moment before smiling cryptically, "Well, I *suppose* you completed your errand, at any rate. I forgot that the Magi are being so protective these days. We can't be *too* careful, you know. One of Prince Belgi's Magi could try to slip in without warning and cause who knows what sort of trouble."

"Yes, milady," Katherine said with another bob. Prince Belgi's Magi? What was the woman talking about? She didn't know very much about

Jonas Belgi, but Aleksei had never mentioned anything about the man associating with the Voralla.

A knock sounded at the door and Katherine jumped.

Lady Delira chuckled, "Calm down, girl, it's alright. The Palace is as safe a place as you're likely to find these days. Get the door."

Katherine hurried away, anxious for a reason to be out from under Lady Delira's nightmarish eyes. She opened the door and almost let out a shriek.

A "man" stood on the other side. He was handsome, after a fashion, with bright green eyes and a blond braid draped over his left shoulder. He was almost a head shorter than Katherine, but there was a loathsome aura around him, something she couldn't hope to define. Instinctively, she wanted to be as far from the man as her legs could carry her.

"Ah," Delira's voice came from behind, "Lord Bael. A pleasure, as always."

Katherine backed away, giving Bael a deep curtsey to keep from having to look at him one moment longer than was absolutely necessary. Before straightening, she looked to Lady Delira. She woman was smiling broadly, "You may leave us, Katherine."

Katherine turned to go, but Delira suddenly seemed to remember one last thing. "Katherine?" She turned, trying not to wince.

Lady Delira handed her an elegant ruby gown. "Have this cleaned, I'd like to wear it to dinner tomorrow."

"Yes, milady," Katherine managed, taking the dress with as much care as she could muster before scurrying out the door, giving Bael as wide a berth as possible without being obvious.

When it shut behind her, something else happened. The air hummed, and she could feel the fine hair on her arms and neck lift away. Someone in the other room was using the Archanium. She'd often had the same feeling when Mother Margareta said prayers over crops or lit the fire.

As much as she wished she could have remained in the room and heard their conversation, Katherine simply wanted *away* as quickly as possible. She abandoned all pretenses and raced down the hall, away from the monstrosity that was Bael. She had never seen or felt a more perfect representation of evil in her entire life. His aura clung to her skin, like a revolting, oily film she couldn't wash away.

She was running so fast she didn't even see the man until it was too late. He was walking along the hallway, his attention fixed on a small book, when they collided.

For the second time that day, Katherine found herself on the ground, staring up in confusion. She raised herself on her elbows quickly, looking to see where the man had landed. To her shock, he was still standing, blandly staring down at her.

He had thick brown hair and penetrating, hawkish hazel eyes. She wondered if he was going to yell at her, or perhaps burn her to a cinder. She'd found it impossible to tell who among these people was a Magus until they actually used their power.

To her utter surprise, he started laughing. She just stared at him as he hooted with mirth. Finally, he reached out a hand and pulled her to her feet. Gods, but how had the man remained standing? She felt as though she'd just run into a brick wall.

Katherine curtseyed as deeply as she could, "Begging your pardon, milord. I didn't see you there."

His laughter died down to a chuckle, "At that speed, I'm not sure how you saw much of *anything*."

Her face flushed as she looked at the floor. She caught sight of Lady Delira's ruby gown laying a pace away and bent down to fetch it. The man beat her to it, lifting it towards her outstretched arms. She flushed again as he smiled. She couldn't help noticing how handsome he was.

He was, after all, the enemy.

"If I may inquire," he said after a moment of awkward silence, "where were you off to in such a hurry?"

"Oh! I apologize again. I was trying to get Lady Delira's dress to the washwomen."

His smile turned into a puzzled frown, "For this evening?"

"No, tomorrow," Katherine said, her mind racing far ahead of her words.

"Then why the rush?"

She cursed herself. She needed to keep her mind in the moment. But all she'd wanted to do was get away from Bael as fast as she could. "I'm sorry, I was frightened by something."

He nodded, "That sounds a little more reasonable. Did one of guards give you a hard time?"

She looked up at him as though he were daft, "What? No. It was... something else. A man. He came to see Lady Delira. He didn't say anything, he just frightened me."

He chuckled, "And did this terrifying stranger have a name?"

She swallowed hard, "Bael."

The man froze, watching her face intently. Katherine wondered if she'd just said something wrong. The look in the man's eyes had shifted. She was no longer looking at the mirthful young man she'd nearly bowled over. There was something else in his eyes now.

Something dangerous.

"I see," he said softly.

"Do you know him?" she asked weakly.

He nodded slowly, "He's my master. He's the master of all the Magi in the Voralla."

"Perhaps that's what it was!" she offered, feigning relief, "I've heard that very powerful men give off auras and such. At least, that's what they say on the Southern Plain. I guess I've just never been so near such a powerful man. He gave me shivers! I didn't know *why* I was feeling like that!"

The man's face softened again, but his eyes retained their edge, "No, you're right to be frightened by him. Lord Bael is a very powerful man and...very dangerous." A smile finally returned to his face, "But take heart, he's not interested in nobodies. He only cares about his students and his enemies."

She let a sigh out, "That's a relief. Thank you so much for putting my mind at rest...."

"Ethan," he offered.

She smiled, "Thank you, Ethan. I was beside myself. I'm so happy I ran into you."

He laughed at that. She blushed again. "And I *am* sorry about that."

Ethan shrugged, "I saw you coming. Don't worry about me. I just hope you aren't injured."

She laughed self-consciously, "I'd be lying if I said that was the first time I've found myself on my back today."

He stared at her, and the horror of what she'd just said suddenly caught up with her. "Oh gods," she whispered, burying her face in her hands. "That sounded bad! It didn't come out the way I meant it. I meant...."

Ethan laughed, "It's alright, miss. Really. May I walk you back to the servants' quarters? Just to make sure you don't bowl anyone over on the way?"

Katherine idly wondered if she'd ever been so humiliated in her life. "I would like that, thank you," she finally managed.

Gods, she thought as they walked, and this was only her first day!

When they arrived in the Reliquary, Adam immediately made off towards the libraries where the records were kept. Jonas started to follow, but he only managed to move a few paces before he was swarmed by the Reliquary staff.

"Master Cherub," began one elderly angel, "we were wondering if you'd be so kind as to assist us with a few things."

Jonas sighed, pinching the bridge of his nose as he thought. He finally looked up with what he hoped was a charming smile, "I'm afraid I have some urgent matters to see to just now," watching their faces fall, he went on, "so I'll make a deal with you. Why don't you show me the three relics that you are either the most confounded by, or the most afraid of?"

The elderly angel beamed at him, "That would be wonderful! Please, this way."

Around him, the other staff members burst into excited chatter. Jonas got the profound impression that they'd actually been trying to work up the courage to ask something quite similar to this. Gods, he wondered, why hadn't they simply asked him to do this from the start?

He imagined it would be decidedly more interesting than staring at the monotonous array of frippery they'd presented thus far. He was fairly certain he'd seen some of the damned things in his sleep.

The older angel halted before a small pedestal of white marble tucked away in an alcove. Resting atop the pedestal was an outstretched hand cast in tarnished copper. Jonas felt the power radiating from it and stepped back on instinct.

The excited whispering started again. The staff seemed satisfied that they'd shown him something of actual danger. Jonas stared at the relic, his heart racing. He could feel the power emanating from the hand, the sheer *malevolence*. The sight of the thing made him sick to his stomach.

"Master Cherub?" the angel asked after a long pause. "What can you tell us of this piece?"

Jonas glared at her as though she'd gone mad. After taking in her surprised expression, he realized she had no idea what manner of magic she was standing next to.

"Cover it," he said softly. "In something ominous. Black velvet or the like. No one is to go near this piece. Under *any* circumstances. It cannot be used by any angel, so it wouldn't do anyone here any good. It's best if it's just left alone."

The angel's face became concerned, "Is it dangerous?"

He nodded emphatically, "I can hardly explain it. But as long as no one touches it, its magic can't hurt you."

She bowed her head at his instructions. "As you say, Master Cherub. We will see to it that your wishes are carried out."

As she led him towards the next one, Jonas frowned, "How did you know that piece was dangerous? You can't feel its magic like I can."

"I've seen the effects of that one firsthand, I'm afraid. Had you reacted any differently, it would have cast serious doubts on your ability to determine danger in these relics."

"I'm pleased I didn't disappoint," he muttered sardonically.

The second piece she led him to turned out to be the same basin he'd pointed out to Adam, its attendant pitcher resting to the side of the basin.

"When I was exorcised," he said gently, studying the strange pieces of wood inlaid into the frame of the relic, "were symbols drawn in ash around me? Or the other angels?"

The staff were quick with their nods. He nodded along.

"Where did that ash come from?"

One of the younger angels stepped forward, "It's the ash from our feathers. When we die, our wings divest their feathers. These are burned in a sacred fire. The ash is used to heal those in need."

Jonas ignored the approving nods. "That's a lie," he said simply. "This? *This* is where they put your feathers. They are placed in the pitcher. When they are poured back out into the basin, they are ash. Sacred ash."

The young angel's face scrunched in confusion, "I thought you couldn't understand our magic."

Jonas scratched the back of his neck, "I can't. This tool was created by Magi, not angels. I can't tell you why, only that I know how it works."

This seemed to disquiet them deeply. He offered a cheery smile, "So, where to next?"

The look he received was anything but excited.

"We have one last piece we'd like you to look at," the older angel said.

Jonas bowed deeply, "I'm happy to be of assistance, Angelica."

The woman blushed furiously. "Angelica" was a term reserved for younger, prettier angels. A woman of her advanced years was rarely out of the Basilica, and as such, was unused to being called by anything but her given name.

She did her best to hide her pleasure at receiving such a compliment and hurried off, Jonas only a pace behind her.

She finally stopped before a small wooden stand. A book bound in violet leather rested atop it.

"Master Cherub," she said dutifully, "if you can tell us anything about this book, we'd be most in your debt."

Jonas smiled at her. He gave her a wink, much as he'd seen Aleksei give the servant girls in the Palace. It always seemed to make them happy...or at least a little more diligent. Jonas sometimes became confused between the two with servant girls.

The older angel's face lit up. He assumed his gesture had been effective.

Jonas reached out and lifted the book. It was light, and thin, probably less than two hundred pages. He pulled back the cover to the first page and froze.

The angels gasped in unison. One fainted against the wall, sliding softly to the floor. Jonas was oblivious to it all. His eyes were fixed on the first line, written in shimmering emerald ink.

For Jonas Belgi, in his time of need.

He closed the book gently, but it did little to quell the murmuring that continued to ripple through the stacks and the corridors.

"Can one of you take me to Adam?" he asked, still gripping the book.

A young angel stepped forward, bowing awkwardly, "It'd be an honor, Master Cherub."

Jonas smiled at her, then nodded to the rest of the staff, "Thank you for showing me this. I'll be back later and we can go through some of the other pieces. But I think that's all I can handle for the moment."

There was a flurry of fervent nods. Apparently, they'd seen all they could handle as well.

He followed the young angel through the warren of shelves, finally emerging into a broad, open area full of tables and chairs. Adam sat at one of the far tables, his eyes staring intently at a report.

Jonas sauntered up to the table and sat across from the angel. "Find anything?"

Adam looked up with a scowl, "Nothing that makes any sense." His eyes settled on the book Jonas held and widened. "Where did you get that?" he whispered.

Jonas set the book down on the table, "It was on a pedestal. The staff showed it to me. I picked it up and had a look at the title page."

Adam stared at him in disbelief, "How? *No* one can open that book. We've tried everything we could think of, but our magic just bounces off. What did you do to it?"

Jonas shrugged, "I opened it." He peeled back the cover and spun the book around so Adam could see the writing on the title page. The angel's face blanched. "Do you know what it means?" Jonas asked softly.

Adam shook his head, "I've never seen anything like that in my life. Jonas, that book has been here at least a decade. You would have been little more than a child when we received that. How would anyone know to put your name in it?"

Jonas lifted the book and righted it, reading the rest of the title page. "*Parasitic Energies and Ancillary Transmission.*" Beneath the title was a circle, pierced by four points of an eight-pointed star. He frowned, lost in his own thoughts as Adam stared at him.

Jonas recalled a book he'd read in the Basilica not that long ago, *The Properties and Constructions of Parasitic Energies.* It had been incredibly informative, but incomplete. It had also borne the same cryptic symbol.

His pulse thrilled. The other book had raised a great many questions, but had been painfully short on answers. This could be the key.

He finally noticed that Adam was still staring at him, his deep blue eyes flicking repeatedly to the book.

"What is it?" Jonas asked, an edge of irritation creeping into his voice.

"That book came in the same shipment as the trinkets in the forbidden sections."

"Really? Perhaps this is what they were trying to hide."

Adam shrugged, "Perhaps, but I don't really think so. It was the only book included, and it was enchanted with a spell no one had ever seen before. You said that you thought the trinkets were sent to hide something? That would be a poor way to hide much of anything."

Jonas frowned. Adam was right. He looked back to the book.

"In any event, I think I have what I came for. At least for now." He stood, turning back towards the archway that led out into the rest of the Undercroft.

Adam stood, "Where are you going with that? That has to stay in the Reliquary."

Jonas turned to the angel with a smile, "Not any longer. Or didn't you notice?" He let the book fall open and tapped the emerald writing, "It's *mine*."

CHAPTER 16

A WICKED WIND

Aleksei opened one eye experimentally. Finding himself in his quarters, buried beneath a pile of quilts, he breathed a sigh. He was alive. He'd cheated death yet again. Somehow, he didn't feel triumphant, merely grateful.

He pushed the blankets away, genuinely surprised at the amount of energy he had. Gods, how long had he been out? Given how strong he felt, especially after losing so much blood, Aleksei imagined it had to have been at least a month.

A month!

Aleksei vaulted out of the bed, pulling his trousers on in a rush as he desperately tried to gain his bearings. He had to get out of there. He needed Agriphon, needed to get on the road for Kuuran.

He *had* to get to Jonas.

Aleksei pulled on his shirt, cramming the shirttails into his trousers as he hunted for his boots.

They were stacked neatly by the fire, still drying from their exposure to the snow.

Aleksei froze. His boots were still wet. He took a deep breath, sitting on the edge of his bed. It didn't make any sense. Just before he'd passed out, he'd reached out for something, *anything* that the Mantle could devour. There'd been nothing within reach.

But then how was he alive? How was he *healed*?

The door opened, and a servant entered bearing a tray. "Lord Captain!" she said, sounding genuinely excited to see him awake. "Let me set this down and I'll fetch Magus Aya. She was *most* insistent that she see you the moment you awoke."

Aleksei managed a befuddled nod. He was suddenly realizing that, while his body felt as strong as ever, his mind was still catching up. He sat on the edge of the bed, trying to fit pieces of memory into some sort of cohesive narrative.

He remembered the battle in fragments, but now and then moments came tumbling back to him. Putting it all together into a larger framework was proving more of a challenge than he'd expected when the door opened again.

He looked up as Aya and Raefan entered the room. Aya's face was grave.

"Aleksei," she said with a sigh, "I'm glad to see you up."

He nodded, "Can we make it quick? I need to be on my way to Dalita as soon as possible."

She looked suddenly alarmed, "Aleksei, I'm afraid you can't go to Dalita just now."

He frowned, "Why not?"

Panic welled up in him, but he suppressed it.

Aya pulled up a chair, "What was that creature that came after you?"

Aleksei exhaled slowly, "I don't rightly know. It attacked me on the way here, when I got captured by Krasik's advance force. I think it destroyed half the rebel camp trying to catch me. I got to Agriphon before it got to me and rode into the trees. When I did, it vanished. Well, it obliterated one of the larger oaks I rode under, but then it was gone. I've kept to wooded areas since then and it hasn't shown itself. Until now."

Aleksei looked up with a sudden flash of memory, "Before I passed out, I saw it heading towards you. How did you escape?"

Aya smoothed her skirts, pursing her lips as she attempted a quick explanation, "I didn't. I...stopped it."

Aleksei sat up straight, "*How?*"

She shrugged self-consciously, "When I realized it was coming for us, I...leapt onto a different meridian. I found a path of greater power... and I stopped it."

Aleksei let out a cheer, his spirits rising for the first time in weeks.

His grin faded when she didn't join him in celebration.

"I stopped it, Aleksei. I didn't *destroy* it. I don't have the power to destroy it, and neither do you."

Aleksei suddenly realized what she wasn't saying, "What is it, Aya? Is it a spell? A...a monster of some sort?" She made a face at the word, and Aleksei felt his frustration rise. "Well, dammit, I don't know. This ain't exactly my specialty."

She looked at the floor. "It's a demon," she said softly.

He frowned, "A demon? How's that possible? I thought they couldn't come into our world. That's why they need Bael, right?"

She sighed, "Yes and no. Demons as you and I understand them are locked away in their own world. They can only influence our world through a Magus, like Cassian, or in this case Bael. But this demon was different. I believe it was summoned, *created*, in *this* world. As such, it isn't bound by the same restrictions.

"So, it's not a demon in the strictest sense. I don't believe it has a consciousness to speak of. I've been thinking about this since I woke up, and I believe it has only one...function; to kill you. I think you were closer to the truth when you asked if it was a spell. In a way it is. One crafted to find you, and kill you. Nothing more.

"You have to understand, my knowledge of such things is incredibly limited. You'd be far better served by Jonas than by me. I can tell you that, as far as magic is concerned, this is not a difficult foe to defeat.

"Your vulnerability comes from your lack of magic. Or more specifically, the right *sort* of magic. The Mantle won't save you, just as the Archanium can't really save you. I believe I merely gave it pause. Whatever I did to it in battle scattered its energies. I believe you may have a grace period while it gathers itself, but once again, that's only a guess."

Aleksei's eyes lit up, "Then I might have time to get to Kuuran?"

Aya shook her head, "I have no idea. I know that it was scattered, but it could have already reformed by now. I simply don't *know*. It might take it days, or weeks...or hours. But Aleksei, I do know that if it catches you alone, out on the Madrhal Plain, it *will* kill you. There's nowhere to hide out there, and your powers can't protect you."

"Then come with me," Aleksei pressed, leaning forward. "*You* could protect me."

Aya kept her eyes on the floor, "I'm sorry, Aleksei, but I can't. I *have* to stay with the Magi."

"Why?"

"Because I've reached a different meridian. This power allowed me to stop that...wind demon." She grimaced at the term. "It also allowed me to heal you. Your wound should have killed you in a matter of minutes, and yet I mended it in a heartbeat. I don't have to tell you that power like that is unheard of in the Voralla. You were there in Drava, when the revenants attacked. You saw our limitations first hand. But this is something new...different.

"I believe there might be a way to teach the others how to break through, as I did. If I can teach them *this*, it would make more of an impact than I could ever convey in words. It could change the entire trajectory of this war alone.

"I'm sorry Aleksei, but I can't risk myself right now. This might be our only chance to stand up to Bael and his Magi. If anything happens to me before I can help someone else reach my meridian, we could lose that opportunity forever.

"Please, I'm *begging* for your understanding. You know I'd crawl through the wastes of Fanj if I thought it would help you and Jonas. Right now, there's no greater contribution I can make than this. This will be a far greater benefit to you, to *all* of us, if I'm successful."

Aleksei allowed a smile to soften his mask of concern. He reached out and gripped Aya's hand, "I understand. Forgive me for not thinking this through. You're right. You're needed here far more, and you're far too valuable to risk.

"Stay here, teach the others. If the feats you've already managed are any indication, this could be the most important thing you do in this war."

She returned his smile, "Thank you for understanding."

He gave her a firm nod, "Now, if you'll excuse me, I need to get packed."

Aya shot to her feet, "*What?* Aleksei, did you hear a word I just said?"

He looked up at her, "I did. You said that I *might* have a grace period to get to Kuuran. You also said I was dealing with a demon, but not an especially powerful or intelligent one, yes?"

She frowned, "Well, yes, I did."

He shrugged, "So wouldn't I be safer among the angels? From what Jonas told me, the Seraphima was made to counter the Demonic Presence. If this demon shows up in Kuuran, I'll be surrounded by people who might actually be able to destroy it."

Aya opened her mouth to protest, only to realize that nothing she said would dissuade him. She sighed in defeat, "You'll have to ride as hard as you can to get to Kuuran before the demon finds you again."

"I know. That's why I need to get moving *now*. The sooner I get on the road, the sooner I'll be there."

He stood and hurried around the room, stuffing his meager belongings into his pack while Aya stood silently, watching. She watched him prepare for a journey that could take weeks, not knowing if he even had days.

And yet, Aya knew there was nothing she could say. Another word and she could doom his chances of survival completely. No, better that he believe everything she'd told him.

At least that way he had a chance.

Aya watched as he searched his bed for something, finally coming up with a tattered crimson scarf. He pressed it to his face for a moment, then stuffed in the pack with the rest of his belongings.

Gods, but this was insane. She couldn't believe she was letting him do this. And then she remembered. This could be their only chance at survival.

The alternative wasn't worth contemplating.

"How is he progressing?"

Adam lifted his face from his hands and looked into the Angelus's ice-blue eyes. "I honestly can't say. I want to believe that he's accepted his fate, but every now and then he does something that suggests otherwise. He was in the Reliquary today."

Kevara Avlon stiffened, "Why? Who allowed him access?"

Adam gave a mirthless chuckle, "He allowed himself access, Angelus. Your grandson isn't much for following the rules. I hardly need to tell *you* that."

Kevara Avlon leaned back in her chair, toying with an enormous ruby on her finger. "Did he prove to be useful?"

Adam nodded, "Very much so, Angelus. He discerned the functions of relics in a way I've never seen before. Apparently, there are a great many relics that are little more than useless."

Kevara frowned thoughtfully, "Did he seem pleased to have a purpose?"

Adam nodded again, "I think he finds his time there a worthy distraction. I figured that could only be a good thing. The more he has to keep him distracted, the less time he has to contemplate escape."

"Then let him continue to spend time there. He might even find something useful to us. It would certainly be a waste to let his talents be squandered."

Adam looked away from the Angelus, "There's something else. He opened the book."

Kevara arched an eyebrow, "Did he now?"

"It was inscribed to him," Adam managed.

Kevara shot to her feet, "What? That's not possible. That book is *ancient*. Even if it weren't, it's been here since he was a child."

Adam shrugged, "I don't understand it myself, but he was very excited to find it. He's locked in his chambers with it right now."

"His chambers?" she hissed, leaning forward, "You allowed him to leave the Reliquary with it?"

Adam sighed, "Angelus, as I said, he's uninterested in our rules. He simply said that the book was his now, not ours. I hardly wanted to provoke him."

Her ire vanished and a vaguely pleasant smile returned to her face, "No, of course you wouldn't. It's not your place, at any rate. You're there to keep him distracted, keep him *happy*. We have others who can antagonize him. You just keep doing your job. And I shouldn't have to remind you that Jonas *is* your only job."

Adam nodded, withholding a sigh of relief. He'd feared her reaction. It was a great weight from his shoulders to be vindicated. "I appreciate your confidence, Angelus, and the opportunity to serve."

Kevara laughed, "Of course you do, child. But don't think I'm a total fool, either. I know your reasons for wanting this assignment."

Adam tensed, but she waved her hand through the air dismissively, "It matters little to me how you entice him to complacency, only that he remains in the Undercroft. I don't care what...methods you employ."

Adam's face flushed, but he bowed his head, "As you command, Angelus. I don't suppose there has been any word from his Knight?"

Kevara went back to running her fingers over her ruby ring, "Not yet, but he will come sooner or later. Given the sort of man Jonas is, I don't imagine he bonded one lacking in fire. I anticipate the man soon.

You have the time between now and then to win Jonas over. Because once the Lord Captain arrives, the rules are going to change, and not in our favor.

"The greatest weapon we have is this time, right now, without the Lord Captain's interference. We must be certain that Jonas is fully convinced of the danger he poses. If he is not, I believe the Lord Captain will return him to his delusions. We cannot afford such a calamity."

Adam frowned, "Begging your pardon, Angelus, but why don't we simply keep the Lord Captain from the Undercroft? If Jonas never sees him, it won't be an issue."

Kevara shrugged, "You may be right, child. But I'd not like to risk the safety of our world on whether or not Aleksei Drago can get past our guards. From the accounts I've received, he is a formidable man. And he isn't stupid."

Another thought suddenly struck Adam, "You don't really believe that Jonas could escape the shield, do you?"

"I don't know, child. I would venture to say that escape is impossible, but Jonas is the eye in the storm. He is unpredictable by virtue of his very existence. If anyone were to prove me wrong, I fear it might be him. Best that we don't allow such a thing to occur. I will handle Captain Drago. You see to Jonas. With the One-God's grace, we can avoid any...unpleasantness."

Tamara woke with a start.

She sat up in her bed, looking around the room for the source of the noise. The room appeared to be empty.

She frowned. There was something different, something that her sleep-addled mind was missing.

She realized she was shivering, and pulled the heavy quilt closer. It smelled strange, musty. This wasn't the room she recalled. The window was set into the south wall, rather than the east. The bed was smaller, harder.

The fog of sleep lightened, and she suddenly understood.

This was another room entirely.

Tamara carefully came to her feet, holding the quilt around her protectively. The air was colder than she recalled.

Significantly colder.

She tiptoed to the window and gasped at the jagged mountains staring back at her in the moonlight. It was impossible. It *had* to be. The land around Taumon was mostly flat. There weren't mountains like this for hundreds of leagues in any direction.

Tamara instinctively reached to her thigh. A breath of relief escaped her as she felt the tiny comfort of her knife. She silently thanked Roux for insisting that she keep it there, tied with two leather thongs, at all times.

She drew it and held it the way he'd shown her. She didn't have nearly enough information to know if it would do her any good, but just holding it made her feel calmer, more secure. She wasn't helpless.

Tamara felt her way around the room until she found the door. It was solid, and locked besides. She cursed under her breath and dropped to the floor, peeking out from the scant inch of space between the floor and door.

The hallway outside was dark, but she could hear a low murmuring. There were men out there.

"–at once."

She jumped at the intrusion of words. One set of boots walked away from the door. Tamara cursed again and quickly sheathed her knife. They must have heard her.

She raced back to the bed, managing to curl up and close her eyes just as the lock came away and the door opened.

"Get up," came a bored voice.

When Tamara didn't move, pain streaked through her. It was like being whipped with an iron brand. She gave a screech and sat up.

A man walked into the room. She lifted her chin and glared at him as he advanced. Under the quilt, she kept her fingers close to the knife's handle. If he lunged at her, she prayed she would have the time to draw it. But the last thing she wanted to do was give a hint that she was armed.

The man lifted his hand, and a ball of yellow flame burst into existence. She flinched at the sudden light. At the casual display of power.

She forced herself to study the man's face, his cruel green eyes. His short but powerful stature. She wanted to retch at being so close to him. She felt defiled just being in his presence.

"Ah, Princess Tamara," he said with a chuckle, "I must say, you couldn't have made this any easier."

"Who are you?" she snarled, mustering the best approximation of bravery she could.

He raised his hands defensively, "I'm merely a messenger, Highness. I was asked to reclaim you. When you are more...settled, I will take you to your grandfather."

Tamara froze. Her *grandfather*? What could he possibly be talking about? She decided not to take the bait.

"How did you find me?" she managed instead.

He chuckled. It was an evil sound. "A princess who vanishes into thin air on the eve of battle would be all but impossible to locate. A princess who arrives at the Admiralty in Taumon is quite another matter. It was stupid of your mother not to take such things into account."

"What have you done with her?" Tamara demanded, her hand tightening around her knife.

"Her? What in the Dark God's name would I want with her? She is a deposed queen without a realm or an army. You, on the other hand, are priceless. *You* are the heir to the throne, not your whore mother. She's merely inconvenient. *You* have value."

"I won't help you," Tamara said, keeping her voice steady. "No matter what you do to me."

The man shrugged his shoulders, "That matters little to me. We'll see what His Majesty has to say about all of that. You are under our power. It would be in your best interest to show some gratitude that we don't have you in chains."

The fire whooshed out of existence. "Sweet dreams, Highness."

He turned and walked from the room. She desperately tried to yank her knife free, but found she couldn't move. She tried to scream at him, but her jaw was locked shut. The invisible bindings didn't fall away until the lock clicked back into place.

Tamara gritted her teeth, calming herself. It would do her no good to have an outburst. It would only prove that the man was winning. She refused to allow that.

A thought suddenly struck her.

He knew she had the knife, he just didn't care. Rather than remind her of her own impotence, he wanted her to know how minuscule of a threat she posed. Her pitiful blade was laughable next to the power he wielded, and so he let her keep it.

She'd never felt so helpless in her life.

194

Before it could overcome her, Tamara forced her despair away. What would Roux say if he saw her right then? She cringed to think how disappointed he would be in her. She wasn't using her head.

Rising to her feet, Tamara went back to the window. It was sealed with lead, but in the moonlight she judged it to have been soldered in a hurry.

She drew her knife and began to chip away at the seal. She worked tirelessly for hours before finally hurling the window open into the frigid night. The cold struck her like a fist, but she gritted her teeth and peered out to either side.

There was a ledge. It was decidedly narrow, but it was her only chance.

Tamara turned back to her room, feeling around until she found her clothes. Until she found the rabbit-skin cloak. *His* rabbit-skin cloak. She'd fallen asleep with it, more to be near Roux, near something he'd worn, than anything.

Now she wrapped it around herself, searching the room for her boots. They were nowhere to be found.

She sat back on her heels with an inward groan. Even if she was able to get out the window, her captors weren't going to make escape any easier than necessary. Without shoes, she had little hope of getting very far.

With a sudden gasp, Tamara stood and hurried to the bed. She quickly shredded one of the sheets into thin strips of cloth. She set about tying the strips over her feet, using the moon for light.

When she felt like her feet were sufficiently protected, Tamara hurried back to the window and swung one leg onto the ledge. With a deep breath, she sheathed her knife and swung the other leg over. When she was sure of her footing, she turned south and began the terrifying trek along the high wall.

As she moved, she tried to keep the memory of escaping with Aleksei fresh in her mind. He'd taken her out the window and across the roof of Kalinor Palace. He'd shown her how to do it right.

Now she just had to remember those lessons.

Her left foot slipped and Tamara grasped frantically at the wall, just managing to catch one of the jagged stones. She let out a shuddering breath as she righted herself, fighting to regain her sense of balance. She refused to look down. She just kept finding handholds in the jagged rocks of the wall.

A few hundred paces distant, Tamara could make out firelight. Even though it was still a ways away, she could tell it was at most a torch.

A sentry.

Tamara felt her pulse thrill as she worked her way inexorably towards the light. This was an opportunity she couldn't afford to waste. She had to get this right if she was to have any real chance of escape.

The closer she got, the better she could see. There was only one man, standing on what appeared to be a landing that spread out a few paces beneath her little ledge. She waited until she was only a footstep from the edge, doing her best to control her breathing so he wouldn't hear her.

Sending a silent prayer to the gods, she drew her knife.

She took a slight step, and then leapt into the air above the man. As her feet left the ledge, one slipped on the snow, sending her tumbling towards the landing in a staggering fall.

Tamara kept her knife extended, even as she crashed into the guard. She felt the blade cut into flesh.

The moment they landed, the man rolled, twisting his way on top of her and grabbing her wrist. Tamara rammed her knee into his crotch, clawing at his face with her free hand. He cried out and grasped at his right eye. She took the opportunity, yanking her wrist free of his grip and slicing his throat.

He began to cough and choke around the blade. She pulled it free, gasping at the spray of blood that erupted from him. She scrambled to get out from under him, spitting his blood out of her mouth, wiping it from her eyes.

She hadn't anticipated such a reaction. She supposed Roux must have forgotten to mention that part, or perhaps he simply assumed she would know.

Tamara looked down at the convulsing guard, frowning as she tried to determine her next step. What had Aleksei done?

Understanding flooded through her, and she dropped next to his shuddering body, wiping her blade on his coat. She sheathed it, then awkwardly pulled the coat off of him. He was much heavier than she'd expected, and jerking frantically. After some awkward maneuvering, she tumbled him free of the coat and onto the landing, even as he choked out the last of his life into the crimson snow.

Before she did anything else, Tamara shed her cloak and pulled on the coat. She pulled the cloak back on, thankful for the added warmth, before stripping the man of his boots and gloves, pulling them over her frozen fingers gratefully. The boots were too big for her, but with her make-shift cloth shoes, they didn't fit all that poorly. And they certainly provided better protection than hastily-torn sheets.

As a last precaution, Tamara disarmed the man, taking his belt knife and sticking it in the coat pocket. It seemed like a good idea to have a second blade if anything happened to her little horn knife.

Abandoning the body for a moment, Tamara finally allowed herself to peer over the edge of the wall. The drop was dizzying. Far below, she could see deep drifts of snow. She breathed a sigh of relief.

Grasping the dead guard's hands, Tamara dragged him to the edge of the landing, resting him against the low wall. Using all of her strength, she managed to prop the man's limp back against the wall's edge. Gripping his feet, she gave a mighty heave.

The man flopped over the edge, vanishing into the night.

She peered over, but could only just make out the indentation in the snow far below her. His body wouldn't be discovered till spring, if ever.

With a tired sigh, Tamara did her best to cover the blood-soaked snow with the powder that had built up in the corners. It was hardly perfect, but it might buy her some added time.

Gods, she *prayed* it would.

Tamara started to run down the length of the landing, searching for her next point of descent. She hadn't gone far when she suddenly ran into something hard. Very hard. She gasped as her nose broke and she tumbled backwards. Blood gushed down her face as she fought back the immediate tears filling her eyes.

"Stand up right now, or I won't bother to heal you," came a bored voice.

It was the same man, the Magus.

Tamara pushed herself to her feet, meeting his eyes as best she could through the tears and the blood. Those emerald eyes, so familiar yet so alien, gave her a deeper chill than the howling winter around her.

He came towards her and unceremoniously clapped a hand over her face. The sudden pain was excruciating, although she wondered if she might still be in shock. Perhaps it would have been worse, had he waited.

The pain slowly subsided. She could feel the blood clotting on her face. When he removed his hand, she could still feel her nose throb, but it wasn't anything like it had been.

"That's about the best I can do. A pity Jonas isn't here. His talents are far more suited to this than mine. Let this be a lesson. Anything more serious is far beyond my abilities to heal. It's in your best interest to stay as healthy as possible. If you don't, you're the only one who will suffer for it.

"Now get inside before you freeze."

CHAPTER 17
UNEXPECTED COMPANIONS

A leksei awoke, sitting up suddenly and gasping for breath. The roof of the small tent that surrounded him was just beginning to brighten with the first rays of daylight. He forced his breathing to slow, glancing around in confusion.

It had been a nightmare.

He schooled his racing thoughts, recalling the incongruous images of the tormented dream, trying to make some sort of sense of them. There had been a voice. A terrified voice he knew well.

It was the Wood.

It had been a very long time since Aleksei had received such a message from Her. That experience had been no less terrifying, but at the time he had known the dream for what it was. A warning.

This had been much the same, but now Her voice sounded strained, distant. He racked his brain, trying to recover the words. Aleksei closed his eyes, taking deep, measured breaths and replaying the images, trying to recall her words.

He'd woken only a moment before...the wind.... Before the wind reached him. A cold understanding flooded through him. The demon had managed to collect itself. His time was up.

With a groan, Aleksei fell back against his sleeping roll. He was still at least a hundred leagues from Kuuran, and this part of Dalita was nothing but flat plains as far as the eye could see.

He was a dead man.

Another image from the nightmare drifted across his mind and he slowly sat back up. There had been something else, hadn't there? A light. A cold, blue light. He knew enough from Jonas's descriptions that it could only be the Seraphima.

Aya had said that he didn't have the magic to fight the demon, but the angels would. That was it! He needed to find an angel escort, someone to protect him until he got to Jonas.

Reaching over into his pack, Aleksei pulled out his field map. While he couldn't pinpoint his exact location, he knew he was close to a city. If he could get there before the wind found him, perhaps he could find someone willing to escort him to Kuuran.

Aleksei scrambled around his small tent, hurriedly packing his things. With the sun rising, he had enough light to ride by. He needed to get on the road immediately. As it was, he didn't know how much time he had before the wind found him.

He strapped his pack closed and crawled out into the frozen morning. A chill swept through him as he broke down his tent and pulled up the stake keeping Agriphon close. He felt naked, vulnerable.

The great warhorse whickered as Aleksei swiftly brushed him down and pulled on his tack. Aleksei marveled that his horse wasn't more irritable. After spending so much time being exercised and sleeping in the stables of Kalinor, Aleksei would have thought that Agriphon might have become a bit spoiled. The Dalitian winter was certainly harsher than the stallion would be accustomed to.

But his warhorse stood there stoically while he was saddled, like an obsidian statue. As he did every morning, Aleksei walked Agriphon towards the road. He liked to give the horse a few minutes to warm up before they started riding in earnest.

Normally, he would have walked his horse for a good ten minutes before mounting, but following the nightmare, he knew he didn't have time to waste. When they reached the road, he slid into the saddle and urged Agriphon into a light trot.

By the time the sun was fully risen, Agriphon was moving at a full gallop. By midmorning, Aleksei could make out the prominence of Shangri-Uun in the distance. He knew next to nothing about the place, except that it sat on the fork of the mighty Ylik Water. One fork headed to the east, where it flowed through the Seil Wood and down through the entirety of eastern Ilyar. The western fork became the Tanren River, and ran out its course in the Sulaq Hills just west of Keiv-Alon.

Aleksei thought it a strange idea to build a city on a river's fork, but as he drew closer to Shangri-Uun, he could tell that Angelic cities followed a decidedly different plan from their Ilyari cousins.

The first thing that struck Aleksei was the absence of a wall. He supposed the city must not be as old as Keldoan or Kalinor. Perhaps it'd been built after the great wars. Even so, Shangri-Uun was one of the southernmost cities in Dalita, and would likely be the first target should an invading army attack. It seemed an odd choice to leave it so undefended.

It was noon by the time Aleksei rode into the city proper. His senses had detected no signs of the wind, though he didn't feel safe even in the city. Better a city than open air, though, at least until he could find an agreeable angel.

He rode towards the center of town, looking this way and that for signs of an Angelic citizen. His concern grew as he saw nothing but humans walking around, most in Ilyari clothing.

It made sense, he realized, that a greater portion of the population might be Ilyari or human Dalitians. The city was a mere hundred leagues from Kalinor. This was the primary trading hub between Dalita and Ilyar. He imagined a great many of the people he passed were traders and merchants.

He saw one woman who looked particularly well-to-do and lifted his hand. She frowned, but stopped so that he could approach.

"Afternoon, ma'am. Is there an angel in this city? I'm in great need of their services."

She snorted a laugh, "Aye, there's an angel here. But good luck getting an audience. He's the fourth-born *Seraph*. He owns the manor house in the city square, but there's never a guarantee that he's even there. Other angels come through now and again, but if you're looking for more of their kind, you'll have better luck in Kuuran or Yosa. Most of them don't fancy coming so far south."

Aleksei slumped a touch and nodded his head, "Thank you, you've been very helpful." Gods, but he'd thought there would be more angels around than *that*.

As he wheeled Agriphon back to the main road, he let out a small sigh. The fourth-born Seraph? This was only going to go one of two ways. There would be no middle ground. He didn't even know if the man would know who he was, who *Jonas* was.

Still, it was his best shot.

Aleksei rode deeper into the city, stopping several times to ask directions to the city square. The city's layout didn't make any sense to him. Even if he'd understood it better, Aleksei generally disliked cities. They were confusing, man-made things. His skills as a Hunter made him much more comfortable in the wilds and, until Jonas had summoned him, he'd expected to live out his days as a farmer, or perhaps a cowboy.

Everything made sense to him on the farm or in the wild, with their predictable hierarchies of life and death, growth and decay. Cities possessed the same systems of life and death, and certainly decay, but the ebb and flow of it all still felt alien to him. Jonas, being a city boy through and though, understood such things far better.

He pushed the thought away before loneliness could overtake him. He was on an important mission, one that would eventually reunite him with his Magus. He had to keep his mind fixed on that for now.

Aleksei finally rode into the square and immediately spotted the angel's manor. It would have been difficult to miss. The façade reminded him of the temples in Kalinor; silver marble columns supporting an ornately tiled roof. Behind that initial splendor was a wall of pure white marble. In the center were a pair of heavy oak doors, banded in silver-plated iron.

As he approached, a man came out from the building to the right. He gave Aleksei a perfunctory bow. "Greetings, Sir. Do you have business with the Seraph Xavathan?"

Aleksei frowned a moment, trying to decide the best way to go about this. He finally settled on what he hoped was the surest way to be seen. "I'm Lord Captain Aleksei Drago of Ilyar. I've come to see the Seraph on urgent business regarding his nephew, Jonas Belgi."

The man looked up at Aleksei in surprise. Aleksei held his face still and calm. If need be, he could produce his seal, though he doubted the man would know it from any other seal in Ilyar.

"Yes, very good, Sir. If you'll let me take your horse, the head chamberlain will greet you inside."

Aleksei dismounted, handing the man a silver. The coin startled the man, but he took it with a deep bow of his head. Aleksei frowned as he walked towards the house.

The man was clearly unused to being tipped. Either the people of this realm were unusually miserly, or he had just made some sort of social misstep. He smiled to himself as he tried to imagine the lecture Jonas would have given him.

The doors opened before he reached them. Aleksei schooled his face to keep from looking startled as a man in his sixtieth summer walked out to greet him.

"Lord Captain Drago, it's an honor. The Seraph has been expecting you."

Aleksei arched an eyebrow, following the man into the house. He felt his hackles rise as he walked through a corridor paneled in rich, dark wood. He was expected? What the hell did *that* mean?

They walked through a series of hallways. Aleksei tried to take in as many of the richly-detailed oil paintings as he could without appearing to gawk. The Ilyari favored tapestries to paintings, but the finest examples he'd seen in Kalinor lacked the majesty and scope of even one of these masterpieces.

The older man finally stopped before a set of double doors, "You may proceed from here, Lord Captain. Beyond are Seraph Xavathan's personal quarters. You will find him within."

Aleksei bowed his head to the man as he pulled the doors open.

He was completely unprepared for what greeted him on the other side.

Rather than opulence and splendor, the place had a comfortable, homey feel to it. The walls were painted in light creams, the carpets were soft and simple pastels. He realized as he walked through the entrance that someone *lived* here. An actual person, not a title.

Every room in Kalinor Palace only served to remind a person that they were in a place of wealth and power, including the private chambers of the royal family. This felt as though it belonged to a normal person who happened to inhabit a position of authority.

Aleksei let his shoulders relax. He hadn't even realized how tense he'd been, entering the manor. The simple elegance of this man's personal quarters put him at ease. He quickly reminded himself not to judge too quickly based on appearance alone.

Actions always spoke louder than words.

An angel swept into the room, his angular gray wings draping regally behind him. Aleksei looked at his face and had to hold back a gasp. It was almost like looking at Jonas. Or at least, Jonas in another thirty years.

"I am Xavathan." The angel smiled, "You are Aleksei Drago?"

Andariana Belgi stared blankly at the wall. Her chamber door was locked, providing at least that much of a barrier to the rest of the world. For now, she just wanted to be by herself.

When Tamara had missed breakfast, she'd thought little of it. Tamara could simply be sleeping in, she supposed, or perhaps she was out shopping for things to take on their voyage. The gods knew it was not going to be an easy passage.

But as the day wore on, she had become increasingly aware of Tamara's absence. When she'd finally gone to the bedroom and seen all of Tamara's things there, even her shoes, Andariana had immediately known that something was wrong. The soldiers guarding the room had been equally surprised.

And yet, beyond calling the Legionnaires to sweep through the city and search for her daughter, Andariana was at a loss. She was hardly in a position of power anymore. Even if Taumon was still loyal to her, she had no way of knowing how many rebel spies were among the townspeople, or among the navy for that matter.

Unlike the rebel officers, the naval men would have a difficult time vanishing into thin air without their precious ships. As far as she knew, no one had commandeered any navy vessels.

But now her daughter was missing. Tamara must have been taken by someone, even though such a thing should have been impossible. The guard stationed outside her room had been questioned. He swore no one had entered or exited the room from the time Tamara entered until the following morning.

Andariana heard the sound of shouting in the hallway and sat up, daring to hope that they'd found something. *Anything.* Fear suddenly gripped her. What if they'd found Tamara's body? What if she was already dead? Andariana fought back the bile rising in her throat. She couldn't allow fear to rule her.

There was a silent flash, and she stared in confusion at the red-faced man standing before her. The door had never opened, and yet here he was, as plain as day.

"Ri-Hnon?" she said, coming unsteadily to her feet.

"Where is she?" he demanded. "Where is Tamara? Why are their soldiers sweeping through the city looking for her?"

She wrinkled her nose at the smell of him, "That's none of your concern, I'm afraid. I don't even know what you're doing here–"

There was another flash, and suddenly Andariana was against the wall, a knife pressed against her throat. Roux's golden eyes glittered, "*Where. Is. She?*"

Andariana started to cry. All the emotions she'd been bottling up suddenly rushed forth, "I don't *know*! Why do you think we're sweeping the city, you stupid savage? Do you honestly think I'd bother if I knew where they'd taken her?"

Roux stepped back. "'*They*'? You know who has her?"

Andariana shook her head, unable to speak past her sobbing.

"Has she been seen today?" Roux asked, receiving the same response. He paused a moment. "She was taken in the night, then. Take me to her room."

Andariana just stared at him.

"*Now!*" he bellowed.

When she unlocked the door, she suddenly understood his request. There were close to fifty soldiers outside the door, all armed to the teeth. It suddenly occurred to her to wonder how he'd managed to get into her chamber.

"It's alright," she managed. "He belongs here. Please, get out of my way, I need to show him something."

The soldiers reluctantly parted for their queen, each suspiciously glaring at Roux. For his part, the Ri-Hnon was oblivious. He was consumed by only one thing. Tamara. He *would* find her. He would not allow *anyone* to take her from him.

As he followed Andariana, Roux recalled his immediate panic at seeing the frantic soldiers. He'd only stopped into the city to find provisions for his return home. But hearing that Tamara was missing had sent him into a blind rage.

Even now it coursed through him, the ferocity, the lust for blood. Becoming the Ri-Hnon entailed more than simply being able to listen to the Seil Wood. Until that first moment of recognition, that someone had taken something that was *his*, someone he *loved*, Roux had never really understood that.

Now, it was all he could do to control the feral fury that threatened to overwhelm his rational mind completely.

Andariana reached the room she sought and pushed the door open. Roux swept past her, balking at the sudden stench that filled his nose.

"What is that?" he gasped.

"What?"

"That smell. It's *foul* in here."

"I don't smell anything but you."

He turned to the queen as though she were mad. "How can you not...." He trailed off as he realized it wasn't exactly a *smell*. It was something else. The taint of something unspeakably corrupted.

But it wasn't in the air.

It permeated everything in the room. It almost felt like....

"It's the Archanium," he grunted.

Andariana stepped into the room, looking around for the invisible echoes, as though a more thorough search would reveal them.

"How can you tell?" she whispered.

He could smell her fear. He wondered if he'd just confirmed her worst nightmares. "It's everywhere. It's a feeling, at least for me. I don't touch the Archanium like your Magi, though I recognize it well enough to feel its presence. But this is *vile*. It's unlike anything I've encountered."

"And whoever used this magic, they have my daughter?"

He looked into her wide, terrified eyes.

"Yes."

Aleksei stared at the angel, "How were you expecting me?"

Xavathan shrugged, "I had a feeling you wouldn't be too far behind Jonas. God knows, if you have half his determination, you'd not let much stand in your way. I must say, though, I'd expected you here a bit earlier."

A thousand questions flooded into Aleksei's mind, but all he managed to say was a feeble "I ran into some complications."

The angel's easy smile returned, "Understandable, I'm sure."

"You mentioned Jonas," Aleksei pressed before Xavathan managed another word. "I didn't realize the two of you had ever met."

Xavathan waved him into a sitting room, "Please, Captain Drago, have a seat. I have a feeling we have much to discuss."

Aleksei stepped into an equally-intimate room and took a seat on a tufted sofa. Xavathan sat across from him in a low-backed chair, his wings stretching behind him before lazily folding.

"Jonas was brought to me a few weeks ago. A young angel had come across him doing battle with another Magus. The other Magus invoked a power called the Demonic Presence. Do you know what that is?"

Aleksei's entire body tensed. "I do," he managed.

Xavathan nodded gravely, "When he was brought to me, your Magus was barely alive. I was able to bring him out of the Presence, though not entirely."

Aleksei frowned, "I'm not sure I follow."

Xavathan shrugged, "It's a bit complicated. It would be as though he was trapped in a deep hole. I pulled him most of the way out. But at the point my power faded, he was left just barely holding onto the edge, unable to pull himself out, but no longer stranded at the bottom, either."

Aleksei nodded. "So how did he end up in the Undercroft of the Basilica?"

Xavathan's eyebrows shot up, "How do you know where he is?"

"I wasn't certain until now, but I was told that few other places in this world could neutralize the bond between Knight and Magus. I knew he was in Dalita. Something happened to our bond. It caused me a great deal of...difficulty, I can assure you. And then the bond was simply *gone*. From the little I know, that would require incredibly powerful magic."

Xavathan nodded, "Indeed it does, lad. When I was unable to separate him from the Presence, and when it became clear that his tentative hold on its world made him a danger to himself and those around him, I took him to the Basilica to be healed. Until such a thing could take place, he was housed in the Undercroft, for everyone's protection."

Aleksei leaned forward, "Then why is he still there?"

Xavathan leaned back in his chair, "Jonas's healing was performed. It was mostly successful, but an echo of the Presence still resides within him. The Angelus feels that Jonas is still sufficiently dangerous, and that he must not be allowed to leave the Undercroft for any reason."

"Why not?" Aleksei fired back.

"Because she believes he will destroy this world if the Presence ever gets ahold of him again. That the Presence is still a part of his soul, even a very small part, is enough to keep my mother...cautious."

"Do *you* believe he's dangerous? That he's going to destroy the world if he's ever allowed to go free?"

"I don't know, lad. I wish I did. My mother adheres to some very ancient exegeses of texts which, frankly, have been debated by theologians for centuries. She has a very specific way of understanding their meanings, and I don't always agree with her interpretations. In this case, I am torn."

Aleksei nodded, "Thank you for telling me this. You've answered a great many questions for me."

Xavathan smiled again, "I'm happy to be of service."

"That's actually the reason I came here. I need to get to Kuuran, and I need an angel to come with me."

Xavathan's smile saddened, "I'm afraid my mother will no sooner listen to me than anyone else. She is very...determined that Jonas must stay in the Undercroft. The journey would only end up wasting your time."

Aleksei waved the words away, "That's not what I'm after, and as far as I'm concerned, *nothing* is a waste of my time when it comes to Jonas. But something is following me. A wind demon. I've encountered it twice now, and I've barely escaped with my life each time.

"Our Magi have identified it as being part of the Demonic Presence, so I need an angel to go with me for protection, at least until I reach Kuuran. We don't think it will attack in the presence of the Seraphima, but if it does, that might provide an opportunity to destroy it. Or, at least, it's my hope that someone there may be able to break this creature's tie to me."

Xavathan considered a long moment. "If you've been riding across the Madrhal Plains, how has this demon not found you by now?"

"A powerful Magus was able to scatter it temporarily, but without the magic of the Seraphima, she was unable to destroy it. I think it just took some time to pull itself together.

"This morning I received a warning that it was once again tracking me. My realm is at war. My people need me. They need Jonas. But we can't help them as long as this thing is hunting me and he's imprisoned."

Xavathan's eyes looked pained, "I can't promise that I'll be able to help you free Jonas. I'm sorry, but there are certain bounds I am simply unable to cross. That is one of them."

"I have no problems dealing with that myself," Aleksei said softly, his golden eyes flashing.

Xavathan paused a long moment before nodding, "Very well, I will accompany you to Kuuran. Perhaps this demon will find you on the way and we can simply be rid of it."

Aleksei smiled, "That'd be an unusual bit of luck."

Xavathan chuckled, "I understand from Jonas that the two of you have been having a rough time of things. Why don't you go to my kitchen and get some food? I need some time to gather my things before we can be on our way."

Aleksei stood and bowed his head, "Thank you for helping me, Xavathan."

The angel rose and clapped a hand on Aleksei's shoulder, "It will turn out right, lad. You'll see. Now go on with you. You'll need your strength for what's to come."

Aleksei quirked a half-smile as the angel left the room. He wondered what Xavathan was hinting at. Perhaps it was just a careless comment.

Somehow, Aleksei doubted that.

CHAPTER 18

INTO THE BELLY OF DARKNESS

Jonas allowed himself a satisfied smile. He lay wrapped in a soft cocoon of white feathers, their warmth filling him with a sense of peace that had been wholly absent from his life for a very long time. He basked in the fading memory of a dream of comfort and familiarity.

As he slowly awakened, he sensed a presence he recognized. His heart skipped as he thought of Aleksei. He could feel so many of the same things that always radiated through the bond when Aleksei was near enough to him.

With a frown, he understood that it wasn't his Knight. It couldn't be. There were too many insecurities, too many differences. The longer he felt the presence, the more it made sense to him. This was someone who cared for him, but not with the feral ferocity that always emanated from Aleksei.

Jonas sat up with a jolt, suddenly recognizing who it was, and the origin of these unexpected feelings.

He blinked in the darkness.

Throwing out a hand, Jonas lit the lamps in his bedchamber, being careful not to let his rising anger envelop him. He could feel the angel on the other side of the door.

Adam.

Jonas recalled his reaction when Sariel had cast a dream into his mind. That had felt like a violation, but most of his anger stemmed from his embarrassment at having such a personal moment shared by a total stranger, at the violation of his mind by someone who claimed to care for him, but had no respect for his privacy.

This, he reasoned, was different. This had not taken his old thoughts and memories and twisted them. This had been different. *New*. And while he didn't welcome the dream, it hadn't been entirely unpleasant.

He carefully came to his feet and pulled on a shirt before pushing the door open. Adam sat in the low-backed chair, his face pensive.

Jonas watched the angel for a long moment, studying his face. "Can I ask what that was?"

Adam cleared his throat, "I hope I didn't upset you. You spent so much of yesterday reading that book. I could tell you were tired and sore, so I thought I might try and help you relax. People tend to sleep better when we send the dreams. I tried to summon something general, but comforting."

Jonas frowned, "I thought you had to use memories to conjure those dreams. *My* memories."

Adam shrugged, "We do, to a degree. Memories, images, we have certain latitude with what other elements we add in." A soft, self-satisfied smile settled over the angel's handsome face, "And of course, some of us are better at sending dreams than others. Some lack the delicacy of crafting a properly therapeutic experience for our invalids. They try too hard, delve too deeply, which can upset the inval..." he caught Jonas's murderous glare and coughed into his hand, "people in your...situation, rather than helping them."

Jonas's face heated as he remembered the last dream an angel had sent to him, lying on the shore with Aleksei. That had never taken place, but he knew *very* well where a few of those images had come from.

"For the dream I sent you," Adam continued slowly, "I drew a memory I thought you would find comforting."

Jonas frowned, "I don't have any such memory."

Adam allowed himself a small smile, "You might not consciously recall it now, but at some point in your life, you felt that secure, that safe. And that feeling came from sleeping surrounded by an angel's wings."

Jonas stiffened with understanding. His father. Those had been his *father's* wings? He couldn't imagine how young he would have been when that memory had been imprinted. He felt tears welling in his eyes, but he forced them back.

Adam seemed to catch the sudden sorrow that had swept over Jonas.

He came to his feet and stepped forward, placing his hands on Jonas's arms, "It wasn't my intention to upset you. I just wanted you to get some proper sleep."

The suddenness of skin to skin contact startled Jonas. For a second, he imagined what it would be like to feel Aleksei's touch again. Not in a dream, but in the waking world.

The very thought slipped past his tightly controlled façade, and he felt tears he'd held back before streaming down his face, finally freed.

Adam pulled him closer, and as much as he wanted to be alone right then, Jonas recognized that he'd spent a great amount of his time in the Undercroft by himself. He was exhausted by the crippling sense of isolation.

Adam held him, allowing him to cry out his loneliness. He felt the gentle warmth of Adam's wings wrapping around him. The feeling of absolute security pushed back the loneliness. After a while, he realized he'd stopped crying; he was actually *smiling* for the first time in what seemed an age.

Jonas looked up into Adam's eyes. The angel was smiling warmly. Jonas returned the smile, and then gently stepped out of the angel's embrace. "Thank you for that. I suppose I've been bottling everything up since I've been here."

Adam drew his wings back and bowed his head. Jonas thought he detected a touch of disappointment in the angel's face. "I know you've been put in a bad position, Jonas. I know you feel like we're all keeping you here, but at least you know why."

Jonas sighed, "No, I don't feel like you're holding me captive any longer. If I wanted out, the gods know I would find a way. But I know I can't risk that. I can't risk anything happening to...to the world."

Adam offered him a forlorn smile, "You don't mean that."

Jonas arched an eyebrow, "Pardon?"

Adam shrugged, "You're not here because you fear destroying the world. You don't wish that to happen, but that's not what keeps you here."

Jonas looked away from the angel, "No, it isn't. But I don't want to talk about any of that just now."

"May I ask why?"

Jonas looked back into the angel's eyes, "Because some things are just for me."

It was Adam's turn to look away. His eyes settled on the book Jonas had taken from the Reliquary. "Are you finding the book of interest?"

Jonas walked over the table and lifted the purple leather volume, "It's at once frustrating and fascinating. I mean, there's an entire section on amalgamated nullification barriers. You know, like the one surrounding *this* place. It's less about their construction and more about the potential dangers of any person with a strong magical connection entering a barrier and then suddenly stepping back out.

"According to the text, the rapid return of your presence to the wider world goes off like a heavenflare for anyone trying to find you, be it through location spells or scrying. That's not something angels typically have to worry about, of course, but if *I* were to step back into the wider world, Bael could find me in a heartbeat. I'd rather avoid *that* particular family reunion," he muttered, shaking his head. "Pieces are missing, of course, and my Yazka isn't particularly amazing, so my translations are a bit suspect.

"But there's so much more in here, things my friends on the outside *need* to know. Some of my questions have been answered. Every now and then it hints at possibilities I can scarcely understand. There are implications in here that, if I'm reading them correctly, are staggering.

"Unfortunately, my training hasn't completely prepared me for this. It takes a long time to get through just a few pages. I find myself reading and rereading sections just to make sure I got it right, and then the next page changes everything and takes the whole mess to another realm that I never thought possible.

"Once I understand enough," Jonas continued, "I'm going to need to send messages to my people. They need to know what's in here. It could help them. Gods, it could win the bloody *war*. I still need to learn more, though, before I can be sure. *Any* mistake could prove fatal."

Adam merely nodded, politely taking in Jonas's ramblings.

The Prince finally paused and flipped the volume open, scanning its pages. He looked back to the angel, "With that in mind, I suppose I'd better get back to it."

Adam bowed his head, seeming to recognize his dismissal. "I need to go eat something anyhow. I'll bring you back a tray."

Jonas flashed the angel a warm smile. As Adam neared the door, Jonas cleared his throat. "Thank you, Adam. You're the only friend I have in this accursed place, and I really do appreciate what you tried to do for me."

Adam returned the smile, and then stepped out of the room.

When the door shut behind him, the angel breathed a long sigh, defeated. He'd been *so* close, but there was something deeply powerful keeping Jonas's thoughts and longings strongly tied to the outside world. The Angelus wanted the Prince to be so consumed with his own danger, and with the need to learn what he could from the Reliquary, that such external thoughts would fade.

But he still clung to the past, to everything he'd lost.

Adam started off towards the kitchens. The man couldn't let go of the world beyond the Undercroft. Not the way the Angelus wanted, and not the way Adam *needed*. Jonas could spend as much time as he liked delving into arcane texts and "sending" messages to the outside world for all Adam cared.

But he desperately needed the Magus's heart to stay locked away with Jonas.

With *him*.

Aleksei rode Agriphon through the sprawling markets and thoroughfares of Kuuran, taking in its size and opulence. It was at least as big as Kalinor, but once again, Aleksei had been alarmed by the apparent lack of a city wall. He *knew* the Basilica had been built before the Dominion Wars. How could these people have fought off the Demon Cassian without military fortifications?

The entire concept seemed absurd to him. He'd asked Xavathan about it, but had received only a cryptic "You have your walls, we have ours."

Even after pressing the point, the Seraph had remained quiet on the subject. It was vexing to say the least, partly because Aleksei was facing the very real possibility of declaring war on Dalita if they insisted on keeping Jonas prisoner.

But for the moment, he maintained the uneasy truce. Xavathan still walked beside him, leading his horse.

The angel had complained most of the ride, so Aleksei had walked as much as he could to ease the older man's discomfort. Angles didn't ride because they could fly. The very idea of relying on an animal for personal transportation was alien to their culture. Still, Aleksei didn't mind slowing down if it meant he was safe from the wind demon.

Unfortunately, the demon hadn't shown itself once on their journey. Aleksei had been hoping for an attack, simply so that Xavathan could have destroyed the thing and he could be done with it.

Now Aleksei wondered if, perhaps, the demon was aware of the danger the angel represented. Perhaps Aya had been wrong. Perhaps this *wasn't* a mindless killing machine.

But Aleksei couldn't be surrounded by angels forever. Sooner or later, he would have to return to Ilyar. Sooner or later, the demon *would* find him.

He pushed the troubling thought away, focusing on the moment at hand. He *had* to persuade Kevara Avlon to release Jonas. He had a plan of attack, but it all depended on how convincing he was as an actor.

He'd had extended discussions with Xavathan during their journey, but they had only hammered home how resolved the Angelus was. To hear tell from Xavathan, her obsession with Jonas bordered on madness. It didn't seem to him that a healthy person could *be* that adamant.

If she refused to release Jonas, Aleksei was going to have to think of something else, but he would not leave this place without his Magus. He had vowed to rip it apart, stone by stone, if necessary. He didn't plan on recanting those words.

They approached the Basilica, and Aleksei could hardly believe his eyes. The place made Kalinor Palace look like a beggar's hovel.

Crafted in black and gold marble and towering into the heavens, the Basilica was beautiful beyond measure. Tears nearly came to his eyes, simply gazing at its magnificence.

But he also knew it as something else. This was Jonas's prison, its people his jailers. They were determined to keep him from his prince.

His reverence dissolved.

They passed off their horses at the grandest stables he'd ever beheld, and Aleksei sighed at seeing Agriphon led away. Giving up his horse had a certain finality to it. He wasn't coming back here without Jonas. The thought both terrified and elated him.

Rather than head straight through the majestic foyer, Xavathan immediately turned to the right. Aleksei trailed after him, trying and failing to keep his bearings as they walked.

He felt like a peasant again.

When he'd first come to Kalinor Palace, the place had been beyond his comprehension. It had taken him weeks to learn the labyrinthine passages and corridors.

The Basilica was something wholly different, truly a city within itself. They passed through broad corridors, open air gardens with walkways stretching far above them, narrow cloisters that wove this way and that, on and on and on. By the time Xavathan came to a halt, Aleksei was completely turned around.

He wasn't used to being lost.

"Hold out your arms," Xavathan commanded.

Aleksei frowned, staring at the great pool of water that stretched out before them. In the center sat a small, ornate palace. Aleksei looked around, but saw no bridges leading towards it, no walkways connecting it to where they were.

Xavathan clutched his arms, and suddenly Aleksei was flying over the pool on the angel's powerful wingbeats. The thrill of flight was over almost before it began. His boots struck the smooth stone of the island only moments after they'd touched off. He straightened his coat, glancing at Xavathan.

"I'll admit, I didn't expect *that*," he said with a low chuckle.

Xavathan's face was grave, "It's the only way to the Angelus's inner sanctum."

Aleksei frowned, "You could also try swimming. Though I don't suppose *you* ever considered that."

Xavathan ignored his flippancy and stepped forward, thrusting the door open. Aleksei followed him into the tiny palace, marveling at how inviting the place was when compared with the cold perfection of the Basilica proper.

Of course, where Xavathan's quarters had been stark and pale, this was brightly colored with peaches, greens, and yellows. It had the distinct feel of belonging to someone feminine. And impossibly poisonous. To Aleksei, the entire place stank of rotted fruit, a sort of fetid fecundity.

He tried to imagine Mother Margareta living in such a place and almost burst out laughing. She would no doubt find it garish and cloying. But the environment *did* give him a few clues about the woman he was there to meet.

"Wait here," Xavathan intoned before heading up a narrow flight of stairs.

Aleksei stood by patiently, running various scenarios through his mind. Gods, but why was he so petrified? He'd led an army against a force twice their size and emerged victorious. He'd fought and escaped the clutches of a malevolent demonic force more than once. He'd survived one of the most horrific battles in recent history. So why did Jonas's grandmother strike so much fear and worry in him?

Of course. Because she had Jonas.

Xavathan reappeared at the top of the stairs and beckoned Aleksei up. He took the stairs two at a time, his heart racing.

"She's waiting for you in her office. She wants to speak to you privately," Xavathan said, his face betraying nothing.

Aleksei didn't need to read the man's face to feel his indignation.

He offered the angel a smile, "Thank you. I appreciate everything you've done for me."

Xavathan gave a curt nod, starting down the stairs.

Aleksei walked crisply down the hall, pulling the authority of his office around him. If he had to face this woman as Aleksei Drago, his heart would ultimately betray him. He couldn't afford that just now.

The office itself maintained the color scheme. The only thing lacking color was the woman seated behind the massive burlwood desk. She smiled sweetly at him, but he was staring into the eyes of a hungry viper.

"Lord Captain," she said gently, "do come in. I've been expecting you for some time."

Aleksei walked into the office and stopped just before the desk, hands clasped behind his back. "I imagine you have."

She blinked at him, obviously startled by his response. "I also know why you've come," she said, leaning back in her chair slowly.

"I'm not entirely sure you do. I've come with two purposes. The first is to see if your angels can help me with a small problem."

She frowned. Xavathan had clearly not mentioned this to her. "I'm afraid I don't understand."

"The Demon Bael has conjured a lethal entity...a wind demon.

"It's hunting me, and I need to know if your people can do anything to destroy it, or at the very least protect me from it. My life, Jonas's life, is too important to risk at the moment."

She arched a snowy eyebrow, "Lord Captain, I'm afraid that what you've just described is impossible. Bael wouldn't have that sort of strength yet. Even if he did, how could you escape such a creature? You have no magic."

Aleksei allowed her last statement to slide.

"Nonetheless, I have barely escaped it twice now. Most recently, I was severely wounded and nearly died. Is there some way to...cut its connection to me? I don't believe it will attack me while angels are present."

Kevara Avlon sighed, tenting her fingers together under her chin, "Even if Bael was strong enough to summon such a thing, we can do nothing to sever its tie to you. In order to do that, we'd have to destroy the Demon himself.

"The Seraphima was created to battle the Presence. *If* this creature exists, it is partly of our world. As such, it would have to be directly exposed to our magic to be destroyed. I *do* apologize."

It sounded as though she was apologizing for stepping on his toes, rather than consigning him to death.

"And there's nothing else? No talisman or charm that might help me?" he pressed.

She sighed again, "I won't rule it out completely, but anything that comes to mind would either be sealed in the Reliquary or would require conditions you do not meet."

"Well, perhaps I might have a look around the Reliquary when I go see Jonas," he said simply.

"Ah, yes," she said, leaning forward. "*Jonas.* I'm sorry to inform you, Lord Captain, that Jonas cannot be allowed to leave the Undercroft. I will be sure to let him know you came, but I'm afraid in his current state, seeing you would only complicate things."

Aleksei frowned, "How so?"

She shrugged, her silver wings flaring behind her, "He's in a fragile state at the moment. He has come to grips with some very unsettling realities. Things have happened to him you cannot imagine."

Aleksei snorted, "I assure you, Lady Angelus, nothing that has happened to him is beyond my imagination. We are Bonded. When he was plunged into the Demonic Presence, I felt it too. It had its own repercussions for me."

"Yes, Lord Captain," she drawled, sounding bored, "but no one gave up their *life* to heal you."

Aleksei felt a certain irony at the statement. He could feel the Mantle thrill across his back at the memories of the people who had died to heal him. He could see flashes of their faces as their lives drained away. A cold ripple thrilled through him.

He resisted the urge to give into his frustration. This game was going nowhere. There had to be a way around this.

"I know Jonas Belgi better than anyone alive," he said softly. "If he's troubled, who better to comfort him? To bring him around? How could my presence be anything but helpful?"

"Because, Lord Captain, it would remind him of the outside world. A world he cannot be allowed to visit ever again. It would bring back all the ugly memories and longings we've worked to wean from him. You are the ultimate symbol of his life in this world. He must now adapt to his new life...without you.

"And even if I thought it *could* be beneficial for him, I would still not allow it. You have admitted to being touched by the Presence too, if in an indirect way. Going through the shield could trap you forever, just as he is trapped now, and I would never do such harm to an ally such as Ilyar. Our realms have been close for *so* long."

Aleksei fought a frown. "Lady Angelus, I'm afraid you miss the true subject at hand. You don't seem to understand how much trouble you're in."

Her luminous blue eyes narrowed to slits, "Are you trying to threaten me, Lord Captain?"

Aleksei's golden eyes flashed, "I am *directly* threatening you and your people for the transgressions you have personally made against the Ilyari royal family and realm of Ilyar itself, no matter how...*close* you believe us to be."

She chuckled, but he heard a hint of anxiety. "What rubbish. You sound like a scared little boy grasping at straws."

She did not meet his eyes.

Aleksei leaned forward. "I have an army of nearly thirty-thousand seasoned soldiers, as well as over three hundred Magi. They're all in Keldoan, right on your border. It would be the work of moments to command them to march on Kuuran."

"I do believe you're in the middle of a civil war, Lord Captain. And even if you *weren't*, I have enough soldiers and angels to obliterate your little army in a flash."

"The vast majority of your army *and* your angels are currently fighting on the Trensed Archipelago in the middle of the Autumn Sea. You have ten thousand soldiers scattered across your realm, and the majority of your angels have never been trained for battle. You've spent so long expecting that Ilyar will blunt any possible threat to your realm, and it shows.

"My Magi survived the sacking of Kalinor, and were instrumental in the destruction of the rebel army at Keldoan, and force twice our size. And that was *before* they embraced a major meridian."

"Making up stories won't get you any closer to your Magus, Lord Captain Drago."

He smiled, "The only stories being spun are the ones your eyes and ears in Ilyar have been sending you. Or should I say, *my* eyes and ears. Your spy network is a joke, and the vast majority of them are on my payroll. But you're in luck! I just told you exactly how many men and Magi I have on your border."

"On what grounds are you declaring war on Dalita?" she snapped.

Good, he was getting to her.

Aleksei wanted her uncomfortable, on edge. She was already quite paranoid; that had nothing to do with him, but he was pleased to see his intelligence was accurate, at least on that front. But he'd need to push her further to get a true sense of what she did and didn't know. She clearly had no idea of his gifts as a Hunter, apparently and appallingly including the Mantle.

It wasn't that surprising, he supposed. It was unlikely she'd ever been aware of an actual living Hunter, depending on how old she *actually* was. But even if the last Hunter had lived during her lifetime, he was reasonably certain Garcelle had never travelled far from the Seil Wood, if at all.

Still, Aleksei wasn't immune to his emotions interfering either. Everything about her enraged him, and that was deeply dangerous, especially considering the power she presently had over Jonas.

He had to fight just to keep the Mantle from shredding his coat and draining every last drop of life from the ancient creature for that alone.

"You sent a Dalitian agent into Ilyari territory with explicit instructions to abduct the Prince of Ilyar, second in line to the throne," he snarled. "You then proceeded to *imprison* him in your gaudy mess of a cathedral.

"You also seem to live under the delusion that you've imprisoned him for *life* based on a personally-held *belief.* I don't recall my Queen receiving so much as an epistle from you *or* your Seraphs, much less consenting to such a scheme.

"As I said before, you don't seem to know the trouble you're in."

"You're surely aware, *Lord Captain*," she practically spat his title, "that *if* this wind demon of yours is indeed real, your people would certainly be none the wiser if I simply had you killed here and now. That would put an end to this sad debacle, yes?" she mused.

Aleksei shrugged, "You could try. But if I don't give the signal to my spies within your Basilica in the next three hours, they will immediately report back to my generals in Keldoan, and *they* will march on Kuuran. Our civil war is all but over. I saw to that personally before heading up here, but I assure you, my generals are extremely capable in their own right."

She'd rebuffed the facts he'd provided, now he hoped she bought the lies he'd carefully woven into the truth.

She arched an eyebrow, "Then bring on your armies. Throw your men and Magi at our cities, and see how they perform. Either way, Jonas is staying right where he is. This is not some personal *vendetta* against your Magus, Lord Captain."

"You cut off his wings, named him the reviled 'Gilded Prince', and attempted to execute him when he was four months old. It's hard to believe you're emotionally detached from this issue."

"Believe what you will, Lord Captain, but any fantasies of heroically rescuing him should vacate your mind immediately. Jonas understands the danger he now poses, and would tell you the same thing, were it safe to allow the two of you to see one another.

"*But,* if it would put your mind at ease, perhaps we can continue this conversation when Andariana arrives in Kuuran. She reached the Admiralty some weeks ago. Assuming she followed your 'orders' and took a ship to Zirvah, she ought to be nearly here by now.

"We really ought to postpone our discussion until she arrives. She must be quite flustered, with the Princess missing. But of course you'd know all about that, wouldn't you?

"Once she arrives, we can all sit down and have a nice, family chat about all of this. You're free to ask for her thoughts on the matter then. In the meantime, you're welcome to wait out her arrival at The Sacred Tree. It's an inn in town where we entertain dignitaries and the like. The stable master will give you a writ as you go."

Aleksei fought to keep his jaw from clenching so hard his teeth shattered, "I have no need of your charity."

She laughed, "Oh, my dear Lord Captain, you are entertaining. No, this is merely to ensure your admittance. Without it, looking as you do, I have no doubt you'd be turned away immediately."

He clenched his fists, his nails cutting into his skin. His face remained calm, despite the storm growing within him. She was playing for time while attempting to display the competency of her own intelligence officers. Once Andariana reached the Basilica, she would essentially be Kevara's political prisoner until the Angelus decided to release her.

If she had, in fact, ever left Taumon.

Should Tamara actually be missing, there was no possible way Andariana would have left on her own to come to Dalita. She'd be firmly planted in Taumon, exhausting whatever resources she had, searching for her daughter.

The fact that Kevara Avlon believed Andariana to be on her way to Kuuran suggested that his spies had, in fact, been successful thus far in obfuscating the truth. The account of Tamara's abduction, however, was the most unwelcome news at the worst possible time. And Kevara Avlon certainly believed it. There was no guile in her pronouncement.

He needed to get Jonas back now more than ever.

"If the Princess is indeed missing, it's a grim possibility that you now hold the heir to the throne of Ilyar in your Undercroft. I greatly look forward to our continued conversation once Her Majesty has arrived," he said finally, forcing himself not to grit his teeth. "I can see that this has been very well thought through. I thank you for taking our interests to heart."

She gave a slight nod of her head. Her face dropped into an expression of concern, "I *do* hope to see you again, once Andariana has arrived to clarify the matter. I'm sure you'll understand if I ask you to remain in Kuuran until then."

Aleksei bowed his head. "Completely. My thanks for your time."

CHAPTER 19

SERPENTS AND SERAPHS

Aleksei's response surprised Kevara Avlon once again. He ignored her smug expression, turning on his heel and walking out the door. When it closed behind him, he took a deep breath. He had played by her rules, but that was clearly not going to work. He rubbed his eyes and yawned, his eyes tearing up.

He walked down the stairs.

Xavathan stood, "Well?"

Aleksei gave the angel a sad half-smile. "Let's go," he managed, swallowing, "I just want to be away from this place."

The angel placed a fatherly hand on Aleksei's shoulder and escorted him out of the palace. The flight across the pool was just as swift as it had been the first time, though Aleksei needed all the time he could get to think.

It had to be perfect.

When they landed Aleksei sniffed, acting as though he was on the brink of tears and glanced at the sky. He turned north.

"Where are you going?"

Aleksei turned back, "I assume the Undercroft is to the north?"

Xavathan frowned, "The Angelus warned me that in no way were you to be allowed anywhere *near* the Undercroft. What could you have possibly said to change her mind on such a thing?"

Aleksei looked away from the angel, the slight sob that rippled across him more genuine than he had anticipated. "I asked for one last good-bye. A final chance to tell the man I love how I feel, and how I will cherish his memory till the end of my days."

Xavathan stared at him a long moment, a look of pity manifesting in the wrinkles of his face, "I'm sorry, boy. I truly am, but I can tell when you're lying. And even if I couldn't, I know my mother all too well. I can't let you near the Undercroft *or* Jonas. And that's the way it must be."

Aleksei just stared at the angel. His heart absorbed the angel's words like a punch in the face. He felt the crush of hopelessness and frustrated rage rising within him. And then he fought it back down.

"Then I have no choice, do I?"

Xavathan quirked a confused frown.

Aleksei barreled on. "You know, I could kill you where you stand, before you could even blink.

"*Believe* me," Aleksei's eyes had regained the all-too-easy, murderous glint that required absolutely no strain on his acting abilities, "I've been weighing it from the second you called out my lie. It would look like an accident. No one would be able to name your cause of death, though the gods know they'd try. But there's a small chance I'd never make it out of this place alive, and that does not suit my purpose. So for now, I'll restrain my impulses."

The angel's face darkened with alarm. Aleksei arched a golden eyebrow, "Am I lying *now*?" Xavathan shook his head slowly. "Then come on. I want to be rid of this place and its blind zealots who think they know what's best for everyone."

Xavathan led him back to the stables silently, still visibly shaken by Aleksei's threat.

For his part, Aleksei kept his face as passive and unmovable as stone. With this newest refusal, he had no intention of providing Xavathan anything but the fear of walking with a man who might change his mind, who might still decide to end his life on a whim. Aleksei had certainly intimated as much, with all the gravity of a broken heart.

When they reached the stables, Xavathan bowed deeply to him.

For all his anger, Aleksei was surprised to see such an act of supplication and respect from a Seraph in the halls of the Basilica.

"My boy, for what it's worth, I apologize. I know you believe my family has wronged you and your Magus. Please know that we do it with the best of intentions. For you, and for the world."

"Your family has not wronged *my* Magus," Aleksei snarled, "Your family has wronged your own. As for your intentions, I couldn't care less about that load of horseshit. I'd no sooner treat with you than a sack of serpents. At least serpents are upfront with their intentions."

Xavathan offered a sad smile, "I hope your anger with me will assuage your pain for a time."

Aleksei shrugged his response, "Sure. Goodbye, Xavathan. You've disappointed me." Aleksei could tell from the angel's face that he knew it, yet it did not alter his willingness to change anything, to go against his mother's orders.

Aleksei swung up into Agriphon's saddle, taking a small token from the Stable Master engraved with a gnarled tree. The sort he would have expected to find near the Heart of a Wood.

He gave the man a friendly nod, pocketing the token, then turned his horse, kicking him into a rough gallop and sending the both of them hurtling through the stables. As massive as the place was, he was quickly out and onto the broad road, leading from the Basilica into Kuuran.

As he entered the city, Aleksei pulled Agriphon back into a trot, his mind teaming with potential possibilities, with strategies.

He was waging a war within the Basilica just as much as he was in Ilyar. Yet the prize here was still within his grasp, as long as he played his cards right. It would take a finer level of delicacy and precision, but he was undeterred by his encounter with Kevara Avlon, or with Xavathan's refusal to aid him.

Aleksei stopped at an inn near the Basilica, but emphatically not the one the Angelus had indicated. He ordered a pint and half a loaf of good bread. Both arrived swiftly, and in spite of himself, Aleksei marveled at the quality. Even with the proximity to the Basilica, he had not expected the inns to be so masterful. It spoke a great deal to him about the need for such places among the richer inhabitants, but away from prying eyes.

After settling his tab, Aleksei moved towards the door, pausing to ask about the fastest route on foot to the Basilica.

"You can't go wrong with the Rite of Supplication," the innkeeper muttered.

Aleksei frowned, "What's that?"

The innkeeper froze from polishing his glass before he shot Aleksei a glare, "Is that supposed to be a joke? If so, it's in very poor taste."

Aleksei affected his best mask of confusion, "I'm so sorry, sir. I'm Ilyari, you see. I'm here to learn as much as I can about the faith of the

One-God, to take it back to Ilyar. But so far I can hardly find anything out at *all*.

"The angels refused to tell me anything of much use, but I want all people to know of the One-God. How am I supposed to do that when I don't know anything myself? And how am I supposed to learn anything myself if no one will tell me?"

The innkeeper glared at him for a long moment before apparently being won over by Aleksei's faked sincerity. "Alright, fine. You have the coin enough, why *shouldn't* you waste it on them? Look, the Rite of Supplication is a pathway that leads from the Ylik Water to the inner depths of the Basilica. I hate to say it, but I mentioned it as a joke. Fools seek the Rite, and most don't come back. Not 'cause it's really dangerous, but 'cause they're so shamed by what they find that they don't dare show their faces 'round here again afterward."

"And what do they find?"

The innkeeper shrugged, "A lot of faithful begging for money, I expect. Maybe some challenges to their faith and whatnot. But mostly money. Lots and *lots* of money. Even most rich folk can't afford it.

"I know stories of a number of small lords and ladies who ended up paupered by trying to pass through. And *they* never made it clear to the other side. Coin is the antidote to faith, or something like that. The more faith you got, the less coin you'll need."

"I see," Aleksei said, considering the man's words. "Well, in any event, I appreciate the information." He slid a silver across to the man.

The innkeeper snorted, "Well, thank you kindly. You sure you won't need this to pass the Rite?"

Aleksei laughed, "Mister, you've just saved me a great deal of money. It's worth me a silver to know where not to go this afternoon."

The innkeeper was still smiling as Aleksei stepped out into the frigid Kuuran air. He took a long moment to think about his next move. The Rite of Supplication sounded ridiculous, and expensive to boot. And he knew he couldn't scale the walls. Whatever shielded the cities from attack undoubtedly protected the Basilica too.

And then the answer struck him. He had to laugh at his slow-witted mind. He'd been around powerful people too long, he decided. That was the quickest poison for sense.

Mentally kicking himself, Aleksei went back to the inn's stable and retrieved Agriphon. He mounted the horse, flipped the stable boy a copper, and headed back up the road towards the Basilica. Its black and gold prominence dominated the cityscape, and Aleksei prepared himself for a fight. Not with swords or Mantle, but with wits. He hoped his were up to the task.

He arrived back at the Basilica's far grander stables, much to the Master Groom's surprise.

"Lord Captain? Back already?"

Aleksei flashed the man a winning smile, "I appear to have forgotten something. My apologies, but I should be out of your way momentarily."

The Master Groom scoffed, "Lord Captain Drago, you are always welcome beneath the roof of the Basilica, in the glory of the One-God. We count your visit among the highest of honors. And arriving with the fourth-born *Seraph*! It was a marvel to see the two of you arrive together, fresh off the road, but companions! The stories I will tell my grandchildren, Lord Captain, you can hardly imagine."

Aleksei allowed himself a genuine grin at the man's enthusiasm. An idea hatched in his head. He stepped forward and lowered his voice, "Then can I let you in on a secret?"

The Master Groom sniffed, his large mustache twitching back and forth much like the bristly combs he used to brush down the horses. "You have my strictest confidence, Lord Captain." Aleksei noted that the man had lowered his voice to match Aleksei's secretive tone.

"Well, you see, it's not so much that I forgot something, but rather that something of great value was taken from me."

The groom's eyebrows shot up, "*Taken*, Lord Captain? Who in the One-God's great world would want to steal from you? And *here* of all places?"

"That's what I came to find out. It might take me a few days to locate the thief. It could be anyone, I suppose, but I'm going to need complete secrecy to narrow down the list of suspects.

"So, can you do me a favor? Can you keep my arrival under your hat until this thief can be brought to justice? Or at least until my treasure is returned? Many lives might depend on your discretion."

The Master Groom looked at once giddy and frightened, but he gave Aleksei a sharp salute, "I will give it my best, Lord Captain, Sir."

Aleksei marveled at the man's behavior. "That's an Ilyari field salute. How did you—"

"Begging your pardon, Lord Captain. I was a Legionnaire in my younger days. Married a girl from Kuuran after I got out, and here I stand. I'm much older, but my allegiances know their place. I could *hardly* turn down the Lord Captain even if I wanted to, Sir."

Aleksei's grin resurfaced, and he returned the man's salute crisply, "Your loyalty is most appreciated. But please do not compromise your job on my behalf."

The Master Groom shrugged, "Can't say as I know how such a thing'd happen, Lord Captain. I go about my business, take care of your beautiful horse, keep my mouth shut, and you catch a thief. I'll just be doing my duty, Sir, same as always."

Aleksei smiled broadly and gave the other man a nod before flipping him a gold piece. "See that he's ready to ride when you see me again. And thank you."

The groom saluted again, "For Queen and Country, Lord Captain."

"For Queen and Country."

Aleksei walked through the halls of the Basilica, taking random turns and twists, but scrupulously avoiding any passage that would take him either towards the Fount or the Undercroft. Now that he'd walked the halls and passages of the Basilica, he didn't feel nearly as lost, and his Hunter skills were able to grant him some guidance. It was far from perfect, but at least he had his bearings.

After walking for a rough hour, he stopped a butler as the man headed towards a set of servant's stairs. The man appeared affronted at being approached, which was the first time Aleksei realized how dirty he must be, and how bad he must smell.

"I apologize, sir," he began calmly, "but I'm afraid I'm completely turned around. How would I find the library?"

"And *why* would you be seeking the libraries?"

Aleksei felt his frustration mount, "Because I believe the Angel Leigha might be there, and I would very much like to speak with her."

The butler frowned at that, "*You* want an audience with the first-born Cherub?"

Aleksei blinked in confusion and consternation, "That's what I just said. Yes, I want an audience with Leigha. She's my cousin, after a fashion, and I'm afraid it's a matter of great urgency."

The butler rolled his eyes, "And I suppose this is a matter of life and death."

"Yes," Aleksei said earnestly, "that's *exactly* what it is. Except that if I don't hurry, it's not Leigha's life that will be forfeit. That life belongs to the man I love. A man who means more to me than anything else in this world or the next.

"I have reason to believe that Leigha can help me save him. But she can't do that if I can't *find* her, and every moment I spend talking to *you* is one that could be spent saving *him*. So please, sir, will you help me?"

The butler stared at Aleksei for a long moment in utter shock. Aleksei wondered when the last time was that anyone spoke to him with real feeling, with genuine love, and genuine pain.

"Follow me," the butler said simply after torturing Aleksei for a handful of heartbeats.

Aleksei walked behind the butler, trying his best not to outpace the man, or goad him into walking faster. The journey was a relatively short one, but even as the butler navigated the hallways, Aleksei knew deep down that he would never have found her on his own.

Honestly, he wasn't even sure she would help him. He had liked Xavathan well enough, and yet when the situation had turned not only dire, but grossly unfair, Xavathan had been unmoved by Aleksei's plea for compassion. Faith ruled reason in the Basilica, it seemed. Aleksei had no time for such nonsense, and as far as he was aware, Jonas had less still.

Leigha was his last hope at cajoling any Angelic favor. If she refused him, he would likely be escorted not only from the Basilica, but from Kuuran itself.

It would take a great feat of strength and stealth to get back into the Basilica after such an exile, and greater feats still to get into the Undercroft. He had no doubt that such a place would be heavily guarded, and while he would kill anyone in his way if necessary, Aleksei desperately wanted to avoid taking innocent lives if he could.

The butler stopped before a plain door at the end of a long corridor, populated on either side by doors of every sort imaginable, some decked with gilt and filigree, others spelled so heavily that a pall of cloud blocked any sign of wood or metal. Some shone while others seemed to drink in the candlelight providing the hallway with a gentle glow.

"I wish you luck, sir," the butler said dryly. "The One-God give you strength. You may need it."

And with that, the man turned and walked away, leaving Aleksei uncertain before a simple door in a sea of magic and confusion. He gathered his resolve and knocked.

He heard a rustle from behind the door, and his ears picked up two heartbeats. For some reason, he knew neither were human. Perhaps it was the butler's steady heartbeat, retreating through the corridors and moving further and further from Aleksei. The rhythm and thump of his heart, of Aleksei's heart, were distinctively different from the hearts beyond the door.

Before he could arrive at a conclusion, the door swung open and he found himself staring down into the confused gray eyes of a large male angel.

"What?" the angel demanded.

"Leigha," Aleksei said, in rough challenge to the man, "I'm looking for the Cherub Leigha."

"*Why?*" the angel demanded, before he was gently pulled aside by one of the most beautiful women Aleksei had ever seen. Her eyes were large and warm, bright brown, but a shade unlike any he'd seen before. Warm and brown, like fur, he decided. Soft and inviting.

"You must pardon my friend, sir. Brahm is...protective at times." Her smile was luminous, her voice like silver bells. If Aleksei had not been so deeply in love already, he felt as though he might have been in trouble.

But his better sense finally kicked in, and he proffered a counter smile. "Milady," he said, gazing deep into her eyes, "my name is Aleksei Drago. I am the Lord Captain—"

He had hardly begun when she reached out and gripped the front of his shirt, pulling him roughly into her chambers and slamming the door shut. A shiver ran through him as one of the angels invoked their queer magic.

It was the Archanium, but he'd never felt it used this way before. A shimmer of icy light washed across the door before Leigha turned to stare at him, her eyes flickering between anger, alarm, and sympathy.

"Why," she finally managed, her hands trembling as she raised them and pushed back her voluminous chocolate hair, "why are you here? What are you *doing* here, Lord Captain? Who sent you?"

Aleksei laughed at her confusion. Not out of malice, but because he empathized with her perfectly in that moment.

"I'll make this simple, Angelica. I am here to free Jonas from his prison. No one *sent* me, I came by myself to get Jonas back. I am here for two reasons. The first is because your people have imprisoned the prince of our realm, the man I love, behind an impossible wall of magic. I have a *problem* with that.

"Not only is he sealed away from the rest of the world, but according to your grandmother, he's also sealed off from *me*. I can't abide that. Our bond is gone. Our bond is gone, and I am being hunted by a wind demon. Or spirit, or spell. I don't know. I don't bloody *care*, because without Jonas around, the next time it shows itself I will likely die. *That* is why I am here. That is what I'm doing here. I'm trying to save him, Leigha," his voice cracking, "and I'm trying to save myself."

She stared at him as tears finally welled up in his golden eyes, spilling over his eyelids and dripping from his chin. If she had been confused before, now she appeared merely appalled.

"And why have you not seen the Angelus about your concerns?" Brahm demanded.

Aleksei turned his gaze to the burly angel, his rage returning, "Kevara Avlon and I had our talk. Her logic is flawed, and her decision is to no one's liking but her own. I decided to let the royal family have another crack at the problem.

"I asked Xavathan for his aid. I used reason, I used *love*. He in turn tried to use that love to shatter my resolve." He looked back at Leigha, who was now hiding her true emotions behind a stony mask, one possibly erected out of self-preservation. "So, what do you say, Leigha? I know your name because Jonas never tired of singing your praises, although between us, I'd leave the singing to you. If there's one trait that he didn't inherit through his Angelic blood, that would be it."

He saw a crack in the facade, a twitch that could lead to a smile.

"I know I'm asking a lot of you. This can't be easy, but it's *important*. Gods, I don't think I can possibly explain how important it is, not just for me, or for Ilyar, but—"

"STOP!" Leigha commanded. Aleksei froze, staring at her, watching her face, ready for her eyes to betray her intentions. "For the love of God, stop *talking*!"

Aleksei frowned, truly at a loss for the first time since arriving in Dalita. "Beg your pardon?"

Leigha slumped into a chair, her ivory wings flaring behind her, "Good *God*, but you can talk! You must realize that you're rambling like a madman. A storm of words will not serve you well, or prove your worth to me. I believe, in the midst of all that, you asked me a question. Am I correct?"

Aleksei sat down on the heavily upholstered poof across from her, "I asked you to help me."

She raised a hand, lest he continue his rant. "Well, you never asked me that directly, but *fine*...you want me to help you free Jonas. I know you have many reasons for wanting him back. God knows, *I* want him back. I'd like, at the very least, to be able to visit him. But it is forbidden."

Aleksei straightened, "You're not allowed to see him? That's ridiculous! You're his cousin, and a Cherub on top of that. What harm could seeing you present?"

Leigha shrugged, "I really have no idea. I don't. But my grandmother was quite firm on that point. I think she believes that if Jonas sees anything that reminds him of the freedom he used to have, he'll snap and either try to get out or just go mad in his confinement. Either way, she believes there's a good chance innocent people will die, and an even greater chance that the Demonic Presence might be unleashed through him in a manner never seen before, not through Cassian, and certainly never through *Bael*. Due to his...unusual placement in the Archanium, the Angelus believes he poses a unique threat to our world."

Aleksei snorted, "Kevara Avlon has a *very* limited understanding of my Magus, then. Anyone who knows him, who has seen his abilities, would immediately see how stupid such ideas are."

"Now that's just about enough!" the immense angel snarled, striding towards Aleksei.

With the sound of rending cloth and leather, a thick rope of the Mantle tore free of Aleksei's shoulder and spiraled towards Brahm's face, halting just before sinking in, its taloned paws lightly scraping at the handsome angel's cheek. The angel froze, but Aleksei's eyes never left Leigha's.

"I appreciate your willingness to defend the Angelus, Brahm. But understand this; I am not here to respect the Angelus, nor am I interested in making her *happy*. In fact, what I am proposing will make her infinitely *un*happy. If you have a problem with that, if that upsets you, and you want to run to her right now, then it'll just be faster to kill you. *If*, however, you'd like to hear what I have to say, then I can allow you to live. Am I clear?"

Aleksei felt Brahm's nod through the Mantle. Slowly, he allowed the tendril to unwind and slither back to his shoulder. He hadn't willed the Mantle to strike like that, but he was relieved when it heeded his call to withdraw. This conversation had very nearly taken an inexcusable turn.

Leigha watched the whole thing with an angry pout outlined on her full lips, her eyes studying him.

When Aleksei turned his attention back to her, she arched a chestnut eyebrow, "Lord Captain Drago, while I understand that your situation is painful, it does not give you license to go around threatening my friends.

"Brahm has as much a stake in this as you, whether you believe it or not. It would be to your advantage to treat him as an ally, even if he *can* be a bit coarse."

Brahm looked at her in furious shock, but Aleksei simply watched her. He knew manipulation when he saw it, even when it was as careful and crafted as Leigha's. It reminded him painfully of his prince.

"Tell me," Aleksei said, his voice rumbling into a growl, "exactly how it is that *you* have as much at stake as *I* do."

It was Brahm's turn to offer a superior smirk, but one haunted by a mirror of Aleksei's own pain.

"You aren't the only one whose love is trapped behind a prison, Lord Captain. When the Angelus crafted her trap for Jonas Belgi in the Undercroft, she knew that unless she found a replacement for you, the trap would never completely close. So, she selected an angel she thought might sway Jonas from your bed."

Aleksei felt rage flare inside him anew. From the tear in his coat, angry threads of the Mantle oozed out, black and blood-red, licking the air like serpents on a scent. He felt the desperate need to *feed*, to steal life, and watch the spark of animation slowly extinguish in his victim's eyes.

And then, with the greatest of efforts, he forced it all far away from his rational mind. He couldn't afford such carelessness now, not when he was this close to Jonas.

"And this angel," Aleksei said finally, "this angel is...."

"As important to me as Jonas is to you," Brahm finished. "Adam is my world. He is *everything* to me, and I to him. But, because he was so well suited to *me*, the Angelus decided he would suit Prince Belgi just as well. So she took him from me."

Aleksei's frown deepened, "*Took* him from you?"

"The Angelus has enormous power, not only over the Host as whole, but over every angel," Leigha said softly. "Sometimes, when the need is great, the Angelus will order an angel to perform a duty or task or rite, whatever is required.

"In Brahm's case, the Angelus commanded Adam to find Jonas and bring him back here. Adam did as he was told, and at the time, he thought that was the end of his trial.

"But once Jonas was safely behind the shield, she decided that he needed an anchor, something to keep him occupied...*satisfied* while he was newly in captivity. So she sent Adam to be that anchor, to satisfy Jonas and to give him someone to hold onto when the loneliness threatened her plans. Jonas already knew Adam, so—"

"So she took him from me," Brahm grunted. "She didn't ask. She literally swept into our rooms and commanded him to get dressed. And then she took him away. I haven't seen him since. I'm not *allowed* to see him."

Brahm kept speaking, tears gathering in his eyes. "Because it might disrupt his focus. He might start thinking about the outside world and forget his mission.

"For that reason, I've been banished from the atriums in the Undercroft. I'm allowed to guard them, and to venture into the outer corridors, but nothing beyond. Sometimes I walk the corridors just hoping he might walk by, but so far...."

Aleksei nodded slowly, "Alright, I understand. *Believe* me, I understand. But this is why I need your help. If I can get inside that shield, I'm certain I can fix all of this."

"How?" Leigha asked, quirking her head to the side in a display of genuine curiosity.

Aleksei ran his hand through his golden hair, longer now than he preferred, nearly past his eyes and tangled with road dust and sweat. He was so very tired, so sick of missing Jonas, missing their bond, missing the other man beside him in the night. Half of him was absent. It was all he could do to bring the words forth.

"I don't know."

CHAPTER 20

ON A WING

A ya sat on the bed, her knees crossed. She looked into Ilyana's watery blue eyes and smiled. She hoped her smile reassured the other woman. She hoped it conveyed a sense of confidence and expertise, because Aya felt none of those things. She was terrified.

For her part, Ilyana sat with her back straight and her chin raised. She sat as she would have for their previous master, Sammul, as one waiting to receive knowledge. And yet what Aya was about to attempt would have enraged Sammul, even as he quaked in his boots.

"I'm not quite sure how to go about this," Aya finally admitted.

Ilyana smiled warmly, "Just do whatever feels natural. You aren't actually afraid this will hurt me, are you? You're the one who had the divine initiation, Aya, and you're perfectly fine. Just use your instincts. If it feels like it's going in the wrong direction, just withdraw from the Sphere."

Aya returned Ilyana's smile, glad that the other woman was so understanding, hoping her trust wasn't misplaced. Aya had spent sleepless nights, worried and scared about teaching this new method to others.

What if she couldn't? What if she tried and failed? There was a far greater power along this new meridian, but there could be greater danger as well. She desperately wanted to protect her friends while gifting them this new-found faculty. But she was terrified that in trying, it might destroy them.

That Ilyana had volunteered to be the first to learn only increased her anxiety. She was no longer just risking an ally, but a dear friend. She and Ilyana had arrived in the Voralla only weeks apart, and had spent years rooming together. She might as well be trying to train her sister. A sister she might be about to accidentally murder. Even should Ilyana survive, she might never touch the Archanium again.

"Stop fussing," Ilyana snapped playfully. "We've discussed the para-meters, and they all work out fine. Just cast the spell as we discussed, and we'll see what happens. If it starts to go wrong, you can always sever the tie."

Aya sighed, trying to mask her hesitation. Ilyana made it sound so simple, yet the woman hadn't felt the power Aya now commanded. She didn't understand its complexities, its nuances, its potential. The gods be cursed, *Aya* hardly even grasped how it all worked. She felt like she was flailing in a sea of sharks.

Ilyana, riding along her minor meridian, never having felt the glorious maelstrom of a major meridian, couldn't possibly grasp what Aya was dealing with.

Clenching her jaw, Aya finally made up her mind. She could hardly rail against a woman who was so eager to join her, even if she didn't know what she was getting into. If Ilyana didn't understand what it was like, Aya simply had to show her.

Aya reached out her hand and clutched Ilyana's delicate fingers. The other woman's eyes snapped wide as the binding spell flooded through her. Aya inhaled stiffly as Ilyana's power twinned with her own. She felt like a mother bird coddling a fledgling into flight. The difference in their abilities was staggering.

And yet there was a similarity.

Aya dove into the Great Sphere, searching for the common thread that connected Ilyana's meridian with her own. It was disorienting, viewing Ilyana's weaker connection to the Archanium in such a way. It was like being held upside down in a raging river. She gasped as she reached towards the spark that was Ilyana's own presence in the Archanium.

Ever so gently, she invoked a second spellform within the Sphere itself. Such spells were generally difficult to perform, but she and Jonas had spent some time exploring them. She had seen him use similar magic to kill enemy Magi, snuffing their connection to the Archanium. She conjured a similar spell, hooking Ilyana's spark and dragging it towards herself.

Aya took care to guide Ilyana's spark through the routes where their meridians intersected. It was like pulling a wagon across a pathway, if that pathway was carved across a treacherous, icy cliff.

With the suddenness of breaking glass, Ilyana's spark leapt onto her meridian, power previously unknown infusing her spark with celestial luminosity.

She gave a cry of relief as their tie dissolved. Even as Aya dropped onto her back, she heard Ilyana gasping for air.

She was far too tired to lift herself, but even from her position she could still see the light infusing the other woman's flesh. Ilyana glowed like a distant star, her mouth open, gasping as the power of the Archanium crashed through her. Tears seeped from her eyes, but the woman seemed oblivious to everything but the sheer rapture surging through her.

"It's like touching the *gods*...like *being* a god!" Ilyana whispered.

Aya allowed herself a small, satisfied smile. She understood the sentiment completely. It was certainly like touching the divine in a singularly peculiar way. She took a deep breath and finally managed to push herself back up.

Ilyana stared at her for a long moment before lunging forward, tackling Aya in a heartfelt hug. Aya burst out laughing at the sudden display of childlike affection.

Ilyana kissed her cheek a dozen times, her own mirth bursting forth.

"You *marvelous* creature!" Ilyana cried, clasping Aya's exhausted form against her, "You glorious woman, what have you *done* to me? How...how is this even *possible?*"

Aya's laughter faded into a smile, "I think you're now worthy of your title, Magus Ilyana."

Ilyana's face lit up with understanding. "You're right. This must be what it means to *truly* command the Archanium. Gods, what foundering whelps we were before the might of *this*. I worked so hard to master Sammul's basic exercises, and all along we could have been using *real* magic, mustering true *power*."

"And now we can, sister."

Ilyana beamed back at her, "We must show the others. We have to show them what *potential* we all have!"

Aya opened her mouth to speak, but Ilyana suddenly held up a hand, "But not yet. Not until we know more. Not until we have more experience...more *control*. I've hardly *touched* this meridian, and even *I* recognize its inherent danger."

Aya frowned, "What?"

Ilyana's eyes were now lit with a different fire, "Aya, how well do you understand the power you now command?"

Aya shrugged, "I'm not sure. Not all that well, I suppose. There's so *much* to it. So much I have yet to learn."

Ilyana nodded, her eyes distracted. "Precisely. We ought to study this a bit more before we teach the others. We need to know what it is we're handing out, to understand the nature of this beast before we unleash it."

Aya shrugged, "I suppose that's as sound an idea as any."

Ilyana nodded. Aya could feel the other woman still tenaciously clinging to the Archanium. "We are now the keepers of something greater." She took a deep breath, her brow creased in concentration, "I think I'm going to spend some time alone, practicing."

She glanced up, her eyes now piercing in their intensity, "Nothing more than a day though."

Aya frowned, "Only a day?"

Ilyana nodded, her eyes now distant, as though she were scrying the future like a Prophet. "Aleksei said he wanted all those rebel corpses to vanish, right?"

Aya nodded, trying to see where Ilyana was going with this. Gods, but she was exhausted. "But I'm not sure he was in his right mind when he gave that order."

"Perhaps before, yes, that would have been near impossible. But *now?* Now, we have the perfect training opportunity!"

Aya's eyes lit up as it hit her. "Gods, you're *right*. For every Magus we usher onto this meridian, there's a perfect training exercise just waiting to be exploited. If we have each of them work out how to use their new gifts on those bodies...they could all keep notes with coordinates and particulars for every spellform they discover, and its effects. And since they're experimenting on the dead, it's not like they can hurt anyone. There are so many potential applications...."

Ilyana giggled, "You're already off to the races, aren't you?"

Aya snapped back to reality, frowning, "What? Is there something I'm missing?"

Ilyana shook her head, "No, dear girl, I think it's *perfect*. And you're right, there are so many possibilities. I never imagined I would be so excited to have tens of thousands of corpses for the entire Voralla to experiment on, but here we are, and there *they* are. Aleksei ordered us to make those bodies disappear. Before this, I had no idea how we were supposed to accomplish that. But now...?

"Let's take a day to recover, and to experiment. And then we can start bringing the others onto this new path. And once they recover, it'll be down the road to help deal with all the frozen corpses the Legionnaires so conveniently piled up for us. Only following the Lord Captain's orders, of course."

Aya laughed, even as her head swam with fantasies and fatigue, "Of course."

Ilyana's smile brightened. She leaned forward and kissed Aya's cheek again, "Thank you for the gift, sister. I could never pay it back."

The whisper was so honest it brought tears to Aya's eyes. She lay back against the heavy quilt, drifting in and out of sleep long after Ilyana left.

After a while, Raefan walked into the room, stripping off his shirt and crawling in next to her, enfolding her in his big arms. She knew he was fresh from sword practice. She could smell his sweat, could feel his hot breath on the back of her neck as he cradled her.

It had never felt so good to have him next to her.

Unlike any other, he understood what she'd just done, and what it had cost her. She dissolved into his arms, feeling the protection he offered surrounding her, cradling her. In that iron embrace, she finally allowed herself to drift into a deep and dreamless sleep.

"Are you sure you're ready for this?"

Aleksei returned Brahm's earnest question with a glare. "I'll be fine."

Brahm's sincerity evaporated in the heat of his own irritation, "You could die in this attempt. If I can't keep you aloft—"

"Then I'll have something to hold onto on the way down," Aleksei snapped. The thick black cords writhing across his chest and tearing at his wrists with blood-red talons served as an unsettling reminder that only a fool could ignore. Their effect was not lost on the angel.

"Easy, boys," Leigha said calmly, pulling on a suede boot. "Brahm, you're not going to drop him and you know it. You've flown this pattern a thousand times. Aleksei, if he drops you, you have my permission to drain every drop of blood, or life, *whatever* it is you drink with that demonic thing on your back, out of his feathered husk."

Brahm stared at her in alarm, but she met his gaze with an ice-cold return.

"We all have a stake in this, I no less than the two of you. I'm taking great risks here. Risks that could likely bear just as dire consequences for me as for you. It's all well and good for you two to talk about tortured love, but you aren't the only ones who could have your lives changed by what we do tonight."

"Then why are you doing this?" Aleksei asked, strapping the leather harness across his chest. "You have no real stake in this."

Leigha laughed harshly, and for the first time Aleksei saw her as a vulnerable individual, not as a priestess or an impossible princess. She was putting herself in harm's way, one way or another. And she was doing it for Adam. For Jonas. For him. He loved her for that alone. Whatever happened as a result, he knew he would protect her. He was honor-bound to her now, whatever the outcome.

"I should be able to walk past the exterior guards without question, but getting into the Undercroft itself is going to be a challenge," she continued, apparently ignoring his remarks.

"Why can't I just run past the shield?" Aleksei asked, keeping his tone as calm as her own.

"Because," she said softly, pulling on a second boot, "*you* still have a lingering thread of the Presence linked to your bond with Jonas. When you pass through the shield, your bond will be connected again. If you try to leave and the shield recognizes the Presence, which I daresay it *will*, you'll be as trapped as Jonas. And there'll be no guarantee that we'd be able to get either you out, much less the *both* of you."

"I could live with that," Aleksei growled.

"No, you *can't*," Leigha snapped, silencing Aleksei's forming rebuttal. "You can't because *we* can't afford to lose you. It might be sunshine and rainbows for you to be with Jonas again, but your possible, permanent imprisonment is *not* a viable option.

"Besides the rebellion in Ilyar, the Demon is roaming this world, free of challenge. Except for you. You are the only man who has withstood his attacks, has fought him face-to-face, has challenged him and *survived*."

"Except for Jonas," Aleksei reminded her.

"Jonas has fought the Demon, but Jonas was wounded in his fight. You've been wounded, yes, but only by association. You are invaluable in this war. You possess unique gifts that *cannot* be locked away for eternity, no matter how deep your love.

"And one way or another, as it grows in strength, *believe* me, the Demon will come for you. He hates my cousin, and you, from what you've told me of this 'wind demon' and its attacks against you. It will come for you eventually, and you will be powerless against it."

Aleksei looked down at the floor, angry that he'd been dressed down so effectively. He had no words to rebut her. She was right, and he silently resented her for putting words to truth. At this point, all he wanted was to be with Jonas, but she had sharply reminded him that there was so much more at stake here than his ultimately selfish yearning to be reunited with his prince.

"So, if I don't run in, how are we going to get past the guard at the shield?" he demanded instead.

"One of us will distract the guard, depending on who it is. Hopefully, either Brahm or I will know the angel well enough to effectively draw them from their post. Whichever it is, the other will enter the gate with you. Our presence will confuse the shield so that you can enter without it recognizing you specifically.

"The shield is powerful, but it has no mind of its own. An Angelic connection to the Seraphima is enough to cancel out the fledgling connection you hold to the Presence. It won't notice under the circumstances. Just make sure you're touching whichever one of us you enter with. That should be enough."

"*Should* be?"

Leigha matched his gaze, "As I said, we're all taking risks here."

Aleksei secured the last leather strap across his chest, tightening the buckles and rolling his shoulders in the uncomfortable contraption. His arms, back, and chest were covered in thick leather straps, each one fastened together to provide Brahm adequate grip.

When Aleksei had asked Brahm about the contraption, he'd been curtly told that they would be flying between the upper layers of the shields that protected the Basilica. One ill-timed move could kill one or both of them. The training harness gave Brahm a better grip for the more delicate maneuvering.

"How did you even figure out you could *do* this?" Aleksei asked, as Brahm plucked out loose feathers and pulled his boots on.

Both Brahm and Leigha glanced at each other before Brahm answered, "When you grow up here, you figure out certain...technicalities. Bored children will find a way past nearly anything. I'm placing a lot of faith on the idea that the Angelus won't have considered such a possibility. If she's shifted the shields, we'll both be dead before you have a chance to drink me dry.

"We've talked it over, however, and we're both confident that such an eventuality likely hasn't occurred to her. Neither of us were caught dodging shields when we were fledglings, and she has no reason to think you'd come to either of us after Xavathan dismissed you from the Basilica. But we're taking a lot on faith here."

"You're telling me," Aleksei grumbled. "So why is it called the Undercroft, of all things? Isn't that supposed to be where you take your dead?"

Leigha rolled her eyes, "Because calling it the 'Eternal Prison for Tainted Magical Persons and Enemies of State' sounds less enticing. And the people we, *she,* imprisons there aren't exactly expected to come out alive. Also, we place many of our dead in crypts, yes, but those are located in the catacombs. If you ever return for some reason, do *not* go into the catacombs. *Ever.* If you think going into the Undercroft is dangerous...."

She walked to the door and embraced the Archanium. As always, Aleksei felt a small shiver pass through him. Summoning the Song was nothing like having his Magus dive into the Great Sphere. No matter how often he felt them embrace the Song, he still found the effect strange and disorienting. *Unnatural.*

"Alright, Brahm, take him from the balcony. I'm going to head towards the library. Unless someone stops me, I should be walking past the guards roughly at the time you're landing in front of the Undercroft. I'll meet you there. I'll try to spot the guard before I head for the fountain."

Brahm nodded. Aleksei just wished he had any idea what they were talking about. The Basilica was enormous. The more he saw of it, the more he realized it was really a city unto itself underneath the same roof. Kuuran was merely where the peasants and human nobility lived.

But for the angels, the Basilica was home in so many more ways than he'd first imagined. For Leigha and Brahm, it was the only world they'd ever really known. He just prayed that their familiarity got him that much closer to his goal.

He followed Brahm to the balcony, placing a boot on the marble railing. The Basilica stretched downwards towards the flood plain, nearly three hundred paces beneath him. The idea that he was going to entrust his life to Brahm's steady grip suddenly filled him with terror. It would only take one slip for him to vanish into the void without anyone knowing.

He wondered if Jonas would even know.

The Mantle rippled across his flesh. It was particularly unpredictable of late; he felt less in control of it than ever, especially since reaching Kuuran. He supposed he'd have to ask the Wood about that the next time he was close enough to speak with Her.

Brahm stepped behind him and gripped the harness. "Ready?"

Aleksei gave a curt nod, pushing any thoughts besides those of his mission from his mind. He had to stay focused.

Brahm's golden wings flapped experimentally a few times, and then with a gut-wrenching jolt the two men were aloft, the earth spinning dizzily beneath Aleksei's boots. He watched the balcony fade away in the midnight mist, watched the precipitation cling to his boots and his bare skin as they broke through the clouds.

Despite his dislike for the angel bearing him, he was impressed that Brahm seemed to be showing no signs of real exertion yet. He supposed he ought to be grateful that Leigha happened to be childhood friends with such a large, powerful angel. Anyone smaller might not have been able to bear his weight through the trial that was to come.

"You might want to look ahead for this next bit," Brahm grunted in his ear. "Try not to get sick on the way."

Aleksei frowned at that last statement a heartbeat before Brahm gave a powerful push with his wings, and they went spiraling down towards the Basilica at a terrifying rate. Riding the fastest horse imaginable at a full gallop couldn't possibly compare to this. There was a taut snap as Brahm pulled his wings behind himself, and he and Aleksei plummeted towards the Undercroft of the Basilica.

As they fell, Brahm opened one wing and then the other with frightening speed, sending them both into a corkscrew, only to suddenly be righted with the next snap of his wing. Aleksei felt ripples of heat and cold flash through him as they fell. He could feel the intense electricity of the shields passing between them, and Aleksei had no doubt that what Brahm was doing was exceptionally dangerous.

Brahm suddenly dropped a few hundred paces, then stretched his wings out to stop them so sharply, Aleksei could feel his teeth rattle in his skull, his weight pulling heavily on the harness.

The flight felt like it lasted hours, even though Aleksei knew it was only a few minutes. By the time they landed smoothly beside a gloriously large fountain, Aleksei felt like he was going to retch. Brahm had not lied in his warning.

The angel patted him roughly on the back, "You handled that rather well."

Aleksei managed a smile, the swell of pride he felt at the compliment clashing with the nausea coursing through him. It had been the singularly most terrifying moment of his life, and that included running from Demon fire, standing on the highest tower of the Drakleyn in a snow storm, and battling a Salamander in the dark.

Leigha stepped gracefully from the shadow of the fountain, startling both men with her silent arrival.

"I'm afraid I have bad news," she said softly.

Aleksei tensed for what he was about to hear.

"I saw the guard," she continued. She turned her brown-eyed gaze to Brahm, "I'm sorry. I'm *so* sorry, but it's Adam."

CHAPTER 21
KINDNESS CAN BE CRUEL

A leksei glanced between the two angels, "So what does this mean, exactly?"

"*I* have to go. I'll have to be the one to distract him," Brahm's voice came out as little more than a dry rattle. He was still staring at Leigha, "He's never going to forgive me for this."

Tears were brimming in her eyes, "I know, darling. Believe me, I know. But you know why this has to happen."

The big angel gave a curt nod. Aleksei recognized the look on his face. He'd worn the same mask many times himself. It was a face that spoke of duty above base human concerns, one that sought to be something nobler than the mere man who held it, and one that spoke volumes of pain, of love.

Brahm stepped past Aleksei without a word. Through the cascades of icy water, Aleksei saw Brahm approach the other angel. Through the water, Aleksei saw Adam, and he understood Kevara Avlon's insidious nature on a different level.

The man was handsome. Too handsome. He was youthful and seemed untouched by the world beyond. This was not a man hardened in the heat of battle. This was a *boy*. The sort who could make Jonas forget about the world beyond.

And, given time and desperation, the sort who could make Jonas forget about him.

Aleksei felt his rage erupt, cannoning through every wall he'd raised, every barrier he'd erected to keep his emotions in check, to maintain his sanity in such an impossible situation.

The Mantle wriggled and writhed in anticipation of the violence to come. It was only with the greatest of efforts that he forced the Mantle into the back of his mind. There would be no feeding, not now. Not here, with Jonas so close.

But he was also quickly realizing the flaws in Leigha's plan. His mind raced as he calculated the distance between himself and the shield. It would take Adam only a thought to throw him back if he was detected. And from the looks of the conversation Brahm was attempting with the other angel, he doubted he would slip by unnoticed, even with Leigha. *Especially* with Leigha.

"This isn't going to work," he growled.

Leigha glanced over at him, startled. "Excuse me?"

He turned his golden-eyed gaze on her, his irises flashing in the moonlight, "We're too far. There's too much open ground between the fountain and the shield. Adam could sound the alarm before we're halfway there. He might try to stop me. If he does, I *will* kill him."

That last statement finally bought alarm to Leigha's face. "Good God, Aleksei. You never mentioned *killing* anyone."

His response came out as a feral growl, "Your people are keeping Jonas from me. Be thankful there hasn't been any bloodshed thus far. Count yourselves lucky I didn't march on Kuuran with an army. At this point, I would count a single fatality as a victory for your side."

Her hand gripped his bare shoulder painfully. He glared at her and saw her luminous eyes boring into his. "I am on *your* side, Aleksei Drago. I am risking more than your tiny Ilyari mind can possibly appreciate to get you past that shield. So stop comparing me to Kevara Avlon and tell me what you want to *do*."

Aleksei allowed himself to be reprimanded, using the time to think. He watched Adam's body language, his chest puffed out as he argued with Brahm. He watched Brahm's larger form as the man tried to reason with the younger angel.

He glanced at Leigha, "I want you to walk right out from behind the fountain. I want you to approach them, and I want you to try to resolve their argument. Be reasonable. Be sweet. But for the love of the gods, get Adam as close to that archway as you possibly can."

Leigha frowned, "Why?"

Aleksei heard the word from far away, whispered through the eddies of the fountain. He slid through the shadows, dancing around the moonlight and gliding through patches of twilight. As he neared the other side of the black marble archway, he saw with relief that Leigha was engaging the two men.

Her tone was perfect, her pitch just right. Both men relaxed as she started to resolve their bickering.

Adam never saw Aleksei, even as the Knight crashed into him. The angel had been turning to face Brahm, when suddenly he and Aleksei were hurtling into the darkness together.

Jonas stared at the arcane diagrams laid out before him. He checked his notes, searching for anything complimenting the constructed spell scrawled in exacting detail. This particular chapter's title, "Juxtaposition of Base Origins", had piqued his curiosity from the moment he'd opened the violet leather volume in earnest.

If he understood what he was looking at, and it was a big "if", the construct involved uniting two completely different sources of magic to craft something wholly impossible for either to accomplish alone. Such things were conventionally considered impossible and ill-advised to even attempt. Yet according to the book before him, they weren't impossible, just improbable. Improbable, extremely delicate, and devilishly dangerous. The slightest pressure or variance could cause the entire thing to detonate, if applied incorrectly.

A fire blossomed within him and Jonas gasped, clutching at his chest as his notes fell from his hand and scattered across the floor of his chamber. He coughed in surprise, blinking as his vision threatened to black out. And then he straightened, a familiar feeling flooding through him.

It was *back*. The bond had been reforged.

Tears sprang to his eyes at the sudden return of that sacred intimacy, that inexplicable connection that felt at once new, yet innate as drawing breath. Its sudden presence made him wonder how he'd survived so long without it. As he collected himself, Jonas felt Aleksei moving towards him, a thunderhead on the verge of exploding into a storm.

A flash of fear shot through him. His Knight was enraged, and just for a moment Jonas thought that terrible anger was directed at him. Taking a moment to collect himself, he recalled the sort of man he'd bonded the year before. The gods only knew what Aleksei had gone through to find him in the Undercroft, but Jonas found it entirely unreasonable that Aleksei would have journeyed all the way to Kuuran just to yell at him. Which meant the sparking rage bursting from his Knight had to be directed at something, or more likely, some*one* else.

Jonas sprang to his feet, a mixture of joy and trepidation swirling within him as he made his way out of his quarters and towards the atrium. The intensity of Aleksei's emotions threatened to melt his joy into panic. His heart hammered in his chest as he ran barefoot through the Undercroft.

He halted at the entrance to the corridor labyrinth, waiting, breathless as he felt Aleksei draw closer. But when the man finally came into sight, it was *not* what Jonas had anticipated.

Aleksei marched implacably down the corridor. He was shirtless, wearing a complex harness of leather and buckles Jonas had never seen before. The Mantle was on full display, restless and roiling beneath his skin. Aleksei's face was dark, as dangerous as Jonas had ever seen it. Adam jogged next to him, shouting angrily.

"What are you even hoping to achieve? It would take a miracle from the One-God for Jonas to safely leave this place!"

Aleksei abruptly stopped and rounded on the shorter man, "The only 'miracle' here is that you're still *alive*. I've had more than enough of you people hiding behind your ridiculous god to justify the abduction and imprisonment of *my* Magus. But if you get in my way again, you'll be face to face with your 'god' real quick."

"You *can't*! He's in no position to–" the Mantle struck out. Adam staggered before collapsing in a heap on the cold corridor floor.

Aleksei continued forward, ignoring the insensible angel. Jonas stood there, transfixed as Aleksei marched straight at him, the Hunter's emotions a perplexing tumble, until they burst clear through the bond like a thunderbolt.

In one fluid motion, his Knight pulled Jonas hard against him and kissed him with fervor and abandon. Jonas felt like his knees would give way if not for Aleksei's tight grip around his chest. The sheer feeling of contact was staggering. In that one moment, every shred of loneliness, every ounce of pain tormenting him evaporated.

He thought his heart would burst.

When Aleksei finally pulled away, it was too soon. Over the

Knight's shoulder, Jonas saw Adam woozily rising, gawking at the two of them.

"What are you doing here?" Jonas managed.

Aleksei gave him a quizzical smile. His voice dropped low, "I'm breaking you out."

Jonas felt the blood rush from his face. "You can't! I...*I* can't," he choked.

Aleksei's smile ghosted away, "Why not? You don't belong in here."

"Because it's too dangerous," Adam said from behind, a triumphant smirk now plastered across his perfect face.

Aleksei twisted like a viper. The Mantle ripped free of his arm, crimson talons darting into the startled angel's neck. Adam's eye's rolled back and he collapsed with a distinct *thud,* his wings flopping to either side of his suddenly-prone form.

"What did I tell you?" Aleksei growled, his golden eyes hard.

"Aleksei!" Jonas yelled, hurrying around and forcing his Hunter's arm down, lest the Knight make good on his promise of murder, doing his best to ignore Adam's twitching form.

The Mantle's paws stroked lovingly at Jonas's wrist as he took in the alarmed looks of the patients and healers alerted and drawn out by the sudden altercation. "We should speak in my quarters."

Aleksei allowed Jonas to lead him away, but held his murderous glare locked on Adam as the angel staggered slowly to his feet, a wounded expression painting his handsome face.

Jonas led his Knight down a labyrinth of hallways before pulling him into his finely-appointed chambers. The Magus shut the door and threw every ward around it he could conjure.

The last thing he wanted was a bunch of nosy angels spying on them.

He turned back to his Knight, only to find Aleksei emerging from his bedchamber with the large canvas sack of clothing Jonas set out each week for the staff to launder. As he watched, Aleksei moved throughout the chamber, sweeping up books and notes he'd left out on the desk.

"What are you doing?"

Aleksei crouched, collecting the notes Jonas had dropped earlier, "Packing your things so we can get out of here. Speaking of which, what *is* this place?"

Jonas was caught off-guard. "The Undercroft? It's a hospital for people afflicted with magical maladies. I'm surprised you even *found* it without learning what it was."

Aleksei glanced up at him, a half-smile softening his golden glare. "I *know* what the Undercroft is, Jonas. Leigha and Brahm filled me in before they brought me here and helped me break in."

That took Jonas by surprise.

Leigha had brought Aleksei here? He immediately admonished himself. He'd been away from Aleksei for so long, he'd forgotten how focused the man was. At the very least, he needed to give his Knight more credit before he started making assumptions and accusations.

"What I *don't* know," Aleksei continued, rising to his feet and carefully stacking the pile of notes together, "is why this place is practically bursting with Wood magic."

Jonas frowned, again taken aback. "Wood magic? What are you talking about?"

Aleksei pulled the volumes from the desk and carefully laid them in the bag, "When I tackled Adam through the shield, I felt it pass through me, and while there's a veneer of the Archanium to it, there's also an enormous amount of Wood magic underlying it.

"Walking through that labyrinth, the feel of the Archanium faded the farther I got from the shield. But even standing here now, I might as well be standing in Seil Wood for the sheer weight of Wood magic that infuses this entire place. I didn't even know the two could be combined."

"You *tackled* Adam through the shield?" Jonas began before he stopped himself. "You can't combine two different magical origins like that. I mean, it's theoretically *possible*, but I've only discovered that prospect recently. Even then, it's extremely complicated, not to mention dangerous. No one has attempted it and succeeded in probably thousands of years. Well, attempted it and *survived*. It's simply too volatile."

Aleksei grunted as he hefted the canvas sack and walked into the bedchamber. "Well, that shield didn't seem exactly *new*. I had no idea there was a Wood in Dalita. Or rather," the Hunter paused, closing his eyes and inhaling deeply, "there was *once*. I suppose your charming ancestors and their people leveled it to build this...monstrosity."

Jonas was so startled that, for a moment, he forgot what they were even talking about. "As much as I'd like to delve into that just now, we other matters to discuss."

"I'm not going anywhere. Well, not without *you*," Aleksei's voice was a step above a growl. "And, as long as I'm in here, I don't have to worry about that damned wind demon tracking me down."

"What?" Jonas asked before he could help himself. He still wasn't sure what they were talking about. "Aleksei, stop for a second and tell me what's going on."

Aleksei set the sack to the side, taking a seat on Jonas's bed. The prince stood there, trying to keep his jaw off the floor as Aleksei took his time recounting the events of the past several weeks. Had Jonas heard the story from anyone other than Aleksei, he would have dismissed half of it as fabrication, and the rest of it as sorely steeped in hyperbole.

But his Knight didn't treat in flights of fancy. Even without the bond, Jonas believed every word Aleksei spoke. He was also aware of his Knight's exhaustion. Aleksei's voice held an edge Jonas had heard too many times to misinterpret.

The man was bone-tired, likely functioning through sheer will and adrenaline alone. As Aleksei's story moved past the battle in Keldoan, and Aya's miraculous leap onto a major meridian, Jonas found himself unconsciously drifting closer and closer to the man.

By the time Aleksei was detailing his meeting with Leigha and Brahm, Jonas was sitting next to him, his head resting against Aleksei's powerful chest, the Hunter's arm around him, holding him close, his rough cheek resting against the top of Jonas's head, his deep voice rumbling in his chest.

Jonas fought and failed to keep the tears from his eyes. His fear, the crushing loneliness he'd endured since arriving in the Undercroft, had been carefully controlled, always obscured from the angels' sight. He'd refused to allow them the satisfaction of watching his emotional descent.

But with Aleksei, all of those defenses, the lies he'd told himself since arriving in Kuuran, melted away, leaving him open and vulnerable for the first time in weeks. He finally understood exactly what Kevara Avlon had been so afraid of. Learning of the world beyond his little cage, people he loved and cared for struggling just to stay alive while he was safely tucked away, where he could be closely monitored, set his blood aflame.

Even something as simple as Aleksei's arm wrapped protectively around him made Jonas feel infinitely safer than all the arcane wards and barriers insulating the Undercroft from the rest of the world.

As Aleksei finished speaking, it took Jonas a moment to realize the story had ended. He'd been so lulled by the cadence of Aleksei's voice and the comfort of having the man near that, for a blessed moment, he'd managed to forget where he was, or how finely-tuned a cage the angels had crafted to keep him trapped here for the rest of his days.

"So," Aleksei rumbled after several moments of silence, "*why* can't you leave?"

Jonas jumped at the question. He remembered insisting he stay, by reflex as much as anything else. Weeks of Kevara Avlon's relentless mental programming weren't quite so easily dispelled.

He chose his words very carefully, weighing each to ensure he wasn't parroting any of the drivel they'd been force-feeding him since his internment in the Undercroft.

"After Kalinor fell, I tracked Sammul north onto the Madrhal Plain. But before I could catch up to him, I was overtaken by a wind storm. It forced me to land, and that's when Bael caught up to me. I got a few hits in, but he ultimately plunged me into the Presence."

He'd expected a larger reaction, but Aleksei merely offered a single nod. "I know. I'm pretty sure that's when our bond warped, and I lost all control of time. It nearly got me killed a few times. From the moment you were plunged into the Presence to the moment you were thrown in here, I could hardly tell what was happening. Sometimes days flew by in seconds, but other times everything just froze in place. It was *maddening.*"

Jonas looked away from his Knight's handsome face, "I'm so sorry. If I'd been faster...."

Aleksei gripped his chin in his rough fingers and gently turned Jonas's face back to his. "Gods, you don't own me an *apology*, darlin'. Standing your ground was incredibly brave, and I dare you to name another Magus in all of bloody *Ilyar* who has tangled with the Demon and survived. Xavathan said you're the first person in history to be thrown into the Presence and not only survive, but come *back.*"

Jonas's face heated at Aleksei calling him 'brave'. If any man alive knew the definition of that word, it was Aleksei Drago, though it was not a word Jonas ever applied to himself. Still, he needed to properly explain the dangers of returning to the outside world.

Aleksei could be a touch single-minded when something he wanted was in his sights. But sometimes nuance was lost in his dogged determination, and Jonas felt it was his duty to educate the man on the complexities of his situation, a reality he knew Aleksei did not want to face.

"I survived the Presence," Jonas allowed, "but it left a...*shard within me. In here, I'm cut off from its influence. I can access the magic I was born with, but no external force can command me. But the moment I walk through the archway, there's no telling what could happen. For all I know, the Presence could take me over and force me to do unspeakable things. To kill you. And that's just an example of a million different possibilities my grandmother has...brought to my attention."

Aleksei stared at him, a golden eyebrow finally arching, "And the Angelus is convinced that through that sort of magic, you might end the world, correct?"

Jonas sighed heavily, nodding.

Aleksei burst out laughing.

Jonas jumped, taken aback by the sudden explosion from his Knight. He shrank away from the man. Was Aleksei mocking him?

The Hunter, noting the shift in Jonas's body language, again wrapped his arm around the prince's shoulders and pulled him close. "I'm sorry, I don't mean to make light of the dilemma you're facing, but that is the saddest argument I've ever heard for any action, much less imprisoning someone for *life*."

Jonas frowned, starting to explain the details he was certain Aleksei was missing, but the Hunter was already speaking. "In the past few minutes, we've established that you are the first person in history to return from the grasp of the Presence, right?"

Jonas nodded.

"Yet your grandmother has laid out elaborate potentials, saying a shard of this thing would not only endanger us, but potentially end the world?"

Jonas nodded again, trying to divine where Aleksei was heading.

"Darlin', if you're the first person to ever return from the Presence alive and somewhat sane, how exactly does she *know* all these things will happen? Is she operating from some doomsayer's prophecy? Or just some crazy shit she made up herself?"

The Magus opened his mouth to explain Scripture, only to recall Kevara Avlon fuming at him for apparently invalidating nearly *all* of the Basilica's prophecies. Nearly. While it was possible she was over-stating the severity of his "situation", she hadn't brought prophecy back up, and certainly hadn't referenced a specific passage keeping her awake at night.

"I'm...honestly not sure." Jonas said simply.

"So, you're supposed to give up your entire life, *our* entire life together, because she's paranoid about what she thinks *might* happen?"

Indignation flared within him. It wasn't *that* simple, was it? There was a great deal of complexity and magical theory that was being left out of this conversation. Wasn't there? Was he indignant because Aleksei was being bullheaded, and leaving out too many important variables?

Or was he angry because he was only just recognizing the web of lies that had manipulated and controlled him, that didn't even make proper sense, while Aleksei had spotted its flaws within minutes. That web had ensnared Jonas for *weeks.*

"Either way," Jonas said finally, shrugging "it's impossible for me escape this place. We'd need a bridge formed between two angels, one on either side of the shield, to get through. Otherwise, I'm still trapped here."

Aleksei nodded slowly, "Right. That's why Leigha and Brahm are waiting for us at the entrance was we speak. Shift into a mouse and hide in my pocket. I'll carry your things, and we'll be out of here before anyone's the wiser."

Jonas had to fight to keep himself from gawking at Aleksei, with his frustratingly triumphant smile. Could it really be that simple? He'd just opened his mouth to acquiesce when the air was forcefully sucked from his lungs.

He choked, gasping for breath. Aleksei's smile vanished, replaced by concern as the Knight laid him back, a thread of the Mantle dipping into the Magus's flesh.

Run! It was a desperate plea to his Knight, and one he knew the man would completely disregard.

Every ward he'd placed on the door had just been casually destroyed in a single, silent, cataclysmic moment. He hadn't been minding them, and the impact had ripped his breath away. He hadn't anticipated any sort of assault, and all of them breaking apart simultaneously had come as a massive shock to his system. There was a staggering swell of power at the door.

He should have known Aleksei would never leave his side, especially given the ordeals his Hunter had endured just to reach him.

Just as Jonas was getting his breath back, he saw Aleksei's form guarding the bedchamber door, sword in one hand, hunting knife in the other. The cords of the Mantle writhed from his shoulders, sinuous lines of midnight jeweled with ruby talons, the deadly tendrils swaying and darting like serpents preparing to strike.

The door exploded, the anteroom flooded with bodies in an instant.

Jonas pushed himself up, diving into the Archanium. He could still touch the Great Sphere, but he was having a devil of a time grasping the necessary spellforms. They jolted in and out of his vision, each swirl of color, sound, and emotion ricocheting away from him just before he made contact.

The Sphere vanished. Jonas grunted as a shockingly powerful shield tore the Archanium from him. Rage unlike anything he'd felt since accepting his confinement flooded into him. Rage at seeing Aleksei, Mantle and blades both glistening in the gentle firelight of the chamber, blocking the doorway to protect him.

Always to protect him.

And yet even as his anger blossomed, it began to wither. That shield was beyond anything he'd ever experienced. No single man or angel was capable of that level of power. As he'd reached for any of the powerfully destructive spells of the Nagavor, he'd felt the press of bodies not just in the antechamber, but crowding in the hallway beyond.

There were at least fifty angels, likely more. And given the incredible strength keeping him from the Archanium, many, if not all of the angels gathered had linked their abilities. He'd never even *heard* of so many Archanium users combining their strength like this. He was fairly certain it was impossible for so many Magi to link their abilities at once.

But angels were not Magi.

He staggered to his feet and stumbled forward, resting a hand on Aleksei's shoulder. The Hunter never looked away from the room full of angels before him, but Jonas felt the question burst into his mind.

There are fifteen in the first room, at least fifty more in the hallway. They're so packed into the antechamber that they can't even move without running into each other. I will protect you with everything I have, but I don't think we can win this one.

Jonas smiled in spite of himself. He straightened and gently pushed against his Knight. Despite Aleksei's far greater height and weight, he slid aside at the slight pressure from his Magus's hand.

Jonas stepped in front of his Knight, glaring at the mass of angels practically tripping over their own wings to reorient themselves in the small anteroom.

"*What* are you doing?" he barked angrily.

Every angel before him wore the golden-filigreed armor that marked them as archangels. Each blazed with the Archanium, yet a single glanced told him that none of them commanded the link.

There was some jostling and apologies as several angels tried to step out of the way of a figure advancing towards him. Jonas didn't have to guess which angel held the combined magic of all seventy archangels.

Adam finally managed to push his way to the fore, red-faced and gasping. Jonas stared at him, his emerald eyes practically aflame with rage. One of the most incredibly powerful feats of magic manipulation Jonas had ever witnessed, and they'd given control of that power to *him*?

The angel took an involuntary step back, caught in Jonas's glare.

He wondered what the angel had anticipated he'd encounter after shredding spells *Jonas* had placed on the doors of his own chambers, before sending in a literal army to...do what? Step on each other's wings and shuffle uncomfortably about, none of them even able to draw a weapon?

Jonas wondered if he was meant to be impressed.

While the angels outside would be a different matter, Aleksei could have carved his way through every angel in that room, barely breaking a sweat.

Except that Adam knew Aleksei would do no such thing. He was clearly certain Jonas would stop the Hunter before it came to that.

But Jonas did have to wonder what sort of response Adam had anticipated.

"What. Are. You. Doing?" Jonas demanded.

But before the angel even opened his mouth, Jonas knew the answer. Adam had absolutely no idea.

CHAPTER 22
DIVINE COMEDY

Adam stared at Jonas a moment longer, his link to the Archanium burning like a bonfire, the power of seventy archangels filling him. The angel made the mistake of glancing over Jonas's shoulder, to Aleksei. Jonas was mollified a touch to see the pure terror dance across the angel's face.

Any trace of smug triumph ghosted away at the sight of Aleksei, clad in his harness of leather straps and buckles, the Mantle on full display, sword and knife at the ready. Standing easily a foot taller than Adam and broad as a bear, the Hunter was intimidating enough to make enemies scatter on a battlefield.

But this was not a battlefield, and both Jonas and Aleksei knew that.

"You knew how this was going to end," Adam said petulantly, as though chiding a child.

Jonas punched him in the face.

The prince was no warrior, but Aleksei had made him practice basic grappling enough that he didn't break his thumb. That didn't mean it didn't hurt, but he was reasonably certain he'd broken Adam's nose, which offered some consolation.

Adam bent over, clutching his bleeding nose and cursing. An archangel behind him tried to step forward and draw her sword, but she only succeeded in bowling Adam over. Jonas stepped to the side, letting the angel sprawl onto his face, splattering blood across the rich Fanja carpets.

Adam fell, but Jonas hardly noticed, a sudden, nearly overwhelming storm of thoughts bursting into his mind.

"The wind," he muttered. Dread shot through him, and he nearly collapsed next to the fallen angel.

By the time Adam had come to his feet, Jonas was standing before him, arms crossed but his attention elsewhere. Aleksei towered behind him, his arm protectively around the Magus. The Hunter's hand still clutched his knife, its brutal serrations glittering in the firelight like fangs.

The archangels' numbers had thinned during the interruption, leaving only five in the antechamber. All eyes were fixed on Aleksei.

When Adam looked at Jonas, the prince was surprised, pulled from his swirling thoughts for a moment. Rather than glare at the Magus, Adam seemed genuinely hurt, as though the tears streaming down his cheeks weren't wholly from the strike the Magus had just landed.

Adam took a deep breath, sensing Jonas's hesitation. He glanced over his shoulder. "Take him," he managed, nodding at Aleksei.

Two archangels stepped around Adam, cautiously grasping Aleksei's arms as the Mantle spider-webbed down his flesh. The Hunter arched a golden eyebrow, looking to Jonas for guidance.

"I'm not sure that's the best idea," he growled.

The archangels looked nervous, but Adam jerked his head towards the door.

"He's not going to hurt you," the angel snapped. His blue-eyed glare shifted to Jonas, "He can't."

Jonas started when he realized that the angel was staring at him. He hadn't given the angels in the room another thought since breaking Adam's nose. There was something nagging in his mind, perplexing him, but it kept flitting away.

Gods, there was *something* there. Something incredibly important, something about the wind, but he simply couldn't grasp it. His mind kept returning to the purple leather text, but its pages and passages were running together.

In his panic, all Jonas could recall was that Aleksei could *not* leave the Undercroft, but how did he even give voice to such a thought? And why was he so certain Aleksei was in danger?

Stall, for as long as you can without getting hurt. You can't *leave the shield, but I don't know why yet.* Gods, but he hoped Aleksei heeded his words, especially as he couldn't even *explain* them.

Not too worried about getting hurt, darlin', Jonas could feel Aleksei's laugh, even as the other man was pulled away, *but I'll certainly take my time. Don't you worry, I'll make them work for it.* The warmth of his Knight's tone flooded Jonas with relief. Gods, but he was glad for his Knight, especially in the midst of all...this.

Of *course* he didn't want Aleksei to leave, but there was so much more there. Wasn't there? He kept darting back to various pieces of magical principle and construction, flying through them as quickly as he could.

Jonas knew with absolute certainty that if Aleksei was thrown out of the Undercroft, he would die almost immediately. The wind demon that had harried the Hunter would find him the instant he left, but how did he *know* that? Why should it matter if Aleksei left the Undercroft?

There was something about the shield's construction there, but he couldn't place it. And as his mind raced, overwhelmed with the flood of knowledge and confusion, archangels were slowly marching his Knight past him and out of his chambers. There were so many of them, and all linked together their power was practically blinding him, his skin itching from just being near it.

Baffled, he followed, watching Aleksei walk away. Towards the labyrinth. Towards the *shield*. Why couldn't he focus? What was his mind trying to tell him?

Aleksei's voice burst through his thoughts. *I'll figure this out. I won't leave you in here. This battle is far from over. I love you.*

Tears streamed down his cheeks, yet he hadn't even realized he was crying. It had been so long since he'd felt Aleksei near him, since he'd heard the man's voice; felt his heat. Kevara Avlon had made the correct decision in keeping them apart; seeing Aleksei had reignited a fight in Jonas that they'd worked very hard to make him forget.

But now, with Aleksei so close and the dread specter of Bael's wind demon clawing at his mind, nothing in this world could keep him here. If he had to destroy the shield to get out, he would.

Jonas jumped.

That was an unexpected idea; woven from new and old information alike. The purple text had taught him the delicacies of magical constructs built from separate magical origins. If the shield was constructed from Angelic *and* Wood elements, that could explain its incredible power, but it also gave Jonas a glimpse of its weakness.

He shook his head. That may be important later, but he had an incredibly short amount of time to figure out *why* Aleksei was in such incredible danger.

His Knight was still in view, though just barely, walking along with the angels. He wasn't making their jobs easy, however. While not digging in his heels or forcing them to drag him, Aleksei was taking his time. The archangels escorting him kept urging him to pick up the pace, both tugging at his arms.

"Hurry up!" one barked.

The Mantle whipped out, grazing both of their necks before recoiling, splashing back across Aleksei's thickly muscled arms. The angels staggered, slumping against the labyrinth walls, gasping and struggling to keep their feet.

Aleksei observed them dispassionately.

"C'mon, get on with it! Don't lie down on the job, boys!" the Hunter barked as the archangels sought to regain their breath.

Jonas noted that both angels wore haunted grimaces as they pushed him into the labyrinth. He swallowed a laugh. Aleksei may be being forced out, yet somehow the unrepentant Hunter managed to remain in control.

"It's for the best. You'll see."

Jonas started at the intrusion of Adam's voice behind him. He turned and found Adam no longer burning with overwhelming power, his face completely healed, only the few drops of blood splashed on his shirt revealing any proof of his broken nose.

Jonas had the immediate urge to break it again.

"Will I?" he asked, quirking a frown, his face skeptical.

Adam sighed, still condescending to Jonas, as though he were some querulous brat, "If you give it time, and truly invest yourself in our teachings, I truly think you'll find your way."

Jonas looked Adam dead in the eye, "I'm not lost. I know *exactly* who and what I am, and the last thing that is likely to sway me from my path is whatever nonsense *you* plan to teach me.

"Also, in case you couldn't tell, I'm very much in love with that man," he thrust his hand towards the opening of the labyrinth, "the one you just ordered marched out of here like a criminal? The one who's going to be ripped apart the moment he walks past that shield? You will never win my heart, Adam, and from what Aleksei had to say, I think Brahm would prefer it that way."

For a fraction of a moment, Jonas saw the hurt, the loss flash across the angel's face. He recovered with remarkable alacrity.

"What are you talking about? No one is going to harm your Knight. As long as he doesn't try to kill one of us first, that is."

"If Aleksei Drago steps through that shield, the wind demon that's been stalking him will find him in a matter of moments," Jonas snarled. "And *you* people, for all your vaunted magical talent and your Seraphima, won't be able to stop it. My Knight will die. And then I'm afraid I'll be forced to kill all of you."

Though unnerved, Adam still seemed unconvinced. "That's a laughable threat," though his eyes betrayed his lie. "Do you even have proof this phantom wind *exists?*"

"I don't need it," Jonas growled, his anger and need rising to a quick crescendo. Siphoning some of Aleksei's strength, Jonas shattered the shield keeping the Great Sphere from his grasp.

The Archanium flooded into him in a torrent of pure power. He ran past the angel, easily dodging Adam's sad attempt to grab him. The gods only knew what would have happened had the angel actually managed to touch him. Jonas's skin burned with the might coursing through him.

He darted out into the corridor, dashing madly for the labyrinth, even as he felt Aleksei growing further and further from him.

Guards were stationed there, of course. Three archangels stood at the entrance, golden swords unsheathed, their wings spreading as they saw him approach. Jonas dropped his shoulders and charged them as they each sank into defensive stands. They were thus unprepared when Jonas shifted into a sparrow and shot over their heads, into the labyrinth.

He turned a few corners before dissolving back into a man, racing forward, casting out his thoughts. *Do not let them take you beyond the shield. You have to stay inside the Undercroft. Use any means necessary.*

He turned the final corner, and even as his boots skidded against the indifferent marble, he felt the jolt of absence as he was cut off from his Knight. It wasn't the first time he'd felt their bond go suddenly silent, but it was so much more painful this time.

Aleksei was gone. Past the threshold of the shield, and just as soon for the axe.

In his rage, Jonas unleashed a wall of air that hurtled the guardian angels waiting for him back into the shield, turning on his heel and darting back into the labyrinth.

He'd been there long enough to have the maze memorized, and it wasn't long before he'd returned to the Undercroft proper. Again he shot over the shoulders of the archangels guarding the labyrinth entrance, his boots striking the ground just outside the Reliquary.

He could no longer protect Aleksei from within, so he'd just have to get out.

Again, passages from the purple text flashed through his head, but this time they guided his every move. The inscription left within the book, *"For Jonas Belgi, in his time of need"*, raked away his rationality. The contents of the book had been sent to him as a tool, and if there'd ever been a truer time of need in his life, he couldn't recall it.

Jonas stalked through the Reliquary. Angels who, mere days before had been clapping with joy at the sight of him, cowered, casting about for an archangel to appear and stop the Magus's rampage.

Jonas didn't spare them a second glance, but rather headed straight for the relic he required, the final solution to his most vexing problem.

He heard the gasps behind him when he ripped the black velvet drape from the shadowed gauntlet. Even in his enraged state, the pure destructive energy emanating from the gauntlet stopped him in his tracks. He'd never encountered a creation of such unbridled destruction. The power of this gauntlet would have given even the Demonic Presence pause.

Aleksei's life was in danger.

There was no other option.

Jonas gripped the gauntlet, fortifying himself as the brilliant copper turned liquid, crashing up and through his right arm, binding to his nerves and searing his skin. He resisted the urge to retch.

The Magus raised his right hand and examined the intricate armored plating, the indescribably wicked force the gauntlet bore feeling so terribly *right*.

As he marched out of the Reliquary, the totem of darkness bound to his arm drinking in every scrap of light around it, he knew he had the power to level entire cities should the mood strike him.

The Archanium lit up around him like an exploding star, and Jonas understood the odious spellform afforded him by the gauntlet. The darkest, most destructive force in the Forbidden Realms was suddenly at his fingertips, granting him the power to negate the entire world, should he choose to.

But he wanted only for one thing.

Angels, healers, the archangels in their glittering assemblages alike cowered in his wake as he sought the labyrinth. Fury fueled his every step. An unspeakable rage, that these creatures would see the man he loved torn apart as a means of keeping Jonas imprisoned, burned through him, singing through his blood.

As he reached the labyrinth, Adam stepped in front of him.

He could have unraveled the angel's entire being with a thought, but Adam stood stalwart, seemingly unafraid of the terrible power Jonas now commanded.

The angel held out a canvas sack.

Jonas halted, his wrath sputtering for a moment.

"Here," Adam said softly, pushing the bag against Jonas's chest.

A softness threatened to break the terrible tempest tearing through the Magus.

"What...?" Jonas managed.

"I can't win you, Jonas Belgi. No matter how hard I try, your heart doesn't belong to me. And it never will.

"But I also want you to be happy. More than anything the One-God has given me, I want that most of all. You say the Demon has conjured a being to destroy your Knight, and I would spare you that pain."

Adam's words threatened to tear through the torrent of power spinning around Jonas, even as it threatened to tear the fabric of reality itself. And yet Jonas felt a strange calm as Adam grasped a thick wing feather, ripping in free.

Brilliant crimson splattered the angel's pristine ivory wing, shocking in its intensity.

Adam grunted in pain, but quickly schooled his emotions, his perfect face now stiff and guarded, "I offer this feather, this sacrifice, so that he might be safe. In turn, I pray for *your* safety. I can't protect you," the angel's voice broke, "but I'm happy knowing someone else can. For now, that's the best I can do."

Jonas fought to steady his breath, to prevent himself from giving in to the storm of his own emotions, or the unstable amount of power coursing through him.

"Thank you. From the depths of my heart, *thank* you, Adam."

The angel looked away, and Jonas recognized his dismissal.

Bloody feather clutched tightly in his hand, Jonas ran through the labyrinth, archangels hugging the walls as he passed.

Reaching the shield, he took a deep breath.

This was the only way.

He wasn't sure what would happen when the gauntlet touched the shield. One way or another, there *would* be a reaction.

He prayed he survived it.

Jonas stopped to consider for only a moment. As long as the shield existed, Kevara Avlon would only hunt him down again and again, to throw him in her little birdcage, if not ultimately murder him outright, on the unspoken orders of a corrupted faith. She was beyond reason.

This was the only way.

The only way to ensure that she could never hold this threat over him again. The only way he would ever truly be allowed to be with Aleksei. The only way he could *protect* Aleksei, consequences be damned.

He gripped his bag in his left hand, thrusting his gauntleted fist into the shield.

The world ignited.

CHAPTER 23
REACHING FROM THE ABYSS

Aleksei sat on a bench fifty paces from the Undercroft's black marble archway, his head in his hands. Frustration and despair kept warring to overcome him, but he battled them back.

Even as a Hunter, even with the Mantle, he couldn't have possibly bested seventy archangels, whether they were linked or not. He knew that. Jonas knew that. But as much as that enraged him, it didn't solve his problem.

Jonas was still locked in the Undercroft, and he outside it. Perhaps he ought to investigate the catacombs Leigha had so strongly warned him against? If there was *that* much Wood magic in the shield between him and Jonas, if a Wood had indeed once grown where the foundation of the Basilica sat today, then going beneath it might give him more answers into the shield's nature, perhaps even a way to break through it.

Leigha and Brahm had vanished during the altercation in the Undercroft, likely hoping to save face. He didn't blame them. He blamed himself for being weak, but he *was* certain of one thing now... now that he was back where he'd started.

He was not leaving without Jonas.

The entire Host could come at him, all at once. It didn't matter, Aleksei refused to give up. He would find another way. Of course, they'd been interrupted before he could completely bring Jonas around to reality. What if he couldn't convince his prince to return to the outside world?

He could always plan another assault, this time with the plants he'd need to drug Jonas. Once beyond the bounds of the shield, Jonas would have little choice but to go along. If he soon saw evidence that his magic wouldn't envelop the world, perhaps he would come around.

Or Aleksei could just rush back through the shield now. If Leigha was correct, he might become as trapped as his Magus. That could force the Angelus to stand down and free the both of them. Refusing would absolutely plunge Dalita into a war with Ilyar, and while the angels had powerful magic, they really had no armed forces to speak of. If Aya could teach the rest of the Voralla to access her new meridian....

Aleksei groaned and rubbed his face.

It was wishful thinking, and he knew it. What was it that his father had always said? Live your life through logic, not wasted on wishes. He had to think. Not about what he wanted, but about what he could actually accomplish.

Aleksei's head jerked up as an explosion shattered the sky. He stared, mesmerized, as the dome of stained glass sheltering the Undercroft erupted into a trillion rainbow shards.

It was like watching vividly-colored falling snow. Somehow, he could hardly tear his eyes away from the beautiful chaos enveloping him.

"*Aleksei!*"

His head snapped down to the archway, staring as Jonas ran towards him. The bond swelled inside him. He could feel the bizarre, perplexing tangle of emotions raging through the prince. Jonas's right hand was clad in a copper gauntlet, wreathed in a deep darkness Aleksei innately feared, the other clutching a single, bloody ivory feather.

Aleksei leapt to his feet, catching the Magus and pulling him close. He could feel the heat of exertion radiating from the man. But he felt something else. Something ominous

A feeling that left him shaken.

"What...how...." Aleksei fought for words. Jonas urgently pressed the feather he held to Aleksei's chest.

The feeling of apprehension grew unbearable.

With sudden comprehension, Aleksei threw Jonas to the floor, rolling out of the way as the wind demon suddenly materialized. Aleksei leapt to his feet, reaching out with his senses for the creature. He could feel it mere paces away, twisting, racing towards him.

The air erupted with lightning. The wind demon wailed as it swerved and tumbled through the atrium, away from him. Aleksei's head snapped around to see Jonas on his feet, his face red.

The demon gathered itself, once again screaming towards Aleksei. There was an impact in the air as Jonas lashed out again with a fist of thunder. The demon paused, allowing the knot of lightning to slide *through* it.

It barreled on its way, unharmed.

"Aleksei!" Jonas shouted. "The *feather!*"

Aleksei looked around wildly and finally caught sight of it, lying paces away.

Shift. Even as the demon came within striking distance, Aleksei dove beneath it, hands scrambling.

The moment his fingers closed around the bloody feather, the demon froze.

It hung in the air for a moment longer, before vanishing with an ear-piercing shriek.

Aleksei lay on the marble floor, panting and clutching the feather in his hand, looking around in confusion.

Jonas was there a heartbeat later, gasping for air as he crashed onto his Knight's chest. "Are you alright? Did it hurt you?"

Aleksei took a moment. His hand and thigh ached from where he'd struck the marble, but beyond that he was uninjured.

"I don't understand," he said finally, ignoring the crowd of shocked onlookers gathered around them. "What just happened? I didn't think it would attack me *here*. Why did it stop like that?"

Jonas smiled sadly, "The feather."

Aleksei glanced down to the blood-spattered white shaft in his palm. He looked into Jonas's eyes, "Where did you get this?"

"It was a gift. From Adam."

Aleksei could feel Jonas's confusion and aching sadness course across the bond. Whatever had transpired between Jonas and Adam, Aleksei immediately knew that he couldn't take this gift lightly.

"Jonas!"

The Magus stood and turned slowly. "Uncle."

Aleksei came to his feet as an enraged Xavathan pushed his way through the crowd, "What in God's name have you *done?*"

Jonas glared at him coolly. "I'm sure I've committed some sort of blasphemy, Uncle."

Xavathan stared, then turned to the black archway. "It's gone," he whispered. He turned back to Jonas, "You've destroyed the shield! How could you manage such a thing? That shield predated the bloody *Basilica!*"

Jonas lifted his copper-clad forearm. He shuddered, lowering his arm as the gauntlet fell away, clattering impotently onto the marble, its malevolence seemingly spent.

"I didn't have much of a choice. It was either that, or I let Aleksei die."

Xavathan stared at him in shock.

Aleksei could tell that the man's world had just been turned upside down. He'd seen the same incredulous expression on the faces of his own men during the invasion of Kalinor.

"You have no idea what you've done," Xavathan whispered finally.

"I've saved my Knight from certain death, Uncle. I've also ensured my grandmother no longer has a prison to keep me in."

"You think this is all just about *you?*" Xavathan demanded, his anger rising.

Jonas arched an eyebrow, "Isn't it? Your bitch mother is certainly insistent that I believe that. She spent a *great* deal of time reminding me of my duty to the world, of how vitally important I was, how dangerous my presence in this world could be. That the Undercroft was designed to protect the world from *me*. She made some perilous leaps of logic, certainly, but she *was* right."

"You know nothing of Scripture, of *prophecy*," the angel shot back.

"You're right, I'm no expert. But a Prophet's word is not the same as an addled interpretation by a paranoid old woman."

The Magus turned away.

Xavathan grabbed him by the arm, hauling him around, "Don't you *dare* walk away from me!"

The Seraph stiffened as Aleksei's hand closed around his throat. No one had seen Aleksei move. One moment he'd been standing paces away, and the next he'd simply appeared at Xavathan's side.

Angry red claws spiraled from the Aleksei's wrist and caressed the angel's carotid artery.

"*Stop*," Aleksei growled. "You're angry, but I'm showing *enormous* restraint right now. I'll warn you, my patience is wearing thin."

The angel stared back at him with wide eyes. "I'm on your side, lad. I'm only trying to do what's best for all of us."

The angel's wings flapped desperately, though he gained no traction.

"You have an interesting interpretation of what's *best* for me. For Jonas. And let me remind you, you're in no position to threaten anyone at the moment."

Xavathan gave a curt nod.

Aleksei snarled. "We are leaving this place, and we're leaving *now*. If anyone tries to follow us, or seeks to hinder us in any way, I will kill them."

Aleksei opened his hand, the fourth-born Seraph crashing to the ground unceremoniously.

"You still don't understand," Xavathan insisted, pulling himself up and rubbing his neck, "Jonas is dangerous."

"So am *I*," Aleksei roared. "And now that your little cage is busted, I don't see what more you can do to 'help' him. So leave well enough alone." Aleksei turned to walk away, but then thought better of it. "And Xavathan? I *will* keep my word, so don't test me."

He glanced over his shoulder as he walked away, fixing the older man with a hard glare.

Aleksei wasn't about to let Jonas's life, *his* life, be dictated by these people and their misguided theology. He finally had Jonas back, and they were getting the hell out of there.

Hade trembled.

He now truly grasped the power of Sammul's connection to the Archanium. He could feel it as every thread that ran through him rang out in agony.

Hade's back arched and he screamed, sobbing. The trees above him spun in a dark vortex of confusion. He could have shrieked his lungs out, but no one would hear him this deep in the woods. The lights of Keldoan glimmered indifferently through the canopy.

"*Stop* it!" Sammul snarled.

Hade gritted his teeth. He had to be careful. Vadim could feel the things he felt. But as long as he was alive, Vadim would be held under his spell. His pain and fear would manifest as nightmares, as they had a hundred times since their arrival in Keldoan.

Aleksei's victory over the rebel forces had only confirmed Vadim's foolish belief that the Hunter was indeed in command of their futures. Vadim had nearly punched Hade out to go and join the fight, but Sammul had not given Hade permission to return to the others yet. He'd wanted to see how the battle went, and Hade had done a fair job of gathering information for his master, despite being cut off from the others.

When Vadim became too aggressive or unhappy, Hade used Sammul's secret spells to settle him down. The hardest of it had been during the battle, especially since Vadim could see some of the fighting from their inn. It had taken everything Hade had to quiet the Knight, but he now commanded far more power in their bond than Vadim. Still, his Knight was growing increasingly frustrated and suspicious.

Hade badly wanted to tell his Knight all the things that had been revealed to him, but he didn't dare. Vadim's confusion was warranted, but his safety was all Hade cared for. Every time Vadim had tried to get near Aleksei, Hade found a reason to keep him away. The Master had made that last command imperative.

Hade's relief had been immeasurable when Aleksei had fled Keldoan following the battle. If *anyone* was going to discover their presence, it would have been Aleksei Drago. Despite his own misgivings, and Vadim's apparent infatuation, Hade was also aware of Aleksei's skills as Hunter. As yet, no one was aware of their presence, and having Aleksei gone had made such detection far less likely.

But Hade was hoping that Sammul might finally let them come out of hiding tonight.

Hade was only too pleased when his Knight had finally succumbed to exhaustion. He'd allowed Vadim to fall into a peaceful sleep, and then he'd wrapped a spell around the man he professed to protect.

No one noticed or cared as Hade slipped out of the inn, and out of the city walls.

And now Hade was ready to die, to release his Knight from the silent torture he'd been putting both of them through.

He sank to his knees, feeling the wet thickness of the mud beneath.

"So?" came the demand again.

Hade didn't want to speak. He didn't want to tell Sammul anything that would place Ilyana in danger. He cried out as lightning crackled across his skin. He could smell himself burn.

He hoped the Master would heal him before he was sent away. If the Master didn't heal him, Vadim would notice. Hade was beginning to care less. He *wanted* Vadim to notice. Perhaps Vadim could help him. He wanted so badly for Vadim to save him. At the moment, he just wanted Vadim.

The lightning crackled through his teeth.

"*Aya*," he gasped. "She's found a new meridian. I heard she banished a wind demon. She's *stronger*."

"A new *meridian*?" The Master finally calmed himself, "You must learn how she did this, Hade. I want you to uncover this new...meridian, and then report back to me. Do you understand?"

An invisible lash whipped across his back. "*Yes!*" he screamed, "Yes, I *understand*." The pain faded and he was left burned, bleeding, and naked. "Just leave her alone. Please?"

There was a moment of silence from the Master.

"Who?" Sammul asked finally.

"Ilyana," Hade panted, his throat hoarse from screaming. "I told you, I want her clear of all this."

The Master glowered, but gave a single nod. "Do this task, and I will see that she is not harmed."

Hade felt the breath leap from him. He held back a whimper as his body was released from Sammul's power. The sobs would come later. For the moment, he stowed them behind the curtain of shame he'd cultivated.

Hade's hatred for his fellow Magi was newly stoked by their disgustingly perfect love. He had purposefully bonded a skillful man in the hopes that Ilyana would finally recognize him as a true Magus, as a true man himself.

Instead, Ilyana had bonded someone much older. A man in his fiftieth summer even then, who claimed to love her as much as Hade did.

For his part, Hade had shared no affection for Vadim. They'd been bound by their profession. That was it. Vadim had provided him a service, and he provided Vadim with station. It was long ago worked out, but now their friendship, their bond was getting in his way.

Sammul smiled, "And you'll do as I command?"

He dared glare back at his master, "What*ever* it takes."

They were several leagues outside of Kuuran before either spoke.

Jonas rode the brown gelding that Xavathan had left in the stables. He kept his horse as close to Agriphon as he could. Aleksei welcomed the proximity to his Magus, even if the man was still a few paces away. It was a decided improvement after being separated by distance and deceit.

Aleksei could feel the tangle of emotions Jonas was giving off. It was for that very reason that he'd held his tongue. The Magus was a conflicted ball of confusion, anger, and determination. He'd speak when he was good and ready.

As dusk fell, Aleksei could wait no longer. He had to tell Jonas of the *other* matter at hand. "Darlin', I don't know how to say this, but it's possible that Tamara has been abducted."

An agonized groan escaped the prince, "You can't be serious. When did you learn this?"

Aleksei sighed deeply, "Your grandmother mentioned it when I was...bargaining for your release. I don't know how accurate her information is, but it's a possibility."

Jonas was silent for a time, and Aleksei left him alone, trying not to read too much into his shifting emotions or the barrage of his thoughts.

Finally, the Prince looked at Aleksei, fire burning in his eyes, "How close do you have to be to track someone?"

Aleksei frowned, considering a long moment before answering. There were elements of being a Hunter that he didn't entirely understand.

In the past, every time he'd uncovered one of his abilities, it had been through instinct. Once he grasped the nature of something, he was able to replicate it. But he hardly understood all the facets of his unexpected birthright.

"I'm not entirely sure," he admitted, swaying with Agriphon's trot. "It depends on what, or whom, I'm tracking. I can follow tracks for leagues, provided they're fresh enough. Scents are harder because they disperse on the wind easily. I've tracked heartbeats from a goodly distance, but never over a league. They get too muddied with all the... confusion of life." He eyed his Magus curiously, "Why?"

Jonas shrugged, "I was just thinking, wondering if there was some preternatural way you could track her. I'm not sure how she could be abducted from the Wood, but—"

"She's not in the Wood," Aleksei said, his own emotions suddenly roiling. "Before I left, I ordered Andariana and Tamara to go to Taumon and take the first ship to Zirvah. I told them to seek sanctuary with the Angelus."

"*What?*" Jonas squawked, "Why would you tell them to do that?"

"Because I didn't want them that close to Kalinor. Because I didn't want Bael to burn down the Wood looking for them. Because no one would expect them to take that route in winter. Krasik and his lackeys would never attack the Basilica, and the angels are the single greatest threat to Bael and the Presence. I was *trying* to keep them safe."

Jonas exhaled sharply, and Aleksei couldn't miss the sudden fury flaring in the Magus.

"Well," Jonas said finally, "how were *you* to know what was going on up here?"

Aleksei prickled at the intimation of his ignorance, but let it slide. This was not the time to get into a shouting match over petty jibes.

"Did they at least get there? To Taumon?" Jonas finally asked.

"From what I understand, yes. The Angelus seemed to be under the impression that Andariana had continued on alone, but—"

"She would never do that," Jonas snapped.

Aleksei took a deep breath of the frigid twilight, his eyes scouting for a suitable campsite. "I'm aware. That claim made me doubt the reporting in the first place. But then I've been sending her misinformation for months now."

Jonas straightened in his saddle, "Why?"

Aleksei shrugged, "Because I deeply dislike her, and the way she's treated you. Do I need a better reason?"

Despite his apparent anger, Jonas chuckled softly. "I suppose you don't."

"But misinformation aside, Tamara's abduction ain't the sort of thing my people would've made up. It's an imperfect system. Some actual truth was bound to slip through.

"Now, would you care to explain why...*how* you destroyed the shield on the Undercroft? Before Adam showed up with the most ineffectual army ever, I wasn't sure you even *wanted* to leave."

Jonas sat atop his horse, dry-washing his hands, "I...found a book in the Reliquary. It had been there for years, at least a decade, but it was inscribed to *me*. Some of the magical theory inside warned me about the wind demon finding you."

Aleksei's hackles rose.

"After you told me about the wind demon, I realized you were going to die the moment you left unless I found a way to protect you, a way through the shield. There was a relic that I recalled. I can't even describe what it was meant for. It was a weapon, something meant to...disrupt...or *erase* everything around it. I think it was meant to kill people. Vast numbers of people."

Aleksei's eyebrows shot up in alarm, "That was the gauntlet you were wearing?"

Jonas nodded, "I've never encountered anything that felt as dangerous as that copper gauntlet. The shield was ancient, but you were right; it was comprised of an Archanium composition and an enormous amount of Wood magic. So I figured that if I thrust that *thing* into it, the energies would be disrupted or negated long enough for me to get through. I wasn't sure if it would work, or if I'd even survive. I didn't know what would happen.

"Of course, now that I know, I think I understand it. When the shield was destroyed, so was the relic. By the time you saw it, it had little power left. I think its energy erased the Archanium element in the shield. The explosion was from the Wood magic...or *entity*, being freed."

Aleksei considered the idea. While he was far from an expert on magic, certainly not on the scale Jonas was talking about, he inherently grasped the need for balance. The gods knew he had to balance life and death as a Hunter, even more so through the Mantle.

"And the feather?" he asked after a pregnant pause.

"It's from Adam."

Gods, but the Magus sounded guilty. Aleksei swallowed, not sure he wanted to hear the next bit. "I know. I learned everything I could from Leigha and Brahm before entering the Undercroft. But why would he give it to *you?*"

Jonas looked away, "In the book, it says there are few talismans against the Demonic Presence, but one of them is an angel's feather, freely given.

"There are conditions, of course. In this instance, the feather was given to me in the spirit of the great personal sacrifice. Adam gave up something precious so you could live."

Aleksei smiled sadly, "And by protecting me, he protects you."

Jonas nodded silently.

Aleksei exhaled, watching his breath steam from his mouth. "I didn't realize there'd been so much...*happening* in there."

"There wasn't," Jonas said frantically, "he just...finally realized there were certain things he couldn't have. Things that already belonged to someone else."

Aleksei watched the road, not daring to meet Jonas's gaze just then. "Jonas, if you ever...I *understand* that you didn't think you'd ever leave that place. When I arrived, they had you pretty turned around, jumping at phantoms and shades, spouting nonsense...."

Jonas raised a hand, halting Aleksei's tumble of words.

"I won't say they didn't try to pull me from this world. The gods know, they tried everything they could think of. But I *never* let them forget who my heart belonged to."

Aleksei smiled at that, a reassuring warmth blocking out the oppressive cold.

The sun finally set, plunging them into the gloom of afterglow. "We might as well make camp," he grumbled. "I wanted to get a lot further south than this, but it'll have to do."

Aleksei led the way off the path and through the snow, following the lay of the land to an area off the road where the ground dipped into a dry riverbed. He slipped from his saddle, turning to his Magus, "Can you clear a space for us? Maybe a circle of about five paces?"

Jonas chuckled, "How'd you manage without me?"

Aleksei rolled his shoulders, pulling down his saddlebags, "I used a shovel."

As Aleksei pulled out his small tent, the Archanium hummed behind him. There was a soft *boom*, and the snow scattered from around his feet, billowing out into fragile clouds that sparkled in the emerging starlight. Aleksei shot his Magus an appreciative smile as he unrolled the waxed woolen tent and went about setting things up.

Jonas slid from his horse's back and pulled his meager bag over a shoulder. He wasn't about to risk the book inside; it was far too precious. He startled pulling off the horse's tack, suddenly exhilarated to be doing something with his hands again.

He'd spent too long locked in the Undercroft, reading and arguing Scripture. He even embraced the biting winter cold as a welcome change from the perpetual, unremarkable warmth of the Undercroft, at least for the moment.

He turned to see the fully-erected tent and fought to keep his laughter contained. The tiny woolen structure was hardly big enough for one person. How did a man of Aleksei's size even fit into such a minuscule vessel? Aleksei apparently felt his mirth across the bond.

"It was the smallest one I could find on short notice," the Hunter grunted. "I didn't see the need to be overburdened."

Jonas watched as his Knight set about digging a fire pit. He almost stopped Aleksei, but it would take about as long to explain how swiftly he could have accomplished the task as it was for Aleksei to finish the job.

There was a keen awkwardness to their situation.

They'd spent a year perpetually together, but in the last few months they'd hardly seen one another. This was the longest he'd been around Aleksei since returning from the Drakleyn at the end of the autumn.

Even their time together during the invasion of Kalinor and the brief siege that followed felt ephemeral, built from fear and desperation.

Of course, Jonas thought ruefully, they were hardly in better circumstances now. They knew Tamara was likely gone, but not *where*. They didn't have to guess at who took her, though. Their home had been overrun by a madman, leading their own people against them, and the Demonic Presence once again extended its claws into their world.

Still, until Jonas was sure of exactly what they needed to do next, he was determined to enjoy his time with Aleksei.

The gods only knew how long it would last.

CHAPTER 24

BLOOD MERIDIAN

K atherine rushed through the servants' quarters, her arms wrapped around a large wicker hamper. She was late, and if her lady's things weren't put away promptly and tidily, she knew she'd get the strap.

She'd only been in the Palace a few weeks, and she was already well aware of Lady Delira's reputation. Girls had been put out for nothing more than failing to arrange her dressing table the way she liked.

And now Katherine had a bundle of her wash, fresh from the racks, and she was late.

Never mind that it wasn't her fault. Never mind that the wash-women were more likely than any other servants in the Palace to gossip rather than do their jobs. Never mind that Lady Delira had only sent her things out mere hours before, yet required some of them for dinner that evening.

None of it mattered, because it was *Katherine's* responsibility. And now she was late.

As she rounded a corner, Katherine's toe caught a rough floor-stone. She gasped as she tripped forward, the tidy stacks of laundry spilling out.

She threw her arms out, trying to protect her chin.

She hit hard, waiting for the hamper to come crashing down on top of her. She frowned, glancing up at all the chemises and colorful petti-coats frozen in midair, along with the hamper.

Katherine came to her feet, staring at the bizarre sight. Then she methodically began pulling the pieces out of the air, refolding them, and positioning them in the hamper. She heard a low chuckle, but she didn't turn from her duty until the hamper was just as it had been before she tripped. She grasped it firmly in her arms, but couldn't seem to budge the thing.

With a huff, she turned to find Ethan standing there, a smug grin plastered across his handsome face. When he caught sight of her with-ering glare, his smile faltered.

"I'm sorry," he said hurriedly, "I saw you trip and thought you'd appreciate a little help."

Katherine tried to dismiss her frustration, tears welling around her eyelids. "Yes, thank you, but I'm so late as it is. Now Lady Delira is prob-ably gonna have me sacked because the bloody washwomen weren't fast enough, and because milady doesn't realize how long wool takes to dry. Either way, I'll get the blame. And while I *do* appreciate your help, it's only made me the later."

The tears started to trickle down her cheeks, and she saw no way to hold them back...not that they'd do any good.

Ethan's face fell. She could see the concern buried in his deep brown eyes. "I'm sorry," he said softly, "I was only trying to help."

A thought came to her.

"Well," she said, trying to pull herself back together, "perhaps if *you* told Lady Delira what happened, about you running into me and all, she might be more forgiving."

Ethan stared at her in confusion for a moment before he burst out into a deep laugh, "*I* ran into *you*?...Well, I suppose Lady Delira will have to make an exception for my bumbling ways." He leaned forward and gave Katherine a wink, "Besides, she doesn't frighten me so much."

Katherine looked up at him in genuine surprise, grabbing hold of his giant arm. "I thought everyone was scared of her."

Ethan chuckled as he took the hamper from the air and started down the hallway.

Katherine had to jog to keep up with his long-legged stride, "Ser-vants and nobles, perhaps, but not Magi. Delira enjoys a...favored posi-tion at the moment, but the Magi don't pay much attention to her tantrums."

Katherine dared a glance at his face. His smile remained as fixed as ever.

"And what is *your* position, Ethan?" she asked softly.

He paused with a chuckle, "That's not something to worry yourself about, miss. Just know that you won't have to fret about punishment from Delira as long as I'm around."

Katherine's face flushed, but she immediately suppressed her flash of excitement.

This was hardly the place to seek out flattery, but in Ethan she might have found a valuable ally that she could use to her benefit. One of apparently higher ranking than the woman she'd been assigned to.

Perhaps she could coax Ethan into providing her even more useful information, but for the moment it was smarter to play along as the simple, simpering maid. Whatever it took to gain Ethan's trust and further her goals.

They reached Lady Delira's door, and Katherine gently pulled the hamper away from the Magus. When he frowned, she gave him a playful smile, "And how would Lady Delira feel to see *you* show up with a hamper full of her underclothes?"

His face froze for a moment before flushing red. "I see your point."

Katherine knocked gently, then stepped into the room.

She breathed a sigh of relief when she saw that Lady Delira had yet to return for her dinner preparations.

Leaving Ethan in the corridor, Katherine rushed to the massive oak wardrobe and put the Lady's things away, careful that they all appeared neat and tidy. Well, she supposed, nothing had actually touched the floor, so there was no reason they would be soiled.

She closed up the wardrobe and turned, gasping as she found herself only inches from Lady Delira's black eyes.

"*Katherine*, my dear," Delira said with a wicked smile. "I see you've finished your chores."

Katherine gave a short curtsey, "Yes, Milady."

"I feel like dressing myself this evening. There is a man outside who has asked the pleasure of escorting you around the South Lawn for an evening stroll, and I find it to be a *marvelous* idea!"

"Mi...milady?"

There was gleam in Lady Delira's eyes that Katherine could hardly miss. "I am *most* interested in hearing this man's opinions on a number of things. Be a dear and take a walk with the Ox, listen *carefully* to what he has to say. I want you back here by midnight, and I want to hear *every* word of it. Do you understand?"

Katherine felt her face flush again, so she played it off as embarrassment, "Of course, milady. I will do exactly as milady commands."

Lady Delira leaned forward and lifted Katherine's chin with a finger. Katherine suppressed a shiver as she was forced to meet the woman's black eyes again. "Be sure that you *do*, child, and I will see to it that you have a long, steady career in the Palace."

Her soft face twisted into a menacing snarl, "*Fail* me, and I'll have you thrown out into the gutters with the other trash." Her voice turned syrupy sweet again, "Do you *understand?*"

Katherine offered her most convincing smile and curtseyed, "Of course, milady. As you command, milady."

"Excellent," Delira said brightly. "Now, on your way. You'll want to shed that tattered rag for something more...*befitting* an evening with a Magus of Ethan's stature."

Katherine stared at Lady Delira with genuine confusion, "But milady, this is all I have."

Lady Delira threw her hand carelessly in the air, "That's *non*sense, dear. Your shoulders look a bit wide, but I'm sure you could squeeze into one of my larger gowns. Fetch me the burgundy wool."

Katherine hurried away to find the dress, her mind racing. What was Delira playing at? She wanted Katherine to spy on Ethan? The very concept drew a silent chuckle from her. Spying on Ethan was no different than spying on Delira.

In fact, that would just be more information she could relay to Declan. In a way, Lady Delira was doing her a favor. And she got to wear the woman's gown, besides! She wondered how badly she could sully it without drawing reproach?

Katherine rushed back with the dress, and Delira pulled it from her hands, holding it up to Katherine's chest.

"Yes, I think this one will do *quite* nicely. Tighten your stays and put it on, dear. If it pinches a bit, well, that simply gives you a goal for the future."

Katherine smiled again and curtseyed, "Yes, milady, thank you, milady."

Delira offered her a self-satisfied smirk and walked away, seeming to vanish into her enormous oak wardrobe.

Katherine hurried to the dressing mirror, pulling off her starched livery. She glanced around every now and then to be sure that the lady wasn't watching her.

She didn't know why Lady Delira would have any interest in such a thing, but she was still unsure whether this entire exercise was meant to humiliate her, or if the Lady was somehow sincere. Regardless, her mistress had her motives.

She managed to get the woolen gown buttoned up her back, but she found the last impossible to reach with her stays this tight. As it was, she was shocked by how much of her décolletage was on display. The idea of allowing anyone to see this much of her in the daylight felt scandalous.

But then again, she'd seen enough of the courtiers and sycophants who flooded the Palace every day. Their dresses made the burgundy wool look matronly by comparison. Katherine's natural modesty aside, it would have to do.

When she turned, Lady Delira stood not two paces away, a rapturous smile on her face, "Oh, dear girl, you fill that out *marvelously*." Delira thrust a dark, fur-lined cloak at her. "Put this on, but don't draw it too tight. And we want our young Ethan to be *full* of imagination when he sees you."

Katherine emerged from the ordeal, her hair done up with an elaborate pin, which Lady Delira insisted was all the rage, and her shoulders barely covered by her cloak. The gown's fit had emboldened Lady Delira to declare it "even more daring than I'd imagined."

Katherine felt like a sow dressed up like a swan.

"Now, dear, your young man has been waiting patiently enough. Go and have a walk with him. You're a good Southern Plain girl, you know how to ask *prying* questions. I have faith in you. Show me how *smart* you are."

Katherine heard the conspiring hollowness in Delira's voice. She was hoping to net a spider with a honeyed fly. If her plot failed, Delira lost nothing.

Katherine could name quite a few things she might lose if she didn't handle this just right.

Toma's eyes brightened. Her mouth opened, and Aya could feel the power of the Archanium blossom inside her. She squinted as the radiant light bubbled up from beneath Toma's skin. It was the same as the last three Magi she'd helped crossover.

Aya felt the effervescent joy radiating from the other woman. Ever since she'd leapt onto a new meridian in the Archanium, she'd felt it too. It was like breathing in air for the first time, or tasting the full sweetness of life. It was intoxicating.

Saliva dripped from Toma's chin as Aya watched her friend experience the true majesty of the Archanium for the first time. She knew the feeling well, pleasant enough before but this...this was *rapture*.

Aya allowed herself a heady grin at Toma's expression. The ecstasy of touching this meridian was eclipsed only by the joy of sharing it with others. She pushed away her fatigue. Her personal joy came with a price.

Aya remembered her trepidation at teaching the others. She had stumbled onto the new meridian by sheer accident, in a flash of panic. How could she possibly instruct other Magi to perform the same feat? She hadn't accomplished anything through skill or knowledge, merely terror.

And yet, when she'd sat down with Ilyana the week before, the process had been surprisingly easy. She'd thought there would be mighty barriers to break, or paths of arcane magic to haggardly traverse. Yet when she simply explained what she felt to Ilyana, casting out a hook to guide the woman's spark, the other Magus immediately grasped the nature of what Aya was working to accomplish.

After a simple binding spell granting Aya control over Ilyana's link to the Archanium, she'd easily guided her sister Magus onto the proper meridian.

The results were stunning.

Unlike Aya, who simply wanted to share her newfound knowledge, Ilyana had set about studying the bounds of the new meridian. She was obsessed with learning its strengths and weaknesses. She craved an understanding of her new boundaries, and the extent her new powers afforded her.

Ilyana had spent the next day cloistered in her room with Marrik, testing her abilities until she finally had a grasp of her expanded potential. When she emerged, Aya saw a transformed woman, forged by a deeper power and understanding. Even after all that, Ilyana confessed there were new regions she could reach, yet struggled to understand.

Tragically, in their first days of teaching others, they'd suffered a loss.

A young Magus who'd only just touched the new meridian had attempted to pull yet another onto their new path. The young man had died quickly, and Aya hoped, painlessly.

From that moment forward, however, she had instituted a new rule: only she or Ilyana were permitted to perform the spells that could bring the others over. They'd both had time enough to grasp the basics of their abilities and their limitations. Ilyana taught Aya surprising, even shocking things, things she hadn't even yet *considered*. And Ilyana, for her part, had taken to her new role like a duckling to welcoming water.

Aya suspected Ilyana had an easier time of guiding Magi onto the new meridian than she. Her sister Magus never seemed quite as tired as Aya after bringing over a Magus, as each time a newly initiated Magus radiated with light, the newfound connection seemed to bolster Ilyana rather than drain her. Aya wasn't sure if she were doing it wrong, or if they were just accomplishing the same ends in different ways.

For her part, Aya was more than happy to let Ilyana take charge. She found it simply too exhausting, and there were still hundreds to initiate. But as many as Ilyana was converting, it still wasn't happening it fast enough. And so Aya was once more guiding Magi onto the new meridian, albeit at a much slower pace than Ilyana.

After Toma's blissful praise and thanks for the initiation, and after Aya had sent her down to experiment on obliterating the rebel dead, she sat back against the pillows Raefan had set behind her. She took a long drink of water and breathed slowly as the next Magus took his place across from her. She closed her eyes for just a moment, luxuriating in the feel of winter sun on her face before she sat up again and looked into Hade's tentative gaze.

Aya jumped in surprise. "Hade? I hadn't heard of your return!" She leaned forward and hugged the scrawny Magus tightly, "When did you get here?"

Hade offered her a crooked smile, "Today, actually. When we arrived, we were told to come see you straight away. I expect that Vadim is surrounded by pretty girls and ale by now. They're probably having quite the time." He laughed nervously.

Aya offered him a small smile in return. She didn't feel anything from Raefan that suggested happiness, but then again, she rarely did. Raefan was a man wholly committed to his duty. Since his duty was protecting *her*, she supposed he could be out with Vadim, learning all he could of the other Knight's journey. She doubted he would be drinking much ale.

She'd only seen Raefan drunk twice, and those had been extenuating circumstances to say the least. Generally, Raefan had rules for everything. He was a man committed to structure and efficiency, and thus the escape alcohol provided some was not something he sought. Once in a great while, he would make an exception. Her face heated as she recalled the last exception.

Aya rolled her shoulders, trying to loosen the tension building in her neck and draw attention away from her blushing.

"You don't have to be so scared," she said casually, noting how nervous Hade seemed. "This is nothing to be frightened by. It's simply a little jump from where you are now. It only takes a moment."

Hade managed another furtive smile, "I trust you, Aya. Ilyana offered to help me along, but I'd rather work with you. There are fewer... complications with you."

Aya felt a moment of confusion and doubt at his odd phrasing, but she kept her frown to herself.

Jonas opened one eye experimentally. The waxed wool of their tent was dully lit with early morning sunshine. He yawned. Sleeping on the hard, frozen ground was a decided departure from his cozy bed in the Undercroft.

But Jonas relished his sore muscles. The discomfort was proof he was free of his grandmother. Free from that entire nightmare, and that realization brought him only warmth and contentment.

The scent of woodsmoke drifted into the tent, and Jonas caught the tantalizing aroma of breakfast. He sat up abruptly, almost taking down the tent in the same instant. Careful to mind his head, Jonas crawled his way out of the tent's opening.

Aleksei was dutifully skinning something small. There was a cheery fire going, though where the man had found wood in this desolate plain was anyone's guess. And improbably, Jonas realized that Aleksei was already well into cooking their morning meal.

The Knight turned sharply when he realized he was being watched.

On seeing Jonas's bleary eyes, Aleksei broke into a broad grin, "You're up! Didn't expect to see you quite so early."

Jonas glared back playfully, ducking back into the tent to pull on his boots. He groped around the tiny space for a bit before he finally found his coat. It was always seemed unusually cold in the mornings. While he disliked a great many things about traveling, the frigid winter mornings were at the top of his list.

When he finally ambled out into the snowy dawn, he was dismayed to find his clear campground buried under a handspan of snow. Glancing back at the tent, he suddenly realized the brilliance of the whole thing.

From the road, their tent was barely visible. The snow served to camouflage their presence entirely. Even in the crisp morning, Jonas could hardly distinguish the cozy tent from the rest of the landscape.

His face flushed. Despite the covering of snow, the tent had proved plenty warm enough for two fully-grown men.

"Here," Aleksei said absently, handing Jonas a small, horn-handled knife and a side of bacon. "Can you carve that up? I can only cook a little at a time."

Jonas took the meat and the blade, glancing down at the small cast-iron skillet Aleksei was using. He frowned at the blackened iron.

"Where did you *find* that?" he asked, slicing off hunks of bacon.

Aleksei smiled brightly, "It was among the supplies in Keldoan. My father always used something like this to cook breakfast. I figured it was the easiest thing to take along, since I knew how to use it better than anything else they had."

Jonas enjoyed a moment of silent pleasure, cutting hunks of bacon while his Knight waited to fry them on his peasant's skillet. One would hardly recognize him as a prince, he thought, cutting bacon by a rude fire.

With a curse, Jonas felt the blade go too far, biting into his thumb.

Aleksei looked up sharply as Jonas clenched his jaw, dropping the blade away from his bleeding thumb.

The Hunter immediately grabbed his hand and held it steady. Jonas felt suddenly nauseous as pain swept over him. He wasn't unused to the sight of blood, though he was a little embarrassed at swooning so easily in front of Aleksei.

"It's not too deep," Aleksei said gently, his fingers pressing down on points across Jonas's hand while holding pressure against the base of Jonas's thumb.

His pain and nausea were fading a bit, but Aleksei's face seemed strange and distracted.

"I might need to close this," Aleksei grumbled.

Jonas frowned. Close it? Gods, Jonas was not looking forward to the Mantle crawling about inside his skin again, especially not for such a minor cut.

Aleksei paused, his aureate eyes going out of focus. He relaxed the pressure, letting Jonas's blood flow forth again.

Jonas could feel it pump from his finger with the beat of his heart. The nausea returned.

Aleksei held up a hand.

"Quiet," he commanded.

Jonas wanted to protest that he hadn't said anything, to remind Aleksei that he was presently *bleeding*, but he instinctually obeyed his Hunter. This was certainly unlike anything Aleksei had done before.

The Hunter sniffed experimentally at Jonas's hand, licking the blood welling from of the cut. And then, to Jonas's utter fascination and horror, Aleksei pressed his mouth against the wound, pulling in hard. Jonas winced as the added pressure pulled more of his blood forth.

A moment later, Aleksei's head turned to the west, his rough hands still gripping the prince's wrist. Jonas watched the Hunter cock his head to the side, Was he...*listening?*

Jonas gasped as the Mantle poured over Aleksei's fingers and into his hand.

Even though it lasted only moments, Jonas knew the feeling. It mirrored the time Aleksei healed him after their fight with Bael.

He glanced down at his thumb, finding it whole and unmarked. And then he looked up into Aleksei's eyes, the normally-soft gold of his irises threaded with crimson.

The man was staring off into the distance.

Jonas wasn't sure how long they sat there in silence. He supposed it might have lasted hours, but when Aleksei finally came back to him, the sun was still hardly above the horizon.

Aleksei's eyes finally met his, the red threads gone.

"I know where she is," he grunted.

Jonas frowned, his hand reaching to touch Aleksei's face. "What?"

"Tamara...I know where she is."

Jonas leaned forward, "How?"

Aleksei shrugged, his eyes once again finding that faraway spot on the horizon, "The blood meridian."

Jonas simply stared at his Knight. "Can you start making sense?"

Aleksei snapped out of his trance, "Your blood."

When Jonas blinked at him, Aleksei sighed, "When you cut yourself, I could *smell* it. I could smell your blood, and I felt the connection. You're linked to Tamara.

"You share the same blood. When I...*tasted* your blood, I sensed her, I heard her heartbeat in my ears. I could feel it in my bones."

Aleksei sat back on his heels and closed his eyes, searching for the words. "Once I tasted your blood, I knew I could find anyone linked to you, *through* your blood.

"And then I felt it. It's weak, and it's *incredibly* distant, but I can feel her pulse."

Jonas leaned forward, grasping Aleksei's shoulders, "Where? Where do you feel it?"

Aleksei pointed immediately. Jonas's heart sank as he followed the line of Aleksei's arm. Exactly the direction his gaze had followed.

West.

"And how far is she?" Jonas asked.

"Leagues," Aleksei said definitely, "Perhaps *hundreds* of leagues. It will take weeks, maybe months to reach her. But she's there, Jonas. There is no one within that distance more strongly related to you."

Jonas's mind raced as he tried to calculate the distance between Taumon and Kuuran. It was vast indeed, but if Aleksei was pointing in the direction he thought....

"Are you sure?" Jonas finally asked.

Aleksei looked into Jonas's eyes with such certainly, he could scarcely breathe.

"If we go in that direction, we *will* find her. Her heart beats almost in time with yours. She shares your blood as keenly as anyone in this world."

Jonas sighed, "If she's that far away, there's no way anyone else will know where to find her. We *have* to go after her."

Aleksei's jaw set grimly. "Then we go into Fanj."

CHAPTER 25

PERFECT ILLUSIONS

A pall of mist hung over the rasping woods, shrouding the great spruces in a ghostly cloak. Lillian stepped forward tentatively, her hands wrapped in every scrap of cloth she could beg, coerce, or steal from the others in the King's army camp. All around her, trees groaned with the weight of winter dragging down their mighty limbs.

She listened intently, searching the gaps of quiet for any sign of the men and horses she *knew* must be camped somewhere ahead. Fifty-thousand men had marched out from the camp, yet not a single soul had returned in the days since.

She refused to believe so many could have perished without a single man making it back to them with news, good or ill.

The liberation forces had to be camped in the woods, *somewhere*, surrounding the city, preparing their next assault. Perhaps they'd over-come Keldoan already, as some of the other cooks had suggested, and were too busy enjoying the spoils of victory to bother with the camp followers.

Lillian refused to believe that.

She had followed her Eric to Kalinor, a welcome change from living beneath the frightening countenance of the Drakleyn, and he would never desert her.

She'd seen the column of cloud erupt when the Demon had

conjured his fel magics to cut through untold tons of snow and stone, freeing the King's army from a desolate, desperate winter, trapped in the valley of the Drakleyn without food or supplies.

Demon perhaps, but Lord Bael had been no less their savior that day. She smiled at the memory, recalling the excited, boyish glee on her beloved's face as he'd leapt about with his fellows, waving his cap in the air and praising the gods for sending them their divine protector.

While she herself was no great lover of the Demon, she couldn't help but be grateful for his mercy and godly power that day.

She'd followed Eric and the King's army to the very gates of Kalinor, when the King himself had sprung his ingenious trap in retaliation for the affront in the valley. She'd marveled as the mighty gates of Kalinor itself swung open without so much as an arrow launched, as the King's men poured through the opening, spilling into the city, purging the people who had dared to stand defiant against the one true king.

Against his Demon.

Snow crunched under her boots as the road grew ever steeper, pulling Lillian from her reverie, gawking at the sight before her. For as far as she could see, the snow lay light and smooth across the road. It was pristine. Not a single man nor beast had disturbed it.

A touch of panic snatched at her heart, her breath catching in her throat.

How was that *possible*? There had been so many men, more than in any city she'd ever beheld save Kalinor. Hundreds of horses had ridden towards Keldoan. What of them? How did one make a mighty city of soldiers and their mounts simply vanish?

With a start, Lillian realized that she could hear something beyond the sigh of trees and the crunch of snow beneath her boots.

Someone was riding towards her, through the fog. Fast.

She cast about, searching for the nearest escape, but the trees were at least a dozen paces in either direction. Even if she reached them before she was spotted, her bootprints would betray her in the freshly fallen snow.

Lillian swallowed hard, hoping that it was a friend barreling towards her. Otherwise, she was good as dead.

She'd heard too many stories detailing the savagery of the Legionnaires and their wicked Lord Captain. More beast than man, they said. She'd heard the tales of Legionnaires loyal to Aleksei Drago dining on the flesh of the dead, sometimes preferring to cut their dinners from men who still drew breath.

Gods, but she prayed such a fate had not befallen her Eric.

The mists suddenly parted, and an older man on a scraggly excuse for a horse scrambled into view. His face was haggard and flushed, his eyes wild as he cast about behind him, as though some fearsome horde were closing in on him.

He seemed to see her a just moment before his horse ran her down, and reined the beast in, lest she be trampled.

For a long moment he simply stared at her, his muddy brown eyes blinking at the sight of her cowering on her knees in the snow. He breathed hard, as though *he'd* been running down the hill, not his lathered horse.

He watched her as he caught his breath, the chipped sword in his left hand twitching.

"Sir?" she ventured, taking in his tattered uniform, the leather of his saddle cracked and rotten.

This was no Legionnaire, fattened on the flesh of his foes. This was a freedom fighter, just like Eric. From the insignia pinned to his lapel, she realized she was looking at a major, and she quickly bowed her head.

"Apologies, sir," she whimpered in the snow. "I...I didn't *realize* I was in the way of your horse. Please, sir, I've come from the camp. Do you have news of the campaign?"

He stared at her a moment longer, wiping at the snot running freely into his ragged beard. And then, unexpectedly, he slipped out of the saddle, taking a step towards her.

He paused when she turned away with a cry, closing her eyes as she waited for his retribution for standing in his path. Lillian had seen this play out in the camp enough times to know what to expect. She just prayed the gods reunited her with her beloved in the Aftershadow.

"What're you doing?" he barked gruffly.

She slowly opened her eyes, stunned he was speaking to her, rather than just kicking her out of his way or casually running her through with his sword, leaving her to bleed out in the snow.

"I sincerely apologize," she began, not daring to lift her face from the turned-down cuffs of his boots, "it truly wasn't my intention to—"

"Stop," he said sharply.

Lillian winced again, but then felt something unexpected.

His gloved hand wrapped around her wrist, and he pulled her to her feet. *Almost gently*, she thought in wonder. Gods, but she'd never imagined this happening. What horror did the gods have in store for her now? Perhaps she'd caused an even greater affront than she'd feared.

Behind the major came distant shouts and the thundering of hooves.

"Gods be *damned*," he spat, pulling her to his horse. "Get on. We have to hide from 'em."

As he practically shoved her into the saddle, Lillian noted how heavy his brow was, his eyes grotesquely bloodshot, as though he hadn't slept in days. She herself knew she'd lost count of the days since the King's men marched for Keldoan. Was it three? Ten?

"Major Rickard Surrley, ma'am," he muttered, never meeting her eyes, instead scanning the tree-line.

"Lillian," she managed.

Major Surrley nodded slowly, as though she'd just said something profound. "Can you run, Lillian?"

"Pardon?" It came out as more a squeak than a question.

The major nodded at the tree-line, "If they find us, you'll have to run to live. 'Less you plan on making one last stand right here on the road?"

She suddenly realized she was shivering, and not from the oppressive cold. "N...No, sir. I...can run, if need be."

"Good enough."

Lillian jumped when the major took the reins and turned the lathered horse towards the woods, cursing under his breath as he stumbled through the freshly fallen snow, doggedly making for the tree-line. She looked behind them, certain that any moment the enemy would crash through the mists and rip them to shreds, devouring them even as their blood stained the virgin snow.

Miraculously, time stretched on, and no men appeared to rend them to pieces. The trees enveloped them, and for the first time since she'd set out towards Keldoan by herself, Lillian allowed herself a small sigh of relief. She didn't know *why* this man was being so kind to her, but she was grateful for every moment that she still drew breath.

They traveled deeper into the woods for an interminable period before Major Surrley spoke again. When he did, she had to strain to hear him at first, the low gravel of his voice both alien to her ear, yet unmistakable amidst the ghostly groaning of the woods.

"We thought we knew what we was doin'," he grunted, and Lillian wondered if he was speaking to himself or to her. "Fifty. *Thousand.* Men."

She winced at the pain, the sorrow and bafflement heavy in his voice.

"We didn't know *what* we was gettin' into. The generals told us that the last dregs o'the Legion was backed in a corner. The Demon's Magi would tear the walls apart, just like in Kalinor. We'd be saviors, freeing the good people of Keldoan. Gods, what fools we were."

He fell silent, and Lillian found her desperate need to know Eric's fate finally outweigh her caution. "M...Major Surrley, what happened? Please, sir, even a *hint* would be such a gift just now."

"Happened?" the major practically barked.

Lillian winced as the word burst forth with a dark, empty laugh. She glanced behind them once more, but heard nothing. Perhaps they were deep enough into the trees that the Legionnaires hadn't heard his outburst.

"I'll tell you what happened," he grunted, trudging forward, pausing every now and then to listen before altering their direction. "It were a *trap*. They must've had spies in our ranks. We was told it would be easy, just like Kalinor. We were such bloody *fools*."

"And the other men?" she asked weakly.

"Other?" he stopped and turned to look up at her.

Lillian felt a whimper rise within her at the despair in his eyes. She thought she detected tears.

"There *ain't* no 'other men' no more," he said bitterly.

"Are...are you certain?"

He snorted, heading off once again, pulling the reins behind him. "'Bout as certain as a man can be. I saw 'em, all those men. All them *boys*. So bright, so full of life. And then, it was like a wind from the Aftershadow itself, it was."

Lillian was suddenly aware of how cold she was. Sitting on the horse, her tired muscles were growing colder, stiffening. But the tone of Major Surrley's voice sent a shiver through her colder than the deepest frost.

She was about to press him for more when he jerked to a halt. From her perch in the saddle, she was too high up to see much ahead of her. But something about the way he stood told her this was more than just him collecting himself, or checking their bearings.

Carefully, Lillian slid out of the saddle, reaching to her belt for the familiar handle of her kitchen knife. As her frozen fingers wrapped around the wooden handle, she shuffled forward.

And then she saw what had caused the sudden halt.

Before them stretched a clearing, the center of which was dominated by an achingly blue circle of ice. Eric had told her that the woods around Keldoan were dotted all over with glades just like this one, each one home to a pond, or even occasionally a proper lake.

But she'd never envisioned one to look like *this*.

This deep in the heart of winter, the pond was frozen solid. Yet unlike the peaceful glades of her dreams, she now stood on the edge of a nightmare.

Perhaps forty men filled the clearing, standing on the unearthly blue ice, each frozen in place. Some had their hands raised, as though warding off a great evil. Others were in mid-step, attempting to run. None looked like the proud, virile men she'd watched march off to battle.

Rather than the bright, eager eyes of men heading off to deliver the King's Justice, she now stared into horrified frozen faces. These weren't frozen men, but rather the *shapes* of men conjured from ice, streaked with deep whorls of purple and muddy swatches of brown, their eyes white.

"What...what are they?" she stammered, looking from one lifelike face to another.

The major stared down at the snow, crushing his cap in his hands, trembling. After a long moment, Lillian realized he was sobbing.

"M...Major? Major, what *are* these?"

He wiped his face with his crumpled cap, shaking his head.

"These, miss, are our men. What's left of 'em."

She stared at the frozen faces, contorted with pain, some mouths wrenched wide open, frozen even as they screamed.

"But that's...that's not *possible*," she managed haltingly, taking an involuntary step back.

Even as she tried to understand what she was staring at, a light burst into being above the glade. In a heartbeat, the frozen figures of the men turned to liquid, striking the frozen pond below with wet *thwacks* that reverberated through her. The pond itself melted an instant later, the water bubbling, steam writhing up in misty tendrils and billowing out from the edges.

Lillian gasped at the overpowering stench, vomiting in the snow even as tears froze on her face.

"No time for that, girl!"

The major's voice cut through the miasma filling the glade.

Even as she stumbled back, he gripped her shoulders, shoving her towards the horse. She caught the reins in her hands, staring around in confusion, unsure of what to do next, trying to pull her eyes away from the terrifying sight unfolding before her in the clearing.

Major Surrley bodily lifted her into the saddle, and as she lost sight of the glade, a sudden sound filled the forest. Loud, guttural clicks and exuberant, resonant hooting sounded to the north.

"*Bastards*, they're closer than I thought!" The major roared, pulling his chipped sword free as he turned towards the terrifying cries.

"Get out of here, girl! I'll hold 'em off long as I can. Ride south. Stay to the trees, you outta come out on the road west of the camp. Get back to them! Get them out of here! Go back to Kalinor, go south, it doesn't bloody *matter*! Just *go*!"

He struck the horse's backside with the flat of his blade. It reared, but she managed to hang onto the reins without falling into the snow. It charged south, Lillian barely hanging on for dear life.

She couldn't look back, even as she heard Major Surrley issue a challenge. Seconds later she heard an anguished cacophony as the man was torn apart by the gods-only-*knew* what horror. In the frozen snowscape, Lillian was shocked by how *wet* his death sounded.

Tears streamed down her face, freezing to her face even as new tears formed. But she didn't dare let go, not for a moment. She *had* to get back to the camp. She had to tell them what had happened to the men. She had to *save* them, before they all shared the same grim fate as poor Major Surrley.

⚶

Back in the clearing, Marrik brushed the snow from his coat as the illusion of Major Rickard Surrley melted around him.

"What was *that*?" Raefan demanded, stepping into the frozen glade and crossing his arms. "And who in the blazes is 'Rickard Surrley'? Did you just make that up on the fly? Because it's a piss-poor alias if you did."

A shadow flickered across Marrik's face, if only for an instant. "No, he's very much a real person. Well, *was*."

Ilyana stepped out to join Raefan, both her gloved hands practically shoved in her mouth, her eyes watering as she fought the laughter threatening to burst forth.

Marrik chuckled darkly, turning his head from the Knight to his Magus.

Raefan fixed the both of them with a disgusted look, "Aya said to make it *convincing*. Ice soldiers melting into a boiling pond in the dead of *winter*? Who's going to believe a story like that? And gods, man, what *was* that accent?"

Marrik shrugged with a smirk, "I thought I'd try it out."

Raefan scowled, "Where were you even supposed to be *from*? You better not let Aleksei hear you mocking him like that, and that man can hear a gnat pissing on blotter."

"Excellent, you got the reference," Marrik chortled,

Raefan sighed, laughing in spite of himself, "Barely. And yes, he goes home for five bloody seconds and walks away sounding like a stablehand from the wrong side of Mornj. Then he sees Jonas for an hour, and suddenly he's Sir Prim-and-Proper."

"I believe he calls it 'blending in'."

Raefan snorted, his shoulders relaxing, "I'm not sure how you figure. He's got eyes like a coyote and a living black tattoo that drinks the souls of his enemies, or whatever the bloody thing actually does."

Ilyana wiped tears from her face as she finally reined in her laughter, "To be fair, it wasn't all just on Marrik. I hardly anticipated just how convincing that illusion would be. I've toyed with misinterpretation before, but it's never been that *real*."

Marrik wrinkled his nose, "I don't even want to *know* how you conjured that stench. It was like stepping onto a field of openly rotting corpses in the heat of summer. Was that from memory? Gods, woman, what secrets have you been *keeping* from me?"

Raefan held up a hand, "I don't want to hear the answer to that. And Marrik, that wasn't exactly the script Aya prepared."

Marrik shrugged, "I was in a pantomime or two in my younger days. I was only trying to give life to Aya's wonderful thoughts."

Raefan grunted in the gathering gloom, the sun finally sinking behind the mountains to the west and wrapping the forest valley in shadow. "Let's just hope you didn't scare that girl to death. This doesn't work if all our little 'messengers' die of fright before they get back to the others with their stories."

Marrik allowed himself dry chuckle as they made their way back to their mounts.

"If they can tolerate following Bael to Kalinor, or tagging along with that great band of villains across half of Ilyar in deep winter, I think they can handle a few good-natured spooks. I'm more interested in what's for supper. I'm hungry!"

CHAPTER 26

BOUND

When Katherine stepped back into the corridor, Ethan clapped a hand over his gaping mouth. She stood straight and proud, despite the excruciating restriction of her stays. Delira appeared to be pieced together from delicate bone, minimal muscle, and careless cruelty. It had required a great deal of contortion to squeeze a cooper's daughter into a gown fashioned for a walking skeleton.

"Do you find something amusing?" she asked pointedly.

The Magus coughed uncomfortably, "My apologies, miss. I simply didn't expect you to come out in such...such *finery*."

Finery? I suppose that's a polite enough euphemism for it. she thought.

She nodded down the hallway and began walking. Ethan followed her, frowning.

When Katherine judged that they were out of Delira's earshot, she allowed herself a small smile, "It was hardly my idea. Lady Delira insisted that I 'look the part'. She wants me to flatter you, hoping that you'll divulge all your secrets to me."

Ethan stopped and blinked at her, "Why would you tell me that?"

Katherine turned to face the big Magus with a shrug, "Why shouldn't I? You've spoken with me before, you know my status in the castle. If I stepped out in a dress that's clearly far above my station, obviously designed to inflame your passions, and started acting like some simpering sot, you wouldn't find that the *least* bit suspicious? You wouldn't think me disingenuous, or even naive and silly?"

Ethan struggled to form words; obviously startled. He was clearly unused to anyone being this frank with him.

She wondered if he was of noble birth.

"I suppose you're right," he allowed finally. "It didn't really occur to me until you put it like that, but yes, I would have noticed."

Katherine nodded and started walking again. Ethan had to jog to catch up to her.

She continued, "How likely would you have been to speak to me ever again, had I put on such a display? You'd either have thought me one of Lady Delira's spies, or at the very least a simpleton with no mind of her own. Either way, I doubt you'd find me *charming*."

Ethan quirked a smile at her, "Is that what you want? To be found charming?"

Katherine silently cursed herself. "I think you'd be hard pressed to find a woman in this palace who doesn't desire that on some remote level."

Ethan smirked, bemused as they descended the stairs. He didn't say anything as they traversed the confusion of corridors that led towards the South Lawn.

Katherine didn't force conversation.

The silence was valuable; it allowed her time to plan her responses, her parries and maneuvers. A plan was forming in her mind. If she could execute it, this evening would prove quite valuable, even entertaining.

As she stepped onto the Lawn, Katherine tripped on the hems of her too-long petticoats and pitched forward, nearly planting her face in the snow.

She caught herself, but only just. Lady Delira had tried to force her feet into a pair of platformed slippers that looked to have been made for a doll, but to no avail. As a result, the gown and accompanying undergarments were decidedly too long, and *gods* was it heavy.

At least it was warm.

Upon straightening, Ethan was watching her with that same idiotic grin plastered across his handsome face. Katherine shrugged, hiking up her voluminous skirts around her ankles, "Lady Delira is a fool if she thinks I'm well-versed in walking in these frocks."

Ethan chuckled as they walked towards the lone structure on the South Lawn.

"I've met many women who would have paraded around, trying their best, but looking all the more foolish for it. I think your decision does you great credit."

When she didn't respond, Ethan kept talking, "So, what exactly did Delira want to know?"

Katherine shrugged, "I'm not entirely sure, honestly. She had a list of questions, but most of them didn't make any sense to me. She wants to know where Master Bael has gone off to. Apparently he didn't see a need to tell her."

"Master Bael rarely feels the need to inform *any* of us to his comings and goings. She of all people should appreciate that. What else?"

"She wanted to know if you'd had any encounters with the King."

Ethan snorted, "Krasik? So, she's jumped on the wagon of fools calling him 'king' now?"

Katherine faked her confusion, surprised to hear him call his compatriots "fools". "But I thought he was crowned after the sacking of Kalinor."

Ethan shrugged, "Even if he was, the Queen hasn't been found yet. Neither has the Princess, *nor* the Prince. A military occupation doesn't make you a king. A big army doesn't make you king. Right now, he's little more than a despot with a city of hungry peasants to feed."

Katherine gasped, "*Ethan*, what if someone hears you say such things? They could charge you with treason, king or no."

Ethan snorted, "Unlikely. The people occupying the Palace make a grave mistake if they believe that Krasik's victory proves his legitimacy. Master Bael is in command of Kalinor, not Krasik.

"Krasik is merely a puppet, and Bael pulls the strings. Our Magi have little to fear from pawns like Krasik or Lord Perron."

Katherine blinked in genuine astonishment. Lord Declan had told her that Bael was dangerous, but he'd never given her the sense that Bael was in *command*. In fact, her goal up until now had been to find a way into Lord Perron's service, so that she might have access to the choicest intelligence.

"At any rate," Ethan said, "Krasik keeps to his chambers. No one sees him, but I know of several Magi who have gone to treat the man for his headaches. I think it's difficult for someone of his power to have so many people around all the time."

Katherine frowned, "I didn't realize that power weighed so heavily on him."

Ethan scoffed, "Not the power of rule. Krasik has his own magic. *Ancient* magic that allows him certain...advantages. He can hear thoughts. He can make you see things that aren't there. That's how we breached the outer walls of Kalinor."

Katherine kept her eyes on her feet, "I was still on the Southern Plain when Kalinor was sacked."

Ethan stopped and turned to her, placing a hand gently on her shoulder, "Be very happy you weren't here to witness it, Katherine. It was horrifying. The things I saw...and the things I saw done to people. *Innocent* people...it was horrible. Prince Belgi was a force unlike anything we expected.

"Many of the Palace staff were slaughtered without a care during the initial fighting, and if I do say so, he very rightly exacted retribution on those responsible. Mistakes are made in war, but there's *never* an excuse to murder the innocent."

Katherine flinched at the look on Ethan's face. She could almost see the memories ghosting across his eyes.

He misread her sudden silence. "Don't worry, it's over now. This palace is the safest place in Ilyar."

The words did little to comfort her.

They reached the lone structure on the South Lawn, and for the first time since their walk began, Katherine strayed from her mission.

The Cathedral of Mokosh.

"Ethan," she said with just a hint of excitement, "would it be alright if we went inside?"

The Magus quirked a smile, "Of course. Any particular reason?"

Katherine nodded as she started for the simple oak doors, "In Voskrin, the village I grew up in, Mokosh is particularly revered. We have a priestess there, Mother Margareta. She's like a second mother to me, and I would always go along with her to bless the fields and heal the sick."

Ethan arched an eyebrow, "She can heal the sick?"

Katherine nodded, "And many other things. She is as good a woman as I have ever known. It would bring my heart great joy to someday bring her to this place. I never imagined I'd get to see it myself."

Ethan's perfect smile brightened at her girlish glee. He thrust one of the doors open, holding it for her as she stepped reverently inside. She stared at the barren stone walls, the simple, rough altar. The pews looked as though her father could have carved them.

Ethan frowned when he realized that she was crying. "Katherine? What's the matter? I thought you'd be *happy* to see this."

Katherine turned to him and smiled, even as tears flowed down her cheeks. "But I *am* happy, Ethan. This is wonderful beyond anything I could have imagined."

She could tell from his expression that he didn't understand.

Her smile fixed, Katherine walked down the center aisle, her hands brushing the rough wood of the pews. "This is a simple, modest place. Everything I've ever learned about the Goddess says that She would want nothing more than a space built from the fresh earth, from raw woods.

"The first time I came into Kalinor, we passed between two great Cathedrals. The Cathedral of Stribog was all golden lightning and silver clouds, onyx dog faces glowering from the shadows.

"The Cathedral of Volos was terrifying, black and cold, cows with gilded horns grimacing down from blue torches. Both were luxurious to a fault, but both completely heartless.

"But this place...this place feels like *home*. Amidst all the finery of the Palace, that this humble place *exists* brings joy to my heart."

Ethan's smile returned at seeing her so happy. "I'm glad you approve."

Katherine paused at the rough altar, placing her hands reverentially on the stone. "And yet, this is the only cathedral housed within the walls of the Palace."

Ethan joined her at the altar, shrugging his massive shoulders, "Perhaps it was the first they built?"

Katherine frowned, "I don't think it was. Look at the Palace, Ethan. Look at the Voralla. These weren't built by people who were unaccustomed to beauty."

Ethan glanced around the rough temple, his brow furrowed, "But then why build it like this?"

Katherine wiped her eyes and turned back to the big Magus, "I think it's meant as reminder."

When she could tell he didn't understand, Katherine kept talking, "It would be easy to live in the Palace, or the Voralla, never setting foot into the rest of the world. I think this place is meant to remind the powerful of the weak. That the weak need to be considered, too. That the entire world doesn't live in finery, just because the monarchy and the Magi do."

"That's a very astute insight."

Katherine gave a yelp of surprise at the sudden intrusion of a new voice. She turned to face the source and immediately worked to suppress her shock.

Bael stood at the door of the Cathedral, a leering smile on his face. He turned to Ethan, "And who would *this* lovely young woman be?"

Ethan began to open his mouth, but Katherine brushed past him, looking Bael in the eye before dropping her gaze and flowing into a deep curtsey, "Katherine, Milord Bael. My name is Katherine. I am but a humble servant in the Palace."

Bael stared at her a long moment after she'd straightened. "A servant in such a fine gown?" he asked finally.

She nodded, keeping her eyes demurred, "Lady Delira allowed me the pleasure of wearing her frock so that I might take a turn around the Lawn in more than my simple livery. It was so very kind of her."

Bael sneered, his dead lips pallid and cracked, "Indeed. Tell me, Katherine, where do you hail from?"

"The Southern Plain, Milord Bael. I was fortunate enough to receive employ here only a few weeks ago."

Bael stroked his chin, glancing from Ethan's face to hers. He finally smiled, "Tell me, Katherine, how do you like working for Lady Delira?"

Katherine blinked at the floor, "It's more than I could have hoped for. Lady Delira is very kind to me. She is strict, but I work hard. I don't shirk my duties to gossip, and I am always prompt."

"Are you? If I ask Lady Delira, will she put a lie to your boasts?"

Katherine stiffened in indignation. The first time she'd laid eyes on this man, her fear had sent her running. But standing before him now, she no longer felt afraid. She did a good job, she was honest when it suited her, and she was rarely late. Even one so evil as he had nothing to hold over her on that account.

"If she does then she is lying," Katherine said, looking into his face defiantly.

Bael burst out laughing. "Very good, milady. Very good indeed." He glanced over her shoulder to Ethan, "I see you've found quite a gem, boy. Well done."

Katherine risked a glance over her shoulder and found Ethan looking at the floor, his cheeks flushed.

Bael stepped forward and peered deep into her big brown eyes, "I like you, Katherine. I've been looking for an honest girl such as yourself for a while, now. You see, from time to time, the Palace entertains... special guests. In the not-too-distant future, we will be graced with such a visitor. You would see to their needs when they arrive."

He arched a golden eyebrow, "Will you do me this favor, Katherine? It will, of course, be in addition to your duties to Lady Delira, and a lady's needs must come first. What do you say? Would you be willing to take on a little extra work?"

Katherine lowered her head and curtseyed again, "It would be my honor, milord."

Bael nodded, raising his hand and pressing it against Katherine's forehead.

Hard.

She stifled a whimper, but it seemed over as soon as she'd felt the pressure.

The Demon stepped back, glancing over at Ethan with a cool smile, "Thank you, child. You do your realm a great service."

Thunder shook the windows in their casements. Andariana paced back and forth before the hearth, her concern growing. Roux had been gone for hours, and while that in itself was not unusual, the violence of the storm raised new concerns.

This was a man who had spent the majority of his life in the Seil Wood, shielded from the sky and protected from violent storms. What would he know of such a storm as it approached from the sea? Had he ever been caught out in such rain and fury?

Lightning flashed, and for a moment Andariana caught a glimpse of shadow flicker across the brilliance.

Roux materialized out of the air in the far corner of the room, dripping wet. Andariana breathed a sigh of relief as she rushed towards him. She could see in his face how exhausted he was.

Gods, she wondered if he'd actually slept last night, as he'd claimed. While she found his single-minded determination to find her daughter truly touching, she was beginning to grow concerned for the young man.

He looked around the room, and she thought he must be partly stunned by the force of the rain. She hurried to a nearby chair and pulled away a blanket. He stood, dripping in his Ilyari woolens, shivering ever so slightly. She threw the blanket over his shoulders and led him to the fire.

While winters in Taumon were not nearly as severe as they were in Kalinor, the rain would only serve to sap his strength, and his heat. Sometimes a dry, bitter cold was better than the damp chill of Taumon in winter.

Roux stood before the fire a long time, warming his hands and trying to rub the chill from his bones before he said anything.

Andariana took the opportunity to pour him a mug of hot mulled wine. She hoped that it might relax him.

What with his exhaustion and the sudden storm, she was *determined* to see him get some sleep.

But not before he told her what he'd found.

When she returned to the hearth, she found that Roux had shrugged off her blanket, but accepted the mug from her readily enough.

Andariana stepped away and allowed him his space. She had come to learn that he was not a man to be trifled with. Most men in her realm would bow and scrape when she caused enough of a fuss, but she had lately found herself surrounded by a different breed entirely. It was hardly surprising that Aleksei Drago's cousin was even less accommodating than Aleksei himself. Then again, Aleksei was Ilyari, and bonded to Jonas besides.

Roux Devaan was something altogether different.

"I think I'm getting closer," he said finally.

Andariana's concern rose as she heard the gravel in his voice. Gods, but she hoped he wasn't falling ill. Fever could kill him just as surely as any blade. She glanced to the window again and grimaced. The wet would only serve to exacerbate a fever.

"To what?" she asked, pushing aside her concerns for the moment.

He turned to face her. In the firelight, his woolens clung to his muscular frame. She thought he looked more like a drowned rat than the Ri-Hnon just then.

"I don't believe for a *moment* that Tamara is being held in the city," he said gruffly. "Even if she were, she's no longer here. But that doesn't mean the trail is cold."

Andariana poured herself a glass of wine and frowned at him, "Meaning?"

Roux shrugged, turning his back to the fire. Faint steam rose from his shoulders. "Whoever took Tamara knew *exactly* where she was. They knew her room, and they managed to get her out without anyone ever seeing her *or* them. Even a Magus, no matter his power, would have to be given information to do such a thing. So, there must be *some*one in the Admiralty working with the enemy. Perhaps more than one, but that does little to help us at the moment. I've spent the last week trying to determine how any information gathered *here* got to a Magus out *there*.

"It's hardly a secret that many different nobles and factions have their eyes and ears scattered throughout places of import. I'm simply trying to find the thread that led the Magus to Tamara. If we can find the contacts, I can get information from them."

Andariana nodded. His logic was sound. But there were still questions nipping at the back of her mind.

"And how do you know that any of these spies will have the information we need?" she asked calmly.

He shrugged, "I don't. But this is the most solid, perhaps *only*, connection to Tamara's kidnapper that we have. Without this thread of information, we only know that she's gone and that she was taken by a Magus. I'll keep following it as far as I can. Most of the people I've encountered have loose loyalties. A silver here or there seems to go quite far. When I find someone who knows something, I'll just make them talk. Through bribery or through...other persuasions."

Andariana watched him carefully caress the small horn knife strapped across his chest. She didn't for a moment doubt his resolve, but she did occasionally wonder at his techniques. After all, this was not a man hardened to questioning criminals and torturing the treasonous. This was a leader of a village. Granted, the Wood was a place of powerful magic, but forceful interrogation was not amongst his many skills.

Yet had she not seen his keen wrath already, she wondered how comfortable she would be right now, knowing that her daughter's life could very well hang on Roux Devaan's ability to coerce the right answers.

He paused, finally thrusting his hand into a pocket and carefully withdrawing a thin piece of paper. It was drenched, but he peeled it apart and laid it before the hearth.

She stepped forward, a frown creasing her face, "What is *that*?"

Roux glanced back at her, "I'm not sure. It might be nothing. I was walking through the market and someone thrust it into my hands, mumbling something about a holy Forge or some nonsense.

"The man looked like a fanatic. I wanted to take a better look at it when I had a chance, just to make sure they weren't in any way connected to Tamara."

Andariana glanced down at the drying pamphlet and let out a sigh, "I'm afraid not."

He arched an eyebrow, "How are you so sure?"

She shrugged, flicking her hand at the smudged shield that occupied the first page. "That's the sigil of Winter's Children. They've been reported in Kalinor as well. From what I've heard, they're entirely harmless.

"Just another cult of some sort, preaching another doomsday message. The gods know such nightmares are common enough these days. But I doubt they'd command the sort of influence necessary to attract the attention of an enemy Magus."

Roux frowned at the pamphlet, "Still, I'd rather be certain. I'll look it over, make sure it's nothing too incendiary. The last thing we need is another lot stirring up trouble."

Andariana chuckled mirthlessly, "I'd say we're up to our neck in trouble at the moment. We hardly need any help from *their* ilk."

CHAPTER 27

AN UNEXPECTED ARRIVAL

The doors of Colonel Walsh's office burst open, and everyone looked up with a start as Aleksei and Jonas stepped into the room. From the astonished looks on the faces of the people gathered around the Colonel's desk, this was an unexpected arrival.

A cacophony of questions shattered the stunned silence until Aleksei slammed his hand down on the desk, casting the room into an uneasy quiet.

Colonel Walsh jumped to his feet and saluted, "Lord Captain, this is a surprise! We hadn't received word of your arrival."

Aleksei casually returned the salute, taking in the gathered group. All were people of import. He saw Colonels Rysun and Ander standing next to Aya and Ilyana, accompanied by their Knights. And beside Raefan stood, of all people, his father.

"I'm afraid I have some grave news," Aleksei began without preface, "and we don't have much time."

The room was silent as those gathered shared concerned glances. Colonel Walsh sighed, looking down at the map of Ilyar spread across his desk. "I've been expecting this for a while now. Can you show us how close the enemy is, Sir?"

Aleksei frowned, "The enemy? No, Colonel, this is a concern of a *completely* different nature. Rather than strike us with their soldiers, the rebels have struck us in our hearts."

When he was met with frowns, Aleksei continued, "Princess Tamara has been captured." He waited for the shock and angry oaths to die down before proceeding, "We believe we know her location, but I fear it will take us great amount of time and trouble to recover her."

Colonel Walsh clenched his square jaw, "We will send whatever men we need, Sir, you can rest assured."

Jonas stepped up next to Aleksei, offering the Colonel a rueful smile, "Your dedication to the Crown is most appreciated, Colonel, but I'm afraid all the men in the Legion can't help us now. The enemy has taken my cousin into the depths of Fanj."

At this, curses and angry protestations rang out anew. Jonas and Aleksei stood silently, letting the Magi and officers around the desk vent their frustrations.

As the furor died down, Jonas spoke again, "The Lord Captain and I will go into Fanj. *Alone*. We will be far less conspicuous that way, and more likely to succeed. I believe the enemy is relying on the strength of their secret to keep the Princess from us. They won't risk the security of that secret by surrounding themselves with soldiers in the depths of a foreign realm. This is a job for a Magus, not an army."

He opened his mouth to continue when he suddenly froze. He looked around the room in confusion, before turning to Aya with a frown, "Gods, what has happened here? Every Magus in this room has...*changed*. What have you...you're *all* on a different meridian?"

Aya beamed with pride, "I discovered it by accident, when the wind demon was nearly on Aleksei. When it left him, and charged at me..." Her face grew solemn "I knew I'd just doomed myself. Doomed *Raefan*. I just...I just couldn't accept the thought of him dying because I acted rashly.

"And all of a sudden, there were a thousand spellforms around me I'd never seen in my life, this...well of power within me. More *importantly*, while Aleksei was off searching for you, Ilyana and I discovered how to guide the others onto this new meridian. Now we all command the same magic. It's a *miracle*, Jonas!"

Jonas looked at the Prophet with a newfound respect, "I should say so. This is *incredible* news, Aya. Aleksei mentioned your discovery, of course, but I didn't realize you could help the others make the same leap. This will go a *long* way towards evening the playing field."

Colonel Walsh raised a hand, "With all due respect, Highness, what are we to do now, while the two of you ride into the wastes of Fanj?"

Aleksei leaned forward, looking down at the map, "While we're gone, you're going to have to do your level best to defend the cities we still control. I've given this a great deal of thought, Colonel, and it is now clearer than ever to me that we can*not* just hole up in Keldoan. We have to show Krasik that we're a force to be reckoned with, to be feared. He got lucky in Kalinor, and we made a strong showing with our victory here, but we can't rest on our laurels.

"I'm dividing the force *and* the Voralla."

A cry of protest went up from both the officers and the Magi.

Aleksei's golden glare swept across the small gathering, silencing any immediate complaints. "Keldoan is not the only city worthy of protection. And the more we can keep from the rebels, the better our chances of winning this damned war. I know there is strength and comfort in numbers, but we must separate our forces to have any hope of success.

"First of all, the senior generals abandoned their Queen to follow Perron and Krasik. Therefore, effective immediately, we have our *own* generals."

Eyebrows went up around the desk. Aleksei looked at each of his colonels in turn, "Walsh, Rysun, Ander, congratulations. You are now the commanding generals of Her Majesty's Legion. I will leave it to your discretion to appoint your new colonels and lieutenants. Choose carefully."

A brief wave of applause swept the room for the three men, all of whom appeared to be stunned. For the life of him, Aleksei couldn't understand *why*. They'd all been functioning in that capacity for a good amount of time now, especially Ander and Rysun.

"As to the division," Aleksei continued, using the brief burst of excitement to press his more unpopular decision, "I want at *least* fifty Magi to immediately head towards Taumon, led by Ilyana. Father, you will accompany them, along with General Rysun and five thousand men." Henry opened his mouth to speak, but Aleksei held up his hand, "The Queen is still there, and until you get there, she is vulnerable to assault. I want you to make sure she gets on the water and out of the city as swiftly as possible. You march tomorrow."

Astonished silence met his words, so he plowed onwards, "General Ander, you are to take fifty Magi and ten thousand men to Keiv-Alon. Major Jeran already commands a force of around six thousand there, and with the combined weight of your forces, you ought to be able to hold the city against anything Krasik can scrape together and call an 'army'. The Magi can fortify the walls against the Demon's Magi."

Once again, silence. Aleksei glanced up at Aya, "I want you to stay here with the remainder of the Magi. General Walsh will also remain here and make sure the city is kept safe.

"There are valuable things in the Betrayer's Bastion, things I'd like you to study and protect while you're stationed here. I want to know if there's anything in the library we can use. We no longer have control over the Voralla and its treasures, so we need to find aid wherever we can."

Aya frowned at him, "How do you know about the library? I've never mentioned it before."

Jonas smiled, "I told him what I knew on the ride down. Anything you find could prove to be an enormous boon to our cause. Of the Magi here, you're the most well-read. I don't have to tell you, now more than ever, we need *every* advantage we can get. Besides, it's highly probable there are relics secreted around the Bastion; we just haven't been looking hard enough."

Aya sighed, "I'll do my best, Jonas."

The Prince nodded, "I have faith in you." He turned his attention to the others, "Any other questions?"

Aleksei sensed that there were a great many questions indeed. After all, they'd both been absent for quite some time. To sweep into the command center and immediately start telling them what they were going to do next was a bit arrogant, but he and Jonas had thought about this long and hard on the journey south.

Even before Jonas had learned their Magi's newly acquired might, he'd known they had to be divided. It was too great a risk to have them all bunched together. With their new abilities, Aleksei was even more certain of that decision than ever.

General Rysun cleared his throat, "I believe both you and the Lord Captain were quite clear, Your Highness."

Jonas smiled grimly, "I'm glad to hear it, General. If that's all then, I believe we all have quite a bit of work to do and too little time."

Recognizing their dismissal, nearly everyone hurried from the office to get their people in motion. Jonas caught Aya as she turned to leave. "May I speak with you for a moment?"

She glanced at the retreating backs of the officers, waiting until they were out of the room, "Of course, what is it?"

Jonas reached into his pack and withdrew a slender volume bound in purple leather, "I...found this in the Reliquary. I want to know if it will open for you."

With a curious frown, Aya opened the volume and began to flip through the pages. Her eyes widened as she saw the diagrams. "Great *gods*, Jonas, this thing has to be thousands of years old," she glanced up at him. "So why is it inscribed to *you*?"

Jonas offered a soft smile, "When I found it, there was some sort of seal holding it shut. Honestly, I wasn't sure whether you could open it or not. It was left for me a decade ago. In the *Reliquary*, of all places, but I don't know by whom."

Aya frowned, her fingers tracing the emerald ink of the inscription. She closed her eyes, and Jonas watched her closely as she embraced the Archanium. She stood still a moment, her brow creased in concentration. A slight gasp escaped her as her eyes snapped open.

She stared at the inscription a long moment, her eyebrows drawing down as though she could somehow will the words to reveal something to her before meeting his gaze. "Darielle. It was left by Darielle."

He blinked at her, his head swimming with the improbability of such a statement.

"I didn't say it made sense," she said slowly. "But you said she was a Prophet?"

He nodded.

"Red hair, green eyes that look just like yours?"

He frowned, "I'm not sure I'd phrase it quite like that, but...Aya, she would have been a *child*."

The Magus shrugged, "Unless you know of another Prophet matching that description, it was her. Every Prophet's magic carries a signature. There aren't exactly a lot of us around, but I've encountered echoes on older texts before. Of course, those are normally from people long dead. This one is...very powerful and very alive."

Jonas arched an eyebrow, surprised that she'd been able to identify the other Magus. He doubted he'd told her any more than fleeting bits of information about the woman, but she clearly already possessed a profound dislike for the other Prophet.

"At any rate," he said, trying to push past the dizzying complications such information carried, "I don't want to take something that old and fragile into Fanj. I'm not going to have the time necessary to really study it while we're traveling. Since you're going to be here, I thought you might take a crack at it, see what you can learn."

Aya's face brightened, "I'd be glad to. I just hope I'm up to the challenge."

"You'll have half the Voralla at your disposal. If you run into something you find confusing, consult with whomever you like, anyone you trust. We're not going to get very far if we all keep to ourselves."

Aya sighed, "The gods know *that's* true enough."

"There's something else. Can you use your prophetic talents to see where Tamara is? All we have is a heartbeat, and knowing anything more precise would be a major...." Jonas trailed off as Aya's face fell. "Aya? What's wrong?"

"I'm happy to scry for you, Jonas, but I'm not sure how much good it'll do. Every time I've tried to look into the future, into the *present*, I still see things, but some of them are...wrong."

"What do you mean, 'wrong'?"

Aya blew out a frustrated breath, and Jonas could tell something was deeply upsetting her. "I tried looking into the future before the battle for Keldoan. The vision I saw correctly predicted our victory, but some crucial elements were missing. Aleksei never got injured by that...creature, and as a result, *I* never broke through to our new meridian. Those were both massive events that should have been clear as day, and yet they were absent from my visions. I'm just not sure how...reliable my talents are at the moment."

Jonas took a deep breath, trying not to let the implications of her words overwhelm him. Was it her? Or was it prophecy as a whole? What might cause such an anomaly? "That must be deeply troubling. The gods know, I haven't the faintest idea why something like that is happening, or even that it *could* happen. But truly, anything you see would be helpful, even if it's not completely accurate."

Aya nodded, though Jonas could tell she was lacking confidence. She closed her eyes, and he felt her invoke the Archanium. He watched as she stood there, eyes flickering beneath her eyelids, breathing rapidly.

Her eyes snapped open, and she scowled. "I saw something, but I don't know how useful it is. She's in a cold room. Out the window, there were mountains tipped in snow. I could feel the Demon close by. Her face...she looked as though someone had broken her nose. I honestly don't know what to make of it."

Jonas let loose a tired groan, "Gods, that could be practically *any*where west of here, either in the Askryl Mountains, or on the edge of the bloody Sea of Spires!" When she cast her gaze at the floor, Jonas swiftly corrected course. "But thank you so much for looking for me. I know tapping your abilities like that is taxing, and as we get closer, I'm sure it'll turn out to be vital information."

She offered him a half-hearted smile, "I hope you're right."

Aleksei gently tapped Jonas's shoulder. The Magus turned and looked into his knowing golden eyes.

"We need to get on the road," Aleksei said softly, "I have a servant gathering provisions, but you need to be prepared. Anything you need, fresh clothes, new boots, needs to be taken care of now."

Jonas flashed his Knight a smile, turning quickly back to Aya, "I'll stop by before we leave the city. Let me know if you happen to see anything else. And keep the book locked up in the Bastion. It'll be safer there."

Aya nodded her agreement, taking hold of his upper arm as he turned to leave, "Thank you, Jonas." When he frowned in confusion, she tapped the purple cover, "For your faith. It means a great deal to me."

Jonas's frown melted into a smile, "No one better."

She quirked a smile of her own as he strode from the room. He walked down the corridor, letting out a heavy sigh. Fanj was a hostile, treacherous realm at best. They would be lucky to survive long enough to reach its inner lands, where the wastes finally gave way to cities and civilization, much less return alive with Tamara.

He wondered if he'd ever see her, *any* of them, again.

Hade waited anxiously, trying not to let the nightsounds of forest frighten him. On the one hand, his own power had grown exponentially ever since Aya had helped him reach their new meridian. On the other, he'd lost the ability to access some of Sammul's darker tricks.

He wondered if Sammul would be angry by the loss of his secrets. After all, Hade was the one chosen by the Master. But Sammul had also commanded him to discover what new power Aya commanded. He had only been following orders.

Of course, when it came to the Master, Hade knew that such considerations were easily discarded. If Sammul was angry, it wouldn't matter whether Hade succeeded or failed, he would still be punished.

There was a rustle in the foliage behind him, and Hade's heart leapt into his throat. The Master always simply appeared. Someone was coming, and it wasn't Sammul. His heart stuttered when he suddenly realized who it was, who it *had* to be.

Gods, but he was a fool not to have realized it sooner.

Vadim stepped into the moonlight, his face etched with an angry glower, "What are you doing out here?"

Hade swallowed hard, "Vadim? I thought you were asleep." Well, that was certainly true enough.

"You *do* know that after a few weeks, most Knights build an immunity to spells like that. Especially when they're so hastily crafted."

Hade fought to keep his jaw from dropping. His Knight knew what had been going on. Worse, he was so aware that he could discern Hade's own level of concentration when casting the spell. That was rare, if not unheard of.

Warning flashed through Hade's mind, and he turned angrily on the Knight, "Get out of here! Did it never occur to you that there might be a *reason* I didn't want you tagging along? It's dangerous for you to be here."

Vadim crossed his thick arms across his chest, "Not just dangerous for me, judging from the nightmares I've been having. What happens to you out here, Hade? I'm tired of retching every time I wake up from one of the little naps you force on me. You're risking *both* our lives, and I'm not standing for it any longer."

"*Fine*," Hade growled through gritted teeth, "But like it or not, you need to get out of sight. Now! He'll be here any minute, and he *won't* be happy if he sees you."

Vadim's black-eyed gaze bore into Hade, but the Knight receded into the brush, vanishing into the shadows.

Hade breathed a sigh of relief. Perhaps the Master would be too preoccupied to notice the presence of another. Gods, he wondered what Sammul would do to Vadim if he caught him out here. He wondered what Sammul would to do *him* for his failure to keep Vadim under the sleeping spell.

As if summoned by his thoughts, Sammul burst into the small moonlit clearing in a whorl of green fire. The Master did not look pleased.

"What have you brought me?" Sammul demanded, stepping out of the flames.

"I've uncovered the secret you asked for, Master. I have ascended to Aya's new meridian."

Sammul paused a moment, "What do you mean, you've 'ascended' to it?"

"She...she helped me jump across the void. I now have the power of the Akhrana's outer edge, just as she does."

Sammul crooked a finger, and Hade cried out in pain, "She can *teach* this?"

Hade nodded, stifling the screams that begged for release, "She and Ilyana have trained the entire Voralla. They all command the power now."

Sammul roared.

Hade blinked in confusion. He was now several paces farther away. His head spun and he tasted blood in his mouth. As his senses slowly cleared, he realized that he was suspended in the air, held against the rough bark of a tree. He supposed Sammul must have thrown him there in a fit of rage.

"The Demon has infected them beyond anything I could have imagined," Sammul growled finally.

Hade frowned at that. If they were infected by the Demon, why would they move *farther* from the Presence? After all, Aya's Magi were now so far on the outer edge of the Akhrana that they were practically touching the Seraphima. It didn't make any sense.

"Enough!" came a coarse bark of anger.

Hade dropped unceremoniously to the forest floor as Vadim came charging out of the brush like an angry bull. The Magus managed to glance up in time to see Sammul's expression falter. And then the Master's angry face twisted towards Hade.

"What are you playing at, bringing him here?"

Hade cried out as a lash of air split the skin across his chest, "I didn't! He followed me."

Vadim was ignoring his Magus now. "He's been keeping me under that sleeping spell for weeks. You didn't think I would unravel it eventually? You *instructed* him, Sammul. Surely you aren't that stupid."

Hade gasped at the vehemence in his Knight's voice. Sammul would not be pleased to be spoken to that way.

"I see your Knight has been corrupted as well," Sammul whispered.

Before Hade could open his mouth, green fire shrieked from Sammul's fingertips, enveloping the Knight. Hade cried out in shock. What was Sammul doing? He was going to *kill* them!

Vadim stood stock-still, blinking in confusion at the Magus. Wise as the Master was, it seemed he'd forgotten Vadim's immunity to fire. In one solid motion the Knight drew his broadsword. "Ouch," he snarled, stalking towards the Magus.

Hade threw a shield in front of Vadim a moment before a bolt of lightning splintered it. As it was, the remaining force threw the Knight to his knees. Hade could hear Vadim coughing. He could smell the stench of burnt flesh.

"You are right to kneel before me," Sammul said, keeping his distance from the Knight. Confident or no, Sammul wasn't foolish enough to come within range of Vadim's sword.

Hade pulled himself to his feet unsteadily, "Master, please! Be merciful."

Sammul quirked a wicked smile, "How are you going to effectively serve our cause yoked to *this* ox?"

Hade felt tears spring to his eyes, "He can change, Master. He will learn of his errors, and he will change. Let me try to change him, Master."

Sammul considered as Hade rushed to Vadim's side. He quickly healed the internal burns he could feel radiating from the other man. Vadim finally stopped coughing and drew a deep, clean breath.

Sammul glowered down at the two of them, "I must say, Hade, I didn't expect such a pathetic display. I had greater hope for–"

Hade stared as Sammul halted his speech. The Master seemed to hang in the air for a brief second, and then, as though the strings suspending him had been cut, he crumbled to the forest floor like a broken doll.

Hade winced at the acrid smoke that streamed from Sammul's nose and eyes.

Suddenly shivering, Hade glanced up at a hooded figure towering over them. He couldn't make out a face, but he could feel its presence in the Archanium. It was unholy, almost as though this being was *twisting* the very fabric of the Great Sphere.

The figure pushed away its hood to reveal a strikingly beautiful woman. Her copper hair shone like a halo in the moonlight.

"Rise, my children," she said smoothly. She had the voice of a goddess.

Trembling, Hade came to his feet. Vadim was practically holding him up.

"Who...who *are* you?" Hade whimpered.

"You need not know my name," the woman said softly, "only heed my words."

Hade glanced at Vadim, but his Knight was utterly captivated by the woman's face. He couldn't look away from her piercing emerald eyes. Hade understood the hypnotic attraction. He would be equally transfixed were he not so terrified. In a flush of embarrassment, Hade realized he was pissing himself.

"How would you command us, mistress?" Vadim whispered.

She smiled, and it was as though the sun had blossomed in the midnight sky. "I have an errand for the two of you. Something of grave importance."

"Anything," Vadim answered instantly.

Her smile widened. "Good *boy*," she cooed.

Tears streaked down Vadim's cheeks. Hade felt an instant jealousy that she'd praised his Knight, and not him.

"There are two men, Aleksei Drago and Jonas Belgi. I believe you know them."

Hade and Vadim nodded as one.

"They have left, this very night, for the forsaken realm of Fanj. They are compelled by a phantom they cannot *possibly* comprehend. But whether or not they understand what they are about to unleash, they *must* be stopped."

A frown tugged at the corner of Vadim's mouth, "Mistress? I don't understand."

She smiled and leaned forward, brushing the Knight's cheek with the back of her hand, "You will, my child. Soon, I will make all things clear to you. Will you be my champions? Will you serve your people, and stop them before they unleash this unspeakable evil?"

"Yes, mistress," they both said automatically.

She laughed. It was a light, bubbly sound that filled both men with warmth. "How *dutiful* you are, my children. Remember, you are our only hope. It is *imperative* that you not fail in your duty. You *must* stop them, by any means necessary."

"As you command," they whispered together.

Her eyes twinkled, "I knew I could count on you. Remember, children, you are my champions. Do *not* fail me."

And then she was simply gone.

Hade dropped to his side, gasping for air, as though he'd been afraid to breathe in her presence. Vadim sank back on his haunches, his head bent in contemplation.

Hade suddenly recalled Sammul, standing over them a moment before the woman had appeared. He saw the still form of the Magus lying not far away. Reaching out a hand, he brushed the man's stiff shoulder.

With a light whooshing, part of Sammul's form collapsed into a thin pile of ash, the outer shell of his skin shattering to reveal a hollow, blackened interior. Hade gasped at the sudden stench, at the horror of what he'd just witnessed.

This was something altogether otherworldly. *Unnatural.*

"Who was she?" Vadim finally whispered. *"What* was she? A spirit? A shade?"

Hade felt a certainty suddenly creep into him. "Vadim," he whispered, his voice barely audible, "no mortal being could have touched the Archanium the way she did." He met his Knight's knowing eyes.

"She was a *goddess*."

CHAPTER 28

BLOODLETTING

"Can't say that I know much."

Roux stared at the elderly woman from across the bar. He drummed his fingers across the countertop, fixing her with his wild golden eyes.

"But you know something," he said softly. Beneath his gentle tone lay an unspoken threat. The woman's face showed that she hadn't missed it, either.

"I might have heard a thing or two," she said, straightening, "but it was a while ago. I'm not sure as I could recall *what* it was I heard."

Roux produced a silver and slid it across the counter, "Anything coming back to you?"

The woman's eyes fixed on the silver. Given the look of the place, Roux imagined it was more money than she saw in a fortnight. She looked up at Roux.

"Aye."

Roux leaned forward, keeping his eyes locked squarely on her face, "So what exactly do you recall?"

"Well," the woman said, tapping her chin thoughtfully, "there's a man in town by the name of Ruben. He lives a few blocks down from here. I remember a few weeks ago, he was visited by a very peculiar young man. Short and blond as I recall him, very quiet. Walked about like he owned the place. Ruben took him to talk to people."

"What *sort* of people?" Roux pressed.

The woman considered a long moment, "Mostly servant types. Washwomen, maidservants, kitchen scullions. No one of any import or nothing. From what I heard, those that talked to the young man were *real* shook up afterwards. They didn't like him, but they all know Ruben, so they figured he had to be on the up and up."

"So, this Ruben fellow is well-known around here?"

The woman nodded, "He's a quiet type, keeps to himself. Comes in here a few times a week for a pint. Seems nice enough. People like him, even if he don't talk much."

"When he comes in, does he sit by himself?" Roux asked casually.

She scoffed, "*Gods* no. The man is *always* surrounded by local folk. They like him, 'cause he listens. Don't ask a lot of questions, just lets folk spill their guts. It's almost a *service* to me. People like getting stuff off their chests. Ruben lets 'em do that."

Roux straightened and offered the woman a smile, "Thank you for your time, ma'am. You've been very helpful."

As he turned to leave the inn, the woman came from around the counter, "Now you ain't gonna cause him no trouble, are you?"

Roux paused and turned to offer the woman a smile, "Why do you ask? Has he given anyone cause to harm him?"

She frowned, "No, you just seem awful interested in him. Like I said, he doesn't make trouble. He's a good man."

Roux's smile faded, "I have no doubt of that, ma'am. I'm simply interested in some of the things he might have heard recently."

He could tell the innkeeper wasn't quite sure what to make of that. Or of him, for that matter. He didn't really care; he had what he'd come for.

"Good day to you," he said after a moment of silence, giving her the barest of nods before walking out into the street.

This particular part of Taumon was as squalid as it came, second only to the docks. It was the very reason Roux had come here. The sort of people he sought wouldn't be in places of influence or money. They would be tucked away here, hiding in plain sight.

And from the sounds of it, this Ruben fellow was exactly the sort he was looking for. A collector. Someone who gathered information for the sheer purpose of informing those who employed him. Roux merely had to discern who this man was working for. If his suspicions were correct, he might just have found their first promising lead.

Roux walked down the street, quietly asking a beggar if he knew where Ruben lived. For the paltry price of a few coppers, the beggar pointed out a rundown home, standing thin and tall, shoulder to shoulder with the rest of the squalor. Roux thanked the man, tossing a final copper into his cup. The man practically wept at Roux's generosity.

When Roux reached the house, he quickly realized that no one was there. He tried knocking several times before letting himself in. The hearth was cold. Wherever Ruben was, he'd probably been gone since at least early morning.

He glanced around the small living room, but quickly realized that there was nothing to be gleaned from the man's few possessions besides that he lived a simple, almost monastic life.

Roux headed up the narrow stairway, listening for any signs that the man might still be there. A cold hearth didn't always indicate vacancy, but after checking the single small, cramped room, Roux was satisfied that he was indeed alone in the house.

In the corner of the small upstairs room, Roux found what appeared to be the man's office and started going through papers, searching for any mention of Ruben's employer.

Most of the papers were just notes jotted down in a thin, spidery scrawl. Seemingly unimportant facts about the fishwife down at the wharf, a short tale related by a scullion about the head cook at the Admiralty.

He found notes detailing Andariana's arrival in Taumon.

And then he found it. A name that, while not damning in and of itself, sent off warning bells in Roux's mind.

Bael.

He had never encountered the man himself, but Aleksei had certainly told him enough. This man worked for Bael. The short man with blond hair who walked around like he owned the place.

The front door squealed open and Roux bit back a curse. He dropped the papers where he'd found them and stepped to the nearest window.

He could hear the stairs squeaking. He saw a roof ten paces from the window.

The door opened, but he was only dimly aware of it.

Roux Darted with a thought, reappearing on the roof across the way. He straightened, blinking in the winter sunlight. The roof was higher than he'd judged it from the window. He glanced down at the milling of people and carts on the avenue below him.

And then he turned towards the Admiralty and began to make his way back.

The entire process was actually rather quick. On the rooftops, Roux could travel far faster than he would ever have managed on foot. And unlike Treedarting, it was highly unlikely that he would miss an entire rooftop. That certainty allowed him to move even faster.

He was at Andariana's window in a matter of minutes.

When he popped into her chambers, she merely turned with a hopeful smile. He smiled inwardly at how used to him she'd become. In a manner of speaking, they'd almost become *friends*. They wanted the same thing, each with different but equal desperation.

They understood each other in a way that went beyond convention or rank. Roux was honestly surprised that Andariana was *capable* of such things. He'd always thought her a rather silly woman, so wrapped in her own thoughts and ways that she could hardly see the world around her.

Thus far, she had proved him wrong.

"Well?" she asked, pouring him a goblet of mulled wine.

He let his smile surface as he accepted the silver cup from her. It was their little tradition. When he returned from a morning of searching, she was there to bring him some small warmth and comfort while he explained his progress.

"I found something," he said with a well-earned smile.

Her eyebrows rose, "Anything substantial?"

They'd long ago given up hope of simply finding Tamara secreted somewhere in Taumon. After this amount of time, the best they could hope for were promising leads.

"Yes," Roux allowed.

Andariana's eyes flashed with hope before she seemed to restrain her emotions.

"I found an informant. His name is Ruben, and he lives in the slums. Apparently he's quite the listener. Doesn't say much, just gathers information. I went to his house and found notes on everything from a fishwife's her affair to your arrival. And a reference to Bael."

Andariana almost dropped her glass. "*Bael?*" she hissed softly.

Roux rested his goblet on the hearth and carefully steered Andariana to a chair. The name had a more profound effect on her than he'd expected. She sat and gave him a grateful smile.

"I heard the same story from a few people," Roux finally continued. "A short man with blond hair showed up a few weeks ago and was seen going around with Ruben. They talked to a number of servants who work here. I believe Ruben is the man who told Bael how to find Tamara."

Andariana's expression darkened. "Alright," she said after a measured pause, "here's what we're going to do. I want you to find this man, and capture him. Take as many soldiers as you think you need. Do it yourself, if you think it will be easier. I don't really care. When you have him, meet me at the foundry."

Roux's brow drew down, "The *foundry?*"

She nodded, "Yes. I have some questions I'd like to ask this man. You bring him to me, and we'll find out what we need to know."

"Andariana, I'm not sure that you want to torture this man."

She lifted an eyebrow, "I never said anything about torture. We can only hope it doesn't come to that. But I want answers, and I'm not in the mood to play games. Find him. Once you have him, we'll get our answers one way or another."

Roux felt a chill ripple through him. In the space of just a few moments, the entire game had dramatically changed. He was no longer going out to seek information. He was going to capture the enemy.

He glanced at Andariana. The change that had come over her was dramatic. Her face was set with a foreboding he'd never seen before. Her normally-fiery green eyes were cold. Yet they still burned.

He hefted his goblet and downed the rest of his wine, "I'll be back. It might take a bit to capture him, but I'll bring him to the foundry tonight."

She nodded. There was a harsh finality to the motion.

"Andariana," Roux ventured before he left, "don't forget, this man has been dealing with Bael. You know the Demon will be expecting us to do something like this. We need to be careful about how we handle this situation. *Don't* let your emotions get the best of you."

She offered him a cold smile, "I have no intention of letting that little weasel get the best of me. Now, best you be off. The more time we sit and chat, the more time he has to scurry away."

Roux nodded, recognizing his dismissal.

Aleksei held his head in his hands. A soft moan escaped him.

Jonas looked up sharply, "Are you *sure* you're alright? You've hardly touched your dinner."

Aleksei offered his Magus a soft, loving smile, "I'm fine."

Jonas rolled his eyes, "You know I can feel you, right? I don't buy that for a moment. There's no point in playing the brave, long-suffering Knight with me. If your head hurts that bad, just let me heal you."

Aleksei waved him away, "This isn't something that can be healed, Jonas. This has to do with magic."

Jonas scoffed, "And what would *I* know about magic?"

Aleksei offered a weak half-smile, "You know what I mean. This ain't a matter of trauma and injury. Something's out of balance. I just need to work out what it is, and I'll be fine."

Jonas grunted as he stirred the coals. This far from the sanctuary of the mountains, the winter cold was much more aggressive. It sank into your bones so much faster. Jonas's entire body ached. He knew Aleksei's did, too. But that was nothing compared to the headache Aleksei was enduring.

"Perhaps you just need some sleep," Jonas said, masking a yawn with his hand.

Gods, but they had been riding for days on end. At times he worried that his horse might drop dead beneath him, but Aleksei always seemed to know when enough was enough. There were times when they'd stop, or walk with the horses, or simply slow down a little.

But they were always moving inexorably west, towards the constant pounding in Aleksei's head. Towards Fanj; towards Tamara.

And while Jonas was encouraged by their progress, he was growing increasingly concerned about Aleksei. The farther they'd gone from Keldoan, the worse Aleksei seemed to get.

As it stood, Jonas knew they were on the edge of Ilyar and Fanj. This was the worst he'd seen his Knight so far. At night he sometimes heard Aleksei cry out in pain. He felt it every single moment through their bond. It was excruciating. And yet Jonas knew that his suffering was nothing compared to the pain Aleksei was enduring.

Worse, Jonas worried that if they found no cure for the Knight, he might simply die. If Jonas couldn't heal him, what then? Aleksei could be frighteningly single-minded in his determination to reach a goal. And right then, Aleksei was the only one who knew where they were headed. Jonas couldn't feel the pulse beating in the distance. His own abilities wouldn't help them just now.

It was beyond frustrating.

Aleksei finally stood, glancing at his Magus with what Jonas could only interpret as an apology, "I don't think I can stand this anymore. I'm going to try to get some sleep."

Jonas offered Aleksei a bright smile. "I'll keep watch. Don't worry, just try to get some rest."

Aleksei gave Jonas a weary wink, then climbed into their bedroll and twisted away from the fire. Jonas sat staring at the flickering fire for a long while, wondering whether or not he should simply plunge his Knight into sleep with the Archanium.

The spellform was simple enough, although he wasn't sure how much actual rest Aleksei would get with such a spell drowning out his thoughts. But perhaps some sleep was better than another restless night spent in agony.

Jonas's face was set in grim determination when the first wave washed over him.

He gasped, his mind suddenly sluggish. He tried to rise, but only succeeded in tripping over the firewood pile, his head landing against Aleksei's hip. Contact only intensified the nightmarish effect.

Jonas found himself swimming through the murky waters of a dream, unable to gain his bearings.

He sensed Aleksei close by. Using their bond as a tether, Jonas pulled himself towards the Knight.

It was the strangest sight he'd ever seen.

Aleksei knelt before an entity unlike anything Jonas could have imagined. It was a bizarre creature, moving with bones of branches, a pall of smoke undulating around it. A deep, feminine voice whispered through every fiber of Jonas's being, bringing tears to his eyes as he understood the threat inherent in each word.

He knew without a doubt that this was the voice of the Seil Wood.

But this was unlike anything Aleksei had described before.

Hunter, came the warbling roar, *you come close to straying from Me. You wander from My protection. Should you cross the boundary, you will be at* its *mercy. Please,* Hunter, *return to me.*

Aleksei stood unsteadily, "I'm safe, Mother Wood. Don't fear for me. I'm protected."

You are not. the Wood wailed. *Not if you* insist *on leaving Me. I have granted you great power. Do* not *turn away from Me.*

Aleksei laughed uneasily, "Mother Wood, I only leave for a short time. Your branches have shielded me from the Demon, but I am *protected* now. I will return to You soon, I swear it. But I ask that You grant me a short leave of absence."

This *is how I am repaid?* cried the being of branches. *For the* gifts *I have bestowed upon you,* this *is how I am repaid?*

Aleksei frowned, "I take nothing *from* you, Mother Wood. But I must go into the wastes, to recover someone precious. Were any other worthy, I would send them. But at the moment, I am the one required. I beg Your understanding, and Your leave."

Jonas felt his entire being shake as the Wood began to laugh. The laugh became desperate and thunderous. *Very well, Hunter.* Forsake *your land. Consider* this *your debt repaid.*

Aleksei frowned up at the monster, "I don't understand."

The Wood, still obviously amused, shrugged, *That does not* interest *Me, Hunter. Consider your debt repaid.*

Jonas dissolved into the oblivion of sleep.

Andariana paced back and forth before the forge. She was wearing her riding gear rather than one of the many gowns that had been brought to the Admiralty since her arrival. The forge was no place for such finery. A wayward spark could catch on such a gown in a moment and set the unwary ablaze. She was not nearly so fond of her satins and silks as to ignore good sense.

So, while her quilted linen overcoat and riding leathers were much too warm for the situation, it was far better suited to the danger of her circumstances.

As she stood there, breathing the heavy air, Andariana wondered if she might faint before Roux arrived with her prisoner. She gritted her teeth and steeled her resolve. She would need far more strength to deal with the coming moments. She couldn't afford the luxury of being fragile.

With an effort, she recalled the resolve she'd commanded during the last war. It had served her well then. She prayed to the gods that it would serve her again.

Roux finally appeared, stripped to the waist. He held a length of chain in his hands, dragging a hooded figure behind him. The figure kicked and pulled, but judging from the binding on their hands, leading to the chain Roux held, the prisoner wasn't going anywhere.

Andariana offered a dark smile as Roux came to a halt near the forge. "What do we have here?"

Roux flashed a look, both amusement and rage. Andariana had long since become used to his facial tics. He was pleased, but also grim with the knowledge of what was to come. She knew how he felt.

Even now, her stomach cramped at the very idea. And yet her fear quailed in the face of her resolve.

She *would* have answers.

"Unmask him," she said softly.

Roux leaned forward and ripped the sackcloth hood from the man's head.

The prisoner lurched forward and collapsed on his knees, gasping in the hot air. His face was cut and bruised, no doubt from his earlier encounter with the Ri-Hnon. Andariana couldn't say she was displeased.

She schooled her face, robbing it of emotion as she bent over to look the man in the eye, "And whom do I have the pleasure of addressing?"

She knew the answer, but she wanted to see how hard he would fight her. If he balked at such an easy question, this was going to be much more difficult, to say the least.

When the man snorted to spit on her, Roux kicked him roughly in the side. He fell to the ground with a groan.

Andariana clicked her tongue, "Well, *that* wasn't very polite, was it?" She used the toe of her boot to lift his chin, "Now, I asked you a question. Tell me your name."

"Ruben," the man spat.

She gave him a humorless smile, "Very good, Ruben. Now, tell me, what is it that made my friend here find you so very fascinating?"

"You'll burn for your crimes, witch," Ruben growled.

Andariana flicked a glance to Roux. The prisoner cried out as Roux's knife flashed across his cheek. She'd never even seen Roux move.

"Perhaps, but you'll never see it. I can promise you a *very* slow death if you don't tell me what I want to know. Now, my friend here seems to think you know something about my daughter. True?"

"I'm not tellin' you *nothin'*. And there ain't nothin' your little pet can do to make me talk."

Andariana laughed at that last remark. "Him? You think I'm relying on *him* to make you talk?" She bent down again, glaring into his contemptuous brown eyes, "My dear, I only had him bring you to me."

She straightened, turning to the forge. "You see," she continued nonchalantly, "my friend says you have information. Information I want. You can either surrender it willingly, and we will let you go, *or*...." Andariana shoved her hand into a smith's glove and reached into the forge, withdrawing a long, white-hot iron. "I can *make* you tell me. I care little one way or the other. The second way just wastes my time."

She spun, holding the iron high. Her emerald eyes flashed with a dangerous light. "But don't for a moment doubt my resolve. You will tell me what you know, or I will draw out every scream from your pathetic body until you've given yourself over to Volos Himself. If you tell me nothing, I'm no worse off than I started. I have faith that my friend can find ten more like you. Of course, there will be no trace that you even existed," she said with an obvious nod to the blazing furnace.

She lowered the smoking iron to the man's eye-level. "So, you see," she went on, "it's entirely up to you. Would you like to spend the rest of your wretchedly short life blind and in excruciating pain? Or do you want to tell me what you know about my daughter?"

The man was shaking now. He tried to scurry back from the iron, from Andariana, only to be met by Roux's bracing hands.

"I...I...." Ruben stuttered.

Andariana held the iron closer to his face. She could see the dirt and grime on his skin highlighted by the glowing heat of the metal.

"I'll tell you what I know," Ruben managed, "It ain't much, but I'll *tell* you."

Andariana didn't flinch, "Speak then. And make it quick; this iron is quite heavy."

Sweat rolled down Ruben's face in rivulets. He blinked against the acrid smoke billowing into his eyes. He gulped, then started talking as quickly as he could, "He took her. The dark one, Bael. He came to me a time or two, asked what I knew about you bein' here.

"I told him you was in the Admiralty. I got one of the washwomen to tell me which one was the Princess's room. He was real interested in her. I even pointed it out to him. He told me...he told me...I was to...I *can't!*"

His next word cut off as Andariana plunged the sizzling iron into his right eye. Roux clapped a hand over the man's mouth to muffle his screams.

"*Andariana!*" Roux shouted. "What are you doing?"

She arched an eyebrow, "Whatever's necessary to find my daughter." Andariana held the iron in the man's smoking socket for a second more before ripping it away and thrusting it back into the fire. She returned her gaze to the wretch slumped before her, whimpering incoherently between sobs. "I didn't tell you to cry, I told you *talk!*" she bellowed, backhanding him.

She doubted he could hear her over his own agonized cries.

After a very long bout of howling, Ruben looked up at her with his remaining eye, tears streaming down his left cheek, blood down his right. "He said you'd do somethin' like this."

"Then he was right," Andariana hissed. Her voice crackled. "If the Demon thinks that we'll be merciful, or that we'll balk at what must be done when his ilk will stop at nothing, then he has no idea who he's dealing with."

Ruben cracked a broken smile, "He said you'd say that. I guess that's why he gave me this."

The man opened his palm and both Roux and Andariana stared at the rune tattooed into Ruben's flesh. It was foreign to her, but after a moment it began throbbing with a sickly yellow light.

Andariana knew something had gone horribly wrong. She looked hurriedly around the forge, but she knew she didn't have the time to run for it. The street was a hundred paces distant, and there was no safe cover close by.

Given how quickly the man was taking on the yellow light, she had very little time indeed before whatever magic possessed him manifested. She whispered a prayer to the gods, begging their forgiveness for her cruelty.

Ruben's entire body took on the eerie glow. He started to convulse as rhythmic pulses of light overcame him.

And then Roux's hands were on her shoulders. She only caught the flicker of Ruben's body coming apart in an eruption of light and fire before she was suddenly standing on the rain-soaked street hundreds of paces from the foundry.

Roux was cursing violently. Andariana gasped at the sudden shift from the heat of the forge to the icy rain. She watched, stunned in the explosion's wake, as the foundry ignited in yellow-green light and flame.

"Great gods," she gasped, turning to Roux, "what *was* that?"

"A trap," Roux growled.

Andariana almost crumpled to the cobbles right there. They had possessed an agent of the enemy. For a brief moment, she'd held the answers within her grasp. And now those answers were ash on the wind. She screamed with frustration.

She let Roux guide her back into the Admiralty without a word. He seemed too shocked by her behavior to speak, and she was too angry with herself, with her overzealous need for information, to say much of anything. She had been too heavy-handed. Roux had expressed doubt that she had the mettle to harm someone like that. She doubted he still harbored such concerns.

But he had never seen her twenty years before, during the last war. Gods, if he only *knew* what she'd done to the men who'd captured her Seryn.... The men's screams still woke her some nights, a sorry replacement for Seryn's touch.

Yet when she woke, she still felt the warmth of justice carried out. The sweetness of retribution. But deep down, she knew it had never been enough.

By the time this war was over, though, Andariana knew she'd finally have true retribution, even if it wasn't carried out by her own hand.

Emelian Krasik would pay for what he'd taken from her. From Tamara. This was but an extension of that age-old fight. He'd taken her husband, and now he'd taken her daughter. And she knew why. She shook to think of the things that perverted beast would tell Tamara.

Her jaw clenched so hard she wondered if her teeth might shatter.

She *would* have retribution.

CHAPTER 29

WHITE LIGHT

Hade glanced nervously over the edge. The drop was easily ten or eleven paces, and it still unsettled him to be so close. Such a fall could easily break his legs, if not kill him outright.

Vadim crouched in the shadow of a sumac, carefully watching the road as it careened into the canyon.

From their position, they could see the road in both directions for leagues.

Their divine mistress had returned the night before, warning them that their quarry was changing direction. She had commanded them to come to this place, and to wait. She said they would be rewarded for keeping watch until the chosen time.

Hade was convinced now more than ever that they had been called by the divine. How else could she know such things? How else could her very *presence* cause such ripples in the fabric of the Archanium?

It was the only explanation.

For his part, Vadim was disheartened to learn of Aleksei's betrayal. He didn't believe Aleksei actually *meant* to cause harm, and Vadim hated having to fight the man. Hade knew the prospect terrified him. But the goddess had been *very* clear. This was not an issue that to be discussed, merely obeyed.

Hade was certain he understood her commands better than Vadim, but he kept his smug satisfaction to himself.

331

"How long do you think it'll take them?" Vadim asked absently.

Hade looked away from the edge and shrugged his shoulders. "I have no idea. She just told us to wait."

The order *did* make a lot of sense. The border between Ilyar and Fanj was mostly demarcated by the marching line of the Askryl Mountains. To the west of the mountains, the mighty River Jai'g provided a secondary boundary, delineating the remainder of Fanj's natural internal border.

At their current position, Hade knew they were on the edge of the one of the shortest passes leading into the wild desert realm. If Jonas and Aleksei wanted into Fanj, they almost certainly had to come through this precise spot.

Hade could sense Vadim's uncertainty, and it grated at him. Vadim had never been one to put his whole heart into his beliefs. Well, certainly not until he'd encountered Aleksei Drago. Aleksei had been the first leader Vadim had ever truly respected, if grudgingly at first.

Receiving an order to murder the man, especially from a being as compelling as the goddess, had put Vadim perpetually on edge. For his part, Hade found his Knight's reaction odd. He'd long suspected that Jonas must be doing *something* profane to command such power, so why would it be so surprising that Aleksei would be equally heretical? Hade only felt vindication that he'd been in the right.

Vadim glanced at the road, then back to Hade, "So how are we going to do this?"

Hade shrugged, "You distract Aleksei. He won't want to hurt you. He'll want to talk. I'll throw the entrapment spell around Jonas, and then I'll give you the signal. That's when you take Aleksei. While the two of you are dueling, I'll dispatch Jonas. But remember, the first one to make a kill ends the battle, one way or another."

"I'm *familiar* with the concept, Hade," Vadim snapped.

Hade glared at his Knight. He felt a sudden, unexpected kinship with Sammul, understanding why his former master might *want* Vadim dead. He could feel similar thoughts infecting his own mind.

He pushed them down. There were more important things to worry about now. She had put her faith in them, and Hade wasn't about to fail his mistress. She'd rescued him from Sammul's torment. She'd saved *both* of them, and for that he knew they owed her their lives. If she said that Aleksei and Jonas were about to awaken something wicked, then he and Vadim *would* stop them.

This was the fastest way into Fanj. It was the simplest, and now Hade knew it was the closest to his enemy. They would arrive sooner or later.

And when they did, he would be there, waiting for them.

Aleksei led the way through the canyon.

Upon entering the pass, the road had narrowed to the point that it was no longer possible to ride side by side. Aleksei had explained that it made more sense for him to lead, not only because his Hunter abilities provided a richer idea of the land ahead, but because he was riding Agriphon.

The warhorse had quickly sized up Jonas's brown gelding on the ride from Kuuran, and by now there was little doubt which horse was the alpha. The gelding seemed more than happy to follow Agriphon. Aleksei knew that, were he to reverse the situation, things might not have gone quite so smoothly.

But while riding single-file through the canyon was certainly safer, it was far lonelier. Both men were held prisoner by their thoughts, and Aleksei kept revisiting his dream.

He had never seen the Wood behave in such a way. In the past, She had displayed signs once or twice of something more chilling than Her familiar, maternal aspect, but never like *that*. He'd certainly never witnessed any sort of physical embodiment of Her spirit.

The dream haunted him.

Jonas had mentioned something about witnessing it, but Aleksei wasn't sure how that was possible. The dream had been all-encompassing; the vision of the Wood had filled every crevice of his mind and sight. He wasn't sure how someone else, even Jonas, could have witnessed such a thing.

But Jonas had told him enough for Aleksei to know that his Magus was telling the truth. It unnerved him that Jonas had seen the Wood in such a state, but he also found the knowledge oddly comforting. He hadn't imagined it. It had really happened, word for word as he recalled.

Gods, but how he wished he could convince himself it had been just a phantom of thought. The Wood had never acted so unreasonable. In a way, She had seemed almost *jealous*. Aleksei found the entire experience deeply confusing.

It had never before occurred to him that the Wood would be upset with him straying too far. After all, he'd gone into the heart of Dalita and She hadn't said a word. So why was *this* different? She wanted to protect him, but now that he had Adam's feather around his neck, he was protected from Bael's wind demon.

Perhaps She was simply being *over*protective. As a Hunter, he was rare. He knew the Wood to be unusually possessive of him at times. Perhaps this was one of those times. Yet that explanation felt somehow hollow. She had never appeared in such a way, as a physical being made of branches and smoke. It was an unsettling image to recall.

Aleksei was so wrapped in his thoughts that he didn't see the shadow flash across the ground. A heartbeat later something collided with him, and he was knocked out of his saddle.

Aleksei's head struck the hard, rocky ground. The world spun as he tried to pull himself to his feet. He saw a pair of boots walking slowly towards him; a blade glimmered in the winter sunlight, trailing just behind the boots.

Aleksei managed to look up, but the sun blinded him. He could hardly make out the shape of a man, but his nose didn't lie. He *knew* that scent.

"*Vadim?*" Aleksei coughed.

"I'm sorry to have to do this. I really am," Vadim muttered, lifting the blade.

The world snapped back into crystal-clear focus. Aleksei brought his leg around and swept Vadim's feet out from under him. The other Knight went down hard, dropping his sword.

Aleksei was on his feet in the next instant.

The Mantle thrilled across his shoulders, coursing down his arm, wailing to be released. Aleksei held it back, drawing his sword instead, "What are you doing, Vadim? What's going on?"

Out of the corner of his eye, Aleksei saw that Hade and Jonas were engaged in some sort of dialogue. Or perhaps it was a war of wills. It was often difficult to tell with Magi. Too much that happened went unseen.

"I'm sorry, Aleksei," Vadim said again, coming to his feet and hefting his sword, "But we have orders from a higher power. You can't be allowed to succeed in your mission. If you win, it could spell doom for all of us."

Aleksei faltered for a moment, "What are you talking about? We're trying to rescue Tamara. She's been kidnapped. How could that *possibly* hurt anyone?"

Vadim shrugged, suddenly uncertain, "I don't know. She didn't mention anything about that."

"*She?*" Aleksei asked sharply, "Who is 'she'? Vadim, did *Darielle* tell you to do this?"

Vadim's face dropped into a confused frown, "I don't know who that is."

"Beautiful, strange, red hair, green eyes? Appears out of nowhere? Speaks in riddles?"

Vadim's face betrayed him. Aleksei knew that they had indeed spoken with the Prophet. His blood boiled. "She's a *Prophet*, Vadim. But she doesn't always tell you the truth. She tells you what she wants you to hear."

Vadim looked on the verge of listening when he suddenly shook his head, "No, she *saved* us, Aleksei. She killed Sammul before he could kill me, and she told me what we had to do. About our destiny. Hade says she's a *goddess*. I have to obey her."

Sammul? What the hell was Vadim talking about? Aleksei felt the pain of his headache suddenly return, now compounded by the blow he'd taken. "She's not a goddess," he managed, "she's a *Magus*. And she's toying with you. You attacked us on the word of a total stranger? What's wrong with you?"

There was a loud *crack* behind them, and Hade flew against the canyon wall. Vadim bellowed with rage and lunged at Aleksei. He parried the attack, turning Vadim's blade to the side.

"I don't want to hurt you, Vadim."

A strange light filled Vadim's eyes. This was not a rational man. Aleksei thought he had been getting through to the other Knight, but the moment Hade had lost whatever back and forth he was having with Jonas, Vadim had lost his rationality.

"Then you'll have to kill me. Because if you don't, then I *swear* I will kill you before I let you bring ruin on us all."

Aleksei watched the other Knight, his mind grasping for the best way to end this situation without having to kill a man he still regarded as a friend. A solution presented itself, and Aleksei took it, knowing it was the easiest way to end this quickly.

Aleksei dropped his sword. "Fine. You want to kill me? Take your best shot. Far be it from me to stand in the way of prophecy."

Vadim watched him warily for a long moment before lunging forward. He feinted to the left before driving his blade straight at Aleksei's throat. Time slowed. Aleksei caught the blade between his hands, freeing the Mantle to surge across the blade and sink its talons deep into Vadim's hand.

Vadim screamed in agony.

Behind them, the battle between the Magi suddenly halted. Both men were frozen, staring at their Knights, neither having time to completely comprehend what was happening.

And then Aleksei pulled the Mantle back, ignoring its pulsating need to finish the other Knight. It was wrenching to pull it back before completion, but he forced himself to endure it. He would *not* kill a friend like this, no matter how deluded the other man had become. It would be a terrible waste.

Powerful though he was, the Archanium Knight posed no *real* threat to him, and Aleksei knew that.

Vadim gave a shuddering gasp, crumpling to the canyon floor. Aleksei could hear the man's heart beat. It was slow, but steady. He would recover. It might take some time, but he would survive.

Aleksei turned his attention to Hade and Jonas.

Hade was still plastered against the canyon wall, his clothes rippling against him in some unseen wind. Jonas's face was a mask of confusion and anger. Aleksei realized that the two men had been having a very different sort of conversation.

When Hade saw Aleksei approach, his face contorted with rage, "You *killed* him!"

Aleksei's eyebrows rose sharply, "Killed him? Hade...."

If Vadim had seemed irrational, Hade just came across as insane. The man even appeared unaware of what such a dire pronouncement would have obviously meant for himself. There was something fundamentally wrong here, and Aleksei very much needed to understand what it was.

"I *knew* you were false!" Hade cried out.

Aleksei gasped as a fist of air struck him square in the chest. He felt himself strike the far canyon wall before dropping to the ground. His entire body burned. He knew what it felt like to crack a rib, but this was *so* much worse. He desperately tried to pull air into his lungs, but he only felt fire and pain.

Tears poured from his eyes as he gasped at nothing. He looked up at

Jonas's shocked face, at Hade's mocking triumph. He reached out a hand. Even as his vision threatened to black out, he tried to call the Mantle forth. If he could reach Hade from where he was, perhaps he could survive.

The need for air became unbearable, yet there was none to be had. His lungs didn't work. He risked a glance at his chest, but he could only make out the black-red of his blood soaking into the canyon floor, dripping from his chest. He caught sight of a splinter of bone, and wondered if he could vomit even though his lungs were destroyed.

He looked up again, trying to push away the pounding in his skull. His eyes felt like they were about to burst from of his skull. He reached out again, commanding the Mantle to flood forward and feed.

The tendrils dripped away from his extended wrist, limp.

Panic seized him. He wanted to cry, but he had no air. He wanted to scream, but he had no breath. He was suffocating in broad daylight.

And then it happened.

One moment Aleksei was staring at Jonas's stunned face, at Hade's hateful smirk. And then the world became a blinding ball of light. Aleksei squinted to make something out, but he couldn't see anything beyond the brilliance.

He dimly wondered if a star had just touched down. Perhaps he would be eradicated in its blinding fire. Perhaps it would release him from the screaming inside his head.

When the light touched him, Aleksei opened himself to the merciful embrace of death. But rather than fire, the light felt eerily *cold*. He opened his mouth to gasp. In the distance, he thought he heard someone singing.

Such an odd thing, he thought, for someone to be singing out here, in a mountain pass. He wondered why he felt so cold when the world was so *bright*. Consciousness began to slip from his grasp, and Aleksei figured that this must, at last, be the end.

He tried to find Jonas in the enveloping brilliance. He just wanted to see him one last time, just once more. To say goodbye. But the light was too bright. He couldn't see anything but the light, and he felt only the cold.

And then the light went out.

Tamara sat in the corner of her small room, staring at the door.

Her stomach ached with hunger, but she refused to voice a complaint. That would only prove that they were winning. For the time-being, she clung to every scrap of control she could find.

But she knew it was a losing battle. The hunger consumed her. She had little to do in her room, so she counted her small victories instead. Fighting back was no longer an option. After she'd attempted escape the third time, Bael had used the Archanium to seal her in the room. Even had the door been left wide open, she was still trapped.

At least he hadn't hurt her as he'd threatened. When she'd ultimately decided that losing her beauty was a small price to pay for freedom, the Magus seemed to anticipate her actions, and so now he punished her with starvation rather than physical violence.

Her stomach rumbled, a sour reminder of her gnawing hunger pains. She knew she was losing weight, her once-supple form now deflated. She was determined to bear this burden, just as she bore everything else.

She *refused* to let them win.

And though Bael often spoke about taking her to her grandfather, whatever *that* meant, she had never been permitted to leave the cell. She secretly clung to the hope that there was already a great enterprise working to free her.

She dreamed of seeing the door burst inwards, and Roux rushing into to save her. Sometimes it was Aleksei, sometimes Jonas. Once she'd dreamed of all three of them. That had been the happiest moment of her life in past few weeks. She didn't even care that it had been nothing more than a wishful delusion.

The door swung open, and Tamara jumped at the unexpected intrusion. Bael stood at the threshold with a tray of steaming pheasant and roast potatoes. Her eyes widened at the sight of the feast.

He smiled at her, not the cruel, wicked grin he so often favored, but a genuine, soft smile. She was immediately on her guard.

"Princess," he said with a soft incline of his head as he stepped into the room, "I thought you might appreciate a decent meal."

She watched him carefully as he shut the door and approached, "I thought I was to be starved as punishment."

Bael shrugged as he set the tray down on the mean table beside the window, "That was *weeks* ago, my dear. I think you've suffered enough. And besides, I would hardly want your grandfather seeing you in such a state. He has been working *very* hard to get the opportunity of meeting you, you know. I would very much like him to see his granddaughter in a most favorable light."

Tamara's mind spun, trying to connect the pieces. In the past, Bael had only ever spoken of her grandfather as an ominous figure. This made the man sound almost like prisoner. She wondered where Bael was hiding the lie.

Still, lie or no, she was famished. She walked as gracefully as she could manage to the table and took her time sitting on the three-legged stool, when all she wanted to do was bury her face in the pheasant and stuff the food into her mouth with her bare hands.

As she took delicate bites, Bael kept talking, "You know, your disobedience aside, I don't see why we have to be enemies, you and I."

Tamara refused to look the man in the eye. She just kept eating, fearing that at any moment he might change his mind and take it away. She wasn't good to anyone if she had no strength. She *had* to keep her strength for her eventual rescue and escape.

Rather than rail at him for his insolence and cruelty, Tamara just kept eating. Every bite, she told herself, was her rebuttal. With every mouthful she was striking back, taking something they had and using it to keep her body strong. It was that strength that would lead to her freedom. She kept repeating that to herself over and over as he talked.

"I honestly believe," he continued, "that you might actually grow *fond* of me, should you get the chance to know me."

She was on the border of losing whatever food she'd managed to consume. Did he honestly think this was going to be *effective*?

"After all, we're not so entirely different," he said, reaching across and resting a cold hand on her wrist.

Before she could even open her mouth to say something, another voice intruded, "Keep your hands *off* of her."

Bael tensed and turned. Tamara looked up and gasped in surprise. The door was shut, and yet there was someone new in the room.

"Darielle," Bael said stiffly.

The woman gave him a broad smile. Tamara didn't think she'd ever seen such a beautiful woman in her life. But there was something unsettlingly about Darielle's features. Something deeply familiar about her eyes.

"I'll only warn you this once, Brother." Darielle said softly.

Bael snorted, "You're *warning* me, now?"

Darielle shrugged. Somehow, the woman managed to make such a rough action look sinuously graceful. "I'm not particularly interested in whether or not you heed me. It matters little to me one way or the other. But know there are consequences if you don't afford me the proper amount of respect."

For some reason Tamara couldn't fathom, Bael backed down.

"So you say," he muttered.

Darielle turned her green-eyed gaze to Tamara, "And *you* would be the lovely Tamara. I *do* apologize if my brother has been less than hospitable. He's a bit of a brute, as I'm sure you've noticed."

Tamara started to open her mouth, but found she couldn't speak. Darielle crossed the room and covered the princess's face with her hand. Tamara was so stunned she couldn't move.

Warmth flooded into her, making her suddenly lightheaded. She gasped when Darielle's hand came away, gingerly stroking her cheek. Her face felt exactly the same. At least, she *thought* it did.

Darielle had felt differently, it seemed. The woman rounded on her brother, "You were stupid enough to break her *nose?* Gods, you're more of an idiot than I imagined possible. Why would you hurt one so valuable when you can't even *heal? Simpleton!*"

Bael cried out as he dropped to the floor. Tamara stared as Bael twitched and writhed on the floor, screaming in obvious agony. When he finally relaxed, Darielle gave a heavy sigh. She turned back to Tamara.

"I'm sorry you had to witness that, but I'm afraid it was unavoidable. Sometimes bad boys need to be *punished.* You understand, dear?"

Tamara nodded slowly.

Darielle broke into a motherly smile, "I'm *so* glad. Now, please finish your meal. From the looks of you, you could use a little nourishment. I'll make sure this is just the first meal of many. After all, a lovely girl like you ought to look her best. I'm *sure* you agree?"

Tamara nodded quickly. This was the strangest woman Tamara had ever encountered in her life, and yet she felt completely safe in her presence. She couldn't imagine the power Darielle must command to bring Bael to his knees in such a way, but she felt instantly relieved just knowing that such a being existed.

That someone like Darielle even knew she was alive.

Aya groaned in frustration, pushing the book aside and resting her head against the cool surface of the table. These diagrams were maddening. The complexity of each individual element was enough to give her a headache; deciphering them as an interwoven cryptogram was simply beyond her capabilities.

The fact that Magi had once held such a detailed understanding of the Archanium was sobering. That they were able to elucidate their understanding and *codify* it was staggering.

And now Jonas wanted her to interpret this mess? While she knew he'd had little formal training, Aya always had the feeling that Jonas intrinsically understood the Archanium in a way she simply couldn't.

Perhaps it had to do with his unique position within the Great Sphere. As far as she could tell, he wasn't even *on* a meridian. It was as though he was simply suspended in the precise center of the Sphere. Such placement allowed him to craft any number of unique spellforms, pulling equally from both the Akhrana *and* the Nagavor, while never reaching the farthest meridians, like the one she'd guided everyone else to.

Perhaps he was just naturally gifted. He was certainly better *educated* than most of Ilyar and Dalita rolled into one. Anyway she sliced it, Aya believed he had a deeper understanding of the Archanium, a depth that might even rival the glyphs she'd been staring at all night.

And yet she knew he could no sooner understand this book as he could turn night into day. She'd spent the better part of her life in the halls of the Voralla, reading texts on theory, practicum, and the experimental morphology of Archanial entities.

It was fast proving to be the most valuable time she'd spent in the Voralla. And while her practical training in the Archanium had been a joke at best, her scholarly work had been quite profound.

As a result, she had a leg up on the prince, and possibly on every Archanium Magus in Ilyar, when it came to reading and interpreting magical texts. Unfortunately, the books that would have given her a reference to interpret *this* volume were locked far beneath Kalinor, and unquestionably out of her grasp, in the Voralla. Without them, she was basically blind.

She'd never memorized the numerous declensions and codifications necessary to interpret these forms because she's always had access to the Vault. With a working knowledge of the books in the Vault, it was a simple task to decipher such diagrams. With*out* her books, however, she might as well have been staring at Yrini runescript for all the sense it made to her. She understood bits and pieces, but the larger picture eluded her again and again.

The door opened and Aya looked up, smiling as Toma entered with a tray. Aya caught a whiff of spiced tea, and her body began to relax. They had time.

Jonas was riding into Fanj. It would be hard traveling, and he wouldn't be back anytime in the near future. Perhaps by then she might have figured out why this book was so important.

Toma took a seat across from her, pouring her a cup and sliding it across the table, "Aya, you *have* to rest. You've been here most of the night."

Aya cradled the cup gratefully, sitting back in her chair, "I just wish this wasn't so complicated. The books in the Vault would have answered all the questions I've written down, but I don't have them. It just makes me feel so stupid."

Toma frowned at that. While the tiny Magus was never a brave woman, her mind was sharp. "The Bastion possesses a sizable library, doesn't it? Perhaps there are copies of the books you need *here*."

Aya frowned into her tea for a long moment. In the Voralla, the books she needed were shielded behind enchantments meant to incinerate anyone caught stealing a single volume. Every few decades some thoughtless adept would meet such an end, attempting a moonlight bedroom study session without appreciating the dire power of those wards.

She hadn't encountered any similarly-shielded areas within the Bastion, but that only led her to believe that no such texts were available in the ancient libraries.

"It can't hurt to look, I suppose," she said finally. "But Toma, I'm looking for some pretty esoteric texts."

Toma shrugged, "Like what? Give me an example."

Aya sighed, "*Declensions of the Trinomial Astral Annal.*"

Toma's eyebrows lifted, "Why would you need *that*?"

Aya slid the purple volume across the table, "Read the inset on page fifty-one."

Toma picked up the book, frowning as she flipped through the pages. She gasped when she saw the diagram, "Aya, how could anyone possibly decipher this? This terminology was arcane two thousand years ago!"

Aya scowled, "Thank you for the revelation. I've been staring at that image for hours. And it only gets worse the deeper you go. I *have* to have the right texts. If you think you can find them in the library, be my guest. I spent two hours in there yesterday and came up empty handed."

Toma slid the book back to Aya, her face taking on a defiant cast, "I bet I can find some of them, at the very least. You keep reading the text, and I'll look for the ciphers. Make me a list, and I promise that by this time tomorrow, you'll have every book that you need, provided they exist here."

Aya managed a smile, "Thank you, Toma. I'd forgotten the luxury of a research assistant."

Toma shrugged, "It's the least I can do. You did more for me in one day than I can ever hope to return in a lifetime. Your discovery has revitalized the Magi. I don't know if you ever wanted to be High Magus, Aya, but you're considered the commander of the Voralla now." Toma paused, reconsidering what she'd just said, "Well, I suppose it'd be more accurate to say you're the leader of *our* Magi. But the Voralla be damned. We're now the only thing standing between victory and the Demon. And whether you like it or not, everyone thinks you're the one in charge."

Aya groaned, resting her head against the chair, "I don't *want* to be in charge. And what if Sammul shows up again?"

Toma burst out laughing, "Aya, darling, with what you've shown us, Sammul would be lucky to escape with his life. There's no longer any doubt that we've all been duped. At the time we didn't know any better. But things are *quite* different now. And we've chosen you to lead us."

Aya knew that Toma meant this to be a great honor, but at the moment she just wanted to cry. She was so tired. It all seemed too *much*.

Five minutes ago, she'd just been doing a favor for a friend. And now she was being thrust into the most important position in the Voralla? The gods be damned, even if there was no Voralla to be had, the Magi still felt like it was their home. And it was by right, dammit.

But she didn't want this. Aya realized for the first time in her life that all she wanted was to be left alone, to do as she wished. To have Raefan return to his family's woodworking trade. For him to create toys for their children, to live a life of peace with her wonderful mate.

But instead they were asking this of her? And now? The dreams of Raefan carving up wood rather than men, the dream that she might be fortunate enough to survive the war to start a family with the man she loved, all of those thoughts and dreams withered beneath the cruel sunlight of their current reality.

Aya would hold onto her dreams, but gods, she would be the luckiest woman in the known world if her dreams didn't end in either herself or her love being ripped apart, the other spending their few remaining moments vomiting up blood while they experienced the exquisite anguish of their beloved's loss.

She did not relish her lot.

Aya forced a smile, "I'm honored to be thought of in such high regard, Toma. But unless the assembled Magi want to issue an official proclamation, I'm happy just remaining Aya."

Toma smiled slyly, "I'll tell the others. I'm sure they'll understand."

As the woman stood to leave the room, Aya called out, "Toma, aren't you supposed to help me find volumes in the library?"

Toma gave a soft laugh, "I'm just going to retrieve Tamrix and then I'll be back. It'll go faster with the two of us searching. Perhaps Raefan would like to join us?"

Aya grunted her doubt, "I believe Raefan is trying to figure out what happened to Vadim and Hade. He thinks they've been here longer than we have, even though I told him Hade only appeared a few days ago."

Toma shrugged, her mirth undiminished, "Knights and their hunches."

"Indeed," Aya grumbled, watching the woman leave. She took a deep sip of tea, then turned back to the book.

CHAPTER 30

INTO OBLIVION

Aleksei gasped, his eyes snapping open. His lungs screamed as they expanded, and for a moment he wondered if his heart was about to stop. The pain was almost enough to send him fleeing back into the darkness, but he fought past it.

His insides were full of needles. He could feel the tiny points stabbing into him as he breathed in. The pain lifted as he exhaled, but only just barely.

Aleksei tried to make out the rocky ceiling of what he guessed was a cave, taking short, desperate breaths. He tried to sit up, but his muscles didn't respond. His body shook uncontrollably. Instead, he attempted to twist onto his side. After a delayed handful of seconds, he managed to turn. He coughed violently, blinking at the dark blood that had splattered across the dim, barren dirt floor before him.

It took Aleksei a moment to get his bearings. He looked around for Jonas, but the Magus was nowhere to be found. He pushed back at the suffocating panic rising inside him.

Aleksei had, through necessity, become used to injury, to pain, but this was something altogether different. He could barely move; he could hardly *breathe*. He felt completely helpless. He wanted to cry, but he doubted his body possessed the strength.

He wasn't sure how long he lay there, panting and shaking, before he heard it. A slow, almost rhythmic scraping. It sounded like a body being dragged across stone.

Aleksei's head jerked as he tried to gain a better sense of his surroundings. He was lying against the cave wall, his back pressed to the cool stone. Before him, he thought there must be a bend before the cave opened out into...he wasn't exactly sure. But he could see a hint of daylight, so he knew the rough direction of the entrance.

Gods, but he prayed it was Jonas returning. He couldn't feel the bond very clearly through the storm of pain and fragility, but he knew the Magus was close. Still, if it was anything else, anything unfriendly, Aleksei wasn't sure he'd be able to stop it. Of course, he had the Mantle, but that would do him little good against a swift animal or a crossbow bolt.

He tried to push himself up further. If he could face whatever was coming, he might be able to raise his arm fast enough to let the Mantle loose. But when he tried, his muscles refused to respond. The action just made him shake all the harder. A soft whimper escaped before he could bring his frustration back into check.

The scraping sound grew louder, and in the dim glow of the daylight, Aleksei could make out the shape of a man. His heart leapt into his throat when he realized it was Jonas.

The Magus didn't turn or acknowledge him, but rather concentrated on dragging the large, shadowy shape deeper into the cave. Aleksei stared at the shape, frowning as he tried to understand what he was looking at.

His nose alerted him a moment later. It was an animal. A sort of ox, Aleksei supposed, though he'd never seen an ox that small.

Jonas finally drew the creature within Aleksei's reach and dropped the two limp legs he'd been gripping, "It's not very big, but it's alive. For a bit there, I thought it was going to gore me. I'm amazed I was able to knock it out without killing it."

When Aleksei looked up at the Magus in confusion, Jonas sank into a crouch and grasped Aleksei's hand firmly. He pulled it outward and rested it on the beast's side. Aleksei could feel the beast's slow breathing, the strong pumping of its heart.

The Mantle thrilled across his back, and he felt suddenly, ravenously hungry.

Thick black tendrils coursed down his arm. He couldn't have halted it if he'd wanted to. He gasped as the Mantle sank into the beast, drinking in its lifeblood. Tears streamed down his cheeks as he drew a clear breath, the invisible needles gone.

When the Mantle finally receded, Aleksei's arm dropped away from the beast. His eyes were heavy with exhaustion, but he no longer shook so violently. He frowned. Why didn't he feel more fully restored?

He glanced up at Jonas. The Magus was smiling at him, but there was still a glimmer of concern in his emerald eyes. "Don't worry," he said softly, "I didn't expect this little buck to fix everything. I was just trying to get back to you before your body gave out. This buys us some time to start properly healing you."

Aleksei tried to smile back at Jonas, but he felt himself being pulled inexorably back into the heavy embrace of sleep. He closed his eyes, determined to just rest them for a moment.

Jonas shivered, staring out across the open plain. The sun had just set, lighting up the desert in a dreamlike glow of purples, faded oranges, and blues. This only served to make his task all the more challenging. Aleksei needed so much more than a small water ox to regain his strength. As it was, Jonas was shocked that the Knight had survived. That *they* had survived.

Just the sight of Aleksei's ruined chest, the gaping hole left by Hade's spell and the tattered remains of his Knight's left lung hanging from a wholly incomprehensible chaos of bone and flesh had left Jonas deeply shaken.

So shaken, in fact, that he seemed to have accomplished the impossible. Even now, as he waited in the silence of the unsteady afterglow, he felt an otherworldly chill sweep through him. He had saved Aleksei's life in that single instant, but he still didn't understand *how*.

How had he touched the Seraphima?

His Angelic blood might explain the possibility of such a feat, but he had no training in such magic. He didn't know the first thing about wielding the Seraphima, or even how to reach out to it, and yet somehow he'd managed to restore Aleksei's body enough that the Hunter had survived such an incredible insult. Mostly. He chalked it up to desperation and instinct.

Jonas *hated* relying on instinct. It seemed as though his entire life, every connection he'd forged to the powers beyond himself had been instinctual. He'd pulled off some incredible feats, true, but he desperately wished he understood the methods and techniques he'd employed, so he could replicate the effects at will and with conscious intent.

At least, he mused, the Archanium was finally beginning to make more sense to him. A year ago, he might as well have swung a sword in a crowd of people blindfolded as touch the Archanium with anything approaching *skill*. By now, however, he had a much firmer hold on his abilities, and his limitations.

But touching the Seraphima had opened an entirely new box of questions, and he was many, many leagues at *least* from anyone or anything that might help steer him towards understanding.

Jonas took a deep breath, clearing his mind of worry. There would be time enough for such concerns later. They still had a great deal of traveling ahead of them, and he'd have a chance to muddle through all this then. For the moment, he needed a fresh catch for Aleksei.

His Hunter wasn't out of danger yet. Aleksei was painfully weak, and it was dangerous to try to heal him with the Archanium in his current state. Jonas certainly didn't want to deplete any more of Aleksei's resources than he had to. Fortunately, there was an alternative in the Mantle. Jonas needed Aleksei to be as strong as possible if they were to find Tamara and get her out of danger.

But first they had to get to wherever she was being held. All Aleksei had been able to discern so far was that she was still hundreds of leagues to the west. While Jonas had a fairly decent knowledge of Fanja geography, there was a great deal of wasteland between their current location near the border and the great imperial cities beyond the wastes. Traveling across the desert was difficult in the best of situations, but much more so during the winter.

Winter brought great dust storms to the wastes, and even greater rains to the arable land on the other side. Jonas knew Tamara was most likely being held in one of the great cities, but they wouldn't know which one until they were much closer.

A sudden movement in the brush caught Jonas's eye, and he slowly turned, grasping the Archanium. He prayed it was something larger than the little water ox. He wouldn't be able to drag it down the canyon, but perhaps he could get Aleksei onto one of the horses. Either way, Aleksei needed a much stronger life-force to heal completely.

Jonas sent his senses outwards towards the source of the motion. His hackles rose as he recognized the pulse in the Archanium as that of a human. Why would a person be out here, alone, in the middle of *no*where? He knew immediately that it wasn't Hade or Vadim.

They'd escaped while he was healing Aleksei, but he knew their signatures, and this didn't match either one. This felt entirely alien.

"Show yourself," he called brusquely, holding the Archanium at the ready should he need to protect himself.

A short Ilyari man stepped out of the shadows of a thorn tree, his eyes glimmering in the half-light. He shouted words at Jonas, and for a moment Jonas thought he was hearing the man wrong. He recognized the cadence and suddenly realized that, despite his obvious Ilyari heritage and attire, the man was speaking thickly-accented Fanja.

With a wave of embarrassment, Jonas shouted back. "*I mean you no harm. I simply need to find some game.*"

The man paused, then broke out into a broad grin, "*Then we seek the same thing. I am also hunting for game.*"

Jonas gasped as pain blossomed from his right calf and his left arm, just above his elbow. He looked down in shock at the black shafts now protruding from his flesh. The Archanium boiled up around him in a storm of rage.

He set it loose, hurling waves of pure destruction in a sphere around him.

Nothing happened.

Jonas frowned and tried again, but even as he attempted to touch the jagged shards of crimson and aureate, they slipped from his grasp. The entire Archanium collapsed around him, leaving him cold and breathless. Without his magic, Jonas felt naked and defenseless. His movements were improbably sluggish.

The short Ilyari was still grinning, walking forward with a pair of rough iron manacles. Jonas groaned as he sank to his knees. His buttock brushed against the shaft in his leg and he cried out.

His voice sounded strange to him, strangely distant. His dulled mind realized arrows were poisoned. It was the only explanation. Even his *thoughts* became slippery as the man with the manacles came ever closer.

He felt his face strike the dusty, packed earth. Some of the dust was carried into his lungs as he inhaled. He tried to cough it out, but the darkness was already enveloping him.

It felt like he was drowning. His eyes bugged wide in an effort to fight the darkness. And then he was pulled under, into the black.

Wake.

Aleksei's eyes snapped open in the darkness. He shuddered, realizing that the cave was not only pitch black, but freezing as well. He frowned. Where was Jonas? Surely he wouldn't have left Aleksei alone in the dark without a fire.

Tentatively, Aleksei tested the air. He detected no trace of Jonas *or* the horses. No one had entered the cave for the past few hours at least.

With a groan, Aleksei forced himself into a sitting position. His arms shook with the effort of righting himself. His stomach rumbled unhappily with hunger. Aleksei shoved back the pathetic groan that built in his throat.

Gods, but where could Jonas have gone?

Aleksei focused on his bond with the Magus, wincing at the jumble of information he received. Jonas wasn't far, perhaps less than a league. But the anger, pain, and confusion that washed through Aleksei's mind filled him with immediate panic. And there was something else, something far deeper than any other sensation.

Shame.

The groan building inside Aleksei became a growl.

We can find him. We can save him.

Aleksei started at the intrusion of the voice. He dimly recalled hearing it moments before waking up, but he'd dismissed it as a fragment of dream.

"Who's there?" he grunted weakly into the darkness.

Silence greeted him, and Aleksei felt a flush of embarrassment. His weakness was addling his mind.

Rise, Hunter. We have little time.

Aleksei jumped again. Another wave of embarrassment washed through him as he recognized the particular pitch of a voice not spoken aloud, but rather in his mind.

Hunter. The voice named him by title. For a brief moment, he dared hope that the Wood was guiding him. After their last dream encounter, She had been none too pleased with him. Perhaps this was Her way of offering an apology?

Whatever it was, Aleksei resolved that it was better than being alone. It wanted to help him find Jonas. That was all that mattered.

"Alright," he said. "But I'm still very weak. I don't have the strength to fight. Or Hunt."

It makes no difference. Do as I command. We will find him. We will save *him.*

Aleksei shivered at the sudden shift in the voice's timbre. While it wasn't the same voice that he associated with the Wood, Her appearance in his dream had been entirely different from anything he'd encountered from Her before.

Perhaps he was just experiencing another example of Her many manifestations. Certainly, the way She repeated the same phrases over and over seemed to be echoed in this new voice.

Crawl towards the tunnel entrance. Your horses wait there.

Aleksei sighed and painfully forced himself onto his hands and knees, gritting his teeth with the effort. He might have felt silly crawling like an infant had his body not been so weak. Even that simple motion nearly taxed him to exhaustion.

He followed the cave wall to ensure that he wouldn't run into something in the darkness. His Hunter eyes could see better than most men's in the night, but this deep in the cave there was not even the suggestion of starlight. He would have to rely on his other senses until he reached the cave entrance.

As he went, a musty, fetid stench filled his nostrils. Surely the bull that Jonas had brought in earlier would not have begun to decompose already. Gods, what *was* that? The stench grew stronger the farther he went.

He crawled for what felt like hours, although he was reasonably sure it was only a few minutes. He was beginning to wonder how much longer he would be able to keep this up when the voice intruded.

Stop.

Aleksei froze, breathing raggedly. By this point, the smell was almost overpowering.

Place your hand on the cave wall.

Aleksei frowned, but complied. He gasped as the Mantle slithered up his arm and lifted from his wrist. He blinked in the darkness, confused by the odd command, and the Mantle's reaction.

And then tiny shudders of life flowed into him. Each ripple of energy was relatively small, but as the seconds ticked by there were more and more, until a steady pulse of life poured into him and reinvigorated his body.

Accompanying the flow of life was a strange sound, a series of soft, thumping sounds. The Mantle receded down his arm, and Aleksei managed to stand. His senses sharpened, and with a sick groan he understood what the sound was. And that rank, musty smell.

Bats.

The Mantle had just fed on hundreds, if not thousands, of bats. And yet an entire colony had provided only enough strength for him to stand on his own two feet. He would need still more to feel anywhere close to normal.

It seemed that, though the Mantle could drain animal life, it didn't prove *nearly* as potent a healing agent as human life. The very thought made Aleksei slightly sick, but he pushed his nausea away.

The cave entrance is only few more steps. The night is moonless, but your horses wait for you. Once you find them, follow the bond to Jonas. Once you get nearer, I will help you save him.

Aleksei found himself suddenly irritated by the voice.

"Who *are* you?" he demanded.

Once again, he was greeted by silence. Apparently the voice only issued commands; it didn't respond to questions.

With an angry grunt, Aleksei gingerly waded through the bat carcasses and guano, newly grateful for his boots. His stomach roiled to see the dead bats already being devoured by the incredible variety of swarming insects that lived on the cave floor. The sound of it nearly made him vomit.

He stepped out of the cave finally, and had never been so glad to taste the cold, sweetness of fresh air in his life. Even wading through the Kalinori sewers hadn't been *this* unpleasant.

In the starlight, Aleksei's eyes refocused and he realized that he could see with remarkable clarity. He heard a sound to his left, and saw Agriphon trotting eagerly up to him.

He gave his horse a gentle hug, stroking the great beast's muzzle before pulling himself laboriously up onto his back. Jonas had taken all the tack off the horses, but Aleksei had grown up riding bareback. He used his knees to reorient Agriphon towards Jonas's dull glimmer in the distance.

Aleksei took a moment to study his surroundings.

The cave was located in one of the canyons that made up the pass in the Askryl Mountains. The mountains formed a natural border with

Ilyar, though where one realm ended and the other began had always been a matter of contention.

The canyons and the plain above were generally barren, dotted here and there with scrub grass, low bushes, and rugged rock formations. Jonas had told him that this pass was not natural, but had rather been formed during a great war between the Ilyari Magi and the Fanja Ul'Brek in the centuries following the Dominion Wars.

From the bizarre smoothness of the canyon walls, Aleksei surmised that some unbelievably powerful magic had been unleashed by one party or the other. He shuddered to think what such a spell might have looked like, and to imagine the individual responsible for unleashing it.

With a click of his tongue, Aleksei urged Agriphon into a trot, following the canyon west. He watched the ocher rock turn this way and that, searching for any hint of a path onto the highland. After half a league, he finally found one.

A ramp had formed just behind a tower of jagged red rock. He guided Agriphon carefully behind the monolith and up the uneven slope of stone and sand. The slope broke out onto the plain a moment later, and Aleksei's head snapped towards the only source of light in the vast emptiness.

Firelight on a plain was a tricky thing. Such light could be a mere league or two distant, or twenty. His nose and his bond told a different story.

Through the bond, he could feel Jonas's storm of self-pity and anger. He was in a good deal of pain and discomfort, but that wasn't what was upsetting him. Aleksei realized he was grinding his teeth at the sensations he was receiving from Jonas and forced himself to block it out.

The wind was blowing from the west, and Aleksei plucked a range of scents. He could smell roasting meat mixed with something unexpectedly toxic. He tested the air twice before he was sure of what he was smelling.

His hackles rose.

From the breeze he caught hints of monkshood and crimson cap, but the most surprising scent he encountered was *yuselk*, the pain-killing root used amongst the Ri-Vhan. Yuselk was exceedingly rare even in the Seil Wood, where most things grew quite easily. Worse, the root couldn't be dried. So how had these nomads found it all the way out *here*? And what did they need with a plant as powerful as yuselk, which was given to people only under the most dire circumstances?

And then he understood. These people were brewing a poison. The monkshood and crimson cap together would be enough to incapacitate even the strongest man, should they even *survive* the initial shock to their system. But when mixed with yuselk, Aleksei got the impression that something altogether different would result.

Whatever the actual effects of the poison were, Aleksei was now near certain it was the reason for the pain and confusion Jonas was radiating back through the bond. With a wince, Aleksei recalled the effect yuselk had had on Jonas months before, when he'd been shot out of the sky by Bael and his dark Magi.

The healers who had tended the Magus wanted to heal him in the form he'd been injured in, yet shifting back into a falcon had proven exceedingly difficult under the influence of yuselk.

With enough yuselk in his system, Jonas would likely be unable to touch the Archanium at all, much less free himself. He would also be useless in any escape attempt.

Aleksei forced himself to unclench his jaw yet again. His anger was rising steadily as he rode towards the camp. If he wasn't careful, it would overcome him. He couldn't afford to lose control, not before he found Jonas.

And yet there was a powerful rage growing within him. This fury felt like it possessed a life of its own. It fed into him and he fed into it, as did Jonas's frustration and shame. It was only with the greatest mental effort that he was able to keep it at bay.

When Aleksei judged he was close enough to the camp, he pulled Agriphon behind a low boulder and dismounted. "Stay," he said softly, patting the horse's muzzle.

Agriphon shook his head violently, but didn't make a sound. Aleksei sighed, "I'll be back, old friend. Just give me a few minutes. I have to get Jonas."

Agriphon whickered, and Aleksei offered the great warhorse an apologetic smile before stepping around the boulder's edge. A hundred paces away, Aleksei caught sight of a sentry sitting on a small mountain pony.

A plan unraveled in his mind. There was an ample amount of tall scrub grass and shrubs between Aleksei and the sentry. A quick look to either side showed that the camp had spaced their lookouts too widely. They clearly weren't expecting an attack. And why would they? The closest Ilyari garrison of any size was Keldoan, which was now a good hundred leagues to the east. These men had nothing to fear from the Legion, while any Fanja force was much too far to the west.

Aleksei sank into the grass and took in the air once more. This time he searched for the scent of horses, of *men*. It instantly became clear that there was at least a pony for every man. On a plain this wide and empty, he wasn't surprised.

But at the same time, he understood that these men were likely nomads, traders of some sort. The efficiency of their camp layout backed up his theory. And by the spacing of their sentries, they were more used to looking for wild animals than men.

So what could they possibly want with Jonas? It seemed unlikely that a band of nomadic savages would recognize him for who, or even *what*, he was.

Aleksei's jaw clenched again, this time so hard he was surprised his teeth didn't crack. Had he forgotten so easily? It had been over a year since he'd even thought about them, but growing up on the Southern Plain, and Voskrin so close to the Fanja border, he'd grown up with the stories. The warnings.

These men weren't traders. They were *slavers*.

All of a sudden, the stories Jonas had told him along the way came together with those of his own childhood.

The great cities of Fanj lay on the western edge of the realm, bordering the Sea of Spires. Here, on the outskirts, there was little to live off of, and thus not many people. But as Ilyar traded with Fanj for their iron, gold, and silk, there was a decent amount of traffic along certain routes. Jonas had taken such a route, knowing it to be the fastest way through the Askryl Mountains.

It was also apparently a favorite poaching ground. A hunting ground for humans.

The murderous rage boiled back up into Aleksei, and this time he was not able to suppress it so easily. It roiled just beneath his skin, begging for release, to kill, to *purge*. He only just kept it in check, but it remained, boiling, writhing, *waiting*.

The guard shifted his glance to the south, and Aleksei began to glide through the grass, moving with the wind patterns that sent shivers through the tall, dry stalks. The touch of the wind on his skin made him at once apprehensive and rebellious. Adam's feather, now soaked with sweat and old blood and sticking to the slab-like muscles of his chest, shielded him from the wind demon. Knowing that he was safe from that one evil gave him an odd sense of invulnerability. Of exultation.

Let them try to hurt him. Once he was within reach of this sentry, he would have *two* lives, both man and beast, to restore him. And then *let* them come. These were mere men, possibly no more than twenty. The keenness of his senses and the Mantle that writhed across his shoulders made him so much *more*. Aleksei realized that some of the confidence and rage pulsing through him was coming from the Mantle itself.

For the first time in a long while, Aleksei felt like he was in complete control, even as his fury threatened to boil over. He allowed himself a small, self-satisfied smile as he ghosted through the grass. The sentry was still studying the southern horizon when Aleksei came up beside the pony.

One hand on the pony's leg was all it took. The small beast jerked and opened its mouth to scream, but no sound emerged as the Mantle gorged itself on the animal's life force. The rider's body seized a split second later, eyes wide as the Mantle drank him in. His mouth opened with the same futile expulsion of breath. His last breath.

Man and beast crashed to the ground, and Aleksei rose up. In the starlight, his eyes flickered with the color of fresh blood.

We will find him, we will save him. came the voice.

And Aleksei finally understood the voice for what it was. It wasn't the Wood.

It was the *Mantle*.

"Yes," Aleksei said, "and we will drink *deep*. Until we're sated."

He marched towards the camp, now heedless of the possible danger of exposing himself to so many men. In actuality, the men of the camp were so unprepared for such an assault that they didn't comprehend what was happening until it was too late.

Aleksei reached the edge of their firelight and ripped a torch from the ground. He set the tent closest to him ablaze before hurling the torch to the far end of the camp, where it landed among their ponies. He quickly turned to the burning tent and tied its flaps closed, trapping the men inside.

As the mounts began to shriek, some of the men in other tents came stumbling out of their tents, looking around wildly before running for the screaming horses.

These were nomads, and their tents were well-constructed to stand up to the winds of the plains. That same construction served to seal them in *very* effectively. The screams of burning men mixed with those of the terrified ponies, whose hay had caught fire only moments after the torch had landed.

The stench of burnt hair and flesh filled the night.

Now men were beginning to notice him, marching through the smoke and flames of the burning tent. He grabbed another torch and proceeded to light the next tent in his path. It wasn't worth the effort to seal the men in, he only sought to increase the chaos.

Panic now ran rampant through the camp as men tried to determine the source of the attack. Three slavers who had caught sight of Aleksei ran for him with short spears.

He hefted his flaming torch casually.

Shift. Time slowed as a man rushed at him. Just as the man got close enough to use his spear, Aleksei batted him across the face with the torch, filling the man's eyes and mouth with burning pitch. The man's screams joined the cacophony of panic and pain.

Aleksei chucked the torch end over end into yet another tent, glaring at the remaining men. They paused, startled at their sudden luck. He had just thrown his weapon away. They charged.

Aleksei walked calmly through them, straightening his arms to either side, letting the Mantle loose. Their drained husks thudded to the ground behind him, percussion for his symphony of suffering.

As he approached the center of the camp, where he could now feel Jonas's heart hammering, Aleksei saw that he had at last been fully recognized as the cause of the threat and the chaos.

His blood lust quailed for a moment. There were twelve, perhaps thirteen men surrounding him. In fleeing the cave, he hadn't brought his sword. But even with a blade, he was easily outnumbered. It was possible that, even with the Mantle, these men would tear him limb from limb. His self-assurance cracked.

And then, from the heart of a primitive shell of rusted metal, Aleksei caught sight of something familiar. His heart pumped furiously as his eyes met Jonas's. He had never seen his Magus's eyes so full of pain, of doubt. So full of *shame*. His prince was bound in a literal cage.

Blinding fury erupted within him, and he could no longer dared contain it. He longer *cared* to.

Feed.

Aleksei raised a clenched fist and the Mantle burst forth, ripping into two men simultaneously, yanking them forward. Aleksei caught their spears before they crumpled. As the rest of the slavers converged on him, he rammed a spear through the chest of the first man to reach him.

The second he held onto, jabbing it rapidly through one man's neck before ripping it out and impaling another. The spear went so deep that Aleksei had to pull his clenched fist, dripping with gore, from the man's middle.

Two more came within reach, and time slowed as he caught their heads in his hands, slamming them together. There was the sickening sound of bone splintering. Aleksei dropped the corpses and turned to face the survivors.

Six men remained, slack-jawed at the display of violence and furious mayhem. Two had soiled themselves.

One tried to turn and run, but the Mantle burst from Aleksei's shoulders and struck like a viper, ripping the man's life away.

Five.

As a group, the men charged him with their spears laid out.

Time stopped.

Aleksei heaved deep, panting breaths as he plucked a spear from one man and drove it through its owner. The other four had hardly moved an inch. Rage pumped through him. He drove the spear through each man, darting deep, seeking their vitals and twisting as he pulled away.

As time slammed back into place, five mirrored shrieks burst into the night, completing the choral cadence. Five bloodied bodies collapsed in unison, leaking their lives into the dirt of the plain.

He dropped the spear, his Hunter instinct telling him that there were only a handful of human hearts still beating in the vicinity. He was at Jonas's cage a second later, gripping the bars. He noticed, for the first time, that his hands were red and black with dripping gore.

Jonas stared at him with wide, distant eyes. "What *happened?*" the words slurred from the Magus's mouth.

"Shh," Aleksei said softly, "I'm here. How do I get you out?"

Jonas blinked and looked around his cage, "I...I don't *know.*"

Another face suddenly appeared next to Jonas in the cage, "There's a man with keys on his belt. The keys open all the cages."

Aleksei looked into the man's terrified eyes and nodded, turning back to the line of corpses that he'd just cast into oblivion. He searched a handful of bodies before he found the jailer. Aleksei unceremoniously cut the man's belt and ripped the crude keys from it.

He stumbled back to the cage and found the lock, trying a few random keys before the correct one popped the ancient device open. He yanked the cage open and was shocked to see seven people clustered inside. The cage hardly looked large enough to handle two. His nose alerted him to the overflowing bucket in the corner, a makeshift privy.

Ragged-looking merchants and tradespeople, mostly in their middle years, rushed past him, eager to get out of the cage, and away from him. He idly wondered how long some of these people had been imprisoned.

When the others had vacated the cage, Aleksei reached in and grasped Jonas's outstretched wrist. With a gentle tug, Aleksei pulled his Magus to freedom.

Jonas lurched from the cage and almost collapsed before Aleksei caught him, sweeping the shorter man into his arms. Jonas's eyes were still just as distant, unfocused. Aleksei released the Mantle, willing it to trickle vitality back into his prince.

The gods knew he'd absorbed enough lives to spare a bit.

Jonas's eyes slowly cleared. He coughed violently, but Aleksei kept feeding life back into him. He pulled the Mantle back when the Magus began to violently sob against his shoulder.

"Come on," he whispered, planting a kiss in Jonas's tangled chestnut hair, "Agriphon isn't far off. I want to put as much distance between this place and us as possible before the buzzards and coyotes show up."

Jonas mumbled something against Aleksei's chest. The Knight lifted Jonas higher, being careful not to jostle the man too much. He could only guess what Jonas had just been through. Aleksei might have healed the worst of it, but he wouldn't know until he had a chance to examine and question his Magus.

"It's alright," Aleksei said, feeling foolish for uttering such a statement in a field of burning tents and ruined corpses.

It was only while weaving his way through the destruction that Aleksei fully appreciated exactly what he'd wrought. He felt no remorse, but the sheer violence of it stunned him.

"I'm so sorry," Jonas whimpered.

Aleksei looked down at his Magus, at the man he loved, "Why would you say that?"

Jonas lifted his head and offered a sad smile, "Because I failed you. Because you had to do all these horrible things...for me."

"I've killed men before," Aleksei reminded him softly.

Jonas rested his head heavily against Aleksei's chest, "Not like this."

Aleksei breathed a sigh of relief when the prince drifted out of consciousness a few seconds later. Hopefully when Jonas woke, he wouldn't be nearly so ashamed and self-pitying. They needed each other to survive in this strange, alien realm. Neither of them could be blaming themselves for every misstep along the way.

With a weary sigh, Aleksei headed back to the boulder where Agriphon impatiently waited.

Gods, but even the rocky floor of the cave would be a blessed comfort after the trials of this night.

CHAPTER 31
CLOSET CONFESSIONS

K atherine ducked into the linen closet, setting down an armful of clean bedclothes. She straightened and almost screamed at the sight of Lord Simon Declan standing right in front of her.

"Gods, what is *wrong* with you?" she snapped when she'd regained her breath. "You nearly frightened the life out of me."

Declan chuckled in his fatherly way, "I apologize for giving you a scare, my dear. It's been a while since we spoke, so I thought I might check in on you."

Katherine tried her best to pull back her sudden anger, "A while?" Her snarl seemed to take him aback. "I've been working my way up the ranks, doing drudge work and playing like a dutiful servant wench, and what have *you* been up to? Stuffing your face and frolicking about with your mates."

Declan offered her a small smile.

"What are you grinning at? I'm terrified almost every moment I'm awake. I work for Lady *Delira* now. I am also to be on a special assignment for 'Master' Bael." As Declan's snowy eyebrows rose, she knew she'd got him with that, "Did you *know* either of those things? Do you have any idea the sort of information I've gathered? This place is a complete *mess*."

Declan heaved a quiet sigh, "I'm afraid I have to agree with you on that front. The nobility is hardly organized or functional. But first, tell me what you've discovered."

Katherine glared at him for a moment, but finally began to speak, "Lady Delira is a consort of sorts to Bael. She's a Magus, just like everyone else in this bloody palace."

Declan frowned, "How do you mean?"

"All I ever deal with are washwomen, maids, and Magi. They all have schemes, and they're all suspicious of one another. Whatever transpires between Bael and Lady Delira, she's still keenly interested in learning all his secrets. That's why she has me see Ethan. *He–*"

Declan raised a hand and cut her off. "Who is Ethan?"

Katherine felt herself blush unexpectedly. She was glad that in the dim light of the closet, Declan was likely to miss it. "Ethan is one of Bael's Magi. He's very nice, but doesn't seem particularly *astute*. He's asked me to walk around the Lawn with him on occasion. Lady Delira insists on it every time. She wants to see what secrets he'll casually offer to a servant girl. She has me get dressed up in these *gowns*...."

Katherine realized that she was rambling and looked into Declan's quiet eyes.

He smirked, "Does this boy have feelings for you?"

Katherine threw her hands up, "How should I know? I'm here to get information and pass it on to *you*, not fall for some ox in tight pants!"

"So Ethan wears tight pants?" Declan continued, not bothering to hide his amusement.

Katherine's face reddened all the more. "He's very nice, and he's trying to see things my way. Trying perhaps *too* hard. I don't think he's had to think for himself much in his life. And then *Bael* appears, and after I don't act like a terrified kit at the sight of him, he tells me he wants me to look after some special *guest* coming to the Palace...."

Declan's eyes widened, "He asked *you* to do that? Why?"

Katherine shrugged, "Because I was with Ethan, I suppose. That's why I kept seeing him. That, and Lady Delira threatened to throw me out on my ears if I refused the man. So when Bael asked me to help him, I of course said yes."

Declan watched her face for a long moment, "*Are* you scared, Katherine?"

She stared back at him with big, luminous brown eyes. "Of *course*! I'm terrified to death! Who *wouldn't* be?"

Declan arched an ivory eyebrow, "I disagree. I've *seen* terror. I've seen it on the battlefield, and I've seen it in the eyes of men who knew they were about to die. You aren't truly scared. You're *excited*. You *enjoy* this, don't you?"

Katherine held back a scowl. *Gods*, but she wanted to smack this man.

And then it struck her. Though she was loath to admit it, she wasn't really that afraid. She was uncomfortable, but part of her *was* enjoying this experience. She enjoyed playing the spy, playing the part of the subservient maid. While she was awash with cold dread, she also realized that she even enjoyed her walks with Ethan.

"Oh gods," she whispered. "No, that's very bad."

Declan stepped forward and gripped her shoulder, "You've come to like the boy, yes?"

Katherine let her shoulder fall in disgrace, "What am I thinking?"

Declan patted her gently, "This is not necessarily a bad thing, dear one. You said he tries to see things your way? Encourage that. Who knows? We might have found an ally in the strangest place imaginable. The trick is to use your resources."

He tapped her forehead softly, "And for you, this is the greatest of them all. But you're allowed to possess a heart as well. No one expects you to be inhuman, just clever. From the sound of it, you've done me proud. You've done *Aleksei* proud."

Katherine found her face glowing again at the praise.

But as much as she wanted further praise, she dared not grow overconfident. She'd surpassed every expectation he'd ever held for her, but she had to be cautious. Cockiness could get them *both* killed.

"And you, Simon?" she said quietly, going to the closet door and listening intently. When she was satisfied that they were in no danger, she turned back to him.

His smile remained, "No one but my late wife has ever called me *Simon*." His smile faded. "I've been relatively successful in my endeavors. I was welcomed back as a hero for surviving the explosion in Mornj. They were quick to let me back into their inner circle, or so I thought.

"I know it seems ages since we arrived, but in that time I've mostly been balancing promises and allegiances between one noble or another. Old grudges die hard among my kind, and since many consider the war to be over, they've renewed their bickering. It's not much different than it was before, except they no longer have the Queen to vilify. With Krasik and Bael in command, they don't seem to know whom to attack besides each other.

"Krasik has little to do with governance. He spends most of his time in Princess Tamara's chambers, being treated by Magi for his headaches. He begs for a tonic every now and then, and even then it's just simple saltwater. It would be sad, were it not so pathetic."

"What about Lord Perron? Isn't he supposed to be in command of the nobles?"

Declan snorted. Katherine shoved her hand to his mouth before rushing back to the closet door. No one seemed to have heard him. She scolded him with her eyes and pressed a finger to her lips.

"*Sorry*," he whispered. "Perron has lost his mind, in my opinion. His failure to capture a single member of the royal family during the invasion has made him something of a pariah among the others. He's rather a joke now.

"He was allowed one last hurrah against the remnants of the Legion retreating to Keldoan. It is rumored that the Lord Captain was personally commanding the Legion forces. They estimated the Legion troops to be roughly twenty-thousand. So Perron sent nearly *sixty-thousand* after them, to wipe them out once and for all.

"The rebel advance force also carried a great number of conscripted peasants, meant to break on the swords and arrows of the Legion, to slow and distract them enough for Perron's main force to catch up and overwhelm the Legionnaires."

Katherine could hardly breathe at the thought of such numbers. "What happened?" she whispered.

A look spread across Declan's face, one that was oddly childlike. "We don't *know*! The advance force vanished. The peasants, the soldiers, every*thing* and every*one*. The tactic failed, apparently."

"And the sixty-thousand?" she asked, trying to keep her voice from quavering.

Declan looked into her terrified eyes, "*We. Don't. Know*. It was like some strange dream, or nightmare rather. They just disappeared. Not a body, not a bloody *bone* to be found. There are stories from the army's followers that sound downright insane, pure madness! But they're the closest thing we have to an answer, which isn't saying much."

Katherine felt her hackles rise, "That's impossible. That many men couldn't simply vanish into thin air."

Declan grinned, "I don't know *how* they disappeared, but the Legion now holds the city of Keldoan. Their numbers have not been reported, but that city is impossible to overrun without a great deal of force.

"Perron threw everything they had at the Legion, and now they're simply...gone. That didn't make him particularly popular with Krasik *or* Bael, I can tell you."

Katherine felt suddenly giddy at the entire prospect. "Do you really think Aleksei was leading the Legion forces?"

Declan heaved a sigh, "I know of no one else in command capable of such a feat. He's a very young man, especially by Legion standards, but the boy has a real head for tactics. Anyone who could turn such a rout against an experienced general has an understanding of the art of war that many of our living commanders crave. This apparent annihilation was hardly well-received. And the blame fell on more than just Perron."

"This is *fascinating*," Katherine whispered, "and it could prove useful. I'll have to ask Ethan about this 'rumor' I've been hearing."

Declan grinned, "Good girl. I daresay you're far more savvy at this whole business than I myself."

Katherine quirked a smile and gave the lord a playful wink, "I learn fast."

"Katherine?"

Katherine stiffened. "It's Lady Delira," she mouthed. She gathered the same bundle of bedclothes she'd come in with. "*Hide*," she hissed, and Declan did his best to duck behind a cart of napkins.

Katherine pushed open the door of the linen closet in a determined manner and gasped when she almost ran into her mistress, "Goodness, milady, my apologies! I was just fetching some clean linens to change your room. I pray you haven't been waiting on me!"

Delira snorted, apparently missing the subtle insult, "Hardly, girl. Drop that mess of rags. Others can see to that. I need my sapphire gown. *Immediately*. Something pressing has come up. Now hop to it!"

Katherine ducked a neat curtsey and was about to go when Delira caught her shoulder, "And *who* is that in the closet with you?"

Katherine's face reddened. She was caught. She looked at the floor, hoping that she could force back the tears of her fear.

After a moment, Delira chuckled, "It's quite alright, dear. No need to be embarrassed. You were only doing as I instructed, after all."

Katherine hid her frown of confusion.

"Just make sure he keeps his trousers on," she whispered, "I don't want to lose your...*invaluable* service to such silliness."

"Yes, milady. Of *course*, milady," Katherine said, bowing her head and keeping her face aimed at the floor.

"I must be off," Delira said crisply. "See to it that my dress is laid out *with* shoes and jewels."

Katherine curtseyed again, "Of course, milady. At once, milady."

Lady Delira made a small noise of dissatisfaction before sweeping from the servants' hall.

Katherine kept her head bowed for a long moment, until she was sure Lady Delira had gone. She straightened, gasping for breath.

Her confusion remained. Surely Lady Delira could tell the difference between Simon Declan and Ethan?

"Katherine?" called a new voice.

She whirled at this latest intrusion. A delighted smile blossomed across her face. She could hardly believe the sight of the big Magus as he bounded down the steps of the small corridor towards her.

"What are you doing here?" she asked in genuine confusion.

He shrugged, "I asked if any of the maids knew where you were. I got lost a few times, but finally someone pointed me up here." He frowned as he suddenly took in her panicked look, "Is everything alright?"

She nodded, "Lady Delira just came down here asking me to lay her dress out for dinner. I'm afraid I've suddenly found myself in a terrible hurry."

"Oh," he said, scratching the back of his head and looking crestfallen. "I suppose you better see to that."

"Perhaps another time," Katherine said as she turned to walk away. She paused, suddenly thinking better of it. With a rush, she turned on her toes and gave him a quick kiss.

The Magus blushed as she disappeared up the stairs.

Aleksei opened his bleary eyes into the faint light of approaching dawn. The desert night chilled his face, but the warmth of Jonas's body gripped in his embrace cut the cold.

He frowned as Jonas's shoulders tensed in his arms. He looked down into the Magus's face. Sweat was beading on Jonas's brow, and Aleksei suppressed a sudden panic. It had been several hours since he'd pulled Jonas from the slaver camp. If the prince was still working his way through their poison....

Jonas let out a sigh and crumpled against him. Aleksei gripped him all the tighter, cradling the smaller man in his broad arms.

Jonas's eyes groggily opened as Aleksei shifted his position to accommodate him.

"Are you awake?" the Magus groaned.

Aleksei managed a smile, "Of course I'm awake. You were sound asleep. I'm not about to risk *any*thing coming at either of us again if I can help it."

Jonas coughed roughly into his hand, "I think I might have fixed that."

Aleksei frowned, looking down into Jonas's upturned face, "How?"

Jonas shrugged a shoulder, "I spoke with Aya once about some of the spells she could see, particularly the ones I'd never discovered before. We talked about many of them. Traded secrets, if you will. There were spells she couldn't touch at the time, but she'd studied them. She gave me the general theory and coordinates for one of her gems, so I tried it."

Aleksei felt the hair on the back of his neck stand stiff. "What did you do?"

Jonas chuckled, an unexpected but welcome sound from the prince of late. "I tied a spell around us. Around *me*, technically, using the bond as an anchor. I was worried about being harassed by wild animals, or more slavers. By anything, actually. We stick out more than I'd like, so until we reach the great cities, I thought it might be safer if we weren't seen unless we wanted to be."

Aleksei understood the strange feeling. "So, you basically made us invisible?"

Jonas pushed his head harder against Aleksei's chest and shifted his shoulder. Aleksei was well aware of the maneuver. Jonas was brushing off discussion by going back to sleep.

"Jonas?" Aleksei said with a gentle nudge.

Jonas sighed, "Not as such, I just made us...less noticeable. Making us invisible would require a huge amount of concentration. What Aya described is a much simpler spell. It doesn't really concern *us*, only what other people perceive. It's called an Arrow Spell."

Aleksei waited a moment in silence for Jonas to realize that he didn't know what that meant. Jonas finally continued, "An Arrow Spell is pretty simple. At least I think it is. The idea is that I put the two of us at a point. That allows light to pass to either side of us. So we're still there, but everything that *should* see us looks one way or the other. No one really notices the point, because it's too direct, so their eyes immediately move to either side."

"That sounds brilliant," Aleksei whispered. Then he frowned, "You said you tied the spell around *you*, right?"

Jonas nodded against him, "I'm the stronger link to the Archanium. It made more sense."

Aleksei chuckled lightly, "Are my feet sticking out?"

Jonas frowned for a moment, apparently trying to understand what Aleksei meant. When it finally came to him, he actually laughed out loud. "No," he whispered, giving Aleksei a quick kiss, "your feet aren't sticking out. Sending the spell across the bond ensures that we're both covered."

"And the horses? Are they harder to perceive as well?"

"The spell should affect anything near us, within reason. A horse is small enough to be affected, unless they wander too far away from us at night."

"Are you sure?" Aleksei teased.

Jonas tensed in his arms, "Of course I'm not sure. I've never done this before. Everything I've said is *highly* theoretical at best."

Aleksei kissed Jonas's forehead, "Calm down, I'm just curious, that's all."

"I'm sorry, I'm still a little on edge," Jonas muttered, closing his eyes in the predawn glow.

A chaotic storm of images from the night before flashed through Aleksei's mind.

After observing the slaughter of the slaver camp, Jonas had been shocked. Not so much by the brutality Aleksei displayed, but at the sheer fury and ferocity that had roared across the bond.

Aleksei knew his Magus had never seen him to behave like that, *kill* like that. Aleksei had killed men many times in the past, of course, but this had been different. Again, Aleksei felt a wave of shame from his Magus. Shame that his Knight had done those things on his behalf.

And yet Aleksei seemed to suffer no ill effect as a result of his brutality. He wasn't remorseful, just solidly resolute. He had been grimly determined to get Jonas back safely, to find Tamara. The slavers had been unfortunate enough to get in his way, to take Jonas from him.

Despite the horrors of that night, Aleksei still had the niggling feeling that those men had gotten off easy, their deaths mercifully swift. Had he and Jonas not been in such a rush to find Tamara, he would have staked each of them to the ground, to await the slow cruelty of the local fauna. Alas, they'd each been granted far swifter deaths than they'd deserved.

Jonas lay there, feeling the heat radiating off his Knight, feeling the soft golden hairs on Aleksei's chest brush his face as the Knight breathed. He had never felt so concerned and yet so comforted at the same time.

"Starling," Aleksei said idly.

Jonas opened his eyes, "What?"

Aleksei sat up and turned. Jonas followed suit, shivering as the desert air washed across him. Aleksei was looking at a bird standing not far away. It was a brilliant emerald with patches of purple beneath its wings and across its underside. There was an iridescent quality to its feathers that Jonas had never seen before. One of its beady black eyes was fixed on them. It was at once one of the most beautiful yet ridiculous-looking birds Jonas had ever seen.

"*That's* a starling?" Jonas asked.

Aleksei glanced back at him with a cocked eyebrow, "One kind, yes."

"Why is it just standing there like that?"

"Because it's not afraid of us."

Jonas tensed, "Why not?"

Aleksei shrugged, "No idea. Could just be a curious bird that's never seen a human before."

The bird hopped closer to them, still staring at them with those bright black eyes. The depth in that gaze made it intensely clear that this bird was more than merely curious. It seemed to be *studying* them.

"Hello," Aleksei said calmly, holding out his hand.

"Be careful, Aleksei. What if it's a trap of some sort? Something from Bael?" Jonas said warily.

Aleksei glanced down at him, "I've seen the sorts of things Bael sends our way, and I don't sense any malice from it. Do you feel any magic surrounding the bird? Any Archanium echoes?"

Jonas concentrated and stiffened, "Yes, a little. I can't tell where it's coming from, but this bird has definitely been spelled."

Aleksei didn't seem surprised, "Hmm. Well, if it was dangerous, I imagine it would have done something by now." He turned back to the starling, his hand still extended.

The bird hopped onto his index finger and kept staring at him with those shining jet eyes.

"It's a female," Aleksei said absently.

"How can you tell?" Jonas asked, pulling a blanket up around his shoulders.

"She has a brood patch. See that featherless spot on her belly? It lets her pass heat to her eggs more effectively. Males don't have those."

Jonas cast a wary eye at his Knight's back, "When did you learn so much about starlings?"

Aleksei shrugged, "I don't really know *that* much. I can just tell by looking at her. She just...makes sense to me."

Jonas frowned. Aleksei's Hunter instincts sometimes displayed themselves in the oddest ways, but in this uncertain terrain, he was desperately glad to have them at their disposal.

"She's not here to hurt us," Aleksei announced finally.

"Then what's she doing here?" Jonas muttered.

"I don't know. I think she just wanted to give us a good look," Aleksei said.

The starling abruptly flapped its wings and vanished into the gathering dawn. Aleksei chuckled to himself.

"Whoever sent it was *very* interested in who we were."

"And how do you know that?" Jonas said, only half-joking. "Did the wind whisper that in your ear?"

Aleksei ignored the playful jibe, "No. But when she was looking at me, I got the distinct impression that she wasn't the only one watching."

Aya stepped into the great library of the Betrayer's Bastion, blinking at the rows and rows of books that assaulted her from all sides. Gods, even if she had a century to work through them all, she doubted she could accomplish such a feat.

And yet she needed only a handful of volumes.

Toma stepped in beside her and flashed a cheerful smile.

Aya buried her cynicism. The girl was younger than she, only by a summer or two, but still, Aya had seen Toma under pressure. It had been an unpleasant and embarrassing experience.

Yet without Ilyana there, Toma was the closest to a senior Magus she had to work with. With a tired sigh, Aya lifted her hand.

The lamps all leapt to life at her command.

The power, the *control* she had gained upon attaining use of the higher Akhrana had been immeasurable. Even now, weeks after the fact, she was still startled by the strength of her abilities.

"This should make things easier," Toma said softly.

Aya frowned as the younger woman stepped forward and opened her palm. The air stirred in the library. As Aya watched, the air whipped into a wind that whisked along the shelves and tables, lifting the dust and pulling it into a tight ball above Toma's hand.

After a few moments, Toma closed her fist. When she opened it again, she held a stone, barely larger than a winter apple. Aya stared at the library, now completely cleared of centuries worth of dust and soot.

Aya stared at the younger woman, "How did you do that?"

"It was one of the first things I discovered," Toma blushed, "Thanks to you. I was in a different wing of the Bastion, and I was frustrated by the amount of dust. I reached out for a spell, and this one appeared, so I tried it."

Aya's face became grave, "That could be exceptionally dangerous."

Toma giggled, "I know. But I figured that the Bastion was a very old place, and had probably handled the powers of Magi far stronger than me. So I let it loose, and this is what I got."

Aya breathed a silent prayer of thanks to the gods. "Well, this will certainly save us time. Thank you, Toma."

The younger Magus smirked, "It's a pleasure, High Magus."

Aya gritted her teeth, ignoring the appellation. "Why don't you start on the east end, and I'll take the west? At the *very* least I need *Fractional Divination*, *A Bifurcated System of Arcane Runes*, and *Keller's Grimoire*."

Toma's face went pale, "High Magus, I'd be amazed to find even *one* of those volumes outside the Voralla."

Aya's peridot eyes snapped to Toma's alarmed face, "First, please don't call me that. Second, get looking. Who knows what's buried in this place? We might get lucky. And we'll need *both* of those volumes to clearly understand what Jonas sent my way. Without them, we might as well be blind."

Toma took a deep breath, finally nodding her head, "As you wish, High...*Aya*."

Aya nodded her head wearily, "Let's get to it. This is an ancient library. There ought to be *some* texts here that we can use."

Toma's large eyes glittered, "And if there aren't?"

Aya wiped her face with her hand, "Then Raefan and I will have to infiltrate the Voralla, and find them for ourselves."

Toma's eyes widened in shock, "You can't do that! We *need* you, Aya! We need a *leader!*"

Aya offered a small smile, "Let's have a look around first, shall we? We might have nothing to worry about."

Toma pulled nervously at her collar, "I doubt that."

"Oh, I don't know," Aya said, scanning the titles, "you might find a few surprises in here."

Toma watched Aya for a long moment before turning to the stack on her left, wandering off scanning the titles.

"Aya!"

Aya turned from the stacks to see Raefan and Toma's Knight Tamrix racing towards them. She abandoned her quest for a moment, content to leave Toma to the search while she attended to the Knights.

"We found something you'll want to see," Tamrix said breathlessly.

Aya looked to Raefan, "What do you know of this?"

Raefan fixed her with an arresting gaze. She immediately understood the severity of the situation, "What's happened?"

"Sammul's dead," Raefan stated flatly.

Aya sniffed, "Are you sure?"

Raefan gave a sharp nod.

"Good riddance to bad rubbish then," she spat.

Raefan chuckled, carefully pulling a darkened skull from his pack. "There's this."

Aya glared at the skull. She spat on it before dropping it to the floor and bringing her boot down on the charred bone. It shattered on impact, and she crushed the remaining bits to ash.

She calmly looked up into Raefan's beautiful blue eyes, "Anything else?"

Her Knight nodded to Tamrix, a large man with brilliant red hair,

"High Magus, ma'am," he began, glancing at Toma, who was standing to the side with wide eyes. "I have evidence that Hade and Vadim were living in Keldoan for some time before our arrival."

Aya raised her eyebrows, "And how have you obtained this information?"

Tamrix shrugged, "I spoke to the innkeepers of the town, to the cutpurses and the street toughs. People who know things. I had to bloody a few noses, but they eventually told me what happened."

"And?"

Tamrix sighed heavily, "I believe Hade and Vadim followed the Prince and the Lord Captain. Right after they left, Hade and Vadim quit the city. Their tracks go off in the same direction."

Raefan snorted, "Well, that's hardly worthy of notice."

Tamrix's face fell.

Aya fixed Raefan with a warning glare, "You believe they followed Jonas and Aleksei to *harm* them?"

Tamrix gave a sheepish nod.

"What makes you think there's something nefarious about their departure?"

Tamrix took a deep breath, clearly nervous, "I heard some...disquieting things about the two of them regarding their time here. I started tracking them, which is what led me to...that." The Knight gestured to the remnants of Sammul's crushed skull. "Their tracks were everywhere through the woods surrounding Sammul's corpse. At one point, one of them, I believe it was Hade, was on his knees."

Aya frowned, "How do you know *they* didn't kill him?"

Tamrix looked up and fixed Aya with his dark brown eyes, "When I found Sammul's body...it wasn't so much a body as it was a thin outer shell, but it was almost entirely hollow on the inside. One touch and it all dissolved to ash. Except for the skull. And begging your pardon, but I've never seen a spell like that, certainly not from one of our own, new meridian or no. There was also a third set of tracks that...didn't make any sense."

"Meaning?" Aya asked, leaning forward intently.

"Meaning that there were bootprints from a third person. They were tiny. Either they belonged to a very small woman or a child. But they didn't *go* anywhere. There was no sign of this person entering *or* exiting the area. It was as though one moment she appeared, took a few steps, and then vanished again."

Raefan folded his arms across his chest, "Do you really think Vadim and Hade could harm *Aleksei* and *Jonas*?"

Aya held up a hand, "I do."

Raefan's blinked in surprise, "What? How? I've worked with them. I can't believe they would have any trouble with a pair like Vadim and Hade."

"And therein lies the problem," Aya muttered softly. "They aren't a large enough threat to register, are they? If something convinced them to ambush Jonas and Aleksei, who would stop them? Jonas and Aleksei aren't the type of men to murder their comrades without serious provocation. They have too much heart. A surprise attack would be a definite problem."

Raefan's jaw clenched, "And that could be their undoing."

"Precisely. I'm not entirely sure we can afford mercy under our current circumstances."

Toma stared from Aya to her Knight. "You can't be *serious*, though. We can't afford to lose a single Magus, can we?"

Aya glared at the younger woman, "Toma, we're at war. In this war, some will choose our side, and others will choose poorly. Either way, we have to be prepared to deal with the results. And we cannot sit idly by and allow those who would side against us to put the lives of our friends and loved ones at risk because we're worried about standing up for ourselves.

"In a situation like this, I don't *care* if their motives are misguided. We don't have that luxury. If they try to harm me or those I care about, I will destroy them." She arched a tawny eyebrow, "I would expect you... all of us...to do the same."

Toma's eyes widened, but after a moment she looked away. "I suppose you have a point. I'm just not used to thinking in such extreme terms."

Aya sighed, "Why should you be? These ways of thinking are new to *all* of us. We are unaccustomed to war, to betrayal. But as I said, we don't have the luxury of time right now. We either adapt to our circumstances, or we die. It's as simple as that."

Toma nodded her head, "As you say, High Magus."

Aya bit back a growl of distaste, "That's settled then. Now come on, the sooner we find those volumes, the sooner we'll know what we have to do next. That book must be translated before Jonas returns from the wastes, and if I have to go to the Voralla to make that possible, I will. But in the meantime, we're wasting what precious time we have."

The Knights turned to leave when Aya held up her hand, "Oh, and gentlemen? Take the trash with you on your way out."

She looked down at the ashes of Sammul's skull, and Tamrix immediately set about clearing it up.

CHAPTER 32

STARLING

"How much?" Jonas asked in Fanja, looking down at the array of waterskins.

"*Five coppers each,*" the little boy behind the counter said, flashing his brilliant white teeth in a smile.

Jonas handed the boy an Ilyari silver, "*I'll take four then.*"

The boy's eyes widened. It was unlikely that he'd ever seen that sort of coinage in his life. "*My apologies, sir. I do not have enough to make change.*"

Jonas smiled at the boy, "*Then keep the rest. I'm sure your family could use it.*"

"*Oh, no sir, I could not take this. It is too much. I have not earned it.*"

Jonas thought a moment, ignoring the child's outstretched hand offering him back his silver. Finally, he looked back at the boy, "*What's your name?*"

"*Havar, sir.*"

Jonas leaned forward, "*Well, Havar, can you see those horses there, the big black one and the brown one?*"

The boy nodded.

"*Those horses are very important to my friend and I. Would you watch them for me? A silver for the waterskins and watching our horses is a fair trade.*"

"*Watch them, sir?*"

Jonas nodded, *"Make sure no one takes them?"*

"I suppose so," the boy said uncertainly.

Jonas's face turned serious, *"Have you ever watched a horse before?"*
Havar shook his head.

"Well," Jonas said in a grave tone, *"it's a very important job. If you can watch them while I find my friend, you'll have earned that silver, as far as I'm concerned."*

The boy looked cautiously hopeful, *"Are you sure?"*

Jonas nodded solemnly, *"Very."*

Havar's face grew very serious, mirroring Jonas's expression, *"Thank you, sir. I would be honored, sir."*

"You're doing me a great service, and it's certainly worth a silver to know they're safe."

Havar bowed deeply to Jonas.

Jonas bowed his head slightly, in the Fanja custom, *"Thank you for the water, as well."*

Jonas lifted the four waterskins by their leather thongs and slung them over his shoulder. Behind him, he could hear the sounds of Havar closing up shop.

He smiled to himself. The boy was obviously eager to get to his new job, and with the amount of money clenched in his tight little fist, Jonas didn't blame him. That amount of money could easily sustain his family for months in a place like this.

Jonas turned and squinted in the sun, looking around the tiny village.

The huts that comprised it were all wattle and daub, their roofs poorly thatched or covered by coarse canvas tarps. He doubted the villagers had ever seen proper thatching, but their options were slim. With no source of wood nearby, grass was the only available roofing material, and there wasn't much of it. But, as it hardly ever rained in this part of the world, he doubted they worried much about that. Here the roofs served to block the sun more than anything else.

The market had been built in the center of the village, a great open ring of small booths that appeared to have stood for decades. The wood was gray and sun-bleached. Above each booth was a strip of brightly dyed cloth, Fanja script painted roughly across it alongside pictograms, displaying the nature of the wares available. Everything from water and food to clothing and livestock was for sale.

Jonas looked around, noting that the selection was relatively limited due to the size of the village. He wondered what Aleksei would think when he reached the major cities. Gods, what would Aleksei think if he ever saw *Je'gud?* The crown city was famous for its markets. Jonas doubted there was *anything* in the known world one couldn't find in such a place, from spices to slaves. If one had the coin, of course.

With a sigh, Jonas realized that he didn't know where Aleksei *was*.

His concern rose as he rapidly began to search for his Knight. Aleksei was woefully uneducated when it came to Fanja culture. These were a people of *very* strict rules of behavior and conduct. Aleksei didn't speak their language. Jonas saw disaster looming.

The idea had been simple enough. Stop into a small village, drop the Arrow Spell and resupply food and water for the long trek across the wastes. He had told Aleksei to stay close to him and let him do all the talking. But at some point, Aleksei had drifted away in the market, and Jonas had been too busy bartering to notice.

Now the man was nowhere to be found.

Jonas took a calming breath of the dry, dusty air and focused on their bond. He could feel Aleksei to the northeast, on the other side of a group of huts. Jonas started off at once, righting the waterskins across his back. They were heavy, and he wanted to get back to the horses as quickly as possible.

A boy like Havar might keep some away, but he doubted the boy could keep a real thief at bay. A warhorse like Agriphon was a rare sight in this part of the world, and in such a small place, his black coat and regal stature was hard to ignore.

They were outsiders in this place, and this was a very poor village. He would hardly blame someone for taking their things, but without the horses, they would never get across the wastes.

He followed the bond around the buildings and stopped dead in his tracks.

There was Aleksei, sitting in the red dirt of an alley, surrounded by children. Jonas was instantly struck by the way many of the children kept touching Aleksei, their reddish-brown skin brushing his arms, patting his face, reaching into his hair. He sat there with a handsome grin spread wide across his face, reacting playfully to their questions and words.

It was clear he had no idea what they were saying, but he pretended he did.

Jonas walked closer, and the children stared at him as though afraid they had done something wrong.

Aleksei looked up, that childish grin still plastered across his face, "Did you find what we needed?"

Jonas nodded, then crouched in front of the children. *"Do you like him?"* he asked in Fanja.

The children all nodded, some now suddenly shy and ducking behind the older, taller ones.

"He's nice, isn't he?" Jonas asked.

The children nodded again.

"Why were you touching him like that?"

They all looked to one another before one very brave girl, taller than the others, stepped forward, clasping her hands behind her back, *"We've never seen someone like him before. With straw hair and straw eyes. We wondered what he felt like. If he was pale because he was cold."*

Jonas smiled at that, *"And what did you discover?"*

The girl giggled, *"He's nice. He feels just like us. He just looks different."*

Jonas nodded, *"That's right. What were you saying to him?"*

"We were asking him where he was from, why he looked different."

"He's from Ilyar, in a city called Kalinor. It's big like Je'gud."

The girl's black eyes went wide, *"Are you princes?"*

Jonas chuckled, *"No, just humble travelers."*

The girl slumped, disappointed.

"Well," Jonas whispered with a wink, *"I'm a prince."*

Her eyes lit up again.

Jonas held a finger to his lips. *"Shh. Don't tell anyone till we're gone, alright?"*

She nodded, putting a finger to her lips too. He realized it probably wasn't a familiar gesture among her people.

Jonas winked at the girl before standing. He looked to where some of the other children were already crawling back into Aleksei's lap. They were laughing at his facial expressions. Some of them were still groping his arms, trying to figure out how a man could get to be so *big*. He was playfully flexing for a girl who seemed mesmerized by him in every way.

"Aleksei, we should go."

The Knight looked up, and Jonas felt a stab of guilt at the disappointment on his face.

Aleksei gently lifted the girl in his lap, who had been touching his arm, and carefully placed her amongst the other children. He stood tall and looked down at the motley gang, "I'm sorry, but I have to go. It was an honor to meet all of you."

The older girl Jonas had spoken to turned to him, *"What did he say?"*

Jonas smiled, raising his voice to address all the children gathered, *"He said it was a great honor to meet all of you, but we have to leave. It was an honor for me as well. Thank you."* He bowed his head and the children responded with corresponding bows.

Aleksei watched the whole interchange with a bemused smile on his face.

"What did you tell them?" he asked as they headed back to the horses.

"Almost exactly what you said, and that I was honored, too. How did they *find* you?"

Aleksei hefted a bundle of bright yellow homespun, "I was buying something. The girl you spoke to was behind the counter."

They reached the horses and Havar stood, his eyes wide, *"You've already returned? I thought you would be gone through the* night."

Jonas winked at the boy, *"I told you this was an important job, and I didn't know how long I'd be gone. You did very well. Thank you."*

He nodded his head and the boy bowed before dashing off towards his home.

Aleksei arched an eyebrow, "What was *that* about?"

Jonas shrugged, mounting his gelding, "I paid him a silver for the water and for watching the horses."

Aleksei straddled Agriphon and nudged him into a trot. They were a few leagues from the city before Aleksei turned with a frown, "Why was he guarding the horses?"

Jonas smirked, "That is an *extremely* poor village, Aleksei. Too far from any larger city to receive regular supplies, or protection. Those people don't see horses like Agriphon often, if ever. And some desperate thief could have tried to take off with the both of them while ours back were turned.

"Having a local boy watch them made that a lot less likely. It's one thing to steal from clueless travelers, quite another to hurt one of your own, especially in a place that small."

Aleksei nodded slowly, "And why was he grinning when he ran off?"

Jonas smiled, "Because he's probably never seen a full silver mark in his life. That coin could make that boy's family aristocrats of a sort in that village for some time."

"Ah," Aleksei said, stiffly turning back to the path ahead of them.

Jonas frowned, "Why?"

Aleksei hefted the bundle of yellow cloth, "The girl, the oldest one? She was selling clothes. I thought they looked better suited to this sort of weather, hot as it is in the day. I couldn't understand how much they were, so I poured some coin on the table and let her take what they were worth."

Jonas almost fell out of his saddle, "How much did she *take*?"

Aleksei shrugged uneasily, "Not enough, I'm sure. Nothing close to a silver. But for what I bought...I feel like I cheated her."

Jonas blinked, "What did you buy?"

"Something we need," Aleksei said as he scanned the baked horizon, noting the shimmering waves of heat that made everything look like it was underwater. Jonas noted the collar of his Ilyari woolen shirt was starting to rub his neck raw.

With a low growl, Aleksei pulled the shirt off.

Jonas glanced over at him, his powerful frame sweating in the brilliant midday sunlight. "I *really* don't want to treat your sunburns when we make camp," the Magus said irritably.

Aleksei flashed him an infectious smile and produced the bundle of yellow cloth. While Agriphon trotted at a brisk pace, Aleksei looped a knot in the fabric around his saddle horn. He gently pulled a cluster of white linen from the inside and turned it out. It looked to be some sort of tunic. Aleksei unrolled it in the air before him and pulled it over his broad shoulders.

Jonas watched as Aleksei's powerful arms emerged from the holes in the shirt where the sleeves should have been.

Jonas blinked in the brilliant sun. Aleksei stuffed his gray Ilyari shirt into the yellow bundle and returned it to his saddlebags. The shirt he now wore was made of coarse Fanja linen. Small horn buttons ran up the front, but his arms were laid bare.

Aleksei stretched his back and settled back into the saddle, totally oblivious that Jonas was staring at him. Jonas felt his face flush at the thoughts flashing through his mind.

"How is it?" he called over.

Aleksei flashed him a grin, "Much better. Want to see what I bought for you?"

Jonas blinked again. "You bought me something?"

The Knight held up a hand. Jonas felt his breath catch as Aleksei leaned to the side, rooting around in the saddlebag where he'd stowed the yellow bundle. It always made him uneasy to watch Aleksei perform complicated tasks while riding Agriphon. Jonas had been riding his entire life, but Aleksei looked like he'd grown up in the saddle. His Knight might as well have been walking down the street. He was so fluid, so controlled in his movements. Jonas knew he would never under-stand, or match, Aleksei's natural grace and skill with animals.

Aleksei straightened with the bundle and casually flipped it under-hand at Jonas. The Magus was surprised when it landed perfectly in his arms. Aleksei had judged the distance between them and how far Jonas had traveled in the meantime perfectly.

Jonas's concern rose for the second time that day. Aleksei was usually very confident. And strong. But Jonas was beginning to notice a change in his Knight. Aleksei had never seemed so *cocky* before.

Now, Aleksei was almost acting like he thought he was invincible. Flashes from the night of the slaver camp filled Jonas's mind, the way Aleksei had used the Mantle. Worry crept into his heart as he watched Aleksei, so dashing in his sleeveless white tunic, bound across the Fanja landscape on his magnificent black stallion. They were riding deeper into a strange land, and misplaced confidence could lead to a lack of caution.

The humility Jonas had fallen in love with was shifting into an abun-dance of self-assurance and strength that the prince found at once infuri-ating and intoxicating. But concern still nagged at the back of his mind.

He carefully opened the yellow bundle of cloth and pushed aside Aleksei's woolen shirt. He smiled unintentionally at the emerald green linen tunic underneath. Looping the yellow bundle around his saddle horn, Jonas attempted to do the same as Aleksei had just done. He unbuttoned his shirt and pulled it off. He blushed when he noticed Aleksei staring out of the corner of his eye.

Jonas did his best to push the shirt into the bundle, but a gust of wind hit a moment later and tore it from his hand. He glanced at Alek-sei, but the man had already dismounted and gone back to retrieve it.

While his Knight ran back to grab the dusty gray wool, Jonas pulled out the green tunic Aleksei had bought for him. He was very careful in pulling it on and buttoning it properly, which was quite a challenge even on a stationary horse.

He looked deeper into the yellow bundle and found a second piece, a pale brown lightcoat. Jonas looked over as Aleksei climbed back into the saddle and his Hunter winked.

Jonas pulled the coat on, sighing as his arms slid through the weightless linen.

He looked back into the bundle, but all he found was Aleksei's sodden wool shirt.

"Where's yours?" he called.

Aleksei shrugged playfully, arching a golden eyebrow.

Jonas felt that spark of concern blossom inside him once more as he passed the yellow bundle back to the Knight. What was Aleksei playing at? His arms would be *blistering* in a few minutes, yet the Hunter seemed unconcerned.

And then Jonas realized that he was missing the complete picture. Aleksei's arms were bare, but they weren't exactly uncovered. The Mantle was in full view, talons trailing lazily down to the middle of Aleksei's biceps. This was no accident.

It was a warning, but for whom?

He tried to puzzle it out as he focused on the road ahead. Everything was sunbaked and dry, the earth cracking open with desperate thirst. He felt his mouth water, and he grabbed a waterskin. The water was warm, but it was enough to slake his thirst.

Red sandstone bluffs loomed before them after a few more hours. Jonas sighed when he finally saw the pass emerge from the cliff faces ahead. The journey beyond would be arduous, but he prayed they could find Tamara before someone moved her. Before they *hurt* her. The gods only knew what was being done to her, even as they traversed the wastes.

She was a powerful symbol, one beloved by her kingdom. It was hard to imagine *anyone*, rebel or Loyalist, who would want to hurt her.

Aleksei suddenly stood in his saddle. Jonas glared, but didn't dare try to copy the maneuver.

"What is it?" he shouted as the winds whipped up around them. He followed the line of Aleksei's arm, to where his Knight was pointing. There was a bird, almost invisible against dusky sky and stone, circling at the entrance to the canyon.

Jonas turned to Aleksei and shrugged his shoulders. "So?"

Aleksei sat back in his saddle and smiled at Jonas, "Starling."

Jonas blinked and looked back to the bird. It was indeed circling in front of them, yet it was a completely different bird, cream and alternating shades of brown where the first one had been emerald and aubergine. Jonas wondered why they were being followed by starlings, especially since Aleksei had claimed that someone else was watching them through the birds' eyes.

It worried him, but Aleksei seemed strangely unbothered. His lack of concern was maddening. Where was the Aleksei who was cautious and uncertain? Unsure of the world around him before every situation had been thoroughly assessed?

Jonas froze in his saddle. Why was he so worried? Was Aleksei's increased confidence bothering him that much? And why?

Something just felt *wrong*.

"Stop," Jonas called.

Aleksei didn't seem to hear him and kept riding. Jonas brought the gelding to a gallop to catch up to the Hunter. Aleksei was tracking something altogether different.

"I said *stop!*" Jonas shouted.

Aleksei fixed him with a dangerous look and pointed down the road. Ahead of them, the starling had landed in the road and wasn't moving. Aleksei pulled Agriphon to a halt. Jonas pulled his horse up short, gratefully slipping from the saddle. Whether it was a starling or something else, at least he had Aleksei's attention.

"Listen...."

His Knight raised a hand. Jonas trailed off as Aleksei knelt in the dust, studying the white and tawny-streaked bird standing in their path. Just beyond the starling was the entrance to the pass.

When Aleksei reached out to touch it, the starling took wing, flying above the pass between the red sandstone. It circled a few times, then abruptly dropped like a stone, striking the road in front of the pass with a dusty thud. The two men shared an uneasy glance.

"What was *that?*" Jonas demanded, squinting in the brilliant sunlight. The starling lay ten paces distant, motionless in the red dust.

Aleksei approached the bird. "A warning. A very *serious* warning. Someone doesn't want us to go through the pass. I don't suppose you want to fly up there and scout it out?"

Jonas shook his head, "I wouldn't risk it this close to Ul'Brek territory. One could snuff my connection to the Archanium in a heartbeat, and I'd rather not fall to my death today."

Aleksei sniffed at the air, casting a concerned glance at the range that extended to either side of the pass. "Is there a way around?"

"Not really," Jonas grumbled after a moment's hesitation. "Nothing that's of use to us. Beyond that pass is the only proper route through the wastes."

"Why?" Aleksei asked as he scooped up the lifeless bird and carried it back towards the horses.

"The mountains are impassable south of here. The land to the north is cursed. We *have* to take the pass. It's the only way through, especially if we don't want to die of thirst out there."

Aleksei was silent for a long moment. Rather than question Jonas further, he knelt beside the road and buried the starling in the loose scree. "It's a bad idea," he said finally, coming to his feet. "We need to find another way."

Jonas breathed out in frustration, "Didn't you hear me? There *isn't* another way. These cliffs and rocks stretch north and south farther than you'd care to believe. The pass is the *only* way into the wastes that isn't a hundred leagues distant."

"There's highland to the north," Aleksei noted, reading the terrain.

"We can't go there," Jonas snapped, "I already told you, it's *cursed*. That isn't a word I throw about lightly!" He took a deep breath, calming himself. "This magic is far older than anything we've seen before, Aleksei. It is beyond dangerous. We can't make it go *away* simply because you don't like the pass."

Aleksei arched a golden eyebrow, "Cursed? By what?"

"Prophecy."

Aleksei scowled, "So why do we care?"

"I'm happiest when I can avoid prophecy of any kind," Jonas growled.

Aleksei flashed a smile, "Not always possible. Sometimes we just luck into it."

Jonas grew increasingly cautious. Aleksei had never been fond of prophecy, but Jonas recognized it as be a valuable tool in the proper contexts. He couldn't escape the feeling that this was one time when they'd be better off heeding the warnings passed down through generations of Prophets and Magi.

Aleksei's experience with prophecy was altogether different. The Hunter had been given a prophecy directly from Darielle. Jonas still didn't entirely understand what she'd said to his Knight, but he knew that Aleksei had been deeply affected by the experience.

"Let's just try the pass before we make any rash decisions," Jonas said finally.

Aleksei shrugged. "I can't stop you, but I'm *not* going through that pass, and you're risking both our lives if you do."

Jonas glared at him. Aleksei could be impossibly aggravating at times. He was a beautiful man built of muscle and discipline, tempered by humility, but also power.

Power that was magnetic, difficult to ignore, much less resist. But he was becoming increasingly erratic of late. Perhaps his near-brush with death had affected him far more than he let on. The man was starting to balk at the oddest things, while recklessly bulling his way through others. Since Aleksei had destroyed the slaver camp, Jonas found himself questioning Aleksei's judgment more and more.

He closed his eyes and delved into the Archanium, searching for any signs of life in the steep canyon ahead.

Nothing.

He glanced back at Aleksei, "Can you hear any heartbeats up ahead?"

Aleksei frowned at him a moment, then closed his eyes and listened. After a long moment he looked up, "No, but that doesn't mean anything. I'm sure there are ways to block my abilities, just like yours."

Jonas paused. Why was Aleksei making this so *difficult*? Jonas didn't like the situation any better than his Knight. In truth, the starling's warning resonated within him, too.

Animals didn't just drop dead to offer warnings to random travelers. But Aleksei didn't seem to comprehend the very real danger posed by the land north of the pass. And he didn't take Jonas seriously when the Prince warned him of the danger they would be in should they stray from the road.

Jonas irritably rubbed at his eyes. They didn't have the luxury of stopping for the day so Jonas could educate Aleksei on all the various stories and accounts of those who'd opted for the northern route in the past few centuries. They never ended well, and most involved people riding off from the rest of their party, never to be seen again.

There was no choice but to enter the pass. To go north was to invite certain death, and yet it seemed Aleksei was being obstinate just to prove a point.

Perhaps his Knight just had to see it for himself. With a deep sigh, Jonas swung back into the saddle and rode his gelding into the pass, glancing up at the massive boulders that formed a natural bridge across the path far above him.

Crack.

Jonas flinched and pulled his horse to a stop, but nothing seemed to have changed. Rocks of this magnitude, he supposed, were bound to crack every now and again in the desert heat. Still, the timing didn't fill him with confidence.

A second crack, this one sharper, *deeper,* ricocheted through the canyon.

Jonas looked up and gasped. The natural bridge shattered above him, rumbling down in a deadly cascade. As he watched the mountainous rubble fall towards him, too stunned to react, a surge of cold dread swept through him.

His horse screamed and bolted. His vision blurred as waves of pain and light washed across him.

The pain was so powerful, he wondered if he would even survive. His bones felt like they might shatter at any second. It wasn't even the weight of the stone deluge as much as it was the bizarre, permeating *cold.*

His horse bucked, and Jonas fell out of the saddle, ending up on all fours in the dirt. He was shocked that he didn't shatter on impact. He stayed still for a long moment, gasping and desperately wishing the harsh desert heat would drive the cold from his bones. His skull ached so much it seemed to be crushing his eyes from their sockets. And through it all rang the same unwavering, screeching *wail* blocking out all sound, blinding white light burning his eyes.

It suddenly struck him as odd that he was concerned with trifles like sight or cold when he should have been obliterated *immediately.* The cold ebbed from him, and with it went the piercing wail that had filled his ears. He realized that he was squeezing his eyes shut and did his best to relax.

When his eyes finally opened, he realized that he had somehow made it onto his back. He was staring at the sky, occluded only by the large, shadowy form of Aleksei looming over him. Jonas inhaled sharply and Aleksei kissed him a second after that.

"*Gods,* I'm glad you came around," Aleksei panted, cradling Jonas against himself. "For a bit there, I thought it was over for both of us."

Jonas managed a dry cough. "I'm harder to kill than that, I suppose."

"Apparently so," Aleksei muttered. "I tried to pull you back with the

Mantle."

"That would explain the pain," Jonas grunted, bracing himself on his elbows.

Aleksei shook his head, "You were too far away. The Mantle couldn't reach you in time."

Jonas frowned, "Then what happened? Where are the rocks? They had to land *somewhere*. How are we alive?"

Aleksei watched him cautiously, "You don't remember? *Anything?*"

Jonas's frown deepened, "I remember incredible pain. And the cold. I remember the cold. There was some a lot of light and...noise, I suppose, but it wasn't anything I recognized."

"It was the Seraphima, Jonas. It was *you*. Whatever you did, a column of light erupted from you and the next time I saw you, you were on your knees with rocks all around you. The ones directly above you just turned to dust. I don't know how you did it, but this is *twice* now."

Jonas's mouth went dry. The *Seraphima?*

The first time he'd invoked the Angelic magic, it had been to save Aleksei's life. He didn't remember touching the Seraphima consciously, it had just happened through instinct. Instinct and panic. He supposed this wasn't all that different.

"But," Jonas began again, "the rocks. Why would they collapse like that in the first place?"

Aleksei helped Jonas to his feet and pointed to a nearby boulder, "You tell me."

Jonas stared at Aleksei for a long moment before turning to the wall of stone that now blocked their passage. He opened himself to the Archanium.

He saw the echo, the signature.

Jonas coughed. "Hade," he managed, "It was *Hade*."

Aleksei nodded slowly, "I don't remember everything that happened the last time they attacked us, but as I recall, we didn't do too well."

Jonas stiffened, "We survived."

Aleksei gave a dry chuckle, "Yeah, we survived. *Barely*. Against the two of them. Think about that for a moment."

Jonas stared at Aleksei, his blood boiling. Aleksei didn't back down. "You could have taken Hade to pieces without breaking a sweat. I didn't bother killing Vadim, but it would only have taken a thought."

Jonas frowned, "What are you getting at?"

Aleksei dropped his head into his hands, running his fingers through his thick blond hair, "We should have killed them both when we had the chance. This is the *second* time they've almost killed us."

"*You* couldn't tell they were there, and neither could I. That alone makes them extremely dangerous. I underestimated them the first time. I should have finished it then."

"If I had killed Hade the moment I realized what he was up to, you would never have had to recover from that wound," Jonas muttered.

Aleksei coughed, "Wound? That's an awfully polite way to put it. Half my chest cavity was *gone*." He reached out and gripped Jonas's arm. "You saved me. You saved *us*."

Jonas stared at the dust billowing from the shattered boulders before him, "Not this time. I almost got us killed by ignoring your warning. I thought you were just getting cocky. It never occurred to me something like this could happen."

He looked back at Aleksei, tears welling in his eyes, "Gods, I'm sorry." Aleksei wrapped his arms around Jonas as the Magus began to sob. "I'm *so* sorry. I've been acting a fool, and I ought to *know* better. I should have listened to you."

"It wasn't your fault. There was no way you could have known that he was up there," Aleksei grunted.

"But I could have listened to *you* for once," Jonas whispered. "I could have had *faith* that you knew what you were talking about."

"Shh," Aleksei breathed. "We're both prone to mistakes, me just as well as you. The important thing is that we're *alive*."

"I'm so sorry. I should have listened," Jonas whimpered.

He lay there for a moment, letting the cold reality of their circumstance wash over him. He frowned, "Where's my horse?"

Aleksei nodded towards the pass, "When the rocks split, he spooked and bolted. Honestly, you're pretty lucky you didn't break anything when you fell off."

As if in reply, a wailing animal shriek rebounded out of the canyon. Jonas could feel Aleksei's jaw clench, and he could hear the man's thoughts. Something had just killed Jonas's horse, and it didn't take much imagination to determine whom. The pass was far too dangerous to attempt.

"I'm sorry," Jonas whispered.

Aleksei shushed his Magus, holding him close, all the while watching the sky.

Watching the dark shape of a white starling circling high above.

CHAPTER 33

A BROTHERHOOD OF BONE

Ilyana followed Marrik through the rough brush of the northern Sulaq Hills, her horse dancing around rocks and water-starved shrubs gripping the ground.

Despite having spent weeks searching through the new currents of the Akhrana she now commanded, Ilyana still found it a challenge to be out in the open with only Marrik for protection. She knew she had hold of very different reins now, that she commanded *real* power, but it was still so unfamiliar compared to the way she'd learned to manipulate the Archanium. It made her nervous.

Marrik signaled that he wanted to scout into the shadow of a tall, rocky bluff rising into the darkening sky. She followed reluctantly, hovering on the edge of contact with the Archanium. Holding this tentative grip on the Great Sphere allowed her to notice others nearby, especially those crafting spells, without alerting them to her presence. Of course, it also delayed in summoning spellforms of her own.

Though a short scouting trip, she prayed it would be sufficient. Since they'd learned there were enemy Magi to fear, her people had become a great deal more careful in declaring themselves.

She felt the flash across the Archanium a heartbeat before the lance of red light struck the earth beneath Marrik's mount, throwing man and horse into the air in a spray of earth and flame.

Ilyana immediately pulled her horse behind a large boulder, stifling a scream and slipping out of the saddle, doing her best to calm the animal. As she fought to return her breathing to normal, she realized she could *feel* Marrik through the bond.

He was alive.

Of course *he's alive.* she berated herself. He was still breathing, and that was all she needed to know.

But his pain radiated through her like a hundred arrows, a feeling she'd only experienced once before, in Drava, when the dead had walked. The memory brought a panic all of its own, and Ilyana fought the pain and the terror back as they surged to the fore. It took every mental faculty she had to maintain her sanity.

Stay where you are. she sent weakly through the bond. Don't *move.*

Marrik sent back only a tangle of emotions: confusion at what had just happened, panic at her going ahead on her own, rage at their attacker. The panic threatened to overtake her again. Marrik was stronger than any man she had ever met. For him to be so incoherent meant that he was injured worse than she'd feared.

Fury flooded through her, unlike anything she'd experienced in Drava *or* Kalinor. Even the battle for Keldoan seemed buffered somehow.

With a flare of understanding, she realized what was missing. *Aleksei* was missing. His leadership had made all three battles work themselves out. But he wasn't here. He was out where the gods only *knew*, in the wastes of Fanj. And she was here with her dying Knight and an enemy Magus. Her burning rage came into sharper focus, cast in its new light.

Ilyana did her best to block it all from her mind. The pain, the rage, the *doubt*.

Marrik. she called as she reached into the Archanium and wrapped herself in a pink and silver swath of illusion.

She operated on pure intuition. Those days spent exploring this new meridian had shown her little, but perhaps it was because she'd had so little *need* for magic at the time.

Things were suddenly very different.

The other Magus seemed immediately wary, as they felt someone else invoke the Archanium, but as she stepped from behind the rock, she could tell that her enemy couldn't spot her.

She walked softly and deliberately towards the Magus, taking care with her steps not to make obvious noise, but ever moving towards the wary form high on the hillside.

She stopped behind a short outcropping of stone, startled to see a man younger than herself looking about wildly. He *knew* she was paces away, but he couldn't place her. And without seeing her, it would be impossible for him to fire off another spell with any accuracy.

Had their roles been reversed, she could have simply launched a spell at the stones *behind* him, but the open sky now protected her as much as any shield ever had. That, and the fact that she was moving, likely saved her. He had no link to connect to the Nagavor, and as such had no spell to launch.

Ilyana kept moving. The young man kept glancing from the tangle of Archanium echoes she'd left behind to the new sensations he was feeling just behind him.

He almost had it figured out, too. A heartbeat before her hand clapped over his eyes and she let her light spell ignite.

His scream punctuated the still twilight, and the sweet smell of burning flesh drifted past her face. Still, Ilyana withdrew her blackened, bloodied hand calmly, dropping the illusion and snuffing out her connection to the Archanium.

She wiped her palm on a stone as she stepped past it to stare into the burnt-out sockets of the young man she's just blinded. He was sobbing as he desperately searched about with his hands. She reached back into the Archanium, pulling another swirl of color and emotion into the world. Pausing a moment, Ilyana reached for several others, pulling them through with her as well.

Silence reigned, leaving only the young man and herself to hear one another. Unless his friends had heard his initial outburst, there would be no help coming for this boy.

Ilyana sat on a rock facing the blind boy, hands folded in her lap. Through the bond, she let Marrik know she had located the source of the attack, and that she was close to subduing it. She was met with gruff approval and no small amount of surprise, but also a still-alarming echo of profound pain. She had no time to waste.

"Who sent you here?" she demanded. Her voice rippled and slithered, distorted in the eerie silence.

The boy jumped, whimpering, *"Please!"* he begged, screaming into the void all around him, *"Please* don't kill me! I was guarding them! That's *all!* Watching for trouble!"

"*Who?*" she demanded.

"I...I can't say!"

"I have a knife. I'm going to cut your throat, unless you talk. *Now.*"

"The King's men," the boy said after a long moment, clearly confused. And with good reason. The Magi that travelled with Ilyana were not supposed to be able to do *anything* like what she had just accomplished, certainly not against a Magus as mired in the Nagavor as this boy.

"How many?"

"I'll tell you nothing more!" the boy screamed.

"You *will.*"

Ilyana dove deeper into the Akhrana, summoning a bubbling bundle of turquoise and oily gray. She pulled it forth and forced it into the boy's thoughts. She felt his mind snap; she could see the entirety of the boy's intelligence, limited though it was.

"T—Three thousand, milady?"

"And how many like you?"

"Magi, milady? Five, milady."

Ilyana sat for a long moment, watching the boy's panic rise and fall as he tried to keep away the pain of what she'd done, trying to comprehend what was happening around him.

A wave of pain and panic crashed across her. Marrik needed help *now*. She recalled that, had this boy's spell hit its intended target, Marrik would be dead. *She* would be dead.

Ilyana pulled her belt knife free and dragged it across the boy's throat, thinking all the while about each of the children she'd held dying in her arms after the revenants had attacked Drava. Revenants summoned by this boy's master. If he were allowed to survive, he would *return* to that master.

Part of her wanted so desperately to never become the Demon. But if she offered mercy and Bael offered only death at every opportunity, her people, her friends were destined to lose time and time again. And she would not be a victim.

Never again.

Ilyana held the silencing ward until the boy stopped kicking and gasping, and then she slipped back down the edge of the bluff, where Marrik awaited her, propped against a boulder and bleeding freely. With his sad eyes. "It's alright, Yana. Truly, it is."

She shook her head as he wrapped her in his powerful arms. "For a moment, I was afraid I'd lost you," he whispered.

"You're *about* to, unless you let me heal this mess."

Marrik allowed her to tend to his burns and lacerations, all the while watching her face. She could hear his thoughts flashing like a thunderhead. The sweetest, most delicate women he'd ever known. No longer. He was now looking into the face of a warrior.

She felt his heart break.

As they rode north, passing in the shadow of the great red cliffs that cut them off from the wastes, Jonas reached into the Archanium, searching for signs of life. In the back of his mind, Jonas's shame burned ever deeper.

He sat pressed firmly against Aleksei, his arms wrapped around the bigger man's middle, his head resting on his Knight's broad shoulders.

How had things between them changed so fundamentally?

He recalled a time when Aleksei had been an uncertain farm boy, plagued by constant doubt and worry. He had even looked to Jonas as a mentor of sorts. Aleksei'd certainly had *moments*, breaking away from the humble beginnings of his childhood while still clinging to his inborn convictions.

For the majority of that blissful first year they'd spent together, Aleksei had watched Jonas with an almost-worshipful attentiveness. As though a prince or Magus could somehow explain the complexities and disappointments of his own limited life.

But Aleksei had also grown a great deal in the time they'd spent apart. Somehow, Jonas hadn't even begun to appreciate that. Until now.

Aleksei was in command. Aleksei knew what he was doing, and Jonas feared he'd grown impatient with his spoiled prince. Well, Jonas recanted, that was unfair. He had shown Aleksei a great deal of patience, and Aleksei was returning the favor in kind. He clearly didn't want Jonas to *fail* in any way.

Still, the realization that Aleksei might have outgrown him was disturbing.

He had failed Aleksei twice, now. First as a guardian, when Aleksei was broken and healing. Jonas had foolishly allowed himself to be captured, requiring Aleksei to pull him back into the world of the living from under the pall of the slavers' poison.

Aleksei, who had been at death's door. Aleksei, who had been waiting for Jonas to come back to him, to heal his wounds. Wounds he never would have sustained had Jonas recognized the threat Hade posed in the beginning. That thought burned like an ember in Jonas's heart.

And now it was even worse. Jonas had ignored the starlings, all the omens so obvious to Aleksei. It had almost cost him his life, *Aleksei's* life. His face flushed bright with the shame of it all.

He was supposed to be the one in command. Not because of his abilities, but because of his *knowledge*. They were in an alien realm. He spoke the language, and yet he ignored the advice of a man connected to the very earth on which they trod? Jonas was sickened by his own arrogance.

Can you stop *thinking like that? It's distracting.* Aleksei's voice rang through Jonas's head, the Knight's irritation as apparent as a clarion call.

Jonas's eyes went wide in the moonlight. He sat up and glanced around, suddenly realizing that day had passed into night while he had been mired in self-pity.

Jonas looked up and saw Aleksei glancing back him, his eyes still burning the same ravenous umber. The moonlight glittered across Aleksei's golden irises, reminding Jonas of nothing more than a wild beast appraising prey.

Aleksei was watching him, the way a wolf watched a rabbit.

Jonas shivered, but not from the cold. As Aleksei turned back to the road ahead, Jonas clutched his arms tighter around the Knight. As his head rested again on Aleksei's shoulder, his gaze traveled down the curves of the Knight's arms. A deeper shiver rippled through him.

Aleksei's arms were bare, and rather than sporting brilliantly burned flesh from exposure to the blistering sun, his Hunter's arms only displayed the vivid light-drinking ink of the Mantle.

No longer hidden, no longer discreet, Aleksei's white tunic now served less to cover his body and more to present the Mantle in all its glory.

"Hasn't the sun burned your arms?" Jonas asked.

Aleksei shrugged, "I felt warm a time or two."

Jonas's eyes widened, "You should be blistered by now."

The Magus raised a tentative hand and touched Aleksei's upper arm. The Mantle rippled outward from his fingers before swirling to right itself, but Aleksei's skin was cool.

The Hunter chuckled, "We aren't in the wastes *yet*. And even if we were, I've spent most of my life in the sun. Do you think we covered up for Harvest? Stripped down is more like it. I can hardly remember a summer when I wore a shirt. You get red at first, but then you skin toughens and darkens and you get used to it."

Jonas stared at his Knight in confusion, "But it's been a *long* while since you worked the land."

Aleksei shrugged, "I suppose some things just stick with you."

Jonas kept his thoughts to himself. The *last* thing he wanted was start an argument, especially about something so comparatively trivial. Not now, on foreign soil. No, now they needed to stick together more than ever before.

Aleksei was silent for a long time after that. Even his thoughts were hidden from Jonas. Jonas eventually grew used to the silence. Between the steady rhythm of Agriphon beneath him and Aleksei's warmth, he began to drift off.

There are three men around the bend in the road.

Aleksei's voice in his mind was so unexpected that Jonas jumped. He quickly composed himself, concentrating on the Archanium.

I don't feel anything.

Aleksei gave him a warning look and pressed a finger to his lips. He pulled Agriphon to a silent stop and slid off the mammoth warhorse. Jonas bit back his own feelings. Aleksei slipping away was akin to losing the sun; the sudden vacancy of warmth and security was jarring. He ached for Aleksei to come back, but held his silence.

They were in forsaken lands now, and the gods only knew what sort of people they might encounter. Jonas kept quiet as he watched his Knight scale a small hillock. Watching Aleksei move was always fascinating to Jonas, the way the Knight instinctively avoided loose sticks and stones. It was like a dance, each foot placed deliberately, every move of his body precisely aimed at striking the proper position.

Aleksei drew his belt knife and Jonas tensed. He readied himself to seize the Archanium should violence become necessary. He would *not* fail Aleksei a third time.

The Knight vanished over the small hillock, and Jonas sat back in the saddle, scarcely breathing as he waited for the sounds of battle to emerge.

The Arrow Spell Jonas had invoked long ago suddenly blinked out of existence.

Panic surged through him.

Ul'Brek.

And then screams filled the air. Jonas cringed in the wake of the panicked, desperate cries.

The Prince exhaled slowly. He hadn't known *what* to expect by taking the northern route, but it certainly hadn't been Ul'Brek. They were supposed to be just as superstitious about the cursed northern routes as anyone else, preferring to patrol the main roads.

The people of Fanj used the Archanium just like any other culture, but in a decidedly unpleasant way. Most of the realm was held under the thrall of the so-called Ul'Brek, the Brotherhood of Bone. They were spoken of in legends, and only ever involved in the most fearful tales.

With good reason.

The Ul'Brek used the Archanium not to encourage magic to flower and improve humanity, but to *extinguish* it through the use of their gift. Among the Ul'Brek, Jonas would be as helpless as any mere mortal man.

Jonas tried to control his growing dread. He wasn't *completely* defenseless, even without the Archanium. Aleksei had spent time enough training him to defend himself.

And failing that, he had his emerald ring and a gold circlet he'd commissioned in Keldoan buried in Agriphon's saddlebags. He thanked the gods he'd decided they would be safer with Agriphon and Aleksei. This realm was likely unaware of his abilities as a Magus, and therefore would see him only as the Prince of Ilyar.

There were, of course, ways to hide his use of the Archanium from sight, but they were risky even amongst the most trained Magi. Jonas prayed that his gods would see them through the worst of these lands. Abandoning the pass had winnowed his hopes now to mere glimmers of possibility. He harbored no illusions. He knew that he and Aleksei would be lucky to survive this journey.

As the echoes of dying men reverberated away and to the south along the sheer mountain walls, Jonas shook his head. He knew *precisely* what had happened to those men. He required no special insight into their fate. He saw it embodied in the man now striding down the hill towards him, a wake of midnight tendrils trailing behind him like wings, darker even than the most starless night.

When Aleksei mounted again, Jonas wrapped his arms protectively around his Knight.

"What happened?" he whispered, pressing his face into Aleksei's back.

"They were waiting for us," Aleksei said gruffly. "Three men in black robes, wearing bone masks. They had some sort of magic, I *think*. But it didn't seem to affect me. When they saw that I wasn't affected, they drew blades. I killed them. We can't afford to have people know where we are."

"They were Ul'Brek," Jonas said softly. "We should bury them."

"No need. There are plenty of scavengers in the area. Their remains will be gone long before morning." The complete lack of emotion in Aleksei's voice was disquieting.

Jonas's eyes burned with sudden tears. He let them silently seep into Aleksei's tunic.

The Knight stiffened, "They were waiting to ambush us. They could hardly have made their intentions any clearer. What else would you have me do?"

Jonas sighed. He didn't have an answer, yet he wept for the innocent farm boy he'd lured to Kalinor what now seemed a lifetime ago. The boy was gone. His arms were now, without question, around a man; a man who brooked no compromise.

"Come on," Aleksei said distantly, "we need to make camp, and I'd like it to be as far from those men as possible. Will the Arrow Spell still work?"

"I think so. I can put wards around it to keep them from detecting it, though I don't know how effective they'll be."

Aleksei shrugged, "I can stay awake through the night if necessary. Whatever power these men hold, they still die easily enough."

Jonas shuddered.

"So I've noticed," he whispered.

CHAPTER 34

IMPURE

"Run this by me once more," Frederick Rysun said, rubbing the bridge of his nose.

Ilyana stood before him, her face as grim as he'd ever seen it. Behind her, guarding the tent entrance, Marrik looked like death itself. The man had swiftly changed from affable warrior into a creature of such extreme danger that Rysun hardly recognized him.

Not that he was complaining.

Rysun personally preferred his men to be overly cautious, always expecting the worst. As much like Marrik as possible.

One of the many gifts Henry Drago had given Rysun's men during the farmer's time with them was a proper sense of caution. Rysun was *certain* it had saved them any number of times, when details that might have otherwise been overlooked were suddenly brought to the fore.

But this was different. Ilyana's experience scouting with Marrik brought a very troubling question to mind.

"The boy said there were three *thousand* men camped on the other side of that ridge-line?" Rysun asked slowly.

"Indeed, General. And four or five Magi like himself."

Rysun cursed. "Lord Captain Drago sent us to reach Taumon *intact*, not to diminish our numbers in pitched battle."

Ilyana raised a silver-blond eyebrow, "You want to slip around them?"

Rysun frowned up at her, "No, I *want* to destroy them. But I want to lose as few people as is humanly possible. Any ideas, Lady Magus?"

Frederick Rysun had never completely trusted Archanium Magi. Every time they had been needed, the results had been disappointing at best, and the enemy *always* seemed to have the upper hand.

Ilyana paused for a long moment, but then her frown shifted into a wicked smile. "I may have one or two thoughts, General."

Rysun's frown deepened. Something about the way she phrased her response gave him pause. "You...you aren't proposing anything...*villainous*, are you?" he asked hesitantly.

"And if she is, General?" Henry Drago asked from behind him, amused.

Ilyana composed herself, though Rysun could see her fighting her own amusement. "General Rysun, we are at war. I have my orders from the Lord Captain and from Prince Belgi. And, if the situation demands it, I will open the gates of the Aftershadow and wipe those men from this land with a fury."

She paused, and his face blanched at the ferocity of her statement. "But, I don't think it'll come to that. I will, however, need to speak to your men before they go into battle. I'm going to do something *to* them, General. Nothing harmful, but they will need to be briefed about it so they aren't surprised by the enemy's response. Because *believe* me when I say that it will be fearsome indeed."

Rysun opened his mouth to protest, but Henry put his hand on Rysun's shoulder. When he glanced up into Henry Drago's gold-brown eyes, he saw a look that told him it was time to let go.

"As you command, Lady Magus," he heard himself saying. "Let me know what you need of me."

Ilyana smiled. "Thank you for your cooperation, General. If you don't mind, I'll go prepare for the ritual. I suggest you prepare your men for battle. That boy's death will not go unnoticed, and his comrades will no doubt be alerted to our presence soon enough."

Rysun nodded stiffly, watching both Magus and Knight as they solemnly exited his tent. He thought back to his observation of Marrik, of liking the man's newfound edge.

He understood with new clarity that he had no idea how deep that darkness delved into the both man *and* Magus. It frightened him.

Still, they were in the middle of a war, and given his druthers, Rysun would much prefer to be afraid of his *own* troops over those marshaled by the enemy.

Rysun rose from his field desk, but found Henry standing right before him. When Frederick paused, the farmer merely tipped his hat, "They have new abilities, Frederick. Let them loose. These are not the same Magi we found limping out of the Kalinori sewer.

"It's taken me a great deal of time to accept the man my son has become, but I've come to appreciate the way he wields authority, the way he takes to violence, even if it makes me uncomfortable. Perhaps you ought to try the same sort of thinking; allow these people to *evolve*."

Mere hours later, Rysun found himself standing on a large rock before his force. Ilyana and her ilk had not yet performed their so-called ritual, and Rysun was pleased to be looking into the eyes of his men as they were, before they were altered by the Archanium.

"The enemy lies over that hill," he proclaimed. "By now, they likely know we are here, but that only works to our benefit. The Magus Ilyana has a plan to turn the tide in our favor with the Archanium, though I will leave that explanation to her."

He stepped down, helping Ilyana onto the rock. "Men," she called with determination, "over that hill there are three thousand rebels. Men who think they are safe. Men who think they will be fighting *men*.

"But they are gravely mistaken. We will *change* you, but only to the eye of the enemy. When they look upon you, they will see a horror. If you can, play the part.

"They will scream when they see you. *Expect* it. Use it to your advantage. Your only goal is to kill. Wipe them from this world, and let the rebels know just how dangerous we are. They believe their Demon is dangerous. Let's see how they fare against *our* demons!"

A cheer rose from the men, and Ilyana seemed to luxuriate in their fury.

"Gods, Henry Drago," Rysun grumbled to himself, "you'd better be right."

Jonas was fast asleep, snoring softly near the fire-pit Aleksei had dug into the sandy soil of their camp. Aleksei watched his Magus's face as the man slept. He had heard Jonas cry out for several nights, clearly having night terrors, but each morning he woke without a word. Aleksei was growing concerned, catching occasional hints of the specters haunting his Magus, but until Jonas decided to open up to him, there was little he could do.

He stood, abandoning the rock he'd adopted as a chair, and started scouting the area, searching for any signs of life. He could hear the hearts of various scavengers, but nothing human. On the cliff face above them, he could hear the gentle repetitive coo of a starling.

Aleksei no longer knew what to make of the strange birds. The warning at the pass had been clear enough, yet their continued presence left him uneasy. It not only told him that they were being watched, but that someone *still* felt the need to protect them. At least, he prayed the starlings were indicative of protection. They could just as easily be part of an elaborate trap, though Aleksei's gut insisted there was no malice accompanying the birds.

While he didn't doubt Jonas's warning about the land they were entering, he *had* wondered how much of Jonas's fear was based in fact, and how much was simply ancient superstition.

Their encounter with the Ul'Brek had cleared away any such uncertainties. The very idea that Jonas might be robbed of his abilities at any moment had Aleksei on edge.

He finally turned from the cliff face, staring out into the barren darkness, straining for any human heartbeats beyond Jonas's; from Tamara's several hundred leagues to the west.

Silence.

Tracking other heartbeats seemed more difficult since entering Fanj. While that was troubling, Aleksei wondered whether hearing Tamara's pulse through the blood meridian was masking the others, or if he was simply so used to being surrounded by myriad heartbeats that simply didn't exist in such a harsh climate.

He made his way back to camp, reclaiming his seat on the stone and stirring the coals of the fire. Dawn was still a few hours off, so Aleksei took a moment to close his eyes and listen to the thumping of his own heart, beating out the counter rhythm to Jonas's. The soothing beats, perfectly in harmony, always helped clear his head.

Before he realized it, the twinned beats had gently lulled him into an uneasy sleep, far deeper than he'd intended.

Aleksei's back arched away from a sudden, sharp intrusion. He screamed in pain.

The Mantle writhed across his back, shrieking in twinned agony.

There were men standing over him, screaming in Fanja, but he didn't have a clue what they were saying. One was pulling away a spear, dripping scarlet. His shoulder blade had blocked most of the spear's impact, but the shock of the wound still reverberated through him.

Their small camp was swarming with men in black robes, bone masks covering the upper portions of their faces. Aleksei rolled away from the man with the spear, delving into his bond with Jonas and pulling time to a standstill.

Nothing. The bond was silent.

He couldn't feel Jonas *any*where. It was as though the Magus didn't *exist*. Gods, but he could kill himself for falling asleep.

He stood tall in an instant, startling his assailants. A second later the Ul'Brek were upon him.

Let me feed.

Aleksei instinctively dropped his safeguards and the Mantle roared forth, striking into the hearts of the men surrounding him. They fell to the cruel blood-black talons of the Mantle as one.

He felt no joy in the banquet, only satisfaction at the sound of six bodies striking the coarse dirt road in unison.

The battle was over before it had even begun.

He had won.

Rather, the Mantle had won. *He* had been caught completely unawares, and without the Mantle he could be very well have ended up a prisoner of these men, or simply dead.

Aleksei looked around, desperately searching for any sign of his Magus, but Jonas was nowhere to be found. Aleksei forgot about feeling for the bond, tapping his Hunter instincts instead, testing the air for his scent.

A low, guttural growl built in his throat. Aleksei dropped onto his hands, reading the earth for tracks leaving the camp, but in the starlight and sand, the tracks were nearly impossible to discern, Jonas's scent muddied with those of the dead.

After a few frustrated moments, Aleksei took a deep breath. He was letting his anger get the better of him, and it was clouding his judgment.

"Where would they take him?" he snarled into the void, pacing to make sense of the muddled tracks from the fight. As though asking the dark of predawn would grant him new information.

They will not take him far.

Aleksei's growl deepened. He bared his teeth to the stars, searching for Jonas's blood meridian.

We will find *him, we will* protect *him, and we will* feast.

Aleksei's mouth watered at the very thought.

"Yes," he whispered finally. "We'll find him, and then we'll feast."

The Mantle slithered across his back in expectant undulations.

Aleksei froze a moment, sniffing at the air. Jonas's scent still lingered, though only faintly. He listened, searching for the twin to his own heartbeat, for Jonas's blood meridian. It came to him like a clap of thunder, throbbing through his bones.

There.

Aleksei vaulted onto Agriphon's back, sparing a moment to thank the gods that the Ul'Brek had attacked him before they had thought to steal his horse. The stallion leapt forward, racing into the dark. Aleksei felt his pulse pounding in his ears in rhythmic sympathy to Jonas's frantic hammering heartbeat. He could feel the Mantle writhing across his arms and shoulders, licking the air, tasting inevitable victory. The feasting to come.

It didn't take him long to find the Ul'Brek.

On horseback, Aleksei was far faster. There would be no escape for them. They had forfeited their lives the moment they had dared enter his camp, had dared to take Jonas from him.

The air shattered, as though he'd struck an invisible wall, and Aleksei realized he was staring up at the stars.

He tasted blood. The Mantle shrieked. He tried to sit up, but his body wouldn't obey. Everything ached, and when his limbs finally responded, they were heavy and sluggish.

When he turned his head, Aleksei saw his graceful, riderless stallion vanishing into the night. He allowed himself a bloody grin.

He felt a man's presence nearby, and suddenly found himself looking up into a dark hood.

Aleksei's fist instinctively connected in the next moment, and he felt the man's jaw dislocate as he fell to the side. The man's bone mask splintered as it struck the rocks several paces distant. Aleksei forced himself over and into a crawl, pulling himself over the prone dark form, "Where *is* he?"

Aleksei's snarl was met with silence. He pulled the hood back, revealing a dark, bloodied man, "Where is he? Where did you *take* him?"

The man's terrified black eyes were strangely sympathetic. Aleksei stared at the man, his lower jaw almost completely unhinged, as he stared back into Aleksei's glowing golden eyes.

The man tried to form intelligible words, but with his distended jaw hanging to the right, it was impossible. Even had he been able to speak, Aleksei realized he wouldn't have understood a lick of it.

The Mantle drilled into the man's chest, and Aleksei relished the ear-splitting scream that issued from his prey. Aleksei breathed out a sigh as the man went still.

He rose, walking a few paces to the top of the nearest ridge and staring out over the encampment that fanned out before him. It wasn't at all like the slaver camp.

Beneath his feet stretched an actual *village*, constructed of hide tents that were clearly permanent. Here and there, Aleksei noted a surprising number of Fanja, and peppered throughout the village were the dark-robed figures he'd come to recognize all too well.

But by far the most intriguing thing about the village was its center. Carved into the rocky landscape was a deep, nine-sided hole. Surrounding the strange pit were torches that illuminated carved bits of stone, and a towering redstone spire rising from the pit's center.

Aleksei's fascination was broken by a soft whimper from behind. He spun, thrusting out his hand and sending the Mantle forth, but even as the tendrils ripped away from his wrist, he pulled them back.

He was looking into the horrified eyes of a child, crouched over the man he'd just killed and staring up at Aleksei.

She couldn't have been more than ten summers from the look of her. Her large, dark eyes were shimmering with unshed tears in the moonlight. It took Aleksei a moment to notice that she was cradling the dead man's head in her hands. Her entire body was shaking.

Unlike the man's black robes, she wore a brightly-dyed red dress. Her raven hair was swept back and tied with a pale blue scarf. This girl was no Ul'Brek.

So, what *was* she?

"P...Please?" she managed in thickly-accented Ilyari.

Aleksei kept the Mantle at bay, though he was not willing to lower his hand just yet. This could be a trick. After all, *something* had knocked him off of Agriphon. He had felt the Archanium used against or near him enough to recognize its unique aura by now, but Jonas had never mentioned Ul'Brek using the Archanium in that manner.

"Who are you?" he asked slowly.

The girl blinked at the question, then lowered her gaze, "Ramla. I am Impure."

Aleksei took an aggressive step forward, and the girl cringed in fear. "Explain," he hissed.

She blinked at him again, wiping her eyes on the backs of her hands. "I...am *dirty*. I touch the Darkness."

Aleksei lowered his hand and crouched near the girl. "Do you mean the Archanium?"

Ramla's eyes went wide when he said the word. She looked at the dead man beneath her, then back to Aleksei. "Yes. Archanium."

The word sounded forced and alien coming from her, as though she'd heard it before, but never spoken it out loud.

"Who was that man?" he asked, changing the topic. It was becoming clearer that she had a better command of Ilyari than he'd first imagined.

"He is gone," she said softly, returning her gaze to the dead man. Her voice broke, tears finally flowing down her cheeks. "He was my father."

Aleksei's jaw flexed. "I'm sorry I had to kill him. Your people raided my camp and stole my companion. I only came here to get him back. Your father attacked me."

Ramla's eyes returned to him. Tears slipped down her cheeks, but she didn't make a sound. After a long moment, Ramla dried her eyes and spoke, calmer now. "He didn't attack you. *I* did. He told me to stop you."

"You mean *kill* me," Aleksei spat.

She shook her head, "He wanted to keep you from the village. They are setting traps for you. They know you will come for the Impure we stole."

Aleksei felt his hackles rise, "You're very calm for a girl who's just seen her father murdered."

"Because it's *you*," she said softly, her face now hard. "Because he told me this would happen. He knew he would die, just as I knew you would not kill me. This is what the prophecies told us long ago."

A deep chill swept through Aleksei.

"It is why I studied, to learn your language. My father made me do my lessons every night, so I would be ready when you came."

"And what does your prophecy say will happen *next*?" Aleksei asked, shaken, his voice barely above a whisper.

Ramla shook her head, "I cannot tell you. You are the key to its function. But the Magus *must* be tried by the Nine."

Aleksei reflexively checked to make sure that his sword was clear in the scabbard.

"And where do I find these Nine?"

The girl stared at him as though he were the stupidest man alive, "Where else? In the Pit."

CHAPTER 35

A NAMELESS BLADE

R oux was tired of the rain. Beyond tired. Tired of being cold, tired of being wet. Most of all, he was tired of being *wrong*.

It had been two weeks since he'd uncovered anything new. Tamara's trail was quickly growing as cold as the freezing drizzle that pelted him from his position on the windowsill.

Whatever lead he'd had seemed to have been destroyed with Bael's spy. That spy had very nearly succeeded in taking both Roux and Andariana with him. But while they had at least escaped with their lives, whatever information Ruben might have possessed had burned with him at the foundry.

And now Roux stood outside the window of Commander Yegor's chambers, shivering in the freezing rain. Roux had been following Yegor for the last week, asking questions about the man, following his routes from his offices at the Admiralty to his estate, all the while trying to pin something on him.

All this, of course, based on the muttered confession of a single scullery maid. A maid who only *thought* she might have overheard something a week previous. But the man she described as being in the commander's office sounded very similar to Ruben. If Roux could trace Ruben to Yegor, perhaps Tamara's trail could be picked back up.

Roux just prayed to the gods that Yegor wasn't going to reveal a glowing yellow rune and destroy the entire Admiralty. Such an explosion could easily eradicate Ilyar's best naval commanders before they'd even been mustered. Then again, Roux didn't have any intentions of burning out the commander's eyes with hot irons.

Not this time.

The light from the window fluttered, and Roux snuck a surreptitious glance into the office. The commander appeared to have stepped out for the moment. Roux growled under his breath, feeling the hot rage that warmed him even in the rain.

That rage had sustained him throughout this entire search. Without it, he might have easily succumbed to his own depression long ago. But he refused to abandon Tamara.

Roux Darted through the scant inch of glass keeping him from the room. The sudden warmth of the office made his body ache. It was a welcome relief from the frigid rain, true, but not one his body had experienced for hours.

He took quick stock of the chamber, the layout, where the commander kept his papers, his books. He spotted a shadowed rafter just above the fireplace. The commander was only of middling importance among the officers, and as a result, his offices were not nearly so grand as those of the admirals themselves. Roux preferred the grandiose offices; they were far easier to hide in.

Unfortunately, the bare rafter would have to do.

He Darted onto the rafter, steam rising from his cold, sodden clothes in the heat above the hearth.

Roux let out a slow breath and slid out of his dripping coat. The wool wasn't nearly as warm as the rabbit cloak he'd given Tamara, but it dripped less and didn't carry the distinct stink of raw leather. Even if he couldn't be seen, Roux knew anyone in this place would have been able to *smell* him.

After an hour, he shifted position to keep his muscles from locking. He needed to be as agile as possible. While he didn't count on anything necessarily happening, he always liked to prepare for the worst.

The door opened and Roux started. He caught himself a heartbeat before he fell off the rafter. Gods, but his time away from the Wood was taking a toll on his balance.

Roux slowed his breathing to a soft pant. He carefully glanced over the rafter's edge and saw that the commander had indeed returned. With a guest, this time.

He clenched his fist in triumph. He'd checked the commander's meeting schedule this morning. He was supposed to be inspecting the trade roster for his ship, *The Firebird*.

"This has to be fast. I'm *late*," the commander growled at the short woman standing before him.

"I apologize, Sir, but he said it was urgent, Sir," the woman mumbled.

"Well give it here then. Let's have the message," he grunted impatiently.

"I'm...I'm sorry, Sir, but I was pushed into a puddle on my way here. The message got wet, and well, there's not much of it left."

"I beg your pardon?" the commander's voice dropped to a deadly hiss. "Then why would you bother coming here, unless you were hoping I'd have you *executed*?"

"I read the message, Sir. I know what it said. He *made* me read it, Sir. Trouble is, I don't remember every word."

Yegor exhaled angrily, "Out with it then, you worthless trollop."

"He said about the prisoner, Sir. The prisoner is being moved from the South to a more secure location."

"That's it? She's being moved? What are you forgetting? *Think*, woman!"

"That's *all*. I swear it, Sir. That's all I remember."

Yegor stared into the fire a long moment before glancing back at the woman, "Get out of my sight."

Roux watched the man carefully bolt the door behind her. He returned to the fireplace and began to pace back and forth, muttering to himself. Roux decided it was about time the commander answered a few questions.

When Commander Yegor turned away from the fire he found himself staring into the feral eyes of the Ri-Hnon. Yegor's mouth dropped open as he took in the full sight, Roux sitting in the commander's chair, his muddy feet on Yegor's table.

His surprise was short-lived. "What are *you* doing in here?" Yegor demanded, his hand going to his sword.

Roux sighed. He was starting to be recognized at the Admiralty. Rumors had certainly been circulating since the explosion at the foundry, about the Queen and a strange man being found by city guards near the explosion. They had quieted since the incident, but the officers were still clearly on their toes.

"I'd like to know what that was all about, Commander," Roux said conversationally, rolling his small horn knife through his fingers.

"What, the errand girl?" Yegor snorted. He shrugged his broad shoulders, "We captured a rebel captain in southern Ilyar. They're moving her from Bereg Morya to Taumon, where she can be questioned. And why does this concern *you*?"

"Because everything you just said was a lie, Commander," Roux groaned, flipping the knife into the air and catching it gracefully by the blade. "A poor excuse for a lie, at that."

With a flash, Roux had the commander by the back of his coat. Another flash, and the commander hung over the fireplace. Roux above him, perched on the rafter's edge. Roux's clenched fist holding his coat collar was the only thing that kept the Commander from crashing to the floor ten paces below.

"Now, tell me what that message meant. Who were you talking about? *Who* is the prisoner?"

"I *told* you," the commander choked, "a rebel officer. That's all. Let me *go!*"

Roux opened his fist and watched the man plummet. He Darted just as the man struck the carpeted marble before the fireplace. He was there the moment Yegor's femur snapped.

The Commander shrieked in pain as he collapsed in a heap.

Roux gritted his teeth against the Commander's cries, grabbing the man and locking him in a headlock, clamping his jaw shut. "You're about to go into shock, Commander. You need to stop your bellowing and give me some honest answers if you hope to survive this. Am I clear?"

The Commander stared at him with a stunned, glazed expression and slowly nodded.

"Good," Roux said soothingly. "Now, I *know* you're lying because I saw you speak with the errand girl, and you hardly knew what to think of that message. It had nothing to do with a captured rebel officer, but you understood it. *Didn't* you?"

The commander nodded slowly.

"Good. *Who* is the prisoner?"

Roux Darted away from the commander, letting him find his voice again. While Yegor tried to pull himself together, in spite of his broken leg, Roux continued to roll his short knife from knuckle to knuckle.

"He'll kill me if I say anything," the Commander gasped finally.

Roux caught the knife by its curved blade and cocked his arm back.

"That's funny, because *I'll* kill you if you don't. And if you try to use any of his Demon magic, you'll die in a far more painful way than you can possibly imagine."

While Roux wasn't entirely lying, he certainly hoped it never came to that. It was one aspect of his magic he was not entirely comfortable with. It was also the deadliest. "Now, tell me where she *is*."

The Commander's eyes widened, "You...you think that...?" The man's face flashed from agonized to pained mirth so quickly it was shocking.

Roux had the man pressed against the floor a heartbeat later, the small knife at Yegor's throat. "You know where she is. Where is she? Where is *Tamara*?"

Yegor's face froze, "Tamara?"

Roux felt the rage inside him explode outward. He teeth snapped a scant inch from Yegor's face, "Where is she? Tell me, or you're a dead man."

"*Guards!*" Yegor roared.

"No one's coming to help you, Yegor," Roux snarled. "You know yourself. The guards won't round for another five minutes. You wanted privacy, and you found it. Now, where is she? You said the prisoner was in the South. *Where* in the South?"

"You'll get nothing from me, you savage," Yegor spat. He reared up at Roux, but the Ri-Hnon's knife cut too deeply into his throat, severing his windpipe and finally catching in his vertebrae. Roux slid the razor out of the dying Commander and Darted back into the rain. His brain was already flashing through endless levels of possibility. Where could they have her?

The South. The Relvyn Wood. He could reach the Seil Wood far sooner than he could travel all the way to southern Ilyar, but if the Wood allowed him transport, he could make up for weeks of lost time. If the two forests could shift Aleksei so easily, surely they could grant him the same passage.

He had to tell Andariana.

Darting back to her chambers had become so routine he hardly even noticed the exquisite beauty of the carving he was climbing across, the majesty of the building he was scaling. It had long ago become yet another set of obstacles between him and the woman he loved.

He finally caught sight of the high, bright window where Andariana spent most of her time. He flashed through the crystalline glass and stopped dead in his tracks.

Andariana Belgi, Queen of Ilyar, was suspended in the center of the room, a chain wrapped around her neck. Roux's golden eyes saw the man just in time to see the crossbow bolt fly towards his heart.

"It's around this way."

Aleksei watched Ramla slide around a corner. He followed, grimacing at the smell of drying blood permeating his hood.

Ramla had insisted he wear her father's cloak. Despite the obvious size difference between Aleksei and the Ul'Brek present in the village, it drew far less attention than his blond hair and lighter skin would have.

When he'd asked Ramla about her father, and whether or not he should be buried, she had simply shrugged, responding with a calm, "That was never mentioned."

She opened a tent flap in the shadows and beckoned him in. He followed her into the tent as quickly as possible. The last thing he wanted was someone spotting him and asking questions.

It was late, and most of the villagers had gone to bed. A few Ul'Brek were on patrol, but they had been easy enough to avoid. Even if they were spotted, Ramla had insisted that the guards would merely think she and her father were going home.

The tent was spartan, only a few odds and ends, a pile of rags, and two bedrolls. There was a heap of scrolls against the far side of the tent.

Ramla walked purposefully across the tent floor and lifted the rag pile reverently. She turned and thrust it towards Aleksei. "This is yours," she said solemnly.

Aleksei frowned at her, accepting the rags. They were much heavier than he'd imagined. As they fell away from the long bundle, Aleksei realized that they concealed a sword.

He found the handle and delicately extracted it from the rags.

It was the oddest sword he'd ever seen.

In many ways, it was unremarkable. The length was average for a one-handed sword, but the blade was crafted from a silver steel that was dull and pitted. It resembled an ancient, unpolished Legionnaire blade.

But the carvings were an entirely different matter. Etched deep into the blade, swirls and dramatic taloned claws swept forward from the hilt with an almost liquid quality.

Moving unbidden, the Mantle slithered down his arm and flowed into the valleys carved into the blade. Aleksei stared at the sword, now whole with the Mantle filling in the filigree.

"What's it called?"

Ramla stared at him blankly. "It has no name, Hunter."

He looked at her sharply. She had called him by his title. "How do you know what I am?"

She frowned, "The Hunter? It is part of the prophecy."

Aleksei suppressed an involuntary shudder. Gods, but he *loathed* prophecy.

"Do you know my name? Or the name of the man your people captured?" Aleksei growled.

"Prophecy doesn't know names, only events and titles," she responded calmly. "But it said you were an angry man. A deadly man. A *rare* man."

"Right now, I'm a *very* angry man, Ramla. Your people took someone extremely precious from me. More precious than you can imagine. Someone I *love.*"

"I know," she said simply. "And that sword will help you get him back. But first he *must* be judged in the Pit."

Aleksei's golden eyes narrowed, "Why? I could go rescue him right now. We could be gone before anyone even knew I was *here.*"

"No, they would kill you," Ramla said absently.

Aleksei glared at the strange little girl before him, "How?"

"I don't know. But if you go now, at night, before he is judged, you will die. You have to stay here. You have to sleep here. You have the sword, now you must rest until morning. Until he is judged."

He wiped a hand across his face, frustrated. "And where am I supposed to sleep?"

"Right there," she said, pointing to her father's bedroll.

Aleksei stared at the space, his mind whirling. She wanted him to sleep where her father had slept? A man he'd killed only an hour before? The idea of taking a dead man's bed was not one he relished. It was bad enough wearing the man's blood-stained cloak.

"He said this would happen," Ramla repeated for the fifth time since Aleksei had met her. "It's alright. He knew this would happen."

"Stop saying that," he growled back.

"But he did."

"Well, if we have to wait till morning I might as well get some sleep," he grumbled. When she didn't offer any argument, Aleksei picked up the rags that had covered the sword and laid down on the dead man's bedroll. He laid the sword beside to him, covering it.

"Good night," he murmured as she snuffed out her lantern.

"Don't be afraid," she whispered in the darkness. "They won't find you. I know how to shield us. Father taught me how to work *around* the Ul'Brek. They can't find me."

Aleksei frowned, "Your father was Ul'Brek?"

"Yes. That's how he taught me. He taught me how to hide my Darkness. I am Impure, like your companion, but Father taught me how to help serve the light."

Aleksei didn't care enough to ask her what she meant by that. He would just be glad if it worked.

"I'm very sorry," she said suddenly.

Aleksei turned and glared at her. "Why?"

She met his glare with her calm black eyes, "Because tomorrow, the man you love is going to be thrown into the Pit. And he will die."

The crossbow bolt slammed into the wall, flashing through Roux as he Darted towards the man. His knife cut clean across the archer's throat, sending a spray of blood across the room. The man dropped to the marble floor, gurgling as he bled out on richly-woven carpet.

Roux Darted to the rafter and frantically unwound the chains. Andariana's weight unraveled the rest a few seconds later. He Darted in time to catch her falling body.

Roux carefully laid her down on the carpet and began breathing into her mouth. His hands pressed on her chest, forcing blood through her heart, just as the Healers had shown him. Sometimes, they said, it was too late to bring back a life. It depended on how long the person had spent in the Aftershadow.

When Andariana started coughing, Roux finally relaxed. He had pulled her back.

He carried her to her bed and fetched a glass of water. She stared at him the whole time, almost as though she couldn't believe he was real.

"*Thank* you," she finally croaked.

"Who was that man? What was he doing here? What *happened?*" Roux snarled, his blood still boiling from the fight.

"I don't know," she admitted, her voice still raspy, her throat lividly red. "Someone brought me tea. It must have been drugged, because I fell asleep in my chair. When I woke, that man was hoisting me from the rafter. I fought as hard as I could, but...." Andariana dissolved into a fit of coughing.

"What are you doing here?" she asked when her voice finally returned.

Roux blinked at the question, "I just questioned Commander Yegor. I think I know where Tamara is, but I have to move fast."

Andariana sat up straight, "*Where?*"

Roux sighed, frustrated that she wasn't recognizing the significance of what had just happened to her, "In the South. I don't know exactly where, but I think I can travel through the Seil Wood to the Relvyn Wood, and that will save us time."

"How do you know it's her? Did Yegor *say* it was her?"

Roux frowned, "Well, no."

"What did he say?" she asked, taking another sip of water and massaging her neck.

"He was talking to an errand girl about an important prisoner in the South being moved. He was angry when she didn't remember what the message had said precisely. After she left, I questioned him. I kept asking about Tamara, but he seemed surprised by the question." Roux paused for a long moment, "He never actually *confirmed* anything I asked him."

"And now he's dead?" Andariana asked critically.

Roux averted his eyes, "Yes. After I told you, I was going to move his body and dump it in the sea. Make it look like he was robbed on the wharf."

"Well," Andariana said, slowly regaining her composure, "whether or not he confirmed that it was Tamara being held, *whomever* it is must be important. They don't send messengers for nobodies. And even if it isn't Tamara, it could be someone we need."

"But where would they keep someone like that?" Roux muttered.

Andariana arched a chestnut eyebrow, "The Drakleyn, of course. That's where Krasik launched his campaign. I'm sure it's still heavily defended, so that would be the obvious place."

Roux's eyes glittered, "That's not far from the Relvyn Wood. If I can travel through the Seil Wood, I can be there in days. Moments, even."

Andariana frowned, "*Moments?* The Seil Wood is almost two hundred leagues from here."

Roux nodded, the fury that sustained him resurfacing, "Two hundred leagues doesn't matter in the Archanium. I just have to know the place I'm Darting. And I *know* my village."

"Have you ever attempted such a thing?"

Roux frowned, "Not exactly. But it'll work...in theory anyway."

Andariana looked suddenly panicked, "You could be killed."

Roux chuckled, "Would that upset you so much?"

Her emerald eyes commanded his gaze, "*Yes,* Roux Devaan, it *would*. We want the same thing. I may have been critical in the past, but you have proven yourself a true friend to my family. Considering that my nephew and your cousin are Bonded, and I daresay a great deal more, I would go so far as to say you *are* family."

Roux smiled in spite of his confusion. Perhaps the blood hadn't completely returned to her brain, or perhaps the failed attempt on her life had made her suddenly sentimental. But at that moment, Andariana Belgi seemed far warmer than the icy queen he'd come to know.

"Thank you, Andariana," Roux said softly. "But what about you?"

She smiled, "Now that I know they aren't above killing me, I can take steps to ensure that I'm better protected and never alone. Go find her, Roux. As fast as you can. I'll handle things here." Her gaze shifted to the fresh corpse stiffening by the fire.

Roux straightened and gave her a wink, "Wish me luck."

And then he vanished.

Katherine was exhausted.

The day in and day out of Palace work was *far* more demanding than life in Voskrin. Of course, the Palace itself was also several times larger than her tiny village, and the hectic activity never ceased. Katherine guessed that on any given day she went from the lowest basements to Lady Delira's rooms on the upper floors at least three, sometimes four times. And during those treks, she was usually burdened by a good deal of washing, be it clean or soiled.

And then beyond that were the endless errands, sometimes to the

Voralla, sometimes to the various lords and ladies scattered across the grounds. And when all of *that* was finally seen to, there was Ethan.

The man had a good heart, but it was difficult to notice when she was supposed to be remembering every word he uttered so that she could convincingly spy for her mistress. Sometimes she'd make up comments he made or things he alluded to just to satisfy Delira's insatiable desire for intelligence.

She opened the doors to Lady Delira's quarters and walked swiftly across the room, placing her large basket of linens on the floor next to the dresser. When she looked up, she was surprised to see another maid in the room.

"Who are you?" she demanded, more out of surprise than anger.

The girl flinched, and Katherine realized that she was speaking to a child. The girl could only have been fifteen, perhaps sixteen summers at the oldest. She was pretty enough, which wasn't always a good thing in a place like Kalinor. She looked on the verge of tears.

Katherine sighed, "I'm sorry, I didn't mean to snap at you. I'm just not used to seeing other maids in the Lady's room, and you startled me."

Her eyes fell on the folder of papers in the girl's trembling hands.

"What do you have there?" Katherine asked softly.

The girl burst into tears, "Please don't hurt me!"

Katherine strolled across the room and wrapped her arms around the girl's shoulders. "Stop that immediately. I'm not going to hurt you."

The girl hiccuped in surprise at Katherine's command. "Miss?" she mumbled in confusion, staring at Katherine through tear-filled blue eyes.

"What's your name?" Katherine asked gently.

"M...M...Marina, miss."

"Alright, Marina, why don't you tell me what those papers are."

Marina started trembling again, so Katherine reached forward and gently took the papers from the girl's hand. She straightened and pored over the documents, her eyes widening as she read the contents.

It didn't make complete sense to her, but she got the general idea of what she was reading.

She turned sharply to the girl, "What were you going to do with these? Tell me the truth."

"I was...I was going to take them, miss," Marina admitted.

"Where?" Katherine demanded.

Marina was so startled by Katherine's vehemence that she just answered without thinking, "The Seil Wood, miss. Some of my family escaped there. But I couldn't leave the Palace until I had something of...value."

"You're a spy," Katherine said finally.

Marina looked like she was about to dissolve into sobs. Katherine took the girl's face in her hands and stared into her bleary blue eyes, "Marina, listen to me carefully. It is *very* important that you get these papers to the Seil Wood as fast as you can. Do you understand?"

Marina stared at her in confusion, "Miss?"

"There are dangerous things in here. *Very* dangerous things. There are people in the Wood who will understand what these words mean, but you have to get them into the right hands."

"You want me to *escape*, miss?" Marina asked blankly.

"Immediately," Katherine said, glancing over her shoulder as though Lady Delira might materialize at any moment. "Hide them in your blouse and leave. *Now*. Don't stop for anything until you're well past the tree-line."

Marina stared at Katherine for a long moment, then tucked the papers into her livery and tearfully headed towards the door. As she reached for the handle, the door flew open and Lady Delira stormed imperiously into the room.

She was so absorbed in her own thoughts that she bowled Marina over. The girl fell to the ground and Katherine held her breath. Marina scrambled to her feet, "Begging your pardon, milady."

She hurried out the door and disappeared.

Katherine exhaled sharply. Lady Delira was staring at her. Katherine averted her eyes and curtseyed, her brain racing.

"Care to explain what all *that* was about?" Delira asked sharply.

"Of course, milady," Katherine said, adding a hint of acid to her words, "I caught that little rat snooping around in here. She claimed she was in here to keep the fire going.

"She had oil and rags, but she was hovering by your desk when I walked in. She said she was curious, so I gave her a beating and sent her on her way. She was just leaving when you arrived."

Delira's eyes widened, "Snooping around my *desk*, you say?"

Katherine cursed her own stupidity. Why hadn't she said the *jewel-box* instead?

Delira stormed across the room and began rifling through her papers. Katherine took a deep breath and began counting the seconds that Marina had before Delira noticed that she was indeed missing some of her documents.

After a minute or two of frantic searching, Delira let out an angry shriek. "That little *bitch*!"

"Milady?" Katherine asked, feigning confusion.

Delira whirled, striking her hard across the jaw.

Katherine dropped to the floor with a shocked cry. Her face stung from the slap, "I'm sorry if I caused offense, milady."

"That girl *stole* something from me, you simpleton. You didn't even have to the brains to *search* her?"

"My apologies, milady," Katherine managed as she pulled herself back to her feet, "when I caught sight of her, she was still paces from your desk. I hadn't thought she'd had time to take anything. I can go find her, if it pleases you."

"*Find* her?" Delira sneered, "Do you have any idea how many maids are in this palace? She could be in the city by now, all because *you* were too stupid to search her. No, you stay here and make sure no one else comes in here after her. I must sound the alarm before she gets too far."

Katherine bowed her head and curtseyed again, counting every second that she kept Lady Delira from sounding the alarm, "As you wish, milady."

Delira scowled and rushed from the room in a panic. In the hallway, Katherine heard her hysterical shouting. "*You* there. Yes, *you* Perron. Get over here. *Now!*"

Katherine's eyebrows raised. If Delira was commanding Perron about, he must be quite out of favor. She offered up a silent prayer to the gods that Marina make her way safely out of the city and reach the Wood.

It was only a few of leagues away, and one girl on foot could easily hide in the tall grass and snow long enough to get there ahead of her pursuers. Katherine only hoped that the Ri-Vhan would find her before Lord Perron and his men.

CHAPTER 36

THE PIT

"*Get up.*"

Jonas lay there for a moment, trying to shut out the pain. His hands were bound behind him with bonds woven from *suul*.

He only knew of the black vine because its thorns produced a toxin that made accessing the Archanium near impossible. Those same thorns had been cutting into his wrists all night, which had in turn made sleep equally elusive.

A whiplash landed across his back, and he cried out.

"*Up, swine!*"

Jonas staggered to his feet. His face was bloody from the beating he'd received on his arrival to the village, before they'd tossed him in the pig stall. He'd spent the night bound, and lying in hog shit.

With their bond severed, he had no idea what was happening to Aleksei, or if the Knight was even still *alive*. At first he'd hoped the Ul'Brek were simply shielding him, but his hours in solitude had allowed him plenty of time to think, to reach for the Archanium in spite of the *suul* thorns.

He'd even managed to brush the surface a few times, and while those fleeting touches were never enough to invoke a spell, they had given him some small insight. The bond was gone.

Not dormant, *severed*.

As though it had never existed. The horror of that realization had nearly broken the tattered remnants of his spirit. In the depths of his heart, he knew Aleksei had to be alive, but without the bond it was impossible to be sure.

He had half-expected Aleksei to appear as he had in the slaver camp, like some divine vision of death incarnate, beauty and horror bound in the same skin.

Instead, he'd spent the night in the pig stall, shivering in the cold and increasingly convinced that he really *was* all alone.

And now a man with a whip was forcing him to his feet.

He faced the man with the whip, his mind racing as he was forced to march through the village. "*Do you have any* idea *who I am?*" he shouted angrily. "*I'm the Prince of* Ilyar. *If you harm me, my realm will marshal its armies and* decimate *this tiny hamlet. Think about what you're doing.*"

"*We know what you are,*" the man sneered. "*You are Impure.*"

Jonas froze. "Impure?"

"*You touch the Darkness. You are Impure, and you will be taken to the Pit for judgment.*"

Jonas cursed. The Pit? "*Judged by whom?*" he demanded.

"*The Nine.*"

Jonas clenched his jaw. The Nine? He was at a loss. He felt a surge of hopelessness well up within him as he marched, stranded in an alien land, surrounded by alien words and strange people, unable to access the one thing that might give him a fighting chance. He was lost.

He was also rapidly running out of time. Where was Aleksei? Would he be able to track Jonas without the bond? What if he *couldn't* track Jonas? He certainly wouldn't have left Jonas to languish in a pig stall all night, his wrists bound and bleeding, if he was nearby.

If anything, the Knight's continued absence only served to convince Jonas that Aleksei had not survived the Ul'Brek attack.

He immediately regretted the thought, pushing it away, even as sorrow threatened to drown him.

No one was coming to save him. Perhaps he truly *was* forgotten.

"*Let's get this over with,*" he grunted.

The Ul'Brek seemed surprised by Jonas's behavior. "*Impure usually struggle.*" He goaded Jonas to walk faster.

Jonas didn't offer a response. He refused to give the man the satisfaction. He walked silently with the man towards the center of the village, flanked now by Ul'Brek in black cloaks and bleached bone masks. They passed through a few rows of hide tents before bursting out into the crowd.

Jonas was astounded to see the number of people who had turned out to watch him be judged. There were easily three hundred Fanja gathered. He couldn't believe a village of this size could support that many people, especially in the middle of such Gods-forsaken country.

As the crowd parted, Jonas finally caught sight of the Pit.

It dominated the village center. As Jonas neared, he paused, studying the markings that had been carved into the stone surrounding the Pit.

The whip landed across his shoulders, driving him to the Pit's edge. He glanced down into the depths as an Ul'Brek stepped up behind him and sliced away his bonds.

The crowd was silent, staring down in the Pit as the Nine emerged. Jonas stared at them in shocked surprise. He *knew* these creatures.

They were shaped like men, but rather than skin, jagged whorls of horn and bone covered them. Their jaws clacked and flexed on horn hinges set into nightmarish faces. The sight of the creatures conjured only one word to Jonas's mind.

Revenants.

And then the crowd surged forward. *"Impure,"* they shouted as they moved in an unstoppable wall.

Jonas was one footstep from falling in when he suddenly heard screams from the people at the outer edge of the crowd. He pressed back against the throng of bodies, trying every trick Aleksei had ever taught him to avoid being thrust into the Pit with the revenants.

The screams grew increasingly louder, and closer.

For just a moment the crowd parted, and Jonas caught sight of Aleksei. His heart skipped a beat at the sight of his Hunter's handsome face, contorted in his singular rage as he shoved aside the Fanja keeping him from his Magus. When they raised a weapon or a fist, they fell to the bizarre sword he wielded.

But he was too far away.

The crowd pressed against Jonas even harder, their desperate need to escape Aleksei's ravenous blade forcing Jonas ever closer to the Pit. The crowd surged forward and Jonas's boot slipped on the edge. He dropped three paces down, landing roughly on his back and grunting as the wind was knocked from him.

Jonas coughed violently and tried to catch his breath, but the dust only made him cough more. He rolled onto his knees and staggered to his feet, coughing the dust from his lungs and gasping for air.

As the revenants circled around him, Jonas realized that the screaming and yelling above had ceased completely. All eyes were fixed on him.

Despair welled up within him. It warred with the hatred he felt for the people staring down at him, eagerly anticipating his death like spectators at a festival.

The Nine circled, a queer clicking emanating from their pronged horn jaws.

One darted forward and swiped at his arm with a serrated claw.

He cried out, covering his torn flesh with his free hand, having nowhere to go, no wall to back up against. Once they attacked in earnest, Jonas knew they would tear him apart in seconds.

Hatred tore through him, almost *comforting* as he stared his death in the face. Faces from a hideous nightmare.

The Nine kept circling, clicking to one another. Gods, what were they *waiting* for?

The screams from Aleksei's rescue attempt intensified, now much closer, but Jonas knew his Hunter wouldn't be in time. He could hear the man's bestial bellowing over the screams.

"*Jonas!* Jonas, I'm coming! Hold *on!*"

"I love you," Jonas shouted back.

"Jonas, *no!*" Aleksei's voice was getting closer, and increasingly desperate. "I'm getting you out of there."

"I love you," Jonas called, a bitter tear crawling down his face and dripping from his jaw, "and I'm sorry."

The Nine all struck in the same moment, but Jonas was no longer concerned about their jaws or their wicked claws. Time stood still, and Jonas idly wondered if this was what it felt like when Aleksei had tapped their bond.

Their bond. Severed. *Gone.* Aleksei would survive him. He no longer had to fear for his Knight. Aleksei was strong, *so* much stronger than he. And he had grown. *Gods*, he had grown into such an amazing man, a leader, a warrior.

Jonas felt his heart swell with love for Aleksei Drago, with pride, and with bitterness for the fact that he'd told his Knight he loved him for the last time. Saying the words alone wasn't near enough, but it was all he could do. He'd never see his Hunter again in this life, but at least he'd professed his love one last time.

And then Jonas let it all consume him. The shame, the fury, the hatred, the spectacular *failure* that had been his last moments. He let them burn through him, *from* him. A conflagration erupted from him even as he wholly surrendered to it.

He could hear Aleksei shouting his name, but his Knight's voice now seemed so far away, almost as though it were from another world entirely.

These people had taken the Archanium from him, but he had touched the Seraphima twice, reaching *outside* the Archanium when he'd needed to.

But he didn't need the Seraphima now. He didn't need the cold light and the piercing Song. He needed *destruction*.

He wanted to *punish* them, any and everyone intent of taking his life and his love from him.

Jonas forfeited his last shred of humanity, and the full force of the Demonic Presence flooded into him, through him, *out* of him.

The black fire of his judgement spiraled through the Pit.

First Private Danel Bront was stationed at the pass, bored beyond comprehension. The other men were gambling around the fire, but Danel knew better than to bet wages he may never see. Joining the rebellion had seemed like the right thing to do at the time, but he now understood how he'd been swept up in the cause, in the friends cheering him on when he'd torn off the Queen's colors to don the sigil of the crow.

It was a decision he regretted, but one he couldn't take back. And now, with the talk of a Loyalist band somewhere in the Sulaq Hills, he needed to be especially vigilant. His friends, or the men he'd *thought* were his friends, had all accepted the Demon's deal too easily, and they believed they were living the high life for it.

But he had never been as confident as his friends, and they had rejected him in favor of the new men that had infused the unit with the fervor befitting a rebellion.

Now Danel stood alone, guarding one of the many small passes that threaded through the Sulaq Hills. His friends would have nothing to do with him, and he was too committed a soldier to abandon his post, no matter *how* much he regretted the choices that had led him here.

As such, he was the first man to see the sky change.

"Sergeant T-Talbain? *Sergeant?*" he shouted, watching bloody red eat away at the gray of the low-lying snow clouds dominating the sky.

"Gods, what is it man?" the Sergeant called.

"There's something I think you should see."

Danel heard cursing behind him, and he shuddered to think at how the Sergeant would punish him if he was wrong about a threat encroaching on them. But gods, the *sky* was changing. Surely that merited a mention to the commanding officer?

"And?" Sergeant Talbain demanded as he watched the crimson surge eat away the gloom of gray.

"My apologies, Sergeant. But this shouldn't be happening. What if we're being attacked?" Danel cowered away even as the Sergeant cuffed him sharply across the ear with his half-empty tankard.

"By *who?*" the Sergeant shouted in his face. "The *sky* isn't attacking us, half-wit. Your stupidity might be a threat, perhaps. Unless you see the Queen's men charging the hill, you keep your mouth shut, you got me?"

Danel nodded, his hand reflexively touching the place where his ear had been partially torn by the blow. The blood was pouring freely, but in the cold it would clot before he lost too much.

Danel returned to his post, taking only a moment to check in on his watch partner. Jarvis was passed out, as usual. The man had been part of the gambling and drinking earlier in the afternoon, so the Sergeant had sent him to stand watch with Danel until he sobered up.

As a result, Danel was the only man to see the beasts.

At first, he thought he was imagining it all. Perhaps the blow to his head had addled his senses. A red sky, and grotesque, other-worldly beasts hooting and screeching their way up the mountain, strange weapons in their claws?

"*Sergeant!*" he screamed, scrambling back from the hillside.

Sergeant Talbain glared up from his game, finally picking up a fire-brand and stalking towards Danel. "Boy, I warned you!"

Danel looked between the advancing sergeant and the hooting demons rushing towards him. "Can't you hear them, Sergeant?"

"Hear *what?*" Talbain demanded, just as a sword ripped through the man's belly. He dropped to his knees, grasping at his entrails as they spilled across the ground.

Danel clambered beneath an overhang in the rock, curling up but unable to keep his eyes shut as the demons tore though the camp and cut the other men, his *friends*, to shreds.

He saw men who had told him that he was weak and foolish beg for mercy as they were cut down. He watched the bravest men he knew soil themselves before being decapitated.

He couldn't explain *why*, but as each member of the command fell, as they screamed and begged and died, Danel found himself laughing. His laughter grew louder as his comrades were silenced and the screams of the beasts faded.

When one of the demons finally found him, sword dripping with gore, Danel was hysterical. He wasn't sure if he was laughing or crying any longer. The demon who found him seemed to have the same question.

The sky cleared, and he found himself looking into the clearest blue eyes he'd ever seen.

"Who are you?" the woman asked.

"Private Danel Bront, miss. I *tried* to tell them the demons were coming. They didn't listen. They're all dead, aren't they?"

She paused for a moment, before nodding slowly, "They are."

He started weeping, "I *told* them to listen. They never listened!"

The woman frowned, then looked to a grim, gray man behind her. "Send him back to his masters. They might as well know what we've done here."

As the gray man advanced towards him, Danel felt liquid warmth spreading out in his trousers and rushing down his leg.

The gray man smiled.

Roux couldn't breathe.

He felt himself flashing through space, but unlike traditional Darting, the experience was lasting much longer than usual. His lungs screamed for air, but there was no end in sight. White and gray shapes whipped past him, seconds dragging slowly, interminably by as he hurtled through the void.

His vision grew dark around the edges as his need for air grew increasingly desperate.

His mind panicked, begging him to draw just one breath, but he couldn't. He was frozen in place, locked in the void even as he moved through it.

He briefly wondered if he was going to die.

With a sudden explosion of light and sound, Roux slammed into the platform of his village, the air trapped in his lungs forcefully expelled by the violent impact. He writhed on the harsh wood of the platform for a long moment, trying to force his body to draw the breath it so stridently craved.

After an eternity of gasping at nothing, Roux's lungs expanded and filled him with the sweet, heady rush of fresh forest air.

Welcome back, Ri-Hnon.

The shock of the voice rippled through Roux like a thunderbolt. He was once again left gasping on the platform, pulling air desperately into his lungs. What cruel trickery was this?

"Who's there?" he shouted weakly.

You know me, Ri-Hnon. You are my Child. I am your Mother.

It was the *Wood*, Roux realized. But that was impossible. The Wood never spoke to him directly. Not like *this*. He could interpret Her voice from small motions in the Wood, a falling leaf, a twist in the wind, a ripple in a pond.

But She only ever spoke to Aleksei.

It had caused him a great deal of anger towards his cousin when Aleksei had first come to the Wood and been proclaimed their Hunter.

So why would She suddenly begin speaking to him *now*?

I don't understand. he thought, just as he had all his life.

You need not understand, only obey.

Roux frowned, pushing himself to his knees.

Aleksei had spoken with him about the voice of the Wood, but he'd always made Her sound motherly. Odd, but comforting. At times, even childish.

Roux heard none of those things now.

I need to get to the Relvyn Wood. he thought, stressing the importance in his mind. *Can you help me get there?*

If I wanted to, yes, Ri-Hnon, I could. I do not want to now.

Roux pushed himself to his feet and staggered before righting himself. The platform of his village was empty this early in the morning, for which he was deeply grateful.

Why not? he managed, wincing at Her caustic retort.

Do not question!

Her mental roar hurled him to his knees. He shook his head in shock. Something was wrong. Something horrible had happened, and he needed to find out what. But he also *had* to get to Tamara before she disappeared forever.

What do You want? he demanded, trying and failing to remain calm.

I want My Ri-Hnon. My Warden. I want My Hunter back.

I don't know where Aleksei is. I'm sorry. Roux began.

I know where he is, Warden. He is the one who freed Me of My shackles.

Roux froze. Shackles? Hearing Her voice was odd enough, but he had never heard anyone mention the Wood being *shackled*.

I don't understand. he admitted.

Your understanding is not important, only obedience.

What do You want from me? he asked again, pleading this time.

I want to show you something.

Roux nodded, pulling himself to his feet a second time, *Show me.*

Go to the tigerlily pond by the breaks.

Roux frowned, but gathered himself and Darted to the forest floor, turning south. As he moved through the Wood, he felt the familiar shift in the forest as it shaped his path. He arrived at the edge of the tigerlily pool and stiffened.

Across the pond stood a girl. She looked to a mere fifteen summers at most. Her back was to him, but before her stood a contingent of soldiers. There looked to be near thirty men closing in on her.

One man sat atop a horse, his face twisted in a smirk. "You ran well, girl, but not fast enough. Now hand it over."

The girl backed towards the pond, "No. You'll have to kill me first."

The man on the horse sighed, "Don't make this difficult, girl. Just hand over the documents and we may let you live."

The girl pulled a pouch from her pack and held it over the water, "I can just destroy them."

The man chuckled, "Go ahead. See how that turns out for you."

Why are you showing me this? Roux demanded angrily.

The mixture of fear and confidence in the girl's voice reminded him of Tamara the first time he'd met her. It made his heart ache. Roux felt the sting of tears in his eyes and tried to blink them away.

And then Roux heard another voice. Alluring, silky, seductive.

"Lord Perron, it was *very* brave of you to come chasing after this girl. But are you *sure* she has what you truly want?"

Roux turned sharply at the sound. A stunningly beautiful woman was emerging from the water, dripping and naked, only just barely covered by pond moss. The men all stared at her with mouths agape, Marina apparently forgotten.

"Come to me, Lord Perron. Bring your men, and I shall give you what you *desire*."

The man on the horse slid out of his saddle and stumbled towards the woman in the pond. "You will?" he asked, his voice now dramatically different. Worshipful.

"Of *course*, my love. Come, and I shall give you *all* what you seek."

Roux could only stare as Lord Perron walked into the water, his face now light and joyful. The woman slowly drifted back into the water, drawing Perron further in. His men followed, their expressions increasingly excited yet vacant as they followed their commander into the pond's cool embrace.

Roux stared at the creature, at the rusalka, luring these men to their deaths. A chill shuddered through his bones.

A moment later, he Darted across the pond and appeared beside the girl. "Who are you looking for?" he asked quickly.

"The Ri-Vhan," Marina said flatly, her eyes still on the men. On the rusalka.

Roux reached forward and touched her hand.

They reappeared on the platform, the girl suddenly free of the rusalka's spell.

Marina stared at him for a moment before the full weight of what had just happened seemed to crash in on her. She collapsed.

Roux caught her fall, his own head swirling in confusion.

What was that? he asked the Wood, his confusion rippling through his thoughts.

Justice, Warden. Those men deserved a far crueler fate. But I was lenient. The girl has suffered, but now she is here, with you. With Me. Safe.

CHAPTER 37

ANOMALY

The first of the Nine lunged at Jonas.

It had only grazed him when it released a shriek, crumpling to the ground. One by one they came at him, their hooked claws cutting at his flesh. But the moment they made contact, each fell away screaming. In mere seconds, the Nine lay on the floor of the Pit, motionless.

Aleksei was beside Jonas in the next instant, his sword at the ready. A tendril of the Mantle bored into his Magus's neck, healing his injuries in a heartbeat. Jonas shuddered as it slithered from beneath his skin.

The Nine were still on the ground, but Aleksei eyed them as though they might pounce any moment. Knight and Magus stood there, side by side, panting as they waited for the fight to resume.

Above them, the crowd had grown deathly silent, their eyes fixated on the two men in the Pit.

One of the Nine stirred.

Aleksei held his blade at the ready, intent on the creature.

It raised its head and Aleksei paused, his surprise outweighing his caution. The creature's face had changed. Aleksei realized he was looking not at a nightmare, but at a man. Traces of horn and bone were still in evidence, but they were fading.

The creature uttered a sound. Beside him, Jonas tensed.

"What?" Aleksei asked, his hackles rising. "What is it?"

"He said 'please'," Jonas whispered.

"In Fanja?" Aleksei panted.

"No," Jonas muttered, clearly disquieted, "in *Yazka*."

Aleksei frowned, "In what?"

"It's an ancient language. *So* ancient that no one has spoken it in nearly a thousand years."

"Then how can you understand it?"

Jonas met the Knight's golden-eyed gaze, "It's the language of magic."

When Aleksei's face remained blank, Jonas let out a tired sigh, "The oldest texts in the Voralla are written in Yazka. The Magi who defeated the Kholod would have spoken it. Over time, it evolved into the language you and I are speaking now."

Aleksei returned his gaze to the creature. He shuddered. Most of the horn and bone had vanished from the man's face now. Around him, Aleksei could see that other revenants were stirring, growing less monstrous by the moment. Some, however, remained as they were. Unmoving and seemingly lifeless.

Of the Nine, five were already changing.

"Who are they?" Aleksei asked, not taking his eyes off the creatures that were growing more human every second. Jonas translated the question in halting, awkward Yazka.

The creature who had spoken made a sound and Jonas translated, "He says they are the Impure."

Aleksei frowned, "The Impure are what these people call Magi. Is he a Magus?"

Jonas rephrased the question to the creature, now mostly human. The creature responded with a stream of almost-familiar syllables.

"He calls himself a Magus," Jonas said slowly, a trace of hesitation in his voice.

"What?" Aleksei asked, "What's wrong?"

"He didn't use the common phrase," Jonas said softly. "At least, not the way we use it. The Magi of old didn't have Knights. In many ways, they *were* the Knights. That word is different from our idea of Magi. But that's the word he used."

"Who are you?" Aleksei demanded, stepping forward and pointing his blade at the half-man, half-revenant.

Soft golden eyes met his own. A frown crossed the man's face.

Aleksei pointed at himself. "Aleksei." He pointed at the creature.

Understanding came into the creature's eerily familiar eyes. It flexed its jaw, and Aleksei's eyes were drawn to the thin white scar that ran from its right eye, almost as though tracing the path of a teardrop. It smiled.

"*Richter.*"

Roux sat in his bedroom, his face in his hands. The low crackle of the fire was the only source of sound in the room, providing little warmth or comfort.

Something was happening to the Wood. He had spent the last few hours scouring every scroll in his library for any mention of the Wood's true nature, of anything that might have been sealed away, but had found nothing.

Yet there was no question that something deeply wrong had happened since he'd been away. Even the Ri-Vhan themselves were acting strangely.

Gone was the jovial warmth and camaraderie he knew so well. In its place was an unusual coldness, an absence of emotion that sent shivers through Roux every time he looked into yet another set of dead eyes.

A soft knock came at the door, and Roux looked up to see his father framed in the firelight. "Thought you could use some company," Theo said softly.

Roux managed a smile. Thank the gods for his father. Of all the Ri-Vhan, Theo was the most like himself, the least changed. Not that he was unaffected, but rather than emotionless, he just seemed resigned.

"Come on in. The fire's not much, but it's better than nothing."

Theo nodded and took a seat next to his son. "You're troubled."

Roux nodded, eyes fixated on the low dancing flames, "More than I can say, Father." He took a breath and turned to look into Theo's tired eyes, "What *happened* here? I haven't been gone all that long, and yet it's like I'm in a foreign land."

Theo shrugged, turning his eyes to the fire, "After you left, things were fine for a long time. Nothing unusual. A few border skirmishes with the Ilyari rebels and the like, but we were mostly left alone. And then...I don't know. The Wood began to change."

"Change how?"

Theo shrugged again, "I'm not sure how to put it, Son. The Wood used to be so vibrant and alive. But then it suddenly seemed like She was holding Her breath. The wind no longer stirred the trees. Deer became even harder to come by than before. And then we all had the *dream*."

Roux's brow creased, but he didn't interrupt.

"One night the entire village was going about its business, same as any other night. The next thing we knew, we were all picking ourselves up off the ground. It was morning. And stranger still, every single man, woman, and child in the village recalled the *exact* same dream."

"What was it? What did you see?" Roux asked, trying to rein in his alarm.

Theo frowned as he remembered, "It was a terrifying thing to behold, Son. We saw a...a *thing* made of smoke and branches. It was the Wood, but She wasn't as we know Her. She was a horrid apparition... terrifying. And She was *angry*."

"About what?"

"We don't know," Theo said after a pause. "No one has been able to figure that one out. But ever since the dream, things have been different. People grew colder. Careless. And some speak of hearing Her in their heads."

Roux stiffened, "Ri-Vhan are hearing the voice of the Wood?"

Theo scoffed, "Some claim to, but no one really believes them. Such a thing is impossible for mere Ri-Vhan. You know that as well as anyone. She only communicates with the Ri-Hnon and the Hunters. Not common folk like the rest of us."

"I'm not sure I believe that anymore, Father."

When Theo regarded him with surprise, Roux explained, "Before my return, the closest I ever came to communicating with the Wood was expressed in the movements of the forest. It was subtle and indirect. Since my return, She has spoken directly to me. And She doesn't sound anything like Aleksei described in the past."

Warden. Her voice crashed through his head, drowning out his father's response. *The girl has woken. See to her.*

Roux blinked and realized that he was on the floor of his bedchamber, his father staring down at him in concern, "Are you alright, boy? What was all that about?"

Roux pushed himself to his feet warily, his head spinning, "That was the Wood. She wants me to see to someone."

Theo followed him out of his chambers and down the hall, raining questions on Roux that he didn't stop to answer. He wasn't about to keep the Wood waiting, not in Her new incarnation.

When he reached the bedchamber he'd placed the girl in, he was surprised to the find the door already open. The girl sat on the small cot, a pile of papers in her lap.

He knocked awkwardly on the doorframe and stepped into the room.

"Good morning, ma'am," he said softly, offering a reassuring smile.

The girl stared at him, cringing back as he entered. "What do you want?" she asked timidly.

Roux dropped into a crouch a safe distance from her, "Well, first I'd like to know your name."

She watched him for a long moment, as though he were about to pounce on her. When she finally seemed satisfied that he was going to stay where he was, she relaxed a little, "Marina."

He nodded, "Marina, my name is Roux Devaan. I'm the leader of the Ri-Vhan. Welcome to our village."

She looked around her small room suspiciously, as though she was scrutinizing the entire village, "How did I get here?"

"You may not recall, but I spoke with you at the pond, before you fainted. You told me that you sought the Ri-Vhan. In my haste, I brought you here. You were so exhausted that the jump was a bit more than you could handle. You've been resting here ever since. Don't worry, you're safe here."

Marina relaxed a bit, "She said you could help me." She lifted the papers in her lap, "She said you needed to see these."

Roux knitted his brows, ignoring the papers for the moment, "Who is 'she'?"

Marina fidgeted on her cot, and Roux reminded himself that he was talking to a girl. A girl who was likely unused to being questioned by someone like him. "I don't know her name, milord. She was a maid in the Palace. She caught me stealing these papers from her mistress. But when she saw them, she told me to get here as soon as I could."

Roux frowned at that. There was a spy in the Palace? Well, that was more welcome news than he'd expected.

"Why did she want you to come to the Wood?"

"I told her I was coming here. Some of my family made a run for it when they could. We promised we'd all try to meet up in the Wood. I was hoping to find them, milord."

Roux offered her a sincere smile. "May I see those?" he asked, nodding to the papers in her lap.

Marina held them out stiffly. "I hope they can help."

Roux took them gingerly, his smile unwavering, "I'm sure they will. Thank you for your bravery."

She blushed, seeming suddenly unsure how to react to the compliment.

"Father?" Roux called into the hallway.

Theo appeared in the doorway a moment later, "What is it, boy?"

Roux stood and turned to Marina, "This is my father, Theo. You tell him who you're looking for, and I promise he'll do his best to help you find them."

Her face lit up at that.

Roux winked at her, then turned to his father. His voice dropped low, "She's looking for her family. Can you see to that while I read what she's brought us?"

Theo nodded and turned back to Marina, "Well, shall we be off, my dear? I'm sure your family is worried sick about you. Let's see if we can find out where they ended up."

Marina came shakily to her feet and managed a curtsey, "Thank you, milord."

Theo laughed at that, gently guiding her out of the room, "Oh, my dear, I am *far* from a lord. But I'm happy to be of assistance."

As their voices faded into the recesses of the house, Roux stared at the spidery scrawl that decorated the stack of pages in his hands. The more he read, the wider his eyes grew, until a sense of true panic settled over him.

"Great *gods*," he whispered.

The moment his name escaped his lips, Richter's head dropped back into the dust. Aleksei stared at his body a long moment, until he was satisfied that the man was still breathing. There was a heartbeat there, too, but it was so faint and thready that Aleksei could barely make it out.

"Aleksei!" Jonas shouted, pulling the Knight's attention back to the moment at hand.

A small door had opened on the far side of the Pit, and Ul'Brek were flooding into the chamber. Aleksei swallowed hard as he realized just how outnumbered they were.

He raised his sword, the Mantle flowing seamlessly into the tiny cracks and crevices carved into the strange, pitted metal. The blade's tip throbbed a deep, pulsing red, an echoed reflection of Aleksei's heartbeat.

The men fanned out around Aleksei and Jonas, each drawing a thin, silver blade.

A screeching whistle sounded from above, and the men all dropped to a knee. Aleksei looked up in surprise, and found himself staring into Ramla's black eyes. She looked away from him, shouting to the Ul'Brek in Fanja.

A few called back to her, but she stared them down. Aleksei watched the entire proceedings, perplexed. Jonas stepped up next to him. "What is she talking about?" the Magus whispered.

Aleksei frowned, "How should I know? I can't understand a word she's saying."

Jonas arched an eyebrow, "She's talking about *you*. She's saying you are the living embodiment of prophecy. You bear the sword. The Impure have been cleansed. And...I have been...sacrificed?"

Aleksei winced at that last part. "She said you were going to die," he grunted.

Jonas sighed, "Depending on how you look at it, perhaps she was right."

Aleksei's hackles rose. His head whipped around to stare into Jonas's eyes. Jonas's midnight eyes, pulsing with crackles of yellow-green light.

"Good gods," Aleksei whispered.

"It will fade," Jonas said softly, but Aleksei could tell the Magus wasn't entirely sure of himself.

"What's *happened* to you?" Aleksei breathed, pulling his love into a tight embrace.

One of the Ul'Brek stood and shouted angrily at them. Aleksei fixed the man with a venomous glare. The Mantle lifted from his shoulders and pawed the air, pulsing a vibrant scarlet. The man faltered and finally dropped back to his knee, frowning into the dust.

Aleksei pressed a kiss into Jonas's hair, "What did you *do*?"

Jonas released a breath against Aleksei's chest, "What I had to.

What they *needed* me to. I summoned the Demonic Presence. That's what saved me. When the creatures touched me, they were touching the Presence itself. I was able to cut my connection to it before it consumed me, but I have no doubt there will be a price."

Aleksei glanced back up at Ramla, now staring calmly back at him. "There's always a price," he muttered.

"You can come up now," Ramla said gently. "It's over. The prophecy has been fulfilled."

In that moment, the Ul'Brek apparently withdrew their shields over Jonas's connection to the Archanium, because he suddenly poured the bonding spell back into Aleksei. The Knight opened himself up to the familiar warmth, allowing the magic of the Archanium to blossom within him once again.

Aleksei led Jonas carefully from the Pit, feeling renewed, restored, as they stepped around the bodies of the Nine. The Ul'Brek rose as one and made a path for them. Aleksei's eyes never left the men, daring any one of them to make a move. No one budged.

They walked through the small door that that allowed the Ul'Brek into the Pit. Ramla met them at the end of a sloping ramp, her eyes bright. When Aleksei reached the top of the ramp, Ramla bowed to him. "You have helped free us of our burden, Hunter. We are in your debt."

"I don't understand," Aleksei said calmly, keeping as close to Jonas as possible. He imagined it would be a good long while before he was comfortable letting Jonas get too far from his side. "You never mentioned a burden."

Ramla spread her hands before her, "You were told what you needed to know. You fulfilled your part in the prophecy. And you, Magus," she said, turning to Jonas, "you performed your part admirably. It is because of you that we are truly free. When you freed the Darkness in you, you freed us all."

Before Jonas could respond, Ramla turned to the assembled villagers who now stared at her in shock and confusion. At her shout, the villagers erupted into giddy applause and cheering. Aleksei stared at their celebration in the same fog of confusion he'd been mired in for the past two days.

"She said we've freed them from the Nine," Jonas said softly. "The Darkness has been banished from their lands."

Aleksei frowned, "She called the Archanium 'the Darkness'."

Jonas shrugged, "They might have the same word for the Archanium and the Presence. This isn't a particularly sophisticated village, Aleksei. Those who can touch the Archanium here typically learn how to shut it away, not embrace it."

"Except her," Aleksei said, nodding to Ramla.

"What do you mean?"

Aleksei smiled at Jonas, "Surely you can feel it. She's a Magus. She knocked me off Agriphon last night with a spell. Her father was Ul'Brek, but she was raised to touch the Archanium."

Jonas stared at the girl, "Then she was brought up with a very specific purpose."

"I'll say. She even speaks Ilyari."

Jonas smiled at him, then stepped forward and introduced himself in Fanja. Aleksei watched the interchange with a small degree of envy, wishing he could understand what they were saying to each other.

But even without language, Aleksei could tell that he was observing two people born into power. People who respected each other, not as equals, but as individuals, marvels in their own unique ways.

"Jonas," Aleksei called, feeling suddenly uneasy, "I'm going to find Agriphon."

Jonas held up a hand, directing a few more questions at Ramla. Aleksei stood impatiently, waiting for his Magus to finish. If Agriphon was lost in the wastes, he could already be dead. Fulfilling prophecy was all well and good, but now that it was over, Aleksei needed to find his horse.

Jonas finished his conversation with Ramla and turned to Aleksei, "She thinks her people captured Agriphon. She's going to find out."

Aleksei glanced at the crowd of villagers, still staring at them uncertainly. The Ul'Brek remained in the Pit below. From the edge, Aleksei could tell they were all still on one knee. They seemed to be praying.

"What's going on here?" he asked, meeting Jonas's nightmare eyes.

Jonas sighed, "I told you, these lands were dangerous because they were cursed by old magic. By prophecy. I know because that's what I've been told my entire life. But my knowledge of specific details is limited at best.

"The Fanja are a secretive people. No one who has ventured this far into their northern lands in the past few centuries has returned."

Jonas turned and pointed at the Pit, "And that is why. Every time these people catch an outlander, they've thrown them into the Pit, to be 'judged'. Unfortunately for those travelers, the only person who had a chance at surviving was someone who could touch the Demonic Presence."

"And the Presence was sealed away until Bael released it," Aleksei growled.

"Exactly. So, it wasn't even until last year that anyone had a chance. Even then, they had to wait for someone who had been touched by the Presence and survived. No one in this world is born with a connection to the Presence; it's not like the Seraphima."

Aleksei frowned as a sudden realization struck him, "But you've touched *both* now."

"Correct."

Aleksei leaned forward, his voice dropping to a whisper, "When was the last time something like this happened?"

When Jonas looked at him again, Aleksei felt his heart break just a little, "It's *never* happened, Aleksei. No one has ever been able to touch both magics at the same time. Until very recently, no one even had the chance."

"So why now? Why you?"

Jonas pinched the bridge of his nose, closing his eyes and exhaling forcefully. Through their newly-forged bond, Aleksei could feel exactly how exhausted his Magus was.

"Fantastic question, but I don't know. I wish to the gods I did, but I don't. It doesn't make any sense. And worse, now that I *have* touched the Presence, I'm afraid I know what happens next."

Aleksei felt his pity evaporate with those words. Anger roared up in place of anguish. He turned and grabbed Jonas by his shoulders, turning the Magus to face him.

"Don't you *dare* say that," he snarled. "You can't know the future any better than I can."

Jonas looked up at Aleksei, his black eyes pleading, "I told you what Kevara said, Aleksei. I was willing to put aside her fears before, but now...."

"Nothing has changed, Jonas. Did you destroy the world? Did you destroy me? You touched the Presence, but you *controlled* it. If you hadn't, we wouldn't be standing here now."

"We just fulfilled prophecy, Aleksei. How is that any different from the prophecies my grandmother is reading back in Kuuran?"

Aleksei thought for a moment before seizing the answer, "Richter."

Jonas frowned, "What?"

"When Richter was speaking, you understood him. You said he used a word that meant Magus, but not the way we use it. The same way Ramla called the Archanium and the Presence 'the Darkness'."

"Aleksei, what does this have to do—"

"*Everything*, Jonas," the Hunter said, his excitement growing. "Prophecy is magic, but it's magic grounded in *words*. Words can have different meanings to different people." Jonas was staring at him, trying to follow where he was headed. "What's to say that your grandmother hasn't misinterpreted her own prophecies? How old are they? Who translated them?"

"I...I don't know," Jonas admitted after a moment.

"Then how can you place so much stock in what they say? Did you read the words for yourself? The original Scripture? Or did she simply recite them to you?"

"Well, I never saw the source texts themselves."

"Which means that you don't know what they actually say, only how Kevara interpreted them. You've got to forget it. Forget *all* of it," Aleksei commanded.

Jonas stared up at his Knight in surprise.

"I mean it, Jonas. For all you or I know, she was reading you a fairy story. She was making up a night terror so you would do what she wanted. She believes her Scriptures say what she *wants* them to say, but that's her interpretation. It has nothing to do with actual fact, or even the actual text. You believed that before. I need you to believe it *now*."

Jonas looked into his golden eyes for a long moment, then leaned forward and gave him a grateful kiss.

"Thank you," he whispered.

"Hunter."

Aleksei turned to find Ramla striding across the dusty earth, her face as serious as ever.

"Your horse is at the northern outpost of the village. Magus," she turned to take in Jonas, "you are needed in the Pit."

Aleksei frowned, "He's not going back in there without me."

To his surprise, she shook her head, "You are to collect your horse. He comes with me. *Now*."

Aleksei turned to Jonas, but the Magus smiled back, "It'll be alright. Make sure Agriphon's safe. I'll be there shortly."

Aleksei watched helplessly as Jonas followed Ramla back into the Pit. He turned north only to find a crowd of villagers still standing there, gawking at him, as though he hadn't just killed any number of them trying to get to the Pit.

"Don't you people have anything better to do?" he growled, striding forward as they parted and respectfully let him through.

CHAPTER 38

RICHTER

"These are of the utmost importance, do you understand?"

Theo stood staring back his son, a stormy look on his face, "Yes, yes, you've repeated that ten times by now, boy. I know how important they are. But you still haven't told me *why*."

Roux shook his head, running a hand through his tangled curls, "It's not important that you understand them, Father. But if Aleksei or Jonas returns to the Wood, I need your *word* that you will give them these documents. Immediately."

"And I promised I would. Now answer me. Where are you off to? You've only just rejoined your people, and you're leaving them already?"

Roux turned and glared at his father, "I have to convince the Wood to let me travel to Relvyn."

Theo sighed, "Yes, I'm well aware of your mad plan. But let's be reasonable, boy."

"*No!*" Roux barked. "I've wasted enough time here dealing with this mess. I've got to get to the Relvyn Wood before they move Tamara. If they take her away...." He stopped and allowed himself a moment to push the thought to the back of his mind. "I *have* to find her, Father."

He turned and set off for the center of the village.

"And what if she's already gone, boy? What if she hasn't been there in ages? What *then?*"

"Then I'll follow her trail until I find her," Roux shouted over his shoulder.

Theo tried to shout something after him, but Roux Darted to the forest floor before the words reached him. He'd had enough of listening to his father. He loved the man dearly, but he was different from the father Roux remembered.

Something had changed him, changed *all* of them.

And Roux had no time for it. He only wanted to find Tamara.

Mother Wood, I wish to travel.

Her voice roared up from the roots beneath his feet, *Then you must satisfy Me.*

I am yours to command, Mother.

There was a palpable silence. Roux waited, forcing his muscles to relax before the next barrage of soundless words assaulted him.

You wish for passage? Then you go bearing a gift, *Warden. Travel to the Wyrmwell, to the Qoorenmir. I will grace you with my gift, and permit you passage.*

Roux stiffened.

Is there no other way?

He was greeted only by silence. After waiting for moments that felt like hours, he realized that the Wood had given him Her answer.

Roux sank to a knee.

He was a dead man.

Roux took a few minutes to compose himself. Yet another thing now stood between him and Tamara. True, he was working on limited information at best, but finding a lead to her location was the only thing that had kept him going these past few weeks.

And now this.

He took a deep breath and walked into the forest, heading south. Not that it mattered. She would take him where She pleased. But the Heart lay to the south, so he might as well make his intentions clear.

Once more, the forest shifted around him, reorganizing itself into the unfamiliar darkness of the Heart.

No one traveled the Heart.

Aleksei had been there once, or so the story went. He had defeated a Salamander hatchling, and had earned the Mantle as his reward. Roux had often wondered whether or not it had ever really happened. He had never heard tales of Salamanders living in the Heart.

But then again, the Wood had only *now* chosen to speak into his mind. The gods only knew what secrets She had imparted to Aleksei.

Roux walked among Her twisted roots and broken stones with more confidence than he felt, trying to put a brave face forward. The Ri-Vhan had many legends surrounding the Heart, and most of them ended in the death of one hero or another.

Those same stories tumbled through Roux's consciousness as he made his way deeper and deeper, relishing the faint light even as it was slowly snuffed out high above him.

He stumbled in the darkness for a few minutes, waiting for his eyes to adjust to the black. After a few moments, he began to hear the unsettling laughter and clapping of the leshii.

Roux shivered, pressing forward as his eyes adjusted. He may be master of the Ri-Vhan, but the leshii were masters of the Wood itself, and all the fey creatures that dwelt within it. They were older than time, as far as he was aware. And they could be as helpful or harmful as they chose.

Worse, they had only returned a year ago. For eons they had been trapped within the Cathedral of Dazhbog, far to the north. The first Hunter, Richter, had used their demonic natures to lure the Demon Cassian into the angels' trap, binding them together. When he fell, the angels had locked them in the Cathedral with the Presence to serve as a warning, should anyone ever try to release the Presence back into the world.

The Magus Bael had inadvertently released them in his apparently never-ending quest for power and dominance. A nightmare which, Roux noted with smug satisfaction, had not yet come to fruition. Roux hadn't been there the night Bael had tapped into his newfound powers and razed the spelled gates of Kalinor Palace, but he had witnessed the sacking of Kalinor.

It was the night he'd met Tamara.

The laughter drifted closer, and Roux shivered again. He could feel the leshii's breath across on nape of his neck. He kept moving.

After a while, the leshii seemed to tire of the game and left him alone to plod and stumble through the darkness. Hours seemed to drift by, but he had no way of judging time.

The leshii appeared here and there, winged things covered in coarse dark hair watching him from the trees. Swallowed by the near-black of the Heart, Roux found the creatures deeply unsettling. Even in the sinking dimness, he knew that they cast no shadow.

He was dwelling on that unpleasant thought when his bare foot struck a jagged stone. Roux howled out a curse as a wave of pained nausea crested over him. He remained still for a moment, finally determining that he'd only broken a toe. He breathed a sigh of relief. Gods, but he wanted to Dart away from here, as far as bloody *possible*.

But Darting was thought to be impossible in the Heart. Without light to see, how could anyone Dart safely? It was the conventional wisdom of every Treedarter he'd ever known, but Roux knew better. He'd Darted across two hundred leagues, though it had nearly killed him.

But he couldn't escape this place until he had what he'd come for.

He kept walking, ignoring the splintering pain racing up his left leg every time he took a step. He was close. He *had* to be close. His next step landed on hard marble and Roux called out in triumph.

The Wyrmwell.

The Heart echoed his exuberance back at him in a menacing cacophony. Roux smiled in spite of himself. *These* were the true beasts of the Wood. Deadly to any but the chosen few. But he *was* chosen. He and Aleksei.

Roux stared into the endless darkness that expanded before him.

And then he began his descent.

Tamara screamed.

"What are you *doing*?" she demanded angrily.

Bael ignored her, tightening the restraints painfully around her wrists. He shifted the apparatus and secured her ankles.

"*Answer* me you little worm!" she shrieked.

The past few weeks had been uneventful for the most part. Tamara had attempted escape twice more, but she hadn't been able to use her hands quite as well since they'd torn off her fingernails.

That was when she'd lost her knife. She didn't remember dropping it, but shortly after she noticed its absence, she had been moved to a different room; one without windows and only guttering tallow lamps for light. She had no idea where her knife was now. It had been the most precious thing she'd ever been given, and now it was gone.

That one moment had been enough for her to stop caring whether they hurt her or not. Now her only goal was to escape, or die trying. Of course, that was becoming increasingly complicated.

The last few days had been filled not with monotony and silence, as she'd become accustomed to. Rather, she'd been frequented by more guests than she'd received in the whole of the interminable days since she'd been taken.

Darielle had only appeared once since they'd tortured her, but this visit had been less encouraging. The Prophet had refused to heal her again, saying that this time Tamara needed to learn her lesson.

And once Darielle had gone, there seemed no end to the *tests*.

Most of it made little or no sense to Tamara. She sat stiffly in a chair, her hands bound, while strange people watched her and jotted notes. This went on for hours with no seeming purpose or conclusion. And then, abruptly, she would be removed from her chair and thrust back into her cell.

That very morning, they had come for her again. And Tamara had been ready.

The first guard took the full force of the wooden stake to the gut. These men wore armor to protect their chests, leaving their bellies open, and she had taken full advantage of that. Once that stake was ripped from the first guard, she'd managed to club the second with the blunt end, doing little damage but still sending the man sprawling headfirst into the wall of her chamber.

But, as always, the second she placed a foot outside her cell the pain came, rendering her unconscious as it had time and time again. While she could fashion a number of weapons from her shoddy wooden bed and blankets, she could never escape the Archanium.

And now she was somewhere new.

There were windows this time, that much was welcome. From their crystal panes, Tamara could make out tall mountains dusted in snow. She craned her neck, trying to get a better idea of where she was. She saw *something* far below. She saw towers and turrets gleaming in the winter sun.

Her head fell back, her muscles aching. It was a world like none she'd ever known. Whatever lay beyond her prison, it wasn't something she could escape from. If she hadn't learned that lesson already, the impossibility of her circumstance was finally sinking home.

She was in a wilderness of foreign structures and forsaken lands.

She was lost; she prayed she hadn't been forgotten.

Bael finished tightening the last restraint, "Well, I see you've finally calmed down. I promise, Princess, that this is all in your best interest."

"She *does* possess quite a bit of spirit, doesn't she?"

Tamara jerked her head in the direction of the new voice. She made out a form of straight black hair and pale white skin. Tamara wasn't sure whether she was looking at a woman or a serpent.

Bael chuckled, "More than you know, my dear. She's maimed or killed more than her share of guards since we arrived."

The woman huffed, "But did you have to bring her all the way out *here*, Lord Bael? Everything is so *dusty*. I *do* hope all this is worth my efforts."

"As do I, Delira," Bael said with a snarl, "because if you fail me, I'll see you fare as well as your predecessors."

Tamara stiffened, waiting for the response, but none came. Rather than allay her fears, Tamara realized that the woman called Delira must be almost as terrified as she was.

"My apologies, Lord Bael, but it seems my notes on the procedure have been...stolen. However, the past few attempts have been successful enough, and as I engineered the process, I have high hopes."

Bael's rough laughter filled the room, "As long as your high hopes return the desired result, I doubt I'll have cause to complain. Now get to it."

The woman called Delira came fully into view, and Tamara realized that her estimation of a serpent hadn't been too far off. Delira's straight black hair flowed around her waifish white form. Her eyes echoed the darkness of her locks, but Tamara saw past the façade.

"So which sort of errand girl are *you*?" she asked tightly.

Delira paused, "I beg your pardon?"

Tamara managed a snarl of her own, "He has enough strumpets filling these desiccated halls. Which one are *you*? The *whore* or the *servant*?"

Delira's eyes filled with a sudden rage. Her hand moved so fast Tamara hardly saw it move before she felt the jaw-rattling blow across her face. Tamara grinned in response. "Is that the best you have to offer? His *other* whores were much more inventive. Which gutter did he pluck *you* from?"

The woman moved to strike her again.

"*Delira!*" Bael roared.

Tamara cursed herself. For a moment, she thought the woman might be of a mind to burn her from existence. Without her, Bael would have nothing to bargain with. Her mother, Roux, Aleksei, Jonas...they would all have to abandon saving her in favor of saving the realm.

Assuming they were *trying* to save her. Tamara cursed herself for the thought. These monsters were clearly getting to her if she thought that any of her loved ones would abandon her.

When Delira's face finally returned to its pale white, an unexpected smile graced the serpent's features. "Well, you *are* more spirited than I gave you credit for, Princess. Let's see if we can correct some of your more serious *flaws*."

Tamara screamed again.

She could feel the claws of the Archanium sinking into her, tearing at the very fiber of her soul. By the time she blacked out from the pain, Tamara was praying for the sweet embrace of death.

Jonas followed Ramla back down the ramp, pulling deeply on the Archanium and wrapping himself in its power.

"*That isn't necessary,*" Ramla said, giving him a disapproving glare.

Jonas arched a chestnut eyebrow, "*I'll be the judge of that,* especially *after everything you just put me through.*"

Ramla's face tightened, but Jonas met her black glare with his own. "*Then, if you* insist," she said curtly, "*try to be less obvious about what you're doing. You may have fulfilled prophecy, but you're still subject to the laws of my people. They don't like being pressed.*"

"*I'm not here to perform for you. I'm here because your people abducted me for a barbaric ritual. Your prophecy has been fulfilled. What more do you want with me?*"

"*You freed us from the shackles of an ancient magic. Now you must tell us what is to be done with our prisoners.*"

"*The Ul'Brek?*" Jonas asked, frowning.

"*The Nine,*" she corrected. "*We have held them captive since time began, waiting for you to free us. Now we are free. You must tell us what to do with them.*"

Jonas took a deep breath. The Presence was still there, in the back of his mind, banging against the door he had slammed shut when the Nine had fallen. If he gave in to his frustration and anger now, he risked letting it loose. And this time, the consequences could be cataclysmic.

"*Then get out of my way,*" he growled, pushing past her and stepping into the Pit.

The Ul'Brek were still there, but they had come to their feet. The bodies of the Nine were laid out around the redstone spire that rose from the Pit's center, each body laid across a panel of the nine-sided foundation.

One man walked forward and shook an angry finger in Jonas's face, "*You are the cause of our suffering, Demon.*"

Jonas caught hold of himself. For a split second, he had considered breaking the finger that was so coarsely pointing at him. But that would only delay them all the longer in this forsaken place.

He brushed the man aside and walked around the spire until he found the man who had named himself "Richter". The man now bore little trace of the twisted horn and bone that had constituted his entire body only minutes before.

He pressed a finger to the man's chest, releasing a flutter of the Archanium into him. Richter's golden eyes opened wide.

The Ul'Brek shouted angrily, but stood back, raining curses on both Jonas and Richter. Jonas turned angrily, "*Unless you want me to embrace the Demon again, get out.*" The men hesitated. "Now!" he roared in Ilyari.

His alien shout had the desired effect. The men turned and ran for the tunnel entrance, cursing him as they fled. Jonas took another breath, expelling his surging anger.

The implications of what was happening, of who this man promised to be, were so much more important than a few overzealous fanatics cursing him from their tiny island of ignorance and superstition.

Ramla stood a few paces away, observing him through her stony countenance. He supposed it was natural enough for her to dislike him. She had guided Aleksei through the ways of her people's prophecy. It was likely that she had been brought up to believe that particular events would happen in a specific order. In a way, he wasn't nearly so different from her as he'd originally supposed.

But things had changed. He was supposed to have died, at least according to her. Yet here he stood. He was supposed to have freed them, which he had, in a manner of speaking. Yet the Nine still drew breath.

And now he was supposed to tell these people, the ones who had captured and tortured him without any sign of remorse, how to live their lives; now that he had *destroyed* the one thing that bound them all together.

Jonas looked away from Ramla and found the man called Richter staring at him.

"*You touched the Demon?*" Richter asked incredulously.

"*I did,*" Jonas responded. "*And it did not consume me. My father was Angelic royalty, and the Archanium flows strongly through the veins of my mother's people. I believe that offered me a measure of protection.*"

"*You cannot think to have* mastered *it,*" Richter growled angrily, trying to push himself off his back.

Jonas placed a firm hand on the man's chest, "*Stay. Reserve your strength. These people are not your friends; they have merely kept watch over you.*"

Richter watched him carefully, "*And what are* you *called, Magus?*"

"*I am Jonas Belgi, a Prince of Ilyar. I released you from your curse.*"

Jonas winced at his clumsy use of the man's language, but he had never been taught how to speak it. It was primarily studied to understand texts, not hold conversations.

"*And you, Magus?*" Jonas asked, his eyes narrowing. "*You call yourself Richter. I know of one by your same name, but you cannot possibly be him.*"

Richter frowned, "*There may be many by my name. I can only be myself, Jonas, Prince of Ilyar. I am the Hunter.*"

Despite the intense heat in the Pit, Jonas felt a chill sweep through him. Whether or not this man was who he claimed to be, there were a *great* many problems with him lying there before Jonas. The most obvious being that this man would be well over a thousand years old.

"*You were the first Hunter, the first chosen by the Wood?*" Jonas whispered.

Richter's golden gaze grew deadly, "*There are no others. I am Her Hunter. Her champion.*"

"*Richter,*" Jonas began softly, "*what is the last thing you recall?*"

Richter's face grew haunted, "*Cassian, my love, lying within an arm's reach. Dying, even as the Seraphima was invoked to trap the Demon that possessed him.*"

Richter's voice broke, and Jonas was surprised to see a tear wind its way down Richter's cheek, tracing the white line of his scar. *"I thought I'd gotten him back, in the end, even for just the fraction of an instant."*

He turned his face away from Jonas's black-eyed gaze, *"But I was wrong. The man I loved was gone, consumed by the Demonic Presence. As it will consume you, in time."*

"I did not release the Presence back into this world. That crime was committed by another. He struck me down with the power of the Presence, tried to imprison me in its hell, as you were imprisoned. I carry its curse, but also its counter. When the Demon struck you down, did you enter that place of dust and pain? The harsh buzzing voices and the yellow-black sky?"

Richter nodded slowly, studying Jonas's face. Gods, but those eyes were so like Aleksei's.

"Richter, how much time passed after you were pulled into the Demonic Presence?"

Richter looked at him sharply, *"Time? There is no time there. But it felt like an eternity of pain. The pain they inflicted on my body was a tickle compared to the pain they brought me in that last moment with Cassian. Next to the agony of losing everything, losing him so completely, the torment my spirit endured was but a jape."*

Jonas nodded his agreement, *"I know a piece of what you speak. The pain makes time lose meaning. But now you're free of it. All of you are free of the Presence."*

Jonas managed a half-smile. This man would likely never see those closest to him again. Their bones would have long since turned to dust. The only love this man had known now lived in infamy as one of greatest monsters in history. He himself had passed into legend as both a hero and tyrant, savior and betrayer, Hunter and prey.

Richter watched Jonas's face carefully, *"And what sort of world have I awoken to find?"*

"One far worse."

CHAPTER 39

A BLIGHTED BLESSING

When Aleksei returned to the center of the village, Agriphon freshly watered and brushed down, he was surprised to find the Pit empty save Jonas and the Nine. Ramla was waiting for him at the Pit's edge.

"Your Magus is among them now. He demanded to be left alone," she said.

If Aleksei hadn't known better, he might have thought she was pouting. "You don't sound very happy with him," Aleksei said with an apologetic smile.

"He was supposed to free the Nine, and then instruct us on their fate, on *our* fate. Without the Nine, my people have no purpose. The prophecy foretold that he would provide us new purpose, but he hasn't. He's being stubborn."

Aleksei fought back a laugh. She thought Jonas was being stubborn? She hardly knew the half of it.

"Let me ask you a very fair question. Does your prophecy give you any sense of *when* he's supposed to do this?"

"Of course not. Prophecy does not dictate time, only that which must happen."

Aleksei shrugged, "Then you have your answer. If Jonas is indeed the man you think he is, then he will fulfill his role when the time is right. You don't want to rush this, do you? If your father taught you

453

about prophecy, then he probably taught you that it can be dangerous to expect the people involved to 'perform' the way you want or expect them to. I know you're still a child, but a little patience wouldn't be amiss about now."

He ignored her scowl. "Besides, I know him better than anyone alive, and I can tell you that whatever your people *think* is supposed to happen is of no interest to him. What you need to do now is give him the space to do what he has to do. Be patient."

Ramla stared at him for a long moment before looking away, "You sound like my father. And without him, the only thing I have left is the work he raised me to do. Once this is over, once you leave, what will there be for me here unless your Magus fulfills his duty to us?" She glanced back at him, and Aleksei thought he detected tears in her eyes.

Worse, he wasn't quite sure how to respond to that. This little girl acted so grown up at times that he had to remind himself of her youth.

Not only her youth, but her new-found desperation. Their arrival ended any and all certainty for her, and she was desperate for one of them to give her an answer. A future.

He breathed a sigh of relief when Jonas emerged from the Pit, gently supporting one of the Nine.

"Aleksei," Jonas said, panting at the exertion of supporting the much-larger man's weight in the heat, "this is Richter. *The* Richter."

Aleksei could only stare at Jonas, dumbfounded. When he'd first arrived in Kalinor, Jonas had given him a book, a biography of this man. Over time, Aleksei had come to idolize the hero.

The first Hunter, the first to bear the Mantle. It had never occurred to him that he might stand before the legend *himself* someday. When Richter had given his name in the Pit, it had never occurred to Aleksei that this man and the Hunter of legend could be one and the same.

Richter looked at Aleksei and his eyes widened. Aleksei found himself staring into a mirrored reflection of his own wild golden eyes once again. Richter took in Aleksei's arms, the writhing black of the Mantle, and his eyes narrowed.

Aleksei watched as Richter's hand moved tentatively forward, stroking the black tendrils on Aleksei's bicep. He ripped his hand back as a talon whipped away from Aleksei's flesh and clawed across his forearm.

Richter muttered something in his language. Jonas frowned as he listened.

"What?" Aleksei asked, now suddenly alarmed, "What did he say? Why is he *looking* at me like that?"

Jonas glanced at Aleksei, his eyes still dark and shadowed. Before he could translate, Richter grasped Aleksei's arm. Aleksei tensed, but the Mantle didn't lash out again. Instead, it stroked Richter's wrist, much as it had touched Jonas in the past.

Richter's gaze bored into Aleksei.

Aleksei found himself transfixed by the other man's eyes. The man said *something*, but Aleksei couldn't understand a word of it. When Aleksei blinked in confused silence, Jonas haltingly explained, "Richter was the first Hunter. But the Wood has obviously filled the void he left.

"I think he's having a hard time understanding how much time has passed. Seeing the Mantle, having the Mantle lash out at him like that...I think he's finally realizing that his world is gone. And now he's trapped in ours."

Richter was watching Jonas carefully, clearly trying to understand what he was saying. Aleksei felt something across the bond, something confusing. Jonas wasn't telling him everything. Richter looked past Aleksei, his eyes settling on the sword Aleksei wore. His face went white.

He looked into Aleksei's eyes, his own narrowing into shimmering slits. He said one short phrase, then turned and walked slowly back towards the Pit.

Aleksei stared at the retreating form, feeling as though he needed no translation. It wasn't difficult to hear hatred, to *smell* it. By virtue of his birth, Aleksei had taken everything from his own hero, and had earned the other man's enmity as payment.

Aleksei turned to Jonas, watching the uncertainty on Prince's face. "I think it's time to go."

Jonas nodded, "Let me get cleaned up and we can get out of here." He started towards Agriphon, his shoulders slumped.

"*Wait*," Ramla said angrily, "You have given us no new purpose, no instructions. What are we to *do*?"

Jonas turned to the small girl, "Whatever he may think of Aleksei, or me for that matter, Richter is an important man. Any of the Nine could be equally important. Nurse them to health. Take care of them. Bury your dead. And when they are strong, guide them from this place. I expect the world is very different from the one they inhabited. That is your purpose."

Aleksei watched Jonas walk towards Agriphon, his own spirits sinking. He'd never seen his Magus so dejected before.

We'll protect him, the Mantle hissed in his mind, *we'll feed, and we'll protect him. Always.*

"Always," Aleksei echoed softly.

As he descended into the Wyrmwell, Roux heard the sound of water dripping, the musty perfume of rella fungus, and something else.... Something new.

It was a rustling, *prickly* sound, like snakes slithering through dry leaves.

Roux descended the ancient stone stairway, being careful with his footing on the slick steps, breathing a relieved sigh when he reached the nadir.

The starlight that drifted through the canopy had long since been snuffed by the true black of the underground. This far down, he was alone amongst whispers of history and long lost echoes of a bygone age. After all, there was a reason no one ventured into the Wyrmwell. Those who tried seldom returned.

"They're still bloody *here,*" Roux muttered, striding confidently through the tunnel before him, the weight of past adventurers and Ri-Vhan alike pressing down upon him. His heart was pounding in his ears, but the Wood had sent him into this pit, and it was unlikely She would to send him into danger without warning.

That was not his role. That was for Aleksei to undertake, to risk life and limb battling Salamanders, no matter how small. A Salamander hatchling was nothing to laugh at, and Roux had been amazed when he'd heard the tale. But such was the duty of a Hunter, *not* the Ri-Hnon.

Thus, Roux walked resolutely forward, his golden eyes bright in the darkness. He could not so much see in the traditional sense as he was intimately aware of every pebble, every jagged break in the floor before him. The walls of the tunnel around him seemed to respire, drawing breath as he approached and breathing out as he passed. It was an eerie, unsettling experience.

To be raised Ri-Vhan was to live in insecurity. There was no guarantee of a long, happy life. There was *hope* for one. But the Wood could all too capriciously decide to end that if She chose.

Seeing his people for the first time in weeks, Roux had a feeling that the Wood had been taking more than Her fair share of late.

As he continued ever onward, ever *down*ward, Roux recalled the tale he'd been taught as a child. That the Ri-Vhan didn't truly die when they fell to the forest floor. That it was not a matter of mistake, but of sacrifice. He wasn't sure which fiction he preferred.

On the one hand, he led a community of people who traveled by basic rote teleportation, a form of travel they used almost as frequently as walking. The idea that some of them, sometimes quite accomplished, would miss their mark by so much *and* would be unable to recover in time to save themselves struck him as ridiculous. He'd certainly had his near-misses, as had they all, but never to the point of missing a jump by that *much*.

Yet the alternative was somehow deeply worse. That the Wood was sacrificing chosen Ri-Vhan for some ulterior purpose.

He would have to see how many men they had lost, compared to how many women. That alone would give some truth to the mythology.

In legend, the sacrificed women became a part of the Wood Herself, giving life to Her spirit, giving voice to Her words. More than anything, granting the goddess-like force of magic and nature that embodied the Wood true, nearly-human compassion.

After all, if such a faerie story were true, the Wood would be consuming feelings, *memories* of real Ri-Vhan women, memories of their loves, their children, their longings and desires, as much as their failures and disappointments.

If the Wood wanted to understand Her Children, what better way?

More puzzling still, the sacrificed men of the Ri-Vhan were not meant to educate or feed the Wood. Their lives, their deaths fed into something that was supposed to be far more important, far more serious than the Wood's compassion for Her Children.

Roux came up short as the tunnel ended and he stepped into a great atrium, the entire space illuminated in the blue glow of rella fungus. Just from a glance at the bizarrely intricate chandeliers of glowing blue, Roux had no doubt in his mind that all the rella fungus in the Wood originated from this single central position.

And there it stood before him. The reason his mother had explained why men were sometimes sacrificed. They strengthened it. Gave it a life of its own, a strength, bravery and ferocity imbued into inanimate stone.

The Chymrian Gate.

Roux realized he was shivering, staring at the enormous stone edifice, carved into the very living rock that supported the entirety of the Seil Wood. Etched into its facade were carvings he had seen depicted hundreds of times as a boy, and then as a man in the sacred texts entrusted to Ri-Hnon.

This time, the world-tree carved into the stone filled him with dread.

The branches of the tree were made up of twisting, writhing forms, tendrils that terminated in tridents, each prong a claw, undulating in an unseen wind.

It was the Mantle.

With a start, Roux realized that the queer rustling sound had grown in volume.

He turned his head just in time to see a thick, rope-like tendril of pure black whip towards him. He dove to the side, but the tendril wrapped around his ankle, sinking blood-red talons into his flesh.

He screamed.

"Where is my gown?" Lady Delira demanded in an agitated hiss.

"The cleaning staff promised that it would ready within the hour," Katherine said meekly, keeping her eyes on the floor. But even being as deferential as possible didn't spare her the harsh slap across her bruised face.

It had happened slowly over the past few weeks, but Delira was becoming increasingly abusive with every passing day. She had begun by belittling Katherine as often as possible, landing the occasional blow for good measure.

At the moment, Katherine was confident that almost every inch of skin covered by her uniform was black, purple, or yellow with repeated bruising.

Delira would lash out at her, sometimes with an open palm but more often with the Archanium. Before Katherine left, her face would be healed to hide the abuse from anyone who might squeal to Bael that Delira was growing more and more unhinged by the project he had her working on.

Katherine knew only basic things from the notes she had scanned, but the project sounded literally monstrous to her. The very idea of using the Archanium like that, tweaking the basic elements of what made someone human until the 'desired effect' was reached, made her sick to her stomach. And she had yet to even *witness* the fruits of their twisted labor.

She prayed that she would never *have* to.

"Apologies if I caused offense, milady," she responded stiffly. Another slap, this one significantly harder.

"Did I *ask* you to speak, you little piece of trash? *No!* Mind your manners or I'll flay you alive where you stand, am I *clear?*"

Katherine nodded, staring at the floor intently.

A third jaw-cracking slap, "*Answer* me, you stupid *bitch.*"

"I understand, milady," Katherine said woodenly, awaiting a fourth hit to land at any second. But Delira appeared to be finished with striking her for the moment.

"*Good.* Your new charge is here, so I'll fix your face one more time, and then you'll need to go attend her. Send another maid in to take care of all the things *you've* obviously forgotten to do."

Katherine curtseyed, "Yes, milady."

She turned and walked towards the door when a crippling pain wrapped around her body. She fell to the floor in an agonized heap.

"Did I dismiss you? No, I did *not.* I swear by the gods, the way you act, you might as well be queen of the bloody realm. How many times must I remind you of your station? Or are you simply too *stupid* to comprehend the simplest instructions?"

The pain continued for what seemed an eternity, each slow second dragging itself along, as though time was also afflicted. Finally, it abated to the point where she could stand.

"Now get over here so I can put your dog face back together. I'll not have you parade your punishment about, trying to garner sympathy."

Katherine came to her feet and walked dutifully back to Delira, standing as still as she could. In her mind, she had determined that if she didn't move during the healing it would hurt less. It was patently false, but she felt a bit better to be in control of even the smallest aspect of the ordeal her life had become.

Delira gripped her face, her long nails biting into Katherine bruises as she summoned the weakest glimmer of her various magics. The pain was nothing compared to the spell Delira had just unleashed upon her, but it left her even more sore and tender than the bruises.

The experience was mercifully short, though, and soon enough Delira was withdrawing her hand with a look that reminded Katherine of a contented cat that had just devoured a family of mice. "I suppose there's nothing magic can do to make you even the least bit *attractive*, but you don't look so ridiculous anymore. I'm satisfied. Now get out."

Katherine curtseyed and turned back to the door with trepidation. She kept expecting the hammer to fall, but it never came. She made it safely into the hallway. She took a moment to compose herself, taking deep breaths to calm herself down as much as possible. It didn't work, but she did it anyway.

Then, with severe determination, she made her way towards Declan's quarters.

Declan himself was sitting by the fire with a glass of brandy and a book. It probably looked very cozy, even charming to an outsider. Katherine felt the seed of resentment, and a little bit of hatred within her grow at seeing him enjoy himself while she had to put up with such hellish circumstances.

He smiled when he saw her, "Katherine! Gods, but it's been ages. How long has it been since we last met?"

"Three weeks and two days," she said automatically. Each day that passed was a reminder that she was hardly progressing their mission along while absorbing Delira's abuse all the while.

"Truly? I suppose time got away from me, what with all the bizarre reports we've been receiving of late. Three thousand troops killed to man in the Hills, and by *demons* of all things. Ridiculous nonsense if you ask me," he muttered to himself before seeming to remember that she was in the room. "And how are you doing? How's your part of the mission going?"

She pulled down the shoulder of her livery, exposing angry purple-yellow flesh, "This is what I look like all over. It's a miracle if I can walk into Delira's quarters without at least receiving a slap or two. At most she'll torture me with the Archanium for a few minutes, but I'm not sure how much longer that will satisfy her. It seems to be getting worse as the deadline for her project gets closer."

"Ah yes! The project. Have you found out anything else on that front?"

Katherine shook her head, "I know the premise, but that's all. I'll let you know if I find anything else out, but if I wind up dead in a gutter because I spoke out of turn, you'll be on your own."

Declan chuckled uncertainly, and she returned his levity with an icy stare, "That was *not* a joke. I only have so much time before she snaps and just stops my heart, or however these Magi kill people. She's growing increasingly unstable. I never know what she's going to do next."

"And any word on your new charge?" Declan asked leaning forward in his chair.

Katherine pointedly poured herself some of his Dalitian firebrandy and downed the glass in one scorching swallow. She poured herself another. "It's apparently a woman, but that's all I know. She's here, and Delira sent me to take care of her for the rest of the day, but at this point Simon, I just don't know that I can *do* it."

"But you *must*! This could be an *excellent* turn of events for us."

Katherine burst into tears, taking a slower sip of the firebrandy. "I just want to go *home*," she whimpered.

For the first time since she had arrived in his quarters, Declan responded appropriately. He patted her hand and refilled her glass, "I know you do, dearheart. I sympathize with the lot you've been given. I know it must be very difficult, but we've also been blessed with an important opportunity. I would hate to leave prematurely, especially without something concrete we can deliver to Aleksei. Surely you agree with that?"

Katherine drained her third glass and managed a nod. Her head was already starting to swim, "I wouldn't still be here if I didn't think it was important. But as of this moment, I'm letting you know that my remaining time here is limited. And based on the severity of Delira's attacks, I have a few weeks at the most. And then I'm leaving. I can't help Aleksei if I'm *dead*."

Declan thought for a long moment, "Well, then I suppose you'd better come up with something we can use in that time."

She stood, "I'll *work* on that, milord."

"Katherine...."

She turned and walked out without acknowledging him. If he was going to ignore her obvious pain and her pleas for his understanding, *she* was going to ignore him.

She walked back towards Delira's quarters. She stopped one of the other maids on the way and passed along Delira's instructions. And then she kept walking. Her head was definitely swimming now. She realized she was good and properly drunk.

Hardly the state she needed to be in to take care of her new charge.

She wandered the hallways and ended up at his door. If he was even in the Palace. It seemed that with the increase in Delira's abuse, Ethan had been increasingly unavailable. Like Declan, she hadn't seen him since Delira had become physically violent.

She didn't bother to knock, pushing her way into his quarters. The door opened easily enough.

He was home.

And then he was in front of her, big and *so* handsome. He wore a ready smile, but it faded when he looked at her face. "You've been healed. Poorly, but I can tell. Why would you need to be *healed?*"

Katherine let her tears flow free again, knowing that an actual display of her misery would be more effective than explaining it. He took her into his powerful arms and planted a kiss in her hair.

"Tell me what's going on," he said softly, leading her to a chair by the fire.

She repeated everything she'd told Declan, except this time Ethan had a visible reaction to her story. By the time she had caught him up, his face was a mask of rage. He looked murderous.

"What can I do for you right *now?*" he asked gently, taking her hands in his. Her hands looked so fragile and delicate in his large, calloused paws.

She started to cry again. It had been so long since anyone had expressed *any* interest in her wellbeing that it took her a moment to respond. She had to think about herself on an immediate level, and she had done so little of that, spent so little time taking *any* care of herself that she'd almost forgotten how.

"Can you heal?" she asked, hoping he was better than Delira.

Ethan nodded, "It's not my strongest suit, but I'm far more able than many of the Magi who follow my same meridian through the Archanium.

"It's been theorized that personality has some impact on which talents each of us possesses. It would explain Delira's cruelty. Her lack of compassion would certainly explain her inability in the art of healing. Though I suppose that would be true of nearly *every* Magus who follows Lord Bael."

Katherine blushed at the thought of what she was about to ask. But if he could even scratch the surface of the pain she was in, she just might be able to stand staying in the Palace for a little while longer.

"My whole body is covered in bruises and welts," she admitted. "If you heal even just my back or my feet, I would be forever grateful."

Ethan offered her a sympathetic smile, "I think I can do a fair sight better than that. Come over here." He helped her to her feet, and she allowed him to use his immense strength to support her. She needed as much help as she could get at the moment.

Ethan led her to his bed. Despite her present state, Katherine was a touch surprised. Her surprise mounted when he sheepishly said, "Alright, first we need to get you out of that dress. I can't do anything if I can't *see* your injuries."

Katherine turned and allowed him to unbutton her dress. He gently slid the dress off her shoulders, letting it fall in an undignified heap on the floor. He proceeded to do the same with her stays and her shift, leaving her standing naked, her face flushed.

"Great gods," he muttered, "what has that woman done to you? This is going to take some time. Fortunately, I have all the time in the world at the moment. Now get into bed and we'll begin."

Katherine steeled herself and turned to face him. Her face was flushed with embarrassment, but if his spells worked, it was worth feeling ashamed and self-conscious for a few hours.

He leaned forward and gave her a long, slow kiss. "Even when you're bruised all over, you're still indescribably beautiful."

She clung to those words as she slid onto the bed. Ethan came around the other side and climbed next to her. Much to her surprise, he had stripped to his small-clothes. He lay on the bed, practically naked, his muscles clearly defined and covered with thick, light brown hair. He really *was* a beautiful specimen, and despite her initial reaction, she found that his near-nudity put her more at ease.

"Turnabout is fair play," he said, his voice thick with humor. He leaned forward and kissed her again. As he did, Katherine could feel the euphoria of proper healing wind its way through her. That in and of itself was such a relief that the tears returned unbidden.

"It's alright," he whispered, "You're safe. You don't have to hide your feelings. And I'm going to do everything I can to make you feel better, alright?"

She managed a small smile, "Alright."

He kissed her again, longer this time, and Katherine wondered if there was any better feeling. By the time the sun rose, shining through the windows of his chambers, Katherine had learned decidedly that there were indeed better feelings. *Immensely* better feelings.

Rise, *Warden. You have reached the Qoorenmir.*

Roux's eyes snapped open.

He wasn't certain how much time had passed, and there was no sky to tell him. His mouth was dry. He tried to lift his arm but found that he had no strength. His body refused to respond to his commands.

Rise, Warden. You are a breath from failure.

The voice rumbled through him to his core, gripping his heart in icy claws. He felt Her displeasure. Her condemnation.

Roux looked helplessly around the great chamber, his mind trying to process what was happening in the soft blue light of the rella fungus.

The prominence of the Chymrian Gate was ten paces away, solid and sealed just as it had been since the dawn of time.

Before him rose the Qoorenmir, the world-pillar, the root that fed the entire Seil Wood and burrowed through the very core of their world. He had seen it depicted countless times, but never like *this.*

The root's white flesh gave off a faint, throbbing glow. But corrupting the pulsating ivory pillar, winding its way through the core of the root itself, was a midnight morass, moving like liquid, rippling and roiling as it splashed across the skin of the Qoorenmir.

The Blight.

Its black briars were buried in his wrists and ankles, rings of red light slithering up the thorns and across the inky tendrils as they fed on him. He didn't know how long he'd been unconscious in this underground hall. How long it had *feasted* on him.

Amidst the pain thundering in his head, a shining bolt of clarity broke through. He was going to die. He was going to die down here like all the others, and he would never see Tamara again. She was lost to him, to everyone, and it was all his fault. He had failed her.

But with that thought came a rage unlike anything Roux had ever known. He felt blood pump through him, bitter blood that forced the black tendrils to recoil in disgust as he gathered a new kind of strength.

Rise, Warden. the Wood cooed in his mind.

He struggled to his feet, haltingly managing to stand. The Blight roared forth, splashing across his chest and piercing him. He screamed, barely remaining upright as it tore through the very fiber of his being.

He could feel the depth of its corruption as it tainted his very soul.

The Blight surged, hurling him back as it released him.

Roux crashed to the floor, skidding painfully across the rough stone. He panted in the darkness, trying desperately to catch his breath. His broken toe throbbed, but not nearly as painfully as his chest.

His head was swimming as he fought back to his feet.

Roux tried to ignore the other pains, the skin of his shoulder, rubbed raw nearly to the bone by his landing, the broken toe, the hellish infection burning at the core of his being.

You have done well, *Warden.* The booming voice of the Wood nearly knocked Roux to his knees. *Escape the den and return to Me. If you survive, I will grant your request.*

He wearily made his way back through the tunnel to the Wyrmwell's stairway.

Now climb.

Roux glanced at the ancient, spiraling stairs and shuddered. The climb would be arduous at best. Still, he struggled towards the steps, gasping in pain the whole way.

You please *Me, Warden.*

Roux nearly wept at the statement. As a younger man, as the new Ri-Hnon, he would have been flattered beyond belief. But to receive a benediction from this new, disturbed creature was more cause for concern than joy.

He fixed an image of Tamara tightly in his mind to bolster him when his courage faltered as he ascended. Slowly, laboriously, he made his way up the spiral towards the cold starlight.

He lost track of time, but after minutes or hours, he collapsed onto the indifferent marble stones of the Wyrmwell. Such vulnerability was deadly this deep in the Heart of the Wood, yet Roux had lost the energy to care. He had done as the Wood requested, had performed according to Her expectations.

That *thing,* the Blight beneath the Heart of the Wood, was part of his cousin? Was bonded to his *flesh*? Roux couldn't fathom a world where being possessed by such a vile entity would do *any*thing except ultimately corrupt any and everything it touched.

Carry this to My Brother Wood, Warden. Wake Him from His slumber, and confer My gift. My blessing.

Roux opened his mouth to thank Her, but his exhaustion got the better of him. As he slipped out of consciousness, he had the distinct impression that the very world around him was changing. *Shifting.* At the very least he knew where he was headed.

Finally.

CHAPTER 40

THE CLAWS OF CORRUPTION

Jonas woke to a cry in the oppressive night.

He twisted in their bedroll, feeling Aleksei's entire body contract, feeling him *seize*. He gripped his Knight's arms, shaking him urgently.

"*Aleksei!*" he shouted, suddenly disinterested in the danger of raising his voice, isolated as they were in the middle of the wastes.

Aleksei's eyes were fluttering, and from the familiar magic that rippling through the Hunter and into Jonas's hands, the Magus recognized the distinct presence of the Seil Wood.

But this felt as alien as it did familiar.

Jonas realized that he *understood* the alien feeling. It was still new. Still fresh, but the Wood magic pulsing through his Hunter felt wholly Demonic.

This time, however, he kept himself secure in the bond, kept himself from being pulled in to Aleksei's vision. Instead, he sent his own magic into the Knight, seeking to counter the Wood's hold over the man.

She bore a powerful presence inside Aleksei, but given their distance from Her, Jonas thought he might be stronger. As he pushed, bearing down on the bond, building pressure to disrupt Her hold, he saw flashes of the images consuming Aleksei.

Roux screaming. Something black, as black as the Mantle, burrowing through a great white root. A massive stone door with an intricate tree carved into its surface. A world-tree. But from its branches, the carving appeared to be less of a tree and more like the Mantle itself, talons extending where the leaves ought to be.

The pressure of his magic built, and in his desperation, Jonas felt the intensity of the Seraphima surge within him. He released it, allowing it to burst through, prying the Wood's stranglehold from his Knight. Even as he fell against Aleksei, gripping the other man tight in his arms, his formidable Hunter shook and convulsed.

The convulsions dissolved into wracking sobs, and Jonas held Aleksei for what felt like hours. He whispered lovingly in the other man's ear, reassuring him that everything was alright.

He tried to wake Aleksei again, only to find him staring blankly ahead.

"Aleksei! Do you know where you are?"

"Huh...." Aleksei breathed.

"Where *are* you?" Jonas begged again.

Aleksei's eyes met his own, and Jonas felt the distinct impression that Aleksei was searching for the words. But something was blocking his mind from connecting to his body, keeping him from fully waking.

"Who am I?" Jonas asked firmly, fixing Aleksei's golden gaze with his emerald eyes.

Aleksei's brow knitted, staring up at him. "J...Jo...*Jonas*?" Tears sprang to the prince's eyes at hearing Aleksei's difficulty forming his name.

"And where *are* you?" he whimpered.

"Huh...ho...home?" Aleksei managed, a hand absently brushing Jonas's tear-stained face.

Jonas dissolved against his Knight, the terror and uncertainty crashing through Aleksei cresting over him through their newly-reforged bond.

He hugged Aleksei tight, tears pouring from his eyes as he held the most precious thing in his world to him, kissing his Hunter's golden hair, whispering, "That's right, darling, you're *home*."

All the while, Richter's parting words to Aleksei ricocheted in his mind.

"*You broke the truce, Brother. When Her sickness grows too strong, find me.*"

Roux cried out in shock as he plummeted into ice-cold water. The force of his traveling must have been intense indeed, because even as he fought his way to the top of the crystal-clear water, he realized that he had to be at least ten paces beneath the surface.

If indeed there *was* a surface. With the way the Wood had been behaving of late, he wouldn't have been all that surprised to find that She had 'misplaced' him in the Autumn Sea, and chosen another Ri-Hnon in his absence. Perhaps he was still *in* the Seil Wood, and She had simply transported him somewhere out of the way, where he would drown quietly.

He felt instant relief when he broke the water's surface, gasping in fresh forest air. Still, his trepidation grew with every passing stroke of his arms.

Roux finally spotted sunlight streaming in from the outside, and set out for it, trying to gain his bearings as he swam. The chamber was massive, gilded carvings arching up the ceiling far above.

The ceiling itself was strangely barren, revealing only earth and vines. The walkway surrounding the cave pool was ornamented with friezes and murals of shocking beauty.

By the time Roux reached the edge of the pool, he was exhausted. Still, it had been less of a trial than enduring the corruption of the Blight.

The Wood called that a *gift*?

Plunging him into a giant pool of freezing water hadn't exactly been the kindest thing She had done for him, either. But then again, neither was sending him down into the Wyrmwell as Her experimental sacrifice.

He prayed to the Woods and the gods that Brother Relvyn would treat him kinder.

He stood and pressed as much of the water from his clothing as he could, ignoring the vague discomfort of dampness. One of the few advantages to being born Ri-Vhan was his natural affinity for the elements. Dampness didn't bother him much.

With the exceptions of life-threatening cold or heat, he and his people both were comfortable in most natural circumstances. And as Seil Wood was nearly the same temperature every day, locked in endless spring, there was little they had to worry about in terms of temperature extremes.

Roux took mental note to remember as many of the friezes and frescos as he could. He promised himself that once this was all over, he would bring Jonas and Aleksei here, *any*one who might be able to help him decipher the ancient artwork.

He knew there was no doubt in Jonas's mind that the Ri-Vhan and the current order of Magi had been spawned from the same movement against the Kholodym. That they were branches off the same root.

Roux had his own concerns with that idea, especially when it came to the history and identity of his people. But he couldn't just disallow his cousin's consort because he didn't like the questions the Magus presented.

Finally, he climbed up the rudimentary stairwell and came out into the filtered daylight, clambering from a cylinder of stone that most closely resembled an Ilyari wishing well.

He wandered the Wood for a while, listening, and seeking signs of life. After an hour, he smelled wood smoke and headed straight for it.

Roux stepped onto a crude path directly in front of an elderly man. The man froze, his rheumy eyes wide at Roux's sudden appearance. Finally, he greeted him with a toothless smile.

Roux took in the man's unkempt appearance, the reek of his unwashed flesh. He had clearly been living in the Relvyn Wood, but poorly.

"What are you doing here?" Roux asked softly.

The man shrugged, "Ever since the destruction of Drava, lots of us folks have run into the Wood. The Relvyn Wood has supplied us with many good harvests, and now He's caring for us in our time of need.

"It ain't a perfect way o'doing things, but it's worked for us. Ri-Sul, we started callin' ourselves. We know about you Ri-Vhan to the north, and we ain't got no claim on the thousand years you've got on us, but we wanna be *like* you. To help you too, if we can."

"And what do you ask of the Ri-Vhan in return for your 'help'?" Roux asked wearily.

"Oh, you know, all sorts of stuff. How your township *works*, for instance. Do y'all have a mayor or council or—"

"A Ri-Hnon," Roux said, "who can really be any individual, even occasionally very young. The Ri-Hnon is not elected by general consensus or affability, and it doesn't matter who your family is. They lead as long as they live. The moment a Ri-Hnon passes to join the Mother Wood or bolster the Chymrian Gate, a new one is Chosen that same moment."

"And where were *you* when you was the last one chosen?" the man asked cautiously, no doubt noting the authority in Roux's voice, the particular inflections he placed on words like *gate* and *wood*.

"In the arms of a very beautiful woman, if you must know," Roux replied with a wry smile, genuinely surprised by how perceptive the man was. "One never forgets an...intrusion like that. I knew exactly what was happening, and yet I was absolutely terrified."

The little color left in the man's face whispered away, as he seemed to realize who he was speaking to. "Begging your pardon, Ri-Hnon, your grace...er, Sir! How may I serve you?"

Roux had only recently become acquainted with Ilyari custom, first when Aleksei's people had taken brief shelter in his village, then of course during the weeks he'd spent with Andariana. And, most importantly, on the road to Taumon with Tamara. For everything he had shown Tamara about hunting, fighting, and killing, she'd returned that favor and more by instructing him in the ways of Ilyari culture and authority. He'd found every subsequent conversation more confusing than the last, but it was those very lessons that had allowed him to gain Andariana's trust to begin with.

The memory of Tamara's face was a jagged thorn into his heart, far darker than even the Blight that lurked beneath the Wyrmwell.

The Ri-Hnon smiled ruefully, pushing past the memory. He was not here to make this man his friend. He was here to rescue Tamara from Bael and the rebellion. "I have a very important question. Two, actually."

"Ask away!" the man said jovially, his knees shaking.

"How many of you are willing to die?"

As far as Roux was concerned, the only use these people could be to him were as fighters. It was a grim thought.

"Die? Well, sir, plenty of us died when the dead came alive in the forests. It were a horrible thing, it was!"

Roux took a deep breath before answering, "Is there someone else I might speak to? Perhaps your leader?"

The old man nodded, becoming less and less intimidated as Roux's easy manner calmed him.

He led Roux through the mess of primitive signs and poorly-cut pathways that led deeper into the Wood, while somehow running roughshod over natural game trails, missing obvious gathering sites completely.

He saw yuselk growing in the wild, and was sorely tempted to harvest it right then and there, just for the opportunity.

But as long as it was alive and thriving, it wasn't being used by these...*children*. Or worse, wasted.

The people had erected tents of canvas or leather. His nose had alerted him to the presence of uncured hide a league back, but it had hardly registered at the time. Now he realized the hide wasn't cured because these people didn't know *how*.

"Where's your tanner? Your woodsmen? Your hunters?" Surely such people would know better. The woodsmen would certainly have known better than to build the small village in a clearing without the protection of the trees.

"Died. Lots and lots died," the man muttered, looking away pathetically.

Roux sniffed at the air and, beyond the stinking hides, he could make out the scent of fresh-cut timber. Horror blossomed across his face as he realized that these people hadn't built their village in a glade; they had leveled the glade to build a *village*.

Roux reached a larger tent, and the elderly man stepped back. "Sorry, Sir. This is far as they let ones like me go. His lordship Erron Conrad should be just inside."

For the first time in weeks, Roux thought he might actually manage a chuckle. He ducked under a flap of stinking hide to see an average-looking Ilyari man flanked by two poorly-armored soldiers, each armed with crossbows and swords. He recognized the metal in the weapons, if not the designs. Aleksei had weapons like these.

"Who or *what* are you?" the man in the armchair asked, sounding bored and sipping a glass of brackish wine.

"What are you?" Roux asked in honest confusion.

"A wildling *and* impertinent?" Conrad demanded, banging his glass on the table and sloshing thin red liquid across his filthy cuff. "I'll not have it!" None of the men in the tent appeared to have bathed in days. Excepting Roux, he thought with a sardonic inner smile.

"Wildling?" Roux asked, arching an eyebrow, "What kinds of people have you encountered in this Wood beyond yourselves?"

"And now he asks *questions* too?" howled the man in the chair.

Roux stared the man down, "My name is Roux Devaan. I am the Ri-Hnon of Seil Wood. My cousin is Aleksei Drago, the Lord Captain of Her Majesty's Legion. He has filled me in on the particulars of when the dead walked in Drava; I believe you'll recall him as the man with the *scythe*.

"Lord Captain Drago is the master of this Wood, as he is a master of Seil Wood. He's the Bonded Knight and Royal Consort to Prince Jonas Belgi. In his name, I *demand* to know what is going on here. Who gave you the right to cut down this glade?"

The man stared at Roux woodenly before giving a great belly laugh, "Boy, you've been reading too many stories, or drinking too much ale. Aleksei Drago is either dead or about to be, and even if he isn't, he's never coming back *here*.

"Sure, back in Drava he saved us, then *doomed* us just before Perron's army showed up and gutted the village whole. They took our food, our winter supplies, they took *everything*. Even our animals and some of the younger girls. It was a betrayal, it was!"

Roux restrained himself. Something was deeply wrong with this place. It felt *rancid*.

Roux stood there, his blood boiling. "How many did you lose?"

"Girls or goats?" Conrad said with another chuckle.

Roux Darted, and in an instant he had his knife against the other man's throat.

"I think we might have a problem," he growled into the trembling man's ear. Above the stale smell of sweat, the stinking of the hides, and the raw lumber outside, he could still pick out the reek of fresh urine.

For the first time in weeks, Roux smiled.

"Gods, what is that *smell*?"

Jonas took a deep breath and almost choked. "It's the off breeze from the spice markets, mixed with unwashed flesh and rotting meat. It's the smell of too many people and animals packed into the same place."

Aleksei arched a golden eyebrow, "No, this smell is all too familiar."

Jonas shrugged, "You're the Hunter, I'm sure you'll figure it out."

"It's shit." Aleksei announced.

Jonas winced, "Well, it might be, but *try* not to shout it too loud?"

Aleksei smirked at him, "Most of these people don't speak our language, and if I've learned anything from you about Fanja culture, it's that the people who *could* understand me would never have entered by this gate. Am I wrong?"

Jonas managed a weak smile, feeling both a sting at the slight rebuff and triumph at the compliment, "Nobles and scholars don't typically enter the city at this....cultural level. Je'gud is easily one of the most educated cities in the known world, but every city, no matter how rich or enlightened, has slums."

"But it's also not without its charms. This *is* the City of Clouds. You can see why."

Even Aleksei would have to acknowledge the stunning architecture of the city, with its monolithic spires and minarets, each filigreed, adorned in bright colors and daring embellishments. Standing on a cliff hundreds of paces above the Sea of Spires, Je'gud was one of the marvels of the known world, and a place Jonas had long wanted to visit.

"Some of the most beautiful flowers are also the deadliest," Aleksei mused as he watched people scatter before Agriphon's majesty and the foreign men riding him.

Aleksei tensed, and Jonas realized that his Knight had spotted the reason the air reeked of human excrement.

Jonas glanced up at his handsome Hunter to find the larger man's attention fixated on a platform several hundred paces away. "What's that?" the Knight demanded sharply. "That's where this stink is coming from."

Jonas sighed inwardly, though he already knew the answer. In the distance he could make out a platform packed with people chained together. Slaves.

The same sort of nomads who had captured him were auctioning off their "wares". And Jonas knew immediately that Aleksei had picked up on the distinctive smell of fresh, hot human leavings, shoved into fly-ridden piles next to the platform.

Before Jonas could say a word, Aleksei was steering Agriphon straight towards the slave platform. Jonas gripped Aleksei's arm as though clinging to the last stone before plunging over a waterfall. "Aleksei," he said in a soft, measured tone, "where are you going?"

Aleksei turned a golden glare at him that almost made Jonas shrink back, "I'm going to put a stop to this."

Jonas's fingers dug deep into Aleksei's arm. The Mantle licked at his fingers, thread-thin crimson talons that communicated affection, but also danger. He was coming very near to crossing a line that the Mantle would not abide.

"You *can't*," Jonas hissed into his Knight's ear.

Aleksei twisted in the saddle, his glare now murderous, "These people are *monsters*. And I have the power to stop them."

Jonas stood his ground, pulling back on Aleksei's formidable muscles, "No, you *don't*. Not like this." Aleksei opened his mouth to counter his Magus, but Jonas bulled ahead, "If you attack these men, more will come. The slaves you free will merely be taken by the crowd. They will be forced into far harsher labor than if they are paid for, because they will have no *value*.

"You will die, I will die, and nothing will change. You'll only have served to make a few miserable lives that much worse.

"Your heart is in the right place. You have the heart of a lion, but it *must* be tempered. That's what I'm here for. I could speak to the people in charge of the markets. I might be able to convince the ruler of this province to end the slave trade in the region.

"But even if I do, it will only create a black market that will end in the same result as you charging in right now, except more will suffer and we'll live. Especially since the moment we're gone, that same ruler will begin taking half the money from that same black market.

"That is how this *works*, Aleksei. This is a culture foreign to you. *I* understand it, at least to a degree. I speak the language, but I know far more than just words. I understand these people as well as any foreigner can.

"And right now, that is our most powerful weapon. So, before you go charging off without thinking, remember that there is a time for all things. At this time, I am the more effective weapon. You are a brilliant strategist. Use your arsenal, but use it *wisely*."

Aleksei stared into Jonas's eyes for a long moment, but Jonas could see the heat slowly seep from him. "I still don't like it. It's wrong to treat people like this."

"I didn't say I liked it," Jonas muttered. "I merely explained the reality of our situation. This isn't Ilyar, and it's not our place to enforce *our* cultural mores onto these people, even when we disagree with them."

Aleksei was still extremely tense, but he turned Agriphon back towards the main market road, leading them out of the poorest part of the city. Jonas breathed a sigh of relief, but his inner panic was slower to subside. If he'd needed any proof that a worrying change had come over his Knight, this outburst was the worst sort of confirmation.

The Aleksei he knew so well, and loved so deeply, would never have attempted such recklessness. It didn't fill him with confidence for whatever was to come.

"I can hear her heartbeat, even over this ridiculous commotion," Aleksei declared after half an hour of riding in silence. "It's constant. Like a drum throbbing in my skull. We're close."

Jonas scanned the crowd churning around them. The fact that Aleksei could isolate anything at all was remarkable in and of itself. The market teemed with people haggling over small wares. Children ran carelessly among the mule carts, nimbly navigating the general bustle.

It looked like complete and utter chaos, and yet there was an unspoken rhythm to the market.

He knew that he and Aleksei stood out sharply amongst the locals. They were hardly the only Ilyari or Dalitians in the market based on clothing alone, but Jonas knew it was entirely obvious they were new to the city.

At least Aleksei's sleeveless tunic had turned his arms a burnished bronze. The openness of the vest, too, left little to the imagination, and Jonas was unsure what else one would want to imagine about Aleksei Drago that wasn't already on display.

He was hardened through work and battle, but oddly unscarred. He moved with the grace of an acrobat, yet Jonas had often seen him heft hay with the rough mechanics more befitting his past life. Jonas had seen Aleksei dispatch men with those same rough mechanics, and the same cool intensity.

It was unsettling to say the least.

But in all things Aleksei did, he was dedicated. If it was worth the work, it was worth doing properly.

The Mantle writhed in the presence of such delicious innocence and lifeblood on full display. It screamed a silent warning, like a viper waiting to strike, that even Jonas could sense.

Danger. Do not approach. So far, the only people who seemed oblivious to it were the children.

As Aleksei guided Agriphon through the city, homing ever more towards the beat of Tamara's heart, Jonas became increasingly nervous. "We're heading towards the Ul'Faa. Basically the Basilica of the Ul'Brek," Jonas warned.

"And?" Aleksei snarled.

Their experiences with the Ul'Brek had been less than pleasant, true, but Jonas didn't want to *think* what an encounter with the Ul'Brek elemental Scions might look like.

"We might want to see what the local governor has to offer," the Prince offered. "If he could help us gain access to Tamara, it would be well worth the delay."

"I'm tired of waiting," Aleksei growled.

"You've crossed the wastes of Fanj. Another day isn't likely to change much, is it?"

"It's a risk I'd just as soon avoid," Aleksei muttered, turning Agriphon away from the towering silhouette of the Ul'Faa in the distance; towards the great palace dominating the city center.

As he rode away, Aleksei glanced back at the temples and ziggurats of the Ul'Faa. There was the heartbeat, but something else too. Something sinister. Something that could touch the Mantle.

Something the Mantle *feared*.

The entirety of the palatial compound radiated Wood magic. But just as the shield over the Undercroft had possessed Wood magic that felt entirely different from the magic of a living Wood, so too did this magic feel strange and disquieting. Not like the shield exactly, but also nothing like what he'd experienced in Seil or Relvyn.

They rode through progressively wealthier districts of Je'gud, Aleksei doing his best to ignore the juxtaposition of exquisitely beautiful estates and luxurious sedan chairs all clearly operated by slaves, though at least these slaves looked well-fed and cared for.

Jonas reached his arms around his Knight, but there was nothing he could do to protect Aleksei from the reality that was Je'gud, that was *Fanj*; accepting unpleasant realities was the nature of being an Archanium Knight.

Of being *Jonas's* Archanium Knight.

The palaces were staggering in their beauty, as the slums had been shocking in their deep and abiding neglect and rot. Aleksei tried to focus solely on reaching the governor's palace.

Jonas said the population of Je'gud was estimated at around ten million people, a number Aleksei had difficulty even grasping. He disliked being surrounded by all the people living in Kalinor, but that seemed quaint compared to the sheer mass of people inhabiting Je'gud.

Riding through a city with a population five times the entirety of Dalita made his head swim.

When they finally reached the grounds of the governor's resplendent citadel, Aleksei felt ready to retch.

Jonas leaned back in the saddle and gazed into his Knight's face. "Talk to me. How are you feeling?"

Aleksei swung out of the saddle and cleared the two swords he now carried; his bastard sword, the same simple soldier's blade he'd carried at his hip since being promoted to the station of Lord Captain of Her Majesty's Legion, and strapped to his back, the corroded blade that had been lying in wait for him for centuries.

The unnamed blade tied to Ramla's village, awaiting a Hunter wielding the Mantle, arriving with his Demonic Magus to free the beasts of the Pit.

The Mantle filled the channels of the blade, but the very *idea* of the sword filled Aleksei with a unique sense of loathing.

"*Angry.* I want to be away from this place as fast as possible," Aleksei growled, radiating his disgust through the bond.

A groom stepped forward and bowed as he took Agriphon's reins. "*This is a beautiful horse. May I tell the chancellor whom is arriving?*"

Jonas thought for a moment on how best to announce them. "*Inform His Highness, Sabra rem Darshak Rai that Jonas Belgi, Crown Prince of Ilyar, is seeking an audience. Prince Belgi is attended by his Archanium Knight, the Ri-Vhan Hunter Aleksei Drago, Bearer of the Mantle. The Hunter will remain with the beasts.*"

His command rang clear enough across the bond. *Stay here. I'll translate for you, so listen through me, and wait for my instructions. Do not act until I give you permission. Act as an animal, that's what they're expecting.*

The groom chuckled at Jonas's pronouncement of station until he saw the gold piece between Jonas's fingertips. Even as the groom pocketed it, Jonas opened one of Agriphon's saddlebags and withdrew a ring, golden ram horns encircling a large, flawless emerald, and a thin gold circlet. He slid the ring onto his left hand, setting the circlet firmly on his brow.

While his official circlet held a single hexagonal emerald which matched his eyes perfectly, the thin ring of unadorned gold still accomplished what it needed to.

The groom disappeared, and for a long moment Jonas feared that the man wouldn't believe him. He was not looking forward to having to fight their way out of here, as if that were even possible. But then the chancellor appeared, wearing robes of azure and sun-colored silk. He bowed deeply to Jonas, then nodded to Aleksei.

"If you will follow me, Prince Belgi, His Highness will see you promptly," he said, bowing again to Jonas.

Heel. Jonas ordered across the bond, as Aleksei stepped up to follow them.

"You're going to have to get me a crown or something so they don't look at me like that," Aleksei called.

To Aleksei's surprise, the chancellor turned at his comment, responding in Ilyari. "The Mantle you bear is worth more than a thousand crowns, Master Hunter. You carry a very old magic. Few can boast of the sacred power afforded you.

"If you please, wait here while your prince is occupied."

Jonas cast his Knight a meaningful glance. It was met by Aleksei's obvious consternation, but he remained with Agriphon.

Jonas followed the chancellor through a labyrinth of twists and turns before he stepped into the opulence of the throne room. For the first time in his life, Jonas was beholding splendor exceeding the Basilica and the Voralla combined. The gold and silver-embroidered silk draperies alone were priceless.

But Jonas had been surrounded by luxury his entire life, and his eyes quickly slid past the finery, resting on the man occupying the throne, carved from ivory and jade, inlaid with flawless turquoise and intensely-indigo lapis.

He approached, noting the guards on either side. To his surprise, beside each guard was a leashed tiger. The great cats snarled at him as he stepped forward.

"Your Highness," Jonas said with a deep bow. *"I've sought an audience with the sincerest hope that you might help locate a relative of mine in the city."*

Sabra frowned, *"A Belgi? In the city? Who of your blood would have sought the refuge of Je'gud, if I might be so bold?"*

Jonas bowed his head, *"My cousin and heir to the throne, Princess Tamara. I actually believe her to be housed in the Ul'Faa."*

478

Sabra tensed at that, as did his guards. Jonas stayed exactly where he was, acting as though he'd said nothing incendiary. Sabra might believe himself to have the upper hand, but then he'd never encountered Jonas Belgi before.

Keep listening. he insisted across the bond. *They could silence me at any moment, but listen and hopefully you'll understand.*

I don't like this. Aleksei's angry echo came back.

You're going to have to trust me. But be ready. We'll only get this chance once.

"Prince Belgi," Sabra said in Ilyari, surprising the Magus, "know that if you press this issue, you will likely be immediately taken to the Ul'Faa to...encounter the elemental Scions. The Ul'Brek are most sensitive about anything regarding their business."

Jonas bowed his head, "I sincerely thank you for the warning, Your Highness. But I'm afraid I have no choice to press this issue, as you put it."

Sabra's face shifted from warmth to regret. *"I am aware, Prince Belgi, of an Ilyari captive within the Ul'Faa, but must express that I am most surprised that you would come here and question me about such matters. Are such inquiries not better taken to the Ul'Faa itself?"*

Jonas bowed deeper this time, playing along, *"I apologize if I am breaking with decorum, Highness. It seemed most prudent to come to you first, before beseeching the Ul'Brek themselves, as I know of their history with outlanders."*

Sabra studied him for a long moment before he burst out laughing, *"Well, you are a brave man for requesting aid from a man such as myself. The Ul'Brek hardly deign to tell someone of my import about their inner goings on."*

Jonas withheld a smile.

"So indeed, it seems my inquiry involves the inner workings of the Ul'Brek?" he asked, keeping his head bowed.

He knows more than he's letting on. Aleksei whispered across the bond.

"Well," Sabra managed, *"I suppose...."*

Jonas frowned and raised his voice. *"Who else is listening now? Please, show yourselves."*

Ul'Brek. Our bond could be compromised at any moment.

The curtains rustled and several Ul'Brek monks emerged.

The expression on Sabra's face was pained. *"I am sorry, Prince Belgi,*

*but I believe you've been asking some questions that make the Ul'Brek...
uncomfortable. As a high-ranking Ilyari and an Archanium Magus yourself, they've been most interested in your presence within Je'gud since
your arrival."*

Jonas shrugged the apology off, *"Not a problem in the slightest."* He
turned to address the Ul'Brek, standing solemn in their voluminous
black robes and white masks. *"Where are you keeping my cousin? Where
are you keeping Tamara Belgi?"*

When the men glanced at each other in what seemed confusion,
Jonas realized the inherent problem with his gamble. They had to know
what he was talking about before they could betray information. But he
was certain they knew something.

He looked back to Sabra, *"If they had an Ilyari prisoner, how would I
get to her? Where would she be?"*

"I'd imagine the southwest tower," Sabra said, surprised by Jonas's
straight-forward interrogation.

"I don't need directions," Jonas said simply, *"but instructions. How
do I gain access to the southwest tower?"*

The Ul'Faa, southwest tower.

*"The southwest tower is where they meet. The Scions of the Ul'Brek.
If you wish to reach her, you'll have to go through the trial."*

Jonas stepped forward, *"Trial?"*

Sabra fanned his face irritably, *"Those seeking entrance to the upper
chambers of the Ul'Faa must go through the purification process.*

*"The nine great Scions of the Ul'Brek are permitted to test you. From
what I have been told, it may be quite gruesome. Is this woman worth that
to you?"*

Trial. I am going with them. Follow, but not too close.

"Yes," the word erupted from Jonas without second thought.

"You will be taken immediately from here for preparations," grunted
one of the Ul'Brek.

Jonas shrugged, *"Lead the way."*

CHAPTER 41

ONE BY ONE

Another rush of ice-cold water splashed across Jonas's bare flesh, but he refused to cry out. Were they trying to break him down before the actual trial? Was this *part* of the trial? He had survived the horror of the Demonic Presence; had been healed in the blazing light of the Seraphima. As such efforts went, this wasn't even close to the mark.

Yet.

The Ul'Brek were playing at children's games compared to what he'd faced, even in just the recent past. Perhaps they meant to chip away at his resolve, or weaken the spark within him they found so abhorrent?

Perhaps they just wanted him washed, albeit in a decidedly unpleasant manner. The cleansing ceremony had been deeply uncomfortable, but feeling his bond with Aleksei severed had been the only true torture thus far.

He wondered how many had been tried by the Scions. He'd read stories of such trials taking place, but struggled to recall whether anyone had succeeded.

"You will now be anointed, as all offerings are anointed," muttered a young woman as she began to rub balm into the fur on his chest.

"What's your name?" he asked idly.

She looked up, apparently startled that he spoke Fanja, *"Qurin. What's yours?"*

He was taken aback by the way she stared him down. *"Jonas,"* he answered, unsettled.

"Jonas," Qurin said smoothly, *"it sounds like you have questions."*

"Many. What is the point of this trial? Are you a captive?"

Qurin stifled a laugh with the side of her arm, *"'Your Highness', that's what I've been told to call you. But no, Jonas, I am no captive. The Scions are a fearsome group, but also lovely people. I hold no fear of them. I hold fear for you. I have anointed many such aspirants. Individuals who believe that they are the ones to succeed the Scions and ascend to the greatest throne."*

Jonas frowned, *"Which is...what exactly?"*

Qurin smiled, as though instructing a very slow pupil, *"This trial exists to draw out one who will end the accursed Darkness."*

"Which is...."

Qurin's smile faded, seeming surprised at Jonas's continued confusion, *"The Archanium is a wicked engine, built on the souls of the dead. It takes so much, yet returns nothing. It is the Darkness that steals away the hopes of the living, and offers only oblivion in return. Even now, the Archanium has brought you to us. Will you disappear, becoming ash on the wind? Will you triumph? Grow darker still by being the one to finally eradicate the sin you bear upon your shoulders?*

"Should you defeat the Scions, you prove their point. If you lose, you die, as many have before you. Which will you choose, Prince Belgi? Can you choose? Or does your sainted Hunter have to do it for you?"

Jonas started. *"What does my Hunter have to do with this?"*

"This has far less to do with you, really, and more to do with your Hunter. In these halls, we worship the Wood, and everything They require of us. And you, you have a Hunter, hailing from a distant Wood. The Scions wish no harm upon him. They are intrigued by the Magus he drags alongside him. So, to answer your question, no, I am not afraid of my masters.

"They are all kind, caring, and powerful people. I am afraid of what will happen to you, however, because you at least seem kind and caring. I suppose the strength of your Hunter will determine the outcome. This trial is for the both of you. But know that if you succeed, the Scions wished it from the very beginning."

Jonas stared at her for a long moment. He had never heard any of the ideas she'd just put forward. His head was swimming with the possible implications of what she'd said. He was suddenly deeply uncomfortable with the way Qurin stared at him.

She pitied him. He could see it in her luminous black eyes.

She pitied him, and he thought he understood why. He was, as he'd discovered, testing the mettle of the gods themselves. Nine Scions, each one the master of a natural element. As a council, they ruled over all Ul'Brek.

Even without his own plans in play, Jonas wondered how many could have tried to defeat such powerful foes alone. The odds hardly favored the challenger. In fact, Jonas was hard-pressed to think of a single living Magus capable of such a feat. Even Bael would likely be torn apart, weak as the Presence remained within him.

He had placed his own wards around the shard of the Demonic Presence still within himself, but in the brief time Jonas had accessed the magic, he had *seen* things.

Just as the Presence had tormented him, he'd caught glimpses of its connection to Bael, its foothold in the realm of the living, and it was tenuous. For all his bluster, Bael was hardly the harbinger of destruction he pretended to be.

He had his pretty tricks, and they were not to be discounted, but it would be some time before the Presence reached its full strength in this world. For all his storied power, the Demon Cassian had spent nine *years* inhabited by the Presence, only to be defeated the first time he'd encountered the Seraphima.

Jonas turned his thoughts away from Bael, from the Presence. The challenge facing him was far from over. Were Qurin's words meant to distract him? They sounded so outlandish that he wondered at her intent in invoking them. Yet there had been no mistaking the calm in her voice, the steadiness of her gaze. This was not a woman lying, unless she was unusually practiced at it.

He forced her strange words from his mind as well. His trial had only just begun, but he knew the seeds he'd cast, and he was confident in what he'd sown.

He was Jonas bloody Belgi. If *he* couldn't manage this ordeal, he dared any other Magus to make the attempt.

Shielded though he was, it didn't stop Jonas from pushing one last thought through the void where the bond had been. A prayer, of sorts.

Gods, Aleksei, please find me in time.

483

Both guards leveled their crossbows at Roux, but by the time he heard the sharp *twang* of the bolts being launched, he was already standing in front of Conrad's chair once again, watching the chaos unfold with obligatory curiosity.

Conrad cried out as one arrow struck him in the gut, the second piercing his bicep. "Who the hell are you *shooting* at, you idiots?" he screamed.

"That would be me," Roux said firmly. The guards stood there, dumbfounded by the whole event. It would take them some time to reload their crossbows, but from the looks on their faces, Roux wasn't convinced they knew *how*.

"Great *gods*," Conrad whimpered, sliding from his chair and onto his knees, "I'm a dead man."

"Not necessarily," Roux said, concealing his amusement at the ridiculous spectacle he was witnessing. "I can save you."

Conrad's bloodshot eyes widened as tears of pain dripped free from his chin, "*How?*"

Roux shrugged, advancing towards Conrad. "The Wood has powers beyond my ability to Dart or Aleksei Drago's Hunter birthright. As Ri-Hnon, I have access to certain magics. One of them can save you from certain death. It can also bring you great honor, should you wish it."

The guards finally snapped out of their fugue and pulled their swords. Roux's eyes narrowed, "Did you not see what just happened? I can snap both your necks before either of you even sees me move. I will, and I won't care. Not one bit."

"Put the bloody swords *down*, you fool!" Conrad barked. He looked up at Roux pleadingly, "Yes, I accept! Just do whatever you have to. *Save me!*" The words came out as a command more than a plea, but Roux was anxious enough to perform the rite and get out of the village before he lost any more daylight.

He thrust out his hand and gripped Conrad's temples between his fingers, silently calling out to the spirit of the Relvyn Wood. It took a moment for any echo of response to sound. When the Wood answered, it was with a sleepy groan. Relvyn had been slumbering for far too long.

You have a new charge. Roux announced. *Let this measly man serve as Your link to Your new Children. Grant him the gift of the Wood. Grant him life anew.*

Relvyn shuddered. Wind gusted through the tent, carrying a scattering of scree and dead leaves along with it. Roux almost interpreted the message as a yawn, but he knew better. With his words, Relvyn had awakened.

He looked down at Conrad. The man's eyes were wide and white. "How do you feel?" Roux asked out of sheer curiosity.

"Strange," Conrad panted. "I...I feel *different.*"

"The Relvyn Wood has awoken," Roux said calmly. "He has agreed to accept your people as His own. *You* will be the physical link between the spirit of Relvyn and your people."

Conrad looked at his hands, though Roux could only imagine what sorts of sensations were rushing through the man's body just then

The transformation process had already begun, and Roux could see early signs of the rough bark taking over Conrad's skin. He'd never had an opportunity to witness a transformation like this. The link in Seil Wood was ancient, far older than the Ri-Vhan themselves. It resided in the depths of Her Heart, but the gods only knew *where.*

"What's happening to me?" Conrad gasped.

Roux shrugged, "I made a bargain with the Relvyn Wood. In return for saving your life, Relvyn claimed you as His own. He's now ensuring your continued safety. You are being clad in the armor of the Wood, so that no harm can come to you. You have saved your people from the fate my cousin consigned them to, when he commanded the Wood to envelop Drava. You will live on forever in the legends of the 'Ri-Sul'."

Budding branches were emerging from Conrad's scalp now. There was an account of the transformation in the ancient texts. If it was accurate, Roux knew that Conrad's body would go through each season before settling on permanent spring. It was for this reason that Seil Wood was unaffected by the seasons occurring beyond Her borders.

Petals rained from the branches, thicker green leaves emerging to replace them. Within seconds those same leaves were on fire with the colors of autumn. As they drifted to the ground, Conrad turned his stiffening neck to his guards, who, like Roux, were now transfixed by his transformation.

"Kill me!" he begged.

"Oh no," Roux said, doing his best to sound conciliatory. "I'm afraid that's quite impossible. Once the transformation is complete, you will endure on this spot for the rest of time, keeping watch over the people you've cared for so well."

The horror of what was happening settled permanently on Conrad's face, his skin now completely transformed into iron-hard bark.

But then a curious thing happened. Rather than the branches growing from Conrad settling on spring, they continued to age. When they reached the blaze of autumn, the transformation stopped entirely.

Roux frowned in confusion. He left Conrad and stepped out of the tent, staring in wonder at the trees that encircled the camp, blazing in the same autumnal colors that decorated Conrad's form. The whole *Wood* had been affected by the transformation. He idly wondered what other lasting effects the Lord of Relvyn had bestowed upon His people.

It was an experiment Roux would have to observe for himself. There were no texts to compare this to. He supposed he would have to write them himself, as he was the only Ri-Vhan to witness the event.

The old man who'd brought him to Conrad was still standing outside, wringing his hands. When he saw Roux, he broke out into a broad, toothless grin. "I was hopin' you'd come outta there without no harm."

"Not that they didn't try," Roux said, offering the man a smile.

"It's a miracle, it is," the old man continued. "The Wood, it's all different colors and all. Happened in the blink of an eye!"

"You have Lord Conrad to thank for that. He decided it was more important to save the rest of you, so he offered himself to the Wood to help protect you. The spot where he made that decision ought to be a place of peace and reverence. Great magic has occurred here, and it should be remembered."

"He dead?"

Roux actually laughed at that, "Great gods, no. In fact, he'll live forever. It'll just be a very different life than he's used to."

"Can he talk?"

"No. He can't even move, actually. Think of him like a statue. Just take care of the statue."

"And he'll be like that for*ever*?"

"Yes," Roux conceded.

The old man considered this for a long moment before grinning again, "I guess that's even better than him being dead. Good job, son."

Roux just stared as the old man clasped his shoulder, then turned and ambled away down the mud pathway these "Ri-Sul" used as a road.

Roux might as well have told the old man that the sun was going to rise in the morning for all the impact it seemed to have on him. Except for the glee. *That* was new.

He wondered if he ought to find someone to put in charge, but the sun was setting. He needed to get out of the Wood as quickly as possible before nightfall. He wasn't exactly sure *where* he was going, and it would be much more difficult to Dart with only moonlight to guide him.

In a blink he was atop the nearest tree, scanning the Wood to the southeast. He Darted from tree to tree, moving so fast that his feet hardly even registered the impact of landing before he was gone again.

After a handful of minutes, Roux stood at the edge of the Wood, panting with the exertion of Darting so rapidly. He gave himself time to recover by walking towards the pass he'd spotted a few leagues back. The weather was colder outside the bounds of the Wood, and it was clear that winter held the land surrounding the Relvyn Wood in its frozen grip. That was doubly true for the pass and the mountains beyond it.

Before long, Roux was shivering. His coat was thin, and while his natural comfort with his surroundings was dampening the effects of the cold to *some* degree, it couldn't cancel out the chill of winter completely. The sun was now dipping behind the mountains. He would need to move faster to reach the Drakleyn before sunset.

With a heavy sigh, Roux chose the farthest point he could visualize and Darted. He stood at a bend in the pass, his feet buried in the snow. He Darted again, gaining more ground.

After that first rise, the pass descended into a deep valley, surrounded by towering mountains. The Drakleyn had been actually built into one of them, or *from* one of them, before the Dominion Wars.

During the war with the Kholodym, a Magus named Elise had broken the adjoining mountain, crushing critical parts of the structure.

Roux wondered how the inside was still habitable after such an insult, but according to Andariana, half of the fortress was still in heavy use by Emelian Krasik and his forces. So where *better* to keep Tamara captive than a remote, heavily-fortified castle held by the enemy?

The sun had nearly set by the time the ruined castle came into full view. He had mere minutes to get to the structure, and from his vantage point he could tell that the valley floor was a shifting sea of rebel troops.

Their roads were well-formed and well-travelled. There were even some permanent structures that looked newly built.

Obviously, this camp had been here for quite a long time.

Looming over the camp was one of the oddest structures Roux had ever beheld. The architecture of the Drakleyn looked to have been designed by a madman. But here and there, he spotted balconies. And sentries.

Unless he was just going to walk in the front gate, Roux decided that a balcony would be his easiest entrance into the fortress. He would need to kill a few sentries to do it without being noticed, but he hardly considered that a deterrent.

He concentrated on the highest balcony he could see. At its ridiculous height, he would have to be very precise with his where he Darted. This might be worse than Darting through the bloody dark!

He took a deep breath and locked the image in his mind. He thought about Tamara, and how she could be one Dart away from being in his arms.

Blink.

Aleksei woke well before dawn. He'd bedded down in a barn, half a league from the Ul'Faa, for a steep fee. The gold ensured that the chicken-man didn't report his suspicious presence. He'd made no promises about the man's safety if Aleksei was found out.

We're going to fix it. The Mantle whispered. *We're going to feed. We'll protect him. We'll find the girl, but first we find the boy. First we drink their nectar.*

Aleksei knew exactly where Jonas was. Even if the bond had been silenced by the Ul'Brek, they could never mask the blood meridian.

That was far older magic, Wood magic, and while it was practically pulsing from the Ul'Faa, it didn't seem to have any effect on his talents as a Hunter.

Feeling their reforged bond within him had filled Aleksei with more joy than he could possibly give voice to, but having it silenced again so quickly was miserable. Aleksei would cut down every Ul'Brek in Fanj if it meant having that connection, that sacred intimacy restored.

He pulled on a pair of dark gray cotton trousers and matching shirt, but left his boots behind in the shadows. He took a brace of throwing knives, strapping the nameless blade across his back, and a length of rope. He always seemed to need rope.

Aleksei had no real idea of how this was going to go, but it was better to face it head-on, as properly equipped as possible. At the same time, he was infiltrating a heavily-guarded fortress.

In the gloom of predawn, the gray would serve to hide him in the shadows far better than black.

It was a basic precaution, but the fewer people he had to kill this morning, the faster he could free Jonas and retrieve Tamara. Then they could be away from this cursed place.

He stepped out into the chill pre-dawn morning, leaving Agriphon well-hidden in the shadowed barn. Je'gud was still sleeping, it seemed. He didn't see a single citizen as he made his way to the Ul'Faa.

When he finally reached the wall, Aleksei was genuinely surprised not to see more guards posted. There was a contingent of fifteen stationed at the southern gate, but approaching from the north, he didn't spot a single sentry.

Aleksei climbed the northern wall, his hands and bare feet finding easy purchase in the uneven sandstone blocks. He sniffed the air and listened for alien heartbeats, reaching the wall-walk apparently unseen.

It was difficult to separate out the pulsing of anyone besides Jonas and Tamara in the thunder of the blood meridian, but after a few moments, Aleksei was sufficiently confident that there were no guards in his immediate proximity.

Aleksei trotted along the top of the wall towards the southwest tower, scattering a murmuration of starlings. He prayed to every god he could think of, and found himself concentrating on Perun and Volos; gods of thunder and death. Warring gods, yes, but gods he'd placed his faith in before. He expected quite a bit of both thunder and death in the coming dawn.

He stepped up to the southwest tower and searched for handholds. Unlike the wall, the tower was polished, almost smooth as glass. Aleksei cursed, searching for another point of access.

If he were to attempt to enter at the base of the fortress, that might give the elemental Scions a chance to prepare and defend. They'd almost certainly relocate Jonas. He wasn't exactly sure what these elite Ul'Brek were capable of, but he was reasonably certain he wouldn't be able to fight them all at once, not as a unified front.

Even the Mantle, powerful though it was, had its limitations.

Finally, he spotted a thin minaret within range of a window he had identified earlier as the location of twelve heartbeats. Eleven were steady, but Jonas's stood out, a nervous throb against a sea of faint flutters. Tamara's beat just as loud, but she was either still asleep or completely unaware of what was about to take place in the tower beneath her.

The minaret was constructed from intricately carved pieces of white marble, leaving it hollow in places. It served for a quick ascent, though the higher he got, the more precarious his handholds became. In its own way, the climb reminded him of being a boy, climbing trees to hunt squirrels.

Bit by bit, Aleksei pulled himself up. He knew his point of entry. He'd sighted it before he'd ridden through the Gates of Heaven. He hadn't expected it to come to this, but the drumming in his head, the pulse that was now so familiar that it seemed a part of him, *demanded* satisfaction.

He reached the precipice. Before him stood a stained glass window, the highest entrance he could find.

Aleksei prayed that the violence he was about to commit would be enough to shield Jonas, to protect him from the trials he was about to endure.

Jonas had mentioned that most of the people in the Ul'Faa were Ul'Brek, and thus could nullify Jonas's access to the Archanium. Without magic, Jonas was a *far* less formidable opponent on the battlefield, and was more likely to be a liability during the fight than an asset.

A gust of wind threatened his footing, and Aleksei snapped his attention back to the moment at hand. Sabra had told Jonas that he must complete the trial to even *see* Tamara. Aleksei saw it differently.

He saw a religious oligarchy that tore apart each precocious adept for the apparent sake of their combined personal enjoyment. But he was no adept.

Behind the stained-glass window, softer than the thundering heartbeat that had dominated his thoughts since arriving in Je'gud, beneath the throb of Jonas's blood meridian, he could feel nine weaker hearts, confirming his earlier suspicions.

Aleksei had tried to work out how a religion devoted to extinguishing the Archanium was ruled by magic users, what Sabra had called *Scions*. At first it had seemed contradictory. But a disturbing theory had been tumbling around in his skull since he'd passed the Ul'Faa the day before.

There were nine people surrounding Jonas within the tower. Not a single one of them was touching the Archanium. Rather, an enormous well of Wood magic thrummed through the tower's entirety. The majority of it surged up from beneath the ground, but within the tower it branched out, its power ending in nine brilliant flares.

These Scions were each imbued with heady amounts of Wood magic.

That alone made him question a great many things regarding what he was about to do, but in the end, he supposed the details didn't matter. Whatever magic they commanded, the Scions were standing between him and Jonas. Between them and Tamara. Whatever purpose this trial served, it was irrelevant to Aleksei. He was not a Magus. He was something far more dangerous.

He was the Hunter.

Aleksei pulled the rope from his shoulder and tied a loose knot, searching for a place to land it. He winced when he finally caught sight of his only real option. It was a small horn of stone jutting out just above the window.

Aleksei whirled the knot around experimentally, getting a feel for the heft and balance of the rope. And then he released it with a gentle thrust, watching it glide across the span between the minaret and the tower.

The knot fell short.

Aleksei whispered a curse, pulling the rope back into a coil and launching the knot again. This time it caught on the horn of stone, though the grip appeared tenuous.

Aleksei took a deep breath, pulled on the rope to ensure it had caught, checking that his brace of knives and his swords were secure. And then he leapt from the minaret.

The knot tightened and he swung across the gap, bursting feet-first through the stained glass. He felt the sharp sting of the glass and solder a moment before he landed in the center of a large circle.

Next to Jonas.

The stunned look on the faces of the Scions was all Aleksei needed. He returned their shocked stares with a grim smile. He was not here to have a conversation with these men. He was here to kill them. They were about to tear his Magus to pieces, and he would *not* abide that.

The Mantle roared forward like a river, shredding Aleksei's shirt as it plunged crimson claws into a wizened Scion's chest. In the very next moment Aleksei's chest burst apart in a fiery blaze, disintegrating a lung and exposing his beating heart.

The Mantle claimed another life, making him whole even as a lightning bolt obliterated his left leg. The Mantle consumed a third Scion, and even as Aleksei started to fall, his leg was there to catch him, restored. The pain of destruction and instant regeneration was indescribable, and yet there were still six men remaining.

As he turned to face the Scion directly behind him, a knot of air blasted off the right side of his face. He could feel the blood gushing from the opening in his skull, even as the Mantle struck, restoring him once again.

Five.

A geyser of flame swirled up from the floor and devoured one man, his agonized screams echoing through the chamber.

Even with the Mantle's power, even with Jonas now aiding him, Aleksei knew he couldn't hold out much longer. He saw the four remaining men group together. He reached out, but even as the Mantle sought one life, a conjured spike of ice pierced his chest.

Aleksei felt his heart stop as it was torn in two.

Jonas opened a pit in the chamber's floor. The ice-casting Scion vanished with a cry. Jonas slammed the pieces of marble back together, cutting the man's scream short.

As Aleksei dropped to his knees dying, the Mantle flowed from his hand, crawling *through* Jonas, plunging its tendrils into the nearest Scion and drinking him dry.

A heartbeat later the Mantle was feeding life *into* Aleksei through Jonas. Aleksei reached up and ripped the blood-slicked ice from his chest, his heart suddenly pounding in his ears.

The Mantle reached for the two remaining men, but when it bit into the first, searing pain shot back along the tendrils and into the Hunter. The Scion held a thick golden armband. At once, Aleksei knew that this was what the Mantle coveted. Coveted and *feared*.

Aleksei was perplexed, even as the towering stone column behind him shattered with an ear-piercing *crack*. A massive chunk of marble tumbled forward, slamming him to the ground. He felt his spine splinter, his legs go numb as the stone crushed him to the floor.

The Scion holding the band looked perplexed when Aleksei's throwing knife suddenly sprouted from his belly. The man opened his mouth to cry out in pain, but before any sound escaped him, Jonas forced the man to ground, battering the back of the Scion's head. The thin marble floor tiles and the Scion's skull cracked in unison, freeing the

Mantle to feed life into Aleksei's shattered back. Jonas rose, hands bloody, and hefted the heavy gold band in triumph.

Aleksei worked to get out from under the crushing weight of the stone as the last remaining Scion held out a plain wooden staff. From his position, Aleksei knew that the man was out of the Mantle's range. He *had* to get the stone off of his back if he was to survive the coming attack.

Summoning every ounce of strength he still possessed, Aleksei finally rolled the stone off of him, the muscles in his back ripping in the effort. He stood, finally free of his bondage. The last Scion's staff shattered into several large, slender splinters, all of which flew towards Aleksei with incredible speed.

In a blinding flash, Jonas threw up a wall of liquid fire, burning the shards to ash in an instant. The liquid fire flowed forth as though alive, enveloping the last Scion. *Consuming* him.

As Aleksei crawled towards Jonas, his body slowly, sluggishly following his commands, he realized that the entire battle had occurred within the space of a few excruciating seconds.

A door on the far end of the chamber creaked open, and he was suddenly entranced by a dream-like vision. There she was, glorious golden hair sparkling in the dawn light streaming through the shattered window.

Aleksei managed a smile, "We found you. I *told* him we would."

Behind the woman came an older man dressed in tattered Ilyari wool. Aleksei idly wondered who he was, even as he felt the all-too-familiar threat of oblivion press harder upon his mind and body.

"Yosef, get over here. *Hurry!*" the woman shouted.

And then Aleksei slowly realized something was wrong.

The man called Yosef knelt next to Aleksei, and he was suddenly plunged into the Archanium. Aleksei screamed at the intrusion of pain, but seconds later, the warmth of healing flooded his entire being.

As he gave into the agony and exhaustion, Aleksei was dimly aware of the woman looking at the man called Yosef. The man was clearly a Magus of some sort.

In a mental fog, a thought came swimming out of his unconscious; Gods, where was *Jonas?*

Aleksei noticed Yosef's troubled frown as he looked over to the blond woman, "Who *is* he?"

She looked deep into Aleksei's golden eyes, frowning even as she whispered, "I have no idea."

Roux crashed into the first sentry, his short knife cutting out the man's throat before Roux's appearance even registered on his face.

By the time the man hit the ground, the second sentry was already dropping, a torrent of his blood staining the snow.

The third sentry drew his sword and looked about wildly in confusion. Roux stood outside the firelight. The men had been watching their fire for too long, and were now blinded to the darkness.

The third sentry bent to look over the side of the railing. Roux wasn't sure what he expected to find below him, but a heartbeat later he supposed the man would find out first-hand. The sentry's terrified scream faded into the darkness. It terminated abruptly, and Roux smiled.

He peered over the railing to see if anyone had taken notice of the falling sentry. He knew he ought to be more careful and not draw attention to himself, but it had been all too tempting, just a quick shove and his job on the balcony was finished.

He dumped the other two bodies over the edge. The snow piled up under the Drakleyn was *incredibly* deep. Those bodies wouldn't be found for months, if ever.

As he started to walk away, something in the far corner caught his eye. He stepped over to a stretch of snow, a few weeks old at the most. The snow had hardened into ice. From the looks of the railings and the balcony, it had been quite a while since the last snowfall.

But there were strange prints, and a dark patch that he recognized as old blood. It was too dark, too congealed in the snow to be from his recent massacre.

He prayed it didn't belong to Tamara. But as he followed the tiny prints, impressions left not by boots, but irregular stripes he recognized as being from strips of cloth, he saw with relief that they continued beyond the blood. If she had been bleeding, there would have been a trail. And those prints.... He knew them, and he knew the woman who had left them.

She was *here*.

He scanned the windows above the balcony. There were no lamps shining through the glass, but from their different points, there could only be one that would structurally lead down to the balcony without resulting in a *very* nasty fall.

Roux cursed that he couldn't see inside or he would have simply Darted into the room, dangerous though it was. Instead, he had to find a way to get up there without raising the alarm. He cursed again, this time at his own stupidity. He could have stolen one of the uniforms from the sentries and passed for a rebel easily enough. But those men were now beyond his reach.

"Gods, that was sloppy," he groaned to himself, seeking another path.

Finally, he came to the conclusion that there was nothing for it but to enter the Drakleyn and use the bloody *stairs*.

He pushed through the heavy wooden door, finding himself in some sort of antechamber. Cloaks and heavy boots lined the walls. He passed through the room to the next door, which opened directly onto a stairway.

The area appeared to be deserted.

He hurried up the stairway, his heart hammering the higher he climbed. By the time he reached the landing, Roux was running.

The landing was as empty as the stairwell. He had lost his bearings a bit on the stairs, so he selected a room at random and pushed his way inside. Nothing. He crossed to the window and saw the room he had identified as leading to the balcony.

Running back to the landing, he crossed to the door that *should* correspond with the window. He tried the door, but it was locked. Taking a deep breath, Roux Darted just a pace ahead and found himself in a dark, barren chamber. Except for the small bed and threadbare blanket, there was hardly anything in the room at all.

He walked towards the window. If the casement was cracked, it could mean she'd escaped from this desolate place, but somehow he doubted they would have given her the opportunity to make it out of the camp below, even *if* she escaped the fortress.

A flash of pain shot up his leg, and Roux cursed vehemently under his breath. He looked down and his heart skipped a beat. A shallow cut ran along the sole of his foot. It was bleeding, though being in the snow again would fix that problem shortly. But his attention wasn't on the gash in his foot, as his heart hammered in his ears, punctuating his confusion and rage. Lying on the floor and stained with his blood was a bone-handled knife he instantly recognized.

Tamara's knife.

He bent down and lifted the blade, sniffing it experimentally and catching her scent on the handle. It was cold, but she *had* been here.

Roux turned to the window and saw that the solder around the casement had been recently repaired.

That single detail cut through his hurt and brought a smile to his face. She had been here. She had been *thinking*, and had taken a risk to get away. She had used her knife, and her head.

His rage roared back into place as he realized the logical conclusion of her actions. Her knife was on the floor in an empty room. She had been here.

But now she was gone.

Katherine woke several hours after sunrise, disoriented. When had Ethan moved her back to her tiny, modest room? And to her own bed?

She had dreamed of the night before while she slept, and she couldn't help but feel the pang of loss at waking up without him. She realized, much to her alarm, that she *never* wanted this to happen again if she could avoid it. She never wanted to wake without him.

"Great gods, Katherine," she muttered to herself, "you're supposed to gather information. Falling in love was *not* part of the plan."

But in the back of her mind, gears were already shifting. Ethan had unlimited access to certain areas, and information that she and Declan could scarcely *dream* of. If she could somehow bring him over to her side without risking his displeasure, without him turning his back on her, or turning her in....

She knew she couldn't take such a risk. Yet what was she to do? What would *he* do if she vanished in the night, never to return? The very idea of the hurt that would cause him nearly broke her heart.

No, for the moment she had to keep playing both sides, taking Delira's abuse and Ethan's adoration in the hopes that one or the other would carelessly let something slip, some vital piece of information that she could give to Aleksei. Something of *value*.

The worst part was that she was *so* close to cracking the nut. She just needed a little more time.

Her door banged open and Lady Delira stormed in, "Where the *hell* have you been? Your charge was left waiting all *night* long *without* you.

Do you have any *idea* the *chaos* you've caused? Though I shouldn't be *surprised* by your *constant* stupidity."

Katherine braced herself for the abuse that was to come, but a slap never came. Rather, Delira appeared to be watching her very closely.

She felt like the woman was about to devour her. For all she knew, Delira was absolutely capable of such an atrocity, as long as it didn't spoil one of her treasured gowns.

"You know," Katherine snapped, her anger bubbling over, "you keep reminding me of *my* stupidity, but every time you say something horrible to me, it seems like you're really speaking about *yourself*.

"What's *upsetting* you so much? You haven't been acting like yourself in the past few weeks, and I'm quite troubled by this stranger you've become."

Delira stared at her for a long, excruciating moment, hatred burning in her black eyes. And then she dissolved into a burst of tears, "Great *gods*, but you're right."

The pale woman slumped into a pile of toile and tears. "I'm a bloody *mess*. No matter what I engineer, he always wants *more*. But I don't hear *him* coming up with any brilliant ideas."

Katherine hesitantly stepped forward and knelt, giving Delira a tentative hug. The other woman stiffened, but after a moment she relaxed into Katherine's arms and continued sobbing. Katherine knelt there, her knees aching on the cold flagstone, her arms wrapped around a woman she loathed. A woman whose throat she *dreamed* of ripping out.

"It's alright to cry, milady. But you can't keep hurting yourself because Lord Bael is unreasonable. I'm sure whatever you've achieved is remarkable, because you're clearly extremely intelligent."

Delira snorted, and Katherine released her. "Gods, now the *servants* are counseling the nobles? What will be next? Mice eating cats? This is *ridiculous*."

Katherine shrugged, "I apologize. I know I stepped outside my bounds. But it seemed to me if I waited for anyone to really *care* for you as a person, I'd be an old maid in no time. And I hate to see you suffer for something that isn't your fault."

Gods, what was she *doing*? Katherine hadn't a clue, but she felt as though her night with Ethan had restored her to who she really was. It was a constant reminder, along with his healing, that she really *was* worthy. She wasn't anyone's to abuse. Least of all the privileged trash that was Delira.

Money, power, and a fake title didn't make anyone *noble*, as anyone from Voskrin knew very well. Trash was trash. No matter how you tried to cover up the midden heap with silk and jewels, it still stank.

"*Well*," Delira said, her imperious tone now back in full force as she clambered to her feet, "I don't know *what* you did, but this morning *Ethan* paid me a visit. I was most startled by his intrusion, but he *is* one of Bael's favorites, so I had to hear him out.

"He actually had the nerve to *instruct* me to come down here and *apologize* for my behavior. At any rate, I *do* feel partially to blame for taking my frustrations out on you. I *know* you try your best, even *if* your work isn't always to my satisfaction.

"Now," she said, smoothing her gown, "you'd better get to the North Tower before *she* wakes up. You risk her displeasure the more you dilly-dally, and were *I* in your shoes, I would not start off by making her an enemy. We have rather grand plans for her, once she is properly broken in. Keep that in mind?"

Katherine stood and curtseyed, still unnerved by Delira's complete reversal of behavior. She was curious to see how long Ethan's commands held sway. But even being granted a temporary reprieve made her stronger by the hour. She would not be "broken in" like the woman in the tower. She would die before she allowed that to happen.

Delira swept out of the tiny room, patting her eyes dry on the cuff of her gown as she went. Katherine dressed quickly, stepping out and locking the door, not that she had anything of value in the room beyond some dried flowers Ethan had given her on one of their forced walks around the Lawn.

When she reached the North Tower, she was startled to see the entrance heavily guarded. Ten men stood outside. From the looks of them, five were Magi, the other five soldiers.

Her interest was piqued.

"You the maid for our little princess upstairs?" one of the Magi asked, looking her up and down in a way that made Katherine's skin crawl.

She curtseyed, "Yes, Katherine, milord. Lady Delira sent me to see to her needs, milord."

"Well, get on up there. If anyone comes in to ask her questions, you are to leave immediately and wait at the base of the tower until you are told you can return, is that understood?"

"Perfectly, milord." Her interest rose even higher. Who could be up there that would require this level of security? Unless they had the Queen herself, which would present a whole *new* host of problems for her and Declan.

Katherine was suddenly very nervous at seeing who they had taken captive. It could very well spell doom for her entire mission.

She climbed the stairs with mounting trepidation, dreading each step that led her closer to this mysterious woman.

When Katherine reached the uppermost landing, she was startled by what she found. The woman was in a chair, her hands mangled and strapped down. She was wearing a bloody blindfold, her lips cracked and dry. This certainly wasn't the "special guest" she'd imagined.

"Mi*lady*?" Katherine asked, cautiously stepping closer to this wretch of a person.

The woman looked about, despite having her vision obstructed, "Who's there? Who are you? Another one of Bael's little *puppets* come to question me? Just kill me already, because I'll *never* cooperate with the likes of you."

Katherine found the diatribe fascinating, "No, milady. My name is Katherine. I'm to be your maid during your...stay here."

"A maid? Well, I won't deny *that's* a welcome change. Can you remove this bloody blindfold?"

"At once, milady," Katherine said, trying not to laugh at the woman's curiously imperious nature.

As she pulled the cloth away, she had to suppress a gasp. The woman's eyes had been cut out. The bruising around her empty sockets was a deep purple, yellowing sourly at the edges. Katherine glanced at the blindfold and forced down a gag. It was covered in pus and writhing maggots.

"Might I ask your name, milady? Or would you prefer to keep that to yourself?" she asked, pushing past her nausea.

The woman laughed harshly, "My name is hardly a secret around here, Katherine. I've always loved your name. I've thought of calling my daughter by that name, someday. I don't suppose that will be happening *now*, what with all the supposed 'tests' they've been performing. But what am I saying? If you're working for them, you must be on their side."

Katherine took a deep breath. For all her fancies of telling Ethan the truth, she had been sure that admitting her true purpose in Kalinor was a horrible mistake.

And yet she felt such sympathy for this poor, tortured woman that she couldn't stop the words from pouring from her mouth. "I wouldn't be so sure of that, milady. I personally am here on a very different errand for the Lord Captain of Her Majesty's Legion, whatever is left of it."

The woman sank back in her chair, incredulous. "You work for *Aleksei*? If I had eyes, I would be crying right now. Gods, but I love that man. Of course, he only has eyes for *Jonas*. It's a shame, really. He would make such a good husband, and a wonderful father."

"Oh yes, milady. Aleksei and I are friends from the same village. We grew up together, and I had designs on marrying him myself. But he left to come up here, to become Jonas's Knight."

"Truly? Thank the gods! Then you know what I'm talking about. At any rate, Katherine, it's a pleasure to meet a potential ally for once in this nightmare.

"My name is Tamara. Tamara Belgi."

CHAPTER 42
DRIPPINGS TO FOLLOW

F*ather Relvyn, I apologize that I must leave You so soon, but with Your guidance, Your new Children will learn and adapt. Soon they may well rival the Ri-Vhan in strength and ability.*

Not without you, but you'll be back. I'll need you back.

Roux concealed a wry smile, *I'm sure I'll return, Father Wood. In the meantime, it might be best to choose a Ri-Hnon for Your people, someone with a strong heart and the ability to lead, to inspire.*

You'll be back.

Now Roux was getting a little irritated. *Yes, of course, Father Wood. Now may I travel to the Seil Wood? I am sure She will have much to tell me.*

Seil is sick. Her spirit has been poisoned, Child. Do not hold that against Her until She has been cleansed.

Roux tried to mask his surprise. So, Relvyn knew about the strange changes in the Seil Wood? Things were either far worse than he'd originally thought, or he didn't understand the nature of the bond between Woods at all.

Father Wood, Roux said haltingly, *She instructed me to give You a gift.*

It is no gift, Child. You well know what it is. It is the Blight. It is a piece of poison, one that was seeded and has grown in Her for aeons. Her first Hunter trapped it, kept it away, but he has been absent from our branches for too many seasons.

I'm sorry, Child, but you now carry that burden alone. I cannot aid you in this.

Roux stood at the Relvyn Wood's core, an inch from the pool he'd initially risen from. He could feel the corruption warring inside him, *infecting* him.

Will you let me return to Her? he managed, his last hope to divest himself of Seil's Blight dashed.

Dive into the pool, Relvyn responded, *and I will aid your transport.*

Roux sighed. Why couldn't he just travel like Aleksei, with the Wood reshaping itself around him? He stopped himself, recalling the services Aleksei had rendered to the Seil Wood. The infant Salamander he'd killed, earning the Mantle in the process. Some of the intricate friezes covering the walls of the cavern depicted many similar battles, and Roux did not begrudge his cousin's reward, even if he'd only killed a hatchling. Salamanders had not been seen for a thousand years, and with good reason.

The Kholod had cultivated them as weapons of pure destruction. A fully grown Salamander could decimate an entire city without even exerting itself. When the ancient Magi had triumphed over the Kholod, they had purged the continent, destroying the lairs of the beasts and pulling down every one of the adults, though almost nearly as many Magi died in the attempt as were lost in the whole of the Dominion Wars. After all, the Salamander Aleksei had killed couldn't even *fly* yet, and Roux considered that a mercy.

He pushed his thoughts aside and dove into the frigid pool, just as Relvyn had instructed. As he swam downwards, the water rushed past him, the ice piercing his bones. And then he broke the surface of a pond in the Seil Wood.

It was always disorienting to dive into one pool only to find himself rising in another. At least the water in Seil was somewhat warmer. He swam as quickly as he could to the pond's edge, scrambling to the shore and Darting to a tree.

He had no interest in entertaining the rusalka that occupied that particular pond. It was *that* pond that had spelled doom for Lord Perron and his men. He supposed their tortured souls were still down there, providing a distraction for the rusalka as she exacted her revenge on men such as Perron, so like the men who'd betrayed her in ages past.

Roux Darted through the trees, reaching the village in a matter of moments, still dripping. Before everyone started recognizing him, or *approaching* him with that same haunted glaze over their eyes, he ducked into his home and shut the door. No matter how he tried, Roux couldn't reconcile the change in the Wood, or Her people, since he'd been away.

"Greetings, Son," Theo said from the central room.

Roux stepped in the room and looked his father over. Theo had the same glaze over his eyes, though it didn't appear to have taken him over completely. "Father, are you well? You seem...different since my last visit."

"It's the Mother Wood, Son. When She changed, it was only a matter of time before Her needs spread to us. We have always held Her in a state of reverence. If this is the direction She has decided to pursue, the Ri-Vhan will follow." Theo's voice was a flat monotone.

Roux arched an eyebrow. He wondered briefly whether or not he would have changed just like the rest of them, had he remained. He wondered what protected Theo from being so unthinking, so *like* the others.

Theo cocked his head, almost as though he'd been listening to Roux's thoughts. After a moment, Theo nodded and turned to look at Roux. "She asks a question. She says, 'What am I going to do with you?' She's *angry*."

"So am I!" Roux snarled. His frustration hit the boiling point. "If You want to talk to me, talk to *me*," he roared at his rooftop. "And explain what You've done to my people."

"*Your* people?" Theo chuckled darkly. "Well now, that's rich. You have been gone too long, Son, that I daresay you hardly remember *your* people. That's why the Wood selected me as Ri-Hnon in your place. So you can chase all the skirts you want, without having to worry about *your* people."

Roux glowered at the ceiling, as though She could see him where he stood. He didn't *care* in that moment. "I awakened your Brother Wood. Aren't You the *least* bit pleased by that? He has people of His own to tend to. He called Your 'gift' *poison*, Mother."

Theo hissed, clapping his hands over his ears. When he looked back up at Roux, blood poured from his ears, from his eyes.

"Great *gods*," Roux whispered, Darting to the kitchen to grab towels to mop up the blood. When he reentered the central room, Theo was on his feet, staring into the fire. There were bloody smears all over his chair and clothes, but he hardly seemed to notice.

"She is displeased by your transgression, Son. *Disturbed*. But if you continue in this folly, She presents you to Her Brother as a gift. A gift, She says, laced with sweet, dark Blight."

"It's called reason, Father. Can't you see? She's lost hold of it." He glared up at the ceiling, "What *happened*? Why the sudden change? You've never acted like this before. I'm *confused*."

Theo cocked his head again, then looked to Roux. "It was *Aleksei*, Son. He escaped the bonds of Her control. When he escaped, the Blight was unleashed. It has been teaching Her *many* new things. Dark things, Son. Let us bask together in Her glorious shade."

Roux Darted immediately outside, before She forced him and his father into an altercation, Darting again to the eastern edge of the forest. As he stepped away from Her sphere of influence, he wiped stinging tears from his eyes.

Relvyn knew.

He'd known the whole time, yet He let His Sister tell Roux Her terrible secret instead. And He'd been right, Roux *would* be back. He had no other choice.

The sun was again sinking past the horizon. Roux cursed himself for wasting time. He needed to get to Taumon, and fast. He needed to tell Andariana what he had discovered, start planning their next steps to find Tamara. He visualized the strong wooden beams that crossed each room of the Admiralty, doing his best to recall the specific details of her room.

And then he Darted.

It was worse this time. He passed black shadows in a world of white and smoke. He was suffocating, but once more there was no breath to be had. His head pounded, his vision darkening.

His limbs went numb as blood rushed to his core to protect his vital organs, to his brain to keep him from passing out entirely.

With a terrific *crack,* his body smashed into the beam. His leg snapped, a hot wave of nausea flooding his senses. His body went into shock as he attempted to Dart down to the floor. He crashed onto the carpets, gasping. Startled, Andariana sat up in her bed, staring at him.

"Roux? What happened? Did you find her?" Andariana asked, hope rapidly turning to panic in her voice and demeanor.

"She *was* at the Drakleyn," he whispered brokenly, "but by the time I reached it, she'd already been gone for weeks.

"I'm sorry, Andariana. I did everything I could, but I wasn't fast enough."

The same burning tears from earlier clouded his vision. He wasn't sure if it was the excruciating pain of his broken leg, or the Wood stripping him of rank and title. If it was the consequence his people were facing without him, or rather finally admitting that he had failed Tamara. And now he was back in Taumon, where he'd started, and he *still* had no idea where she was.

Surprisingly, Andariana climbed out of bed and slipped on her dressing gown. She came to sit on the floor beside him and wrapped her arms around his chest.

"Shh," she whispered, "it's alright, Roux. We did the best we could. But sometimes it isn't good *enough*, and that isn't your fault. I certainly don't see it that way, and I would ask you to adopt the same view. We *will* find her, it's just going to take some time."

"But..." Roux whimpered, "but I don't know where she is, Andi. I have no *idea*. Gods, how I miss her, but that counts for nothing if I can't even *find* her.

"The Wood stripped me of rank completely. I am no one to Her now. She's lost Her damned mind. I simply don't know what to *do*." His voice failed as his body was overtaken by wracking sobs.

Andariana patted his leg, but frowned when he jumped violently. "Are you alright? What's happened to you?" she asked, her clear green eyes boring into him.

"I Darted directly here from the Wood, and I think I broke my leg," he managed. "Dangerous, but I had to get to you, to tell you what I found as fast as possible. Every day that passes is one where they could be doing any manner of terrible things to her.

"My leg may be broken, but I swear, Andi, I *swear* that when I find the bastards who did this, I will kill every single one of them. They won't even see me, but I swear they will drown in their own blood for the crime they have committed against us. Against *her*."

Andariana hugged him tightly again, "I *know* you will, you brave boy. Just don't get yourself killed trying to save her. She would be devastated to lose you. That would be far worse than any form of captivity; for her, she would always consider your death her fault."

She smoothed his hair back from his brow and gave him a motherly kiss on the forehead. "And she is not *nearly* as fragile as she looks. She tries to be brave and fearless, but only because you and Aleksei showed her heroism in Kalinor and in the Wood. And on the road to Taumon after that. Had she never met you, she would be so lost right now. So without hope. She *trusts* in you. You gave her strength.

"And she knows you will bend the heavens to find her. I'm sure that if you put your mind to it, you *could* bend the world to pluck her out of oblivion. But for now, we have to get you well. I'm sure they have local healers here. I'll be right back."

Andariana rose and hurried from the room. Roux took the opportunity to lay his head down on the carpet. He wondered if he was more in shock from his leg, or from Andariana's motherly affection.

They had come a long way since Tamara had been taken. Despite the pain radiating from his leg, his exhaustion won the war and he fell into a troubled sleep. A nightmare which repeated itself over and over. Tamara screaming, being pulled away from him time and time again into the darkness.

Until she *became* the darkness. Just like the Wood, as sinister as the Ri-Vhan had become. Worse. Roux howled at a broken sky above, enraged at losing her in an endless cycle until finally he had her, only to find that she had been replaced with a monster of indescribable horror.

As he tore out its throat with his teeth, the anguish of losing her burned like a red coal in his chest where his heart should have been. And then it happened again. And again.

It was a malevolent, swirling mass of air, a soul with a singular purpose.

It should have been a simple assassination job, but it was quick becoming a royal headache. Bael stared at the construct, throbbing with unwieldy life imbued by the Presence.

He was the first point of contact between the Demonic Presence and his world. As a result, the Presence could act through him with less hindrance than anything he brought forth into world on his own.

So far. It would change with time, he was assured. But for now, this crude creature was the best he could do. And it should have accomplished its job *months* ago.

So why was it taking so bloody *long*?

"I see no flaw," he grumbled, searching through the fibers of the Presence woven into the Archanium. He knew it was an imperfect system, but how hard could it be to assassinate one Archanium Knight? It had not been that long ago that he'd sent archers to assassinate Princess Tamara.

While his efforts to kill her had been thwarted, and notably by the same Knight he was now trying to end, arrows had been sufficient to drop two Archanium Knights without either drawing steel.

Bael didn't care *how* talented or skilled Aleksei Drago was, he should still be a meaningless pile of flesh and bone, picked apart by wild animals and shat out ages ago. Yet he persisted in living.

He is protected. the Presence buzzed in his mind.

"By what?" Bael demanded.

The Seraphima blinds Us to him. The construct will never find him as long as he is protected by filthy angel magic.

"Jonas can't touch the Seraphima like that. He's only a half-blood. Perhaps in moments of crisis, if he's lucky. But whatever his breeding, he is still just a Magus. He can no more command the Seraphima than *I* can."

Your protestations are invalid and unimportant. Your plan has failed, Pilgrim. Unless you can find a duty for this sad little puppet, extinguish it.

Bael ground his teeth. He would *not* let it end like this.

A slow smile spread across his face as an idea hatched. "No, not yet. If we cannot kill Aleksei, if he insists on hiding in his protective little shell, I'll simply give the construct a different task."

Bael ran his jagged fingernail down the inside of his left palm, stepping to his writing desk and allowing thick, old blood to drip into a crusty inkwell. He dipped his pen with his right hand, pulling the full power of the Presence into his bones, and began to write.

In the corner, the construct writhed and shimmered as Bael scripted a secondary set of instructions into the fabric of its being.

Bael stood after a long moment, healing the slash in his palm back into the ugly scar it had become with repeated use. His experiences with pain were many and varied, but his own blood was becoming increasingly precious.

Yet it was *essential* for the most difficult spells he had to conjure. With his own blood now a limited resource, he wondered what he would do when he ran dry.

Of course, if it was Belgi blood he needed, he always had his dear cousin in the tower.

Bael stepped over to the construct and inserted the rolled piece of parchment into its center.

"Deliver this swiftly. The sooner you return, the sooner we can move against him again. Do this, and he *will* step out from his sanctimonious shadow. Then we will have him."

Jonas could only stare.

An older man and a woman of near her fortieth summer were hovering over Aleksei's prone form. Both were using the Archanium, though in very different ways. The man was healing Aleksei. The woman was using her own ability the way a small child used newly-acquired language.

It was instinctual, but not particularly graceful in execution. And yet he got the distinct impression that she was casting her spell on everyone around her. She exuded an otherworldly presence of grace and authority that he had to consciously resist, lest he be sucked into it.

Whoever she was, Jonas couldn't help but be impressed by her expression amplified through the Archanium. She was clearly very strong, though deeply untrained.

When she caught sight of him making his way towards them, her face faltered. The presence she was exuding snuffed out.

"Who are you?" Jonas asked in genuine confusion.

The woman offered a secret, private smile, "You and your Knight came in here and single-handedly *executed* the entire Council of Scions. When that happened, the shield guarding our cloister faltered."

Jonas glanced over her shoulder, noting a simple wooden door set into the buff stone of the far wall.

"Yosef and I were going to use the opportunity to escape, but then we stumbled upon this young man. Yosef said he was never going to survive his wounds without our help, and it was miraculous that he doesn't have more, given the men he just defeated."

Jonas watched Aleksei's muscular chest rise and fall, and he breathed a sigh of relief. And then he saw the tatters of his Knight's clothing, part of a pant leg that ended far too high, its frayed ends singed.

He took in Aleksei's shredded shirt, soaked in drying blood with no wound underneath. The exposed parts of Aleksei's chest and leg were smooth, devoid of the soft golden fur he was so accustomed to. He was sure there was more he was missing, but it was enough to tell its own gory tale.

Aleksei had come here in the dark hours of the morning to execute these men before Jonas even had a chance to begin the trial.

His Hunter had decided to take matters into his own hands, exactly as Jonas had hoped. And when Aleksei had landed in this chamber, the first thing he had done was lash out with the Mantle. As each spell struck him, he regenerated with the Mantle; at the cost of another life. But in the end, it hadn't been enough to keep him collectively intact.

Jonas was suddenly so thankful for the two strangers standing over Aleksei. Without Yosef present, his Knight likely would never have woken up at all. Jonas suppressed a deep shudder and turned to the two strangers.

"What are your proper names? I would like to personally offer my thanks for the aid and service you have provided us."

Yosef bowed deeply, "My name is Yosef Halbers. I am an Archanium Magus, and retainer to Her Highness."

The woman chuckled. "So *formal*, Yosef," she was being playful now, which was a definite shift from the grim look she had carried moments before.

"It's a pleasure to meet you, Sir," she said earnestly. "I am Rhiannon Belgi. Thank you for freeing us of that awful place, even if it was by accident. We've been trapped in that tower for an eternity, but Yosef assures me it has only been a mere twenty years, or *something* like that."

"Twenty-*one* years, or near enough," Jonas whispered knowingly. He noted their startled, confused expressions.

"I apologize, how rude of me." He made a sweeping bow to her, looking up and keeping the tears from his eyes with an effort. "My name is Jonas Belgi, Crown Prince of Ilyar, and the third-born Cherub. Or *something* like that."

Rhiannon seemed about to collapse. An inescapable smile warred with shock for control of both their faces.

Jonas sought the words, and finally they came to him.

"It's wonderful to see you again, Mother."

The man was ancient. He hobbled on a cane that looked as unsteady as his knees. Yet Tamara knew who he was without having to ask.

This man was her grandfather. He had murdered her father for betraying him during his last, bloody campaign for the throne decades ago. Her mother still carried that ancient hurt, buried deep down inside her. As did she.

Bael followed, almost reverential in his stance, his head bowed as he trailed Emelian Krasik across the long room, ever towards her.

They had made a special provision for her visit with her grandfather. Her eyes had been regrown in their sockets, though after seeing herself in a mirror, not only had she lost a ridiculous amount of weight, but her eyes had gone from clear sky blue to muddy reddish-brown.

At Bael's insistence, Katherine had done her best to make Tamara look presentable. She'd done Tamara's hair, and applied enough makeup to hide the obvious bruising and scarring. They'd even dressed her in one of her old gowns, though at her current weight it practically swallowed her whole.

She looked *awful*.

But at least she could see again. It was bittersweet, knowing they were going to cut them out again the moment Krasik was out of earshot. It wouldn't do for His Majesty to hear her screams. Perhaps when they grew back next time, they would return to her lovely blue.

Somehow, she doubted it.

When Krasik came within paces of her he stopped stock-still, just watching her watching him.

He finally broke into a broad, crooked smile, "Child, but it *is* good to see you." He shambled forward at twice the speed from before. "It was such a *shame* when I had to kill your father. He was such a good little boy. But good little boys aren't traitors, now *are* they?"

"They are if their father is a madman," Tamara sighed dismissively. "Go *away*, Krasik. And please, have a stroke going down the stairs. It would be fitting for filth like you. I am *not* interested in your pronouncements, even if we happen to be accidentally related.

"As far as I'm concerned, you are the enemy. And when my love finds me, you'd better hide, because he's faster than *anyone* in this room. But if you fancy a swift disemboweling, by all means stay."

Krasik stared at her a long moment before bursting out in a rasping laugh, "My, but you *are* spirited, aren't you? That comes from your mother's people. They always think a little too highly of themselves to be concerned with the health of the realm. One of the reasons I wanted Marra disposed of from the beginning. Of course, she didn't die like she should have, and as a result we have *this* cursed chap behind me."

Tamara stared into Bael's emerald eyes, shocked. "You're telling me *he* is supposed to be my cousin? And *Darielle* as well? You make me sick to my stomach, the *both* of you. But what a lark! My own cousin abducted me, and has been subjecting me to torture for weeks! Well, try all you want, *Cousin,* but you won't break me."

Bael shrugged, stepping around Krasik. "We aren't trying to break you. We're trying to *change* you, to keep you from ending up like him. After we accomplish that little feat, we won't *have* to break you."

She snarled at the Demon, "I'll never cooperate with rot like you."

Bael snorted, "Yes you will, but I'll not argue with you about something destined to happen. And offer your grandfather some respect. Even in his seventieth summer, he led the sacking of your precious Kalinor."

Krasik smiled wistfully, "Oh *yes*, that takes me back. You wouldn't remember it, dearie, it was *months* ago. You'd have been too young."

Tamara stared at her grandfather with incredulity. "You really *are* mad, aren't you?"

Krasik's face easily contorted to an expression absolute rage. "*Mad?* I'll show you mad!"

His crystal blue eyes narrowed, shifting sideways. Bael cried out as blood gushed from his nose. Tamara just stared at the both of them in confusion, then started laughing.

"Was that supposed to impress me? Giving your monster a *nose*bleed? I'm pretty sure a street gleeman could do much the same. Or a mercenary at any tavern. You really are pathetic."

Krasik began to laugh as though she'd told a very funny joke. "That's a *good* one, lass. You *liked* it, didn't you Bael? I thought it was *brilliant!*"

Bael glowered at her, mopping the dead blood from his face even as it drooled from his nose. "Very funny, Sire. Very funny indeed. Perhaps *I* should try telling a joke."

Krasik spun on his heel, staring Bael down, "You will do no such thing, or the next thing that comes out of you will be the bits of your brain I have melted. We don't want to cause a *mess*, now do we, Katherine?"

Tamara lit up when she heard Katherine's name. The maid hurried up a stairwell that seemed far too deep, now that Tamara was able to see again. Then she finally realized where she was.

She was in the bloody North *Tower*? It was a place where the highest priority prisoners were kept, but it had never occurred to her that *she* might someday be in the same position as those prisoners from long ago.

Katherine reached her side and curtseyed deeply, "Highness, it is always a pleasure to serve. What would you have me do?"

Bael glared at her, "You might start by explaining why were you *eavesdropping* on this meeting between the Zra-Uul and Princess Tamara."

To his obvious surprise, Katherine shot back a narrow glare of her own. "I was hardly eavesdropping, Lord Bael. I am merely here to serve the Princess, as you commanded. If I happen to hear something I wasn't meant to, you must understand that as a maid, I have no power in this world. You have more power than I by a thousandfold. *Ten* thousandfold! What would someone like *me* do with such meaningless information?"

Bael stared back a long moment before nodding to himself. "Very well, be useful and help the Princess as necessary, but speak of what you see and hear to *no* one. Do you understand? If I find out you have—"

Katherine rolled her eyes, "Yes, yes, you'll flay me where I stand or stop my heart or turn my blood to bile. I was wondering where Lady Delira was hearing such pronouncements. They sound like something a bully would say to a little child, not the sort of thing I'd expect to hear from a man, *certainly* not one as powerful as you."

Emelian Krasik burst out laughing. Tamara did too. Bael's face was an obvious mask of rage and humiliation. Arrogant insolence from a bloody *maid*. Perun's thunder-wielding cock, but he looked angry.

Krasik howled, "She's got you there! Bow down to your intellectual superior, boy."

Bael stood still, blood clearly boiling. The room filled with yellow and black smoke, a sinister chuckle booming above them all.

The Demon crumpled to the ground, screaming. The smoke and the voice instantly dissipated. Krasik tortured Bael for a handful of minutes before allowing him to come to his knees, but no further. Now he was kneeling before the bloody *maid*, just as Krasik had commanded. It was likely the first time Emelian Krasik had done something Tamara actually appreciated.

3333

"The only one here who can resist me is *her*," Krasik chuckled, thrusting a wizened finger at Tamara. He turned a grandfatherly smile on her, "When I pass on, someday not that far off I fear, *you* will inherit all the gifts that I currently possess. But, unfortunately for you, Bael will be immune to your powers. As will Darielle, Azarael, and Prince Jonas. The magic has to have *somewhere* to go, but it can only travel along bloodlines. You are my only kin, so there's no question that you will receive these marvelous gifts upon my demise."

"So," Tamara said cautiously, "I could use these powers the way *I* wanted to? Without going mad like you?"

Krasik smiled, "Quite, child."

But Bael shook his head, "Not unless our experiments are successful, or you are on the water when it happens. Water disrupts the flow of the magic from the earth into the Zra-Uul. This is old magic. *Kholod* magic. Power that mortals were never meant to possess. My father was standing right next to His Majesty at the time, and the concussive aftershock drove him near as mad. The man was never the same. *Neither* of them were.

"Father left documents to aid his successor in tracking down Krasik's location, which I used to start the campaign against Andariana, and eventually take her throne. That silly chair is no longer of interest to me, however. Now I serve a greater power, one far beyond this midden heap of a world. And one day, I will sit amongst the ancient ones, higher than a god."

"Well," Tamara said, after considering for a moment, "I suppose it's always nice to have goals. *I* want to protect my people, to protect my mother, and my darling Jonas, as much as I can."

At that Bael chuckled, "Good luck with *that* one, Princess."

She frowned, "Why? What does *that* mean?"

Bael shrugged, "I realized, try as I might, that Jonas would best me until the Presence grows stronger. So I summoned a *karigul*, a wind demon, to track down and kill Aleksei Drago.

"He has eluded it so far, but that can only last so long before it rips him to shreds. And as Jonas will die as well, my mission of retribution against your beloved prince will come to an end. Then I can focus entirely on my experiments with the Presence in this world." Bael's face was positively gleeful with this announcement.

Tamara was always surprised when the wicked people in fairy

stories crowed about their wicked plans. With a hidden smile, Tamara hung her head and began to cry.

Krasik huffed in disgust and shakily turned. "I was bored anyway," he declared. He hobbled away, Bael following with a triumphant smirk.

When they were finally gone, and the deep *thunk* of the steel lock turning over reverberated up the stairwell, Tamara abruptly stopped crying. She sat up and looked Katherine in the eye, "Did you get all that?"

Katherine nodded, her soft brown eyes wide with understanding.

Tamara smiled, "Good, that ought to be enough to get you out of this place. Head for Taumon. My mother ought to be there, and with any luck, so is Roux. I don't think they'll try to move me again in the near future, so if he can find me in the North Tower, I might be able to escape.

"But either way, you *must* get that information to Taumon. Aleksei and Jonas might also be there, and there are quite a few things a strategist like Aleksei could do with information like that. Things we had no access to the last time."

"Highness, I don't know that I'm comfortable just leaving you here. I *know* what they do to you in this room, and it makes me sick even to think about it."

Tamara sighed, "I know it's hard, Katherine. No one ever said being heroic was easy. That's why no one with a brain ever *wants* to be a hero.

"But there are really only two options; either you succeed or you fail. But if you do nothing, you've already failed, and I'm *not* willing to risk anything this important because we're afraid. And you feel the same way. Or am I mistaken?"

"No, Highness, you're not mistaken," boomed a new voice.

Katherine jumped and turned around, the blood draining from her face as Ethan stepped up to her and glowered down, his eyes radiating hurt and anger.

"I think we need to have a little chat."

CHAPTER 43

FADING AWAY

"Jonas?" Rhiannon whispered.

Tears sprang into her eyes at the dawning recognition. She rushed forward and wrapped him in her arms. "Great gods, can it really be *you*? It's been so long...I thought you'd forgotten all about me. I wasn't even sure you were *alive*, after the horrible things your grandmother said about you. *Did* to you. I'm so sorry you were left alone, without either of us. We loved you *so* very much, and then your father...."

Her emotions seemed to overwhelm her, and Jonas felt the aura she cast become volatile, unpredictable, fluctuating wildly from joy to sorrow to deep concern. It was all he could do to keep his own emotions in check.

"Kevara Avlon decided *I* caused your father's death," Rhiannon rambled in his ear. "She forced me into exile *here*. She made some sort of deal with the Fanja. I never knew what it was because she laid a trap for me. By the time I came to, she'd me locked up, along with Yosef.

"I'd reminded her several times that I had a young son, her *grandson*, but she insisted that *you* were the problem. The wicked Gilded Prince, she called you. My exile was designed to keep me from ever having children again. She was so *afraid* of you."

Jonas's face grew stormy, "She told me you died."

"Who died?" Aleksei grumbled as he sat up from the floor. Jonas slipped from his mother's embrace and hurried to his Knight, wrapping an arm around his shoulders and helping him to his feet. Despite the battle he'd just barely survived, Aleksei seemed remarkably recovered and cognizant of what was happening.

Rhiannon, however, was still apparently recovering from Jonas's last comment, though she calmed herself with remarkable speed. "I wouldn't put *anything* past that horrid creature," she growled.

"If you're talking about Kevara Avlon, I couldn't agree more," Aleksei said, offering a small bow. "Aleksei Drago, ma'am. Lord Captain of Her Majesty's Legion, Knight to the Crown Prince, and Ri-Vhan Hunter. I'm also...uh, well how would you say it?"

Jonas slipped his arm around Aleksei's waist, taking on some of the man's considerable weight. "Mother, this is my husband. Or he *will* be once we have a chance to get married."

Aleksei beamed down at him, "I knew you'd have a better word for me."

Jonas just grinned, taking the moment to reforge the bond between them. His head swam for a moment, but Aleksei was there to steady him, as strong and stalwart as ever.

Rhiannon studied the two of them for a long moment before sweeping across the marble and gripping Aleksei's face in her hands. She stood on her toes, planting a firm kiss on his cheek, "I have no doubt that my son is extremely lucky to have you in his life."

"Ah, ma'am, *I'm* the lucky one. Once upon a time I was just a farmer. Until Jonas found me."

"I literally showed up in his dreams," Jonas proclaimed.

"We laugh *now*," Aleksei noted soberly, "but at the time, it was terrifying."

Rhiannon watched the interaction between to two men, finally letting out a girlish giggle, "My, but you suit each other. And Aleksei, dear, from the looks of this room, I would have to insist that it's time to give up the idea that you were ever *only* a farmer."

"Well...." Aleksei mumbled, averting his eyes in embarrassment.

"Farmers don't typically become Lord Captains, or Hunters for that matter. *Maybe* Archanium Knights. No, my dear, you must be a rare breed indeed. I can see that my son has inherited very discriminating tastes, but know that he comes by them honestly."

Aleksei blushed, "You're too kind, ma'am." He glanced around the room and stiffened, "But I'd advise us all to get out of here as quickly as possible. There's a number of people making their way towards this room, and from what I understand about your captivity, they would *not* be pleased to see you out and about. Certainly not with all this." His hand swept towards the carnage that he'd made of the Council of Scions.

Rhiannon's eyes widened, "You're right. Everyone, up the stairs! Yosef, seal the door behind us."

Aleksei frowned, "*Up* the stairs? Begging your pardon, Highness, but we don't want to get trapped or boxed in by the enemy."

Yosef clapped a hand on his shoulder, "Trust her. We've been planning this for a while."

Jonas looked from his Knight to the narrow stairway rising up behind the small wooden door. He shared Aleksei's concern. Shouldn't they be trying to go *down*?

Then again, he didn't have a clue how many Ul'Brek had been alerted to their victory over the Scions. For all he knew, they were coming to congratulate him on his victory, but he wasn't about to take that chance. Aleksei was still weak from the last battle, and there was no way he could take on an untold number of armed combatants. And, with the Ul'Brek able to silence the Archanium, neither Jonas nor Yosef would be very effective in a fight.

They reached the top of the small staircase, stepping into a vast chamber that resembled an alchemist's laboratory more than an apartment. Rhiannon stalked imperiously around the tower top, ripping drapes off a series of tables and pedestals. For every drape she removed, there was at least one unusual object underneath to behold, some bearing as many as ten.

She gave Jonas a pointed glance, "I thought you might be interested in our little collection."

Jonas immediately began following her, his curiosity growing as he sensed of the nature of each item, all of them relics. She eyed him curiously, but stayed silent. For Jonas's part, he raised his eyebrows at the power radiating from the relics. These were not the trinkets kept in the Reliquary. One in particular emitted an otherworldly energy that pricked at his skin.

"How many relics are up here?" he wondered aloud.

"Fifty-five," Yosef grunted, finally making his way up the stairs. "They tried the door. For now, they seemed satisfied the seal is intact, but we don't have long to dillydally. They'll probably return to check on us soon enough."

Jonas gazed out of a massive crystal-paned window, the city sprawling beneath him, the Sea of Spires glistening in the distance. "How many of these relics do you want to take with you?"

Yosef snorted, "Take with me? *All* of them, if possible. What are the bloody *Fanja* going to do with them? They don't even *believe* in the Archanium. And there's a Kholodym artifact in here that I can't even decipher."

Jonas glanced at Aleksei, "I think I might be able to help with that."

Yosef frowned, glancing down the stairwell nervously, "The Kholod artifact?"

"All of them," Jonas said enthusiastically.

"Boy, if you can get them out of here along with us, I will sing your praises from dawn till dusk. Speaking of which, you need to see this."

Aleksei seemed to be growing more concerned by the moment. "What is it?"

Yosef smirked, "Our deliverance."

Jonas followed the older Magus to a black metal gear sitting upright with no base. He hefted it, surprised by how light it was.

"Do you know what this is?" he asked.

Yosef chuckled, "Half the relics in this room are a mystery to me. Some I only understand because I've tinkered with them, and there was a shield that I *very* much wanted to destroy. Through my trials, I came to understand them somewhat.

"But I *know* the purpose of that particular piece. It's the reason we came up here, rather than fleeing the tower. But until you showed up," he looked pointedly at Jonas, "I've never had a chance to use it. Tried to train your mother to touch it, but that was a losing game."

Rhiannon sniffed in irritation. Aleksei stood there, glancing between them as though they'd all gone mad.

Jonas held out the gear, his excitement building, "Grab the other end."

Yosef reached out, hesitantly gripping the gear. "Now what, lad? I've been trying to get this thing to work for twenty years, and you've already figured it out?"

Jonas gave a sharp nod, "We both have to channel the same spell into it. Anything will do, but it has to be identical and it *has* to be the both of us at the same time."

Rhiannon stepped forward, concern written across her face, "And how do *you* know what this does, Jonas? Couldn't you be injured, messing with these things?"

"Call it a talent," Jonas muttered as he embraced the Archanium. "*There.* Yosef, can you see a milky blue spellform in the northwest higher quadrant of the Nagavor? About four point three degrees right ascending?"

"I see it, lad."

"On the count of three."

Aleksei and Rhiannon stepped back as the two men counted down, finally casting identical spells into the gear. There was a flash of cold light, frost spreading across the marble in an ellipsis around them.

The gear started turning, even as both men gripped it tightly.

As it spun, Jonas and Yosef studied the air in front of them, watching the swirls of the Archanium spilling out and contorting into an incredibly complicated construct.

"Great gods," Yosef whispered. "Lad, we've *done* it!"

"The Fading Spell," Jonas said, an air of contented superiority clinging to his words. "I knew it the moment I touched it. But it had specific requirements to unlock properly."

"Aye, there had to be two Magi to access it. I can't tell you the days I spent trying to train your mother to activate it with me, but to no avail. Do you realize what this *means*?" Yosef panted, turning to Rhiannon and Aleksei.

They looked at each other, Rhiannon clearly perplexed. Aleksei gave a knowing chuckle, and through their renewed bond, Jonas knew his Hunter had figured it out.

Rhiannon threw up her hands, "Alright, very well. Am I'm the only one in the room who has no idea? Jonas, what does it mean?"

"It means we can leave the tower from this room. The Ul'Brek will never have to see any of us again."

Her eyes widened in amazement. She looked at Yosef accusatorially, "Why didn't you *tell* me what this did?"

Yosef shrugged, "I didn't want to give you false hope. It requires two experienced Magi to open it, so that it could never be used by accident or by an untrained adept. That would be you, Rhi—erm, Your Highness. If you don't know what you're doing, it could be disastrous. You certainly wouldn't want to accidentally Fade into a wall."

Rhiannon's eyes widened further, "Is that even possible?"

Jonas nodded gravely, "And horrifying, from what I've read."

"So, what's keeping the two of you from making the same mistake?" Aleksei asked, clearly uneasy.

Both men looked at him as though he were insulting them.

"Training," Jonas laughed. "We're not *idiots*, love."

Aleksei blushed deeply, looking down at the floor. Jonas walked over and lifted his chin with a finger. "There's no reason to feel ashamed or embarrassed. You've *seen* me try to fire a bow. I'm a nightmare."

Aleksei rolled his eyes, "Yeah, we're going to have to work on that a bit more."

"Ahem," Yosef said, clearing his throat and bringing the men back to the matter at hand. "I believe there is still the issue of getting us and these artifacts out of this accursed place."

Jonas walked over to the wide bed, pulling off the sheets. "Wrap them all up in these, but don't let any of them touch the others. Aleksei and I have a safe place to store them until we have a little more time for research. In the meantime, I want the two of you to head to Taumon. If I know Andariana, she hasn't left, and won't until Tamara's found."

Rhiannon frowned, "Who is Tamara?"

Jonas smiled, "Andariana's daughter. She was born after you'd already been exiled here. She's heir to the throne.

"But she was abducted from the Admiralty under...mysterious circumstances. We came out here because we thought Aleksei was tracking her heartbeat. It never occurred to either of us that he could be tracking *you*."

Rhiannon met his eyes, "Because I'm supposed to be dead?"

Jonas nodded, tears finally springing to his eyes. She stepped forward and swept him up in her arms. "It's alright, darling. I'm *overjoyed* you came all this way, even if only by mistake. I'm sorry I wasn't the person you were seeking. But I'm so glad you're here, my sweet little starling."

"Don't *ever* apologize for that, Mother. I *found* you. Well, Aleksei found you. It's the greatest miracle I've ever witnessed." He paused a moment, "Did you say '*starling*'?"

She smiled that special smile, as though her secrets were trapped behind those ruby lips, just begging for release. "We'll get to that later."

Aleksei walked up to the two of them. "Ready." He turned to Jonas, "We'll need to grab Agriphon before we leave. Can that spell take two men and a horse?"

Jonas nodded slowly, turning back to his mother, "You remember what we told you? Taumon. Don't take any detours, don't... 'dillydally'. The realm is a *very* different place than it was last time you were there."

"I promise," she said earnestly, pulling him into another heartfelt embrace. He hugged her back with all his strength, as though afraid that she might turn to vapor at any moment.

Yosef walked up with a large improvised sack, "I've packed up everything of value. I'm leaving my clothes here. I've been wearing them for twenty-one years. I need some new things."

Rhiannon snorted, "And I don't?"

Yosef smirked at her, "The very reason I didn't bother to pack your things, either."

The older Magus walked up to Jonas and gave him a hearty embrace, "We'll see you in Taumon, boy. Thank you, again, for coming for us. You've given us our freedom; there's *nothing* more sacred."

Jonas smiled, "Once again, Aleksei did most of the work. Now get out of here. And keep her safe. We'll see each other again soon, I have no doubt."

Yosef saluted Aleksei, nodding to Jonas. He stepped over to Rhiannon with their meager sack of possessions. "Ready?"

She nodded sadly, kissing her fingers and waving them at her son. "I am. Let's get to Taumon as swiftly as possible."

Yosef grinned, "Just you watch *this*."

There was a surge of light, outlining their forms and enveloping them. And then they simply faded away.

Aleksei stepped forward, stunned. "That was *incredible*."

Jonas nodded, a broad smile on his face. "Agreed. So, I've figured that we're going to need to make several stops. Am I correct?"

Aleksei returned the nod.

Jonas smiled, "I'd suggest Keldoan first, to drop off the relics, and then we can head to Taumon and see how everyone is getting on."

Aleksei considered for a minute before answering, "I'd like to stop by the Wood for a moment to see what's wrong with Her. I've had some *very* strange dreams ever since leaving Ilyar. I want to see if there's any truth in them."

Jonas sighed, "Alright, let's start *small*. I've never done this before, so we'll just take it one step at a time." He put his hand on Aleksei's shoulder and piercing light flared around the two men as they Faded, leaving the tower top vacant and still.

Aya scribbled out her translation, double-checking her notes to make sure she'd converted the text properly. She heard the door to the library open and sighed.

"Just put those references to the side for the moment, Toma. I'm knee-deep in these charts."

"And which charts would those be?" a very different voice responded.

Aya dropped her pen in surprise, looking up slowly. It was too early in the afternoon to be hallucinating.

Jonas Belgi stood there, with that infernal grin she knew so well plastered across his face.

"Great gods...h...how are you here? Did you turn *back*?" she asked, realizing that her questions sounded more like demands and not caring one whit.

"We did not," Jonas responded, walking cautiously towards her.

She realized she might sound a bit hostile, though if he'd spent the past several weeks cloistered in the Bastion's library, he might as well. "Then how are you *here*?" she pressed.

"We Faded from the Ul'Faa in Je'gud. It's...a long story."

Aya could only imagine. She stood shakily and stepped around the desk. For a moment, Jonas's whole body seemed to tense, as though she was about to attack him. Aya lunged, but with a heartfelt hug.

He laughed, clearly surprised as he hugged her close. "Gods, but it's good to be back in Ilyar," he murmured.

She stepped back, straightening her dress and meeting his emerald eyes cautiously, "Did you find her?"

Jonas took a deep breath and shook his head. Her heart sank.

"We found my mother instead."

Aya blinked at the prince. "Princess Rhiannon has been alive this whole *time*?"

He gave a sharp nod, "Apparently. We learned...a great many things on our journey."

She shook her head, "I can only imagine." Raefan's investigations came to mind, and she winced. "You didn't...happen to run into Hade and Vadim on your travels, did you?"

A shadow crossed Jonas's face, "We did. They nearly murdered us, actually. The first time they attacked, I knowingly touched the Seraphima."

"The *first* time?"

Jonas waved it away, "There's an enormous amount I need to tell you, but it's going to have to wait. How are things here? The city is still intact, at least."

She nodded, "Whatever the enemy is doing, they haven't mounted any new assaults. I don't know if it's just the depth of winter, or the fact that they sent fifty-thousand soldiers who simply vanished...."

Jonas quirked a smile, "You actually *did* it? Made fifty-thousand men disappear?"

Aya chuckled darkly, "Well, once we started sharing the new meridian with the rest of our Magi, we had to come up with some sort of training ground. Without the various rooms and relics in the Voralla to work with, we decided to use that gruesome mountain of frozen corpses instead. Aleksei *did* say he wanted them to just vanish. Between accomplishing that and scaring off the camp followers, we had our hands full."

Jonas blinked at her. "Gods, but how did you *accomplish* all that?"

Aya shrugged, "We set the Magi to practicing on the cadavers. It took a few attempts to figure out the process, but we made sure every Magus kept detailed notes on the various spellforms they found, as well as the coordinates of each one. Eventually, Rostam realized that we could just pull all the water from each body. The water had mostly turned to ice, of course, but the effect was the same.

"Without any water, the bodies basically became slabs of dried meat. Well, except for the bones. But then Lucil figured out that their dried flesh and bones could be pulverized and packed into sacks. There are quite a few villages to the south of the forests, and we've been selling them the corpse powder as fertilizer.

"The clothing the men were wearing was heavily boiled and cut up for use as bandages. We gathered all the weapons, all the metal really, and every scrap of leather for our craftsmen. Some of the leather had rotted, but the weapons and the metal we stripped from them have either been repaired or just melted down.

"The Legionnaires had plenty of equipment in need of repair, and we were able to fill so many orders with what we took from the dead. We followed the Lord Captain's orders, and helped our own people at the same time."

She'd gotten so excited about all of their projects that she hadn't really been paying attention to the prince. She paused when she noticed that he'd grown pale during her speech.

"Jonas?"

He snapped out of whatever thoughts were holding court in his head. "I...I don't know what to say," he managed, sounding a bit strangled. "On one hand, I'm a bit shocked and appalled...and deeply disgusted." Her heart sank. "On the other, that was bloody *genius*."

Aya sighed in relief, "I was afraid I'd gravely offended you in some way."

He laughed, "I must admit I was surprised at first, but that was so...*efficient*. You're brilliant for working all that out."

Aya felt her face heat at his praise, "It was a group effort, honestly. And besides, Ilyana came up with a lot of it, especially the part about stripping the bodies and reusing every scrap we could find."

"Far better for our Legionnaires to benefit from all that material than to toss it away in mass grave that'll just become a monstrous sinkhole in a few years' time," Jonas allowed.

Aya snorted, "As though you could *dig* a mass grave so far north in the depths of winter. Or burn them, for that matter, surrounded by forests as we are."

Jonas chuckled, "You know what I mean. Now come along, I was only meant to collect you for a meeting with Aleksei and General Walsh."

"And then you'll teach me to Fade?"

Jonas grunted, "I hardly have a mastery of it yet. I'm still working out some of the kinks. But I *promise,* the moment I understand it better, I will return and share it with every Magus here."

Aya sighed inwardly. She knew her friend well enough, and if he was guarding this particular revelation closely, it was likely with good reason. The man attracted danger like a moth seeking flame. Even if he didn't want it, it would pursue him until he either burned up or the flame guttered out.

Still, the prospect of wielding such an ability was exceedingly enticing.

The Prince paused. She stopped, her heavy woolen skirt swirling as she turned to him, watching the frown on his face transform into a resigned smile, "Well, I suppose there is *one* thing I ought to show you."

"That about wraps it up," Ilyana said cheerfully. "We ran into a few dilemmas, but at each turn we just did what we assumed *you* would have done. In the end, I'd say it turned out quite well. We're making back a decent amount of the money our presence has cost the city, those dead rebel troops no longer exist in any meaningful way, and honestly their...cast-off possessions were a tremendous boon to our healers and craftspeople.

Aleksei thought he might be sick. He'd wanted the bodies of their enemy to vanish, certainly. He'd even given the order to make it happen. But somehow, hearing about their thought processes, that they assumed *he'd* have thought the same way was...unsettling at best.

Still, she was right. A massive funeral pyre would have done nothing but burn down half the forests, even *if* winter had Keldoan by the throat, and the earth was far too frozen to dig an effective mass grave. Besides, either method of disposing of the rebels' bodies would have left tell-tale traces, and he *had* left orders that the rebel corpses should simply disappear....

Perhaps he was most mortified that they'd assumed he would have ordered the same response for the newly-empowered Magi. In all likelihood he might have, but others intuiting how he would have acted was a dangerous precedent to set. Gods, Ilyana was still looking at him, no doubt expecting praise for the Magi's more...imaginative means of following his rather vague orders.

"Well done," he managed. "I doubt I'd have been as...clever in figuring all that out."

She beamed at his praise just as the door opened to allow Jonas and Aya in. Aleksei breathed a mental sigh of relief. He hadn't wanted to go into the vast majority of their time in the wastes, or Je'gud for that matter, without Jonas present. The Prince would know far better how to debrief the others on some of the more...sensitive portions of their journey.

"Aya," he said, trying to keep his voice brighter than he felt, "I understand you've been toiling away in the Betrayer's Bastion while everyone else has been studying this new meridian at the expense of the enemy dead?"

To his surprise, Aya let out a laugh, "See, Jonas? That's *exactly* how your face looked when I explained our methodology concerning the rebel corpses."

"How interesting," Jonas muttered, looking for all the world like he wished to be anywhere in Ilyar more than General Walsh's office just then.

"So, what's the plan?" General Walsh cut in, much to Aleksei's relief.

"The plan," Aleksei sighed, "is for y'all to stay put."

When he saw Walsh's black brows draw down, the Lord Captain continued, "As I've already mentioned, Jonas and I will be heading to the Seil Wood, then on to Taumon. Given that our foray into Fanj yielded...unexpected results, we need to see what the Queen has been up to in our absence.

"For all I know, the Princess has already been found, and is safely back at the Admiralty. Or, gods willing, on a ship to Zirvah, as I ordered from the start. If Jonas's hunch is wrong, and Andariana has already headed north from Taumon, then we'll regroup and figure out our next steps moving forward.

"The fact that the rebels haven't mounted a counter attack leads me to believe that they exhausted most of their resources when they tried to take Keldoan. If that's the case, the moment spring is upon us, we could march on Kalinor.

"There is, however, still the complication of retaking Kalinor. As long as Emelian Krasik is alive, a full-on assault could be defeated just as easily as the city was taken in the first place. We don't *know*. We don't know the span of his abilities. Kalinor's not exactly an easy city to take without wielding surprise tactics like he did last time. However, with all of them holed up in there, the rest of Ilyar is open to us.

"We could send our soldiers to take the ancestral home of every lord and lady who threw their lots in with Krasik, ensuring that they have nothing to return to. They conscripted so *many* men from the southern territories that it's unlikely we'd meet much resistance down there. Our Magi are much more powerful than they were the last time we fought, and they bested Bael's Magi in that battle as they *were*.

"With their expanded abilities, and our apparently superior forces, the hardest bit should be marching our men across such distances, establishing proper supply chains, and the like. There's not much point in holding the capital of the realm if that's *all* you hold. We can cut off their supply chains, and then our positions will be properly reversed, with them trapped behind the city walls, hoping to outlast us in a siege that we don't even have to engage in.

"But with spring, then summer, approaching, our troops will have access to far greater foodstuffs than they will. Eventually their people, not to mention *our* people left within the walls, will revolt. If everything goes right, this war could be over by Harvest, if not before, unless they can summon enough troops to make a decent showing, and with us controlling the ancestral homes of their nobles, and thus their lands... well, that's not likely to happen. Between the explosion in Mornj and the massacre at your gates, General, we've killed too many of them at this point."

General Walsh nodded to himself as he scribbled down Aleksei's battle-plan. "Makes sense. But this all hinges on Krasik, doesn't it?"

Aleksei sighed, his shoulders falling, "It does. As long as he's safely in Kalinor, the capital is off-limits. I'm not wasting the lives of good men because of his parlor tricks. Still, as long as Krasik is holed up in Kalinor, it doesn't matter. And based on some reconnaissance Jonas did during the sacking of Kalinor Palace, we know that using his abilities severely drains him. So even if they wanted to, it's not like they could Fade him from place to place to use his...peculiar abilities. That would likely prove far too taxing.

"The enemy also doesn't know that we can Fade yet. Thus, we can carry information as quickly as they can, which they won't be expecting. If Jonas and I get to Taumon and find the situation completely different from anything I just laid out, Jonas can Fade back here in a trice and let you know what to do next."

Walsh held his hand to his mouth before finally nodding. "Seems sound enough. Either way, I'd appreciate knowing what you find in Taumon."

Beside him, Jonas offered a comforting smile, "You'll be the first to know, General. Now, as much I wish we could stay and catch up, things are a bit pressing at the moment."

Jonas gripped Aleksei's upper arm, and a moment before he felt the sunlight reach for him, he called out. "Please take care of Agriphon for me. He's in the stables, but it's vitally important that you keep him fit for the battlefield. The gods only know what tomorrow brings."

Walsh saluted smartly, "As you command, Lord Captain."

Aleksei's smile unraveled into threads of waning daylight. Gods, he hoped he found good news in Taumon, but at least he didn't have to worry about Keldoan.

Aya sat down at her desk and sighed.

It had been good to see Jonas and Aleksei, even it was only for a short time. She was properly amazed by Jonas's ability to Fade. So amazed that she actually *begged* him to teach her how to access it several times before he left. At least he'd shown her where the cache of relics from Je'gud were hidden. And he was right, that wasn't the sort of secret he needed to keep to himself. If anything happened to him and Aleksei, the gods only *knew* how long it would have been before they were rediscovered, and there was no guarantee that such a discovery would belong solely to their side.

Thinking of Jonas, Aya pulled his violet book from its secret pocket under the desk, laying it beside the cypher she'd finally assembled. She was getting better at reading it unaided, but it certainly helped for the more obscure diagrams.

This section was particularly dry, discussing battle formations the Kholod had used during the war. A word popped out at her, and Aya frowned. She'd seen it before. She checked the cypher and found the index. The same word was recorded right where she'd expected.

Beside it she had written "Emelian Krasik". She suddenly recognized the word as the phonetic equivalent of "Zra-Uul". Aya scanned the page for more references to the construct, and found that the word cropped up multiple times in the span of a few pages.

She groaned.

It was going to take days to decode that much raw text. Especially without the star charts and spell representation analogs she needed, which were helpful, but also took up multiple volumes with their complexities.

There was no access to any of that here.

Aya stood and arched her back. She needed sleep before she tackled this particular monster. She replaced the book in its secret pocket and quickly overlaid a spell to keep others from finding it.

She left the Bastion, enjoying a breeze that felt like spring was finally on the way. The moon dangled bright and full in the sky, casting light across the broad field that stretched between the Bastion and Keldoan proper. She luxuriated in the new smell of snowmelt and revitalized grass as Spring's children drank the remnants of Winter's harsh remonstrations.

Aya spotted Raefan across the field and headed towards him. She had been spending so much time in the library that she hardly ever set eyes on the man any more.

Yet even after all these years, the thought of his smile still turned her knees weak. His arms were as strong and powerful as oak when she needed to be protected from the rest of the world.

The full moon and hints of spring brought back memories of the two of them growing up together. They had arrived at the Voralla as children, she six and he seven. That first day, a group of boys began picking on her, though she could hardly recall *why*. Without hesitation, Raefan had put himself between her and the group of bullies. They had beaten him bloody. They only stopped when she had managed a spell her mother had shown her that created booming thunder.

They'd scattered in ignorant terror, and she had used healing for the first time, trying to mend wounds that she now knew were far beyond her abilities back then. But the Magi at the time had been impressed by his bravery and her quick thinking and use of the Archanium at such an early age.

From that day, they had been inseparable. When her prophetic talent had manifested, he was the first to notice her headaches, the way she'd locked herself in her room, refusing food and water until the day he picked the lock. She'd only been fifteen summers at the time, but he had learned some very questionable skills from the older boys.

He had climbed into bed with her and wrapped her in his arms, kissing her forehead. He promised he'd be there all night, and he'd kept that promise.

When morning broke, she'd found him snoring softly beside her. It was one of the sweetest things anyone had ever done for her, especially because he hadn't been told that she was feeling poorly. He just *knew* when she needed someone to cling to.

He had crawled into her bed again that night, and shortly thereafter they were Bonded. From that night forward, he had never left her side or her bed. It suited the both of them quite well, she thought with a smile.

As she came upon Raefan, she noticed something was wrong. Her Knight was actually hovering a scant inch off the ground. On the other side of him was some sort of construct that she couldn't see.

But she *felt* it.

It was Aleksei's wind demon.

Aleksei had just passed through, and she had seen the angel feather still bound around his neck, the sacrifice of another man, meant for

Jonas to remember him by, but used instead to protect Aleksei from the demon.

So, what was it doing with *Raefan?* She rushed to the other side, ready to banish it with a spell, but it dissipated in a twist of air. Raefan collapsed in a nerveless heap on the lawn. He wasn't breathing.

"*Help!*" she screamed, straightening his airway and pressing her lips to his mouth. She tried to breathe life into him, but something was blocking the air's passage into his lungs. She clapped her hands on his bulky chest, searching with the Archanium for anything unusual.

There.

Something was in his throat. She opened his mouth and reached in with her delicate fingers, finally finding purchase on a rolled bit of parchment. She carefully slid it out and cast it aside, trying again to breathe the life back into her love. A few moments later he started coughing and breathing on his own.

When he'd gotten his breath back, Raefan just stared at her for a moment, as if he didn't know her. And then he lurched across the grass and gripped her in his arms, kissing her passionately. He kissed her again and again. By the time he was done, everyone who had heard her scream had surrounded them.

Aya's face went scarlet. Tamrix looked at the others gathered, "Looks like she took care of whatever it was. Show's over, back inside, folks."

As the crowd dissipated back to their respective dwellings, Raefan shook his head, blinking furiously and tapping at his ears. She wondered if he could even make sense of what was happening around him. He coughed roughly, pounding his chest to break whatever was caught there loose.

He met her eyes and shook his head again, "*Gods*, but that hurt. Is that why you came so fast?"

Aya stared into his face for a long moment, her eyes watering, "No. I didn't feel *anything* across the bond. That thing masked your pain and panic. I have no idea how such a thing is even *possible.*"

Raefan rubbed his throat, "This is the worst. It felt like I was put through a meat grinder."

"Oh!" Aya exclaimed crawling across the grass and retrieving the scroll. "*This.* This was...in your throat. I couldn't understand what was blocking me from filling your lungs until I found this."

"What is it?" he croaked.

She unrolled the parchment and gave a small scream at what she saw.

"A message," she finally managed.

Tears sprang unbidden to her eyes. Raefan moved quickly, resting his arms around her. For the first time in her life, Aya struggled free of him, stepping out into the moonlight. She *had* to be sure.

A whimper escaped her lips. "Oh great gods, *no!*"

Tamara squared her shoulders, "Katherine, get behind me."

Ethan gave a mirthless chuckle, "And what exactly are you going to do, Princess? Protect her? Because it seems to me that *you're* the one trying to get her killed."

Tamara arched a golden eyebrow, "What am *I* doing? This coming from a man who follows an undead corpse animated by *demons* and calls it *righteous*? At least *I* belong here. At least *I* didn't slaughter innocent people for some madman's vision of glory, simply because I was *told* to.

"*I* can call out a lie without fear, and *I* can sleep at night when your so-called master isn't torturing me. Can you say the same? Because if you can't, you're a lower lifeform than I had previously anticipated, and I was thinking *you* were about as low as pond scum."

Ethan's face burned with rage. He embraced the Archanium, but Katherine shoved his hand down, pushing against his chest. She was hardly strong enough to move him, but her exertion was startling.

Then, for the first time since stepping into the North Tower, he noticed the tears streaming down Katherine's face.

"You don't *get* it, do you?" Katherine looked up at him, her brown-eyed glare violently accusatory, "You're doing what you've done all your life. And now you're about to attack an innocent woman, a woman who has been abused and horrifically tortured, because she told you the *truth?*

"You really are like the rest of them, aren't you? And here I was thinking you were *better*. But *no*, you're like every other tyrant in this gods-forsaken place.

"And by the way, the Princess isn't trying to get me killed. This is what I came here to *do*. I came here to gather information that would help Aleksei *defeat* people like you."

"Aleksei?" Ethan said with a frown, "*Drago?* The Lord Captain?" Now he was actually laughing, "Why would the Lord Captain listen to a *maid?*"

She slapped him hard across the face. The strike hardly stung, but it was the insult that damaged his pride and doubled his anger. Yet when he turned back to her, the intensity of her glare was a fraction from hatred.

"I'm not a *maid*, you idiot," she snarled. "I'm a cooper's daughter from the Southern Plain. I'm from Voskrin. The same town the Lord Captain grew up in. We've been friends since we were three.

"But just so you know, Aleksei isn't the sort to go thrusting his weight around because he's important. He *would* listen to a maid, just as soon as a general, if she had something important to say, so don't you *dare* act like you know who you're talking about."

Ethan was now more confused than angry, "So *every*thing you told me was a lie?"

"Can you *blame* me? I've been terrified from the moment I set foot in this city. The woman I work for is *almost* as psychotic as your 'master', and yet *I* have to wash her small-clothes and let her beat me in the hopes that I'll hear something useful. But I put up with all that horseshit because I'm here for someone I *believe* in.

"I don't have to wonder about it, or justify my actions. If Aleksei Drago is on one side, that's the *right* side as far as I'm concerned, because he is the most just and fair person I have ever met in my life. Can *you* say the same about anyone here? Can you argue that *Bael* is fair, or bloody *just?* Are *you* just, Ethan?"

A war of emotions stormed through him. She was challenging him on principles and ideals that he had never really questioned. His entire life, he'd been taught not to question, not to get higher than his station afforded him.

When Bael had passed through his village, he'd been selected by a great man to fight for a great man. It sounded like the stuff of legends. So, he'd gone to chase his fortune.

But as Katherine spat his decisions back at him, she made him sound like a tyrant and a villain. The other Magi were always congratulating each other on being righteous warriors for Lord Bael, a man so pious and dedicated to his cause that he had sacrificed his own life for the power to defeat the evil that pervaded Ilyar.

Katherine pushed past him, walking defiantly away. His rage roared back to the fore. "Where do you think you're going?" he demanded.

"*I'm* going back to work, you big ox. Because *I'm* doing what I came here for, and then I'm getting the hell out of here."

"Don't take another step," he commanded, holding his hand out and embracing the Archanium.

She glared at him again, but this time all he felt from her was a deep and abiding sense of disappointment. "Or what? You're going to kill me and prove us both right?"

She stood there for a long moment, glowering at him, her obvious pain and disdain a match for every power he commanded. And then she vanished down the stairwell. He stood there for a long minute, lacking direction in every sense of the word.

"And you thought a woman that smart would fall in with your ideology because you're *pretty*?" Tamara sneered behind him.

He turned to her, his rage barely under control. "This is all your fault," he spat, tears brimming in his eyes.

She laughed at him, "Oh please, by all means. Use your magic to kill me, or strangle me with your own hands. Please, prove every word we've said to you completely true. *That* should make you feel better about your decisions."

Ethan couldn't believe he was being spoken to like this, like he was some naughty schoolboy deserving of punishment. The derision in her voice matched that in Katherine's tone for tone. Yet she had only been in Kalinor for a handful of days. He had been there for *months*, months he'd spent talking with Katherine.

He thought he'd been impressing her with his connections, his obvious power, his *compassion* when he healed her.

He found her absolutely fascinating, because she had no trouble voicing her opinions, and while he found a number of them to be blasphemous, he didn't *care*. He'd never met a woman like her.

This most recent revelation had him completely turned around. He had expected her to hold on to her ideas until she heard his. He had been convinced that if he just explained the way things *worked*, she would change her mind.

After all, he *knew* she wasn't stupid. But how could she so easily take him apart like that? She had analyzed his own belief system far more astutely than he ever had. That alone was unnerving.

He liked talking with her because she made him *think*. But the moment he realized that he'd made *no* headway with her whatsoever, the implication became insulting.

Ethan had been criticized his entire life for being thick. He was always bigger than the other boys, so that alone made him ripe for ridicule.

When he first touched the Archanium, he'd felt very smart indeed. Until someone explained to him that power in the Archanium was a trait people were born with, and it really had nothing to do with his mind.

Just now, when Tamara and Katherine had been talking back to him, was the first time since he'd joined Bael that anyone had dared speak to him that way, had made him *feel* that way.

"I don't understand," he admitted softly. "What am I supposed to do now?"

He felt lost and bewildered. He felt stupid. Although he felt the pain of what had just happened, he still didn't entirely comprehend it.

"If I were you, and thank the *gods* I'm not," Tamara hissed, "I would go after her before she leaves this palace and *you* forever."

Ethan stood stock-still for a long moment, the war of ideals still raging inside his skull. But with each argument he could hear Bael pushing, he could now imagine Katherine dissecting it, making him feel indescribably stupid for not having come to that same conclusion years before.

He had stood at the gates of the Cathedral of Dazhbog. He remembered how giddy he'd been. How much of this whole endeavor had been built up by Bael and the acolytes from Bael's hallowed Commune? Such people were held in the highest esteem, but the rest of his followers were practically salivating at seeing their dreams about to come to fruition.

When Raim was chosen as the fortunate one to open the Third Gate, Ethan had been so excited for his friend. He had been shocked when the explosion of demonic energy had burst free from the Third Gate. When it was over, he had seen Raim's body near the end of the misty platform, at the edge of death.

The rest of the party had entered the sept, blithely stepping over Raim's broken body, eager to open the Second Gate. He had reluctantly joined them as they sang songs about how they were the chosen, hand selected by their Dark God to bring sanity to a world gone mad.

Someone had clapped him on the shoulder and told him what a hero Raim had been, how he would always be remembered. And yet, they hadn't even stopped to see if Raim needed help. When the Second Gate opened, and Stephen had gained the construct to create revenants, Ethan had wondered if they hadn't been right. After all, the first thing Stephen had done was to resurrect Raim.

But the Raim who had returned was not his friend. It was something entirely different. Just a thing to be *used*. Something devoid of a soul, possessed of an unnatural hunger for life. It was the opposite of resurrection; it was death incarnate. Stupid, but dangerous.

Just like me, he thought bitterly.

Ethan ran after Katherine hurriedly. "Thank you, Princess."

Tamara watched him, still strapped to her chair, knowing they would be back in a few hours to cut her eyes out anew. "You're welcome," she whispered, tears leaking out of eyes that were hers for only a little while longer.

CHAPTER 44

GREETINGS AND GOODBYES

Katherine nearly slammed the door to Lady Delira's quarters, stopping herself only at the last moment, as reason kicked in and set off warning bells in her angry mind.

Gods, but why did Ethan have to be so *thick*?

Katherine had often heard the women in Voskrin complain about their men, how one's husband would spend half the farm's income at Redman's Pub every fortnight, and another would never take a sensible crop to market because he was just sure that there would be far too many leeks that week, and *this* would be the week they made that fortune he'd been promising for the past three decades.

She'd actually had *dreams* of being part of those discussions, because being present in that group meant she would be a woman, not a little girl with two big, protective brothers who wouldn't let a decent boy within five hundred paces of her house, and because it meant she would actually *have* a man to complain about.

And on the Southern Plain, it was hard to have dreams aside from marriage and children. Though, looking back on it, Katherine found herself quite surprised how bitter she was towards the whole endeavor, and the future that had been prepared for her.

Of course, her first mistake had been marrying Pyotr, Aleksei's boyhood friend. Aleksei had gone on to become the Lord Captain, to invade the Drakleyn with only the Prince at his side. *Her* husband had ended up drowning in bar tabs and gambling debts, finally joining Perron's army to skip town and get away from his creditors. To get away from *her*.

It was a grim irony that both men ended up in the same place at the same time. Except Aleksei had been holding the sword, while Petya received the blow.

She felt a sick, sad chuckle mounting in her chest. It took everything she had to suppress it. It wouldn't do for passersby to hear the maid in Lady Delira's room cackling like a madwoman.

In all likelihood, they might have just assumed Katherine was pretending to *be* Delira. That would probably earn her a swift caning. Or an execution, she could hardly keep it straight it anymore. Everything around her seemed to grow more capricious, more dangerous, by the hour.

She sat on the floor in the corner, feeling a little silly that she kept hoping Ethan would follow her, that any moment there would be a knock and she'd see him standing in the hallways, looking sad and pathetic, and just a little like a lost puppy.

The moment stretched on and on, until finally she pulled herself to her feet and retrieved a small bag from beneath Delira's bed. Items that she had been steadily collecting: notes, confidences, some of Delira's actual personal findings from her project.

All of it was meticulously organized each night when she turned out her pockets and turned down the bed, while Delira was safely at some dinner or other. Katherine slid it into the pouch she had sewn into her livery right where her apron crossed her waist. She removed the small pillow of rags and placed it where her bag of clues normally rested so there was no change in her appearance. When she straightened, she was startled to find Lady Delira standing in the room with the door closed.

"Well," Delira said with a cruel smile, "how very interesting."

A chill swept through her, but Katherine was determined not to let the woman throw her off, "Milady? Another day of tests?"

Lady Delira tossed her hand in the air nonchalantly. "Oh, of course. Those will continue for some time. But then, you already knew that."

Katherine busied herself turning down the bed, "Well, as long as it isn't like the last few weeks. They can't keep making you work such ridiculous hours."

"No," Delira said, dragging the word out, "no, it certainly won't be like the last few weeks. Of *that* much I can be certain." She snapped her boney fingers and a shimmer crossed over the door.

Katherine heard the lock turn over with a terrifying *thunk*..

"I was curious," Delira said, once more drawling her words while slowly circling the room, touching various objects out of habit as she moved. "I'm *always* curious. It's gotten me into a great amount of...*trouble* in the past. I fear that you are more like me than you know, Katherine. We've got to learn how to keep our noses fixed on the prize, *don't* we? Or else we can oh-so-easily find ourselves...led astray."

Delira's path had led her to the other side of the bed. The side where Katherine was gently fluffing pillows and smoothing over the velvet duvet drooping lazily across the bed.

Katherine finished her work on that side and, suppressing a shudder, turned to Lady Delira with a bright smile, "I couldn't agree more, milady. And I can't think of anyone I'd rather spend that time with than a Lady such as yourself. Is there anything else I can do for you before I turn in for the evening?"

Delira looked down at her pale, balled up fist. Katherine saw blood dripping from between her fingers. "Oh! Milady, are you alright? Did you cut yourself? Here, let me get you something to—"

Katherine's words were violently cut off as she slammed into the wall behind her. Her head struck the rich panelling, bouncing off the wall as a blast of bright light flashed behind her eyes.

Her vision slowly cleared as she stared into Delira's face. Or what remained of it. Here and there, the skin looked tattered, like leather nearly rubbed away. Her hair moved with a stiff fragility, and as she swayed Katherine could see the stitch marks where thick thatches of black hair had been sewn into her scalp.

"What are you?" Katherine managed before the force holding her let go and she dropped through the fragile side table, sending ruined pieces of gem and crystal across the carpets. Katherine smelled blood. Far more than the tiny amount dripping from Delira's hand.

She looked up at the walls. All around the room were swathes of thick, clotting blood that Delira had smeared across every surface she came in contact with. It dripped from the hem of her gown, and Katherine realized that the woman had no feet. Had she? Had she ever had feet? She had shoes....

Katherine's head ached powerfully, but she had the presence of mind to grasp a jagged shard of glass from the rug and push herself back from the Delira creature as quickly as she could.

"What *are* you?" she screamed.

A light laughter filled the air, and Katherine blinked to find herself in the corner of Delira's room, the other woman's misshapen hand outstretched to her, humor fading into faux concern, "Dearie, are you alright? You've had me worried, what with your emotions so fragile."

Katherine struggled to her feet, glancing at her hand to find the shard of glass gone. She turned her gaze back to Delira and found the sharp, yet motherly gaze she recalled. Distantly she smelled something.

Something terrible.

Delira sniffed the air and laughed again, "Oh, darling, there's nothing to worry about it. Just a little fear is all. Delicious fear. Delicious delirious deleterious...*fear*."

Rhiannon stepped gracefully from the carriage and took a deep breath, relishing the fresh breeze coming in from the open sea. It was an odd luxury to be outside after twenty-one years of being held captive with only Yosef for company. Not that he was the *worst* company, but after the first decade, she felt they had to know each other better than anyone else alive.

She had told him everything about her life before the birth of her son and the death of her husband. The series of months that had followed would have been a fog were it not for Joel's older siblings, Forfax and Barbelo. And Jonas. Even after the initial shock of the tragedy faded, raising a precocious three year old without her husband presented far less of a trial than many supposed.

In fact, she had found an enormous amount of solace in her son during that time. He'd so often reminded her of Joel. That had been the only part that stung, but she had loved him for it, too. She didn't believe, then or now, that remembering loved ones long lost was ever a bad thing. Painful, but never bad.

Whether the memory was good or bad rarely mattered, as actions or behaviors that once had seemed irritating took on a different cast after the person had been gone for a handful of years. Andariana was particularly prone to overstating Seryn's more charming qualities.

Well, she had been the last time Rhiannon had seen her.

Porters came to help her with her luggage before she reassured them that she had none. In fact, she reflected, there were quite a few things she didn't have. Gold or silver being the most pressing.

"Yosef," she whispered, "I don't have any coin. Do you?"

The Magus shrugged helplessly.

Rhiannon rolled her eyes, "Oh, *this* is going to be entertaining."

She turned and smiled at the carriage driver, "It will be just one moment, sir." Surprisingly, he smiled, tipped his hat, and sat contentedly atop the carriage.

She turned her attention back to the Magus, "Keep him busy. I'll be right back." She flashed a smile and waved once more to the driver before heading down towards the Admiralty.

Behind her she heard Yosef, "Sir, those are some mighty impressive hubcaps. I've never seen them in solid gold myself, but...."

The driver's exclamations of shock and wonder left her groaning. She didn't slow her pace, but moments later Yosef was beside her. He caught her arched eyebrow and shrugged haplessly. "It was going to take all day. And—Rhi, don't look at me like that—and the last thing you want to do is arrive, see your sister for the first time in two decades, and immediately beg her for money."

She quirked a frown, before finally allowing that he made a good point.

The doors of the main entrance were being opened to allow out several messenger carts. Rhiannon smiled at the guards and gave them a wave as she confidently sashayed in.

"What are you doing?" Yosef asked in confusion.

"What could you possibly mean?" she asked, adding in a wink for the guard captain.

"Well," Yosef whispered, "from this angle I'd think you're a princess just away from her nursemaid's skirts long enough to act a fool. When was the last time you looked in a mirror? You don't exactly look like a darling young princess. Your behavior is highly confusing for these young men."

She let out a bubbly laugh, "Oh, no, Yosef, this is the Admiralty. These 'young men' aren't nearly as innocent as you think." She pitched her voice conspiratorially low, but still loud enough where she could be audibly heard, "They're *sailors*. *You* know, port to port?"

"No," Yosef whispered irritably, "and neither do *you*. Remember, Rhiannon Belgi, I know everything there is to know about you."

"Yes, Yosef Halbers," she said, smiling, and without even seeming to move her mouth, "and I know everything there is to know about *you*. So, if the very first thing you wanted *me* to do was find your lady wife down in Voskrin, you're about to get your long-awaited wish."

Yosef grumbled to himself, but lost his accusatory tone. After a few long, uncomfortable moments, he picked back up again. "We *were* on an important mission, you know. Grigori sent us out of the Voralla because he was so fearful of some dark, sinister force emerging from within.

"I was never sure if he meant a coup, or if he thought the actual Voralla was getting darker...he was a complicated man. But the point is, he wanted Margaret and me to be where the most important action was."

"Yes," she said disdainfully, "and yet, instead, you ended up trapped in a tower with me for twenty years. However did you manage *that*?"

"That was a grave miscalculation."

"On your wife's part?" she said, baiting him for the amusement of how red his face always became.

"Of *course* not on my wife's part! *She* did exactly what she was supposed to."

"Meaning she ended up where she was ordered to go by the High Magus and then proceeded to carry out her mission." Rhiannon said, leading him towards her ultimate destination.

"Rhiannon...."

"I'm just curious where you were supposed to be, if you weren't supposed to end up locked away with me," she continued.

"Rhiannon."

"Because I'm pretty sure you told *me* the answer was—"

"*Rhiannon!*" he hissed in her ear.

"*What?*" she demanded.

He looked her square in the eye, his small brown eyes glaring up from his spectacles into her luminous sapphire irises.

"Where are we?"

Rhiannon blinked, looked around, and realized to her chagrin that she'd been walking and smiling and goading the little man, but she really hadn't been paying attention to where she was going. They seemed to be in the middle of Admiralty.

She caught sight of a maid down the hallway and swept towards her. "Excuse me? Miss?"

The maid turned, her eyes widening in awe, "Yes, Mistress?"

Rhiannon flashed her a disarming smile, "I'm ever so sorry, but could you possibly direct us towards the chambers of Andariana Belgi?"

The woman blinked as though trying to wake up. She caught Rhiannon's eyes again, the look of reverence returning, "The Queen, Mistress?"

Rhiannon gave a light sigh, "Yes, my dear. Where might I find the Queen?"

The maid stretched a hand out to the left, "Two hallways to your left, one to your right. Fifth door on the left."

Rhiannon smiled again, "Thank you *so* much, my darling girl. It is greatly appreciated."

She started off towards the hallways the maid had indicated, Yosef a half-step behind her, hissing in her ear, "What was *that*?"

"Courtesy, Yosef. Sometimes people like to feel important."

"Like you?"

She scowled, "I *am* important, Yosef."

"I'm not so sure," he said, glancing around the inner halls of the Admiralty. "It seems like they've gotten on well enough without you for twenty years."

"Twenty-one," she corrected, "and no they haven't. If they had, they wouldn't be fighting a repeat of the civil war that was still raging when I was captured. Does that sound like success to *you*?"

Yosef was silent for a moment, so it gave Rhiannon a chance to return to her favorite game. One of her own invention, of course. "So, as I was saying, where were you supposed to be while your wife waited in the gods only know where?"

"Voskrin. It's a tiny village in the Southern Plain," Yosef practically spat. "And I was supposed to be with you."

"*Whom* were you supposed to be with?"

He sighed heavily, as though begrudging every word, "Gods, we've been over this a thousand times. Jonas! I was supposed to be with Jonas. Happy now?"

"Not even a little bit," she growled. He was taken aback back at the ferocity of her response. "Although I will say, *Margaret* seems to have done *her* job beautifully."

"Now how could you possibly—"

Rhiannon turned on him quick as serpent, hypnotizing him with her eyes, "A man, a Ri-Vhan Hunter, is working on a farm in the Southern Plain, in the same insignificant hamlet? That same man who now bears the Hunter's Mantle, which he used to set us free from an impossible prison. A prison he found by tracking me through my son. Through my son's *blood*."

"Well, coincidence could play a part—"

"Coincidence?" she snarled, "The only 'coincidence' that took place is that my son, through no guidance of your own, found Aleksei in the Southern Plain through instinct, which is about as precise as throwing knives while blindfolded." Her face hovered closer to his, "Which is to say, someone might very well lose an eye."

"Excuse me?" came a new voice behind them.

Rhiannon straightened, smiling at a young man who hobbled out towards them on crutches. Her smile flashed into a frown, "Are you quite well, young man?"

The man's face remained impassive, "Is there something I can help you with?"

Rhiannon sighed, as though she'd been waiting for someone, *anyone*, to ask her that question all afternoon. "Yes," she admitted weakly. "I am looking for my sister. I can't seem to find her in this labyrinth, but I have been told that she's in here *somewhere*."

"If I can presume to ask a question," the young man said, remaining very still on his crutches, "you were just mentioning a man named Aleksei? From the Southern Plain?"

She nodded, "What of it?"

"Do you know him?" the man asked warily.

"Only ever so briefly, but I have it on the best authority that he's to become my son-in-law, once this war foolishness is over with."

"And your sister is—"

"Andariana Belgi. Have you seen her? Oh, I believe she's the Queen now."

The man's golden eyes widened.

"Yes!" Rhiannon exclaimed, "Just like that! Are you Ri-Vhan?"

The man on crutches seemed surprised by the question, but gave a stiff nod.

"You see, Yosef?"

The Magus looked decidedly uncomfortable, "What?"

"Aleksei's eyes. They were just that shade of gold. I *told* you it had something to do with the Wood."

She turned back to the man on crutches, who was suddenly standing right in front of her. "Well," she said breathlessly, "aren't you just the

543

cutest thing?" She kissed the tip of his nose, "but I like Aleksei better. Nothing against you, but you're not marrying my son."

Rhiannon swept past him as he turned a startled glance at Yosef. The Magus shrugged, "It's easier to get out of her way and let her go where she pleases."

"Was that...Does Jonas know...*Who are you?*" Roux choked.

The Magus smiled apologetically, "Sorry about that. If that's Andariana's room, they'll be a while...it's been a long time. Let's find a room and I'll have a look at that leg for you."

Ethan hurtled down the hallways, ignoring the startled glances and angry glares as he pushed his way past servants and Magi alike. But no one thought to question or hinder the big ox thundering by.

He reached Delira's chambers and halted, immediately unsettled by the ward skittering across the door. This was no mere locking charm. It was one of the most complex shield spells he'd ever seen, and there was a hidden element to it he didn't entirely understand. But even while he was studying it, he heard Katherine's scream.

Panic and rage consumed him.

He plunged himself into the Archanium and hurtled as deeply as he dared into the Nagavor. He lost himself in the torrential storm, flickering past shards of lightning and pain until he locked onto the spell he needed.

With an electric *boom,* the door shattered. Threads of light ran up and across his arms, singeing his flesh in a scattershot of angry burns and blackened skin. His white-hot rage burned hotter than the pain.

He stepped into a nightmare.

Delira was hovering over Katherine.

The magic emanating from Delira filled Ethan's heart with foreboding. He had heard rumors that she was part of the weaponizing tests, but he had no idea how successful they had been. The form hovering over Katherine was far closer to a tortured miscreation than a woman. And it was feeding on Katherine's life, and on her terror and madness. Madness it was presently inflicting.

At the sudden intrusion, Delira's head snapped towards him, "What are *you* doing here?" she snarled.

His fear and fury burning ever hotter, Ethan hurled forth the same spell as before, not thinking for even a moment, driven only by a primal need to protect Katherine.

Delira erupted.

Every fiber of her being stretched and rent. She burst apart in a spray of blood, viscera, and bone. It splattered across the walls, covering Katherine and himself in her gore. Ethan wiped a hand across his face and then flicked the black-scarlet slop contemptuously to the carpets. He rushed across the room, where he found Katherine staring blankly at the wall, shaking uncontrollably and whimpering.

He didn't bother to ask her questions, but rather scooped her up in his arms, hurrying her back to his chambers. Once again, no one dared challenge him.

It took him a while to wash Delira's remnants from Katherine's hair and skin, and then get her into a clean shift. As he did, Ethan thanked the gods that she had left clean livery in his chambers.

When he had her cleanly dressed, he checked on her again. Her eyes remained vacant, her expression slack. He picked her back up and, rather than bother running through the hallways again, he pulled the candle and firelight around him, Fading the short distance he could manage with such limited resources, directly into the East Wing corridor Simon Declan shared with the other minor lords.

He wandered for a few moments before he found a maid. "Excuse me, I believe this maid belongs to Lord Declan." He made sure his voice brooked no questioning. The maid was already frightened enough of his size and the catatonic maid in his arms to bother asking many questions. "Where is he housed?"

The maid pointed to a door just over Ethan's shoulder. The big Magus nodded his thanks, then turned and kicked down the door.

From the other room he heard the crash of shattering crystal. He stomped through the first room and into a small parlor to find Declan shaking in front of the fire, his eyes wide.

"You're Simon Declan?" Ethan demanded.

Declan nodded, slowly taking in the tableau before him.

Ethan nodded curtly, "Good. We need to get out of here. *Now.*"

Declan recovered a touch of his dignity, "'We', lad? Who, exactly, is *we*?"

"You, me, and Katherine," Ethan said shortly. "Gather what you hold precious and follow me."

Declan disregarded the goods in the room, stepping boldly forward and examining Katherine. "What did this to her?"

"Delira. Her best attempt at feeding in her new form, I suppose."

Declan looked up at Ethan, curiosity glimmering in his eyes, "And where is Lady Delira now?"

"In her room," Ethan growled, "and somewhat across the front of my shirt and trousers."

Declan stepped back, taking in the evidence literally painted across the large Magus. Ethan knew he smelled like a butcher's, except the black smear across his front was quickly hardening into an unrecognizable tar.

The Lord seemed to assess the situation with surprising alacrity. "Very well. What's your plan of escape?"

"The stables. There will be plenty of carts leaving the city today to collect grain and lumber from the villages surrounding the Wood. If we can get you and Katherine out in one of those carts, would you be safe in the Wood itself?"

Declan considered before nodding, "Seems reasonable enough. Even if Lord Captain Drago isn't there, I've heard word that the Queen found refuge there following the sacking of the city."

"Then let's not waste time talking," Ethan grumbled, turning sharply and leading Declan down towards the stables.

"Is there no magic you can perform to simply take us there?" Declan demanded. "I've heard that you lot can move anywhere with a thought."

"It doesn't work like that," Ethan grunted, hefting Katherine a little higher to gain a better grip, "We need light to Fade. Lots of it. And besides, it leaves a traceable echo. Bael would simply follow us. But if we take a cart, and if no trail leads him to the stables, he will have no more knowledge of where we went than anyone else."

"Clever lad."

Andariana was growing nervous. There had been an awful lot of noisy chatter in the hallway. Roux had gone to check on it, but he'd been gone longer than she was comfortable with.

When a figure appeared in the doorway, it was decidedly not Roux Devaan. She squinted to make out the features beyond the impossibly long hair, the stand of imperious command, the movement like liquid grace.

Her heart leapt into her throat as those elements reassembled themselves in her mind. The figure stepped forward, and Andariana was glad she was already seated, lest she fall straight to the floor.

"Rhi?" she choked, staggering to her feet on shaky legs.

A second later she was caught up in her younger sister's embrace. It was as warm and heartfelt as she recalled, and she felt that warmth reflected in the tears falling freely down her cheeks.

"How?" she mumbled into Rhiannon's shoulder. "You were dead. They said you were *dead*."

Rhiannon softly kissed her cheek and stepped back, "Yes, I've been hearing the most interesting things about myself since I've been 'resurrected'."

Andariana just stared at her sister, still so youthful and bright, but also decidedly older. This was not a woman who had stepped out of the past, nor one reborn. This was her sister, but a sister time had never forgotten, though she'd tried her best to.

"From whom?" Andi managed finally.

Rhiannon laughed, the lilting sound reminding Andariana of a lark as it had when they were but children. Rhiannon had always seemed to be a bird of some sort to Andi, always flitting from this branch to that, singing as bright as the morning sun, while her attention was constantly diverted by a thousand different things at once. Being around her had always been invigorating and exhausting at the same time.

Rhiannon gave a light chirp of a chuckle, "Who would you think? My son, of *course*."

Andi blinked in surprise, "Jonas? You've already met Jonas?"

"And Aleksei. Aleksei is the reason I'm free, actually."

Andariana held up a hand in self-defense, "Sister, I'm afraid I have yet to get over your return, much less the manner in which it occurred." The Queen took a moment to right herself, "Where the hell *were* you?"

Rhiannon cackled, "There's the Andi I know. Queen! Well, you're far more suited to the job than Marra ever was. Gods, whatever became of our little problem child?"

Andariana averted her eyes towards the fire, "It isn't a pretty story, Sister. I'm afraid neither of us have done you proud, as we'd hoped. Neither of us ever set an example worth following. Marra made a bloody mess of things before she tromped off into the swamp with that zealot Rafael, and I hardly fared better."

Rhiannon raised a hand, commanding silence, "You forget I've missed the last twenty-one years, Sister. The last thing I really recall from that time was Joel's death. The Inquisition I suffered under Kevara Avlon, Jonas being taken from me, and being trapped in that bloody tower for ages all to blur a bit together. I must admit, my knowledge of the war was thin by that point, being imprisoned up in Dalita."

Andariana sank back in her chair, running a hand through the snarls in her chestnut hair, "Gods, but it's been a long time. Rhi, it's been an absolute nightmare. I hardly know where to begin! And it's all my fault. *All* of it."

She didn't want or expect to dissolve into a sobbing fit, but the moment she felt it overcome her, Rhiannon was hugging her again, holding her gently and rocking her while whispering kindnesses in her ear.

"It's alright, Andi. I'm here, just like when we were girls. Jonas is coming soon, with Aleksei. That's a wonderful young man you raised. Perfectly splendid. I'm so sorry I couldn't be there for him when he needed it," Rhiannon kissed the top of her head, "but *you* were. And that is a debt I can never repay you. Because of what you did, because of the man you raised, I am free again. And I will never let that be forgotten."

Andariana clung all the tighter to Rhiannon, rocking gently back and forth for what seemed hours. When Andariana opened her eyes again she was in her bed, and Rhiannon was sitting in her chair, watching the fire speculatively.

"How did I get here?" Andi asked gently.

Rhiannon turned and offered her a bright smile, "You fell asleep. Poor thing, you were so exhausted! So I put you to bed. But I've been here the entire time. I'm not about to venture back out into that bloody maze, and I'm *not* about to leave you alone."

"Where's Roux?" Andi asked, sinking back into her pillows.

"Who? Oh, the young Ri-Vhan on crutches with the golden eyes?"

"Gods, he's been such a blessing in all of this."

"And he's with you because...." Rhiannon pried.

"Because he's fallen madly in love with my daughter, Rhi. With Tamara. They'd didn't spend very much time together, so 'love' seems like a stretch. But whatever you want to call it, his...infatuation with

Tamara has made him a tireless crusader bent on getting her back, and I can hardly fault him for that. She's been missing for weeks. Months, perhaps. I've lost track of time since she's been gone. I don't even know what *season* it is."

"It appears to be the end of winter or the beginning of spring," Rhiannon said dryly. "Andi, I must confess, I have no idea either. Until yesterday, I was a prisoner in Je'gud."

Andariana sat upright at that, "*Je'gud?* But that makes no *sense.*"

Rhiannon's face darkened, "It does if you're Kevara Avlon, apparently. At any rate, Jonas and Aleksei freed us, a Magus named Yosef and myself, only yesterday morning."

Andariana regarded her sister with suspicion, "Sister, if you left Je'gud yesterday...."

"And arrived here yesterday afternoon," Rhiannon pressed.

Andi chuckled, "Did those years in captivity drive you mad?"

Rhiannon's smile grew wicked, "Nearly. But when Jonas arrived, he made a few...'discoveries'. Yosef and I Faded here, Andi. *Faded.* Like in the stories!"

Andariana froze, "Jonas knows how to Fade?"

Rhiannon nodded, studying her sister's expression. "Is that bad?"

Andariana snapped out of her brief reverie, "Bad? Not necessarily. Jonas is indeed a wonderful man, but he is...unpredictable. Aleksei is no different. In that way, they are perfectly suited. Jonas possessing such an impossible ability...it makes him very dangerous, until he learns to *control* it."

Rhiannon laughed, "From what I can tell, he is already quite formidable."

Andariana gave Rhiannon a look that spoke volumes, "Sister, you truly have no idea."

Ethan laid Katherine in the hay, stepping back and locking the cart's gate into place. Declan finished strapping in the horses and swung himself into the driver's seat. Ethan followed him, gently shoving him aside.

"With all due respect—" Declan began.

Ethan took the reins in his powerful hands and cracked them once. The horses charged out of the stables and down the road towards the ruins of the Palace Gate. "You stay in the back with Katherine," Ethan said gruffly.

"She needs someone with her right now. It doesn't have to be me, but it needs to be someone who cares about her. Her mind has suffered a bad insult. She needs reassurance. She needs love. I can drive this cart better than you, and I'm much less likely to draw suspicion than you are, Lord Declan.

"But that means you need to be with *her* right now. Talk to her. Say anything you think of, just try to remind her who she is, why she matters. Why she matters to the Lord Captain, to me. Why she matters to you. *Anything.*"

Declan stared into Ethan's fur-brown eyes for a long moment, then clambered in the back of the cart. When Ethan passed through the Palace Gate unmolested, he checked over his shoulder. From what he could tell, the alarm had not yet been sounded. There was no pursuit. He glanced down into the cart and saw Declan cradling Katherine's head in his lap, stroking her hair, whispering gently in her ear.

Ethan turned his attention back to the road, guiding the horses through the thick crowd, dodging Kalinori on foot, soldiers on horseback, wagons and carts much like his own returning with their daily haul.

It took longer than he would have liked to reach the outer edge of the city. By then, he knew the alarm must surely have sounded. Bael would not appreciate the way he had dispatched a valuable lieutenant. He didn't imagine the Demon was far behind them.

That was the primary reason he had wanted Declan in the back of the cart. If Declan was fresh after the run through the city, he would have a better chance of making the run to Seil Wood. Ethan didn't have any illusions of escaping with Katherine.

It was a lovely dream, but after seeing the pain that Princess Tamara endured, seeing the sacrifices Katherine had made just to gather information for her people, her friends, it had become shockingly clear to him; he wasn't worthy of her, of people like her.

These were good people, people fighting for something they truly believed in. Believed in enough to put their lives at stake in the hopes of defeating insurmountable odds. Ethan had never believed in anything like that, not anything that required true thought. But he believed in Katherine. If she truly cared about a cause, about people that much, he couldn't help but care too.

That was why he knew he'd have to stay behind.

They approached the East Gate, and Ethan whipped the horses into a dead run. He caught the shimmer of the Archanium a moment before they would have crashed into it. Ethan hurled a counter, shattering the ward, looking over his shoulder to see Bael flickering in and out of existence behind them.

He was surprised that their flight would have roused the Demon himself, but that only confirmed the importance of the cargo he carried.

Ethan shattered yet another barrier, this one considerably stronger. Bael was getting closer, his aim and strength increasing with every flicker. Their only advantage was the night; the weak torchlight wasn't much to Fade with.

He imagined the effort Bael was expending was exhausting in and of itself. Still, Ethan had to slow the horses lest he encountered a barrier he couldn't destroy. Bael would be on them in a matter of moments. He took a deep breath to steel himself for what was to come. He would die, that much was obvious, but if he could buy them to time to run, it would be well worth it.

A hand clasped his shoulder, "Take good care of her lad. I'd have liked more time with the both of you."

He heard Declan's words before he registered that the man was no longer in the cart. He saw Katherine sit up, her face a mask of confusion and pain. "What's going on?" she moaned.

She turned her head just in time to see Declan making his stand before the Demon.

Just in time to see Declan's head fall casually away from his body.

CHAPTER 45

RIDDLES IN INK, RIDDLES IN BLOOD

Aya sat at her desk, Jonas's book opened on one side, the parchment that had nearly killed Raefan...nearly killed *her*...on the other.

Raefan stood guard, as he had for the past three days, his sword but an inch from his grasp. She wasn't exactly sure what he was expecting to *do,* should the wind demon make another appearance. Through their bond, she knew he didn't either.

But she also knew that it didn't matter. She felt his humiliation, his horror at letting her down. At exposing her to danger like that. She had nearly been killed, and Raefan burned with the full brunt of that shame. Never mind that it was a creature of air, fully beyond his ability to fight.

No thought for his own life, only for hers.

Which was why Aya did her best to remind him that his life *was* hers, just as hers was his. One could not survive without the other. It was a cruel bargain, but she had never questioned the benefits.

The closeness, the sheer intimacy of being Bonded for the past fifteen years. She could hardly count the moments she'd doubted herself, had nearly given up, only to be buoyed by his strength and fidelity. Those were things she never questioned.

She knew he did not stand beside her desk to guard against attack, but to remind her that he was there, not just in thought and feeling, but for *her*.

He was protecting her from far more than a simple wind demon. He was protecting her from doubt and uncertainty. He was her stone in the storm. A reminder that should she ever falter, he would catch her. Just as this time, she'd been the one to catch him.

Aya forced her eyes from Raefan's straight form and perfect posture, from his broad shoulders and pert rear. She made herself focus once more on the parchment she'd pulled from his throat.

It was a list of names. From what she could piece together, since the wind demon had failed to kill Aleksei, and therefore Jonas, Bael had sicced it on those around them. The sangualligraphy was finely shaped and shaded. She doubted anyone in Ilyar besides herself could have read it. Perhaps that was the joke. Kill the Prophet, kill the message. A lot of people would have died.

Could *still* die.

The demon wouldn't have used the parchment to suffocate Raefan if it was required to hunt down the targets listed in blood. But as she traced the shapes, images flashed through her. People, people she knew and loved falling, or bursting apart as they were discovered and destroyed by the demon, a creature Bael referred to as a *karigul*.

Of course, it was more of a boast than a plan. Likely, the wind demon had found her first because she had used her magic to defeat it once before.

It *remembered* her. And, in remembering its defeat at her hands, had sought out Raefan instead.

But the others, Henry Drago, Andariana Belgi, Roux Devaan, Ilyana and Marrik, Hade and Vadim, those would take longer, those threads harder to unravel. And if it believed, if it *could* believe, or think, that she was dead, perhaps it wouldn't be able to anticipate her next moves as she made them. Perhaps it would follow a set pattern without care as to whether she lived or died.

Perhaps she could lay a trap.

"It wants to draw him out," Raefan said, startling her.

"What?" she asked, rubbing her eyes.

He turned suddenly, for the first time in days, "Why come after *me*? Who am I to the Demon? I'm no one, except I'm linked to *you*. Killing you has become a priority for the Demon, it seems. But if I can't fight it, I can't kill it.

"That's where you come in. We've been mostly apart while we've been here, trying to hold things together. It caught me unawares because I wasn't focused my job protecting you, and it used that against us. But even if we both dropped dead tomorrow, it still hasn't killed Aleksei."

Aya's mind was foggy from lack of sleep and too much time staring at parchment in weak firelight. "So?" she managed, stifling a yawn.

"So," Raefan said slowly, "if it kills enough of us, Aleksei will get the message. He'd end up exposing himself to danger, lest more of us die."

"Us?" Aya asked in confusion.

"Yeah, *us*. Anyone who has fought by their sides, anyone who's ever helped them. Anyone who has been their friend. Their family. That's what you said, right? We're expendable. But once we're gone, our loss will drive him mad."

That last word burst in Aya's mind and she sat bolt upright, "What did you say? About going mad?"

Raefan watched her face carefully, "'Our loss will drive him mad'? Was that it?"

Her eyes flickered to Jonas's book, to the last phrase she had yet to translate. "Great gods," she whispered, "that's it. I've got to go. *Now!*"

Aya snapped the book shut and ran past Raefan. He grabbed the blood-etched scroll and charged after her, his steel a breath from being drawn.

Aya was in the stables, saddling a horse when he caught up with her, "*Aya!*"

The inherent anger and confusion in Raefan's voice brought her up short. Her pale green eyes shone, golden flecks glittering in the silver starlight.

"What are you doing?" he demanded. "Where are *going?*"

It took him a moment to realize that she was saddling Agriphon.

"To Taumon," she panted, struggling to fit Agriphon's tack correctly. "I have no idea where better to deliver this information. Perhaps they'll know there. But I *am* going. If you're coming with me, you'd better hurry up."

"Aya, I'm not sure he's the horse for you. Do you even *know* how to handle a warhorse?"

Aya glared at him, and Raefan clearly felt her rebuke hot across the bond. She turned and stroked the black mount's nose, standing on the tips of her toes and leaning forward to whisper to him. "I need to get to Aleksei. I need to find him. *Fast.* Will you take me?"

The horse whickered, shaking his head aggressively.

She glanced at Raefan, "What do you think that means?"

The Archanium Knight threw his hands up, "Are you losing your mind? I have no idea! I don't speak 'horse'! And from the looks of it, neither do you. We aren't Ri-Vhan Hunters. We can't pretend he'll understand us like he would Aleksei."

Aya ignored Raefan to the best of her ability. She didn't know if she'd be able to reach Taumon fast enough, but she was certain that if she took a regular horse she'd never make it in time. Finding Agriphon in the stables had been a burst of unexpected luck. She deeply believed that he possessed the stamina she needed, but every second that passed was a second she lost. A second that could lose them the bloody *war*. Gods, why hadn't she forced Jonas to teach her Fading when she'd had the chance?

"You try it, then," she said helplessly, taking a step back.

Raefan rolled his eyes, muttering under his breath, and stepped forward, fixing the warhorse with a stern gaze. Agriphon knew Raefan. He had ridden next to Aleksei enough times that the warhorse knew his voice, his posture, his presence.

He looked into the horse's eyes and said, "Can you take us to him? We have a desperate need. The whole war could depend on us getting to Taumon. To Aleksei. Can you understand me?"

Agriphon didn't move. When Raefan reached forward to place a hand on the horse's ebony coat, the stallion snapped at him. He yanked his hand back just in time to keep his fingers. With a stormy expression he turned back to her.

"This isn't going to work. You're going to have to come up with something else."

"Great gods," Katherine cried, "oh great merciful gods, *why?*"

Ethan cracked the reins and the horses dropped into a flat-out run, clattering the cart down the road towards the Seil Wood. "He saved us," he shouted over his shoulder. "He saved *you*."

Ethan glanced over his shoulder and saw Katherine slumped into an ungainly heap, her chest heaving with sobs. "Katherine? Katherine! You can't go back there. You've *got* to stay with me. Stay *here*, Katherine! If you don't, he died for nothing!"

She raised her head and looked at him with bloodshot eyes, her face a wreck.

"You've *got* to stay with me," he roared, his voice going hoarse from screaming into the wind. "And right now, I need you up here with me. I can't drive *and* protect you if Bael decides to follow. I need to be able to see you."

Katherine pushed herself to her knees and clumsily climbed into the seat, nearly falling in the attempt. He reached out to steady her, and she clung to his arm for support until she was finally able to make it onto the bench.

"How's your head?" he asked, trying to sound as gentle as he could despite the deafening thunder of his heart pounding in his ears.

She blinked several times, trying to regain her bearings, "I'm having trouble remembering things. I remember the fight we had. I remember the Princess." A look of horror crested her face again. "Oh gods, Tamara!"

Ethan raised a hand, "She told you to leave her. She told you to get word to the Queen, and that someone would come for her."

She gave him an accusatory glare, "What else did you overhear?"

Ethan shrugged, "That's about it. But from the way you acted, the way *she* acted, I could tell that whatever you two were discussing was highly treasonous." He stole a glance into her accusatory eyes, "Treasonous, but important. Gods, Katherine, if it wasn't important, would I be in this cart with the bloody *Demon* chasing me? Would Lord Declan have sacrificed his *life* to give you that extra moment to escape?"

She turned her eyes away from him, onto the road.

The Seil Wood was only a few leagues distant from Kalinor, and they had already made more than half that distance. The horses were fresh and the cart was light. With the time Declan had gained them, they had easily outdistanced Bael and any others. The farther they got from Kalinor, the less light was available for Fading.

He could feel her relax in the seat. "So, we're going to the Wood," she said, so softly he could barely hear her. "What happens once we get there?"

Ethan shook his head, "I honestly don't know. I know the Ri-Vhan have helped Aleksei Drago in the past. I believe he's one of them, or something to that effect. If we can find them before something finds us, we might be able to get word to the Queen in Taumon. Whatever it is Tamara told you, you wanted it out as soon as possible. If the Ri-Vhan have a way of communicating with the Lord Captain, it could be the key to ending this damned war."

Katherine closed her eyes and rested her face in her hands. "Gods, my memory is playing tricks on me. I can hardly remember my *name* right now, much less whatever secrets Tamara imparted to me."

Ethan's hands tightened on the reins, his knuckles white. She couldn't remember? Gods, he was risking both their lives, Declan had lost his, and now she couldn't *remember*?

"I'm sure it will come to you in time," he managed.

Seil Wood loomed large before them as he closed the final league. The Archanium spiraled and raged in his vision as he guided the horses along the road. Katherine might be hopeful that they had left Bael behind, but he had no such illusions.

His master was not so easily bested. He was just waiting. Ethan watched the Archanium for any sign that the Demon was following them, but thus far he'd seen nothing.

As Ethan closed the last hundred paces, everything changed.

He felt it like thunder tearing across, *through,* the Archanium. He knew what it was before he saw the Demon appear. Very few individuals made such an impact on the Great Sphere. Katherine gasped, but Ethan simply handed her the reins. "Ride into the Wood," he commanded. "He can't hurt you once the Wood has you under Her protection."

She stared at him pleadingly, "What about you?"

Ethan shrugged again, "I suppose I'll find out." He leaned over and gave her a quick kiss. "I love you, Katherine Bondar."

And then he leapt from the cart, running forward until his momentum was spent. Bael stood before him, blocking his path into the Wood. He knew what he was facing. He harbored no illusions.

"You stupid child," Bael said with a shake of his head. "Was that silly girl really worth it?"

Ethan squared off against his former master. "More than you could imagine, Demon."

Bael snorted.

Ethan heard Katherine cry out. He turned his head to see the cart empty as it vanished into the Wood. Katherine struggled to her feet and began limping towards the tree-line, her face braced in pain.

He turned back to Bael and found the Demon staring at Katherine in consternation. Ethan felt the Demon reach for a blaze. He ran forward and lashed out, not with the Archanium, but with his fists. He dealt Bael two solid strikes across the face before the Demon managed to throw him back.

Blood ran freely down Bael's face, and Ethan was surprised to see the look of panic in the other man's eyes. Ethan hurled a rumble forward, cracking the soil and stone beneath Bael's feet, hurling the Demon back. He dodged a poorly-aimed flare and rushed forward again, punishing Bael's torso with blow after blow. Bael's eyes were glazed, so he gripped the Demon's head and drove it into his knee for good measure. He felt bone break.

The earth erupted under his feet.

Ethan landed on his back, the air forcibly ejected from his lungs on impact. Still, he managed to roll to his feet as the space he'd just occupied burst into a sphere of fire and thunder.

He sucked in air and held on to his tenuous grip on the Archanium. He spared a glance to the side and noted with relief that Katherine was nowhere to be seen. He prayed to every god he could think of that she'd actually reached the Wood.

That she was safe.

Bael stared at Ethan in genuine disbelief. "You've more talent than I gave you credit for. It's a shame you have to die."

Ethan ignored the Demon, sending out one spell, a weak series of blaze phantoms that flew at Bael from multiple directions. Bael laughed as he easily waved the spell away. That was why he completely missed the whisperwind Ethan cast just behind the blaze.

The air resounded with the shattering of bone as the Demon went flying back towards the Wood. He slammed into one of the mighty oaks making up the tree-line with punishing force.

The tree burst forth with wicked, thorn-covered tendrils, its vines wrapping Bael in a quick coffin as the trunk opened itself and swallowed the Demon whole.

Ethan didn't spare a second more to stare. He raced past the bulging tree and into the Seil Wood. He saw Katherine a heartbeat before the forest floor gave out beneath her feet. There was a deep vibration beneath him, and the earth yawned open.

He fell into suffocating darkness.

Vadim sat high above the pass. He and Hade had worked their way across most of the Askryl Mountains, dropping impassable avalanches into every pass they found. This was the last. If Aleksei and Jonas wanted to get out of Fanj, if they *made* it out alive, they would have to come through here. There was no other option.

At the same time, food was becoming scarce this high on the steppes. They had nearly run through all their supplies, and hunting was becoming harder by the day.

Vadim was beginning to think that this whole mission had been some sort of bizarre setup. They should have succeeded the first time, while Jonas still underestimated Hade. With that element gone, their only other option was to hide and create an impossible circumstance. The rupture of the pass had nearly been enough to crush Jonas, but once again he'd tapped into the Seraphima, miraculously surviving their trap.

Even as they sat atop the bluff, Vadim was at a loss. His own gift from Hade would do little against Aleksei. The Hunter was a superior warrior and tactician. It wasn't admitting defeat, as Hade so often claimed, but merely acknowledging his opponent's very real prowess.

Hade was napping in the shade, trying to maintain his strength and mental acuity should they spot Jonas and Aleksei on the horizon. Somehow, Vadim doubted they would.

Not today. Perhaps not ever. Deep inside, he hoped he never saw either man again. That he would never be forced to complete this ridiculous crusade. It had to end, either with his own death, or with the deaths of people he respected and admired. There was no good outcome, as far as he could see. He was also starting to doubt his memories of the supposed goddess who'd set them on this wild goose chase. What if she wasn't divine at all, merely a supremely talented Magus? What was this all *actually* for?

Hade sat up suddenly, his ear cocked to the side.

"What is it?" Vadim grumbled, staring out over the horizon.

"I don't know. It's strange. It *sounds* strange. It feels...like...I don't know. It's like the wind is *twisting* somehow."

Vadim turned to regard his Magus with a frown. Hade didn't normally speak with uncertainty. As of late, every statement had been more certain than the last.

But then he heard it.

The fine hairs on the back of his neck lifted as he felt the charged air suddenly shift. He could even *see* it, a whorl of distortion, air that warped and contorted the wrong way. It tumbled towards them with shocking speed.

"Vadim, get back!" Hade managed, just before the tumble of air drove into his Magus. He watched in helpless horror as Hade burst apart into a bloody haze. He hadn't even managed a scream.

The bond snapped.

If Vadim hadn't already gone into shock, the pain might have been too much to handle. His half of the bond crashed into him with a heart-shattering impact. He insides tore apart, even as his vision started to black out.

Bloody foam poured from his mouth as he doubled over in the extreme agony of death. The broken bond cut through everything, through the shock, through every defense he'd ever managed. The pain was everything.

And then it stopped.

Vadim blinked as his chin was lifted by two fragile fingers. He blinked through his tears, and saw the "goddess" standing over him, her emerald eyes blazing brighter than the sun, coursing with an inner fire.

"I'm not done with *you* yet, little sparrow," she purred. "So *sorry* about your friend. A tragedy, to be sure. Imagine, if he hadn't been so *rough* with my precious Aleksei, he might still be alive!"

He tried to form words around the thickening blood in his mouth, but found himself incapable of even that simple action.

"But I have *plans* for you," she continued as though nothing had happened. As though she wasn't standing in the remains of his Magus, of his friend. "Such *delightful* plans, my little sparrow."

Aleksei took a step, his boot sinking into the thick moss that dominated the floor of Seil Wood. He noted with surprise that Jonas's Fading had brought them only to the Wood's edge, rather than the Ri-Vhan village as he'd requested.

He turned and found the Magus on his knees, grasping his head.

Aleksei dropped to a crouch next to the prince, "What's wrong?"

Jonas's eyes were pressed closed, the veins at his temples standing out from strain.

"That one hurt," Jonas allowed. "A *lot*. It's like the Wood pushed me *out*. I knew where I was going, I knew where to land the spell. But

She shoved us to the side. I'm fine. I'll be fine. It was just...unexpected."

Aleksei rose, his face a storm of anger and confusion. She shouldn't be acting like this. And goddess or child of a goddess, or whatever She called herself, Aleksei was beyond caring. If She was hurting Jonas, Aleksei was *not* happy. And if he was unhappy, he would make damn sure the Wood was keenly aware.

My Hunter returns!

Her ebullient trumpet sounded in his mind, blocking any other thought. He could hear Her giddiness, Her laughter. And a sort of... playfulness he didn't recall.

Nothing like the nightmare creature who had invaded his dreams for weeks. No smokey pall, no bones made of bone. It was the voice of the Wood he remembered, mostly. The mother, the mentor who had guided him when he doubted himself, when he'd needed Her most.

Mother, why would you push us out? he demanded.

Jonas remained on the ground, still clutching his head in his hands.

Questions, too many questions. I've had my fill. Venture further, my Hunter. Should you still be worthy, perhaps I'll deign to proffer an answer.

Aleksei stood there, stunned by Her response. He clenched his jaw in frustration, wanting for all the world to bark an angry retort.

Instead, he dropped into a crouch and put his arm around Jonas's hunched shoulders. The Mantle rippled forth and a single scarlet talon dipped into the other man's neck, spilling life and vitality into his Magus's veins.

With a gasp, Jonas looked up. His emerald eyes glittered as he turned his head to stare at Aleksei. He leaned forward, giving Aleksei an appreciative kiss. "You didn't have to do that."

Aleksei winked at his prince, "You didn't have to move us across the entire bloody *continent*, but you did it anyway."

Jonas returned his smile, pushing himself to his feet. "Well, that setback aside, we should probably find Roux and tell him what's happened."

Aleksei nodded slowly, "No doubt he'll have more recent news from Taumon. If Andariana is set on staying put, I hope she's at least communicating with him. We wasted enough time in Fanj as it is."

"Wasted?" Jonas asked, the hurt showing on his handsome face.

Aleksei groaned as he stood, "Not wasted. At all. We brought back

Richter for the gods' sakes! We found your *mother*. I fulfilled some kind of bloody prophecy.

"But we didn't find Tamara. For every good thing that's happened while we've been gone, I only hope we don't reach Andariana to discover ten thousand horrors have happened in our absence. That's all I meant."

Jonas smiled, his eyes twinkling as he stood on his toes and kissed Aleksei again, harder this time. "I know. And I'm sorry. I'm still trying to decide how I feel about all of this. I'm trying not to be disappointed by not finding Tamara, but I am.

"And I'm confused, honestly, by finding my mother. I don't know how to feel. I want to trap her in a room all by myself and just *talk* to her, but I know we don't have time for that right now. I find myself praying for a few moments' peace so we can just discover who the other *is*."

Aleksei wrapped his arms around Jonas, pulling him close, "When we get to Taumon, I have no doubt there will be meeting after meeting. Everyone will need briefing on everything, every which way you can imagine.

"I can handle all of that for the both of us. And you can use that time, short though it may be, to be with your mother. I could hardly ask anything else of you when something so important is at stake."

"But—" Jonas began.

Aleksei pressed a finger to Jonas's lips, "I'm not joking. I lost my mother, years ago. I *know* she's not coming back. Gods be praised, my father is still alive and well.

"But believe me when I tell you, you have to take every moment you can, especially with something as delicate as this. The last thing I would ever wish for you is that you find her, only to somehow lose her, that you never get the chance to know each other. I *refuse* to let that happen."

Jonas stared at Aleksei for a long moment.

"Thank you," he said finally.

Aleksei hugged his prince tightly to him, "I wouldn't be much of a Knight if I didn't pay attention to this sort of thing." There was a pregnant pause. "Also, you mentioned that we're getting married?"

Jonas blushed, "Sorry, I had actually thought of *asking* you. You're not angry, are you?"

Aleksei quirked a smile, staring into Jonas's seeking emerald eyes, "As long as I get a proper proposal, no, I'm not angry. Though you might want to ask my father if he's alright with the whole setup. He's a very traditional man, as far as Southern Plainsmen go. He'd appreciate the courtesy."

Jonas's uncertainty melted into an abashed grin, "Consider it done."

Aleksei noted the sinking sun on the horizon, "We should probably move deeper into the Wood. The sooner we find Roux, the sooner we'll have an idea of what's going on."

Jonas smiled, "Well then lead on, Master Hunter."

Aleksei's smile matched his prince's as he stepped into the Wood proper. It felt odd to be without Agriphon after having his horse as a constant companion for so long, but Jonas had said it was faster and easier to Fade without the stallion, and as much as he hated leaving his horse behind, Aleksei had to agree.

If he was going to be bouncing across the whole continent, he'd rather Agriphon be securely stabled, cared for, and exercised, so that the warhorse was ready when Aleksei needed him. Better than leaving Agriphon to wander the Wood while he ricocheted about with Jonas.

He felt a stab of guilt at the thought. His old draft horse, Dash, was still somewhere in the Wood. He'd asked Her to watch over Dash, and She'd promised to protect him. When the war was finally over, Aleksei would come for him. For now, there was no safer place for old gelding.

As he walked beneath the canopy, Aleksei breathed a sigh of relief. He'd forgotten how secure he felt under Her branches, how the entire aura of the forest soothed his spirits. He turned to say as much to Jonas, only to find the other man missing.

"Jonas?" he called, hearing his own voice reverberate back to him.

He frowned. The tree-line wasn't visible from where he stood. Either the Wood had shifted and left Jonas behind, or something very strange was going on.

Either way, Aleksei was having none of it.

"Where is he?" he called.

My Hunter has returned! I bask in the warmth of my Hunter's protection!

Aleksei's patience evaporated, "Where *is* he?"

You have no need of him. You are Mine. You will always be Mine.

Aleksei glared at the canopy. And then he began walking.

Do you go to Hunt? You have no bow. How will you accomplish your task, Hunter?

Aleksei ignored Her, his sense of direction drawing him inexorably towards the Heart of the Wood. He felt the forest twist around him, diverting him to the south. Aleksei reoriented himself and struck out once more for the Heart.

Hunter, why do you defy Me? You do not need to hunt the Heart.

Aleksei stopped walking, "Will you give him back to me?"

You have no need of him. You are Mine. You will always be Mine.

"Then I'm not interested in Your opinion," Aleksei barked.

He stalked off once again, keeping the Heart in his mind as he walked. Begrudgingly, the Wood moved to his desires and the waning gloam was snuffed out. He found himself in a land of pure black, his heightened senses the only thing that kept him from tripping over his own feet.

Aleksei kept walking. He wasn't sure if She was keeping Jonas in the Heart, or if he was heading there by instinct. But he made his boots move forward as he heard the unsettling clapping of the leshii, the chilling swish and swirl of the vodnoia in nearby pools of mist and stagnant water.

Finally, his right boot struck a painfully abrupt intrusion of stone and soil. He kept his howl of pain to himself, bending instead to examine the ring that made up the entrance to a darkened stairwell.

He glanced up at the black canopy. "What is this place?"

You have no need of him. You are Mine. You will always be Mine.

Aleksei continued to ignore Her, stepping over the ring of rigid stonework and setting himself down the curling stairway.

Hunter! If you go down into the darkness, you may not return.

"Will you return him? Will you give Jonas back to me?"

You have no need of him. You are Mine. You will always be Mine.

"That's what I thought," he snarled as he made his descent.

The stairs went on and on for longer than Aleksei could have possibly imagined. He wasn't sure if it took hours or just a handful of inexplicably dark and terrible minutes. Whatever transpired, Aleksei let a sigh of relief escape when his boots finally touched down on solid earth once again.

The chamber was crudely built, a tower inverted into the earth that ended in a poorly dugout tunnel. He broke off a piece of rella fungus and rubbed it between his hands to activate the hyphae into glowing. They would burn themselves out faster this way, but then again, he didn't intend to spend that much time in the belly of the Wood.

He stalked down the corridor, expecting to be attacked at any moment. He didn't know what She might send at him, but he was fairly certain She wouldn't let his insolence pass unpunished. But an attack never came. The rella glowed a healthy blue, filling the corridor and giving Aleksei more confidence with every step.

He advanced into a yawning cavern. The ceiling seemed to be made of nothing but giant rella fungi. With only one look, Aleksei knew where he was. This was indeed the Wood's Heart. The structure he was staring at was the Qoorenmir, the taproot that fed the Seil Wood, and possibly the Relvyn Wood as well.

Blighted.

He knew from the moment he saw it, saw the seething black that punctured holes in the Wood's prime root. It writhed and lashed, but Aleksei ignored everything but the root itself. He knew at once; this was why She hadn't objected to his insistence. *This* was why She allowed his impertinence. She was infected. And at least some part of Her wanted to be clean.

As Aleksei neared the taproot, the black infection lashed out at him. The first time, he thought it might just be an accidental slash across his arm. As he stepped closer, he realized he'd been mistaken.

More and more, the blackness reached for him, tried to wrap around him, to pull him in. But each time the Mantle met the whips of blackness, intertwining with them, merging with them until there was no distinction between the two.

Aleksei came as close as he dared, hundreds of tendrils now matched to the ebony that clung to the Qoorenmir. Slowly, he backed away, the blackness dripping away with the Mantle, clinging to it, following him.

With an audible *snap*, the Mantle's claws withdrew from the taproot.

The understanding of what he had to do sickened him, and Aleksei recited every curse he could recall as he strode forward, waving off the blackness as it lashed at him. He reached the taproot and planted his palm firmly against the rough skin of the root.

The Mantle roared forth and braided itself around the taproot, soaking the darkness into itself, into Aleksei. The Hunter grunted as the full power of the darkness flowed into him. He could feel the poison, the malignant energy that suffused the black. He took it on without question, allowed it access to his body and soul, a feverish battle raging throughout his being as he ripped the corruption from the root and pulled it into himself.

Time slowed to a crawl, torment twisting within him, like nothing he'd ever felt or imagined. The whole of existence dwindled, until it was just him and the Blight. There was nothing else. He was the Wood's protector, and he mercilessly removed the rot, until the Qoorenmir was clean of corruption.

"Where *is* he?" he croaked, finally ripping his hand away from the root, his voice dripping with danger.

I am sorry, Hunter, but there's nothing left.

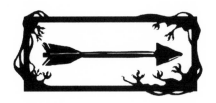

CHAPTER 46

DEVILS AND GODS

"I want him back. *Find* him!"

Aleksei's roar reverberated around the cavern, even as he stepped past the ivory root, the Wood obediently shifting around him. It was no longer a matter of request, it was a command that the newly-purged forest obeyed without question. His rage quaked about him, leaving tangible cracks in the firmament supporting the tunnel above him; flowering under the floor beneath his boots. He paid it no mind.

He was beyond caring.

He wanted Jonas.

If the Wood answered his demand with anything less than his prince, he would blast the bitch to splinters until he found what he sought.

You will not be happy. She finally conceded.

"I'm not happy *now*," he snapped. "I didn't think it possible for You to truly disappoint me. But as always, You've exceeded my expectations."

The Wood trembled. He knew the impact his words had, his every fiber rippling with the Blight he'd just absorbed. He did not speak them flippantly; She didn't receive them lightly, either.

A year ago, he would have been the one quivering. A year ago, he didn't have Jonas. A year ago, he hadn't *fought* for Jonas. Now, her protestations fell on deaf ears. Until he had Jonas, alive and well, he wasn't leaving. And if Jonas was somehow gone, or damaged, or changed beyond recognition, he would end the Seil Wood with his wrath, without thought or hesitation.

Aleksei was done apologizing.

He was done with the questions that arose from even the most difficult actions. Either it aided Jonas and himself, or it didn't. He was done with outlier possibilities. If something separated him from Jonas, the reckoning would be swift and severe.

The tunnel wall yawned open and Aleksei paused, staring at the profane scene unfolding in the chamber before him.

Jonas hung from the wall, yet Aleksei felt no pain or fear emanating across their bond.

Only paces from Jonas, Aleksei was astonished to see Katherine Bondar, and beside her a stranger, a man roughly matching Aleksei's own height and build, yet one ensorcelled with Archanium echoes. This was no mere man, he realized. This was a Magus.

As Aleksei studied the newly-revealed chamber, he realized that thick, gnarled roots were snaking into each of their veins. As he watched, the dark roots embedded in each captive throbbed, draining the very life from them, feeding that life into the Wood Herself.

"What are you *doing?*" he roared, afraid to move lest he disrupt some exchange he didn't fully understand.

Your love for Me has diminished.

That was *not* the response he'd expected.

"*What?*" he demanded.

The first one, the woman. She reeks of affection for you. Her knowledge of you permeates her entire being. So I took her. The boy loves her. I took him too. If she loves you, he must reek of that same affection, that same delicious confusion. Your Bonded tried to Fade into Me. I didn't allow it. I wanted to see what you would do. Foolish, selfish boy. I took him too.

Your love for them blinds you, diminishes your love for Me. You can't love them. They can't love you. They will pass. I will love you for all of time. I will love you through centuries, through epochs and aeons. And you will be My Hunter. Always My Hunter. And they will be gone.

"*No!*" Aleksei bellowed. The Wood rippled in displeasure. "If you refuse to hear me, I will leave this place, and I will only return to cut you down. I will personally see to it that you are forgotten in the ages to follow. You will die. I will break Your soul until You have nowhere to run but to me, and I will reject You."

The spirit of the Wood crested up around him. Aleksei felt Her anger, Her fear of his rejection and hatred, Her rage at his defiance bombarding him from the great oaks and tsugas far above. He fought to maintain his composure as the weight of a demigod collapsed down upon him.

He had no defense against such power. Except....

He had something She *wanted*, and it had nothing to do with their pact. She was trying to rob the most precious thing from him, but he would deny Her, no matter what She took from him, until Jonas was returned.

The Wood was fighting a frightening war, but he refused to be bested. He met Her anger with principled reason, with his father's earthy logic. The shock alone of seeing Katherine and the strange man with her only strengthened his conviction.

Whatever spirit had infected the Seil Wood, he wasn't going to fix it with a grand gesture. The Wood had irrefutably changed since he'd entered Fanj. She had warned him, and he'd ignored the warning. Now he understood the nightmares for what they had been from the beginning. Now he was ready to take action.

"Let them *go*."

If I release them, you will no longer love Me. Each one possesses something, elements *that make Me that much more desirable to you. I want it.* All *of it!*

"I don't care!" Aleksei howled into the darkness. "Return them to me. Now!"

The heat in his voice was enough to start a forest fire, even deep in the Heart.

If I give them back, you will abandon Me again.

"I didn't abandon You, Mother Wood. But the world is falling apart. I need my Magus. I need my friends. And no amount of Your magic, no amount of You robbing the inherent essences from those I love, from *Jonas*, is going to change that."

I must keep you.

"If you want to keep me, then let them *go*. Release Jonas. Release Katherine. You will never earn my love by stealing it from them. All You will ensure is Your own destruction. I *swear* it!"

At the harsh certainty in his voice, the Wood convulsed yet again. *As you wish, Hunter.*

Aleksei ran forward to catch Jonas, watching with uncomfortable consternation as the deep roots withdrew from the Magus's veins, leaving gaping holes in his pale flesh.

Katherine collapsed into a nerveless heap next to the unnamed Magus, both only weakly stirring.

"What *is* this place, Mother?" Aleksei demanded as he helped Jonas find his footing.

You left Me. You abandoned Me. They know you. They love you. I consumed their love, so you could love only Me. I was drinking them in when you insisted on taking them back. Now, you have taken that away. Selfish, selfish Hunter.

"You nearly killed him," Aleksei snarled. "If you wanted to make me hate You, congratulations."

There was a crack, and Aleksei felt the forest around him writhe in agony.

No!

"It's not a question or a command," Aleksei spat. "If you *ever* harm Jonas again, I will burn You to the ground."

The Wood grew instantly belligerent, bearing down on Aleksei once more with the full weight of Her being. He stood over Jonas, bracing himself, his mind threatening to shatter at any moment, as he stared down a god. In a fit of desperation, Aleksei threw out his arm, freeing ebony threads of the Mantle, of the *Blight*; allowing them to spiral into a vortex above him.

"I have taken something from you. Something dangerous. Poison that now lives with *me*. You should be *grateful*, at the very least."

The threads of the Mantle broadened and wrapped around the exposed roots that had only just been pulled from Her captives, drinking in the blood that dripped from their ends. And then drinking deeper, drinking *Her*.

The Wood quailed, withdrawing Her threat.

What do you want, Hunter?

Aleksei hauled the Mantle back. "I want to be free of this place. I want to be free of *You*. If I return, it will because You have redeemed Yourself to me. In the meantime, think about what You've done. What wrongs You've perpetrated with your blind lust for my love."

The Wood wailed at his words.

"You look terrible."

Delira smiled. If the tangle of pallid lips and fangs that wriggled across her face could be called a smile. The rest of her appeared much as Bael recalled, her hair black and tangled across the thin, fragile form floating a handspan from the floor, her legs dissipating into a light-sucking mist at the base.

Her transformation had been quite remarkable, drawing the demonic qualities from rusalka and vodnoia both to create something new.

Something uniquely Delira.

But what the water and air demons lacked, what his brother Azarael had been unable to manipulate and refine into a single essence, Delira had more than made up for with her own flesh. And her capacity to both inspire and devour fear had made the process complete.

Now she was wholly beautiful and terrible, a creature, a *weapon*, unlike anything the world had ever seen.

Bael was pleased.

And disgusted.

"Congratulations, you managed to pull yourself back together. I did wonder how Ethan would handle your torture of his little whore."

Her face crumbled into a hideous hole of shock. It was like seeing art through the eyes of a madman. The very idea brought out a grin in Bael.

"He destroyed me," she rattled, pulling her features back together.

"And you righted yourself. Well done. Our experiment was a success."

"What happened to you?" she asked, her eyes bugging out to take in Bael's skin, the deep gashes from the thorns of the Wood's nasty little stunt.

"I ran afoul of a tree. Ethan turned out to be surprisingly resource-ful. It also helped that he had a demigod to aid him. I suppose Seil is less than pleased with my...sampling of Her more enticing and dangerous denizens.

"We seem to disagree as to who owns such creatures. She was less than pleased by my ingress, though She tolerates *Azarael*. Women!"

Delira chuckled as a ripple ran through her entire form and belched from her mouth and nostrils.

"You *would* know so much about women," she gurgled.

His nose wrinkled, "I know enough to find you repulsive. Make yourself presentable, then join me in the tower. I've had a visit from one of my sources in Taumon. I think you'll find the information most entertaining. His Majesty is departing for Bereg Morya immediately. You will be in command of all projects until I return, and I cannot have you looking so repulsively...hungry."

The horror before him shivered, then began to fold itself inward, features warping and bones snapping as the creature Delira reshaped itself to resemble a human woman. She shrieked as the transformation righted her into the alluring illusion of her former self.

Bael stepped forward and gripped her fine porcelain jaw, turning her face this way and that until he was satisfied, "Good girl. The next time I see you looking like that horrid mess, I'd better be wiping your insides from the ceiling, is that understood? You are only to reveal your true nature when I command it. And never in my sight again."

Delira lifted her wrist and reset her bone, licking the blood from the wound as it closed up. "As you command, Lord Bael."

The Demon smiled.

Aleksei rubbed his temples, squeezing his eyes shut against the wailing of the Wood.

They were camped several leagues beyond Her boundary, but Her howling still easily reached him at this distance. The air with rife with apologies and laments. Aleksei did his best to shut them out, but it was proving an impossible task while they remained this close.

Neither Ethan nor Jonas had been in much condition to hold a trickle of the Archanium after Her assault on them. By the time Jonas had even been able to find the Great Sphere again, the light had been far too low to Fade even a handspan away, or so the prince claimed. Ethan seemed to agree, so Aleksei had stopped pushing Jonas to try harder, settling instead on hiking as far from Seil as possible before they lost the light.

Aleksei's head throbbed far too much for him to focus with anything resembling clarity. But he trusted Jonas enough to know that the prince would have done anything in his power to deliver Aleksei from his misery.

He forced himself to shut out the wailing Wood, keeping an eye on

Katherine's sleeping form and concentrating on the conversation the two Magi were having just a pace away.

"I'm afraid I don't understand at all," Jonas grumbled. "It makes no tactical sense that I can see. If Krasik knew where Andariana was this entire time, why hasn't he attacked the city? He could have had Taumon under siege for half the winter by now!"

"He didn't learn the truth nearly so fast, actually," Ethan countered. "In fact, I suspect that Lord...that *Bael* only had a hunch when he went to abduct the princess. He basically got lucky. But he also didn't share this information with Krasik until long after the fact.

"You have to understand, Highness, Bael and Krasik are hardly close. Bael tolerates Krasik like an irritant. Krasik is useful to him, so Bael maintains the fiction that he serves the man. But ever since the Lord Captain's humiliating defeat of Krasik's primary force, the real power in Kalinor has been Bael and the Magi. We're the real muscle behind Krasik's throne."

Aleksei could feel Jonas's delight glitter across the bond, cutting through the Wood's tantrum. It was like watching a wolf eyeing a kit, licking its chops in anticipation.

"What of the forces at the Drakleyn?" Aleksei managed.

"There's still a sizable force in the South, Lord Captain, but Bael is adamant that they be held in reserve until you're dead."

Aleksei had to laugh at that. An army was cooling its heels until *he* died? The idea was so ludicrous it hardly warranted a second thought.

"With all due respect, Lord Captain, you've been single-handedly credited in Kalinor with delivering a killing blow to Krasik's glorious rebel army. Additionally, it is known that you command an impressive force in Keldoan, though our...*their* numbers aren't very good. Bael believes that if he puts the forces in the South on the field, you'll just wipe them out. That would effectively end the war, and Bael's bid for power."

Jonas snorted, "I hardly think that would be enough to stop the Demon."

"No," Ethan said patiently, "but it would end any hope he had of gaining legitimacy."

"And since when has he cared about that?" Jonas demanded.

There was a pregnant pause, and Aleksei finally looked up to see complete confusion written across Ethan's face. After a long moment, the big Magus cleared his throat, "Begging your pardon, Highness—"

"Don't call me that," Jonas snapped.

"Uh...Jonas, then," Ethan growled back, growing quickly exasperated. "It's clear that you have a very poor idea of who Bael Belgi *is*."

"Says his former lapdog."

"Jonas," Aleksei grunted, "just let the man speak."

"Bael plays at being the pious prince in exile to his people. He is viewed with a divine devotion. The highest among his people are from his father's commune, in the marshlands north of the Wood. They are the most fanatical by far. You must remember, I've been following Bael for a good while now. Long before the sacking of Kalinor.

"I was with him the night he opened the Third Gate. The Third Key had been in his father's possession, before Bael killed him and assumed control of his father's people.

"Bael led them from being a grotty little cult, worshiping some 'Dark God', into the ruling class of Magi in Ilyar within the span of a year. But he based a great deal of his authority to lead on the fact that he is, in fact, the rightful heir to the Belgi throne."

"And he's not entirely wrong," Jonas said softly.

Aleksei felt sad irritation radiating from his prince. If Bael was in fact Jonas's first cousin, and Tamara's as well, he could potentially be older than either of them, Bael's mother Marra being the oldest of the three Belgi daughters.

He might have as much claim to the throne of Ilyar as Andariana. Or could have, until he gave his soul to the Demonic Presence. Aleksei didn't understand the laws of succession like Jonas, but he was reasonably certain that you had to have a beating heart to be a viable heir.

"He's dead, Jonas," Aleksei said softly into the night.

"And he's very aware of that fact," Ethan continued. "He would never have been able to rise to such heights without the Demonic Presence, but he had to sacrifice his humanity in the process. Bael is not a man who readily accepts compromise, so he's seeking to make himself *seem* like a legitimate heir.

"But in order to do that, he has to have a populace who are, at the very least, generally not terrified of him. He has had some small success in Kalinor by holding back on the brutality, and by staying out of the public eye. The less people see of him, the more forgiving they can be towards his inhumanity, and the more fanciful the stories about him being a walking corpse sound. And since he's not eating babies in the public square, it's difficult to put truth to his monstrosity."

"Alright," Aleksei said finally, "so he has to maintain the war if he wants to be king, and he can't put a proper army in the field until I die because he thinks I'll always win. Why not just kill me right out?"

"That's what the wind demon was supposed to do," Ethan said simply.

Aleksei heard Jonas inhale sharply. He forced himself to pay closer attention. "You know about that, then?"

"We *all* do. All the Magi, at least. It's been one of Bael's more obvious failures. He was supposed to be divinely chosen. He conjured an avenging wraith to hunt you down and devour your traitorous heart. That's what he told the lower Magi, at least. And then you survived. The more time that passed, the stranger it became that we never heard about you or Jonas being killed.

"Eventually, we all realized that whatever Bael had created to kill you had failed. And the idea that he could be bested like that was a revelation for many in his flock."

Aleksei let out a sigh, "So it's gone?"

"The *karigul*? I assumed you'd destroyed it somehow."

Aleksei groaned, "No. I've been told that it's impossible to destroy without destroying Bael himself. I've been hiding from it with this." He pulled Adam's feather from his shirt and spun the thread-bare filament in the firelight.

"Ah," Ethan said quietly. "You've hidden yourself, then? That won't work forever, Lord Captain."

"And what would *you* suggest?" Aleksei snarled.

Ethan paused a long moment. "I don't know," he conceded. "None of us ever thought that hard about how to *beat* the Demon, just how to strengthen him. Since we took Kalinor, he's had the lot of us working nonstop in the Voralla, trying to unlock a series of forgotten secrets, weapons from the Dominion Wars. Each of his captains oversees a specific project, and we're given very little time to do anything but work with our teams to bring our projects to completion.

"More and more, it almost seems like Bael has forgotten that the war isn't over. He doesn't concern himself with troops or tactics like he did before. Now he focuses on our projects with a sort of single-mindedness."

"He has Kalinor," Jonas said, "And the Voralla. Aleksei and I have been in Fanj for weeks. There haven't been any flies biting his flanks like there were, not for a while."

"Which is why that needs to change," Aleksei said, looking up and forcing the Wood's voice from his mind with a final and concentrated push. "We need to remind Bael that we haven't gone quietly into the night. But I don't want to take a bite." The Mantle rippled across his arms and chest, pawing at the air, talons bleeding with need.

"I want to *feed.*"

Morning light flitted lazily across the shadows of the room, casting a roiling mosaic of bright and dark across the slumbering couple. The sunlight brightened and flashed across Aya's face, bringing her back to the waking world with a yawn and a slow stretch.

She sat up, gently sliding Raefan's arm from across her bare chest and guiding it back to the down mattress. She could tell from his face nearly as well as their bond that the man was exhausted.

Her face reddened as she recalled exactly how he'd become so worn out. Their bond afforded him stamina unlike any mortal man, and it probably hadn't been the best idea for them to have engaged in such an...*athletic* demonstration of affection when they had been so weary, but the results spoke for themselves.

Her head was clearer than it had been in weeks, *months* perhaps. She couldn't remember feeling this energetic, or her mind being this acute, since she'd broken through to the higher realms of the Akhrana.

Since she'd made that discovery, so much of her time had been taken up either training the other Magi, teaching them how to find the new path across the Great Sphere, or researching the book Jonas had left under her protection.

She'd worked her mind to the breaking point, but her body had seen little activity. Raefan had erased any such deficits the night before, and now it felt that her mind and body were both thanking her for the respite.

Well, *most* of her body, at least.

She'd finally decided listen to Raefan, at least on the folly to riding for Taumon like a madwoman.

Jonas was supposed to report back to General Walsh once he reached Taumon, and when he returned, she'd be able to tell him all about her discoveries. It pained her to wait, but it would be ultimately be faster than trying to ride hundreds of leagues in winter. Perhaps he would finally relent and teach her to Fade....

She slipped out from the covers, shivering in the chill of another Keldoan dawn and casting a ripple of fire into the hearth.

The logs burst into a merry blaze, and Aya shook her head in wonder, stepping to her changing screen and pulling down her dressing gown.

This time last year, it would have taken the better part of her concentration to accomplish such a feat, but now it took no more effort than summoning a spark.

She shrugged her arms through the silk, lighting the lamps above her desk and the door. The light was bright enough outside, but the chill of dying winter still clung to the stones of their chamber. While there were hints of spring's arrival, the winds curling down from Dalita remained biting as ever.

Aya took a seat at the small desk. She tended to keep notes of particular import with her at all times, but in the chaos that was her desk, she doubted a spy could find anything of worth without carting off the whole lot.

And at any rate, she had crafted enough loose ends and false notes to throw anyone particularly thorough off the trail for a month before they recognized her ruse.

A trick from an old friend, she thought warmly, her thoughts briefly resting on Aleksei Drago. For a supposed farm boy, he was a ready equal to his Magus in the laws of deception and illusion.

Behind her, Aya heard Raefan stir. She glanced over her shoulder, wrapping her cascade of honey-colored curls into a tight bun and pinning it carefully as she watched him fumble for her in the mountain of snowy down that was their bed in the Betrayer's Bastion.

He finally looked up, blue eyes bleary. He rubbed at them absently as he finally caught sight of her. He glanced around the room for a long moment before sinking back into the avalanche of down. There was no danger, not here, not now. The man would be aware and ready should he be needed, but Aya had given him no sense of urgency, so he stole a few more moments' sleep.

Aya smiled to herself as she turned back to her notes. She picked up a sheaf of papers that chronicled her time studying Jonas's book, but tossed them aside when her eye caught something further down in the mess of texts.

She pulled the note free, frowning as she realized how recently it was dated. She would have do better about keeping things organized.

Written in Jonas's hand, it was something he'd given to her in the brief moment he and Aleksei had passed through on their way to Taumon.

With a start, she recognized it as a hastily scribbled note. There was mention of researching a new topic, but the lines that followed read like a madman's screed, citing the creation of the Archanium, and whether necromancy had been employed when ancient peoples had conjured it.

Aya blinked in utter confusion, scanning past that bit of insanity to a list detailing the cache he'd brought her, the relics from Fanj. She hadn't paid it much mind when Jonas had handed it to her, being far too busy persuading him to teach her to Fade. Somehow, it'd been lost amongst sheafs of parchment and precarious towers of tomes from the library.

There were too many items for her to understand every single one, and they had been in a terrible rush to get to Taumon. But now, as Aya studied the parchment closer, her eyes widened.

Theoretical weapons, and bits and bobs serving obscure purposes that made little sense to her crowded the list. She almost felt like a peasant reading prophecy, attempting to decipher the possible applications of some of the relics listed. And while it seemed Jonas had a gift for reading these intentions of magical items, his descriptions made little sense to her.

Except one.

Light, move. Shadow, stay.

Excitement flooded through her in a rush. It made sudden and absolute sense, and she cursed herself so violently for missing it that Raefan bolted out of bed, strapping on his sword-belt before he bothered finding his trousers.

"Gods, Aya, what is it?" he shouted, yanking the blade free and holding it at the ready, his body bare and bootless.

"Nothing!" But then she collected herself, "Not exactly nothing, but we're not being attacked. I'm just a very stupid woman."

Raefan frowned, leaving his trousers in a heap on the floor as he walked over and kissed her forehead, wrapping an arm around her, sword still at attention. "I don't believe you."

She smiled at his affectionate embrace before her eyes caught the silvery curved blade hovering mere inches inches from her face. The reality of the situation returned. "The fact remains that we're wasting time."

Raefan sighed as she pulled away from him, the bond radiating confusion and just a little bit of hurt.

"You were right to keep me from riding Agriphon to Taumon," she said softly. "That would have been silly. I was just out of ideas. I was going to wait for Jonas to return, but now I may not have to. Jonas Faded here, Raefan. *Faded.* That kind of magic hasn't been seen in centuries, but he managed it.

"At first, I chalked it up to Jonas being Jonas, but then I thought about it. *Really* thought about it. Jonas wasn't likely to just stumble upon magic like that. Unless he found it in Fanj. Unless it had been hidden away for a *reason.*"

Her eyes glittered green and gold, "Unless it the spell was housed in one of the relics he brought back."

Raefan blinked, and then understanding lit his eyes. "One of the relics he left here. But why wouldn't he tell you?"

Aya shrugged, "I don't know. Perhaps he didn't think they had enough time. Perhaps he was afraid that one of us would try something dangerous and get ourselves killed before he could come back and show us how it worked. That wouldn't be at all unusual for him."

Raefan scowled, his blond eyebrows knitting together before he sighed, "No, it wouldn't. For *either* of those blasted men."

Aya chuckled, pulling herself back into the moment and observing her Knight, standing in the middle of the room naked but for his sword belt, his blade drawn.

"Well, what do you say? Let's get properly dressed and see if we can find something in that cache he left."

Raefan nodded, stalking back to the bed and pulling his trousers up. He slipped on a shirt as she poured water into the basin built into the corner. She sent a trickle of flame into the water, steam rising from the bowl, rather than the icy chill she'd been expecting.

It was becoming more apparent to her every day how much this new path through the Archanium was improving their lives. And bit by bit, she was beginning to understand the Magi of old a little better.

How different their lives had been. How their world had worked once the Kholod had been expelled, and they'd been free to build and create the world *they* wanted. And how their use of the Archanium was a function of living, rather than a tool designed simply for survival.

Aya stripped out of her dressing gown and washed herself quickly, rinsing her hair for a moment before pausing. She stood before the mirror, reaching into the new river of Akhrana that rushed past her vision.

She chose a tumbling cascade of white and silver, drawing it into the room and running it through her hair. And just like that, the dirty water poured into the basin, leaving her hair clean and dry.

"Good gods," she whispered.

She backed away so that Raefan could shave and wash himself, watching the man relish in the warmth of the water, watching the cloth slide across his muscles and the runnels of water trickling down his body.

He turned to her, his face flushed, "Gods, woman, are you alright? I haven't felt you look at me like that since we were just bonded."

Aya blushed, "Sorry, I've just been feeling a little...clearer of mind recently."

Raefan arched a red-gold eyebrow as he lathered his face, "Not that I'm complaining, mind. Just surprised."

She felt a flicker of thought across the bond and her cheeks shone scarlet. She had forgotten that she was standing there naked while watching him.

Before things could escalate any further, Aya turned and threw open the stout cedar wardrobe that dominated the chamber near the door.

She dressed quickly, pulling on the warmest clothes she could find. Jonas had not secreted the cache in a pleasant place. Rather, he had placed it somewhere no one would think or *want* to search for it.

She would need help.

As she released the latch to step outside, the door burst open. Aya didn't have time to jump back as the soldier charged into the room, crossbow at the ready. The only thing that saved her life was that he hadn't expected her to be so close. The man crashed into her, throwing her back into the sturdy footboard of the bed. Her head cracked against the heavy wood.

She tried to reach for the Archanium, but it kept slipping from her grasp as she fought to remain conscious.

Above her, she saw the short fight as the man clambered to his feet and fired his crossbow at Raefan. She felt the impact as the bolt struck the Knight, then saw the soldier hoisted up by his hair, Raefan's sword ripping through his throat.

He dropped with a heavy *thud* only inches from where she lay, his body heaving as blood gushed from his neck. The blood stank of rot and decay. With muddied alarm, she saw the soldier's yellow-green eyes stare into hers as possession and life abandoned the man together.

She wished she'd had the strength to spit in his face, before Volos took him.

CHAPTER 47

REVELING AND RECKONING

"M other?"
"Jonas!"
The light of a sunrise burst in the air around him, despite it being well past midnight. He looked into her azure eyes and saw no sense of the shame he'd felt as a boy for performing spells inappropriately, for flaring up with the Archanium due to his emotions.

She raced forward, wrapping him in her arms. And in that moment he seriously considered shifting into a mouse or a bird, anything to end the unbearable emotional tension building within him. This was not something he was especially adept at or used to.

He wondered how Aleksei handled it.

But here he was once more, this time in Taumon, this time with the ocean crashing around him and his mother kissing his cheek as though he were a boy of three again.

They stood there for a long moment, her holding him, he stiff at first. He had no reference for this but, slowly, he relaxed. And as he did, each wall crumbled, each barrier he'd erected over time falling until he was a sobbing wreck in her arms.

And, just as he'd wanted since he'd been that boy of three summers, at once orphaned and yet surrounded by family doing their best, she smoothed his hair, kissed his forehead and whispered, "It's alright." into his ear.

"But you're here," he whimpered. "You're still here. The world doesn't make *sense*...but you're still *here*." He clung to her now, not the other way around. He clung to her for sanity.

He thought she'd laid another spell across him, but after a moment he realized that nothing had changed.

What *was* this, this feeling of warmth and security? So peculiar, so foreign, yet he didn't dare fight it. Being with Aleksei had become his definition of *home*, but these were emotions he had no name to give.

He stepped back and stared into her eyes, so warm, yet so strange to him. Staring at his woman who, like him, was powerful in so many unusual, unexpected ways. She had a palpable magic to her, and yet she clearly had no idea where she fit into his world. At least not the world he'd so carefully crafted around his intrinsic loneliness.

"I'm here," she managed through her tears, smiling all the while. "I'm here, and I'm not going anywhere. So I guess you're stuck with me."

"Oh, great gods."

Aleksei glowered at his queen, standing in her doorframe, "Why are you still here?"

Andariana had known this was coming. She had spent evenings pacing before the fire, trying to decide how she would respond, but she'd known it was inevitable.

And that he would *not* be happy.

She rose, her hands stiffly at her side, "My daughter was kidnapped, Lord Captain."

She practically spat the title, but it might as well have been bluster and breeze for as much as it impacted his broad frame.

"*Why* are you still *here*?" he repeated, calm and yet somehow menacing.

She'd never heard the man properly growl, but she was quickly gaining an appreciation for why his golden eyes unnerved her so. Those eyes, and the wicked, black claws that were rising from his beneath collar, tipped crimson and snatching at the air like snapping serpents, sent shivers through her.

Something was wrong. *Different*. This was not the Aleksei Drago who had sent her on her way from the Seil Wood.

This was a man changed.

"It seemed prudent to wait until we found her," she managed, despite the heat of his glare.

"*We?*"

Andariana attempted to muster a smirk, "Your cousin and I."

"*Roux?*" he demanded, incredulous. When he saw the truth in her eyes, his face stormed all the more, "Why would you listen to that *Treedarter* over *me?* Have you lost your damn *mind?*"

She raised her chin in defiance, "You are speaking to your Queen."

"I am speaking to a *fool*," he snarled, moving effortlessly forward. "You ignored *every*thing I told you. You might as well have spat in my face for all the credence you gave my efforts to keep you both *safe*. And, may I remind you that you are not a queen *now*, Andariana Belgi. You were *deposed*. You have lost your throne to a lunatic, despite my better efforts.

"I have spent the last two months trekking through sand and stupidity to find your daughter because *you* refused to get on a ship when you were *told* to. When *I* told you to. If you had, Bael would not have stolen her, and you would now be in Dalita. With the angels. Protected by the *Seraphima*, where the Demon is too weak to dare *any* assault. Where you would have been *safe*. Like I am."

He lifted a bloodied and beaten feather from around his neck and thrust it forward. "I have bested demons and armies to go to the other side of the world and back searching for your daughter. I have left a goddess trembling in my wake, and yet you cannot listen to one bloody word I *say?*

"So I ask again, 'Majesty', *why* are you still here?"

Tears welled in her eyes.

"What was I supposed to *do?*" she demanded. "I had no way of knowing how long it would take to find her. Gods, it took long enough to even divine who had taken her. Or where. You weren't here, *Lord Captain. You* were off trekking into nowhere rescuing my sister.

"It's charming and lovely, but not exactly helpful at the moment. Oh, except that it conveniently makes *your* prince heir to the throne as long as Tamara is missing."

For a moment, Andariana feared he was going to strike her. The moment flickered and faded, but his eyes thundered.

"He can't be king of a realm you already lost," he snarled.

Aleksei didn't wait to be excused. He turned on his heel, stalking to the door without another word. And then he was gone.

The sting of his final rebuke was so much more damaging than his initial outrage.

She sat down, tears clouding her sight.

Gods, but why did his anger hurt so *much*? What had happened to that man in the desert? She had never seen him like this, the Mantle writhing and burning in plain sight, his rage on full display towards *her*. She had never seen him truly angry, it seemed. She had seen him frustrated with her, but any hint of anger was always tempered with a soft sort of deference. Even when she had been making a clear mistake, he had been gentle with her.

That man was gone now, and something truly terrible had replaced him. Something hard, raging and strong, but never gentle. *Cruel.*

"Majesty?"

Andariana looked up to see the face of a girl, dark brown hair wreathing her face. She wore stained Kalinori livery. Andariana wiped her eyes, mustering what was left of her dignity.

"What is it?"

"Could I speak with you for a moment? Aleksei said it was important."

Andariana's eyes widened, but she waved the girl in. "What's your name?" she asked as the girl stepped into the room and shut the door behind her.

"Katherine, your Majesty. Katherine Bondar. I'm a very old friend of the Lord Captain."

At hearing the man's title so soon after his rebuke, Andariana felt her chest tighten. Her tears roared back to the surface, and it took all of her training to master them.

"And why are you here, child?"

Katherine blushed and glanced at the floor, "It's an odd story, Majesty. I found a man in a field several months back, near death. In the Southern Plain, near my village. His name was Simon Declan."

"*Was?*" Andariana stressed.

Katherine's eyes flitted to the carpet, "Yes, Majesty. Lord Declan died saving me, trying to buy me time to escape Kalinor."

Andariana stared at the girl. No, *woman*. This was not some silly slip of a farm girl. This woman had suffered, but had become stronger for it. Andariana had seen it enough in the last war. She could see it in her eyes. There was pain there, pain she'd *earned*, and an understanding that came from enduring trials Andariana could only imagine.

She waved to a chair, "Please, have a seat, dear."

Katherine gracefully sat across from her, and then launched into the most improbable story of what she'd seen and heard working whilst posing as a maid in Kalinor Palace, working as a spy with Simon Declan. Andariana had a difficult time maintaining her composure, trying to neither laugh nor cry at each new twist in the bewildering tale Katherine spun.

"And that's how I came to find the Princess, your daughter, in the North Tower, Majesty. But she was most insistent that I get this information to you at any cost. The bit about water weakening him...well, we hoped it might be helpful," Katherine stammered, her large brown eyes directed down at the carpet. Andariana saw tears glittering in the firelight, dropping freely to the floor.

"How do I know any of this is true?" Andariana asked, trying to keep her voice gentle. "You could just as easily have been sent by the enemy to lure me into a trap."

Katherine looked up startled, defiant, the edge in her voice cutting into Andariana. "Every word I speak is the truth. I suffered, Lord Declan *died*, to bring you this information. I have no interest in proving my worth to you, or *any*one. Ethan was working for Bael until I showed him the evil he was supporting. We nearly died any number of times just to tell you this, in the hopes that it may help you. Help *Tamara*.

"Whether or not you believe me is none of my concern. I have done as your daughter asked, and I have given you all the information I can recall. I apologize that some of it was...damaged when Lady Delira tried to destroy my mind, but then again, I wasn't exactly in *control* of that."

Andariana sat back in her chair and considered for a long moment. The woman's combination of bravery and bitterness was convincing enough for the moment. "Did Tamara tell you what she wanted me to *do* with this?"

Katherine shook her head, "No, Majesty. She only said that I should get this information to Aleksei—to the Lord Captain, as quickly as I could."

Andariana sighed, "I see. Unfortunately, I fear Lord Captain Drago is not particularly *pleased* with me at the moment."

To her surprise, Katherine snorted, "Majesty, begging your pardon, but whether or not Aleksei is *happy* with you has nothing to do with how much he *cares* about you.

"In fact, I would dare say that he is angry *because* he cares about you so much. Since he was a boy, he has only *ever* tried to protect me. Sometimes, when I'd do something stupid or dangerous, he would get so cross with me, but only because I'd put myself in harm's way."

Andariana frowned. The girl was right. Of course she was right. The man's heroics during the sacking of Kalinor alone put the truth to Katherine's words.

"Very well. Can you call for him? I would very much like to learn his thoughts on all this."

Katherine stood and offered a shaky curtsey before making her way out the door. Andariana stared into the fire, trying her level best to keep her thoughts from running away with her sense of reason.

To finally know where Tamara was, how cruelly she was being treated, and yet be so unable to reach her, to help her in any way, was nearly all Andariana could stand. But, to at long last find a chink in Emelian Krasik's armor was an opportunity too rich not to capitalize on. Gods, but what was she going to do?

The door opened again, and Aleksei stepped into the room, along with an even larger man she'd never seen before. Jonas and Roux were behind them, each man's face eager and angry.

"I don't recall summoning a mob," Andariana commented dryly.

Jonas stepped next to Aleksei, "Nevertheless, that's what you're getting."

She turned her gaze to Aleksei, standing there stoically, his arms folded across his chest.

With a resigned sigh, she sank back in her chair, "Very well. Lord Captain, I assume you know everything your...friend told me?"

Aleksei nodded gravely, "I do. You now know where Tamara is. You know of Krasik's weakness. The question that we now face is what do we do next? Where would you like me to start?"

She fought the smile that twitched at the edge of her frown. Katherine was right, his anger didn't signal hatred.

Quite the opposite.

"How do we get Krasik on the water?"

"That's the easy part. We set a trap, and we use you as the bait."

"*Me?*" It came out as a squeak.

Perhaps he hated her after all.

"When they sacked Kalinor," Aleksei said, his tone softer now, "you told me that Krasik was triumphant, having you in his control. You said he wanted you dead more than anyone else. That he blamed *you* for his son's murder.

"So, we make it easy. We use his obsession with you against him. We act as though you *had* followed my orders from the start, with a few modifications. We send you out to sea, pretend you're hiding out there, that it's a secret. Then we leak that secret out.

"Roux told me about the man that you tortured. One of Bael's eyes and ears in Taumon, with a rune burned into his hand? He apparently said that Bael could hear everything? Well, we have two such individuals with us right now. Ethan," Aleksei nodded to the giant standing beside him, "and Katherine. We let the secret out through the same sources, and Bael thinks he's breached our intelligence. He's not stupid, but he *is* enormously impressed with himself. Krasik wants you. Bael wants Jonas. If we put both of you in the same place, they might not be able to resist."

She frowned, "That is a lot of risk on a *maybe*, Aleksei."

His gaze hardened, "I regret to inform you, Majesty, that our intelligence is rather thin at the moment. We have few enough spies within Kalinor as it stands, and fewer in the Palace. Katherine's report and Ethan's standing knowledge are by far the two most valuable weapons we have at the moment."

Andariana sighed, motioning for Aleksei to continue.

"Bael marked Katherine as one of his own, and Ethan has been part of his retinue for the past year. He knows they're here. Katherine was present when he revealed Krasik's weakness. Documents stolen from this 'Lady' Delira's quarters support all of this. But Bael *doesn't* know what Katherine's told you."

Andariana opened her mouth to protest Ethan's very presence at this meeting, but Jonas raised a hand. An icy chill swept through her. She'd only felt the Seraphima once in her life, but it had left a distinct impression.

"Bael can't see everything, Andariana," Jonas noted. "If we're careful, I can manipulate his intelligence through Katherine and Ethan. He'll hear what we *want* him to hear."

Andariana nodded, acknowledging that there was a vast amount about her nephew and his Knight she had yet to understand.

"Once they come for you on the water, Krasik won't have an army to hide behind. And he won't have his...abilities to rely on, either."

"But he'll have Bael," she countered.

"And all the Magi Bael can muster, most likely," Aleksei agreed, "But Krasik only controls the port at Bereg Morya, and the ships there are dwarfed by those commanded by the Admiralty. They can only field so many ships, which can only hold so many Magi. In the meantime, we have Yosef, Jonas, and Ethan, here."

The big man next to Aleksei dropped to a knee, "I've worked closely with the Demon, Majesty. I know how he thinks, and I know his limitations. His and those who serve him. I humbly offer my talents and abilities, such as they are, in your service."

Andariana withdrew from the big man, "And what would possess me to trust a traitor who, until very recently, was working with my greatest enemies?"

Ethan shrugged his shoulders, "Nothing, Majesty. But you have only two other Magi, including your nephew, who can even *touch* the Naga-vor, from what the Prince has told me. Begging your pardon, Majesty, but at the moment you need every able Magus you can *get*."

Andariana blinked at him, at once shocked and intrigued.

"Adequately stated," she allowed.

Ethan stood and stepped back, seeming surprisingly embarrassed after such a pronouncement.

She turned to Aleksei, "Very well, Lord Captain. You seem to have that part of things well underway. What of my daughter?"

Roux stepped around Aleksei, "I'm leaving at first light. With any luck, I can infiltrate the Palace and get her out of there without anyone sounding the alarm. Once we're done here, Katherine has offered to give me a precise description of where she's being held. I just have to get to Kalinor. The rest should be relatively simple."

Andariana could scarcely credit what she was hearing. It sounded too good to be true. Too perfect. She knew Krasik's weakness, and he would almost certainly fall into their trap.

Roux could get to Tamara in a matter of days. In less than a fortnight, she might very well be rid of her greatest enemy *and* have her daughter back. The prospect of either was hardly to be believed.

To have both was incomprehensible.

"Very well," she said finally. "Lord Captain, the Admiralty is at your disposal. Do whatever you must to set your trap into motion. My dear Roux, the gods grant you a safe and expeditious return. Bring her back to me. *Please.*"

Roux nodded, exiting the room. Aleksei offered her a sad smile. He turned to follow the rest of them out when she stood and gripped his arm. He halted, pushing the door shut and turning to her.

"Aleksei, when we get them on the water—you *have* to kill him."

Aleksei frowned at her, "I thought that was the entire point."

She shook her head, "No, I don't mean in some pitched naval battle. I mean I want you to slip across the water, board his ship, and execute him. I don't care how you do it, or when. But I want Emelian Krasik dead, and I want it to be certain. I want this *over*."

His golden eyes searched hers for a long moment, but he finally nodded. "As you command, Majesty."

And then he was gone.

"Gods, but it's *bitter* out here," Toma complained.

"I told you it would be a hike," Aya shouted above the howling wind.

They'd been in Keldoan for months, through the heart of winter. Any woman who hadn't thought to procure proper undergarments deserved whatever she got, in Aya's estimation.

"And we're looking for *what* again?" Toma demanded.

"Something hidden," Aya barked.

She didn't dare tell Toma what they were actually looking for. Not after the attack. If the Demon could possess a man in their guard, she refused to risk her safety, or the security of Jonas's cache, on Bael's ability to infect those around her.

Likewise, Raefan was at the back of their small party, keeping Tamrix firmly in his sights. Toma's Knight seemed mostly oblivious, but she knew Raefan when he was stalking something, and at the moment she feared for Tamrix should the man make even a questionable move.

"It ought to be coming up just beyond those boulders," she continued, blinking back the snow flurries that flew into her eyes.

She knew spring was nearly blossoming in the South, but this far north it was still weeks away. Gods, but she was ready for its arrival. General Walsh consistently reminded her of how harsh winter was this high in the mountains, though she was no fonder of the general for it.

She halted as she reached an outcropping of boulders. The stones were at least the height and width of two men a piece, seeming to have fallen from high atop Mount Richter centuries before. Emblazoned across the stones were deep tones of the Seraphima, and echoes of the Archanium. Echoes Jonas had left for her just before his departure.

Aya stepped through the snow, embracing the Archanium and dissolving Jonas's illusion. The path revealed, she passed between two massive rocks cracked down the center only enough to allow a single person through at a time. Jonas had brought her to this strange place before obscuring the split in the stone.

Toma marveled as she passed between the boulders. "Gods, Aya, what have you *got* back here?"

Aya remained silent until all four of them were within the hollow ring of rock before conjuring an illusion to hide the crevice once again.

Toma turned to her, her eyes now deeply suspicious, "Aya, what are we doing out here?"

Aya sighed, noticing Raefan and his stance behind Tamrix. "Jonas left me with a cache of relics from his journey into Fanj."

Toma gasped, and it was all Aya could do not to roll her eyes. Now that they were protected by the rocks, within Jonas's wards, she could be certain that no signs of possession emanated from Toma or Tamrix, but the precaution was necessary.

"I believe one of these artifacts will teach us how to Fade. If that's true, I need to figure out which one it is so I can Fade to Taumon. I've never been out that far east, but I have critical information I must get to Jonas *immediately*.

"But Toma, until we know more, until we know who can be trusted and who can't, we can't allow this information to be general knowledge. Do you understand?"

Toma nodded gravely, "Like the man who attacked you. That hallway still reeks of the Presence. You're wise to take precautions." The Magus paused before understanding flitted across her face. "That's why you brought the two of us out here alone, isn't it?"

Aya nodded grimly.

Tamrix caught on a heartbeat later, turning to see Raefan leaning nonchalantly against the rocks. His face colored in the cold.

Aya pressed forward, "Since neither of you seem to be possessed, however, you'll be invaluable in helping me. Not just with this, but with what happens next."

Toma nodded sharply, "Very well. Let's get digging."

Aya turned to where the stones met the mountain. After a small manipulation of the spell she'd left there, the stones at the base of the mountain vanished and revealed a large, lumpy canvas covered in snow.

She brushed the snow away until she found the seam, peeling the tarp back to uncover a cluster of cloth bundles.

"It's in here somewhere," she said softly.

Toma reached into the bundles and pulled one out, uncovering a pitcher and bowl set, both cast in a cloudy crystal. Aya touched it and frowned. It didn't feel like any relic she'd ever touched in the Voralla. Generally, even if she didn't know what something did exactly, she could get a general impression of its purpose or function. With a frown, she shook her head.

"I don't think this is it. But make a note of it, I'd like to study it later."

The Knights began unwrapping objects, showing them to Toma and Aya so either Magi could take a moment to touch them. Again and again, both women shook their heads. It was beyond frustrating, never having seen the Fading Spell itself.

Tamrix hoisted a black gear and all but tossed it at Aya, "What about this?"

The moment she touched it, Aya knew he was on to something. She touched the Archanium, and while she noticed that certain spells seemed brighter to her, she was blocked from accessing the relic.

Toma frowned, "What is it?"

She stepped over and touched it, opening herself to the Archanium.

"Ooh!" Toma said, "I've never seen any of these!"

"Like what?" Aya asked, watching the swirling morass for anything unusual.

"Lots of them. That bright green and gold growth spell is usually a lot harder to find. That burning yellow-brownish one? The spark spell Sammul made me seek out for six *weeks* before failing me in *Advanced Energy Conduction and Provisional Sciences?* I can see that clear as day."

"I can too," Aya said with no small surprise. She and Toma had spent nearly as long searching for the same spell, only to have it evade them again and again.

"Gods, I haven't seen this for years. If nothing else, I'm going to cast it at the stones for practice."

Aya actually found herself laughing, "No, not now. Wait until we're done."

"Oh Aya! Just let me *try* it? I haven't seen that spell even since jumping to the new meridian."

Aya frowned, "Neither have I."

One of the threads she'd been following in Jonas's book suddenly popped into her mind. It was a rule about protecting certain spells from common or inadvertent access. She felt the fine hairs on the back of her neck raise. "Toma, I have an idea. I want you to cast that spellform at the boulder. I'm going to cast it at the same time. Alright?"

Toma chuckled, "Very well. Let's see who gets the best color out of it."

Aya shook her head, "Don't put a lot of power behind it. Just cast the spell, like a test. I'll do the same."

"If that's what you think is best," Toma responded, though she sounded disappointed.

"On three."

Two identical sparks of brilliance flashed across the surface of the stones, the Knights already standing well clear of their Magi's intended target. The moment their spells faded, the gear began to spin, but despite the grooves in the gear moving faster and faster, it held solid in the women's hands. Aya stared, her mouth slightly agape as a new spellform blossomed between them.

"Oh, *this* is dangerous. Great gods, this is going to be difficult."

Toma's face grew concerned as the spell wove itself out and began to grow dim. "So that's it? That's all there is to Fading?"

Aya sighed, taking her eyes way from the Archanium echo. "Apparently. Its simplicity is part of the problem. We have the spellform, but there are a *lot* of unanswered questions regarding its operation."

"Toma, I have to reach Taumon. But if for some reason I don't make it, I need to know that you can get there too. So, I want you to wait for a day, but no longer. After a day, follow me to Taumon. If for some reason I don't make it, I want you to alert Jonas immediately.

"I might not be fast enough as it is, but I would rather he get the information I have for him and risk it being late than he never knowing what happened, and possibly putting everyone in danger. Is that understood?"

Toma frowned, "You're not making a lot of sense, Aya."

Aya paused, breathing in the frigid air, her mind warring with itself. Finally, she realized she had no other choice. "If Emelian Krasik is killed, Tamara will inherit his power. Immediately."

Toma blinked in confusion. She stood there, silent as a statue for a long moment before glaring at Aya with unexpected defiance, "How do you know this? Do you have proof?"

Aya reached into her coat and pulled out a parcel. "Take this and guard it closely. Everything I've discovered is in this book. Watch as I Fade, and tomorrow, you do the same, and bring the book to Taumon. It is beyond precious. If you can't find Jonas, find the Queen. She won't understand like he will, but at least it might find its way to him."

Toma's eyes widened, "Aya, you can't possibly mean to leave right now!"

Aya took a deep breath, "I have no choice. I have to get there as soon as I can. Take care, Toma. Gods granting, I will see you tomorrow, and all will be well."

Toma eyes watered in the frigid air, "But what will I do if something happens to you?"

Aya rewrapped the Fade relic and hid it amongst the others in the cache, covering the whole lot beneath the tarp and replacing her illusion. "You will carry on," she said softly, "and you will help win this war. May the gods protect you."

Raefan stepped behind her and placed a hand on Aya's shoulder. She kissed her gloved fingers and held them out to Toma.

She dove into the deepest realms of the Archanium, pulling the brilliant morning sun into their rocky enclosure and wrapping it around herself, around Raefan.

The light pulled them apart as they Faded.

CHAPTER 48

THE WORTH OF A GOOD MAN

"You aren't listening," Aleksei growled.

Admiral Jefress snorted, "Boy, you might have strong-armed those fools in Kalinor, but the Lord Captain does not command Her Majesty's Navy. No matter how many hare-brained ideas you may have, the final tactics will be left to men who know what they're *doing*."

Aleksei took a deep breath, his every instinct screaming for him to simply end the man's life. The Mantle writhed across his shoulders in sympathy with his thoughts, hungrily demanding retribution for the insult. It took every ounce of his self-control to keep the Mantle at bay.

"With all due respect, Admiral Jefress, I disagree," he said softly, forcing a normal tone, rather than the feral snarl building inside him. "Her Majesty has placed me in command of the realm's defense. That includes the Legion *and* the Navy. It would be best if you'd simply heed Her Majesty's orders and *listen* to me."

The Admiral watched Aleksei for a long moment before sighing, "I'm not saying I don't understand, son. I do. It can be intimidating, taking on a new command like this. Especially when you're so unsuited to the role.

"The sacking of Kalinor was an utter embarrassment. But this is not the way to prove your worth to the Queen. Another failure of this magnitude doesn't only undermine your authority, it undermines the realm itself. Losing the capital was one thing, but *this*? This is madness."

The Mantle rose from Aleksei's shoulders, slicing through his leather coat and spreading into the air in a mockery of Angelic wings. He felt the tattered feather burn against his skin in response. He ignored both magics. He didn't have time for that sort of nonsense at the moment. Or the Admiral's cynicism, for that matter.

"While it is not my job to impress you, I formulated the trap in Mornj and the destruction of that garrison took out at least twenty-thousand rebel soldiers. I led the battle of Keldoan, and a force of fifty-thousand vanished in a single night. In the meantime, *you* have sat here in the Admiralty, safe in the knowledge that no one has bothered to think about you yet because you rank so low on anyone's list of importance that you haven't even registered as a threat or a boon.

"As a result, you've remained unmolested. You have no real value in this war, unless *I* assign you one. You do minimal trade with Dalita, and at best you keep the Yrini raiders from invading southern fishing villages. Significant resources have been poured into maintaining the Navy, and as of yet you have not shown me a single reason why we need you.

"As Lord Captain of Her Majesty's Legion, it is within my authority to divert all funds from the Admiralty to the Legions until such a time as I see just cause to maintain a naval presence. Should I choose to do so, the Admiralty would cease to serve as your home.

"You would be put on leave until such a time as your Queen called you back into service. Your ships would be decommissioned, and you would have to find yourself a comfortable place to retire. So, before you go about calling me 'boy' and leveling imperious claims in my direction, may I remind you to whom you are speaking?"

Admiral Jefress stared at him for a long moment, watching him, his eyes flickering to the crimson webwork of wings undulating behind Aleksei, the faint blue glow of the feather resting on his prominent chest. Aleksei could see the fear and confusion cross the Admiral's face. He was no boy.

But then, what *was* he?

"Very well," Jefress said with a reluctant sigh. "I have made my concerns known. If you kill the Queen in your sad attempt to catch Krasik with his pants down, let it be on your head. But I'll have no part in it."

Aleksei snorted, "Oh yes you will. In fact, you're going to run the entire operation."

When Jefress stared at him in surprise, it was all Aleksei could do not to backhand the man. "As you said, this is not *my* arena. I deal in troop movements across land. The sea is its own theatre. Therefore, who better to orchestrate the mission?"

"But—you just spent half an hour telling me you were in command," Jefress spat, his face flushing red.

"I *am*," Aleksei said coolly. "And I am commanding *you* to lead this operation." His eyes flashed a brilliant gold as he leaned forward and fixed the admiral in his gaze. "It's time for the Admiralty to prove its worth in this war."

The door opened, and Aleksei turned in frustration.

"*What?*"

Jonas stood there, a flicker of surprise crossing his face before vanishing into a mask of calm observation.

"I need to speak with you."

Aleksei turned back to the table, "It'll have to wait."

"It can't, Lord Captain," Jonas shot back.

Aleksei grunted as the bond suddenly burned like a hot coal shoved under his skin. It was almost unbearable. He turned, nodding to the other men in the room before exiting into the hallway as fast as he could. He had never felt *anything* like that through his bond with Jonas.

The door closed, and Aleksei faced Jonas's storming anger.

"You may order everyone else in this bloody world around, Aleksei, but not me. *Never* me. I don't have time to deal with your temper tantrums, however, so I'm telling you that I'm leaving at once for Keldoan."

Aleksei frowned, the animal rage clouding his understanding. "You're leaving before the battle?"

Jonas rolled his eyes. "Yes, I have to retrieve something. If I can find it, we might actually have a chance at *surviving* this."

Aleksei opened his mouth protest, but Jonas forestalled him with a glare that burned hot enough to make his skin crawl with terrified anticipation.

"You do *your* job, Aleksei. I'll do to mine."

The sudden light of Jonas's Fading was so brilliant that it left Aleksei temporarily stunned. He stood there, staring weakly at the violet afterimage where the furious love of his life had stood heartbeats before.

Blood pumped angrily through him, emotions puling with disappointment and hurt across a bond so unlike the intimate connection they had shared for so long, now sharp and hot, a knife perfectly crafted to find his heart with an edge keener than any blade.

Henry Drago swayed in his saddle, the stiff sea breeze and the warm glow of Taumon leagues distant the only things capable of motivating him to continue forward another pace.

The journey from Keldoan had taken much longer than he'd ever expected, but with fifty Magi and nearly five thousand men to feed and hide from the enemy, the challenges of the road had manifested ten-fold from the moment they'd set foot out the city gate.

Handling Rysun's irrational, innate fear of Archanium Magi with Ilyana's new-found power had been an unexpected hurdle, but one eventually overcome, if not easily.

By this point he was merely looking forward to a hot, decent meal and a moment to be separate from the messy machinery of war and personal rivalries.

While Henry appreciated the reasons his son insisted he be surrounded by soldiers and Magi at all times, always on the move so assassins couldn't find him again and the like, he was ready for a rest.

The next two hours ticked by interminably as they made slow, steady progress towards the sea.

At this time in the afternoon, the Autumn Sea seemed to be more fire than water. Henry had only seen it once himself, and even then only as a boy. His father had cut wood and hunted the animals of the Seil Wood for their pelts. On one such hunt, his father had taken down a red Seil wolf. The animals were more legend than fact in his small village, and his father had taken him to sell the pelt in Taumon, where they were told they could command a small fortune for the fur.

He had to chuckle at the small amount of coin it had commanded back then. Three silver crowns. He thought his father was going to drop dead on the spot at seeing so much money. He had ridden the whole way home proclaiming them princes. And Henry had believed him every league of the way.

In a way, those silver crowns *had* made princes of him and his son in the long run. Without that money, he'd never have been able to study woodworking with the Ri-Vhan, and he'd never have met his beautiful

Meraux. Though if she'd ever told him the sort of boy they would raise, he'd have laughed in her face.

He'd always thought Aleksei was special, but his reasoning would never have resonated with the men and Magi who now viewed his son as something of a god.

But those were never the things that made Aleksei special to him. He had watched his son risk himself countless times as a boy, always to protect those who weren't as strong, who couldn't stand up to others on their own.

He had seen his son protect others when it would have been the smarter, safer choice to turn a blind eye. Sometimes those ended with Aleksei's eyes being blackened or his nose bloodied, but the boy had never acted the victim, had never shed a tear except in anger. Anger that other boys would treat his friends without respect or mercy.

Other boys who were now missing teeth thanks to Aleksei Drago. Henry paused at that thought as the memory of Pyotr Krovel flashed across his mind. Some were missing teeth, yes, and others lives.

The thought brought back the very haunting nature of what he'd seen Aleksei do since his son had left Voskrin on their old draft horse. The things his son had become, the magic that had infused him, the violence he'd committed. And yet Henry kept telling himself that his son was a still a good man.

A strong, solid, good man. He was no different, really, than that boy who had taken a black eye to protect a weaker friend. Or that boy who had knocked out his rival's tooth. Never for himself. Only for someone else. Given his own way, Henry knew his son would just as soon be left alone, to work the land, spend time with his friends, with Jonas.

At the thought of the prince, who'd become something of a son to Henry himself, he found himself shaking his head. It was far from a life he'd ever seen for himself or his son, but when Jonas was around, he'd never seen Aleksei happier or more in love.

And while royalty had never much played into his thinking, he couldn't be too upset about the life it allowed Aleksei to live.

Until the war came.

They rode through Taumon's gates following a mercifully short back and forth with the gatekeepers. Henry could feel his back tightening near to the point of breaking, and he knew he could only take so much more of being in the saddle.

Soon enough, a groom came and helped him from his horse. The young man had to help him a touch more than he liked. The ride from Keldoan should have strengthened him, yet Henry felt a good deal weaker than when they'd set out.

As soon as his boots touched the cobbles of Taumon, Henry thought his knees might buckle, but the groom was there to steady him.

"Apologies," he said gruffly.

The groom held his arm, offering him a look of honest concern, "No worries, Sir. Not uncommon after a long day in the saddle, or at sea. Take a moment to regain your land legs, and you'll be right."

Henry took a long moment to straighten. The groom made a show of brushing his mount down as Henry took a few experimental steps, but after a long moment of uncertainty, he felt the blood flowing back into his legs.

He thanked the groom with a silver crown for his discretion and walked stiffly towards the Admiralty. He wasn't sure what he'd find inside, and as ever his heart clutched in his chest. The gods knew, he could be walking into an ambush, or where men in fancy uniforms would tell him in very apologetic tones that his son was dead.

The idea filled him with panic every time he walked into yet another command tent, or gilded hallway, or audience chamber. Everyone else was always fixated on the lord or queen in the room. Henry only ever wanted to hear that his son was alive before he dared care about anything else.

He often found himself surprised at how calm everyone else behaved. After the battle of Keldoan, he'd casually been informed that Aleksei had been grievously wounded, and nearly died. Had it not been for Aya's miraculous transformation, his son would be dead, and yet the news of Aleksei's near-fatal injury was delivered as a barely-interesting footnote.

The tension faded when Aleksei came striding out of the shadows with a bright, broad grin spread across his handsome face. A face that no longer brought Henry pain, despite how much of Meraux he could see in the boy's eyes, in his smile.

Aleksei had long ago become far more than a shade of either one of them. He was his own man, strong, in command of an incredible mind, and heart.

Aleksei's arms wrapped around him a second later, and Henry found himself laughing as he felt his feet briefly leave the cobbles, as his son bear-hugged him tightly to his chest and planted a kiss in his dusty hair.

He found it odd how their positions had so seamlessly been reversed. When Aleksei finally stepped back, Henry just stared at the man standing before him.

He had never thought of Aleksei as being a towering man, but that was certainly what he'd become. More than that, there was an animal threat to Aleksei's entire being that Henry had never completely understood. He knew others spoke of it, and he'd seen his son fight on the odd occasion, but now he gained a deeper appreciation.

His son had not been erased from the man who stood before him, but something else had come into being. Something feral; something wholly otherworldly. Lethal.

"Da? Everything alright?" Aleksei asked, his golden eyes boring into Henry.

Henry shook his head, burying his discomfort at his son's newest transformation, "It's been a very long road, Son. A long road indeed. Could hardly get my feet under me when I dismounted."

Aleksei's brow creased with concern as he immediately began to run his eyes over Henry. "Are you hurt? I heard there was a battle with the rebels, but no one told me—"

"I'm fine," Henry insisted, cutting off his son's worry, "just tired. I don't suppose there's a place to lie down and have a meal before I pass out?"

Aleksei's worry seemed to recede, once again replaced by his handsome grin. A grin that was somehow too perfect, too flawless to have survived the scrapes he knew Aleksei had been in. The gods only knew the things his son had experienced since he'd last laid eyes on the boy.

"Of course, follow me. There's someone very special I want you to meet."

Henry tried to match his son's smile, but as he followed him into the relative darkness of the Admiralty, all Henry could think was, "*Oh, my darling boy, what has this world done to you? And gods, what does it have in store for you yet?*"

The light pulled Jonas back together, and he immediately regretted his rash decision to Fade directly to Keldoan without finding a proper coat.

The cold was biting, but he wouldn't be here long.

He glanced around the stone circle holding the relics they'd taken from Fanj, feeling the Seraphic webwork he'd wrapped around the boulders add an extra chill to the frigid air. While anyone could Fade from the stone circle, he was the only one who Fade directly *into* it. At least, he was reasonably certain that was the case.

He trudged through the snow to the illusory pile stones he'd crafted to obscure their cache of invaluable magical totems. The rocks vanished as he waved the spellform away, digging his hands beneath the snow and gripping the edge of the tarpaulin covering his treasures. The moment he pulled it back, Jonas was keenly aware that someone had rifled through the relics since he'd last been here.

Biting back a curse, he began the finger-numbing search through various cloth bundles, seeking a relic he prayed he recalled correctly. If they were to battle on the open sea, he wanted every possible advantage. Krasik's powers might be muted on the water, but Bael's were another matter entirely.

After a frantic few minutes of rooting around, he finally emerged victorious.

It was less ostentatious than some relics he'd encountered, but still quite a sight to behold. A small, lacquered seahorse, painted in varying shades of ocean blues. Running down the ridges of the seahorse's body were small aquamarines, each section of the tiny, armored fish outlined in gold, its eyes set with rubies.

Not quite a handspan tall, Jonas marveled a moment at the craftsmanship, before his chattering teeth reminded him that his time was limited.

He delved into the Archanium, gently probing the tiny relic. A flood of images rippled through his mind, some of which he had a difficult time understanding. He'd spent precious little time at the seaside as a boy, and even less on open water.

Still, the pulsing echoes emanating from the bejeweled statue were enough to convince him that this relic would come in handy. It might even save his life, if he could determine how to use it properly. But he'd have to be on the water to know for sure, and at the moment, he was as far from the Autumn Sea as he could be while still standing in Ilyar.

He slipped the glittering relic into his pocket, covering the rest in the tarp. A brief twirl of liquid silver and vermillion wrapped around his hands, sending the scattered snow back over the tarp as smoothly as though it was freshly fallen.

The rock illusion shimmered back into place, and Jonas turned away from the cache.

A glimmer caught his eye, and he paused. He squinted at what should have been a wall of buff-colored boulder to see something hazy shimmering in the air before him. Closer inspection revealed it as an Archanium echo, nearly dissipated. He frowned. The spell must have been cast quite recently for the echo to linger visibly, and from its form, he immediately realized what he was looking at.

It was the echo of a Fade, but not his own.

Jonas cursed, immediately harboring strong suspicions of just who had been burrowing through the cache, and why.

"Dammit, Aya," he moaned, stepping closer to examine the Fading echo.

Once again, Jonas fell into the Archanium, allowing the echo to come into sharp focus. He'd noticed that if he was very careful, he could catch images of where someone had Faded.

But where would Aya have gone? The only place he could imagine her needing to reach quickly was Taumon, and the thought filled him with dread. If she'd felt the need to Fade this badly, he could only guess at her intent, her *need*, to reach him.

The Fading echo filled his mind, and he cried out. Rather than any image of the bright sea surrounding Taumon, or the Admiralty's golden spire, Jonas was instead confronted by a blast of searing light. Beyond its brilliance, he couldn't make out a thing. Only empty, oppressive darkness.

An aura unlike anything he'd ever experienced filled his head. He screamed as the entity, the sheer force of *will* roared into him, hurling him back into the snow.

Jonas blinked, tasting blood and staring about the rocky enclosure. Once he'd recalled his own name, he struggled for words to express what he'd just encountered. What had he touched? How was this...*entity* something Aya could have Faded to?

His heart raced, his mind vainly attempting to make sense of the bizarre experience. And he'd only touched a dying memory of the spell. Was Aya even alive? Could *anything* survive the full force of whatever being he'd just barely brushed?

Jonas pulled himself out of the snow, wiping his hands on his trousers and shoving them into his pockets. His left hand wrapped around the seahorse relic, and he breathed a sigh of relief.

He had what he came for. Now, before anything else unforeseen occurred, he grasped at the daylight, desperately ripping rays of light from the sky and wrapping himself in a brilliant helix. As the light broke him apart once again, he found his face wet with tears. His tears evaporated into flashing glimmers as the rest of him unspooled.

"Gods, Aya," he whimpered as he cast himself back to Taumon.

Back to Aleksei and, he prayed, back to sanity.

Roux flashed across the landscape. It was simultaneously exhausting and exhilarating. Why was he just learning to Dart like this? He'd first learned to Dart when he was barely six summers old. He hardly remembered a time when he *couldn't* flicker from one point to another.

Yet the things he'd pushed himself to do in the past few months were supposed to be impossible, or at the very least im*probable*. One of the first rules he'd ever learned was that you never Darted to a place you couldn't see. The consequences were often beyond horrific.

He'd *killed* men using such principles during the Battle of Kalinor. And yet, despite the spectacular danger, he'd risked himself more times than he cared to count in recent weeks.

There was also the law against Darting over a certain distance, which was usually line of sight unless you knew the place *very* well. Roux could think of hundreds of places in the Seil Wood that he could Dart to from memory. But the Seil Wood had always shifted to accommodate him.

Or at least She *had* before She changed...before the schism. He wished he properly understood what had happened to Her, why She had forsaken him.

Even as he pondered that, he caught a distant voice on the wind.

You will return to me.

Roux frowned, stopping in the middle of a meadow on fire with orange crocuses. *You woke me from my slumber. You gave me Children. You forged the link. You will return to me. You are my Champion.*

Roux shivered as the voice flickered and faded from his mind. Relvyn. Relvyn wanted him. His initial reaction was disgust, but then he paused. Why? Or better, why not?

Seil had forsaken him. She had nearly killed him, and for what? He had only ever served Her, and in Her infinite wisdom She had cast him aside for his *father*? A man who was so old and gouty he could hardly stand, much less lead the Ri-Vhan?

No, he was done being tortured for trying to do the right thing. The stories Aleksei had told him, of Seil capturing his friends, capturing *Jonas,* had confirmed his suspicions.

Either something had taken over Her spirit, or a new aspect of Her had manifested. The latter was most likely the case. She knew him. She knew Her people, and She had made the decision to *change* them. Roux refused to change along with them, so he was cast out like nightsoil. She had no use for a tool that would not bend to Her will.

But I have use for you. Many uses. I will be kind. I will bend with you, and through you, My Children will become legendary. But I need you, Roux Devaan. My Berserker.

His breath caught in his throat. That word. That horrible word. He suddenly recalled a text he'd come across years ago. It spoke to the connection between Seil and Relvyn, and the ancient Ri-Vhan's terrible decision.

Like Seil, Relvyn had also once had Children. The Ri-Adyn had been founded not long after the Ri-Vhan. Magi stationed themselves in the southern Wood to continue their assault on the Drakleyn. But unlike the Ri-Vhan, the Ri-Adyn had been consumed not with thoughts of escape or hiding, but with the wrath of war.

They had existed in the South solely to destroy the Drakleyn, or, at least, deactivate it. The texts were hazy on exactly what the Drakleyn did. Roux had a hard enough time imagining that a building *did* anything, besides offer shelter. But whatever it was, the texts were clear that the Drakleyn had been a terrible weapon.

The Ri-Adyn had plotted and planned in secret, but their hearts were hard. Every Magus who travelled to the South had lost something, some*one* to the Drakleyn and the Kholod overlords within. Their hatred, their burning need to destroy had impressed the spirit of Relvyn, and so He rewarded them with abilities quite unlike those of the Ri-Vhan.

So unlike the Ri-Vhan.

The Ri-Adyn didn't have Hunters. At their height, the Hunters had been the ruling warriors of the Ri-Vhan, back when there was one every generation, and they ranged far across the known world. Now, Aleksei was an anomaly, a genetic fluke with rare magic not seen in centuries.

But the Ri-Adyn had Berserkers; warriors who entered a state of absolute rage. Anger so deep, yet burning bright. Fighting with either twin axes or long, curved knives, the texts were very clear. These were creatures driven by bloodlust, with nothing left to lose. These individuals went into battle with the knowledge that they would die, but that they would massacre hundreds before they were taken down.

And now Relvyn wanted him to become one? The Champion of a strange Wood?

It has already begun, Child. Relvyn's whisper brought a shiver. The fact that he could hear the Wood from this distance gave away far more information than Roux cared for. If Relvyn could reach him at this distance, then they were already bound together. Relvyn knew his thoughts.

They were linked.

Roux crouched, feeling as though he might retch at any moment.

The rage. I know you can feel it. Your rage will burn bright and pure, washing away everything else. But fear not, Berserker. I learned much from the last trial.

You did not come with rage and death in your heart. You came with loss, with need. Be my Champion, Roux Devaan. Become my guardian, and I will grant you gifts to rival the greatest Hunter in history. I will make you legendary, and the foes who took your beloved will quake at your approach.

Roux took a deep breath. Every word Relvyn seeded in his mind seemed to resonate in his heart. It all felt...*right.*

Of course, this could all be more manipulative magic from one, or both, of the Woods. That came with the territory when you were serving demigods. At least, that's who Roux *thought* he was serving.

"What do you need of me?" he asked aloud.

Travel to me. Travel to the pool, and I will grant you such gifts as will make my Sister's paltry offering pale in comparison. I will bring you to your destination faster than She ever could, and you will be armed with abilities that will rival any in this world.

"The last time I tried that, I nearly died," Roux shouted, his anger rising that Relvyn would try to distract him like that.

She can be cruel, my Sister. Or rather, the creature that corrupts Her. She allowed you to fall, as She sacrifices others so She can feed, so She can bolster Her Gate to Chymria.

I have no need to murder my Children. My Berserkers always kept my

Gate well fed when their rage burned the brightest. The Kholodym were strong, after a fashion. Now their strength is part of me, part of the Gate. And when it's opened, when it's needed, it will be their undoing.

Roux groaned. Not only was Relvyn trying to make him a ruthless murder machine blinded by bright-burning rage, He was also several thousand years behind.

Roux decided to change the subject back to Darting; the dangers of following Relvyn's request.

"You're sure I won't drown?" he asked skeptically.

A feeling of distinct horror flickered through his mind. It was a strange feeling, swirling though him.

It made him profoundly itchy.

I cradle my Children. I don't break them. You are prized above all others, Roux Devaan. My Sister does not understand your value, but I am gratified to offer you a place beneath My branches, a place where you can teach My new Children.

Teach them to be legendary. Teach them to handle the gifts I provide. It can overwhelm humans who wake to new talents, new lives before them. You will guide them, lead them to rival the Ri-Vhan, to surpass them for the Glory of Mokosh!

"And because You care for me so much, You're going to imbue me with the gift of spectacular rage?"

Worry less about the gift I bestow upon you until it is in your hands. Should you deem it unworthy, I will withdraw it. Now, will you come to the pool? I have something to show you.

Roux turned west, toward Kalinor, towards Tamara. His heart ached for her, ached even more after hearing the terrible things she had endured in captivity.

Katherine had told him of Tamara's ordeals. Every injustice, every torture. Hearing about her eyes alone... Gods, but he couldn't get there soon enough.

If Relvyn offered something that would fortify him, something that would help him better protect Tamara, was it worth the time not spent flying to her side?

Roux closed his eyes, pushing out all other thoughts. He weighed every good against every evil.

Then he Darted.

CHAPTER 49

ALTERED STATES

Aleksei stood at the prow of Her Majesty's *Gray Wolf*, staring out into the open sea. He'd done his level best to remain calm while talking to the admirals about ship movements, never letting it slip that this was the first time he'd ever seen the Autumn Sea...and the first time he'd been on water of any kind.

As it turned out, even docked, he was standing on a wooden ship, bobbing in the vast watery expanse, and it filled him with terror. Terror he had to overcome, if he was to follow Andariana's solemn command.

Assuming Krasik fell for their trap.

Jonas Faded next to him and Aleksei jumped. He still wasn't used to this new ability, and it was starting to unnerve him.

It felt somehow unnatural, yet he knew it was important that their Magi have the same access to travel as Bael's. Still, the strength that one skill alone would grant his battle plan was staggering. It might very well be the difference between winning and losing the war. Indeed, their journey across the Fanja waste might have been accomplished in a moment, rather than weeks.

He was still silently cursing himself for that lapse in judgment. He wasn't sure why; there was no reason he should have expected to find Rhiannon rather than Tamara, and he was reasonably certain that Rhiannon's rescue would be important in ways they couldn't even imagine at the moment.

But he should have been more careful.

He should have thought it out, rather than jumping to conclusions without actual information.

A blood meridian pulse in the distance wasn't really accurate information. It was a clue, and he'd been acting on instinct too strongly too much of late. While that may have worked when dealing with the Angelus, or fulfilling some sort of ridiculous prophecy, it did not work when designing precise stratagem.

He knew Krasik's tactics. He had studied them extensively before the sacking of Kalinor. The problem lay in the fact that Krasik had not become the Zra-Uul until late into the first rebellion. Krasik's transformation was actually the cause of his army's defeat.

And even then, his abilities had been too new, too raw for him to use them to any real effect. That, and the man was crazier than a shithouse rat. So the tactics Krasik used in the first war were useless to him.

That problem was compounded by the fact that, once on the sea, Aleksei was out of his arena. Ships and open water were hardly his area of expertise. The entire setup seemed ridiculous to him.

Placing men in full armor on floating pieces of wood was one of the stupidest things he could imagine. It was one of the first commands he'd issued after stepping on board. A man going over the side in armor was dead, no matter his rank or skill. Covering yourself in metal on a churning sea was just asking to die for all the wrong reasons. The sea could shift, and you were literally sunk.

A man in a pressed leather breast plate and an open-faced helm, however, had a much better chance of survival. The admirals had begrudgingly acquiesced to his orders, arguing that the officers would resent his new armor specifications, being dressed like foot soldiers and archers.

He had argued that the officers in question might appreciate the chance to live, were they to go overboard. He didn't know exactly how to run a military fleet, but he knew what he *wouldn't* do; the very things that jumped out at him as strange, perilous, or just plain stupid.

"Ethan is a very dangerous man," Jonas said absently, and Aleksei started at the sudden intrusion into his ruminations.

The Hunter recovered quickly and chuckled, earning a confused glance from his Magus, "Really? One of Bael's Magi captains is dangerous? Gods, *that's* a surprise! And here I thought they spent all their time picking wildflowers and singing songs about boyhood days long gone."

Jonas frowned, "I'm not exactly enthralled with this new streak of cruelty."

"It's not cruelty," Aleksei clarified, "it's just an observation of the obvious. Ethan is dangerous. So are you. So am I. So is bloody *Ilyana*, now.

"Some of us are predators, and some are prey. From the moment I saw the man, I knew he was a predator. He has the look of a man who has killed. A man who may have questioned himself, but killed the innocent anyway.

"His danger lies not in his strength in the Archanium, or his path through the Nagavor, but in his ability to be *led*. He was led by gullibility into Bael's army, and he was led out of it by the love of a woman who wasn't completely insane.

"It didn't take more than that, mind you. Katherine told me. All she had to do was explain why the Demon and his followers were evil and corrupt, just *show* him she was being beaten daily while they tried to turn Tamara into a monster.

"She just had to show him that he was being used. And then, just like that, he forsook his entire life with Bael and his Commune and followed a cooper's daughter posing as a maid who was really a Loyalist spy out of Voskrin. The man faced down the Demon alone. And won.

"*That's* what makes him dangerous. He's obviously powerful, perhaps more powerful than you when it comes to sheer destructive force, but he'll support the loudest voice in the room, and it's unlikely that he'll question a single word before he follows orders."

Jonas smirked, surprising Aleksei, "Well then, I think we're in luck."

Aleksei took the bait, "Why?"

"Because from what I've witnessed, the loudest voice in Ethan's head is always Katherine Bondar. He ignores everyone around him just to answer her simplest question, or to fetch her a cup of tea if he thinks she *might* be thirsty. Really, he does nearly everything she asks of him, and if he can't see to her needs right away, he can't stop apologizing.

"Mind you, she's hardly running him ragged. But it's quite clear to me that, to Ethan, there is Katherine, and then there's the rest of us. But if she agrees with, let's say me, on any topic, he agrees immediately. Whatever she wants, he will do." Jonas leaned in, dropping his voice to a whisper, "So let's not upset her with your new-found fondness for mockery, shall we?"

Aleksei snorted, turning away from the Prince. Jonas might be a bit jealous at the moment, what with having *two* new Magi on their side who could deliver destruction he could hardly fathom.

It didn't help matters that his mother was suddenly present in a life he'd built out of loneliness and scholarly objectivity. Like a child playing with blocks, even the mightiest walls could be toppled with appropriate force.

Jonas had lost his protective shield, the one he'd erected as a boy to keep out all the darkness that sought to consume an orphan. No matter how highborn, he'd still had to shield himself from the shadows at night, from songs never sung, tales never told, memories never made.

For the longest time, Jonas had believed that this made him stronger. His lack of direct attachment, his depth of uncaring, made him superior because he was not weakened by sentimentality.

Andariana and Tamara were his family, and they were important to the realm, of course. But Jonas was alone. Beyond his royal blood, he was alone.

His grandmother had made that clear when she had exiled his mother, though no one thought to allow *him* such information. Kevara had proved her enmity time and time again. Most recently, she had tried to imprison him beyond a gate so powerful that he would be trapped until he died.

Aleksei watched Jonas's face, feeling his emotions, his thoughts cascading in a torrent across their bond.

No one else had this. No one else had a grandmother who still sought to entrap them because *she* thought they were going to end the world. No one else found out that their mother had been kept from them for twenty-odd years because the same grandmother was either playing political games, simply hated the woman who had birthed them, or both. The price paid for Jonas's existence was not his father Joel's life. The price was Jonas's childhood. His innocence. And now Jonas felt that as deeply as he ever would.

And Aleksei felt something else, something in the shadows of the bond that might have gone unnoticed had he not felt a reciprocal tinge at losing his own mother.

He felt *rage*. A rage he himself knew all too well. The Mantle withdrew from the sheer force of that emotion, crawling down Aleksei's back in an attempt to hide.

It was *afraid*.

Aleksei looked into Jonas's eyes, green matching gold in the blazing sunlight.

And then Aleksei reached forward and wrapped his Magus in his arms, pulling him close and holding him as tightly as possible.

I know. I can't say I know all of it, but I know now. And I'm sorry. But we're going to fix this.

Jonas was keeping back his tears with a will, so Aleksei released him. His prince was unlikely to display emotion in front of so many sailors and soldiers. But then Aleksei caught a different thought.

We will do this. And then we will kill her. I don't even want her to suffer. I just want her dead.

Aleksei did his level best to keep his face straight, as though he was just looking out onto the sea.

I want her dead, Aleksei. And once this is over, she dies. I don't care if it causes a war, at this point what else could go wrong? But I am going to kill Kevara Avlon.

Aleksei was shaken from his connection with Jonas only when an insistent young woman shoved him and nearly threw him off the prow.

He blinked, cutting off his mental conversation with Jonas and turning to face the girl. He was startled to see Andariana standing before him.

"He took the bait," she whispered.

Aleksei had never seen her this youthful and vibrant. Gone were the dark circles and the wrinkles. She seemed rejuvenated, nearly twenty years younger.

Rhiannon graced the deck, and every sailor onboard turned to her, their eyes adoring. Aleksei clapped his hands and broke through the worst parts of the unintentional spell she cast.

As much as he liked her, even admired her, Rhiannon's presence was bad for the sailors' work ethic. So bad that he'd nearly had to confine her to the Admiralty just to keep the sailors on the ship focused on their jobs, and not distracted and enthralled by her very presence. Jonas went to his mother, and as her eyes lit upon him, the mood of the crew shifted from adoring in silence to ebullient.

It was unsettling.

Aleksei looked back to Andariana and quickly set his arms on Andariana's shoulders. She had been bobbing while standing still, nearly about to fall over.

"Are you *drunk?*" he whispered, his eyes widening with alarm.

She giggled.

Aleksei withdrew his hands. His nose confirmed what her breath delivered. The woman was sauced. It was not the first time he'd seen it, but he was hardly keen to seek out and murder a man based on the whim of a daft and drunken woman, queen or no.

He *would* do it. But for all the men he'd lost in this stupid war. For the innocents consumed in that spectacular-yet-fledging display of what Bael had purposefully brought into the world.

He would fulfill her wish, but not for her. Never for Andariana Belgi. Never for her tirades, her histrionics, or her feuds.

He would do it to avenge the brave people killed on that terrible day, the day they'd lost Kalinor. For all those who'd died without ever understanding *why* they were dying.

And, he would do it for Tamara.

For the things Katherine had told him about Tamara. For all the tortures, all the tears, all the horrors those *people* had inflicted upon her. He had saved her life now more than twice. He had risked everything he had, had twisted time itself to save her, to protect her. He had accomplished the impossible again and again to keep Tamara safe.

To hear of the things she endured, the horrors visited upon her while he'd sought her in the wastes, was heartbreaking.

He clutched a hand to his chest and tried to calm his breath, keeping the panic already present from overwhelming him. He'd tried to do everything right. He'd tried to accomplish the impossible yet again, and he had been wrong.

But was she paying the price for his mistakes?

He could still only think of her as Tamara, the sweet, innocent girl he'd saved from assassins, who he'd dragged across the roof of the Palace and then through its foulest underguts. The pain of hearing Katherine's words alone put him in a murderous mood.

Andariana's words were a logical desire for victory, Jonas's a piece of sport. Aleksei would no sooner consider Kevara Avlon human as he would any other winged beast to be brought down. The Mantle relished the promise of drinking her in.

Emelian Krasik would not be an easy mark to kill. But Aleksei knew as surely as he knew the paths and ways of the Wood that Emelian Krasik would die by his hand, and he would smile as he delivered the killing blow.

"It's time to prepare for battle," Aleksei announced to a small group of gawking Magi. "Kindly get this woman off my ship."

"She's moving!"

Bael looked up at the giddy, childish grin plastered across Emelian Krasik's withered face. The man was becoming more and more of a nuisance as time progressed. It was a pity that he was still so badly needed for the cause.

"Calm down," Bael cautioned, looking back into his hand mirror and running a finger across the side of his face, just above his ear.

The Archanium rippled forth and pulled the dead skin back together, repairing yet another of the myriad punctures and slashes he'd endured within the cursed tree. Ethan would pay for what he'd done, even if the Seil Wood Herself had been the who to save him from Bael's wrath.

She would pay for that too, but he couldn't burn Her, not yet. For now, Ethan would be succulent to devour with the Presence. It would be well pleased with one such as he.

"Who is *she* and where is she moving? And also, why do I *care?*"

"Andariana Belgi, you fool," Krasik growled, his glee now rage. "And if you would spend more time hunting that traitorous bitch down rather than patching your stinking corpse, this war would be over!"

Bael blinked and put the mirror down, sitting up to regard his supposed king. "Well, it seems that the *real* Emelian Krasik has finally come out to play. Delightful. So where has she gotten to?"

"The sea," Krasik said, his eyes glittering with anticipation.

Bael frowned, "The *sea?* The Autumn Sea? Where is she going?"

"Nowhere," Krasik whispered. "She's hiding on the waves. We tried to kill her in the Admiralty, but that goat-born Treedarter kept saving her. Who saw *that* coming? But on the sea, she'll be on a ship, and ships can be broken. Ships can be *burned.* And when they're gone, the people who survive just...sink. And I'll be there to watch the water consume her."

Bael regarded Krasik with curiosity. "You are aware what being on the water will mean for you?"

Krasik licked his lips, "I'm looking forward to it. My father was a man of the sea. Never left it, really. The moment he did was the moment he went mad. He didn't survive very long after, and he left me with these visions, these magical thoughts. Thoughts that make people do as I please. But the madness of the land, oh the Madness, Demon. You cannot *possibly* comprehend."

Bael bristled, "Don't call me that."

Krasik smiled, suddenly grandfatherly, "Ah, but Baeli, that's what you *are*."

Bael stiffened. No one had called him Baeli in a *very* long time. In fact, only two people remained alive who had ever heard him called by that name, though unfortunately his siblings were unlikely to die anytime soon.

"My name is Bael," he growled, keeping his temper in check lest Krasik decide to use some of those 'magical thoughts' against him. "I would prefer if you use it."

Krasik chuckled, "Well, aren't we petulant? Very well, *Bael*. Since you won't be my Demon, I suppose I'll have to settle for the living corpse before me, stitching himself back together like a rag-doll to save itself from falling apart altogether."

Bael tried to ignore the barb, but it pierced him nonetheless. *Gods*, but he was ready to be rid of this man.

And then a thought hatched in his mind. Water. Krasik would be on the water. Hunting down Andariana Belgi. Without access to his abilities, those 'magical thoughts'.

And Bael knew exactly who else would be there. Krasik's presence would draw them like wasps to honey. And they would be stuck, adrift in the water, on a boat, all of them, and unable to escape.

"It's a brilliant idea, Sire," Bael said quickly. "Really, your most inspired to date. Ships burn, and people drown. And even if they don't, they don't have far to go, do they?"

Krasik chuckled, "No, Master Bael, they do not. They do not."

There was a tentative knock on the door of her Admiralty chambers. Andariana looked up from the book laying neglected in her lap.

The door opened to admit a middle-aged man with sandy hair, and a handsome enough face. He cleared his throat nervously, "Is this the room for the able-bodied but useless?"

Beside her, Rhiannon frowned in confusion. Andariana studied his face a moment, then rose with a broad smile.

"Henry," she said, stepping forward and clasping the man's hand in her own.

"Your Majesty," Henry responded, bowing his head. "It's a true honor to finally meet you."

When Andariana looked into his soft brown eyes, she realized that he was likely as terrified about the oncoming battle as she and Rhiannon were. On a whim, she released his hand and stepped forward, wrapping Aleksei's father in a gentle embrace. His entire body tensed, but she didn't let go, not just yet.

"There's no shame in being afraid for our boys. Frankly, I'm terrified. For *both* of them," she said softly. "I know I'm asking a great deal of them, but know that I would never put either in harm's way unless I firmly believed in their abilities, not just to complete their missions, but to return to us alive and in one piece."

Henry's stiffness melted. Not completely, but enough.

"Sister," Rhiannon drawled, "tell me this is not some new consort you had spirited down here."

Henry laughed out loud, chagrin coloring his face.

Rhiannon started, arching a golden eyebrow. Andariana stepped back from the man, relishing the look of surprise on her sister's face as Rhiannon stared into Henry's handsome, sun-worn face.

"Consort to a queen?" Henry coughed into his hand, his face still burning. "*That'd* be the day. My wife Meraux was my queen, but I lost her a good sixteen summers ago now."

Andariana sighed, "Apologies, Henry. That uncouth lout is my sister Rhiannon; Jonas's mother."

Rhiannon's eyes flicked between her sister and Henry before the princess sighed in exasperation, "Is one of you going to explain what's going on here?"

Andariana stared at her sister, incredulous, "Are you blinded, Sister? Just look at him for a few seconds; it will come to you."

She herself had never laid eyes on Henry Drago, though she'd heard enough stories about him to feel as though they were old friends. But the resemblance between the Drago men should have been enough to immediately identify him as Aleksei's father.

He turned to Rhiannon, performing a surprisingly courtly bow, "Your sister is quite right, ma'am. Any sane person would quail at the very thought of facing the Demon head-on. But our boys, well, *they* are something special."

Even as Andariana smiled at his folksy manner, Rhiannon rose sharply, finally recognizing who this man was. "It's an honest pleasure to finally meet you, Master Drago. I cannot tell you what your son did to release me from my prison, because I'm not entirely sure how it was even possible, but for me standing here, free.... It was a true miracle of deliverance. The debt I owe him is beyond measure."

Henry chuckled uneasily, "My son is excellent at figuring the impossible, as it turns out. That, and knowing what his men need, on or off the field." His face grew suddenly troubled, "But I'm afraid that when it comes to his own safety, Aleksei'll do just about anything to protect those he loves. And he loves deeply." His worry melted into a mischievous smile, "And, if I'm not mistaken, my son is marrying yours in the not-so-distant future."

Upon hearing that, Rhiannon blushed, "I'm not that fresh on the protocol when it comes to commoners and kings, Bonded and military tradition, but I'm sure you and I are bound to the same thing they all are; don't let them kill each other, and when the gods throw nobility at them, give them a place to hide."

Andariana rolled her eyes. Was there a man her sister had ever *not* flirted with?

Henry turned to the third woman in the room, sitting quietly in the corner. His eyes widened before he again burst out laughing. "Katherine Bondar. Great *gods*, but it's good to see you."

The girl had been quiet until now, but upon hearing Henry Drago speak her name, she was transformed. She bounded out of her chair and rushed forward to give the man an effusive hug.

"Henry!" she gushed.

Andariana was almost embarrassed for the girl before she realized that both of them were laughing like old friends. "Gods, but it's been a long time. I never thought I'd see you again!"

Henry chuckled, "Well, I'm harder to kill than all that!"

"Not you," Katherine shouted, shoving the man roughly, "me!"

Rhiannon and Andariana were both alarmed, but Henry only laughed all the louder.

Katherine only jostled him harder, "I'll have you know that Mother Margareta decided I'd be the perfect *spy*. I went with Lord Simon Declan to bloody *Kalinor*."

For the next half hour, Andariana and Rhiannon watched Katherine and Henry, each glancing at the other while two old friends caught up on topics that nearly made Andariana's hair stand on end.

Yet it was a marvel to watch these two simple people from the Southern Plain adapt so smoothly to the bizarre situation they found themselves in, each lacking any of the training or education that Andariana and her sister had always been told made them so superior to common folk.

And, if Andariana was being honest with herself, she was delighted that her nephew had found love with such a noble and relatively "simple" man as Aleksei Drago. So why would it be such a shock to find his childhood friend and his father to be people she so admired, despite their lack of breeding? She was pleased to see those same feelings reflected in Rhiannon's face.

The door opened, and the conversation came to an abrupt halt as Aleksei stepped into the room, "We need to talk." He shut the door and walked over to Andariana. "I'm afraid I need you to leave."

"What nonsense is this?" she demanded, her mood souring in an instant.

"You want to station me on a burning ship as your assassin?" he growled. "Then you'll do this. If not, I will abandon your mission faster than you can snap."

Andariana moved to slap him, but before her hand could make contact with his face, Aleksei flashed with impossibly casual speed, catching her wrist and delicately returning it to her side.

His mouth was a scant inch from her ear as he whispered, "I'm not your grunt, Andariana. And I'm not your assassin. If I do this, it's for a good reason, but never for *you*.

"However," he said, stepping back and addressing the rest of those assembled, "we're going to have split our people up. They're going to expect us to turn the tables on them. They might think that we'll hide Andariana here, in the depths of the Admiralty. They don't know that we can Fade yet, hopefully, so we could only get her so far. With five thousand troops and Ilyana's Magi and Knights, we make a formidable military force in a city this fortified.

"They know we've grown in power, though not by how much. But if we can Fade now, why would we keep the Queen, the only one Krasik *really* wants, in the city? Why not make use of such a powerful tool?"

"And where were you planning on hiding me? Some shanty halfway in the sea?" Andariana snarled.

Aleksei smiled like a feral dog in a hen house, "No, Majesty. I thought my father's farm might be better suited."

Several voices rose up, but Aleksei raised an angry hand, "*Stop!*"

Everyone quieted.

"It is the *last* thing Bael would expect, and he's going to be looking for you, Andariana, because he wants your throne after he dispenses with Krasik. But if he's under the illusion that we can't Fade, then how would you get a thousand leagues from here, out in the middle of nowhere? Who is going to think to look for you there?"

There were some murmurs of agreement around the room.

"I refuse," Andariana growled.

The door opened, and Jonas stepped through. "Unfortunately, that's not of particular import."

Her eyes went wide, "What are you talking about?"

By the time she understood what they were doing, Jonas and Henry were chatting, and Jonas reached for her arm.

"Don't you dare—" she started before the candlelight, the firelight, the sunlight pouring in through the window reached into her, pulling her apart.

Roux struck the water in a tremendous icy spray. The impact had driven all the air from his desperate lungs, and still he was being driven deeper and deeper into the murky dark.

He lost any sense of which way led to air, and which to his grave. The water swirled around him, powerful and uncompromising. It pulled him along in the darkness, but he had no idea where. The pool he recalled was only so many paces across, and yet he was traveling at an incredible speed.

The need to breathe edged out all other thoughts as his senses returned to him. He opened his mouth instinctively, taking the water into his lungs eagerly, as though gulping down the bright, musty air of the forest far above.

Surprisingly, the screaming terror in his mind abated. He breathed the water out and back in, relieved. He was too weak to question this latest turn. He was in Relvyn's hands now. Whatever His will might be, it would be done, and Roux understood that he was merely a tool.

It was a role he was quite accustomed to.

The water rushed upwards, carrying Roux to the surface and placing him on dry land. He immediately coughed up the water, choking and retching as it was expelled.

Air had never tasted so sweet.

He rested on his hands and knees for a long moment, waiting for the Wood to flood his mind with instructions, benedictions, or even a bare acknowledgement that he'd done as instructed, and had managed not to drown in the process.

Finally, Roux pushed himself to his feet and took stock of the chamber where he'd surfaced. Unlike the one he'd been in before, this was a natural cavern, stalactites of purple and blue crystal clinging to the ceiling; jagged, flaking spikes of aubergine wood erupting from the cavern floor.

Roux frowned. Nothing about those were natural.

He was in the Heart of the Wood, he realized suddenly. The Heart of the Relvyn Wood. And if he was underground, that meant the taproot, the World Root that connected the Relvyn and Seil Woods together, couldn't be far.

He walked through the cavern, his strength slowly returning to him. He found himself feeling more robust than he had in a very long time. It was eerie. The water that should have ended his life seemed instead to have rejuvenated him.

Roux froze, remembering what Relvyn had said to him before he'd Darted into the pool.

Worry less about the gift I will bestow upon you until it is in your hands. Should you deem it unworthy, I will withdraw it.

Relvyn had used the water to bestow his gift. Roux groaned, sinking into a crouch. He searched for the anger that had been building over the past few months. And there it was, just beneath the surface. Naked fury. Terrible rage, capable of consuming a man.

With a frown, Roux focused his intent forward, Darting across the cavern. A heartbeat later, he found himself a hundred paces away. So, he hadn't lost that ability. That in itself was worth something.

The rage is there should you need it, my legendary Child, but it will not consume you. Not unless you drink too deeply. And when you do, and you will, gods will shiver and shudder to behold what you will do. What you will bring about. And I will applaud and sing your praises to the Eternal Mother.

Roux rested his back against the cavern wall and closed his eyes. This was becoming stranger by the second. His heart nearly ached for the Seil Wood, for a return to Her grace.

Nearly.

He had never understood Aleksei's claim of feeling homesick. He had never known what such a feeling might be like. Even outside the Wood, he had always known She was there, guiding him, lending him Her strength.

Until now.

Until he suddenly realized he could never go back, not ever again. He felt it with a pang that threatened to drop him to his knees. His heart ached in his chest, burning with the loss as his idea of home diminished and dimmed to nothing.

But you are home, Child. And this home shall never forsake you. You are my legendary Child, and I will cradle and protect you until the Darkness envelops the land and all things cease to be.

And here, a gift, to show you are above all else, all things in this Wood. A piece of the link. A piece of My connection to My Children. It was fashioned by you, and thus you should be delivered the proper weapon you forged in that moment.

Roux frowned, glancing around the cavern, seeing nothing. He started as one of the red wooden fangs unfolded before him, rising up, spreading into a blossom, revealing a jagged piece of something hard and white, streaked with red.

He looked closer, suddenly recognizing the strange material, fashioned into a brutal knife several handspans long. The majority of the blade was composed of veined bone and hardened maroon marrow, but the edge glistened, a garnet and ruby jewel that Roux grudgingly recognized as crystalized blood.

The handle was wrapped in the iron bark of the link's new skin and thin strips of leather. As Roux reached forward and wrapped his hand around the grip, he suddenly realized that rather than leather, his hand was wrapped around belts of tanned human skin.

The Wood sensed his unease. *He had no need of such fragile flesh. But in this fashion, it will serve to protect you. Far more functional.*

As Roux held back bile, he swung the knife. The balance was perfect; there was no mistaking it. The bone blade, streaked with uncomfortably human veining and slashes of maroon marrow, made for a devastating weapon.

Your rage feeds the blade. The Wood whispered. *When you enter into your Berserker state, the blade will mirror your rage, will feed the fury back to you. It is a formidable weapon, Berserker. It will prove useful.*

Roux bowed his head. He knew better than to question the gifts of a demigod. He started to look for a place to keep it. His small horn knife rested so simply, strapped across his chest. This knife would have to be worn at his hip or across his back, as Aleksei wore his sword. In truth, it was nearer a short sword than a knife.

Another gift, Berserker. To house your blade. The Wood sounded amused. Roux was immediately troubled until he saw the sheath and strap unfold from another red spike. He took it gently, sliding the knife into the sheath. It fit perfectly. The strap was meant to lay from shoulder to hip, keeping the knife just over his right shoulder. He recognized the same...unconventional leather.

Why should a man be different from a deer? Both are prey before you. The Wood mused into his mind.

Roux winced, feeling a man's castoff skin slide against his own. The skin of a man he'd consigned to an eternal death unlike any other.

But as the Relvyn Wood had said, the man in question no longer had need of skin. As Ri-Vhan, he had always sought to be meticulous about using every bit of the animals he and his people hunted. Gut for bowstring, leather and fur for warmth and grips, bone for needles and knives. How was this blade and its sheath different?

Roux found himself wishing, for just a moment, that the spirit of Relvyn was less practical.

You are satisfied with your gifts. This pleases Me. Return to the water, and I will send you back. And I send you back with a message.

Roux Darted to the water's edge and stood, waiting. Finally, he stared at the ceiling, an old habit, and called, "What's your message, Father Wood?"

It is encoded in your knife. Worry not, it will be delivered at the right time.

Roux shrugged and dove into the water, not yet willing to admit that he was ready to be rid of this place and its odd spirit.

You will come to love Me. He whispered as Roux sank into the depths.

622

"How dare you!" Andariana spat.

Jonas just stared blankly at his aunt, "That might sound like a joke if you were sober. Which you haven't been since I've arrived in Taumon. This time will be good for you."

"I will *never* forgive you for this, Jonas Belgi," she shouted as he walked away.

"Yes, you will," he said, keeping his back to her, "and unless you can Fade, you'll be here with Henry until this is all over. Where you'll be safe, gods willing."

He turned to Henry, whose face betrayed a mixture of confusion and anger, "I don't like this, Jonas. If anyone in the village finds out that I've come back with a woman, they'll be swarming around here like cowflies on a dungheap."

"I'd say your bigger problem would be Bael getting wise to our idea and sending a Magus here to kill the both of you," Jonas said flatly.

Henry laughed at that, "You've got me there, lad. That *should* be my bigger fear. Gods be damned if the village finds out, I suppose. We'll be here for a long time or a short time. But no one is likely to leave Voskrin and gossip about the bloody Queen being at Henry Drago's farm."

"Henry," Jonas said softly, leaning conspiratorially forward, "who would know who Andariana is?"

Henry frowned, and then slapped his forehead, laughing nervously, "That's right! They won't have any notion of who she is, will they?"

"Why *should* they? It's not like she's met everyone in the realm and shaken their hand. She was also deposed, so they probably think she's dead," Jonas added.

Henry nodded, his mind seeming to jump a hundred leagues at once.

"I've been around you bloody people too long to remember how to be *me*," he whispered.

"I'm sure it'll come back to you," Jonas offered. "It *needs* to come back to you, Henry, if we're going to convince these people that nothing strange is going on.

"We don't know *where* Bael has eyes and ears, but if I were him, I'd put one in Voskrin. He's already sent assassins here once. He knows where to send more. We're playing a dangerous game. If the wrong person hears something, you might have a day or an hour before someone is here to kill the both of you.

"They can Fade, just as we can. It's a terrifying ability, as I'm fast discovering. For the moment, our greatest secret lies in the fact that they don't know we've rediscovered Fading yet, but that won't last forever. They know Ethan ran away with Katherine; they'll know it's only a matter of time before he teaches the rest of us."

"They know they ran into the Seil Wood," Henry corrected, "not that they ran to *you*."

"Henry, they knew Katherine was from the Southern Plain. They now know she was a spy. Bael executed Lord Declan for his attempt to buy her time. The Seil Wood protected Ethan and Katherine against Bael. He's not going to take kindly to that, or miss the fact that *Her* Hunter is *my* Knight."

Henry frowned a moment before nodding, "Alright, it's obvious that I don't do well with this sort of thing. That being said, I'm not sure I'm very good at dealing with drunken queens either."

Jonas quirked a smile, "All you need is a bed and half a bottle of wine." He paused. "Forget I said that. And don't do that either, unless it's not your bed."

Henry stiffened, "I have no intention of bedding the Queen, boy."

Jonas arched an eyebrow, "Don't call me 'boy', Henry. And I'm not worried about you bedding my aunt. You are not that sort of man. Which is why your son selected you for this assignment. You have a code of honor you live by every day. I know you will protect her."

Henry chuckled dryly, "You have a very high idea of 'codes of honor', don't you?"

"Honestly?" Jonas snorted, "No. I think they're horseshit. I've seen them broken too many times. I've broken my own more times than I care to count." When Henry's eyebrows rose, Jonas chuckled, "And yet your son is still alive."

Henry clapped a hand on Jonas's shoulder, "Well, lad, I can't call you *boy*, but I look forward to the day I can call you 'son'." He glanced over his shoulder and stiffened, "And now, if you don't mind, I need to track down your aunt."

Jonas's eyes went wide, but Henry laughed it off, "Don't worry, lad, she probably ran south, because the land slopes down and the earth is softer that way. But I need to get to her before she slips in pig shit."

Jonas was still laughing when he came back together in the suite he shared with Aleksei. He was surprised to find the Hunter actually present. Flat on the floor, pressing himself up and down repeatedly.

"You know, you don't have to do that alone, right?"

"Did they get there alright?" Aleksei asked, never pausing.

"They did. Andariana tried to escape, but Henry seemed to have a good idea of where she ran. She couldn't have gone very far; she can't run more than a few hundred paces on a good day."

Aleksei stood, pulling a piece of white toweling from the bed and wiping his face and chest down. "And you really think this is a match? Are you sure they won't kill each other?"

Jonas considered a moment, trying not to watch Aleksei strip down too hungrily. "I think Henry will curb some of her more obnoxious behaviors, and Andariana will help him explore some of his perpetual sadness. However, she's a wreck at the moment. If Roux can't find Tamara, or if Tamara's already dead, Andariana's going to unravel so rapidly that we'll be lucky to scrape her from bottom of Henry's chicken coop."

"Well, they'll have Mother Margareta," Aleksei muttered.

Jonas chuckled, "Ah, your 'season witch', or whatever you call her."

Aleksei splashed himself with icy water from the ewer in the corner, "*We* call her Mother Margareta. She is a priestess of Mokosh. *You'd* probably call her a Magus. She might not, but you do *not* want to cross that woman."

Jonas quirked his mouth to the side, "Duly noted. Though I take notes on my behavior from you as much as you used to take them from me."

Aleksei frowned, "What's that supposed to mean?"

Jonas shrugged, "It means you've learned much of what I wanted to teach you. The same can't be said for me."

Aleksei walked towards the bath, mollified. Jonas breathed a sigh of relief. His Knight was growing increasingly unpredictable, and each time the tension between them rose, his fear of the other man's reactions increased. For the moment, Jonas was satisfied that this wasn't going to become a different sort of fight. The sort they'd never had really had before.

The sort that hurt his heart.

CHAPTER 50
LAWS OF ILLUSION

"This is ridiculous!"

Jonas winced at the tone in Rhiannon's voice. "I know you aren't happy about this, Mother."

"*Happy?*" she snapped back. "'Happy' that I'm to be left stranded on the shore while you're being blown to bits in the middle of the bloody sea? No, I'm not bloody *happy*."

Jonas took a deep breath, "I wish you could be there, I really do."

Rhiannon's crystal blue eyes flashed wide, reminding him painfully of Tamara, and not for the first time. "You *wish* I could be there? Well, I bloody don't!"

Jonas frowned, taken aback by her response, "But I thought—"

"I don't want to be within two hundred leagues of the hellstorm that's about to be unleashed out there, Jonas. And I don't want you, or Aleksei, or gods, *Yosef* to be there either. I want us *all* away from this horrid war, and I want us safe and happy and healthy."

Tears filled her eyes, and Jonas's heart threatened to break.

"But I can't have that, now can I?" she whispered, wiping a hand across her eyes angrily. "I've gotten my way a thousand times that never mattered a damn, but if I can't have what I want when it's important, what's the bloody point to *any* of it?"

He pulled her into a tight hug, as though the strength of his arms could crush out her fear and heartache. "That's why I have to fight,

Mother. I have to protect the people I love with everything I've got, every gift you gave me."

Rhiannon hugged her son back before stepping out of his embrace, raising her eyes to meet his. Her face was a perfect mask of bitter anger. It took him aback, even though he knew it was never meant at him.

"I know you do, Jonas. And I would never stop you from using your gifts, or your heart." She leaned forward and kissed his cheek, "Just make sure you never let either rule your head."

He managed a weak smile, blinking back tears of his own, "I promise. I only wish I was here to protect you, too."

Rhiannon laughed, only a trace of bitterness lingering, "Despite what everyone keeps telling me, I'm not *entirely* defenseless, you know."

Jonas chuckled, "Oh, I've heard the stories. But nevertheless, I want you to spend the battle with Katherine, if you will."

Rhiannon's eyebrow rose a hair, "Katherine? You're not telling me to spend every second with my delightful sister, but rather Aleksei's *friend*? What an odd request."

"I mean it, Mother. Katherine has a good head on her shoulders, she's imminently practical, and she's quick on her feet. Andariana is far away, and from what Aleksei has told me about Katherine, she is... formidable. If...anything happens, if Bael sends someone to the Admiralty, or if we're defeated—"

"Stop," she commanded.

Jonas found himself suddenly on bended knee before her, his face fixed on the floor. His hackles rose as he realized that Rhiannon was holding tightly to the Archanium, forcing him into that pose.

"Mother?" he managed, though the word came out as a broken supplication rather than a question.

"Gods, Jonas," Rhiannon gasped, relaxing and releasing the Archanium as she bent to help him back to his feet, "I am *so* sorry, darling. I... I'm afraid I cannot bear the idea of being freed, of being *with* you again, only to have you snatched away. I hope I didn't hurt you."

Jonas righted himself, flashing her a devious smile.

Concern crept across her features, "What is it? What does that smile mean? I haven't had time to learn all your facial expressions, but *gods* I could have mistaken you for your father for a second...."

"Anyone who thinks you're defenseless should probably give you a wide berth indeed."

Rhiannon sniffed, "I'm sure I don't know *what* you're talking about."

And just like that, the wall was back up. The mother, frightened for her child, once more safely contained behind the veneer of the princess. The air around them calmed. His mother was again holding the Archanium, but this time with a controlled familiarity devoid of such powerful emotions.

"I *will* see you again, Mother. And soon."

"Of course you will, darling. I don't doubt it for a second," she said with a smile, kissing him again and pulling him into a hug haunted by pure desperation and longing.

When her grip finally relaxed, Jonas took a step back and gave her a haughty wink. He dove into the Archanium and Faded, the light pulling at the edges of his coat, the tips of his boots. The light tore every fiber of his being apart, before rapidly fitting it all back together aboard the broad foredeck of Her Majesty's *Gray Wolf*.

He glanced around at the bustle of activity, searching for Aleksei through the flash of nameless sailors, tanned bodies lightly covered in white garb, and rough enough to be Aleksei's twins these days.

Jonas finally realized that Aleksei *was* the only figure on the entire foredeck.

The Hunter was flashing from one point to another so quickly that Jonas had seen dozens copies of the same man. Aleksei noticed his presence, stopping long enough to finally allow Jonas a clear view of the Hunter across the deck.

His Knight was handsome as ever, yet every time Jonas left and came back, it seemed Aleksei was getting bigger, thicker. The farm boy Jonas had met had, at some point, transformed into a towering and liquid-fast warrior.

But this was something altogether different.

Aleksei had always been tall and strong. But Jonas had never thought of the man as bulky. Since they'd been in Taumon, however, the Knight's muscles seemed to be bulging, as though they were threatening to break through his skin, thick as they were.

"Are you alright?" Jonas asked softly, stepping up alongside his Knight.

Aleksei flashed a false smile, "Why? What's worrying you?"

Jonas started at the dark tone in Aleksei's voice. "You're pulling on the bond to do deck chores. You're...bigger than I've ever seen you, but the mission doesn't call for you to be strong. I'm just trying to understand what you're doing."

"I didn't grow up near the sea, Jonas," Aleksei said softly. "Frankly, the ocean terrifies me. I need to be strong enough to swim for my life, it is comes to that, or we're *both* doomed. I need to learn how these ships are built. And if I'm going to use my gifts to full effect, I need to know how they move. If I commit to a critical moment and the ship shifts beneath me, it might spell the end for both of us. So, I'm learning everything I can. I'm learning how to fight on a ship."

"No," Jonas said, his voice barely audible above the waves crashing across the hull, "you're learning how to *assassinate*."

Aleksei's golden eyes stared straight back at him, "Yes, that's *exactly* what I'm doing. I'm teaching myself how to assassinate a man while on a boat. And I can tell from the look on your face that you hate this idea."

Jonas bit back a snarl, "How could I *not*? This is Andariana getting revenge, plain and simple. Using you for her own purposes. This is just her fulfilling her own fantasy because she knows you'll do it."

Aleksei arched an eyebrow, "Of *course* I'll do it. You're my family too, Jonas. If I can help my family by killing a dangerous man who is bent on killing you all, I will. I didn't take this mission just because she's my queen. But once he kills Andariana, who's he going to go after next?"

"*You*, Jonas. I'll have to kill him sooner or later. I might as well do it now, when we have him weak."

Jonas pushed himself against his Knight, "But I can't be there to help you. I can't *protect* you."

The rumble of laughter against Jonas's ear made him at once thrilled and terrified.

"I've lived through worse," Aleksei rumbled, "and I've overcome against greater odds than this. But I won't let anyone come for you like this. They have to be stopped. And if I have the chance to end this whole thing, I will."

Aleksei's arms wrapped tightly around him, and for a moment Jonas feared that he might be crushed under the ferocity of the other man's embrace. But big though he was, Aleksei knew the limits of his own strength.

Jonas relaxed against his Knight, taking in the other man's scent, basking in his solidity amongst a world constantly shifting around them.

Roux pulled himself onto bitter soil. The air around him stank, like corpses left to molder and rot in the sun for a season. He sucked the air in anyways, ignoring the stench.

Gods, but he swore the air this near the Heart of the Seil Wood had never been so rank. However, after an experimental sniff of his clothing, he realized he was not helping matters much.

And yet, the water he swam through in Relvyn had been pure and sweet. Nothing like this sickly, sweet decay. This water smelled six months stagnant, at least.

His heart filled with an immediate dread. There were many water-beasts that dwelled within the Wood, not merely beasts of air and tree and root. If the water was bad throughout the Wood, those creatures could in great jeopardy, or gone forever.

"All this for a silly feud?" he yelled into the canopy, stripping away his shirt and coat. The rotted water would have ruined them both. Besides, he didn't want to take anything from this Wood that he didn't have to.

Silly? The word exploded in his mind and knocked him to his knees. Had he been a step closer, he would have gone tumbling over the side of the brackish waterfall. The impact would have been fatal.

Roux straightened and squared his shoulders, resting his hand on the bone sword Relvyn had given him. "Yes, You are behaving like a terrified, spoiled child. This does not become You."

And who are you to criticize?

Roux winced when he heard the voice, but then he paused. He had heard Her, but She had been unable to wreck his mind as She had in times past. In fact, it had only sounded as though someone were speaking from the other room, not blasting into his brain.

Roux took a step forward, willing the Seil Wood to change to his whim. She did not, but neither did She strike at him. He changed tactic, turning a different way and Darting towards the western edge. Before he'd even taken a step into the gray-white of the Archanium, his connection shut off.

He took a deep breath, dampening the rage that boiled up within him. But at the same time, he felt comfort in that ancient anger, the connection he now felt to it through the bone blade. The bone blade, he now realized, that he was clutching to the point that his knuckles ached and blanched in the lowlight of the Heart.

Roux began to make his way west. Even in the darkness of the Heart of a Wood that would seek to banish him, or cut him away from the life he'd always known, Roux Devaan maintained his sense of direction.

He worked his way through the trees for hours before he heard the hooting. At first, he'd taken it as a kind of animal unique to the Heart, but the farther he moved through the Wood, the louder the noise became.

Roux experimentally Darted to the top of a tree nearby, breathing a sigh of relief when the moment of connection occurred. A heartbeat later, a dozen arrows filled air where he'd just stood.

Roux saved his curses, Darting forward without breaking the canopy. That might have been allowable in the sleeping Relvyn Wood, but in the darkness of Seil, breaching the canopy would give him away immediately.

The hooting and laughing soon trickled off as his pursuers realized he was not such an easy quarry. Their silence meant that they'd begun the hunt in earnest.

Roux was genuinely startled. She had mustered the hunting party after him in such a short amount of time, yet in the past he would have been surprised if the men had managed to string their bows and find their quivers before taking up the hunt.

These men did not sound as though they were fumbling about.

Could it be that She knew he was coming, and already had Wood-hardened men ready for combat? If so, surely She had chosen new men for the task.

There was a flash next to his face, and he saw Luc a moment before the arrow was released. Roux Darted directly behind the man, snapping his bowstring with his horn knife before Darting to the floor.

He was away before the other lads notched their arrows, yet seeing Luc confirmed his fears. These were no young bucks trying to show their mettle. At least, not all of them. These were men of the hunting party. Men he had grown up with, men he trusted.

And now they were hunting him.

But try and kill him though they may, *he* was master of these Woods, and that was not an idle boast, nor one born from Her magic making it easier on him.

He could just as soon find the rusalka pond he sought without Her help.

A hatchet thudded into the trunk an inch from his face.

Roux gripped the hatchet handle, ripping it from the tree before

Darting behind its point of origin. He saw two men, boys really, studying the foliage where he had been a moment before. He let the hatchet fly, and heard one of the boys scream as the ax cleanly severed his ear.

Roux was already gone before the scream faded, and when he reappeared high in an ancient elm, he could still hear the boy crying out.

Another man suddenly appeared before him, but he kicked out savagely, shifting his weight to his wrist as the man tumbled towards the forest floor.

"Come on boys, you can do better than that!" Roux crowed before Darting to the forest floor and running east. Based on his call, they would think he was moving west. Unless She was interfering.

He traveled at least a quarter mile without being attacked, but the run had him thinking. The men attacking him were *his* people. Her mind had been altered, or infected, by *something*. Her infection had apparently spread to these men, but did that give him license to kill them?

Roux had been as careful as he could thus far, trying to spare these men their lives. But he would not sacrifice his ability to draw breath so they might keep theirs.

It was not just his own life he was protecting. Someone else was depending on him, someone he refused to let down.

There was flash in the Archanium just before him within striking distance. On instinct, Roux thrust forward with his bone blade as he felt the other figure coalesce around it.

As the form sharpened, Roux froze. He stared at his blade, buried in his father's chest.

"Theo?" he whispered.

His father gasped, staring at the bone buried in his heart, then back to his son.

"Father," Roux whimpered, scrambling around the other man, resisting the urge of pull the blade free. Doing so would only hasten the man's death.

"Mother Wood!" he screamed at the canopy. "This man has been faithful, even when you asked the worst of him. He has been *True*. Do not demand this of him! Return him to his people!"

There was a pregnant pause as Roux felt Theo's heart pump its last through his fingers, through his blade. His father seized and stiffened.

No.

Roux loosed a howl.

It was a pule of pure animal rage, of a hatred darker than the blackest star. And in that moment, he understood what Relvyn had been trying to tell him.

He wrenched the blade from his father's chest, Theo's heart having already stilled. But he could feel them there, the others. The hunters Seil had sent to kill him.

Roux took a deep breath, allowing his blind rage to merge with the bone blade he held. And then it crashed back into him in a torrent of bitterness and bile.

The blade and man moved as dual shadows, splintering in the darkness, reforming behind men as they stalked the gloom to find him. His blade bit true every time, and each life ended without a sound.

With each kill, Roux added a talon of blood to his face. He, at least, allowed them to die properly, on the edge of his sword. He luxuriated in it. It was all he could do not to laugh at the looks on their faces as they fell before him, his rage fueling his blood lust.

Luc was the last to fall.

The man was edging out of the Wood. He'd been running for so long. His breath was as ragged as his clothes, his eyes red from exhaustion.

Roux made sure Luc was aware enough to know what was happening. But he'd been sure to puncture the man's lungs so that there was not a single scream before he truly began cutting.

Luc's mouth only opened wider, no sound wrestling forward. But Roux's blade just cut consistently deeper.

When he was finished, Roux knew he was well-painted in the blood pattern, not of a Hunter like Aleksei, but of a proper Berserker. Something his abandoning Mother Wood could never abide, nor understand.

The feeling was mutual.

"Never speak to me again, Seil," he snarled. "You have cut everything from me, and I would burn You, were it in my power. I divest myself of You. Let the Demon take You for what I care."

But I miss you. I'm so lonely now. You've killed so many of My toys. It grows quiet.

Roux wiped his fingers through the congealing blood on his face and spat, forming a paste. He drew a symbol on the nearest tree. A symbol he knew, only because Relvyn forced it into his mind.

As he walked from the Wood, he heard Her howling in pain. It gave him strength. Strength better used to save someone he truly loved.

Someone waiting for him.

"*Blegsh!*"

The icy water cascaded over her face. Andariana sat up, or rather *was* sat up, by a Henry Drago she seemed surprised to see.

"What was *that?*" she spluttered.

"Pond water."

"*Why?*"

Henry shrugged, "Because that's what I had, and I needed to talk to you."

To her credit, Andariana brushed the longer strings of algae from her gown, stood, wrapped her long chestnut hair over one shoulder, and turned to him. "Are you in*sane?*"

"Breakfast will be served downstairs presently, Your Majesty," Henry said, bowing his way out of the small room.

"You're mocking me."

"How could I *not?*" he snorted as he walked down the narrow steps. "No jury here but me, Princess."

"I'm a Queen!" she shouted.

"Says who?"

Half an hour later, she descended.

"So," Andariana said very slowly, emerald eyes glimmering with anger, "how does this go?"

Henry shrugged, turning in his kitchen and grabbing a knife, "We stay put, we do our level best to keep the townsfolk from ever knowing you're here, and we pray no one from the Demon's camp gets wind of any of this. *That's* how this goes."

Andariana walked to a window, leaning against it, "And what happens if there's an emergency, and you have to birth a pig?"

"Well, you don't look ready to pop, so there's no worry there."

When he felt her eyes boring into his back, Henry paused his chopping with a grunt, "*If* I had a sow in labor, I'd deliver it myself, given that it's not that hard. If all goes well. I'd normally have Mother Margareta here, just in case. She's lived in Voskrin since Aleksei and I came here. He was five, or near enough."

"And how many pigs did *he* deliver?" she asked earnestly.

Henry burst out laughing before checking himself. "Gods, but I haven't had a real laugh in some time. I've been marching with what's left of your Legion for a season or two. This is the first I've been here in half a year. Despite being my home, it wasn't good for my safety, not since Aleksei's promotion. We haven't had much time to tend our farm, so I don't rightly know how many pigs I even *have* any longer.

"My son has been at the sword since your nephew sent him terrifying dreams, calling him to ride north to become an Archanium Knight. A job that should still be part of the nobility."

Andariana frowned, "How do you know that?"

Henry frowned at her, "I'm a farmer, not an idiot. That's why my son is running your military, Majesty." Henry flipped his knife to point at Andariana, "And don't for a *moment* think that I don't know what you ordered Aleksei to do. You try to run away again? You go against what those boys told you, try to tell all the villagers who you are, I'll lock you in the root cellar."

Andariana arched a chestnut eyebrow and snarled, her eyes flaring, "Do you know whom you're addressing, Henry Drago?"

He straightened calmly, "I do, ma'am, and you don't want me to tell it to you. But let me tell you who *you're* talking to. I'm the man who sent his only son on a sad draft horse out of my barn into the wide world *alone*.

"I told him to follow his heart, because I had a dream where your nephew explained who Aleksei *could* be. He said my son could be a 'hero'. So, the better question is whether you know who *you're* addressing, Andariana Belgi."

She opened her mouth to contest his claim, but Henry was ready, "You are not *my* queen any more, Andariana. You've been deposed. Be it by death, abdication, or rebellion, I don't much see the difference. The irony, of course, is that I'm one of the fools trying to get you back on your throne. Might as well have been press-ganged into the job.

"My son loves your nephew. As far as I'm aware, that makes us strangers.

"But, because of our relationship to each other, I have to watch over you. You cannot be trusted, nor found. No one cares if I live or die, except your nephew and my son."

When she snorted at him, Henry hurled his knife into the wall above her head so hard it shattered into a deluge of cheap steel.

"You're in *my* home," he growled. "You just sent my son to *die*." Her face registered surprise. Henry's rage only increased, "I know what you did. I know you sent my son to kill Emelian Krasik. The man backed by an actual Demon. And you tell *my* son, my only child, to find and kill that man, and face down that Demon. Again and again.

"I also understand that the Demon in question had summoned a 'friend' to *ensure* my son dies. Not your nephew, not your daughter."

Andariana started forward angrily, "Don't you *dare* mention my daughter, you piece of pauper trash."

Henry watched her calmly. "*I* didn't lose your daughter, Princess. *You* did. That ain't my fault. I can be blamed for many wrongs, but this ain't one of them, and none of them were thrown your way. So, before you start tossing accusations around, stop and take a look at yourself. Take a look at *your* decisions."

Andariana stammered, her usual ready responses apparently now beyond her immediate grasp. Henry quirked a smile.

"It must be rough, thinking you're right all the time," he muttered, pulling another knife from a block at his hip.

Andariana stopped herself. He was trying to get at her.

And she understood it.

She had long thought that her life was more than slightly ridiculous. She could command a gown made of the rarest gems and silks, and it would be made that day. She could ask for a kitten and be given a tame tiger cat from Fanj. She'd had everything from her mother and father that she could ever ask for, except happiness or attention.

That had never been something they could provide. They'd died together from wasting sickness, but the High Magus present called the death something that was long expected.

Once the civil war for Marra's throne had broken out, she'd hardly had a chance to think about happiness except when she was in Seryn's arms, before she was shoved onto the throne.

Seryn had been her world. She'd never had a love since. His was her first, and he was taken nearly as soon as he announced himself as her consort.

Taken by his own father, who murdered Seryn for "treason", out of pure hatred for Andariana, for her family, and then proceeded to blame her for his own actions. To claim Seryn's murder as a blessing in one of his revolutionary tracts, decrying immorality, with a woodcut of her and Seryn in cheap ink.

The entire process had left her emotionally shattered, but then she had Tamara to look after, to love in Seryn's place, and a war to fight to keep both of their heads from ending up tarred on pikes. And even with all of that weighing on her, she had been mature enough to understand that her daughter could never replace her husband, just as the countless hours she'd spent trying to keep the both of them alive couldn't fill the void of his absence.

Henry Drago wanted to know her life story? She would give him the entirety of it. Everything. What she'd done, what she'd survived, all the times she'd wanted to leap off the throne, and the times she wanted to leap from a cliff.

And once he knew who he was really talking to, he could fling accusations till crows picked at the both of them, but he would also know how little she cared.

"And you're sure this will work?" Jonas asked skeptically.

Ilyana scowled at him, "How should I know? But I know what worked in the forests of Keldoan, and in the midlands against that infantry force. The spells worked well enough on land. And what's more, every Magus with me saw and aided in those efforts. We lost less than two hundred men in that battle, Jonas. And we cut the fifty-thousand enemy down to a man. If we can get it to work properly, it would quite literally turn their own game against them."

Jonas sighed. She was certainly right about that, but the risk if she was wrong was monumental. He thought for a long moment before nodding.

"I have to accept that I no longer know everything you know. You have my apologies, Yana. I can't see what you see. The meridians that you now tread are about as far from the Sphere's center as you can get."

Ilyana beamed with pride at that, "And *that's* what's going to make this work. I ran some of these spells past your new friend, Ethan? He barely knew I was touching the Archanium, much less what I was doing. If he's an example of what we're up against, they should be near enough to blind to what we're actually doing."

Jonas nodded, taking a deep breath to steady himself. As much as he played along with the fiction that he knew what he was doing, this was taking a risk with Aleksei's life in a very major way. And he wouldn't even know if it was working before it was too late.

"I trusted you with my life," she said softly, her voice barely a quiver above the rocking of the waves, "when you were one of the only people there for me. No one else would even speak to me. Marrik was in the brig, and you and Hade were the only two who would come see me. You told me to trust you then, Jonas Belgi.

"Trust me now."

He smiled at that, pleased to see her spectacular confidence despite the glowering shade of war. And he did trust her, because he *knew* her. If Ethan had hatched this very same idea, Jonas would never have allowed it to leave the command room.

But Ilyana wasn't going to put Aleksei or himself in danger unless she had to. And beyond that, the plan was so simple as to be near perfect. Something would likely go wrong, but it was always the simple plans that could handle such a failure without collapsing entirely.

The more complexity a commander added, the greater the chances for error, and the less likely it was that anyone would be able to recover when the winds changed. And they *always* changed.

Aleksei was particularly adept at exploiting those very tactics, triggering chain reactions that broke the enemy to pieces. That she had come to the two of them with such a simple plan only served to excite Aleksei to its applications.

"Very well," he said finally, having gone over every possible change to the plan as it stood, knowing that the moment battle was joined, the whole thing might go up in black fire. "If you're ready to call Admiral Jefress over, we can get through the briefing and get into position."

Aleksei frowned, "And how are we going to know when they're getting too close? If Ethan can't feel her touching the Archanium very well from a few paces—"

Jonas raised a hand, once more a prince, "We know these Magi. They fought us in Kalinor. Even if you can't tell what they're casting, you know they're *there*. But you're right, the same oceanic effect that is going to disrupt Krasik's abilities will likely play some manner of chaos on the Archanium, especially if we're listening for the other side to access it. Which is why I'm going to have my eye on those ships."

Aleksei's face was blank for a moment before a look of horror flashed across it. "No. I forbid it. They will burn you from the sky within moments of seeing you."

Jonas smirked at his Knight, "And how are they going to see me in the chaotic hell that is the Autumn Sea at the onset of spring?"

Aleksei's face slid from Jonas's to the churning gray water surrounding them. "And you're sure you can *do* this?"

"Swim?" Jonas asked, a part of him reveling in Aleksei's immediate displeasure. His Knight had been unusually prickly of late. Perhaps he might rethink his behavior if he got a taste of the same from Jonas. And that aside, Jonas had far more practice delivering derision than Aleksei could conjure in a lifetime.

Aleksei looked out towards the sea. The water was exceptionally cold. Not as lethal as in the dead of winter, but cold enough that a man might survive for a handful of minutes only. Jonas knew what his Knight was thinking. Aleksei had to get from one of the four Ilyari warships to Krasik's ship, and there was no room for error.

If that particular plan didn't work, either he'd be spotted and be so filled with arrows before he reached the prow that he'd look like a hedgehog, or he'd freeze to death before he ever reached the ship.

As a man from the Southern Plain, swimming in the ocean was not something he'd ever done before. Jonas knew from his own childhood the difference between swimming in the ocean and a pond. But swimming in the ocean with land a distant sight and spring newly-minted?

If Jonas hadn't known and trusted Aleksei as he did, he would have forbidden the very idea of his Knight hovering inches over the icy water, open to enemy fire, waiting for a moment when he was well past the first three rounds of archers before doing anything.

But between Aleksei and Ilyana, Jonas was impressed at their rather unique approach to what might have been a straight-forward sea battle. In the past, the strength of the Magi on either side and the ballistae would have settled the matter, unless the ships managed to get close enough to board one another before either was blown apart.

But since Yrinu's great maritime empire had fallen a thousand years past, naval battles had been very few and far between. As only the eastern half of Ilyar touched the Autumn Sea, it was rare that they had to deal with more than raiders from Yrinu.

Dalita and Ilyar had enjoyed a peaceful mercantile relationship since the Dominion Wars. Excepting an incident two centuries ago when a Crown Prince had offended an Yrini ambassador and, rather than apologize, had tried to declare war and seize part of the southern realm for himself, the battle that was about to take place was rare indeed.

Jonas was broken from his thoughts when Admiral Jefress approached, glancing between himself and Aleksei. "And you're confident in this plan?"

Aleksei nodded decisively. "We are, Admiral. While I appreciate that there are a lot of unknowns on your end of things, we believe this is the most effective way to win this fight."

Jefress kept his eyes locked on Aleksei, "I'm putting the lives of my men in your hands, Lord Captain."

Aleksei laughed at that, earning a scowl from the admiral. "Admiral," Aleksei all but barked, "I will not be on this ship, or any save my allotted place on my fireship. And then I will be on *their* ships, the ones you're destroying before they can take out any of our most valuable assets; the Magi, the Prince, and any piece of our mercantile fleet and crews.

"The people you need to speak to are the Prince, Magus Ilyana and...ah, here they are."

Two forms flickered wildly about the deck before forming into tight bundles of matter and light, paces from Aleksei and the Admiral. After only a heartbeat, one solidified into Ethan, the other into Yosef.

The men were smartly dressed, camouflaged to match the ship but not the sea. If the enemy Magi got close enough to target an individual, they could wreak havoc in seconds. This was but one of Aleksei's ideas to hide the Magi against the castle of each ship.

"Very well," Aleksei said, watching the growing apprehension build in Ilyana's eyes, while Ethan's remained passive and powerful, "this is the plan. And we are going to stick to it, am I understood?"

He waited to see every single individual nod before he began laying out what they were each to do.

"And they believed you?" Henry asked incredulously.

They sat before the fire in his house, drinking apple brandy he'd hidden for a special occasion. He seemed to think drinking with the former Queen of Ilyar merited such a vintage.

For her part, Andariana was glad for the fire and the drink. The night was cold, and the heat from the rustic hearth felt somehow warmer than the sweet-smelling fires they lit in the cities.

Andariana giggled, "Why wouldn't they? How likely was it that I could climb down that entire wall in a dress?"

Henry stared at her before he burst out laughing. He paused for a moment, before looking into her eyes, "So, how *did* you climb down the walls in a dress?"

Andariana laughed, "What do you think I spent my childhood doing? Yes, of course I was in lessons and had tutors and all that nonsense, but when we were free, my sisters and I got up to all sorts of trouble. Marra was always a spoilsport, so Rhi and I usually just left her in the dark. But when we grew a little older, the two of us started exploring.

"I found an old knotted oak on the East Lawn. One summer, Rhiannon bet me that I couldn't climb to the top of the wall. So, I did. It took me a couple of tries, of course, and I nearly killed myself half a dozen times, but I did it.

"And once I had, I noticed an elm a few hundred paces away on the other side. There's a wide berth on the outer side of the Palace wall with a garden. The wide berth is for falling soldiers, but it had been so long since the last war that we'd turned it into a garden ages ago."

Henry leaned forward, taking a swig of his brandy and smiling. "So, you'd climb down and get into the city?"

Andariana shook her head, still laughing, "Oh gods no. I would have broken my neck in seconds. But there was a lattice *behind* the elm. The tree hid me from view while I climbed down." She paused, wiping away a tear, "I never told my sisters about my secret way into Kalinor proper. I just pretended I'd been looking down into the city. It really was the first time I'd seen it.

"I used it every now and again over the years, not too often, but I was careful not to get caught. And of course, I only had gowns to wear, so I learned how to do it like a lady."

Henry sat back, a wide grin on his face, "That's a wonderful story, Andi."

She blushed, but she knew Henry was keeping up his guard. As much as they were quickly becoming family, she was still his Queen, at least in theory, and he was still a farmer from the Southern Plain.

"I must admit, I have my share of such stories, but it was hard to secretly meet my wife by climbing trees."

Andariana quirked a smile, "And why would that be?" The moment the words were out of her mouth, she cackled like a girl of fourteen summers. "Good gods, what's wrong with me? Your wife was Ri-Vhan, was she not?"

Henry nodded, that infuriating smirk not suddenly charming. "It's a little hard to outmatch them when it comes to sneaking up on someone," he chuckled.

"Tell me about her," Andariana said, learning forward.

Henry rested his head on the back of his chair and closed his eyes. "The older I get, the more I care to remember. The last thing I'd want is to ever forget a single detail. Every night, before I retire, I recall everything I can about her, anything that may have slipped my mind, or I haven't thought about in a long while.

"Her face, her voice, the way she walked, the way she scowled at me when we would argue. Some might have called her harsh, but I called her perfect. She had a temper, no doubt about it, but a wit to match.

"The way she held Aleksei when he was a boy. The way she moved. The way she *smelled*, gods. So many things, some maybe trivial, I know. But it's hard to build a life with someone you love, and then to have that life randomly wrecked."

Andariana staggered up and walked over to him, wrapping her arms around him and giving him a gentle kiss on the cheek. "I know how you feel, Henry Drago, perhaps better than you can imagine. We've both been put in much the same situations."

She withdrew quickly, blushing, "But we've also survived them. And we've raised wonderful children." She took a deep, pained breath, retaking her seat, "And now we're here, sitting by ourselves on your farm, waiting for someone to reappear from the ether and let us know whether one or both of them survived this madness."

Henry sat up, watching her carefully, "Indeed we are. And as much as I want to blame you for what you ordered Aleksei to do, this really is all my fault. He would never have been in this position if I'd told him just to ignore the dreams. Gods, but that feels like a lifetime ago."

Andariana stared back at Henry, tears streaming from her eyes, "Oh, Henry. Think about it. What would have happened if he'd stayed here? The war would still have happened. He would have probably been conscripted, and would be dead, or fighting for the enemy. Sending him to Jonas might honestly be one of the most important decisions in the history of our *realm*.

"Rhiannon would never have been found. And my daughter. My precious, precious Tamara, would be in the same enemy hands that she's in now. Kalinor would still have been sacked, but your son saved a great many lives that day, mine included. He saved my daughter, no matter what happened after. Every Archanium Magus we saved was due to Aleksei and Roux.

"If Aleksei had stayed here, we would never have been able to take refuge with the Ri-Vhan. Aleksei might never have appreciated his Hunter birthright.

"I honestly cannot count the things that would be different in this world without your son and my nephew having met, having fallen in love."

She leaned forward, wiping a tear from Henry's rough cheek, "Please don't doubt yourself, Henry Drago. Your son is a great man. Granted, one who can be difficult to stand sometimes." When Henry's face darkened, she broke out a smile, "And now I see that he comes by that honestly."

Henry blushed, but she pushed forward, "As I said, your son might be a great man, but don't let that fool you into thinking you're anything less. Because that would be an awful lie."

Henry turned his face away, wiping a tear. "That's very kind of you," he grunted.

Andariana sighed, fighting back a giggle at his embarrassment.

The fire went out.

She stifled a scream.

Henry was next to her in a heartbeat, his hand clamped over her mouth. "We're moving to the kitchen," he hissed in her ear. "It's going to be alright, but I have to get you somewhere safe. Be as quiet as possible."

She nodded.

He pulled his hand back, gripping her hand instead, guiding her confidently through the dark of his home.

They reached the kitchen, and he was just helping her under the cupboards when the windows imploded. She fought back a gasp. If they'd still been up and about, they'd have been cut to ribbons.

She expected to hear the shouts of their assailants as they searched for her, but instead she only heard a queer *whistling*, a shrieking she couldn't identify.

Henry started to crawl away, but she grabbed at him. "Where are you going?"

The man glared back at her, raising a finger to his lips, his face hard in the reflected moonlight.

The shrieking whistle only increased, but now there was something else. Something that chilled her heart. Rather than hearing bootsteps and the sounds of steel, she could only make out the sound of something impossibly sharp. And something that sounded like voices, a thousand growling wordlessly in unison.

The front door burst inwards.

Andariana heard the splinters of wood bury themselves above her. She wanted to cry out, but she kept her mouth shut.

She looked up, tears streaming from her eyes, and saw the point of a glittering piece of steel. A knife, perhaps?

Something entered the farmhouse, a tearing tornado hovering in the living room where they had been sitting, ripping everything to shreds from the sound of it. It was undoubtedly the source of the shrieking, the growling, but made no expected sounds. No footsteps to follow, no panting breath that she could make out.

She reached up, easing the glittering blade she'd noted from the counter, her hand wrapping around the spine of the blade as she eased it off the counter, trying to lift it without cutting herself.

The blade slipped and sliced deep into her hand.

She clenched her teeth and pressed her lips together, dropping the blade into her lap and doing her best to get a better grip on its blood-slicked handle.

Was this Aleksei's wind demon? Why would it be *here*? And what good could a blade possibly do against it?

The whistling drew closer. Gods, where was Henry? Was he still even alive? She hadn't heard him move from his position on the other side of the counter, but with Drago men that didn't seem to mean much.

Whatever was stalking them shrieked out one of the shattered windows, sending whatever glass remained splintering around the room.

She did her best to slow her breathing, counting her heartbeats, listening intently. There was a violent crash from above, more shattering and shrieking.

Glass crunched underfoot as a shadowy figure stepped into the kitchen.

The figure rounded the corner and Andariana lunged. The figure caught her wrist and flipped the knife from her hand faster than she could imagine.

"We have to get out of here," Henry whispered. "I think it's moved upstairs."

She realized she was shaking. He pulled her into a brief hug, "We're going to survive this, Andi. I'm a man of my word."

As he led her out the back door towards the barn, she got a look at the terrible destruction the house had already suffered. It wasn't just the windows that were missing, but entire sections of the lower floor. She was amazed the entire house hadn't already crashed down upon them.

"What is it?" she whispered as he led her to the barn.

"Something that destroyed my door and wrecked my home. That's all I know," Henry growled. "I love that house. I raised Aleksei in that house, and the gods be *damned* if I'm going to let some...some *being* come in and ruin what I put my blood and sweat into building."

As they reached the shadows of the barn, Andariana saw another figure rush into the farmhouse. She turned to find Henry emerging from the barn, angrily gripping a pitchfork.

"Someone just went into the house," she whispered, holding close to him.

He turned sharply, "Did you see what they looked like?"

Andariana shook her head, "It was hard to tell with the moonlight being so weak. But—"

Henry peered into her face in the darkness, "But?"

"I'll sound daft. But it looked like an old woman...a *really* old woman," she whispered.

The top of the house erupted in flames and Henry cried out, rushing out in the moonlight, pitchfork at the ready.

She pulled him back towards the barn, "Just what do you expect to do with that?" she demanded, whispering as best she could. "It doesn't have a *body*, Henry!"

A powerful concussion knocked both of them back against the barn wall. A moment later, a dark figure stalked from the house, and Henry readied for battle. Andariana felt her heart clench in her chest as he charged the figure.

He stopped short.

She frowned, but he motioned her forward.

Andariana stepped carefully from the shelter of the barn, hurrying to Henry, only to find a small, seemingly-ancient woman standing next to him.

"Now let me tell you," she was saying as Andariana approached, "this was a mighty interesting creature here. I'm not exactly sure if it was the sort *I'd* have for tea, but it didn't show up by accident, oh no it did *not*.

"It's gone, by the way. I don't know for how long. And I am sorry about your house. I know it was special to you."

Henry was just staring at this woman, nodding to everything she said. "How...how did you know to come?" he whispered, tears streaming down his face as his broken house burned.

"There, there," the old woman said, stepping forward and giving him a firm hug and a pat. "I've been creating a network around Voskrin since I arrived. The people there are protected from this sort of thing. But your farm is too far away, so I came as quickly as I could once I felt it appear."

"You created a...a *network*? What does that even mean? How could someone like you banish a creature that powerful?" Henry demanded, suddenly angry.

The elderly woman didn't seem at all fazed by his outburst. "It means that I did my job, Henry Drago. I used every field blessing, every death, every birth, to protect the people of Voskrin. More importantly, I did all that to protect you and your *son*. That's what I was sent here to do, protect you and Aleksei. Perhaps now you see why."

Andariana was shocked by how forcefully she was speaking to Henry, as though he was a petulant child throwing a tantrum.

"Sent by who?" he yelled.

"By Grigori. By the Voralla. Years ago, just before the 'new order' came into power. Same as Jonas was *meant* to be protected. Those boys were too important to be left to their own devices.

"Do you really believe I was 'Mother Margareta' before I came to Voskrin? No, my name is Margaret, and you know that. But I had to build trust with the locals, so I adopted a name that sounded more familiar to the folks down here."

Andariana had never felt so out of place in her life.

"It might all feel like doom and gloom now, but you'll get through this. And you'll be stronger for it."

Henry stared at her for a long moment. "I don't even know who you are," he whispered, the rage seeming to leave him in an instant.

Margaret snorted, "You know *exactly* who I am, Henry Drago. I've only ever been myself, only ever watched out for you and your son. Speaking of stronger, is your Aleksei behaving himself?"

Henry cleared his throat, looking abashed, "He's about to assassinate Emelian Krasik. The Demon will be there, too."

"Well, my, my, that boy's got some spunk in him, doesn't he? And just whose idea was that?"

"Mine," Andariana managed to whisper.

"Oh, hello there, dear. And who might you be?"

"My name is Andariana," she said, her voice still barely above a whisper.

"Speak up, girl. And straighten your back. You don't want to walk around like some Yrini swamp witch. What sad folk they are."

"Margaret," Henry said, "you're not being very polite."

"Oh hush. I'm being as appropriate as I can stand at the moment."

Andariana felt the now-familiar shock of having a commoner treat her with disdain. "I'm—"

"Girl," Margaret snapped, "I know who you are. I saw you playing on the Lawn when you were a child. I was curious to see who that child would become, and thank you for showing me. But don't you dare lecture me about *respect*."

Andariana started shaking again. She felt panicked, and she knew she was crying. The dressing down she'd just received matched the way she felt in her heart. And it was the last thing she wanted to hear from someone else.

"Oh, it's alright, dear," Margaret said softly. "You'll get this all behind you. *You* will, at least. But I do so hope you haven't killed my darling Aleksei. Because believe me, if you have, we'll have a *very* different conversation."

"Margaret," Henry said, pleadingly.

"Very well. It's not as bad as all that. And besides," she said, bending to retrieve a small lump from the ground, oblivious to Henry's collapsing house behind her, "I baked you a pie."

CHAPTER 51
GHOST

Roux wasted only moments washing himself in the stream before Darting from the edge of the Seil Wood to the gates of Kalinor itself.

By now, a straight Dart of a few leagues felt like no great feat. He was fixated on a single target, and while he couldn't feel her heartbeat against his own, he vowed that it would be mere moments before he once again held her to him.

His time tracking in Taumon came back to him in an instant as he flashed across Kalinori rooftops, the residents beneath completely unaware as he flicked from point to point.

He made one stop in the city proper, pausing in a back alley to take down a soldier as he would a wounded deer, stripping the man naked. He was careful not to get any blood from the kill on the uniform. It would soon become obvious that he didn't belong in the city or Palace proper, but he wanted to throw as much confusion as possible into the mix, and should he need to hide, it was much easier to blend in as one of them when he wasn't half-naked and wearing a kilt of twigs and leaves, with little else to hide him from the Ilyari rebels.

After his time in Taumon, Roux knew no one would miss a soldier in the middle of a midden heap. Even without the fish guts, it would be a long time before anyone discovered the dead man, if they ever did.

A flash and flicker later, and Roux was back atop the roofs of the city, Darting across them, hiding behind chimneys and steam-pipes alike as he flitted through the city, heading ever inward towards the North Tower.

Towards Tamara.

He cleared the city without a single eye finding him, though with the noise and the bustle beneath, that was hardly remarkable. He'd thought Taumon to be a cacophony of chaos, but Kalinor put the port to shame, even under occupation. It was at least three times the size, and the noise didn't begin to compare.

Roux found himself at the city's edge within an hour, the sun sinking towards the horizon as he flickered from post to post along the wall. It still amazed him how conveniently the Ilyari had built their guard towers to have hundreds of perches within sight of one another, all built of the same white stone. If his every footfall had been over crunchy thatch, it might have been one thing, but the smooth stone and tile ensured that the loud men sitting around fires beneath him never heard a single step, brief though each one was.

Half an hour later, he stood at the base of the tower Katherine had described. Alone. Not a soul to be seen.

Roux Darted to the nearest outpost, perching on its roof in the golden afternoon light and sighting the nearest handhold from where he crouched.

As he flickered up the tower, he felt as though every Dart, every hour that had separated him from Tamara, had prepared him for this moment. Each time he took a risk, it was one he'd already taken countless times before. He knew which traps to avoid, which times a mere toe-touch would help him reach the next handhold, when to wait, and when to Dart.

The tower alone seemed to soak up another half-hour, but he had seen no one since the soldier he'd killed in the Kalinor slums. And more importantly, no one had seen him.

He found himself staring at a window that could be no other than the one Katherine Bondar had described to him. To be certain, Roux Darted to the very edge, praying it would bear his weight, lifting himself easily to peek within.

The bandaged wreck, the room's sole occupant, looked strange to his eyes, but he knew her posture, her bearing.

His heart leapt in his chest even as he Darted into the room, his feet landing silently on the rough-hewn planks of the tower floor.

"Hello?" Tamara demanded.

"Quiet up there!" a voice sounded from deep below.

It was all Roux could do to calm himself and not immediately dispatch the guard who had spoken up so roughly. Instead, he focused on being as silent as he'd ever been in his life, ghosting across the boards to her.

He knew she could hear him, but he couldn't risk her speaking out again. Instead, he drew his horn knife, flipped it and reversed it, placing the grip in her palm.

She started, but as her bound hand wrapped around the horn handle, he heard a soft squall in her throat.

Her mouth opened with a question, but he met it with a silencing kiss, ecstatic and panicked at once. He drew back after a long moment, wincing at the crusted blood that lingered on his lips.

Gods, but what had they *done* to her?

For the first time, Roux allowed himself to take in the whole tableau. The bandage across her eyes was more than a blindfold. The cloth was maroon and yellow with old blood and infection. The air stank of rot.

Her previously-perfect golden ringlets were tangled and matted with old sweat, and his nose told him that she had not been allowed to attend to nature in days. She had wounds that festered; some fresh, some seemingly ancient.

Even as he reclaimed his horn knife and worked at her bonds, he heard someone climbing the stairs. She whimpered. His heart raced as he cut each binding, getting closer and closer to freeing her.

When the guard finally made it to the top of the stairwell, he found the Princess Tamara still in her chair, dejected as ever, and just as alone, just as pathetic.

Then there was a light puff of air, and Roux Devaan dragged his knife through the man's jugular veins.

"Sorry," Roux snarled as the man collapsed, silently fountaining blood, "but we'll be going now."

Aleksei crouched on the small frigate, feet spread to maintain his balance just a handspan from the shattering sea. The ship was old and worn, and its interior was packed not with sailors, but rather drums of oil and scraps of wood and paper. The sails were at full mast, but the sailors had long since abandoned it, leaving only himself and a fidgety young Magus named Ricon.

He glanced at the Magus and gave him a confident smile. The one Ricon returned was anything but.

"When we get within striking distance, you're not going to have much time," Ricon shouted shakily. "It'll be a matter of seconds before this whole ship goes up, and they'll be firing at the illusions. There's really no guarantee the ship will even *make* it to the enemy vessel."

Aleksei's smile remained far more optimistic than he felt, "If the ship starts to break up, Fade us back to the *Gray Wolf*. But not until you're certain I can't make it. Otherwise, stick with the plan."

Ricon looked to be near panic, but he nodded, "Aye, Lord Captain."

Aleksei turned to the horizon, to the enemy warships bathed in late afternoon sun, and past them to the seven smaller Yrini raiding balingers. It wasn't really surprising that Krasik would have hired mercenaries.

The ships in Bereg Morya were smaller than those in Taumon by a good margin. They were made for trade, occasionally engaging in short sorties with the very same Yrini corsairs that now moved past the larger warships.

Those mercenaries are going to be firing at the two of you like mad. Be careful.

Aleksei smiled as Jonas's voice filled his mind. It was strange to feel the Prince nearby, as separated as they were by the vast stretch of churning black water.

True to his word, arrows and firebolts flashed across the sea moments later, some landing glancing blows on the vessel, most flying impotently into the sea.

Aleksei had to smirk at that, knowing the confused consternation of the men and Magi in the Yrini ships as their first salvo flew through the men they could clearly see moving around the deck and preparing to return fire.

At least, that was what Ricon was *supposed* to be conjuring. Aleksei couldn't see the spells himself, so he wasn't clear exactly *what* the illusions held.

A second salvo of burning shafts rammed into the side of the frigate, setting off the barrels of oil on the ship's port side. The deck exploded in flame and speeding shards of wood, but Ricon and Aleksei were protected behind a bulwark built to shield them from the worst of the damage while allowing both a view of the battleships ahead.

Aleksei wondered how long it would serve its purpose.

The flames coursing up the side of the frigate were not missed by the larger ships. Not as six of the ancient boats headed straight for them, all of them now blazing brightly.

The ship shuddered, and Aleksei wondered if they would reach the warships before the frigate capsized and burned away in the sea.

But even as they limped across the water, Aleksei saw that their speed was still outpacing the warships. The seconds dragged on, but every second brought them closer to the flagship. To Krasik.

Aleksei's throwing knives and sword were strapped across his right shoulder, but in case any of Krasik's men managed to get within bow range, he strung his small Ri-Vhan horn bow and checked the quiver tied to his left side.

With Bael's Magi certainly out in force, a long-range weapon was crucial.

His fight with the Scions in Je'gud had taught him his limitations in a very visceral way. He was determined not to make the same mistake again.

He didn't have to execute every enemy on the ship, he just had to be faster than they were. And he'd been practicing for days now, drawing on the bond until Jonas had begged him to stop, slumping down in exhaustion.

The amount of power he was drawing from his prince was exhausting the man. But Aleksei would rather Jonas have to endure a little misery if it meant they both stayed alive.

"Lord Captain?" Ricon called, his uncertainty mirroring Aleksei's own.

Aleksei turned and saw the flagship looming before them, coming on fast. "Get out of here," he commanded. "Your job is done."

Ricon nodded, tears streaming down his face as the ship erupted. The force of the explosion threw both men painfully against the weakening bulwark.

"Fade, dammit!" Aleksei roared.

Ricon pulled himself to his knees. He gave Aleksei a weak salute, blood gushing from a gash across his forehead, as the light pulled him apart. Aleksei breathed a sigh of relief, clawing himself back to his feet.

He pulled out two short, thick knives and stalked out from under the bulwark. With the illusion broken, the fighters on the warship would spot him immediately. He would just have to be faster.

Shift. Time stopped as he ran across the deck, the frigate barreling into the side of the flagship. Aleksei took a running jump, ramming into the side of the great ship, his knives piercing the hull.

As the flames licked their way up the warship, Aleksei climbed, slamming his knives into the hull as he made his way up the ship's side.

He pulled himself over the railing, driving his knives into the necks of two men only now drawing their swords.

He released the blades, pulling his bow from his shoulder and sending an arrow at a conjuring Magus. The arrow pierced her eye before the look of surprise could even register.

He ran across the deck, taking stock of where he was. An arrow passed by his face, but it travelled so slowly, as though the air was too thick for its passage.

He batted it away contemptuously, turning and sending his own arrow into the archer's throat.

The ship's castle loomed before him a heartbeat later. He ripped the door open to the below decks and dove down the narrow stairway.

A bolt of thunder shattered the wood just above his head, blowing a burning hole in the castle. Aleksei's heart skipped a beat as he landed, rolling, and dashing through the dark hallway, flashing past confused sailors and soldiers.

Before the battle, Jonas had made him study the layouts of all the ships stationed in Bereg Morya, so he knew their interiors by heart and wouldn't become trapped in their labyrinthine bowels.

Now he moved like an arrow himself, seeking the place he knew Krasik would be like a bloodhound tracking a scent. The captain's quarters, at the back of the ship. It already felt like he'd been on the ship for an hour, but in reality he knew it had been mere seconds. The amount of power he was pulling from Jonas was staggering. He just prayed that there would be no lasting repercussions.

He turned the corner at the bend in the hallway and lashed out with his boot, kicking down the thin door to the captain's chambers.

The moment the door flew open, he found himself staring into the pale eyes of a very old man. The man's face hardly had time to register surprise, even outrage as Aleksei's arrow rammed into his shoulder, pinning him to the wall.

Aleksei stalked across the room, drawing his knife.

"Who are you?" Krasik whispered.

"Judgment," Aleksei grunted, dragging his knife across Krasik's throat.

The Zra-Uul spasmed, laughing as life gushed from him in red torrents.

"Well *done*, Drago," a voice chuckled from behind him. "It certainly took you long enough."

Aleksei spun to see Bael standing in the doorway, a triumphant smirk on his face.

Aleksei drew hard on the bond, hurling a knife at the grinning Demon.

Bael batted the blade away, but Aleksei was already moving, tearing through the room towards the window at the back. Behind him, Bael drew deep on the Archanium.

Even as Aleksei crashed through the glass, he could feel the black fire racing towards him.

It raked across his back for an instant before time snapped back into place, and he hurtled towards the dark, icy ocean far beneath.

The back of the ship erupted in midnight fury.

Aleksei hit the water hard, bursting through the surface into the freezing depths. A moment later something struck the back of his head.

He opened his mouth to cry out as oblivion overcame him. Briny sea filled his mouth. Blackness consumed him.

The guard's body had hardly hit the planks of the tower floor before Roux was back at Tamara's side, cutting the last of the bonds, pulling her to her feet.

"Do you trust me?" he asked hurriedly, hearing men shout and run up the long stairway.

Tamara gulped back a sob, "Of course. You...you *came* for me."

He pulled her close, "I would break the heavens for you. I'm here, but getting out is going to be the tricky part. Just hold onto me, and keep your eyes shut."

Tamara let out a strange, strangled laugh at that. He wrapped his arms around her, preparing to Dart back to the guard tower far below, when she suddenly shoved him away.

"*Stop!*" she shrieked.

Roux tensed, hearing the men rushing up tower grow closer. "We have to go. *Now!* They'll be here any second."

She froze, as though listening. And then she started laughing hysterically. Roux hesitated at the unexpected eruption of sound, wincing at the volume of her laughter. At the *pitch*. It didn't sound like any laugh he'd ever heard from her.

And then she screamed.

Roux found himself on his knees, his cry matching her own, hands clapped over his ears, warm blood pouring down his cheeks.

Her wail was otherworldly.

Despite the confusion and anguish coursing through him, Roux pulled himself shakily to his feet. If he could get to her, if he could Dart her out of the tower, they could still get clear.

Behind Tamara, the guards finally staggered into view. Roux groped for his knife, but before his hand found purchase, Tamara spun. Her scream intensified, and Roux watched the heads of each man crumple like crushed paper, dropping a score of soldiers dead in an instant.

"Tamara!" he cried out, his mind reeling. He vomited from the vertigo.

"Roux! Gods, what did I do to you?" she whispered, her back to him as her scream evaporated from the tower.

He realized he was panting, his foggy brain still paces behind as he tried to make sense of what was happening. "Tamara, we have to get out of here!"

She cocked her head, turning as a mangled smile emerged across her broken face. "Why?"

Roux shook his head, trying to clear it. Was he going mad? "Because they'll be coming for you. Darling, we don't have much time. I don't know what's *happening.*"

"But *I* do," she purred.

Roux felt a dull explosion in his head as her voice bloomed in his mind.

I love you, but you can't control *me, Roux Devaan.*

The booming in his mind reminded him of the Seil Wood. With an eerie understanding, Roux sank back to his knees. Gods, what was happening?

You believe me a victim, but not any longer. I'm not your plaything. *I am not some whore who will spread her legs just because you once made me wet. Do you understand me, DOG?*

Roux stared at her, his vision blacking out as his head threatened to burst. He'd never felt such a pressure before. He felt like he was at the bottom of the Relvyn pool, with the water and darkness crushing him.

"I love you!" he shouted. "What's happened to you?"

She paused, blindly regarding him, perhaps for the first time since the screaming.

I hear your thoughts. I won't tolerate lying. she whispered into his mind.

"I'm not lying!" he whimpered, hardly hearing himself, "Delve wherever you want! I'm not hiding *anything*."

For a queer moment, he felt *fingers* prying about in his brain. He offered everything up, a sacrifice, holding nothing back. Whatever she wanted of him. It was all there. He had never been untrue. From the moment she had been taken, he had wanted nothing but to find her.

He focused his thoughts on everything that had happened since she'd been abducted, everything he had done, all in the name of finding her, of holding her again.

The silence stretched, but Roux wasn't sure if it was due to his new deafness, or if she was actually witnessing what he'd been trying to communicate in the madness of the past few moments.

He cautiously opened his eyes, surprised to find Tamara kneeling in front of him, her bandages gone, her empty eye sockets dripping blood.

A trembling man stood behind her, though from his clothing he was no soldier. She snapped her fingers, and from the void of silence, the man stepped forward and clasped his hands over Roux's ears.

Lancing pain unlike anything Roux had ever experienced coursed through him, but he never stopped looking into the absence of her eyes. His anger at what they had done to his beloved served as the only buffer between him and the agony.

At some point, Roux realized he could hear his own screams.

"I'm sorry," he choked as the Magus stepped back.

Tamara leaned forward and dragged a blood-crusted finger, absent a nail, across Roux's face. "All better, my darling fawn? I'm *sorry* that man had to hurt you, but it was necessary."

Roux choked again, coughing a thin stream of blood across the floor. "Thank...thank you?"

Her face became a nightmarish smile of missing teeth and glee. "Oh, Roux, I'm so glad you came for me!"

The Magus who had healed him dropped to the floor like a limp rag doll, his head crumpled like the soldiers' near the landing.

"Tamara," Roux finally managed, reveling in the fact that he could hear again, "what's *happening*?"

She shrugged, standing and kicking at the Magus's corpse. "I didn't like the way he looked at you. You're mine, Roux Devaan. *All* mine."

"Of course I am," Roux coughed. "Always."

She flashed the same grim, gleeful smile, and Roux was reminded of a grinning skull. She offered him a bandaged hand. "Come, darling. Take me on a stroll through the Palace, won't you?"

Roux rose shakily. "Where would you like to go?" he managed.

"Well," she whispered, her voice suddenly cold, "I *do* need to rid my chambers of all the vermin infesting it lately. Will you escort me?"

Roux shook his head, trying to understand what he was experiencing. "Yes?"

"Yes what?" she snarled.

"Yes...darling?"

She leaned forward, her previously-perfect face still twisted by torture, and kissed him. "What a good boy you are. I think I'll keep you," she giggled.

Tears streamed from his eyes, tears he prayed she didn't know were falling. Tears that washed away some of the blood clouding his vision.

Roux managed a smile he hardly felt, "Well, you are my princess."

Tamara laughed at that, "Darling, I'm not *only* your princess.

"I am your Zra-Uul."

CHAPTER 52

A RULE OF UNINTENDED CONSEQUENCES

The moment Toma felt herself come back together, she knew something was wrong.

Tamrix snapped back into form beside her, his sword coming out the scabbard as his edges sharpened, his ruddy red hair focusing from a blurry mess into the snarl and curl she knew so well.

They stood in her old room.

Toma had grown up in Taumon, in the Admiralty, and had spent her early childhood wandering the hallways and niches of the grand structure, learning it the way only a child could manage. But her room, her poor, sad little room had seen very little love or care since she'd left for Kalinor so many years before.

It smelled of dust and neglect. She'd only returned a few times since going to the Voralla as a girl, and each time, she'd returned with Tamrix. With the bravest man she'd ever known.

"I don't know what's happening out there," she admitted as the entire building rumbled.

Tamrix flashed a handsome grin, though his voice didn't match his apparent confidence, "As long as we're side by side, there's not much that can stop us."

She managed a sardonic laugh, "I think you might be surprised."

He put his hands on her shoulders, fixing her in his brown-eyed gaze, "We're fighting for the right side. And we're going to win."

She nodded, more for him than from actual conviction. "We'll do what needs to be done," she said, mustering more confidence than she felt, mirroring his bravado just as she had since they were little more than children.

Tamrix gave her a gentle kiss, and in his insistence, she understood what he was trying to say. That this could be the end, just as when the Voralla had been taken despite their every effort. Had it not been for Ilyana's light spell, she would have likely died then and there. *They* would have died.

Gods, but she was glad she'd ignored Aya's command to bring that book. The idea of it falling into enemy hands would have been far too much to bear.

"Alright," she said finally, taking a deep breath, "this is something we have to do, isn't it?"

He gave her a determined nod. "And you can do this, Toma. You're braver than you credit yourself."

Toma wrapped his bravery around herself, doing her best to believe his words, believe their *bond*. And then she opened the door of her room, stepping out into a raging war zone.

The hallway was littered with bodies, soldiers and Magi alike.

She only had a moment to stare agape at the carnage before she caught a quake across the Archanium, turning to see a ball of fire roiling towards her.

Toma reacted instinctively, the Archanium snapping into place around her. She dove into it, snatching a spell and quelling the fireball. A heartbeat later, her countering whiplash of air slammed through the enemy Magus.

To Toma's surprise, it didn't throw the woman back as she'd intended.

Instead, the spell cut the woman from shoulder to hip, bursting her apart. Her scream, short though it was, cut through Toma like a blade.

"Good gods," she muttered, blinking in shock, fighting back the bile rising within her.

Tamrix was beside her a moment later, wiping fresh blood from his sword. "She was trying to kill us," he reminded her sharply. "You defended yourself. You saved us."

Toma nodded, doing her best to pull herself together. "We need to find Jonas, or at least Aya. If either of them is still here, they'll be nearest the command center."

Tamrix nodded, not questioning her for a moment. Her fear aside, Toma knew the Admiralty better than any enemy Magus or foot soldier.

She moved down the hallway, doing her level best to ignore the stunned look of horror on the face of the Magus she'd just broken apart. Doing her best to ignore the stench of the woman's viscera splattered across the walls and floor.

Toma kept the Archanium swimming across her vision, knowing that an enemy Magus could round the corner at any moment. She had to be ready. She had to be prepared to murder a thousand foes if she were to get to the right people in time.

An explosion rocked the Admiralty.

Toma fought to keep her footing. Tamrix was there a heartbeat later, his big hands holding her up.

"What was *that?*" she whispered, looking to him, eyes wide with fear.

"I don't know, but we want to stay as far away from it as possible," he grumbled.

"Alright, we need to head down. Most of the Admiralty is built deep into the cliff overlooking the Autumn Sea, and they would never keep *any*one important this high up. We have to get below ground. If we're going to find anyone, they'll be down there."

Tamrix nodded, following her down the corridor.

Toma navigated the labyrinth of the Admiralty's interior, following its twists and warrens as she worked her way down.

They had just reached the ground floor when she saw Ilyana's Marrik round the corner at a full sprint. The space behind him lit up with red light, fragments of plaster and paint shattering off the wall.

Toma felt the enemy Magus mere paces behind him. She stepped past Marrik, turning the corner and unleashing a simple light spell. It was a small, hot flare of brilliant green light. It blossomed in the enemy Magus's heart.

The man dropped in a gasping heap.

She retreated back behind the bend in the hallway, where Tamrix was holding Marrik up.

"What's going on? Where's Aya? Does Jonas know?" she demanded.

Marrik looked at her, and she saw fear in his eyes for the first time since the Voralla had been taken. "Girl, I've no idea what you're on about. Far as I'm aware, Aya hasn't been seen in the Admiralty.

"Besides, we've much bigger things to worry about at the moment.

There's a flood of Bael's Magi. And some *thing* is with them. I don't know what it is, but it's deadly. We lost five Knights in seconds trying to take it down. We can't afford to lose any more. We're barely holding them off here, but nearly all our Magi are on ships battling the Demon. Ilyana is on the water, and using an *enormous* amount of power. I can hardly draw on our bond."

Tamrix frowned, "Then we've got to get to Jonas, or the Queen. It's a matter of grave importance! What's your plan?"

Marrik stared back at him, "To *survive*."

"Where's Jonas? Where's the Queen?" Toma pressed.

Marrik shook his head. "Gone. Both of them. Far from here."

Another explosion shook the Admiralty. Marrik grimaced. "It's that thing. I don't know what it's doing, but it's killing us."

"Alright," Toma said, doing her best to keep her voice calm, "here's what we're going to do."

Jonas stood at the prow of the *Gray Wolf*, watching the battle. It was going well, from what he could tell. Three of the fireships had hit their marks, and all six Magi had returned. Some were a bit worse for wear, but very much alive.

Ricon had found him immediately on his return, despite his obvious concussion and blood loss. Jonas wasn't sure if he ought to be relieved or terrified that his Knight was on Krasik's ship, facing down some of the most dangerous people in Ilyar, alone. Whatever he was doing, he was drawing a significant amount of power through their bond.

For Jonas's part, he had been raining blow after blow on the flagship, trying to keep their Magi busy. Behind him, four other Magi stood, their magic intertwined with his own. Without them, it would have been impossible to light a candle on a ship that far away. But their added power gave him the strength to shred the flagship's sails, even crack its mast in twain.

That ship wouldn't be going anywhere. Aleksei's fire frigate had done its job as well, setting the port side of the ship ablaze. Bael's Magi seemed oblivious to the danger fire posed to their ships. Besides, their hand was being forced elsewhere.

They were busy focusing instead on shielding their ship from Jonas's attacks. Ethan and Yosef were on their own ships, linked with four other Magi each, and raining down destruction of their own.

Ethan had effectively devastated most of the Yrini corsairs. Of the original seven smaller ships, only two remained afloat, if just barely. The rest were mere splinters in the sea.

Jonas turned and saw the Magus Kirsa sobbing. He frowned as one of the others went to her. While it was possible that she was suffering from battle fatigue, or just from exhaustion from being linked with him, he had a much more ominous suspicion.

The Archanium Knights weren't on the ships with their Magi. They had their own job, patrolling the Admiralty in case Bael sent his minions there, searching for Andariana. It didn't matter that she was safe on Henry's farm, or that Ilyana had been parading around the deck of the *Gray Wolf* for the better part of the battle, her intricate illusion spell making it impossible to differentiate her from his aunt.

Jonas didn't always understand Bael's thinking, but were their roles reversed, he would suspect that Andariana had been hidden in the Admiralty, rather than on the *Gray Wolf*. It was exactly what *he* would have done, had he not rediscovered Fading in Fanj.

But, presumably, Bael didn't know that they could Fade, so Jonas was praying to every god he believed in that the Demon would never think to send an assassin anywhere but Taumon.

Still, his prayers were rarely answered.

Andariana wasn't the only one in need of protection, either. For reasons beyond his control, his mother was still in the Admiralty, and she was very vulnerable. It worked in their favor that no one really knew who she was yet, but Jonas hated taking chances.

As a result, he had commanded, and Ilyana had agreed, that the Knights served no purpose on the ships, and their talents were better suited to guarding against attacks on land. In all honesty, he couldn't care less if the enemy were searching for Andariana; he needed those Knights protecting Rhiannon.

And Jonas would sacrifice every Magus in Ilyar, every angel in Dalita, to protect her from harm.

Katherine Bondar was with her, for which Jonas found himself strangely grateful. He wasn't sure how useful a cooper's daughter from Voskrin was, but she was certainly quick and adaptable.

Even after the wreckage Lady Delira had made of Katherine's mind. Jonas had become *very* curious about this shadowy individual. This

"Lady" he'd never heard of now suddenly so influential and powerful, and a Magus of Ethan's equal in strength, but his master in cruelty.

He hoped he never encountered her. For her sake.

Jonas's connection to the Archanium sharply diminished. He spun to see Kirsha vomiting blood. His heart clenched in his chest, even as his well of power eroded.

He reached for Aleksei, but felt only panic. He knelt on the deck, heart pounding in his chest as Aleksei's thoughts tore though him. He couldn't perceive them clearly, but he knew the feel of Aleksei running from danger, the mindset that snapped into place when the man was saving his own life.

The back of Krasik's flagship exploded in black fire, and for a split-second Jonas thought he was about to drop beside Kirsha.

Aleksei's thoughts cut out.

Panic soared within the prince.

And then he sensed something altogether different.

The Demon was at the helm of the doomed flagship, pulling the Nagavor around himself like the eye of a hurricane.

"He has to have every Magus on that *ship* linked to him," Jonas whispered.

He felt the thrumming, painful film of rot that splashed across the Nagavor whenever the Demonic Presence forced itself into his world. It wrapped the Archanium in a putrid, corrupted shell; immensely powerful.

"What is he *doing*?" Jonas barked aloud.

"He's pushing into the water," the Magus to his left replied weakly.

Jonas caught sight of the spellform, and his gut clenched. With a sudden clash of comprehension, the pieces clicked together. This was no black fire. It was precisely the opposite, yet promised to be far more devastating.

With a wrenching scream, another Magus dropped to his knees, convulsing with the horror of a breaking bond.

Jonas felt his power ebb away even more, the Archanium suddenly that much dimmer in his vision.

"Gods," he grunted, pulling himself to his feet, "not *now*."

"Jonas, we can't fight that level of power. It'll blast us out of the sea!" the Magus Feran yelled in his ear.

From their ships, Ethan and Yosef turned the full force of their destructive might on the flagship, raining down blows that were still fearsome, but not as devastating as they'd been at the battle's beginning. From the feel of it, they were down quite a few Magi as well.

A titanic wave erupted from the churning waters, its backwash hurling the enemy ships away with its force.

Jonas gripped the Archanium with everything he had. He knew he could die at any second. Aleksei was clearly near death, his mind silent, and Bael's tidal wave would shatter the Gray Wolf to splinters.

There was no need to hold back.

He pulled everything he could from the other Magi, ripping them along on the cascade of power he amassed, driving them all immediately past the point of dangerous exhaustion.

Jonas pulled the seahorse relic from within his coat. He'd been saving its power for this exact situation, though he hadn't had much time to practice using it to manipulate the water.

He poured his entire being into the relic, into the *sea*.

And then he felt it. The antipode of the virulent shell Bael had summoned into this world: inverted. *Cold.* A burst of Song, all gloriously high harmonies, danced along sheets of ice and cut straight through him.

He invoked the Seraphima, throwing it against the Demonic Presence, countering the magic Bael had returned to the world, denying it victory with every shred of his ability. As he unleashed his spell, he felt something different, something *other*.

Something Jonas had never felt before.

A power welling from the sea itself, meeting the Seraphima and entangling itself within the Angelic magic.

There was a colossal thunderclap as magics collided. The resulting shockwave flung him back, through the other Magi. They all cried out in pain as one, their link shattering in the concussion, even as the swell of water tossed their ship nearly into the air.

A titanic countering wave rushed through the sea, crushing Bael's wave and crashing into the enemy fleet like divine chaos. Ships fragmented and capsized. Some landed on their side, spilling Magi and sailors screaming into the cold, unforgiving depths.

Jonas lay on the deck, a goodly distance from where he'd been standing, gasping for air.

But alive.

He blinked, gingerly coming to his feet, the Seraphima still firmly in his grip. He took a deep breath, expelling frigid mist from his lungs.

He *was* the Seraphima.

He felt Aleksei, still in the sea, but now much farther away. Incredibly, the wave he'd summoned had pushed his Knight nearly to the far shore, half a league away. He slipped the seahorse relic back into his coat, shifting all his remaining strength to focus on the bond.

Jonas Faded.

Rhiannon paced back and forth across the rich blue and gold carpet, gritting her teeth. Katherine sat in a chair not far away, pensively clasping her hands and staring at her feet.

"What *exactly* are we supposed to be doing?" Rhiannon demanded.

Katherine looked up, but remained silent. She seemed to understand that Rhiannon wasn't addressing her specifically. Rather, the Princess was howling at the void, raging against a storm she knew she couldn't weather.

"I spend two bloody *decades* in a tower, only to be found by my son, and within mere days I'm in a bloody basement about to be murdered while he's leagues away. It's not bloody fair," she spat bitterly.

If Katherine was shocked by her vehemence and frustration, the girl didn't show it. Rather, her face reflected only concern.

"Highness, I don't know your son very well," Katherine allowed, "but I know Aleksei Drago better that almost anyone else in this world, and if there was ever another man like him, I haven't yet found him."

Rhiannon grunted, staring into the dim firelight flickering in the hearth, "I hardly see how that protects *Jonas* at a time like this."

Katherine leaned forward and fixed Rhiannon with a surprisingly piercing glare, "*Think.* Would he be your son's Bonded if Jonas was anything but Aleksei's equal?

"Jonas sought Aleksei out, yes. But Aleksei Drago would never have agreed to be bound to your son, prince, Magus, whatever, unless he saw the same strength he possessed himself. That tells me Jonas is more than capable of taking care of himself."

The Admiralty rocked violently. Katherine glanced at the ceiling as it sprouted hairline cracks. "I'm far more concerned about *our* fate right now than either of theirs," she confided softly.

Rhiannon walked to the door and listened. They had heard the sounds of fierce skirmishes, but thus far no one had tried to force the door.

"I see your point," she whispered.

Heavy footfalls sounded down the hall, and Rhiannon had to restrain her emotions, lest they alert the enemy to her presence. The gods only knew what would happen if she were to lose control of herself with the enemy so close. Would they know? Could a Magus recognize what she was? She could be burning like a fire on a new moon to them and not even know it, *especially* if she lost control.

The footfalls came closer, and she was suddenly aware that this mystery person was only inches away, on the other side of the door.

The lock brightened with a cherry-red glow before falling away in a puddle of slag. Rhiannon jumped back, surprised as Katherine pressed past her, knife at the ready.

When the smoldering door opened, a small woman and two large men stood on the other side of the door. Rhiannon sagged in relief when she saw Marrik standing there, looking worse for wear, but very much alive. She hardly knew the man, but she'd seen him at enough war councils to at least know his face.

"Highness," Marrik grunted, "did the Prince leave any means of reaching him?"

"No. If he had, I'd be shouting at him to come get us out of this mess," she added with a touch of bitterness.

He sagged. "That's unfortunate. But Toma can Fade. She can get you to safety. The Admiralty is overrun with enemy Magi and soldiers. We're taking heavy casualties. The enemy has something new...something we've never encountered."

Katherine whipped her knife around, the spine resting against her wrist, concealing the blade. "That's what's causing the explosions?"

Marrik nodded, "Near as we can tell."

Rhiannon looked to the man and woman she'd never seen.

"And who are you?"

The woman stepped forward and gave a brief bow, "Toma, Highness. I'm a Magus. This is my Knight Tamrix." The big man gave a nod of his head, immediately turning to watch the dark hallway behind him. "I have intelligence of terrible importance for your son, but it isn't worth much if we're all dead."

Rhiannon focused on the woman, ignoring the last part of her statement. "Toma, you can Fade us away from here?"

Toma nodded, "If we can get somewhere with enough light, yes. But we'll need to be in the sunlight. I can't Fade with just candlelight, or even firelight. It won't be enough, not with this many people."

Rhiannon's shoulders fell, "And we're buried underground."

Toma nodded, "Yes, but I was raised in this place. I know it better than any rebel possibly could. We'll just have to be extremely cautious during our ascent."

Rhiannon restrained a surge of hope. "Lead the way."

Toma gave a sharp nod and turned, passing her Knight and stepping into the darkness of the corridor. Katherine passed the Knight next, her blade at the ready. The two Archanium Knights waited for Rhiannon before flanking her on either side.

Frightened though Rhiannon was, she was glad for the protection of the two men, one stalking through the dark like a wolf, the other projecting such power and confidence that it almost banished the terror of the situation completely. It was all illusion, but she girded herself with the false sense of security.

Toma led them through twists and turns that Rhiannon found quickly bewildering. At times, they ducked into rooms that led into other rooms that led out into corridors. Each decision moved them further from the explosions, it seemed, but thus far they hadn't been able to progress *up* very well. Still, whatever kept them out of harm's way was preferable to a mad dash that only ended with their blood soaking the stones.

"There's a small central stairway that goes up through the core of the Admiralty," Toma whispered in the darkened corridor. "It's only used by servants, so it's unlikely that the rebels know it's there. If we can get up to the surface that way, we might be able to get to the central gardens."

"How far is it?" Rhiannon whispered.

"We're nearly there, but we may have to take some longer passages to avoid any fighting," Toma whispered. For the first time, she sounded unsure.

"What's wrong?" Katherine hissed.

"I'm not exactly sure *where* all the fighting is happening. I'm trying to avoid any place where I feel others, but I can't feel every enemy Magus here. We'll have to engage *someone* to get to the stairway. From what Marrik said, there's simply too many of them."

Rhiannon straightened and did her best to project confidence. Perhaps if she believed in her own emotion well enough, it would rub off on the rest of them. "Then we must be very cautious."

Toma started off again, and Rhiannon did her best to keep up, without giving into the urge to shrink back into the shadows and hide. She couldn't afford to be weak and afraid.

Even if she wasn't always the most courageous woman, her son and his husband-to-be had enough to spare. She tried to pretend to be as brave, as selfless as they were. Thinking of Jonas, his drive, his passion, his bravery, she found that she did feel a touch stronger. Her stride quickened to keep up with the rest of the group.

She'd hidden in the darkness for far too long.

Toma was moving at a dead run now, and Rhiannon struggled to keep pace, pulling up her voluminous skirts to keep from falling flat on her face.

A door ahead of them burst apart in a gout of flame. The Magus who emerged had barely registered their presence when she was hurled against the wall behind her, impaled on flying fragments of the door she had just destroyed.

Toma dropped to a knee, gasping.

"*Gods*, that took a lot," she panted.

Tamrix scooped her up, hardly stopping for a moment.

"Where to?" he grunted.

As the Magus opened her mouth to answer, a deep shadow darted through the shattered doorframe. It turned to face them. Even in the darkness, Rhiannon knew she was looking into the face of a nightmare.

"Good gods, what *are* you?" she whispered.

The creature smiled, all putrid flesh, broken fangs, and swirling black mist. "My, don't you all look *delicious*."

Toma started gasping for breath. A flash of fire flickered in the air, but the creature laughed it off. "Girl, you can't hurt me. But I'll enjoy eating *you*."

Tamrix stepped back as the creature floated towards them. Katherine was suddenly behind Marrik, her entire body shaking violently.

"It's *impossible*," she whimpered. "I saw you *die*. I saw Ethan burst you apart into a million pieces."

The creature gave a gurgling laugh, "Why, *Katherine, dear*! I could smell *your* fear from the surface. It was simply too delicious to pass by. I spent so much time cultivating your dread, *growing* your terror for this lovely harvest.

"That big ox of yours was never going to deprive me of my feast. I'm stronger now. Lord Bael made me *better*. I'm not some fragile pretty face. I cannot be destroyed. But I can *consume*."

Toma dropped from Tamrix's arms, "*No!*"

She rose and raised a hand. Blinding light pierced the darkness, passing into the creature and blowing holes through its smokey pall.

The Delira creature recoiled and retched. In that moment, Tamrix growled and darted forward, swinging his sword and decapitating the monster. Its head flopped onto the floor and split like a rotten melon.

He stood there, panting. And then the creature's arm slammed him into the wall of the corridor. The fragmented head on the floor evaporated into smoke, flooding back onto the creature's neck stalk.

"*Delira!*" Katherine screamed, hurling her knife into the flesh of the creature that had once been her mistress. Delira grunted, but held Tamrix firmly against the wall.

Toma was on her knees, seemingly trying to gather whatever magic she had at her disposal, but unable to conjure anything.

Delira reached into her body and withdrew Katherine's knife. "Why thank you, dear," she hissed. And then she tore the blade across Tamrix's throat.

Blood spewed forward in a geyser, drenching Delira in crimson. Toma screamed. She managed an anguished sob, desperately crawling towards her love before their broken bond slammed into her fragile frame. Blood fountained from her mouth, but she kept crawling froward, convulsing, yet determined to reach Tamrix as they died together. She collapsed inches from his limp body, her hand outstretched, reaching for his lifeless fingers.

Lady Delira turned towards Katherine. "You smell positively *sour* now."

"Monster," Marrik growled, starting towards her.

"No," Rhiannon managed, pushing him back towards Katherine. "No, this is too much. This *can't* happen." She stepped forward, confronting the grotesquerie.

Delira's pallid face widened with a pumpkin grin as she took in Rhiannon, "What's this, dessert already? How positively *decadent*. Do you hope to fight me? I am *fear*, darling."

Something powerful pulled at Rhiannon, something that had controlled her entire life; the need to be afraid. To fear this thing, just as she'd always been made to fear herself.

But she wasn't afraid. Not of this thing, and no longer of herself. It *had* devoured those age-old fears. Rhiannon felt untethered; enraged. She'd felt this cascade of emotions before, a lifetime ago. It had not ended well for anyone.

A short burst of her anger dispelled Delira's pall of fear, and the monster tumbled back in an unseen torrent, its face registering shock. Registering terror.

Of her.

Rhiannon planted her feet. "You've made a grave mistake," she snarled.

And then she released herself. She abandoned the restraint she'd always worked so hard to maintain, the shame she'd held for what she was. And all she was *not*.

Her fury at this monstrous creature crystallized in a single point before her, and she fed it her wrath, all the darkness that had once consumed her, that had been practiced against her. Her rage at being imprisoned for so long, rage at this *creature*, and what it had just done to two people who'd sacrificed themselves protecting her. Rage at all those fighting in this cursed place, hellbent on murdering her sister, herself, her *son*.

"Fear *me!*" erupted from the princess not as words, but a howl. Its power tore through Delira, its haunted scream immediately nullified by the power of Rhiannon's cry. Delira's body ripped apart, a cyclonic whorl of mist and flame, banished from existence in a blazing, incandescent instant.

But Rhiannon's words, driven by her explosive fury, didn't simply dissipate. They rippled through the Admiralty, tearing through the rebels battling the Knights and Legionnaires, ripping their flesh to tatters in a horrific typhoon of blood and bone.

The power of her howl bore deep into the foundation of the Admiralty itself, shattering stone and sacrificing the structure to the incursion of the Autumn Sea. Water poured through the walls, flooding the lower levels within moments, washing away the wake of fresh atrocities.

Rhiannon stood there, shaking, as the ocean crashed into the corridor. Marrik and Katherine both pulled at her, trying to turn her in the direction of the stairway, but she could hardly move.

Even as the icy water rushed around her, she remained unmoved. Aftershocks of her power reverberated around her, *through* her, as she recalled flashes of a different eruption, a different moment in time entirely, even as she keenly felt the thousands of lives she had just extinguished.

She relished every detail.

Jonas Faded back together high above the Autumn Sea, as near to Aleksei as he could get.

As he fell, Jonas shifted into a gannet and dove, seeking his Knight.

When he finally caught sight of the Hunter, his heart skipped a beat.

Aleksei was bobbing in the sea, face down. Jonas shot beneath the waves as a bird, surfacing as a man. He wrapped his arms around his broken Knight and Faded to the closest shore he could see.

And then they lay on the beach, surrounded only by gulls, the crashing waves, and salt-rimed driftwood.

He turned Aleksei face-up on the sand, finding the Hunter pallid and cold.

He violently shook his Knight, shouting his name, but Aleksei didn't so much as stir.

He pressed his ear to Aleksei's chest and heard a heartbeat, but no breath.

Jonas turned the massive man over and started slapping him on the back as hard as he could. He'd seen a boy drown before, as little more than a boy himself. He'd seen a man bring the boy back by lifting him and striking him on the back. The boy had coughed the water up.

But he couldn't pick Aleksei up.

He wrapped his arms around Aleksei's middle and attempted to lift him, pulling with every ounce of strength he possessed. Aleksei's body barely shifted from the sand.

Jonas kept trying, determined to save the man he loved.

He strained again and again, the other man's chest cracking inward before violently pushing back against him. Muscles in his own back and shoulders twisted and tore, the deep scars where his wings had been split with the strain, wrapping him in a queer warmth.

He realized he was sobbing, babbling, even as his strength faded.

Aleksei suddenly convulsed, twisting violently. His arm struck Jonas hard across the face, sending the prince sprawling into the surf.

When Jonas righted himself, his teeth significantly loosened, he found Aleksei vomiting, expelling the sea from his lungs onto the beach, even as the waves bathed him in black, brackish water.

Jonas scrambled to his feet, practically tackling his Knight, wrapping his arms around him in a vice grip.

"What...what *happened?*" Aleksei barked hoarsely.

Jonas took a closer look at the man, noting the deep cut that ran around the back of Aleksei's skull. That was when his thoughts had silenced, Jonas decided. He'd been hit by something. Hard.

"Something hit you. You need healing."

"What?" Aleksei managed.

Gods, Jonas thought, *his head's a wreck.*

He reached into the Archanium, bypassing the Great Sphere and diving into the Seraphima. He poured the healing power of his Angelic blood into his Knight, knitting bone and tissue back together with a rapidity the Archanium had always lacked.

Aleksei's eyes snapped open as cold white light blossomed within him. He coughed roughly, breathing out frigid mist as his mind cleared.

"Gods," he grumbled, "what was *that?*"

"The Seraphima," Jonas whispered, "and this isn't the first time it's saved your life."

"Where is it?" Aleksei asked, clutching at his tattered grays in a sudden panic that made Jonas jump.

"Where's *what?*" Jonas asked, watching the bizarre display as his Hunter clawed at his chest.

Aleksei looked into Jonas's eyes with a fear unlike anything he'd ever seen.

"The feather...Adam's feather! It's gone!"

Jonas scanned the beach, trying to keep calm. "It must have washed away in the sea."

And then Jonas's fatigued mind caught up with Aleksei's alarm.

The wind demon.

Without Adam's feather to obscure his presence, it could find Aleksei once more. And here, on this desolate strand, there was nowhere to hide. No trees within running distance, especially not with *both* of them weakened as they were.

Jonas wondered if he could even conjure a spark after the tribulations of the past few hours.

He scanned the shoreline, catching sight of a lone structure, a small wattle and daub fisherman's hut built into a grouping large, weathered stones. It was broken, the roof partially caved in, and ancient besides. It was also the only shelter to be had on the vast beach.

"Come on!" Jonas shouted, helping Aleksei to his feet.

Aleksei had spotted the hut, immediately dashing towards it. Jonas pulled the Archanium, the Seraphima, around him as he desperately chased after his Knight.

Aleksei flashed across the beach, pulling on his bond to an extent that left Jonas breathless and staggering. He could hardly believe Aleksei would just abandon him like that, so vulnerable on the open beach.

Then he heard it.

It whistled past him, the creature ignoring him completely as it sped towards its true prey.

Prey that it had been denied for so long, *finally* out in the open.

Aleksei dove into the hut, a heartbeat before the demon smashed into the small structure.

Jonas kept running, desperately trying to conjure *any*thing to throw at the demon, to disperse it, even *distract* it, but he was far too weakened and too far away. At this level of emptiness, forcing a spell into his world could well cost him his life.

He saw the Mantle burst from within the hut, seething through the cracks in the wall and wrapping around the wind demon. Jonas heard a strange sound, something he didn't recognize. He managed to maintain a staggered gallop through the damp sand, coming up to the shack just as he recognized the sound, intertwined with the roar of the surf and the wind demon's wail. Aleksei's screams.

Jonas fell into the hut and found his Knight on his knees, pressed against the wall, the Mantle undulating from his shoulders into the cracks in the flaking mud and brick.

Thin ripples of chartreuse light slithered across the Mantle's midnight fasciae and into the Hunter. Aleksei sobbed in agony, but the demon was being held back. A handspan closer, and the brief battle would end for both of them.

"It's too much!" Aleksei screamed when Jonas stumbled into the hut. "It's too *much*, Jonas. I can't *do* this anymore."

Tears streamed from the man's eyes. Seeing Aleksei in such pain, such desperation, ripped through Jonas in a tortured torrent.

He had nothing left to give his Knight. He couldn't save his love, or even *himself.* Jonas dropped to his knees and wrapped his arms around Aleksei's chest.

Aleksei gritted his teeth, his arms shaking uncontrollably as he braced against the wall.

"I'm *sorry,* Jonas. I wanted to protect you more than anything in this world. And I failed. Gods, I love you. And I'm *sorry.*"

Tears cascaded from Jonas's cheeks and chin as he gripped the Seraphima.

"So let *me* protect *you.*"

With the last of his strength, he poured the Seraphima into his Knight, holding the man tight. The man he loved more than life itself. Demon or no, *nothing* would come between them. Even in death.

The Mantle quaked and vibrated. The chartreuse rivers of light broke apart, scattered as though dispersed in some unseen gale.

From Aleksei's shoulders, the Mantle flickered, blindingly bright. *White.*

Jonas stared as the cold white of the Seraphima banished the black emptiness of the Mantle, its darkness falling away in the wake of brilliant, opalescent light.

He could feel it, could feel the light flash through the tendrils embedded in the brick, and then bursting beyond.

A seemingly infinite amount of energy surged between the two men, opening a window into eternity that existed in a fraction of time. An otherworldly howl exploded through them as the Seraphima violently rent the wind demon into an earth-shattering thunderclap.

And then it was gone.

A sudden silence ringing in his ears, Jonas collapsed to Aleksei's side, his head bouncing painfully on the petrified floorboards. He could hardly breathe. His heart battered his ribcage in its struggle to keep him alive. He convulsed on the floorboards, coughing savagely even as he desperately tried to gulp in air.

Aleksei's arms wrapped around him, a firm kiss pressed into his sodden hair, both of them lying exhausted and intertwined on the floor of the hut.

"Now let *me* protect *you.*"

He barely heard Aleksei's whisper as a crimson tendril sank into his neck, trickling life back into the dying Magus. He lay in his Hunter's embrace, practically lifeless, his breath shallow, emerald eyes flickering as he desperately clawed at the darkness swallowing him. Even the Mantle's life-energy felt weak; faded.

But it was enough.

He coughed, and his eyes fluttered open.

Gods, where *was* he?

Jonas groaned, attempting to gather his wits.

And then, with lightning certainty, Jonas remembered where he was.

In Aleksei's arms.

Where he belonged.

EPILOGUE

BEHEMOTH

The light brought Aya back into sharp lines and soft curves, piece by piece. Slowly, she began the lengthy process of waking. Her body was cushioned by the softest down, a summer wind gently fanning her face.

Aya's eyes opened languidly, and for a long moment she was completely confused. All around her rose a wall of solid, wild green, undulating in the wind. The air was warm, and the breeze smelled of the sea.

When she remembered where she was supposed to be, she clambered to her feet, pausing to gain her balance and casting about in the grass sea for Raefan, or any sign of Taumon.

The air was far too warm for the fur coat wrapped around her, and she shed it quickly, pulling off her heavy wool sweater and tossing them thoughtlessly to the ground. In the distance, past a sloping green field she saw the mirror-brilliance of the sea, the wind carrying scents of salt and spray.

She frowned, her mind still pulling itself back together. There was no sign of Taumon, or the Admiralty, for that matter.

"Aya!"

She spun, relief flooding her as Raefan forded the rippling grass sea towards her. His hair glittered like burnished gold in the sunlight as he stepped out of a deep shadow.

Raefan broke through the verdant wall, stepping into the tiny tamped-down oasis where she'd awoken. She was still trying to make sense of what she was seeing, and failing.

Raefan was tanned and bare-chested. His trousers had been torn off just below his knees, the edges sandy and frayed.

And then he was wrapping her in his arms and kissing her passionately. She looked up into his glacial blue eyes, impossibly bluer, *brighter* than she'd ever seen them. And, over his shoulder, she saw what was casting the shadow he'd emerged from. Aya stared in astonishment at an impossible thing.

A gigantic, mountainous monolith of whitestone towered above her, dominating the center of what she now understood to be a valley. A valley touching the sea, dominated by the largest statue she'd ever seen.

Her blood ran cold as she stared at it, a chill sweeping through her despite the brilliant sunlight and the warming winds.

"Great gods," she whispered, looking back at Raefan's suntanned face and brilliant blue eyes, now communicating more fire than ice. Eyes a shade brighter than they should be. Just a shade.

"Great *gods*, Raefan!"

Raefan watched her eyes carefully, then followed her gaze up the length of the colossal statue, towering hundreds paces above them.

He chuckled, "You read my mind."

ACKNOWLEDGMENTS

This novel was supposed to come out in 2020. And while the pandemic we all lived through, and continue living through, slowed things down quite a bit, it also gave me the time and opportunity to work with some truly amazing people who helped me refine what this book was into what you now hold in your hands. I would be remiss if I didn't thank the extraordinary contributions of the artists, editors, and beta-readers who brought their experiences, passions, and wisdom to this project, as well as those who kept me sane during the editing phase.

To Bradley, thank you for helping me keep life in perspective, and for offering unconditional love when it felt like the world was crumbling just a little too quickly. I love you.

To Rufus Cactus, words cannot express my gratitude and amazement at the amount of time and passion you poured into this book. There is no doubt in my mind that your extremely sharp and meticulous edits elevated this novel far beyond its humble beginnings, and I am forever in your debt. Thank you for being so dedicated, and for being my friend. You are truly amazing! And to Gena, thank you for letting me steal your husband for so long, as well as for your own contributions. I can't properly express what a gift it was to have Rufus dedicate so much time to this project, and I deeply appreciate your forbearance.

To Sonarix, your incredible artwork brings this world to life in such beautiful and excruciating detail, and it is truly an honor to not only be the beneficiary of your monumental talents, but to be your friend as well. Here's to many more delightful collaborations. I don't know what I'd do without you!

To Dr. Angelo Vu, thank you for your clinical excellence and friendship, this novel literally wouldn't have been possible without you!

To CodyAnne Omori, your editorial acumen and wonderful commentary helped shape this novel into a piece I am deeply proud of, and it wouldn't have been possible without you! You have such a sharp eye, and coupled with your remarkable speed, you're every author's dream editor! Thank you for you talents, and your friendship!

To Amber Yourman, I so deeply loved reading through your comments and edits! You saved me from making more than a few blunders, and for that I am deeply grateful.

To Dr. Melissa and Michael Sherrod, I so deeply appreciate the time and effort you spent going through the final draft, ensuring that, despite the size of this novel, it was as clear and clean as humanly possible. There are so many moving parts in this novel, and getting y'all's stamp of approval means the world to me. Michael, thank you for being the best agent/publisher I could have asked for. Here's to 9 more novels!

On a personal level, thank you to Dr. Thomas J. Garza and Dr. Elizabeth Richmond Garza, both of you influenced so much of my knowledge and understanding of literature, folklore, and life in general. I use the tools you provided me every day, and I love you both.

To Joshua Torres, thank you for providing so much inspiration in the early stages of this novel's creation.

To Charles Boyd, this story wouldn't have taken the shape that it did without your wit and influence. Thank you.

Finally, to everyone reading this, thank you for allowing this world and these characters into your lives. I hope they have as profound an impact on you as they have on me.

CODEX PRONUNCIATION
GUIDE

Akhrana - ahk-RAH-nah
    Aleksei Drago - ah-LEHK-say DRAY-go
    Andariana - an-DAR-ee-ana
    Apsis - AHP-sehs
    Archanium - ark-KAN-ee-uhm
    Arrad Bazin - ah-RAHD bah-ZEEN
    Askryl - ASK-rill
    Aya - AYE-yah
    Azarael - AZ-ah-rail
    Bael - BAY-ehl
    Bereg Morya - BEAR-ig MORE- yah
    Cassian - KASS-ee-an
    Dalita - dah-LEET-ah
    Dalitian - dah-LEESH-ahn
    Darielle - DAH-ree-ehl
    The Drakleyn - DRAHK-lehn
    Drava - DRAH-vah
    Emelian Krasik - ee-MEEL-ee-ahn KRAH-sick
    Fanj - FAN-J (It's a hard J)
    Hade - HAY-dh
    Ilyana - ill-ee-AH-nah

Ilyar - ill-ee-AHRE
Jonas Belgi - JOH-nas behl-ZHEE
Jorna - JOR-nah
Kalinor(i) - KAL-eh-nor/kal-eh-NOR-ee
Keiv-Alon - keev-ah-LAWN
Keldoan - kel-DOH-ehn
Kholod - HOE-luhd
Kholodym - HOE-luhd-eem
Krilya - KRIHL-yah
Kuuran - KOO-ran
Magi - MAJ-eye
Magus - MA-guhs
Makar - mai-KAHR
Marra - MAH-rah
Marrik - MAR-ick
Mokosh - muh-KOHSH
Mornj - MORE-njh
(Mother) Margareta - marh-gah-REHT-ah
Nagavor - NAH-gah-vhor
Oborin (Order)- OE-bohr-in
Perron - PEAR-uhn
Perun - PEH-roon
Raefan - RAI-fan
Rafael - exactly like the painter
Relvyn - REL-vehn
Richter - RIHK-tur
Ri-Vhan - REE-vanh
Roux Devaan - ROO dev-ANH
Sammul - SAM-uhl
Seil - SEEL
Seraphima - serah-FEEM-ah
Seryn - SEHR-ihn
Shangri-Uun - shang-ree-OON
Tamara - tah-MAH-ra
Taumon - TAH-mu
Vadim - va-DEEM
Volos - VOH-loes
Voralla - vor-AL-ah
Voskrin - VOSK-ren

Ylik (Water) - ILL-ick
Yrinu - IH-renn-oo
Yrini - ih-REEN-ee
Zra-Uul - zer-ah-OOL
Zirvah - Zehr-VAH

ABOUT THE AUTHOR

NICHOLAS MCINTIRE PUBLISHED HIS DEBUT NOVEL, THE HUNTER'S GAMBIT, IN 2019. A WICKED WIND IS THE SECOND ENTRY IN THE CRITICALLY-ACCLAIMED ARCHANIUM CODEX. HE LIVES IN FORT WORTH AND FORT DAVIS, TEXAS.

IF YOU ENJOYED THIS NOVEL, LEAVING A REVIEW WOULD BE BOTH ENORMOUSLY HELPFUL AND APPRECIATED!

facebook.com/NGMcIntire

twitter.com/NickMcIntire

instagram.com/nicholasmcintire